Unto
This Last

UNTO
THIS LAST

REBECCA LIPKIN

The Book Guild Ltd

First published in Great Britain in 2020 by
The Book Guild Ltd
9 Priory Business Park
Wistow Road, Kibworth
Leicestershire, LE8 0RX
Freephone: 0800 999 2982
www.bookguild.co.uk
Email: info@bookguild.co.uk
Twitter: @bookguild

Typeset in 12pt Adobe Jenson Pro

Printed and bound by CPI Group (UK) Ltd, Croydon, CR0 4YY

ISBN 978 1913208 820

British Library Cataloguing in Publication Data.
A catalogue record for this book is available from the British Library.

For those I love unto this last:
Mother, Father, Husband.

CONTENTS

PART TWO

PART THREE

PART FOUR

"Ruskin was one of the most remarkable men, not only of England and our time, but of all countries and all times. He was one of those rare men who think with their hearts, and so he thought and said not only what he himself had seen and felt, but what everyone will think and say in future."

Leo Tolstoy

PROLOGUE

RUSKIN CHASED THE OPEN CARRIAGE AS IT THUNDERED across Westminster Bridge. Several times he very nearly lost sight of it, yet still he pursued the landau, drawn by a pair of sprightly grey mares. The tails of his frock coat flapped bird-like as he crossed the gustiest part of the bridge, while he could hardly avoid scuffing his fine leather boots when he stumbled in his hurry, for he had no time to look where he was going.

He did not consider what he would say or do if he should catch up with the vehicle, the simple desire to exchange a few words being enough to compel him onwards. He felt that he was fated not to allow this chance encounter to pass him by without at least attempting to seize it, a belief which fired him up and gave him a rush of energy he had not experienced since his youth.

Despite his limbs making him remember his age, he was possessed with an uncommon, exhilarating vitality, coupled with an excitement at the prospect of finally getting to see and speak to her that made him giddy.

A few spots of rain offered him the refreshment he needed and, though he could only see the back of her head and the fair hair which had ignited the chase, this urged him on when he could barely breathe for exhaustion.

The carriage eventually came to a standstill just after a mile when several milk carts blocked the Piccadilly thoroughfare. As the rain was worsening, the ladies asked the coachman to pull over to adjust the hood, a fortunate event which allowed Ruskin to stagger towards his goal, spent and breathless but ecstatic with success.

The canopy had not yet concealed the passengers by the time he approached, however he saw to his horror that he did not recognise either the two plump middle-aged women, nor the young lady, entirely plain with dull grey eyes, who bore no resemblance to his dear one whatsoever.

On the contrary, the stranger's blank face with nondescript features so repulsed him with its many dissimilarities that he could barely look on her, though she was smiling and blushing at him as though he were a sincere admirer, for she rightly assumed that she had been the reason for his maniacal pursuit.

'Why, I do believe it's Mr Ruskin?' the eldest and roundest of the three women remarked, peering at him curiously and pressing her substantial bosom with false modesty.

'Indeed,' their pursuer admitted shamefully, running his fingers through his damp hair in abject humiliation.

'Well, what an honour! Whatever can we do for you?'

Crestfallen, he stuttered an apology because he believed he ought and not because he felt sorry for causing them delay: 'Forgive me, I mistook this lady for a friend,' and, withdrawing his arm from the door of the carriage on which he had momentarily rested, he fancied that his heart was bound to rupture from both the vigour of the exercise and the heartbreak of the reality.

The stupid-looking girl regarded him searchingly and at last enquired, 'Is *this* how you greet your friends?' prompting her companions to snigger at his expense.

'This is my niece,' the portly woman offered without needing to, her expression and tone having changed from one of warmth to brusqueness.

Ruskin, nodding curtly to the young woman but without taking up the introduction, said, 'What a foolish error. I insist that you ladies go on your way, I have inconvenienced you enough already.' And he turned to go without so much as bidding the startled party farewell. After all, *he* was more baffled by his actions than they.

He was a desperate man, never more so than when he faced the disappointment of having to watch the carriage, without his love in it, rumble down Half Moon Street, taking all hope of seeing her away with it.

PART ONE

EIGHT YEARS EARLIER

FIRST SIGHT

T HOUGH IN HIS FORTIETH YEAR RUSKIN FOUND HIMSELF less awkward in society than formerly, he loathed making new acquaintances. The lady's invitation and her style of address had intrigued him, however, for she had clearly read his works well enough to recognise that *his* views were those she wished her children to adopt.

He nervously straightened his customary sky-blue necktie, chosen to highlight the colour of his eyes, as he was ushered into the richly furnished drawing room adorned with paintings, lined with sculpture and cluttered with volumes on art and architecture he immediately recognised.

It was a room not only showcasing a considerable knowledge but ostensibly endless wealth, yet if Mrs La Touche, who rose to greet him looking slightly flushed, had fashioned it with the intention of cultivating his interest, she did so ill-advisedly, for Ruskin's opinions and tastes generally proved contrary to anyone else's.

Slim and beautifully dressed, despite Maria La Touche being his junior by only half a decade, she looked considerably younger, belying her burning intellect.

'It's so good of you to call,' offered the lady with an appealingly soft Irish accent.

'It was no trouble, I was on my way to the Royal Academy,' he demurred, inadvertently affronting her.

Settling down to converse, she enthused, 'You don't know what it is for me to finally meet you. My Irish acquaintances delight in nothing but horse racing and gambling, so my horizons are naturally turned towards London where I can be sure of intelligent discourse.'

'How long do you intend to reside?' Ruskin enquired.

'For several months, or until my husband's work calls him home.'

'What is his business?'

'It's too dull for words! One of his ancestors founded the Bank of Ireland. I dare say it is very wicked of me to be bored by my life,' she sighed, 'yet, despite all this,' she went on, making a sweeping motion in reference to the opulence of her environment, 'one always needs a sense of purpose. Perhaps I never got over being a disappointment to my mother, who had prayed for a boy and frequently told me so.'

'Whilst I was burdened with being male and an only child, and therefore thought *too* highly of,' Ruskin interrupted, smiling sadly.

'I was raised in the shadow of my half-brother, John, Earl of Desart, whom I believe you were acquainted with at Oxford?'

Ruskin, who did not like to discuss his student days, replied tellingly, 'Yes, he was one of the *few* men I admired there.'

'Perhaps women will attend the university one day. I very much hope so, for I refuse to accept that my daughters are not as worthy of as thorough an education as their brother,' she declared emphatically, 'and I believe *you* are of the same mind?'

The question was put so forcefully as to take Ruskin off-guard, unsure whether she was challenging him or only appealing for support.

'Yes, I have always thought it ludicrous that people speak of the rights of women as if they should be separate from those of *man*.'

'When I was married at nineteen,' she went on, looking lost in thought, 'young ladies seldom presumed to wish for anything and were only expected to have pretty manners and answer questions without asking any, nor imagine for a moment that *they* were persons.'

Having a markedly higher intelligence than the average schoolroom-educated female, it was clear to Ruskin that Mrs La Touche would never be understood by her family, peers or neighbours. She craved stimulation and was too sociable for the strangely claustrophobic environment of her large estate in County Kildare.

Desiring to be part of London's intelligentsia, which she attempted to keep in touch with through a series of correspondents who informed her of all the gatherings she was prevented from attending, she had even dallied with literature by way of a pleasant distraction, putting her husband's approbation down to a lack of cultural refinement.

'Does your husband share your views on education?'

'He is a simple man with few interests save religion,' the lady ventured disapprovingly; 'a Baptist convert, he leads an inner religious life with the sincere hope of not only converting *me*, a stalwart Church woman, but my daughters.'

Mrs La Touche fully intended to imply that theirs was anything but a harmonious partnership, whilst it had been the subject of much speculation in Dublin whether the characters in her novels were based on her own lovers.

Ruskin, who knew nothing of that, nevertheless began to question her motivation in asking him to instruct her daughters. He certainly didn't have the time to teach anyone's children, not even the Queen's should she have requested it.

'You require an art tutor for your girls?' he asked, hoping to ascertain her real agenda.

'Yes, although you must think it impudent of me to ask such a thing of *you*,' Mrs La Touche replied meekly. 'It's just that I've so long been an admirer of your work.'

'I ought to say at the outset that I'm not sure I can be of very much service. Due to being so occupied, I'm unable to commit myself to any further teaching,' Ruskin rebuffed, suspecting that she was not used to being refused anything. 'Will you allow me to recommend my talented pupil, William Ward, of the Working Men's College?'

'But does he live with and *for* art as you do?' she asked pertinently, the very idea of compromise unthinkable to her.

Finding no solution, he made no reply, for it was clear that she had no intention of taking up his suggestion that Ward, or anyone else, would make an adequate substitute. He concluded that she was a good deal more than he had expected, and in all sorts of ways. She was so quick, yet quiet, and he realised that he could not venture a word carelessly before her, for she saw all too easily when it *was* careless.

'I'm so very eager for you to meet Rose, my youngest, whom I hope you will think possesses some power worth developing,' Mrs La Touche declared. 'She is all alone today as my son Percy is away at Harrow and her elder sister Emily is out.'

Walking over to the window, the lady offered Ruskin a first indistinct glimpse of the fair child playing in the garden, unaware that she was generating so much interest.

'Should I send for her?' Mrs La Touche asked demurely, all the while moving towards the bell-pull without waiting for his response.

'If you're sure it won't tease the child?' Ruskin ventured hesitantly, overwhelmed by his hostess's wilfulness.

'As you will soon discover, it is *Rose* who does the teasing in this household,' she announced, prompting him to conjecture how much the girl's character had been influenced by her mother.

He could not deny that he *was* intrigued to meet her, and presently the drawing room door opened and a flaxen-haired girl of ten years entered the room, accompanied by her nanny, Miss Bunnett, who blushed upon meeting the eye of such an esteemed gentleman.

'Well, say "how do you do",' Mrs La Touche commanded the little girl; 'this is the great Mr Ruskin I've told you about.'

'I fear such an introduction can only lead to me being a tremendous disappointment,' he interjected modestly.

'You have already exceeded all our expectations by honouring us with this visit,' she gushed.

But Ruskin's interest had shifted entirely to the child, who looked anything but uneasy, despite being in the company of a stranger and her nanny departing the room, leaving her standing quite alone. After evaluating him for a moment, Rose boldly crossed the floor and offered him her hand as a good dog might give its paw.

'Good afternoon. How do you do?' she asked solemnly, standing a little back and regarding him intently.

'It's a pleasure to make your acquaintance,' Ruskin pronounced with equal gravity, for the child did not smile, nor did he wish to make light of her surprising poise.

He saw at once that Rose Lucy La Touche had a self-confidence quite remarkable for her age, and which he doubted had anything to do with being thought pretty. Her hair was gathered at the nape of the neck, enhancing her look of innocence, and whilst she was neither tall nor short for her age she had a rather stiff and formal way of standing, as if she was always careful to be polite and well-mannered when outside the schoolroom. An obviously thoughtful and observant child, he couldn't help but wonder what she made of *him*.

'Mama gave us lessons from your drawing book,' Rose offered.

'That's wonderful to hear. Do you like drawing?' he asked, removing a small sketchbook and pencil from his breast pocket.

She stared at them warily, while Ruskin looked around the room for an object she might sketch. Eventually, a small vase containing a delicate pink rose caught his eye, and which, being her namesake, he thought might make her more amenable.

Placing the not yet unfurled rosebud in the palm of his hand, he requested, 'Would you sketch *this* for me?'

Rose nodded cautiously, aware that her mother would be annoyed if she should fail.

'Don't be afraid, if you draw what you see you'll never go far wrong,' Ruskin reassured.

After several minutes a good likeness of the flower emerged on the paper, yet the conscientious child only offered it to him when she considered the drawing complete.

Examining the sketch, Ruskin turned to Mrs La Touche and confirmed, 'Your daughter certainly has talent.'

The mother beamed, 'Do you really think so?'

Recognising that his refusal to act as tutor had crumbled with this acknowledgement, he went on, 'Yes, and I would be delighted to further her understanding.'

'She would be fortunate indeed,' the lady replied earnestly.

'On the contrary, I consider myself quite inexperienced in teaching the young, but I will do what I can if Rose promises to be patient with me.' And he looked to the child for encouragement.

When Ruskin qualified this by adding that he could not spare the time to visit them routinely, Mrs La Touche enquired after the state of the roads to Denmark Hill, the home he shared with his parents.

'Rose and Emily might easily journey to *your* house if it would be more convenient?' she suggested, and before he knew what he was about, yet not really minding, a day was fixed for them to call on him.

THE STATE OF DENMARK

ENMARK HILL WAS A HANDSOME THREE-STOREY MANSION set within seven acres of land and positioned at the end of a broad, sweeping gravel road. An immense cedar of Lebanon stood proudly before the house and created an impression of stature and maturity that would otherwise have been lacking, while to the rear of the property a meadow sloped towards the sunrise.

The orchard was bounteous, as was the extensive kitchen garden, while a small farm holding housed three cows, providing the household with fresh cream, and pigs that were so tenderly reared that their main purpose in life, that of providing meat for the table, was often met with considerable reluctance on the part of the Ruskin family.

It was a long way from where Ruskin's father, John James, had started out, but though he would never have admitted it he was not as comfortable in his surroundings as he had expected to be, having acquired the house entirely for the sake of vanity.

Purchasing the lease on his son becoming a student of Oxford

University, along with a carriage and a coat of arms to better enable him to peacock his wealth, he had mistakenly believed that the elevation in standing which the larger house afforded would rid the self-consciousness that had hung about him ever since leaving Scotland.

Whilst John James had felt a sense of pride whenever Ruskin invited his noble friends to dine, neither he nor his wife had ever found as much contentment at Denmark Hill as their former dwelling, which though humbler had been more than adequate, as his son had pointed out just a few months after their relocation.

'None of our new ways are as good as the old,' Ruskin complained one day, looking out on the new team of gardeners gathering the ripe fruit. 'The peaches have not the flavour of the few which our old orchard once granted us, nor are all the apples *here* worth a single sour one of our former home.'

'This house possesses every virtue,' John James had contradicted, determined to defend his decision to upgrade their style of living in accordance with his growing fortune and the ambitions he harboured for his son.

Deciding to let the matter rest, Ruskin had turned away from the window and, taking up the seat beside his father, graciously allowed one concession: 'At least Denmark Hill has the advantage of being far enough from the metropolis as to *almost* feel like the country, and provides a quiet spot away from the factories increasing in the city tenfold every month. They say all this enterprise will come to be regarded as an industrial revolution, and what a ghastly business it *is*.'

The boundless greed of the Empire repulsed and frustrated the young man, who little took into account that the early sparks of such commercialism had saved John James from a life of poverty, and that he in turn had benefited from being educated alongside men of nobility according to his father's hard-earned gentlemanly status.

Unlike John James, Ruskin did not have a mind driven by merchantry or commerce, nor did his father wish to see his son's hands dirtied, and thus he set about studying the way in which such things impacted on society and the life of the common man.

Rather than amassing wealth, Ruskin's talents lay more in encouraging his father to *spend* his fortune, and having avoided the family sherry importing business, which sold the best wine that could be given for the highest price, in favour of an academic path, he had remained serenely under the authority of his parents, trying his utmost to please and convince them that this had been a wise decision. It was this rather than any arrogance which made him initially seek to become recognised and lauded for his opinions on art.

Though not nearly so grand as the La Touches, the Ruskins had hosted a great many artists and men of letters at their modest table ever since the publication of *Modern Painters* which had appeared shortly after their son's graduation from Oxford, a select, yet loyal group of followers joining Margaret and John James in celebrating Ruskin's earliest achievement.

On the subject of pictures their guests were guaranteed an intelligent debate; or if they preferred to discuss the sherry trade, the direct, yet hospitable John James would tell them more about it than anyone else alive, whilst offering them a generous taste besides.

As an only child who had been much cosseted due to bouts of ill health, even into his fourth decade Ruskin still retained a slight air of a petulant infant whenever he was home, and thrived on being the main focus of his parents' attention.

John James and Margaret's love for him, though deep and tender, was always strangely concealed in sternness, however, so keen were they for him to know the importance of discipline and hard work. But although Ruskin inwardly despised this parental autocracy, there was a welcome security in living alongside them at Denmark Hill which seemed destined to remain unbroken.

Even when, during his brief marriage, he had been released from the old order in exchange for independence and his own dominion, it was only to find his new situation much worse, prompting Ruskin to look to them for guidance more than ever, much to the annoyance of his wife.

Reflections such as this regularly troubled him during his daily walks and forced him to turn his attention to work in order to avoid the severest episodes of depression. Yet, as he made his way home following his first encounter with Mrs La Touche and Rose, his mind was filled with happier visions, and the prospect of the lady visiting Denmark Hill with her daughters gave way to an unusual optimism.

Teaching them would offer a pleasant new diversion and he felt sure that it would be gratifying to observe the improvement in scholars so young and not overwhelmed by bad practices like so many of his protégés. Thus he set about adapting the lessons he had delivered at the Working Men's College for pupils as fresh and untouched as the canvas on which they would eventually learn to paint.

Mrs La Touche believed Denmark Hill to be charming long before she arrived, nor could anything allay her delight on sweeping up the drive and finding herself in the spacious hall, where Ruskin greeted her and her daughters and wasted no time in providing a detailed tour of the rooms leading from it.

'What would you like to see first,' he addressed the girls, 'my watercolours or my minerals?'

'Oh, the minerals!' Rose declared boisterously, without giving her sister a chance to express her opinion, and thus Ruskin marched them to his study where he revealed half a dozen display cases filled with a multitude of glittering, dazzling rocks.

'I began collecting them when I was about your age,' he ventured to Rose, who immediately passed her gloves to her mother in order to feel the various textures of the minerals: smooth, rough and jagged.

So very different in spirits from the day he had paid his first call on her, Mrs La Touche was amused on witnessing Ruskin's childish glee in presenting his most precious treasures, which he boasted of as a young boy might flaunt his new toys.

It was almost an hour before they reached the cluttered drawing room where his mother, Margaret, upheld a dignified posture by the fireside in an elaborately carved and vulgarly-upholstered armchair. The room was filled with heavy, old-fashioned mahogany furniture which, although not to Mrs La Touche's refined and elegant taste, she complimented profusely in order to please her hostess.

Margaret, offering her mittened hand and scrutinising her guest with a distrustful eye, enquired almost aggressively, 'How do you do?'

'Your home is enchanting,' Mrs La Touche extolled more loudly than necessary; 'it's like something out of dreamland.'

'Thank you kindly. How pretty your daughters are,' she returned, as Rose and Emily took shelter on either side of their mother, blushing in girlish innocence, 'and they greatly resemble *you*,' she went on, silently motioning her guests to take the sofa.

'Don't tell their father that,' Mrs La Touche responded hurriedly, feeling strangely uncomfortable at the way in which the old woman peered at them.

She was not sorry that the conversation was disrupted, for the three had barely sat down when Ruskin begged them all to rise again in order to view the main feature of not only the room but the entire house: the collection of paintings by J. M. W. Turner.

'I hope you will say that I have left the best until last,' he enthused as he ushered her forth and proceeded to relate many details as to the painter's techniques and intentions regarding composition.

Having been keen to impress his father with his astute connoisseurship, Ruskin had persuaded John James to purchase thirty paintings and countless watercolours by the artist over a period of many years, an assemblage extensive enough to make the drawing room resemble one of the galleries at the Royal Academy, and all the more oppressive due to the dark red flock wallpaper peeping out beneath the impressive gilt frames.

Her host finished by returning to the fireside where he revealed the possession he was most proud of. 'My father rewarded my first efforts as an author by purchasing *this* mighty work,' he explained, pointing to the painting which took pride of place over the mantelpiece, 'The Slave Ship.'

'For many years my son kept it at the foot of his bed so that it should be the last thing he saw at night and the first thing he saw upon waking,' Margaret interjected, affirming her son's devout appreciation of the artist.

Mrs La Touche fawned, 'I can well understand it, I too recall the joy of owning my first painting!'

'The pleasure of a new Turner nobody *ever* will, so it's useless my trying to describe it,' he repudiated, wishing the lady might leave off making pointless remarks and baffled that a woman of her intellect should use such commonplace vernacular.

'I did not wish to offend you, my friend,' she apologised, much taken aback at her host's keenness to prevent Turner being likened to any other artist.

'These pictures are my friends,' he replied curtly. 'I have none others.'

Thus the afternoon progressed, with Mrs La Touche afterwards sitting down to talk with Margaret while Ruskin, whose bad temper soon blew over, several times dashed off with Rose and Emily in order to fetch other objects to show her.

His mother was a ruddy-faced matron, who habitually wore a modest white lace cap and an unfashionable brown dress, and soon revealed herself to be a single-minded character who disliked flattery, and not only knew Chamonix better than Camberwell, but was far keener to journey to the former over the latter.

Mrs La Touche did not think Margaret simply a sweet old lady, but rather that she ruled the house from her low seat by the hearth and revelled in being the dominating influence of Denmark Hill. Often likened to a character in one of Miss Austen's novels, she was accustomed to receiving absolute deference from everyone about her, and, though difficult to understand, she possessed a sharp, decisive tone which made new acquaintances wary of saying or enquiring the wrong thing.

Boasting that she had never dismissed a servant in her life, Margaret felt it fully within her right to complain at length about certain loyal retainers who were almost equal to herself in age and infirmity, and Mrs La Touche was greatly surprised when a foul-tempered but entirely devoted maid by the name of Anne Strachan appeared, carrying a tea tray that was clearly too heavy for her judging from the way in which the china rattled as she edged nearer.

With hair that had long since turned white during the many years of service she had given to the Ruskin family, Anne was wizen, stooped, unsteady on her feet, and could barely accomplish the simplest of household tasks such as dusting her mistress's prized furniture or bringing and clearing away refreshments.

When the servant later returned in order to remove the tea things, her mistress addressed and rebuked her as she might a tiresome child: 'You left without bringing us the spoons!'

'Stop mithering me, woman,' the spinster retaliated, allowing Mrs La Touche to observe that Margaret was well used to such disrespect.

Infuriating her still further by clearing away her unfinished cup which had been placed to one side on a little round table, Margaret grumbled to Ruskin on his return and, before the servant had quit the room, said, 'She might have *seen* that I had some tea left!' before turning to Mrs La Touche and urging, 'I trust you will not judge our incompetent staff too harshly? I'm simply too good-hearted to turn anyone out.'

'You know my theory, Mother, there is only one way to have dutiful servants and that is to be *worthy* of them,' he teased, looking up from a particularly fine illustrated volume that he was preparing to show Mrs La Touche.

'Anne, who was my husband's nurse before my son's,' Margaret explained, 'has a natural gift for not only *doing* disagreeable things, but *saying* them, and can always be relied upon for giving the darkest view of any subject.'

'Yes, if ever a woman in this world was possessed by the Devil, *Anne* is that woman,' Ruskin chimed in, making Rose and Emily laugh.

Not entirely sure if it was appropriate for her to laugh also, Mrs La Touche was grateful for not having to decide, for her daughters diverted all attention away from Anne by expressing their desire to see the garden and the many wonders *it* contained.

Mrs La Touche joined Margaret in standing at the French doors opening onto the terrace and looked on as Ruskin showed Rose and Emily the stables. Bathed in the low afternoon sunshine of late summer, the trees in the orchard were loaded with apples, while the peaches, with their velvety downy skin, glowed cheerfully along the old fruit wall and a blackbird sang merrily on an unseen bough.

'The girls appear to have made a playfellow of your son already,' Mrs La Touche commented.

'Those who show John a little affection get a great deal back,' his mother replied proudly as he meanwhile related the pet name of each animal to the girls.

Both women, encouraged by Rose and Emily's carefree laughter and the mild weather, were drawn onto the lawn, content to look on this charming scene in silence for a time. Margaret appeared to enjoy the lively presence of the children; a welcome antidote, so Mrs La Touche perceived, to Ruskin's academic friends, and they too were surprisingly at ease in the old woman's company, notwithstanding her rather severe appearance.

Ruskin, meeting Emily for the first time, meanwhile found her to be a delicate nymph of fourteen, with dark eyes and an angelic quality that made any place holding her presence the brighter for it. She was not as beautiful as Rose, however, and being far more serious did not possess the quick wit that was the most intriguing quality of both her sister's and mother's personalities.

'It has been decided that the pigs are extremely intelligent and speak excellent Irish!' Ruskin called out to his mother and Mrs La Touche, a broad smile upon his face, but Rose and Emily made sure that his opportunity for engaging the adults was limited, and they pulled at his sleeves in the hope of commandeering him for the rest of the afternoon.

'Will you show us the meadow?' Rose pleaded.

'Hush now,' he admonished her, without being in the least serious, 'I see my greatest challenge is going to be instilling some discipline into you wild Irish girls.'

Though Ruskin had intended the remark to amuse their mother, unbeknownst to him she was already looking on with considerable jealousy as his attention became entirely occupied by her two daughters.

Writing in the most gushing terms the following day, Mrs La Touche thanked Ruskin for his kind hospitality and described the sunset she had noticed on her way home, which had appeared more beautiful than any she had yet seen, doubtless the result of viewing his wonderful collection of Turners, an artist whose interpretation of skies she declared unlike anything other painters had ever been brave or skilled enough to capture before.

Concluding that, as no lesson had taken place due to their rustic interludes and talk, Denmark Hill was too magical an atmosphere for teaching and would surely interrupt her daughters' studies, she suggested that they establish a suitable time for Ruskin to tutor them in their own schoolroom. Yet it was selfish rather than motherly concerns which motivated her, for she had calculated that it would fall to their governess, Miss Bunnett, to accompany Rose and Emily if Ruskin insisted on the tuition taking place at his home.

Mrs La Touche was greatly satisfied when he replied by return of post withdrawing his objections to such an arrangement, and from that time most of Ruskin's London avocations led him to their address on Curzon Street. Thus, within just a few months, a close relationship developed between the two households, with the girls subjecting him to amusing pet names and always attempting to stall him from teaching.

He found it delightful to be constantly teased, especially by the fair Rose, who was by far the more mischievous of the two sisters, and with whom it became silently acknowledged that he shared a special rapport. The only attention he wished to avoid was that of their mother, whose presence he dreaded for any lengthy period and whom he regularly disappointed by declining a steady barrage of dinner invitations.

Having long since decided to avoid devoting himself to any woman, Ruskin hardly gave much consideration to his attractiveness to the opposite sex, and whenever one of his female acquaintances made their feelings known to him he lost no time in brutally snuffing out their admiration, as if extinguishing the first signs of a house fire.

Believing that any woman who professed their love without him having first sought it had lost their mind, when one lady began writing him poetry, penned in an elaborate script on pink notepaper, he promptly advised her, in the frankest language possible, *not* to publish her feeble attempts, although he could not resist reading them aloud to his mother for the sake of amusement.

'What do you think of this, Mother, will *this* stifle her passion for me?' Ruskin asked, holding aloft his response and reading comically, "'I believe you are the profoundest little goose who ever wore petticoats. You write me four pink pages full of nonsense, you fancy yourself in love with me and send me the least excusable insult I ever received from a human being. You little idiot!"'

THE DRAWING MASTER

USKIN ENJOYED THE SIMPLE TASK OF PREPARING THE pencils and sketchbooks ahead of visiting the girls, along with deciding what subject to focus their attention upon, from the laws of perspective to reading aloud some passages from his recently published work, *The Elements of Drawing*; for although he was happy to be petted and made a play-friend, he was also determined that his lessons should provide the framework for how Rose and Emily would approach art and nature for the rest of their lives.

They in turn soon realised whenever he desired their full attention, for his manner and tone would change, commanding them to listen to him with due reverence.'I must explain that I cannot assist either of you if you only want to learn drawing, as other girls your age do, merely in order to boast another graceful accomplishment. I mean to teach you how to set down, clearly and usefully, records of things that *cannot* be described in words. Not only shall you discover drawing to be the most powerful way of obtaining and communicating knowledge, but it is my sole objective to help you see greater beauties in nature and art than you did hitherto, thereby affording you more pleasure in life.'

'None of our other tutors ever talk to us like that,' Rose observed, mesmerised.

'I may not be a regular sort of teacher,' Ruskin replied emphatically, 'but neither do I wish *you* to be regular pupils. Art is no recreation to be learned at spare moments or pursued when we have nothing better to do. It must be undertaken in earnest or not at all.'

Having instructed the sisters to draw a peacock's feather, Rose and Emily worked quietly at studying the object in minute detail, learning through making mistakes how best to convey both its texture and colour. It surprised Rose, who found the task enjoyable rather than difficult, how soon the afternoon turned to dusk, as it did Ruskin who occasionally looked up from the book he was reading in order to observe how much of a challenge his pupils found their work.

'I can't do it!' cried Emily in uncharacteristic impatience, throwing down her pencil after many attempts to perfect her work, a poor second to her sister's.

'Of course you can,' replied Rose calmly, leaning over Emily who was starting to whimper; 'Mr Ruskin says you just have to draw what you *see*.'

Ruskin smiled upon hearing Rose's reassuring words and watched with admiration as she guided her elder sister's hand along the paper in effortless strokes and flourishes.

'There, it's beginning to take shape,' he encouraged Emily as soon as she continued on alone. 'Go first to nature, omit nothing, select nothing, scorn nothing. Go in all singleness of heart and walk with her laboriously and trustingly. Nature paints for us, day after day, pictures of infinite beauty if only we have the eyes to see it.'

Saying which, Ruskin withdrew a couple of his own sketches from his portfolio – the one of a rough, mossy, low stone wall, and the other a bit of ivy round a thorn stem – which he held up in order to better illustrate his point.

'The rule is simple,' he explained passionately: 'if an artist draws something they know and love, be it ever so humble, they are sure to make a good picture. One day I noticed this ivy by the roadside and proceeded to make a light and shade pencil study of it – carefully, as if it had been sculpture. Liking it more and more as I drew, when I was done I saw that I had virtually lost all my time since I was twelve years old because no-one had ever told me to draw what was really there!'

'You have an unusual way of looking at the world, Mr Ruskin,' Emily declared, moved by his words. 'I only wish *I* could see it as you do.'

'You probably never shall, for it's something that can't be taught.'

'How so?' she persisted.

'For a start, *my* childhood was decidedly different from yours. I picked up education in an irregular way, having no siblings or friends, nor many toys due to my mother disapproving of them.'

'No toys?!' Rose repeated in consternation.

'On one of my birthdays, pitying my monastic poverty, my aunt bought me the most radiant Punch and Judy she could find in all the Soho Bazaar, but though my mother was obliged to accept it she afterwards quietly told me that it was not right that I should have it, and I never saw it again.'

'That's terrible!' his pet cried.

'Perhaps it is just as well,' Ruskin observed, 'for I learned to study and appreciate everything which my limited library and garden afforded.'

'I would never be happy without toys,' Rose chimed in.

'We know!' Emily added, sharing a knowing glance with her teacher.

'Ah, but you and your sister have always had one another for company,' he reasoned, 'whilst being surrounded by a glorious landscape I don't expect either of you have ever really stopped to admire.'

'Even if we had, I don't suppose we could ever see things the same as you,' Emily responded, aware of her failings.

'I realised, from an extremely young age, that I saw things quite differently from others and examined even ordinary things with a microscopic level of detail,' he went on musingly. 'I would draw blades of grass as they grew, until every square foot of meadow, or mossy bank, became a world in itself. This heightened sense of awareness permeated into my love of art and made me admire artists like Turner, who could replicate the reality of nature and elevate her glories that we might better absorb her humblest gifts when next we walked alone.'

Mrs La Touche had been right to perceive that it was her youngest daughter who possessed a natural gift for creative pursuits, and it was therefore she whom Ruskin, after just a short time of nurturing, observed undergo the greatest advancement, not only in the quality and precision of her work but in a new-found interest in both art and nature.

Rose's keenness to please her drawing master prompted an openness to discover and understand the world outside the more familiar domain of the schoolroom, for Ruskin's teachings were in marked contrast to the humble lessons of the kind-hearted but intellectually limited Miss Bunnett, whom she and her sister always affectionately referred to as "Bun". Thus Rose pushed herself to learn and practise her new skill in a way she would never otherwise have been compelled to do.

The child's desire to impress Ruskin was only reinforced by her mother's unceasing praise of him and the delight she took in boasting to acquaintances that her daughters were now his sole private pupils. Mrs La Touche felt increasingly sidelined due to Ruskin devoting all his attention to them, however, and she flailed about looking for a way to bring herself back into prominence, naively arranging a sizeable dinner party on an occasion when he had scheduled a lesson, with the intention of cajoling him into prolonging his visit.

The lady's face, which had been radiant with anticipation just moments before, fairly fell when she entered the vestibule and found the footman assisting Ruskin with his coat; she was only relieved to have caught him in time and was adamant that she could persuade him to delay his departure.

'I hope the children aren't too much for you, dear Mr Ruskin?' Mrs La Touche enquired, making every effort to hide her vexation at him preparing to leave without bidding her farewell. 'I could hear their laughter from the drawing room.'

'Not at all, they are already showing considerable signs of improvement,' he answered courteously, yet conscious that she wished to detain him.

'But surely you're not going just yet? My husband and I are entertaining some friends this evening who are all so eager to meet you,' Mrs La Touche urged, unable to conceal her feelings of rejection, whilst drawing his attention to her crimson taffeta gown by casting her eyes down and folding her hands.

'I'm very grateful for the invitation, but I have to be getting home to work on my book,' he answered firmly.

Mrs La Touche, who had turned as scarlet as her dress in annoyance, replied, 'I see,' in her most artfully pathetic voice, but this only encouraged Ruskin to curtail the conversation as soon as he politely could.

Gathering up his teaching materials which he had momentarily placed on the hall table, he therefore took his leave of her, promising to pay another visit to the schoolroom the next day, as he did whenever he chanced to be in the area.

Whilst the lady was bitterly disappointed at the failure of the scheme, her own vanity made her reason that it was not Ruskin's disinterest in *her* but simply his inherently reclusive nature which made him shun formal gatherings. Mrs La Touche realised both her error in trying to parade him in company, and that by giving him far too little notice she had made it all too easy for him to offer an excuse.

Ruskin did not appear to have ever fully broken away from his mother's side, whether from habit or choice she was not entirely sure, yet she nonetheless found it strange that Margaret and John James were included in their son's social circle: predominantly academic men, who were probably no more at home in elegant society than he.

Mrs La Touche amused herself with such reflections prior to the arrival of her guests whom alas she no longer had the pleasure of introducing to her new acquaintance, John Ruskin, whose indifference had the odd effect of increasing her desire to understand him better.

Ruskin returned to the La Touche residence the day following the dinner party he had so abruptly declined, instructing the girls for several hours before acquiescing to take tea with Mrs La Touche for fear of causing further offence.

He did not find this hour unpleasant, and was relieved to find that, unlike so many readers of his work, the lady did not choose to question him on the art he had documented or the architecture he had seen in order to agree with him sycophantically; rather, she seemed happier to express her own decisive views and was unafraid to challenge *his* with some of the most intelligent and perceptive arguments he had ever encountered. He deemed it a great waste that Mrs La Touche appeared to have no other means of channelling her knowledge and interests other than by conversing with him, and he began to feel sorry for having so often shied away from her friendship.

Having rarely spoken of her husband, whom to date had always chanced to be absent during Ruskin's visits, she took this opportunity to relate his extraordinary and new-found religious fervour, along with the unusual determination to assist in reforming the city's fallen women.

'He believes himself to have been touched by God,' she confided, partly in the hope that this confession would prompt more openness from her guest, 'and is, at this very moment, working in the East End preaching the joys of a purer life and trying to convince the most brazen temptresses that there *is* an alternative to their degrading means of survival.'

'It's a noble ambition, however misguided it might be,' Ruskin responded with scepticism on his brow.

'Yes, but though I am obliged to say that I admire his dedication, in reality I can't help but view his kind of charity as being akin to coming into contact with a disease. To me, my husband will forever be contaminated by this underworld, and I secretly mock his sermonising, as do most of the fallen women he preaches to – scorning religion and spitting at his feet in contempt as he makes what they see as empty promises of redemption.'

Shocked at the vehemence of this denouncement of her husband, Ruskin attempted to pacify her by defending him: 'He is an idealist, something I often consider myself, although *my* attempts at helping humanity are not founded upon any religious conviction.'

Ruskin little realised that the mention of religion would steer Mrs La Touche upon another tangent, and she continued, increasingly fired up, 'Due to refusing to follow my husband in Baptism we regularly quarrel as to the religious teaching of our children, and I fear that, having failed to convert *me*, he will next try to convert Rose. He teaches her that the Bible is the only thing she need study and so, even in her playtime, she sits and reads it, hoping that doing so will make her perfect, not only in His eyes but her father's, who threatens to spurn her if she dares to follow *my* path.'

Ruskin was grateful that Mrs La Touche stopped short of calling upon him to advise or agree, as he had no wish to enter into a marital argument or a discussion upon religion, a subject increasingly baffling due to scientific advances which even the most ardent believer now struggled to dispute.

He did go so far as to make one observation, however: 'We should all take care that Rosie, in believing in you, myself and her father, does not become a three-headed monster like Cerberus.'

'How true. It is such a joy to converse with someone so wise, for I live so much alone when I am in Ireland and do not care for the people I am obliged to exchange visits with,' the lady flattered, sensing that their communion was drawing to a close and that she had made her companion feel uncomfortable on subjecting him to so many confidences. 'Oh, Mr Ruskin, I am like a black beetle crouching in the shadow!'

She chuckled at this, but Ruskin did not share her amusement and only wondered if this description was more accurate than she perhaps realised.

Recalling his earliest impression of Mrs La Touche as he made his way home, he considered that her husband must possess a strong will indeed to go against her in anything. Above all though, he pitied Rose for being raised by a mother and father constantly at odds over so vital an issue as religion, for both were equally determined that she should choose *their* faith, with no consideration as to the anxiety they caused their daughter by asking her to favour one parent over the other.

Ruskin was glad when the La Touches announced that they would put off their return to Ireland until the spring, when the capital became too overcrowded for their liking, for the winter was certainly a brighter prospect for their presence.

This news heartened him as he took the familiar four-and-a-half mile walk from Denmark Hill to their house, despite it being cold enough to chill a man through, reinforced by the fact that the sky looked pregnant with snow and prompted him to wrap his scarf tighter around his neck.

He thawed out immediately on entering the warm nursery where he found Rose seated, not at her desk as she should have been in anticipation of studying, but on a large cushion by the fire, a black kitten dozing peacefully on her lap.

Neglecting to offer her teacher a formal greeting, so at ease was she in his company, Rose only smiled at Ruskin in acknowledgement of his arrival, bad manners her mother would have scolded her for but which she decided to take full advantage of in her absence. She knew that Ruskin and Emily would indulge her whims, and so it proved when the two began the lesson without her.

Rose, who had spent her childhood in the small contained world of the nursery and schoolroom, was in no mood for learning that day and alternated her attention between half-heartedly listening to her teacher and drawing the black kitten, which had woken up hungry and was stretching out its paws.

Ruskin accepted that Rose's nature was extremely temperamental and her variable moods dictated the level of concentration she could give him at any time. He therefore resigned himself to the fact that teaching her anything that day would be an impossible feat and continued instructing Emily in the hope that he might pique Rosie's interest if only he chanced upon a subject she found more interesting than her kitten.

Having been set the task of drawing a botanical still life, Emily was soon stooped over her work and straining her eyes to sketch the fine detail she was determined to become more adept at; yet no matter how conscientious she was or how much time she invested in any given subject, her work was poor by the side of Rose's endeavours, and the considerable pains she took were never reflected in the final result.

Ruskin thought Emily a dear and lovable creature and sympathised with how easily she lost confidence on making the slightest mistake and looked to those around her for encouragement or consolation, for he knew that he could only teach her so much. Aside from art, he could see that she possessed a remarkable talent for embroidery and arrangement and could make any flowers look as though they had blossomed together.

But whilst Emily had all the feminine gifts that meant she was almost certainly destined for early wifehood, Rose was still too selfish and wilful to consider anyone else. She was an unusual girl, so Ruskin considered, a firm, fiery little thing who was precociously aware of her own beauty and charms and used them unhesitatingly for her own advantage. Yet, however aware he was of being manipulated, he was both powerless and loathe to resist.

He had been daydreaming thus when Rose, who had been unusually lethargic until then, shot to her feet and screamed, 'It's snowing!'

Dashing to the window, she pulled up the sash and offered her hand to the still air in order to feel the icy flakes upon her warm palm. Emily followed her sister in appreciating this sensation, as did Ruskin, who wondered at them both finding the weather such a novelty.

'It must have been snowing for hours without us noticing. Can we go outside?' Rose pleaded, invigorated by the prospect and reaching for her boots which she had earlier placed beside the hearth. But without pausing for Ruskin to answer she placed her hat on her head in the sauciest manner, making it impossible for him to deny her anything.

Though Ruskin often managed to exert his authority when both girls demanded something, their pleas were too persistent on this occasion, coupled with his own willingness to comply. Requesting their mother's permission for an impromptu dash to nearby Hyde Park, he was as keen as they to gather armfuls of snow and practise sledging.

The billowing flakes, which disappeared before they clung to anything, developed into more determined ones, plump and falling fast, silently, upon their soft, pillowy bed. It felt like a liberty to disturb the serene perfection by tumbling upon the ground or taking up great handfuls, yet Ruskin shared Rose and Emily's delight in scooping up the powdery substance in his bare hands, the wonder of its cold, soft texture a sensation he had almost forgotten and was grateful to know again.

He struggled to recall such an occasion from his own childhood and was therefore immensely excited at being included in such merriment. As if young for the first time, the feeling of trying to run or leap in the snow sparked in him a hearty laughter that seemed to have been dormant within him for years and could not, for many minutes, be silenced.

Mrs La Touche, who had accompanied the three to the park, was much surprised to see him hurling snowballs and cavorting thus and was content to look on as a humble bystander, finding much bemusement on witnessing such an unexpected side of Ruskin's nature, not least when Emily successfully managed to dislodge his stovepipe hat. With both girls and Mrs La Touche laughing, it seemed nothing could disturb his good humour. He simply picked up the article and shook off the snow before firmly replacing it, feigning being cross that he might prolong their amusement, most of all Rosie's.

As pure and gentle as the snowflakes melting on her flushed cheeks and fair eyelashes, all who saw Rose, man, woman or child, loved her as surely as they might treasure a beautiful view or an exquisite painting, and yet all the more so because of her captivating humour and side-achingly witty observations, unusually droll and adroit for someone of her years.

She was, Ruskin realised, impossible not to give one's whole heart to; he only hoped that she would look after it better than the last book he had gifted her, which she had scribbled in the margins of, not with pencil but ink, smudging the pages due to the avid speed at which she read. Whether it was ruining a book or throwing snowballs too vigorously, Rose was forgiven without apology or begging his pardon as surely as that magical scene would be gone by the morrow, as transient and wondrous as youth itself.

Age was a withering, beastly condition, Ruskin complained internally, for didn't one always feel the same, give or take some wisdoms collected through cruel experience? He hated himself for regarding his favourite pupil with an uncharacteristic possessiveness and could not stop racing ahead and foreseeing the day when she would be on the threshold of dazzling womanhood, when surely every eligible young man in Christendom would line up at her door and court her gracious attention?

By evening, a mesmerising hush had quieted the city; footsteps and the sound of children laughing muffled by the dense blanket of snow, while those outside enjoying the respite afforded by the unexpected holiday took pleasure in walking in the middle of the road, making the most of the diminished traffic.

The rain would wash away the snow, that much was certain, leaving no trace of its fleeting beauty other than an abandoned sledge or a frostbitten carrot on the soggy ground where once a snowman had stood proud, yet that snowy day forever ingrained itself in Ruskin's mind, whilst precipitating an unshakeable melancholy and unlocking the door to a childhood that had been withheld.

All that had been prohibited by parents who saw no use in play was magnified on watching the carefree Rose and Emily, although he thought himself ridiculous for trying to recapture his long since vanished boyhood. His heart, so he had always believed, had been broken when still a lad, then mended, cracked, kicked about old corridors and finally beaten.

When all laughter had been exhausted Ruskin went in the direction of his father's office, for he needed the kind of fortitude only John James could inspire. Striding through the bustling yard of Ruskin, Telford & Domecq, he noticed that the workmen were unmindful of the snow falling on their faces and continued to load wooden crates, filled with rattling bottles, onto a wagon drawn up outside the main warehouse.

Ruskin paused to look at the prominent sign above the door for a moment and wondered if his father harboured any disappointment that it did not read "J. J. Ruskin & Son". An impressive coat of arms featuring a boar's head was also positioned above the entrance and, as he stepped inside the imposingly dark, oak-panelled office where the main source of light was that of a roaring fire, he was relieved to find the old man alone. The warmth of the room instantly comforted him and soothed his frostbitten fingers, while seeing his father seated at a large desk piled high with papers eased his earlier anxiety.

Seventy-one years old, the stern-looking Scotsman had an abundance of white hair, whiskers and bushy eyebrows which he raised in surprise on seeing Ruskin, so rarely did he call at his office. Neither man uttered a greeting, nor did John James set aside the order he had been poring over. Instead he continued to examine the document quizzically rather than offer any sign that he was pleased to see his son.

'You're working late, Father,' Ruskin remarked kindly as he took the seat opposite.

'They can't manage without me,' came the martyr-like response as he rubbed his careworn forehead in exhaustion.

Yet the impracticalities of retiring were of his own making, the business being not only a mainstay and a fixed habit but John James's greatest pride after his son's achievements, and he would far rather have died working at his desk than at home in bed surrounded by his family.

His strong, forthright brogue entirely suited his character, nor had his many years of living in London in any way diminished the earlier impression of his Scottish heritage. He was of fair height and size, neither so tall nor as slender as his son, though they looked alike insomuch as they both preferred a style of dress that had been the fashion decades before, continuously adopted by John James due to a self-confidence which had peaked in his prime and had withstood all passing trends.

At last conceding that it was ill-mannered to continue working, he tidied his papers away, reclined in his armchair and frowned, as if preparing to address Ruskin with frank words he had long desired an opportunity for venting.

'How do you find life as a drawing master?' he questioned dourly, stroking his whiskers. 'You must go there three times a week now.'

'I know you think such a thing beneath me,' he replied defensively.

'It is all becoming quite a distraction, and an unnecessary one at that. You weren't put on this earth to teach two girls in a schoolroom,' John James continued matter-of-factly whilst preparing a pipe.

'I don't seem to know what I was born for, only what I was *not*, yet I find that teaching pupils so young makes me understand how to convey my thoughts more clearly to the common man,' Ruskin explained irritably as he rose from his seat and stood by the fire.

'You never did accept criticism graciously, least of all from me,' he chided as his son took up the poker and began prodding the fire in order to avoid his gaze.

The conversation was not proceeding as Ruskin had intended, nor was he quite sure how to move it onto a more palatable topic.

'How is the Turner bequest progressing?' John James provoked, intentionally touching upon another dreaded subject. 'Something else which takes up too much of your time in my opinion.'

'I've finally finished cataloguing everything, thank God,' he sighed, 'and frankly I never felt so exhausted as when I locked the last box of drawings and returned the keys.'

'It seems that Turner managed his affairs in death as haphazardly as he managed them in life,' John James scoffed. 'When I went through his dismal, dingy house shortly after his funeral there was at least eighty thousand pounds' worth of oil paintings, drawings and sketches, his labour being even more astonishing than his genius. Nothing since Pompeii has so impressed me, not least the accumulation of forty years' worth of dust,' he sneered, pausing to re-light his pipe which he had neglected whilst conversing. 'We all admired him, but you can't deny that Turner was a strange man.'

'Who am I to judge what is strange in a man? I expect many would say the same of me,' Ruskin confessed. 'As I look deeper into the mirror I find myself a more curious person than I had thought.'

'I trust that you have no inclination to become as eccentric as our late painter friend,' his father dismissed, waving his pipe in impatience.

Ruskin was highly protective of his close bond with Turner, whose merits he had recognised at an early age and had been determined to promote through the powers of literature. Despite his relative youth at the time and the fact that their relationship had begun as that of patron and artist, it developed into an unlikely friendship, ending only with the artist's death. Senior by over forty years, Turner had been greatly in need, not of financial assistance or security, but of a champion, so fashionable had it become for critics to attack his outlandish style, a role which Ruskin had adopted whole-heartedly.

Nor had Turner felt any apparent embarrassment upon discovering that Ruskin's purchasing powers were entirely dependent upon him being able to convince his father of the merits of each work. Thankfully John James believed his son's claims that almost everything the artist touched could be hailed as a masterpiece, although, not being so ardent an art lover, he had acquired them more for their potential rise in value than the pleasure they afforded him.

Having made an analytical study of Turner's techniques, Ruskin had delved more deeply than anyone hitherto into the artist's seemingly divine ways of paying tribute to nature, intent that the volumes of *Modern Painters* would in turn convince the public to pay tribute to the ageing artist and redeem themselves for their long withheld appreciation.

'I always pitied Turner,' Ruskin explained, sorely put out by his father's lack of compassion, 'for he had no-one to love him in his old age, and any respect and affection, if they came at all, came too late,' he pondered wistfully.

'He didn't seem to appreciate them when they did,' John James harrumphed. 'He never was the kind of man to display his appreciation of your laudatory praise, nor did his agent grant us any special reduction. Far from it; when your writings created more demand for his paintings, it merely gave him the wherewithal to raise his prices!'

But this was of little concern to Ruskin, rather it pleased him to think that any word of his led to the paintings being more highly prized.

'I grant that it is unwise to pay too much for a thing, but sometimes it's worse to pay too little, Father,' Ruskin reasoned. 'When you pay too much you lose a little money but that is all, yet by paying too *little* you lose everything because you take away the worth of the thing in your own estimation. There is hardly anything in the world that *some* man cannot make worse in order to sell it cheaper, but to my mind people who only consider price are the lawful prey.'

'Turner and his agent certainly saw to it that *I* paid handsomely. I may have a boar's head for a coat of arms, but that doesn't mean I love being made into sausages!' John James fumed, biting down on his pipe. 'Fancy making you his executor whilst leaving you nothing but nineteen guineas with which to purchase a mourning ring,' John James goaded, chuckling at the irony. 'No-one can say that *you* were paid to praise.'

Ruskin, who felt the joke to be entirely at his expense, defended: 'I never offered him my support in order to receive any return for it, and it isn't true that he never thanked me. He did, in his own way, whilst I assured *him* that I would not lay down my pen until his name acquired all the glory it deserves.'

His father nonetheless tutted and griped, 'I still can't understand why he didn't leave *you* his collection.'

'I'm only too glad that he chose to gift his life's work to the nation. As for the executorship, I consider it an honour that he thought so highly of me; I just wish that he had entrusted the full responsibility of his estate to my care, for there are too many vultures for it to be entirely safe.'

'I still think you ought to write his biography,' John James remarked, believing himself to be paying his son a great compliment, 'for who could be more passionate about his legacy than you?'

'You'd only complain, for I would take too long about it,' Ruskin dismissed; 'besides, examining a man's history is not in my way, especially as there would be too much I would be forced to leave out in Turner's case. Fear not, by the time I complete the last volume of *Modern Painters* it will be such a monument to his name that there will be nothing left for any biographer coming afterwards but to relate the day on which he was born and where he lived, or with whom he dined on this or that occasion, simple facts that might be stated by anyone.'

Growing weary of such fractious discourse, and finding himself more depressed than when he arrived, Ruskin decided to take his leave and commence the cold, lonely walk home. Unable to persuade his father to accompany him, he was at liberty to re-examine his pater's words regarding, not only his involvement in the Turner bequest, but his acquaintance with the La Touches, recognising that they were doubtless wise and well-intended even if it did make him want to cover his ears.

The snow continued to fall all that night and for several days afterwards, and still Ruskin was unable to shake off the gloom following his last encounter with Rose and Emily, whom it was unfair of him to hope might recompense him for a chapter of life he had never known. Therefore, on the day he next intended to tutor the girls, he wrote to Mrs La Touche making his apologies and blaming his absence on needing to finish his current essay, thus unintentionally heeding his father's caution.

NO WEALTH BUT LIFE

'I DON'T CARE TO SEE YOU ALLIED WITH THE PLATFORM,' JOHN James exclaimed decisively one Thursday morning over breakfast on his son announcing that his evening would again be spent in teaching at the Working Men's College. 'There is a distinct vulgarity to lecturing, and I sincerely wish you would give it up.'

In the two years since Ruskin had begun teaching the La Touche girls he had been inspired by the improvement he was able to bring about, thus fixing his determination to widen his influence over others and set down his core philosophical and social beliefs.

Over the course of teaching Rose especially, with whom he was convinced he possessed a unique and spiritual connection, his ambitions had naturally changed and, rather than believing art to be his only calling, he was drawn to educate others, recording as he did so the subsistence, both intellectual and financial, he believed that every man, rich or poor, should be granted by their country.

He drew considerable inspiration from the weekly drawing classes he gave at the Working Men's College, having been recruited by the founder, F. D. Maurice, early in the institution's history, yet his father felt that he was merely being exploited and his compassionate nature taken advantage of.

'The most helpful and sacred work that can be done for humanity is to teach,' Ruskin defended, 'and I give *lessons* rather than lectures. Either way, you wouldn't be urging me to refrain from doing so if I had chosen to speak from a pulpit *or* if I were receiving a handsome fee for my pains, it is simply because my pupils belong to the lower classes.' And he paused in order to include his mother in the protest. 'As for the vulgarity you speak of, that is only what you associate with the men whom I address.'

'Most assuredly, my worry is that in trying to drag *up* the low you will end by pulling *down* the high,' John James argued, while Margaret sought to distance herself from her husband's stance by avoiding his eye and pouring another cup of tea.

'And where do *we* stand in society?' Ruskin asked boldly. 'It would surely be to your credit if you considered the modest position our own family might hold today had it not been for your extraordinary energies and simple good fortune.'

Increasingly inflamed by the topic, John James chose to ignore this remark and contended, 'This Maurice fellow, whilst he is doubtless a most amiable philanthropist, seems to do nothing but start projects for *others* to work at, and I urge you to cease taking any trouble over it. I am weary of hearing about good and wise people "giving their lives" to some cause when they haven't lives to give.'

Exhausted by this narrow, bigoted way of looking at things, and regarding his father's ignorance with disbelief and contempt, Ruskin discontinued challenging him further and went on with his breakfast in silence, sporadically turning his attention to his newspaper in order to illustrate that he no longer wished to converse upon a subject they were so at odds debating.

He set off for the Working Men's College that evening saddened and troubled that their views were so divided and that no amount of reasoning could apparently reconcile them, yet with more conviction that the project was an entirely worthy one that he should continue in spite of the fiercest criticism.

The term "college" might have led many to imagine that this place of education would be located in a far more salubrious building than that of the derelict townhouse on Red Lion Square in Camberwell which was the most that, being a charity, the organisers could afford to rent.

Yet, notwithstanding the humbleness of the venue, the Working Men's College had gained a serious reputation thanks to Maurice's brave approach and impressive connections, including Ruskin and his protégé, the gifted young painter Dante Gabriel Rossetti, who between them related the foundations of art and painting, alongside a devoted and varied band of teachers who took classes on subjects as wide-ranging as arithmetic and algebra, mechanics and gymnastics.

'Evening, Dante!' Ruskin greeted as he passed Rossetti in the corridor on his way to class, slapping him jovially on the back.

'I may look in on you later,' the portly, unkempt artist replied, 'for I hope I still have the honour of being one of your pupils?'

'I rather thought that I was one of *your* disciples, but come along nevertheless!' Ruskin called after him while making haste.

As ever, when he entered the class Ruskin found it crammed with men of all ages, united not only in their lowly station in life but through a shared appreciation of his philosophy and the support he offered them.

Young fresh-faced workmen, still largely oblivious as to the cares their own fathers had known in raising a family on a paltry income, but would face themselves all too soon, stood in sweet innocence before their teacher, and shoulder to shoulder with men considerably older than they who had clearly come direct from their labours judging from the dirt on their hands and faces.

Most of the audience looked eager for the lecture to commence, others wore an expression of meditative solemnity, while those unable to find a seat crowded in the doorway, unmindful of any inconvenience or weariness after a long day of toil, such was Ruskin's fame and the determination of each man to hear him.

A hush, akin to the awe engendered by the arrival of a king, followed Ruskin's entrance, yet due to the density of the crowd many at the back could only glimpse a slender, excitable figure rushing down the aisle to the front of the room, his movements quick and alert. To those with an uninterrupted view, he seemed cheerful rather than happy, while his whole air and manner had a definite and attractive individuality, with no hint of English reserve or stiffness.

Irrespective of how many times some of the audience had seen him before, they each regarded him with the deepest admiration when once he stood upon the raised platform, as if a prophet were preparing to impart wisdom that would shape the course of their lives, his piercing blue eyes seemingly able to look through each individual and draw them to him.

'Let me explain my motivation in holding these classes,' he began, 'and say that I care not what trade you each work at, for my aim is not to advance you in the occupation you follow, or to make artists out of carpenters, I simply want to help you attain a more satisfactory life and a greater sense of dignity in your work. What right have today's capitalists to take the word "wealth", which originally meant "well-being", and degrade it by confining it to certain material objects measured by money?'

Having resolved that his work should have a much wider reach than the members of the upper and aspiring middle classes who could afford his books, Ruskin had zealously set about producing a series of essays solely addressed to his pupils at the Working Men's College, and he placed the unfinished, ink-splattered manuscript to one side of the eleven immaculately bound volumes standing on the table before him.

Knowing the attention of the entire crowd to be concentrated upon his actions, Ruskin suspended the interest of his audience by pausing for a moment, then, without giving any warning, he rushed forwards and violently flung the books onto the floor with a loud bang, causing the men to jump and mutter to one another in surprise.

Taking up the unbound manuscript entitled *Unto This Last* he had earlier put aside, Ruskin raised his arm high and held the work aloft for all to see, declaring with as much passion as if it were his last opportunity of speech, 'I have something to say which I believe to be true and useful or helpfully beautiful, that I would set down forever, engrave on a rock if I could, saying "This is the best of me. For the rest, I ate, drank and slept, loved and hated like another. My life was as the vapour, and is no more, but this I saw and knew, this, if anything of mine, is worth your memory." I dedicate this volume to *you*,' he went on, as if addressing each man individually. 'If I can leave only one work behind me then let it be *this*. If I can *say* only one thing of any merit or meaning then let me say *this*. There. Is. No. Wealth. But. Life.'

The audience again murmured, so impressed were they by the fervour and power of his words, even if they were not entirely sure of the context or meaning, and just as they broke into rapturous applause Maurice entered, who, having no idea what had produced such a response but not wishing to interrupt Ruskin's flow, remained leaning against the door frame.

Ruskin noticed the college's founder, but was encouraged rather than distracted by his presence, for Maurice was a man he greatly respected, although he believed that his altruism had made him too egotistical. At the age of fifty-three his grave yet noble face, which fully illustrated the struggles he had endured in the name of righteousness, lit up on observing his star educator's immense influence over the men, for, however much he was grateful to all the teachers who gave their time to the college, it was Ruskin above all who best comprehended the glory of true and selfless compassion.

'Man should not desire to be rich, but content,' Ruskin continued in his statesmanlike manner. 'Too long has our society been under the illusion that rising to a different class is the answer to everything and that the main benefit of education is to keep a good coat on your son's back, enabling him to ring with confidence at double-belled doors and eventually possess a double-belled door himself. In a word, education shall lead to advancement in life and this we pray for on bent knees, forgetting that the richest country is that which nourishes the greatest number of noble and happy human beings.'

Ruskin paced the stage as if searching for the answer, looking down one moment or rubbing his chin and shaking his head the next. Then, as if finding the solution all at once, he turned and faced the men again. 'And what *makes* men happy, you may ask.'

He paused fleetingly before offering them the answer. 'To watch the corn grow, to read, to think, to love, to hope, to pray, *these* are the things that make men happy. It is not always just a question of you workmen being ill fed but that you take no pleasure or pride in the work by which you make your bread, prompting you to look to wealth as your only means of nourishment. *I* mean to teach you not how to better yourselves but how to *satisfy* yourselves. It is written "in the sweat of thy brow" but it was never written "in the breaking of thine heart" thou shalt eat bread. I am not taking up the common socialist idea of division of property. Division of property is its destruction, and the destruction of all hope, all industry and all justice. The socialist, seeing a strong man, cries, "Break his arms!" but I say, "Teach him to use them to better purpose".'

He continued to expand on the subject for several minutes as he casually strolled up and down the stage as if he were pondering on an idea that had just sprung into his head. It therefore came to the audience as something of a surprise when their teacher abruptly stopped in his tracks and, scanning each face in the crowd, asked, 'Will you pardon me if I pause for a moment and put what you may consider an impertinent question to you? I can't go on unless I feel, or know, whether you are either with me or against me, I don't much care *which*. In order to establish what you think, will those who admit that love of advancement is your strongest motivation in life, and not that of performing any kind of duty, raise your hand?'

Before the workmen had a chance to respond, however, their attention was momentarily distracted by Rossetti entering and standing beside Maurice, both being subsequently bemused when around a dozen men raised their arms in the air, although the artist was not aware what had prompted them to do so.

While it was impossible for Ruskin to fathom if the men believed him to be in earnest, or if those who had raised their arms really *did* carry out their work fuelled by a class-driven ambition, he was nonetheless pleased to find that only a fifth of his audience were sceptical of his philosophy.

Remarking, 'I see,' he warmly invited; 'now you may ask *me* anything you like.'

40

Most of the workmen shifted or looked to their nearest neighbour in confusion, but after a moment Ruskin noticed that one of the fellows who had recently raised his hand lifted it again in order to do just that, an act he graciously encouraged, 'Please speak, you have my full attention.'

The man, dirty from his exertions as a steam train stoker, cleared his throat, as if he had never uttered a word publicly before, and challenged resentfully, 'How can you claim to know about working men when you've never done a day's hard labour in your life?'

Ruskin, resting his chin on his right hand and cupping his elbow in the left, replied thoughtfully, 'It is a fair point, but though I might live outside your world that doesn't mean I cannot understand anything about it;' and, widening his gaze to encompass the entire room, he went on authoritatively, 'I am the son of a merchant and would far rather be nobly remembered than nobly born. Who do you suppose knows more about the Lake of Geneva, I or the fish in it?'

The sentiment, met with howls of laughter and applause, proved a fine way to conclude the lecture and commence the ensuing art class, with Maurice looking on in delight as if what he had just witnessed was the realisation of all that he had ever worked for.

Rossetti, on the other hand, was more entertained than convinced and felt compelled to nudge Maurice and remark, 'Ruskin's a dear old chap, isn't he? But he does talk such awful rubbish!'

Formless and planless as these classes were, their effect on the audience was immense, as was the popularity Ruskin enjoyed, with Maurice noting that *his* classes, above all teachers, were always the most over-subscribed.

In turn, Ruskin possessed a deep affection for his pupils and was gratified to share such possessions as might assist them in observing the beauties of the natural world, nor was he content for lessons always to be restricted to the poorly lit and draughty college rooms, one day ordering enough hansom cabs to transport all the men to the country for a day's sketching, followed by a hearty supper at a local inn, paid for out of his own pocket.

On another occasion Ruskin went so far as to invite the entire class to Denmark Hill where, after showing them his extensive collections of minerals and Turners, he nourished them with tea and cake, much to the bewilderment of the stoical Margaret who nevertheless played the semi-gracious hostess.

Ruskin's spontaneous propositions were not always supported or tolerated by his parents, however, and he was met with thunderous objection when his father chanced to enter the drawing room on the day he was instructing two men in removing his most prized Turners, which had been a prominent feature for almost twenty years.

Impressing on the men the importance of taking great care with the artworks, Ruskin was initially oblivious as to his father's consternation and moved on to another and yet another work which he ordered them to carry away. Struck dumb by the scene, John James was forced to look on in horror while a collection which had taken him so many years to establish, not to mention a substantial sum of money to acquire, was carried off under his very nose.

'I have decided to gift our Turners to Oxford and Cambridge University,' Ruskin informed his father casually.

'You're going to do *what?*' John James responded, apoplectic.

'I know you're going to be angry with me, Father, but it's something I *must* do,' he explained, as though his actions were perfectly understandable. 'Far from being a good thing, my love of art has become a terrible temptation to me and one which I have become overly self-indulgent in trying to satisfy.'

'Rather *I* have been too indulgent with *you,*' he huffed, following Ruskin about the room as he continued to direct the removal of the paintings, there already being several darker patches along the walls where some of the most prized works had hung.

'Stop this at once!' John James beseeched. 'How can you have the audacity to carry off my property without scruple or remorse?' He paused only in astonishment and in order to better prepare his thoughts before surmising, 'I suppose it's this new book of yours that's done it; accumulation of luxury no longer accords with your doctrines. That's it! You're afraid of being accused of hypocrisy,' he condemned, 'yet, to my mind, forsaking possessions that are not even *yours* to dispense with makes you a *greater* hypocrite. It's a strange form of charity when all you give away are monies you haven't sweated to earn.'

Yet all his protestations fell disregarded and, despite knowing his father spoke reasonably and with words that caused him a considerable pang, Ruskin continued on without showing any sign of emotion for, whilst John James believed himself to have made a valid point, as always his son thought he had made a *better* one.

Whilst composing his latest work Ruskin had been inspired to look more closely at his own life and its potential meaning, with the result that he now felt a sense of shame at having only previously spent time and money on whatever afforded him pleasure. He refused to accept the allegation that he was displaying double standards, for he did not dispose of his father's chattels with any degree of carelessness, rather he would have been *more* generous with his own belongings.

'You always say that you wish to make me happy,' he appealed to John James; 'well, the only thing you can do for me is to let me follow out my work in my own way.'

'When have I ever done anything *but* what you asked?' he replied, astonished at the impudence. 'First you convince me of the wisdom in purchasing Turners and of their certain rise in value, and then, without so much as conferring with me, you take it upon yourself to strip the walls and cart off my pictures I know not where!'

'Turner created these works so that people might look on them, not to ornament drawing rooms or enable us to showcase our wealth.' And Ruskin stopped abruptly in order to direct the removal men before going on with his sermon. 'Like all rich men, when I ask what you want to *do* with your money, you never know. In truth you don't increase your fortune to do anything particular *with* it but only because you *can*, and when I say, "What will you do next?" you reply, "Well, I'll get more money", just as in cricket the sportsman always wants to get more runs. There's no use in the runs apart from to get more than other people in the game and, likewise, you have devoted your life to the great foul city of London, rattling, growling, smoking and stinking – a ghastly heap of fermenting brickwork pouring out poison at every pore – and for what real purpose?'

'You don't know you're born. When I was your age I had slaved for years just to settle my father's debts. Criticising the very hand that feeds you is not only ungrateful but the epitome of superciliousness,' John James railed, severely cross and bitterly wishing that he had not always been so quick to give in to his son's whims, for he regarded this as just another act of wilfulness and blamed himself for not having checked such capricious behaviour while he still had some influence. 'I sometimes wonder that you did not end up a clergyman as your mother always intended, for your talent for preaching is surely greater than any man alive.'

'Far be it from me to teach my own father anything,' Ruskin rejoined sarcastically, becoming increasingly impassioned, 'but I believe that the richest men are those who, having perfected the functions of their *own* lives to the utmost, have also the widest helpful influence, both personal and by means of their possessions, over the lives of *others*.'

Despite vociferously refusing to submit to this argument, John James raged in vain, for Ruskin ended by sending forty-eight artworks to Oxford and a further twenty-five to Cambridge, and no interference could have stopped him, even if he had known that the incident would mark the beginning of a bitter rift between them.

This, so Ruskin later considered, was the consequence of an increasing impatience both men had felt towards the other for some time. John James, now in his declining years, was deeply resentful of having his authority contested by his son, quite aside from seeing items given away that *he* alone had so painfully toiled for and which he had intended Ruskin to inherit. At least then John James would not have had to endure the pain of witnessing his acquisitions scattered to the winds, for it was not that he claimed to love Turner as much as his son but that the paintings had come to symbolise his greatest struggles and were the tangible result of so many years of sacrifice.

Ruskin meanwhile believed that this was ultimately a selfish kind of parental love, which had not and never could help him and was cruelly hurtful without meaning to be.

John James's large fortune, and, more importantly, the means by which it had been amassed, sparked an increasing dilemma; for whilst Ruskin considered himself to share old Tory values, a more radical and anti-capitalist form of political belief was beginning to find its voice.

ROSE ABROAD

Spring was beginning to stir as Ruskin looked out on the frost-covered garden of Denmark Hill from his bedroom window. He had awoken early due to anticipating a visit from the La Touches, yet though he had risen in near darkness he noticed that the morning sun was fast chasing away the chill of night.

It had been some time since the family had last been in London, and Rose had no doubt much altered, so Ruskin pondered while he dressed, amusing himself by trying to picture the various ways in which he might observe changes, for there was a new Rose every six months.

Having turned thirteen in January, Rose had evolved into an ever more animated and precocious girl, yet however much he always longed to see her it was with some foreboding, for he never knew when she would finally be too old to pet him or too self-conscious to be called "Rosie Posie".

It was not fear of her growing up that made Ruskin feel thus, but only a dread that she would withdraw her affection on following the rules of propriety which her mother would inevitably teach her as she approached adolescence and adulthood. The days of tutoring her were also sadly numbered and, perhaps very soon, he would have to content himself with admiring his talented pupil at a modest distance.

He tried to put such thoughts away and carry on with his work until they arrived, but his imagination always brought him around to the imminent visit. Soon enough he heard the sound of their carriage making its way down the drive, and one look from Rose, who was the first to alight, reassured him that her former attachment remained, for she rushed to greet him, as did Emily, in quite their old manner and without the least observance of any formal customs.

Mrs La Touche, who was always the last of the three guests to receive any notice from Ruskin, looked equally well, so he finally complimented her, although he perceived from her caustic response that she was affronted by his lack of attention: 'Yes, I am well, but if only I were young enough to still be petted.'

Saying which, the lady elongated her neck haughtily and offered Margaret, who was standing in the doorway, a posy of snowdrops, which the old woman accepted warmly in the hope of making up for her son's oversight.

Whilst they all took tea in the drawing room, Mrs La Touche, who had almost forgiven Ruskin for his ill-manners, particularly directed her announcement to him. 'This year we're planning to extend our annual tour of the French Riviera to include Italy and the cities of Genoa and Florence, and we'd be grateful for any guidance you might offer on what sights the girls should look out for.'

'I can do so of course, though I would prefer them to discover things for themselves. When I was a young man I wanted to go everywhere and be in twenty places at once,' Ruskin recalled fondly, 'only I never travelled as extensively as I should have liked due to always being obliged to stop in the middle of one thing in order to take note of another. Now I wish that I had simply *looked* more.'

'We have the advantage of being able to look upon everything you suggest,' Mrs La Touche interjected flatteringly, 'and therefore not a moment will be wasted.'

'I don't think it is possible for time ever to be *wasted* in Florence,' he corrected, 'only you'll almost certainly have too little of it. You have probably allowed half an hour for Santa Maria Novella, half an hour for San Lorenzo, an hour for the museum of sculpture at the Bargello, an hour for shopping, and then it will be lunchtime, and you mustn't be late because you are to leave by the afternoon train and must be in Rome the next morning.'

'You are making fun of me, Mr Ruskin,' she protested, arching her neck and looking down her nose in order to show her displeasure, 'but I'd like to think that I'm not the average continental tourist.'

'No, indeed, that was ungenerous of me; it just frustrates me that I have spent days, years, studying art most people will only *glimpse* at on a foreign tour, and that's almost worse than never seeing a thing. Take St Peter's for example. Pshaw! I never saw so much good marble and ground wasted. The Romans don't know what architecture means, it's all bigness and blaze with them. As for the Duomo in Florence, whilst it has an effective exterior, nothing but marble and jasper, it's a regular begin-to-build-and-not-able-to-finish affair, a mere shell with no inside, a fine craniological development with no brains, a Pharisaical piece of ecclesiastical hypocrisy.'

'You don't believe in half measures, do you, Mr Ruskin?' Mrs La Touche remarked, laughing.

'I apologise for the rant but Rose must understand what lies ahead. There is something so amusing in how seriously the Italian devout take themselves. Yet, amid all the solemnity, I will never forget seeing a beggar enter a church with his dog, who, following his master to the holy water stoup, cocked his leg against the pedestal, reminding me that, after all, "dog" is only "god" spelt backwards.'

It took some time for Ruskin's numerous European tales to be exhausted, with Mrs La Touche pressing him to relate which Veronese and Titian paintings they should seek out in the Louvre, while he voluntarily provided enthusiastic descriptions of his favourite views in Southern France, such as the beautiful pass of the Esterel mountains.

On noticing that Rose was beginning to look bored and was impatient for his bluster to be over, however, he suggested that she take a turn with him in the garden, while Emily, now seventeen and more conservative and homely than her younger sister, preferred to remain behind, conversing with the ladies.

They stepped into bright sunshine and Ruskin felt a thrill as Rose took his arm without waiting for him to offer it, but this pleasure only made him resentful that she should soon embark on a journey that would divide them for so long, a self-indulgence which caused him guilt when he noticed her regarding his solemn face questioningly, sensing that something was amiss.

'You seem kingfishery today,' Rose, ever discerning, confronted him.

'Whatever do you mean?' he asked, bemused by her inventive appellations.

'Why, sitting sulkily on a branch! Is it because you gave away the Turners you love so much? It was so good of you.'

Her empathy was the sweetest consolation of all and, touched by her sensitivity, he replied, 'No, it isn't that. I am thankful for the few works I still possess, although I admit that it's more the gratitude of a man who has just seen the destruction of his dearest treasures in a house fire. It requires some philosophy not to think of what I have lost.'

'But if that isn't causing you to be gloomy, what is?' Rose enquired, pausing to consider for a moment before proceeding with her interrogation. 'Because I'm going away next week?' she asked penetratingly.

He could not deny it, such were her powers of reading both his thoughts and his unease in expressing them. 'How is it that you always know what I'm thinking?' he admitted, smiling. 'It quite unnerves me.'

Rose tossed her head airily and teased, 'I can observe more than a silly old still life,' to which Ruskin laughed heartily as they continued winding their way along the path of the vegetable garden. 'This will be my last visit to Denmark Hill for ever so long,' she went on after taking great delight in his amusement.

'Seeing new things will be good for you,' he encouraged, feeling himself generous for saying so; 'you must make drawings of all that you discover and bring them home for me.'

'I will, I promise. You've taught us so much,' Rose extolled. 'I shall send you accounts of everywhere we visit.'

Ruskin, despite hearing his father's warnings resonating as she said this, could not bring himself to refuse a bridge between his desperate loneliness and the radiant reports of Europe which Rosie would be sure to furnish him with, a temptation only enforced by her suddenly standing on tiptoe and kissing his cheek. Rose giggled at his boyish blushes and, tugging his arm, encouraged him to walk further into the garden with her in order to inspect and feed the animals, her favourite occupation at Denmark Hill.

His one consolation was that she not only seemed a little sorry to be going away, but understood, in the most curious way, how sorry *he* was. Having so recently believed that he would never find any person to devote himself to, convinced that he would be content to live out the rest of his existence quite alone and with only work to sustain him, Ruskin now realised how completely this little unsuspecting creature had changed everything. He marked this day as a new epoch of life, in which Rose was always with him and all he did was for her sake.

As faithfully as she had promised, Rose commenced a travel diary on the day the family journeyed from London, with the intention of copying extracts to send to Ruskin as they progressed, first to Calais and Paris, where they were to stay five days, then on to Toulon, Fréjus, Nice, Genoa and Florence.

Yet, like all things overly anticipated, Rose felt homesick and mournful rather than excited at the prospect of being so far from home, especially as the countryside to Dover was not very enlivening for such an impressionable young girl filled with expectation, and who, understandably intoxicated by Ruskin's descriptions of the many beautiful landscapes in store for her, was disappointed on first looking out of her carriage window to see flat, flinty plains and stacks of newly-ploughed hops dotted over barren, desolate-looking fields.

Rose was therefore already in an ill temper by the time she boarded the steamer to Calais, made worse when it turned out to be a rough crossing.

On being deposited safely on the other side, she became unnecessarily hostile towards the Frenchmen in the customs house, who babbled away at her incomprehensibly, and her mother and father shouted at her when she made use of the slang French she had picked up from a couple of sailors.

By the time she arrived in Paris, however, her judgement had become much more favourable and she was subsequently all admiration on seeing the artworks which Mr Ruskin had suggested they study at the Louvre, particularly the Venus de Milo, which prompted her to exclaim, on her mother asking her opinion, 'It's so perfectly lovely, despite her arms being broken off!'

From Rose's reports on the inconvenience of a grasshopper trying to make friends with her whilst she attempted to sketch Toulon Harbour, to an account of Fréjus as "a dirty sort of town", along with countless complaints as to the inn they were staying at and the bad suppers they were subjected to, Ruskin eagerly awaited such snatches of news, along with her amusing, rich and detailed impressions of each new place she arrived at, whether she described her thoughts on the various treasures any given place was famed for or the people she encountered along the way.

Attempting to ignore his father's sneers whenever a letter with a French postmark arrived, it was to his mother that Ruskin appealed when he wanted to share some amusing anecdote written by either of the La Touche girls, and fortunately Margaret delighted in these vivid narratives almost as much as he.

'"We went to the Louvre,"' so Ruskin read aloud to his mother from Rose's latest letter one morning, '"and oh how we thought of you! How we looked and talked about the Titians you told us about". While she thinks Nice too cockneyfied,' he went on, raising his eyebrows and chuckling to himself as he scanned the document for the snippets his mother would find most charming. '"The sun was hot, the winds were strong and the glens one mass of foliage, with every leaf throwing back flashes of sunlight" – isn't that pretty?'

Ruskin was always careful to avoid reciting Rose's most tender passages, however, and would keep these for reading in private, when he would take pleasure in scrutinising some sentences in which she had been particularly affectionate.

Quite aside from the pleasure he found in receiving the first really long letters she had ever written him, he considered Rose's observations well beyond the maturity other adolescents would have displayed, nor did he find any sign of vanity contained within them. Although any well taught girl might have a certain command of language, he doubted if they could have expressed things with the amount of sincerity or intuition that *she* did.

Not only were Rose's letters filled with prettily composed descriptions of pictures, statues, flowers and views, it seemed to Ruskin that there was not a line in which she thought of herself. Despite being hundreds of miles away, she appeared only to consider what *he* was thinking and gloried in retracing the discoveries he had made before her.

It was this sympathy that was the unique quality of her letters, which she now provocatively termed "visits", and from which he took solace in the early hours of the morning when insomnia prevented him from sleeping, brought on by anxiety as to what the future might hold.

Smiling wistfully and allowing himself to lap up the flattery she embellished all her communications with, he re-examined her choicest remarks, such as, "Who but the golden-mouthed author of *Modern Painters* could describe such scenery? Irish Roses can't! Oh I think of you so much and all your dearnesses to me. I wish so very much that you were happy."

Questioning her meaning in every line, whilst doubting his own interpretation, he wondered if he was foolhardy to harbour the notion that Rose might *one* day be his, and chastised himself for picturing her in the guise of a wife, years hence, when he couldn't seriously hope to be attractive to one so much younger, nor could he know how the intervening years would shape her affection. It was as intriguing as waiting for the world to awaken on a summer's morning.

Thoughts of this kind were interrupted precipitously when, several weeks into the family's itinerary, an alarming letter arrived from Mrs La Touche, then stationed in Florence where the maternal-looking, red-roofed

Duomo stood overshadowing the cool turquoise of Santa Croce where Ruskin had instructed Rose to go by the pale light of sunrise and study the Giotto frescoes one by one.

As Rose's mother was by no means Ruskin's favourite correspondent, he did not open the greeting with any particular anticipation or urgency and put the packet, with its elaborate wax seal, to one side for an entire day. He thought it charming to read her daughter's effusive narrations but decidedly idiotic when similar observations were made by a lady old enough to exercise some restraint.

Recoiling at the idea of Mrs La Touche's saccharine tone of correspondence, Ruskin eventually decided to brave reading it in the drawing room after dinner in the company of his parents, for he thought it might at least amuse *them*. It was only when he examined the envelope more closely that he observed her handwriting was not as neat and flamboyantly styled as usual, nor had he expected, on scanning its content, to find it so short and obviously hurried.

Margaret and John James naturally anticipated that some disaster had occurred when his expression suddenly became clouded, and his mother enquired anxiously, 'Has there been some kind of accident?'

Ruskin, stunned, took some minutes to reply while he went over the note more carefully, relating, 'Rose has been taken ill with fever,' before going on to read aloud Mrs La Touche's brief account of the child's ailment, though his mouth became parched with emotion and fear as the full horror of the situation unfolded. The words condensed themselves one into another on his tongue as the tears began to fall unchecked down his face, a display of emotion his parents had never before witnessed.

Margaret, assuming from his reaction that the child was close to death, became frustrated at having to wait for snatches of information while her son attempted to compose himself, and quizzed impatiently, 'Is it very bad, do you think?'

'I'm not sure,' he answered vaguely, rising to his feet in agitation and announcing, 'I should go to her.'

'But she's in Italy!' Margaret exclaimed so incredulously that her pince-nez almost dropped off her nose. 'You can't mean it?'

'Of course, but first I must consider the fastest method,' he returned, resting his chin on his hand as he paced the room, brooding. 'I could walk to Camberwell Green, take a cab to London Bridge and then a direct train. It will only take Crawley a moment to pack a few things and we can be there by tomorrow night.'

'What on earth do you hope to do for her when you get there?' John James challenged, astonished at his son's lack of sense or decorum. 'Her parents will think it most irregular. Have patience and wait for Mrs La Touche to send word of an improvement. Doubtless it is just a childhood illness that Rose will make a complete recovery from.'

Saying which, John James glared at his wife by way of rallying for support, in the hope that *her* words, if not his own, might convince their son to quell such erratic, impassioned behaviour.

'Your father is right; why not wait until there is more news? They will no doubt make their way home as soon as the child is well enough to travel,' Margaret suggested persuasively.

But Ruskin, who could only imagine Rose fading by the hour, refused to listen, and turning to his father demanded, 'How can you be certain that she *will* return?'

'I'm quite sure you won't do any good by going,' he answered resolutely, mopping his overheated forehead with a handkerchief and implying that his son would be disobeying him were he to proceed.

With one unexpected turn of events, Ruskin's feelings had been revealed utterly, and no amount of persuasion would take the root of love out of his heart.

John James knew it not to be a poisonous kind, though how others might perceive it, were it to be discovered by some error of judgement such as him running off to Italy to be by Rose's bedside, ruined that night's repose and many others afterwards.

Taking inspiration from the great Italian mind, St Thomas Aquinas, Ruskin turned to the Book of Wisdom for advice and was struck by the words, "I willed, and Sense was given me, I prayed, and the spirit of Wisdom came upon me…"

***

Rose remained confined to bed in the apartment her parents had rented close to the Piazza della Signoria and the Uffizi gallery, oblivious of the tension she had inadvertently caused between Ruskin and his father or the anxiety her own parents underwent as they watched over her day and night, isolated in a foreign city, ignorant of the language and distrustful of the Italian doctors who approached their daughter's malady with as little concern as a common cold.

Despite their scepticism of the advice, however, Rose gradually began to improve after several weeks, proving that the physicians had been wise to allow the fever to run its course and ebb away of its own accord.

Ruskin meanwhile waited impatiently for Mrs La Touche's sporadic and delayed letters with news of her daughter, having eventually listened to reason, whether his father's, God's or St Thomas's he was not quite sure. He knew barely any sympathy from his mother and none at all from John James who had been greatly dismayed by his outburst and viewed his son's affection towards his pupil as wholly inappropriate.

The days leading up to Mrs La Touche's coveted announcement that her daughter had made a sign of recovery were interminable, with Ruskin barely leaving his study, a room which overlooked the garden he had so recently talked in with Rose, prompting him to recall her sweet kiss and the impression of her gentle, bud-like lips upon his cheek.

John James's lack of empathy destroyed all confidence between them, prompting him to withdraw from his father's company altogether in order to avoid being lectured, for the idea of losing Rose confirmed his love for her irrefutably and made him turn away from anyone who would judge him or mistake his devotion for something corrupt.

But this self-imposed solitude only served to increase his despondency and gave him too many hours to dwell upon the hopelessness of his predicament. There was but one person he could go to with his head in his hands and ask for help, and thus he found himself on his knees one night, praying fervently for Rose to be spared in exchange for promising to quell, or at least conceal, his attachment as best he could.

OF QUEENS' GARDENS

T HE BLOSSOM ON THE CHERRY AND MAGNOLIA TREES OF Denmark Hill was already past its prime, with more petals lying on the ground than on the branches, although it was hardly a loss due to other species beginning to burgeon, while all the borders around the garden were colourfully heightened by the palest pink, white and purple tulips.

The occasion on which Rosie had last taken a turn around the garden with Ruskin seemed like an age when Mrs La Touche came to call with her daughters one quiet afternoon in May, an event which caused him to spend the morning in a state of frenzy and expectation.

His fears of never seeing Rose again had almost driven him to madness and he was so relieved to find her health restored that he struggled to contain his joy during the polite conversation which his mother and Mrs La Touche subjected him to in the drawing room, too stuffy a place for such a jubilant occasion.

He wanted to leap up and express his overwhelming happiness to see his dear one, who looked alarmingly fragile in the colourful dress and hat her mother had chosen for her in Paris which emphasised her white pallor and was of a style far too fashionable for someone of her years.

Nor was Rose's physical appearance the only alteration; her illness and recuperation had taken away a part of her carefree spirit. She was more demure and womanly than before, not least whenever Ruskin happened to catch her Wedgewood-blue eyes, for she would avert hers in uncharacteristic timidity.

How quickly she seems to be growing up! he thought as he scrutinised every hair on her head in the hope of finding something unchanged. *She's only been away three months yet it's like trying to paint clouds at sunrise – just when you think you have captured them, they move to create a new picture.*

Trying to restrain his fascination took a considerable effort of will and he therefore thought it was better to listen rather than talk. Whenever he did speak, he found that his usual eloquence escaped him, and his mother, as matriarchal as ever, would demand that he reiterate anything that did not quite reach her ear.

'John, what was that you said?' she bellowed, or 'John, I'm sure you're talking more softly than usual,' and although he would dutifully oblige her by repeating himself, he felt exhausted at having to do this *so* very often and deemed it easier to remain silent, something both Rose and her mother noticed with surprise.

'We're delighted to see that Rose has made such a good recovery,' Margaret observed to Mrs La Touche, and, turning to her son, added pertinently, 'aren't we, John?'

'Naturally,' Ruskin answered with a broken voice.

Mrs La Touche smiled at mother and son in condescending gratitude before offering them a typically narcissistic account, not of her daughter's suffering but of the anxiety she had undergone.

'It was a great concern, especially being so far from home. I still blame myself, for I fear the itinerary was simply too much for poor Rose. How well I remember being almost killed when I was fifteen years old,' she recalled, placing her hand to her bosom theatrically. 'My mother showed me all the sights of Paris and then we embarked on an instructive tour of Europe's best picture galleries, palaces and cathedrals, yet by the time

I returned home I was reduced to lying on sofas or being pushed around in a Bath chair!'

'Goodness, did you take very long to recover?' Margaret asked without managing to disguise her false interest, for the lady's habit of exaggerating mundane events irritated her.

'Several months. That is why my education stopped so abruptly and I learnt no more than I could discover through reading the words of wiser people than I,' Mrs La Touche stated almost boastfully. 'If only *Modern Painters* or *The Stones of Venice* had been published when I was Rose's age.'

But Ruskin did not catch the compliment due to talking aside with Rose in hushed tones, oblivious that her mother never averted her attention from them and became decidedly interested when he took up Rose's ice-cold hand momentarily and pressed it, so moved was he on noticing the signs of weakness that still lingered.

Forced to let her hand fall away on noticing that the gesture arrested Mrs La Touche's speech and caused her to stare at him questioningly, he became sheepish at his incongruous action and, walking over to the French doors, suggested that Rosie and he might take a turn about the garden as they always did, for he simply could not express his delight at seeing Rose in the presence of either her mother or his own.

The sun shone down on his magnificent Rose as though it had waited to come out expressly to alight its rays upon her hair, golden and slightly tinged with copper so as to make it glint like the most precious metal. It seemed a little lighter for the sun she had already been exposed to abroad and lent her a more angelic quality, like that of Botticelli's Venus, coupled with a new gravity of bearing which he supposed emanated from her gravest hours of illness.

'You frightened me out of my wits,' he confessed as soon as they were safely out of earshot and view, 'so much that I even prayed, begged Him not to take you away.'

'It worked. Does that mean that you believe in God now?' Rose asked provocatively.

'No, but I have more faith than I did,' he conceded; before explaining sorrowfully, 'the irony is that my mother devoted me to God before I was born.'

'But you rebelled,' she returned, smiling sadly.

'Yes, it's a supreme disappointment to my parents that I'm not the Archbishop of Canterbury right now,' he announced facetiously.

'That's nonsense,' she laughed, determined to keep up the light-hearted nature of the conversation rather than humour his tendency towards self-pity.

'It's perfectly true,' Ruskin assured her, looking up at the sky thoughtfully, 'although my father would probably have preferred me to be the next Tennyson.'

'Why aren't you?' Rose teased.

'I couldn't see how it was possible to write fine poetry when all my excitement was drawn from art and not from any *living* passion,' he confided. 'Early on I decided that I would far rather be a first-rate shoemaker than a second-rate poet, though in the end I turned out to be neither.'

'You mustn't say such things; your parents love you so much and are proud of everything you accomplish. We all are,' she encouraged, smiling up at him.

'I've written a few books, that is all,' he argued. 'I can't write poetry, draw, sing or ride.'

'You can't be good at everything, aren't you always telling *me* that?' Rose reassured, taking a folded page of one of his latest essays from her pocket and showing him how well-thumbed it was. 'I would sacrifice all the other talents if I could write like *this*.'

Ruskin smiled and declared, 'Your mother says it is *I* who spoil *you*, but the real hurt is all the other way.'

She looked at the ground solemnly and they were silent for several moments, though it was the quietude which only the most natural companions share and therefore not one either hastened to break. The breeze blowing the heavy magnolia petals onto the lawn offered something they could both observe, whilst Rose even stooped to pick a couple up and put them in her pocket.

'I've been ordered by my doctor to take a holiday,' Ruskin eventually continued, looking towards the horizon and suddenly beginning to feel tired.

'Really? Well, I shan't take any more holidays,' she remarked sarcastically, making him laugh. 'Where will you go?'

'France.' And they stepped into the budding orchard and followed the path around the enclosed walled garden, upon which countless stone-fruit trees rested their spines, their arms fully extended as if resigned to their endless crucifixion.

Creasing her brow out of concern and frustration at again being deprived of his company, Rose asked, 'You're not unwell?'

'I hardly know. My symptoms may be nothing or everything.'

She stopped in her tracks, 'Everything?'

'I suppose it's just exhaustion from overdoing things,' he retreated, touched at her kindness but wary of admitting that her perilous illness had been a greater challenge to his equilibrium than he had at first realised. 'I am better when I can be quiet, yet the least worry puts me all wrong again. The one thing I need, so my physician says, is rest.'

'So do I,' she nodded. 'Let us both rest this summer and when you return visit us in Ireland? I'm sure Mama would be delighted to show you the estate, and you've never had the chance to get to know my father.'

It was the idea of observing Rose in her natural environment and not the prospect of getting better acquainted with the pious John La Touche that appealed to Ruskin and made him rush to agree to the proposal without weighing up the potential folly of doing so.

'I would like that very much,' he replied, shaking the dainty hand she held out to him by way of sealing the agreement, prompting him to recollect their very first meeting when she had boldly crossed the floor to greet him. How much had changed, he thought, regarding her graceful features and frank, open expression. Perhaps it was just as well not to guess what the end would be.

ROSE MYSTÉRIEUSE

T HE COLOURFUL FISHING BOATS OF BOULOGNE HARBOUR were scorched by the July sun as Ruskin, with his shirtsleeves rolled up and no longer restricted by a necktie, sat on a wall that was too hot to touch, sketching.

Trying to keep cool by intermittently fanning himself with his straw hat, a worsening headache across his forehead told him that he had sat in the heat of the day far too long, yet he was transfixed by the scene before him and the desire to capture the lives and livelihoods which those boats signified, for there was something so evocative in watching them going out to sea without knowing if they would return.

Having arrived several weeks earlier, he could generally be found on that same wall or on the beach where he would stare at the sea for hours, yet he felt far from rejuvenated, it being a curse of his nature that he became horribly melancholy whenever he allowed himself any time to think, the very thing he was trying to avoid.

Wherever he turned there were reminders of Rose that took his thoughts on a tangent entirely opposite to that which he went there for; and no matter how ludicrous he convinced himself it was to always be finding symbolism in the ordinary or coincidental, he could not help the tricks his mind continued to play.

Laying down his pencil for a moment, he was distracted by the name inscribed on a small blue and white fishing boat, *Rose Mystérieuse*, and rising from his seat he observed the vessel for several minutes before settling down again and continuing with the sketch.

Acutely alert to every possible reference to his flower, who was now in Ireland for the summer, whilst he had initially derived amusement from the fact that the harbour was ironically named Port d'Amour, this latest observation made him anxious as to whether these signs were merely a worrying indication of his growing obsession, for wouldn't there always be a sign if he desired one?

Not being able to reconcile this, Ruskin tried to take it all, as with the rest of life, as something between a jest and a dream.

Forcing himself to make the best of each passing moment, he no longer chastised himself for recalling Rose and made sure that he was on the harbour, sketching, by sunrise each day, that being the most pleasant time of day to work, both in terms of quietude and temperature.

By the time the sun was fully risen and the fishing boats were coming in Ruskin found that he had been stationary for many hours without even pausing for refreshment.

Presently, Huret, the captain of the largest lugger which had moored alongside the pier, climbed the steps close to where Ruskin was seated and, tilting his head so as to better inspect the highly detailed drawing not worthy of the time he had dedicated to it, raised his eyebrows and smiled, as if impressed by the likeness.

'Not bad, huh!' Huret complimented, his thick French accent hoarse from years of chewing tobacco and shouting instructions to his men.

'Thank you,' Ruskin appreciated, immediately warming to the Frenchman's intelligent and sincere face.

'I've seen you here before. Are you an artist, monsieur?' the captain enquired with disarming boldness, having noticed Ruskin working in various locations during the past week.

'Unfortunately not,' he replied humbly, 'just an amateur.'

'I see that you are being modest,' Huret dismissed, laughing. 'Englishmen are always modest, even when they defeat us in battle. Are you on holiday alone?' he went on, surprised that this obviously middle-class gentleman would travel abroad without either a companion or servant.

Ruskin nodded wistfully in response.

'You are not married?' the fisherman persisted, shrugging his shoulders and sighing on considering how little chance *he* would ever have of escaping his wife by going off on a painting sojourn.

'Alas, not anymore,' he informed his new acquaintance frankly. Then, realising that this might lead him to assume that he was a widower, he added, 'I, rather like your fish, enjoy swimming against the stream and have never found a woman to swim *with* me.'

'I can help you understand your subject much better,' he assured, motioning theatrically to the great expanse of sea in the distance.

'How so?' Ruskin encouraged with interest, for he welcomed such casual and hospitable familiarity.

'You should come fishing with us tomorrow!' his new comrade insisted, as if he had found the solution to a great problem.

'Oh, I don't know about that,' came the reply, his upbringing going against his natural curiosity.

Perceiving this, Huret, slapping him on the back to show that he would accept no excuses, expounded, 'Don't look so worried, *I* am no amateur,' whilst beating his chest with his fist. '*I* have spent my whole life at sea.'

It was an unlikely friendship, irrelevant of class and founded upon a mutual love of nature's most unpredictable force. Far from either party judging the other on their differences, they sought one another's comradeship because of them.

From that night forward Ruskin regularly went out with Huret and his men, whom he joined in helping to bring home the day's catch whilst admiring their boundless strength and bravery, essential requirements of such a perilous occupation.

On one such occasion, when the wind was high and the only light came from the partially obscured moon and a swaying storm lamp, the whole of La Manche appeared to Ruskin as a tumultuous and phosphorescent beast, with foam containing so many mystical currents of blue fire.

There was a solemnity and thrill in leaving one's fate to a power much greater than humanity, and the speed at which the boat made progress, coupled with the motion and sway of the great waves, both invigorated and alarmed him.

Ruskin felt liberated on watching the fishermen exert themselves and declared to Huret as excitedly as a young boy, 'No human being, however great or powerful, was ever so free as a fish!'

'The little bastards shall not be so free in a moment!' the Frenchman replied fearlessly as he assisted his men in hurling the nets over the side of the boat, an action that made Ruskin want to laugh on considering the unusual circumstance of finding himself a trainee fisherman, not least on imagining what his parents might have said in protest if they could have seen him.

After many hours of waiting, during which time the men told wicked jokes, drank from the hip flask Huret handed around and sang bawdy old French songs, they landed an ambitious catch of mackerel which the men used all their might in heaving up through the dark water, the silver skin of the fishes flashing brightly through the white spray.

Being by no means the strongest of the men, Ruskin was encouraged to take the tiller as Huret and the others sorted through the catch, thus affording him, for the first time in his life, the opportunity of experiencing the warmth of true fellowship, each man content in their designated roles and the labour divided between them according to their strengths. As his fair hair flew and his shirt sleeves billowed in the chill breeze, Ruskin experienced an inexpressible rush of energy as he scanned the vast expanse of water before him, with each undulation seeming to contain a new rainbow of colours.

The freshly caught fish writhed in tubs on the deck and, whilst he had always detested any kind of killing sports, it seemed only natural to join in the gratification of the men in landing such a bounty, especially as this was their only means of making a living and each one of them had followed their fathers and grandfathers into this most romantic of trades.

Ruskin marvelled at how the men had been as merry when they began fishing as if they had been in an alehouse, nay, immeasurably more, but by the time they came out of their oily, tarry, salty black hole to meet the day they did so in perfect peace.

At five o'clock the familiar coastline of England came into view thanks to the amber glow of the sunrise and a nigh-on cloudless sky, with Ruskin observing that they had ventured almost as far as Hastings. Yet, rather than being overcome with fondness at the sight of his homeland, he only felt a strange disconnection to it and a desire to remain in France for as long as possible, or at least until he should receive an invitation from Ireland.

Despite often being hosted by Huret and his wife until the early hours of the morning, Ruskin arose each day with a renewed vitality and would stride energetically out of his hotel, located under the sandhills north of the pier, with the intention of spending his morning outdoors sketching some new scene, just as though he were once again a student of Oxford and keen to make the most of every hour.

Whether collecting shrimps on the beach or observing rock pools, he had gladly adapted to this simplistic way of life, like a dream after the stuffiness of London drawing rooms and dinner parties, and he wondered how he might capture such an atmosphere if he should ever have a home of his own.

No longer so obviously an Englishman due to his tanned face and forearms and sun-bleached sandy hair, Ruskin enjoyed feeling slightly intoxicated after taking two glasses of cider with his lunch and adopted the custom of returning to his hotel for a restorative sleep each afternoon.

Strolling briskly into the lobby after lunching at his usual harbourside café on one such cloudless afternoon, he carried his art materials and creased linen jacket under his arm and whistled to himself cheerfully, thus attracting the attention of the overfed landlady who, seated behind the reception desk engrossed in crocheting, looked up in surprise at the remarkable change in her guest's countenance and demeanour. He was positively serene, she observed with wonder, handsome even, and she quite forgot to give him his letters as he tipped his hat to her and began climbing the stairs.

Suddenly remembering herself, however, she rose to her feet and called after him, 'Monsieur, I have letters for you!' before turning to fetch the bundle from his allocated pigeonhole and hoping that her dark skin would hide the blush revealing her admiration for the Englishman.

Ruskin's heart leapt at the news of mail, but he was reluctant to raise his hopes in case it should not be from whom he most desired. He easily identified his mother's handwriting on the first envelope and the second was clearly Mrs La Touche, yet one look at the immature script on the third packet told him that it was Rosie's.

Much distracted, he thanked the landlady vaguely and shot across the hall, taking the stairs two steps at a time and causing the hotelier to raise her eyebrows in further bemusement. He could hardly wait to enter his sparse chamber, despite its frayed and tired-looking flower-sprig wallpaper and uncomfortable wrought-iron bedstead, for although the room had little to recommend it, save the lovely view of the harbour, he realised that it had been a long time since he had felt happier.

Carelessly throwing his jacket and art materials down on the chair along with the two letters he was least interested in, he collapsed on the bed, shoes and all, in order to enjoy reading Rose's communication to the full.

Having attached some of his sketches of Boulogne to the walls in the attempt to make his surroundings more cheerful, he always made sure that there was a small vase of pink rosebuds on the table by the window and now there was one of her love letters to go with it.

"Dearest St Crumpet," she began, long since dispensing with any formal address and having nicknamed him thus in honour of her governess Miss Bunnett's affectionate title of Bun, "We are all so excited, for Mother and Father say they want you to visit us at Harristown as soon as your sojourn in France is at an end..."

***

When Ruskin announced his imminent departure, Huret invited him to dine with his family by way of a fond farewell, and had it not been for the prospect of shortly seeing Rosie he was not sure he would ever have had the heart to part from them.

Madame Huret was a maternal, rosy-cheeked woman who was as welcoming and jovial as her husband and enjoyed nothing more than serving up large cooking pots filled to the brim with seafood, exhaustively rushing back and forth between the small kitchen and dining room in order to place more food on the table than could possibly be consumed in one sitting.

Huret meanwhile divided up the generous loaf of bread and passed around the butter as Ruskin rolled his shirtsleeves up in anticipation of the feast.

How pretty the Huret girls are, he thought as they both helped their mother in serving the feast, *yet neither, not even the fairest, is as captivating as Rosie.*

On later furnishing his pet with an account of the charming Huret girls, he little realised how provoking she would find it. Vexed to think that she had been usurped, Rose was fiercely resentful of any other girls having entertained Ruskin; and although she was still too young to fully understand romantic love, she was old enough to experience the first pangs of jealousy, stemming from an attachment to her teacher that was as unfathomable as existence itself.

Youth protected her from the ability to recognise these early and obscure feelings, nor did she connect them with her desire to punish Ruskin by sending him an equally detailed account of her introduction to the dashing young Prince of Wales who had recently visited Ireland.

Nineteen years of age, Prince Edward had been sent to the Curragh for military training ahead of his mother The Queen's review of the troops and, despite his inexperience, had received a commission as a lieutenant colonel in the Grenadier Guards, a promotion more related to his station in life than any outstanding ability.

Impossible for him to be anything but a sensation due to the many newspapers featuring extensive coverage of the visit, the Irish ladies fortunate enough to catch a glimpse of him in his scarlet uniform and bearskin thought he made a very fine soldier, while Mrs La Touche was almost more enthusiastic than her daughters when writing Ruskin her own giddy and florid impressions of the royal party which had delighted her by accepting her invitation to luncheon at Harristown.

Rose grew weary as the entire staff bustled about in readiness of the esteemed visitors, for she seemed always to be getting in the way. She had never witnessed such peculiar, and to her mind quite unnecessary preparations, and looked on in wonder as the team of gardeners provided the bustling housemaids with enough cut flowers for a wedding. Kept lawns that would otherwise have been severely sun-scorched were watered and lush, the croquet lawn had been rolled to within an inch of its life, and every flower border had been trimmed as precisely as the cook and her regularly scolded kitchen maids prepared the dainty cucumber sandwiches downstairs.

The troop of footmen polished silver and glassware regardless of whether or not they would be used by the guests, while the butler ordered cases upon cases of champagne to be put on ice in the large marquee assembled for the gathering, just as if the La Touches lived and entertained as lavishly every day of the week.

When so many of their neighbours still struggled to put food on the table, such excess sickened Rose, and she retired to her room until her presence was required rather than look on and worry herself over the inevitable waste. It was not as if one could reasonably take leftover cucumber sandwiches, smoked salmon and champagne to paupers whose usual diet consisted of broth and bread, thought she.

The only blessing was that she had not seen her mother all day, for Mrs La Touche most of all was busy flapping and fussing about the prince's visit, the greatest compliment ever paid to her as a beacon of the Kildare elite, and one that she would never cease reminding all the ladies of her acquaintance about.

And then Rose's stomach turned over at what her mother would write to Ruskin about her, for doubtless she would be said to have been just as excited as everyone else, even though she could hardly wait for the royal party to come and go. However diligently she applied herself to her studies, her mother would always seek to show her as a fickle girl who longed for nothing but attention.

"A grand affair with over eighty guests and all the ladies rustling about in their finest silk gowns, curtseying at the least opportunity," Mrs La Touche boasted to Ruskin, still giddy on the excitement, "Prince Edward was most taken by Rose with whom he played several games of croquet," making her correspondent wish that the royal guest had chosen to be stationed anywhere but near Harristown.

The prince's visit, coming when Ruskin had been holidaying in France for many weeks, prompted him to take the next steamer back to England. Despite sending regular letters to his parents, far more preferable to being with them, consuming a great deal of Normandy cider with the Huret family and working sporadically on his recently commenced autobiography, such a life was too happy to be endured for long.

Yet, before he had even stepped foot upon the shore, he longed for the simple, untroubled existence of Boulogne and to be back in the bright, shabby little room in the Hôtel des Bains with only a Rosie letter for companionship.

Below deck in his small, claustrophobic cabin, he lay on the mattress, as hard as resting on a plank of wood, and removed a lock of Rose's flaxen hair which he had taken away with him as a souvenir of his life back in England.

Turning to look through the porthole, he could see the choppy English Channel and the coast of Dover through the morning fog, but his thoughts were very much focussed on the other coastline soon to be within sight and which kept him daydreaming all the way back to Denmark Hill and his familiar, comfortless home.

HARRISTOWN

O N THE DAY THAT RUSKIN RETURNED TO DENMARK HILL, Mrs La Touche and her daughters were out calling on their cottage tenants. It was early August and, as the weather had been stiflingly humid in Ireland ever since the prince's visit, the party chose to do their rounds in an open carriage, being grateful for any breeze which the drive afforded.

The three attempted to shield themselves from the midday sun with parasols and wide-brimmed straw hats as best they could, although the refinement of their voluminous Irish lace and muslin not only worsened the oppression of the temperature but displayed their wealth to such a degree that Rose felt mortified for the sake of the cottagers, over whom her mother sought to exert her superiority in every way. Mrs La Touche was so condescending in manner that whenever she called on them she ensured they were on no more familiar terms afterwards than if they had never exchanged a word.

Rose watched her mother fanning herself and sighing with growing abhorrence as they trundled along, for she perceived that she was not merely weary of the exhaustive heat but the tediousness of having to give up her day to such an occupation. Nor did Mrs La Touche attempt to conceal her reluctance from her peasant hosts whom she spent no more than ten minutes with apiece, thrusting a token of charity into their palm on her way out by way of easing her conscience, much to the shame of her daughters who were forced to trail behind her whenever she decided to go.

As they approached a small, white cottage, Rose waved familiarly to Mrs Casey, a frail old woman dressed in plain mended clothes who stood outside her humble dwelling eagerly awaiting them, reconciled to her own inferiority and viewing the La Touches as no less than royalty whom it was a privilege to receive, however briefly.

Unmindful of the woman's impoverished appearance or the deep lines on her face which made her look far older than she was, Rose kissed her cheek affectionately before going inside without ceremony. There she continued to show herself a regular visitor by taking a seat without waiting to be offered one.

Her mother on the other hand would have preferred to remain standing if she could have managed it, for her crinoline fairly dwarfed the interior of the cottage, though this did not persuade her to collapse her hoops out of courtesy to Mrs Casey. Instead she proceeded to sit as grandly as a queen until she had exchanged such politenesses as she thought fitting, before bidding her hostess farewell and counting the call as one less that she would have to make that afternoon.

'It is surely nobler to die than to beg if you are in want,' Mrs La Touche announced resentfully as she settled herself in the carriage again.

'She wasn't begging, and even if she had been I cannot see any shame in her doing so if she needed our help,' Rose denied, much alarmed at her mother's barbarity. 'Christianity teaches us to trust and love our neighbours whether we are rich or poor. I see nothing blessed in dying rather than letting a neighbour assist you.'

'Neither you nor your father comprehend how tiresome it is for a woman like myself to live amongst such people,' her mother went on viciously, 'always without proper conversation.' To which Rose responded by rolling her eyes in antipathy.

Suspecting that her daughter had insulted her thus, Mrs La Touche went on archly, 'Still, I will have Mr Ruskin to talk to shortly, and what a relief *that* shall be. Are you looking forward to his visit, Rose?'

'Very much. I had a letter from him this morning urging me to be careful not to let my dress catch on fire,' she reported boastfully, withdrawing the letter from the pocket of her dress but not letting her mother snatch it from her as she tried to do. 'He even enclosed the newspaper article which prompted him to fear for my safety, saying he hoped that I would discontinue wearing taffeta altogether.'

While Emily joined Rose in laughing, Mrs La Touche struggled to conceal her irritation at Ruskin not having shown as much care regarding *her* safety. As soon as the girls' mirth had subsided she raised her chin haughtily and remarked, 'What a strange man he is. I don't know what your father will make of him.'

'He can't help but like him,' Rose rejoined innocently.

'Fathers often get jealous when their daughters have favourites,' Mrs La Touche goaded; 'you saw how he minded when the prince took a shine to you. But then, I dare say Mr Ruskin didn't like it either, for I wrote and told him how unfaithful you had been in his absence.'

'He knows it was only in play and that I shall make it up to him when he visits us,' Rose dismissed sharply, flushing in annoyance. 'Besides, he made friends with some French girls when he was in Boulogne, yet he says he still prefers *me*, and I believe him.'

'I have received a very earnest invitation from the La Touches to holiday with them in Ireland for the month of August,' Ruskin began, blurting out his plans to visit Harristown within the first few moments of being home with his mother and father, 'and I can't very well refuse.'

'A month?' John James repeated in alarm, for both he and Margaret were naturally disappointed to hear that their son had no sooner returned than he was preparing to leave them again.

During his absence Margaret had fallen and fractured her hip and was disheartened to realise that it was not *this* that had brought him back in such a hurry, nor would it persuade him to stay.

'I didn't mean the *entire* month but rather just a part of it,' Ruskin corrected; 'I'm far too busy to spare more than three or four days due to my work.'

'But you would if you *could*? Three days will be quite long enough if you ask me,' his father remarked acerbically, unconvinced of the benefit of such an excursion and wary of his son increasing his intimacy with the La Touches.

'I know well enough, much *too* well in fact, that I am forty-two years of age and that neither riding nor dancing is good for me, but I have promised the girls that I shall see Harristown, and nothing will persuade me to break my word,' he defended emphatically.

Despite continuing with the arrangement, his parents succeeded in making him question his intention to involve himself still further with the family, especially Rose, and by the time he departed Denmark Hill Ruskin had worked himself into a low and anxious mood, which deeply troubled Margaret and John James.

During this fit of depression he dwelt upon his relationship with his parents and what chance he had of ever knowing a happy and peaceful home life in future, where *he* and not his father would be master.

Ruskin also tackled the great question of his existence, and how, or rather *if*, it had anything to do with God, for although he was no scientist he was nonetheless sure that the sun would not go down on the century without there being many answers that would go some way to revealing the unfathomable mysteries that troubled him so.

Ruskin's long-serving, and equally long-suffering, valet Frederick Crawley accompanied him on the journey to Ireland and, although they were friends first and master and servant second, Crawley could not prevail upon his employer to be agreeable during the ferry crossing from Holyhead.

'Although most people might term this "a beautiful passage", that is to say, an entirely dull one, I consider this boat to be the most disagreeable floating contrivance imaginable,' Ruskin condemned, 'its enormous fires continually vomiting volcanofuls of smoke through two funnels as big as railway tunnels, while the colossal power of the engines makes one feel that one isn't on water at all, but on a timber framework crushing the sea, roaring and storming along. What I wouldn't give for a healthy wave!'

'I imagine those like myself, who suffer from seasickness, would happily forgo the waves,' Crawley argued in vain.

'Whether its boats or railways, modern travelling is not travelling at all,' his master observed caustically, 'it is merely being sent to a place, and very little different from becoming a parcel.'

'Surely the fact that we can reach a destination faster means that we have more time to enjoy it when we get there?' Crawley asserted.

'That's where you are mistaken. No changing of place at a hundred miles an hour will make us one whit stronger, happier or wiser. There was always more in the world than man could see, walked they ever so slowly. They see it no better for going *fast*. The really precious things are thought and sight, not pace. It does a bullet no good to go fast, and a man, if he be truly a man, no harm to go slow, for his glory is not in going, but in *being*.'

Everything, from the size of the boat to the ugly scenery he found upon landing in Dublin, Ruskin commented upon and complained about in his most colourful and melodramatic language; and although this was nothing Crawley was not well used to, it made him long to arrive at Harristown where he hoped to be welcomed into the servants' quarter with famed Irish hospitality.

'Thank heaven having a train to catch means that we don't have to stop *here* for long,' his master declared upon disembarking in the industrial quarter of the city, without realising that he verged on contradicting himself.

'Quite so,' Crawley replied with a wry smile that he was careful not to show.

'It is quite the dreariest-looking place I have ever seen and joins the filth of Manchester to the gloom of Modena,' Ruskin announced with his usual authority, while his companion remained silent in the hope that he would eventually tire himself out.

With forty or so minutes to spare until the next train departed from Kingsbridge Station, Ruskin decided to cross the street for a refreshment at the Terminus Hotel, yet instead of inviting Crawley to join him, as he usually would, he preferred to take tea alone and therefore dispatched his valet to send an unnecessary telegram to his father.

'I hope you don't mind, but I'm in no mood for small talk today,' he excused as he strode off.

Ruskin remained oblivious to the fact that Crawley was put out at being sent on such a thankless errand, thereby preventing him from taking any rest, nor did he observe his blatant disinterestedness when they later reunited on the train and he proceeded to describe in considerable detail the interior of the hotel and the poor level of service he had received.

'They gave me good tea and good bread, but the squalor of the rooms, of the waitress, of the old prints, of the tablecloth! Far worse than the worst of Italy. A more alehousy, nasty and ignoble place I have never seen,' he raved, 'while what I have seen of the Irish themselves, in just the two hours after landing, will I suppose remain a permanent impression. I had no conception that the stories of Ireland were so true. I had fancied all were merely violent exaggeration, but it is *impossible* to exaggerate.'

Crawley, who had never visited Ireland before, tried not to be influenced by his master's irritable mood and continued to watch the changing landscape flashing past the window with great interest, catching a glimpse of the ancient round tower of Clondalkin and the towns of Hazelhatch, Straffan and Sallins, whilst remaining hopeful that Ruskin's humour would eventually improve when their journey was finally at an end and they were in sight of Harristown.

Just as Crawley predicted, as soon as the wheels of the La Touche carriage, which had been sent to meet them from the station, were in motion, Ruskin suddenly left off grumbling. His posture improved and he began referring to his watch and taking more notice of his whereabouts. Even a smile began to appear at the corners of his mouth for, as he acknowledged to himself during this effort to clear his mind of all recent irritations, his hosts would doubtless be irked at finding themselves stuck with such a disagreeable guest.

Eight miles later and they were passing through the elaborate wrought-iron gates of the estate and proceeding up the lengthy private road to the main house: a refined, three-storey Georgian mansion designed along classical lines, with nine sash windows across, a wide Ionic porch and a dominant position overlooking the River Liffey.

It was gone nine o'clock in the evening when the carriage halted outside the front steps, yet Ruskin was alert and expectant despite any weariness from travelling, and he surprised everyone by jumping down energetically, waving to all who greeted him and bearing gifts, including scarves which his mother had knitted for the La Touche children, whom he was sorry not to see among those assembled to welcome him.

Despite the poor quality of the light he was immediately struck by the scale of the property, which made Denmark Hill appear humble by comparison, as did the impressive line of servants standing outside: a housekeeper, butler and under butler, several footmen and maids, cooks, gamekeepers, gardeners, a lady's maid and the pretty if unremarkable governess, Miss Bunnett, whom Ruskin recognised and acknowledged with a warm smile.

As the two footmen assisted Crawley with the luggage, Mrs La Touche rushed to embrace Ruskin and introduce her husband, who was standing beside her looking bullish due to being extremely tall and stocky, with abundant copper whiskers which drew attention to the severity of his expression.

'We finally meet, Mr Ruskin,' John La Touche said with more than a little reluctance in his tone, yet offering his hand nonetheless and wasting no time in leading the way to the marble entrance hall.

The vestibule resembled more a temple than a hallway, and Ruskin was impressed by the grandeur and sheer scale of the architecture, with two Romanesque columns supporting a beam across the room and the focal point being an impressive life-size Carrara marble sculpture after Canova's 'The Three Graces'.

'You have a magnificent home,' Ruskin complimented, unsure whether "home" was the correct term.

'You are very welcome here,' La Touche announced, 'but it is too late for a tour tonight. My wife, who wishes to retire, will take pleasure in showing you around the house and estate on the morrow, while I shall keep you company now if you wish to partake of some supper in the library?'

Mrs La Touche was not keen to retire at all in fact, yet this word from her husband ensured that she did so without protest, bidding the men goodnight with more than a pang at not being able to participate in their discussion.

Within a short time of admiring his new surroundings, Ruskin felt increasingly awkward on receiving little response to the compliments he paid his host, and it was clear that neither man knew what to make of the other.

Fortunately, just as he had begun to despair, Ruskin heard the sound of a bird coming from the direction of his host's breast pocket, and La Touche smiled disarmingly as he removed a green popinjay from out of his waistcoat.

'It's not only the English who are a little eccentric, Mr Ruskin,' he declared.

Laughing heartily and feeling slightly encouraged that he might be able to make his host warm to him after all, Ruskin looked up to see Percy, home from Harrow for the holidays, peeping between the banisters, for it was inevitable that, in the excitement caused by their teacher's visit, the children had gone to bed, but not quite *into* it.

Alas, the boy was unable to remain undiscovered for long thanks to his sisters, who having heard him sneak out of the nursery were insistent upon joining him, though they both broke into a fit of uncontrollable giggles on attempting to remain silent.

'My children were far too excited about your visit to sleep,' their father remarked to Ruskin before running up a few of the bottom stairs in order to pretend that he would chase after them. This was met with even more fits of laughter and playful shrieks by the girls and allowed the guest to observe a side of La Touche which his wife's unflattering descriptions had not prepared him for.

'You may say goodnight to Mr Ruskin but then you must go back to bed and straight to sleep,' he reasoned with Percy, Emily and Rose, the girls looking angelic in pale pink dressing gowns as they tried to stifle their yawns. Greatly pleased with themselves, they agreed to the bargain and all trooped downstairs barefoot.

Percy, who was a dark-haired youth of fifteen and very much resembled his mother, shook Ruskin's hand formally, while Emily kissed him on the cheek and Rose did likewise, also managing to whisper in his ear, 'I missed you.'

She alone knew how much these words would please him, and they had the immediate effect of lifting any heaviness of heart which Ruskin had felt only a few hours before. Too afraid of their father to try their luck further, the three then climbed the stairs, waved one last time and reluctantly scampered back to bed.

Knowing how much his children appreciated anyone who spoiled them, their father was not surprised by Ruskin's popularity, yet he regarded him warily, especially now that he was an outspoken atheist. Above all, La Touche was deeply suspicious of his influence over Rose, and this furthered his determination to gradually remove him from having any hand in her education.

There would be more than enough opportunity for him to fathom Ruskin's motivation in trying to influence Rose over the next few days, he considered as he poured him a glass of wine when they were settled in the library, and perhaps there would even be an opportunity for confronting him, though he would have to choose his time carefully so as to be out of earshot of his wife.

Meanwhile, a maid entered with the tray of sandwiches Mrs La Touche had asked to be sent up, and although Ruskin felt obliged to partake of them, he anticipated that it would be a far from convivial hour.

His host initially remained silent and stared at the unlit hearth, for it was too warm an evening for a fire, and Ruskin was unsure whether this was simply the Irishman's usual manner, or if he chose not to take any trouble to converse because his wife's over-enthusiasm had caused him to feel a certain amount of animosity.

'Running such an estate as this must take up most of your time,' Ruskin ventured.

'One never thinks of time at Harristown, yet much has changed since I succeeded on my father's death in '44,' La Touche offered, without appearing to take any interest in either the subject or his guest.

'The world has changed.'

'And not necessarily for the better,' he agreed. 'My responsibilities are far greater than my ancestors ever knew. Due to once being Master of the Kildare Hounds I have always been referred to as "The Master", which I hope is testament to the respect my tenants and neighbours feel towards me.'

'And of your riding ability too, I don't wonder,' Ruskin observed lightly, inadvertently touching upon his host's most painful memory.

'I no longer ride,' La Touche corrected; 'my twin brother was killed during a hunt and I swore I would never sit upon a horse again.'

'I'm deeply sorry.'

'I am only sorry that I can't persuade my children to give it up,' he complained as his companion struggled in vain to think of a more agreeable subject.

'What is the La Touche family history in Ireland?' Ruskin began hesitantly. 'The name is clearly French?'

'We were once Huguenots,' his host explained pompously, taking a sip of wine before going on; 'my ancestor established the Bank of Ireland when we were expelled from France, during which time this house became the new family seat.'

'You are fortunate in your birth,' Ruskin observed with sarcasm, amused at how much La Touche seemed to revel in self-glory whilst claiming to be humble.

Being a vain man, his host took the remark as flattery and answered seriously, 'It depends on how you look at it. Managing Harristown is a great burden, and not just a financial one. I feel passionately that one's tenants and labourers should be spiritually content, but it took famine to make me really comprehend the importance of the position God has given me,' he blustered. 'It is impossible not to feel guilt when you have so much more than others.'

'Riches depend entirely upon inequality,' Ruskin remarked; 'the worth of the guinea in *your* pocket relies on your neighbour's pocket being without one. If he did not want it, it would be of no use to you.'

Unsure of whether his new acquaintance meant to insult him or if he were merely peacocking his own wisdom, La Touche became increasingly defensive: 'Whilst many landowners were content to watch their tenants starve to death, along with resisting Gladstone's land reforms, *I* lent him my full support and culled herds of deer in order to provide food for the poor, nor did I keep an extravagant table. My wife certainly had to endure a harsh beginning to our marriage.'

'And was she understanding?' Ruskin could not stop himself from enquiring.

'She was relieved to observe my rescue from a previously low and selfish life,' he answered with surprising self-chastisement, 'just as she was when I was baptised by Mr Spurgeon, though she would not join me in beginning a new path.'

Ruskin was surprised to find himself looking forward to seeing more of Mrs La Touche the next day, for notwithstanding her embarrassing flirtatiousness she at least never failed to provide him with more amusing conversation. He was beginning to see why she so often complained about her life in Ireland, for whenever her husband *did* speak it was generally about himself and the benevolent deeds he carried out.

He perceived La Touche to be fundamentally an unworldly man who possessed neither a great knowledge nor a great intellect, yet he nonetheless felt more sympathy for him on hearing of his acts of charity towards his dependants; his new-found Evangelicalism had clearly increased his respect towards his inferiors, though he commanded the same from them. To Ruskin's way of thinking, an estate on which all the tenants struggled to eat after paying their rent seemed a curious kind of Christianity indeed.

La Touche was too proud to reveal to Ruskin his own enormous financial burden, however, for having been forced to apply for a loan many years ago, thereby mortgaging Harristown, he now found himself unable to pay off the debt. It was this and similar strains which had prompted his conversion after hearing the famed preacher Charles Spurgeon, whom Ruskin regarded as no more than a showman who made up for any lack of religious proof with sheer theatrics, yet La Touche had fallen for all his tricks and continued to embrace religion with as much fervour as he had once led the hounds.

Ruskin recalled that one of Spurgeon's recent sermons, entitled 'The Sinner's End', held at the Metropolitan Tabernacle in London, had drawn crowds in their hundreds, all of whom the preacher had urged to heed the call of Jesus as though he were channelling Christ.

He almost pitied La Touche for believing himself redeemed, for had he not simply been plunged into a tank of water during one of Spurgeon's famous mass baptisms, solely designed to increase his notoriety and line his pocket?

On this and many other subjects both men were irrevocably divided, and Ruskin remarked cynically, 'Rather than preach to people to think about the next world, Spurgeon would be far better to teach them to do the best they can in *this* one.'

'You need only attend his meetings to know the wonders he has wrought on his congregation,' La Touche rebuffed, gripping his waistcoat with his large fingers in annoyance at being confronted.

'Great men do not play stage tricks with the doctrines of life and death, only *little* men do that,' Ruskin went on, unable to leave the matter alone. 'It is my view that baptism is just a very imperfect and unnecessary form of washing.'

On this, his host shot up from his seat as abruptly as if he had just been struck and, looking down on Ruskin intimidatingly, responded, 'Whereas in *mine*, anyone who believes that the act only signifies immersion commits a high sin and treason against heaven.' Saying which, he withdrew and left the visitor to his unappetising repast.

Having slept peacefully, Ruskin managed to shrug off any unease regarding his and La Touche's differences of opinion and rose with a great deal of expectancy on finally being able to see his new surroundings clearly, lustrous in the bright daylight the moment he drew back the curtains and contemplated the wide-reaching expanse of garden, wood and agricultural land.

Exploring part of the house before the family had even risen, he found its long corridors and high-ceilinged rooms opulently furnished, ornamented with grandiose eighteenth-century paintings accumulated by La Touche's considerably wealthier ancestors, but which were, unbeknownst to him, gradually being depleted in order to settle debts acquired by the present custodian.

Ruskin could soon comprehend why the eleven thousand acre estate was often described as the most beautiful seat in all Kildare, for the seemingly vast parkland featured a densely populated woodland of beech, oak and limes, set off to full effect by the glimmering River Liffey, which looked a deal more picturesque amidst these surroundings than when flowing through the noisy, smog-polluted hub of industrial Dublin.

Excusing himself after breakfast with the intention of working for several hours, Ruskin politely postponed Mrs La Touche's suggestion to take a long walk around the grounds until the afternoon when it would be cooler and the light would be softer. Nor was this much of a sacrifice considering that his room was located on the first floor of the house with views of the immaculate lawns and terraces, particularly fine on that first bright, auspicious morning which promised so much, providing he kept from talking about religion with La Touche, who had hardly said a word to him over breakfast.

With books and papers spread out on the dressing table, which doubled nicely as a makeshift desk, Ruskin struggled to concentrate on the map of Mont Blanc he had commenced several days ago.

Gazing out of the window momentarily, he observed the Liffey in the distance, shining like a sheet of solid silver in the sunshine, its banks carpeted with wild flowers and willow trees which lined it on either side and drooped their branches in the water as if quenching their thirst.

The water rippling over the stones was the only sound that caught his ear, and he spied the distant Wicklow Hills through the gaps in the trees of the surrounding woodland. It all appeared as a mirror image of Eden, yet it was a paradise which Ruskin already recognised as possessing its own kind of temptation.

Just as he was about to return to his work, Rose and Emily entered the box-hedged garden below carrying croquet mallets, a sport which both sisters had a revived interest in following the visit of the Prince of Wales, and Ruskin found himself unable to draw his attention away.

Emily, whom he always called "Wisie", had also brought her pet goldfinch Bully out to play, and the bird hovered in the air above her head, holding a thread of her long hair as deftly as a spider grasping the fine silk of a cobweb.

As he was thus observing them, transfixed by their youth and beauty, Rose caught sight of Ruskin at the open window and smiled, signalling him to go down.

'Come and play!' she urged persuasively.

'I can't, I must finish my map!' he shouted down obstinately.

'Please?' Rose whined, taking no notice of Emily, who caught hold of her arm in the attempt to deter her harassment and whispered that she should stop disturbing him.

'I'll play a game later,' Ruskin compromised.

'But you can do your map *any* time,' Rose went on, pouting petulantly on being refused what she considered a simple request.

'I always work after breakfast and today won't be any exception,' he replied emphatically, closing the window. Quite enough time had been spent arguing and he didn't want their parents to overhear the commotion.

But whilst Ruskin returned to his seat, determined to continue with his map, it was impossible not to be arrested by the sounds of Rose's croquet mallet or her jubilant peals of laughter when she successfully manoeuvred the ball. It was the wonderful, carefree mirth strangely confined to childhood, yet one he had only ever known vicariously.

Going to the window once more, whilst being careful to avoid being noticed, Ruskin smiled on seeing Rose cartwheeling across the lawn as she awaited her turn. Bareheaded in the August rays, which seemed to stretch their arms across the entire estate, each strand of her hair appeared to be threaded with pure gold, nor had he ever seen anything more precious.

It was joyous to see the girls frolicking so gaily, as if schoolwork didn't exist, but before they had finished their game Miss Bunnett arrived to summon them inside to their lessons. Ruskin observed Rose throw down her mallet in temper, having failed to persuade the governess to allow them any extension, and he smirked on perceiving her shoulders rounding when she sulked, following Miss Bunnett ungraciously up the path whilst making faces behind the lady's back which were intended to make her sister laugh.

She was understandably reluctant at being forced inside on such a pleasant day, he reasoned, and angry at him for having stubbornly insisted on staying in his room, thereby removing all hope of escaping her studies. He felt guilty on seeing them led away, not because he had refused to join in, but because he had failed to finish his work anyway. He decided never to touch the map again.

Ruskin hoped to redeem himself by going in search of Mrs La Touche earlier than he had promised and asking for the children to accompany them on their mile-long turn about the estate, which was, so he suspected, partly designed to familiarise him with his new surroundings but mainly intended to impress him.

As they conversed whilst strolling beside the river, Percy, Emily, and Rose, who wore a red cap and looked quite wild, ran on ahead and approached any fences, puddles and ditches they came across with flying leaps.

'Somehow I feel older and sadder in looking at these children who are so innocent and good,' Ruskin remarked to Mrs La Touche, 'aside from being the most wonderful combination of frog and deer that ever naturalist was puzzled to define.'

'They do not know how fortunate they are,' she replied regretfully. 'Only in adulthood, and from your teachings, will they realise what it *is* to be raised in such privileged circumstances.'

'What will that achieve apart from to make them miserable? It is not a crime to be rich, only to be idle.'

'They will never be *that*,' Mrs La Touche smiled, as they continued to watch the three making an energetic procession many yards ahead.

'Oh to be young! I don't think any man ever mourned his departed youth as much as *I*. I suffer such a weary longing to begin my life over again, and *would* were it not for Fate forbidding it,' he reflected. 'Am I not in a curiously unnatural state of mind that at forty-two, instead of being able to settle to my middle-aged life like a middle-aged creature, I have more instincts of youth about me than when I was young? When I was a youngster I preferred to sit writing metaphysics all day, only now I am vexed because I cannot climb, run, wrestle, sing or flirt as I might once have. Wrong at both ends of life!' Ruskin proclaimed whilst being too moved by the thought to devote his full concentration to Mrs La Touche's answer which, along the lines of flirting, sorely missed the point.

Recognising that the day was altogether unlike any other, he wanted so keenly to commit the moment to his memory and tried to take in every sight and sound, from the sheep grazing peacefully in the meadows either side of them, to the dragonflies, as colourful as fireworks, dancing on the gentle breeze, yet it was all as hopeless as trying to recall a pleasant dream from which one has just awoken.

'Sometimes, on long summer days such as this, I long to watch, not the sunrise, but the dawn,' the lady confided poetically, 'and so, when the house is quite asleep I often go into an empty room, where I sit and wait courageously alone until first light. Then I steal downstairs, unbar the door and break out barefooted, so as to feel the dewy carpet of grass beneath my feet.'

'I've been known to do the same thing,' Ruskin admitted, intrigued to hear that his hostess delighted in carrying out such secretive pursuits.

'With just the faintest gold-tinted light in the east, the sky is inexpressibly resplendent through the early morning mist, and the trees look almost phantom-like. Even a brief ramble allows me to see and hear a great deal more than I ever could during daylight hours, from the birds making the sweetest sleepiest noises, to the roses, still quite scentless, hanging down their heads, as fast asleep and as oblivious to my actions as my own husband and children.'

Wielding a toy fishing net, Percy chose that moment to interrupt his mother and declare that he and his sisters wanted Ruskin to help them make a bridge across the rivulet.

'Poor Mr Ruskin has hardly had time to settle in and you expect him to build bridges?' Mrs La Touche dismissed lightly.

'I'm sure he wants to,' Percy replied confidently.

'Yes, I should like to, really,' Ruskin assured Mrs La Touche, hoping that Rose, who was still sulking with him, would forgive his earlier refusal to play croquet. 'I used to do the same in Cumberland when I was a boy. Do *you* want me to, Rosie Posie?' he asked winningly.

She nodded with a wry smile and reluctantly admitted, 'Yes please, St Crumpet.'

'You always have such pretty names for one another, yet *I'm* never given one,' Mrs La Touche interjected in an attempt to be included. 'When I was your age,' she addressed her daughter, 'I was a very naughty little girl and always used to be called Polly.'

'That's a silly name,' Rose dismissed, protective of the special clique from which she had decided her mother was to be forever excluded.

Humiliated by her daughter's intentionally cruel snub, Mrs La Touche paused before turning to Ruskin and suggesting coquettishly, 'Perhaps it is, but I shouldn't mind if *you* would call me that.'

Too embarrassed to respond to this, and experiencing a genuine glee at the prospect of engaging in bridge-building with the three youngest La Touches, not least because it allowed him to escape conversing with their mother, Ruskin hastened towards Percy who was waiting for him to commence the project.

Before many moments had passed he was standing in the stream with his trouser legs rolled up, assisting the three siblings in lifting a plank of wood; a most peculiar sight should any of Ruskin's friends have chanced to see him, and one he knew full well would have gained the disapproval of his parents, who believed their son should always remain mindful of his position in society.

He was thus occupied when Rose accidentally allowed a plank of wood to slip from her grasp, making a terrific splash and fairly drenching her companions. This naturally caused Mrs La Touche and Miss Bunnett, who had recently joined the party, to fall about laughing on the bankside.

'I haven't found anything so amusing for a long time,' the lady admitted to the governess; 'it's a wonder we haven't thought to invite Mr Ruskin before now, he's such a welcome change from our usual humdrum acquaintances.'

'Yes, the children are clearly very fond of him, and their own father could hardly be seen in such a position,' Miss Bunnett remarked, smiling at the idea.

'If you realised in what esteem Mr Ruskin is held in London you would be more astonished to see *him* thus,' Mrs La Touche praised.

It was just as well that Ruskin was unaware how much the sight of him in such a relaxed attitude stimulated the lady, or he should have been just as keen to cease participating in the game, whilst feeling deeply foolish for having forgotten himself.

After a time Percy, Rose and Emily lost all interest in bridge-making and degenerated into drenching each another; yet no matter how unruly they became, Ruskin remained indulgent and convivial. Mrs La Touche on the other hand, being a fundamentally self-centred creature, inevitably began to feel left out on being unable to participate in any of the frivolity, restricted both by propriety and her typically elaborate attire.

'Look at you! I don't know why you have pretty dresses; you deserve to wear rags,' she chided Rose and Emily when they were eventually tired and had collapsed on the grass, leaving Percy and Ruskin to continue their boyish pranks. The girls sat up anxiously on being unsure whether their mother spoke in jest or seriousness, and Mrs La Touche, realising that her remark had sounded too severe, began to laugh falsely in the attempt to appear in a better light.

'Let's hang them on the washing line; they'll soon dry out!' Ruskin teased, oblivious of his hostess's irritation on not being the focus of his attention. 'The Liffey is a sweet warm stream and I think being in it has done me a great deal of good,' he enthused as he stepped onto the bank and attempted to wring out his shirt. 'Yes, I feel much more springy!' he said, bouncing up and down and causing the youngsters to giggle.

Like a character in one of her own ludicrously melodramatic novels (not that Ruskin had ever dared to read them), Maria La Touche seemed destined to merely observe the enjoyment of others, for the days of her taking foolhardy risks with servants or wealthy aristocrats had long since passed, albeit more from lack of opportunity than any sense of virtue.

It was a realisation which made her increasingly dissatisfied with her lot; and she possessed an unfortunate aptitude for turning against those whom she once cherished, for she was too conceited to feel glad on witnessing any pleasure in which *she* was not engaged. Easily jealous and enraged by those who excluded her, however unintentionally, she would turn against them as easily as a shiny new penny in a coin toss.

Despite being well aware that it would play to the wishes of her husband, by the time Ruskin had abandoned bridge-making Mrs La Touche had half decided that it would be better if he were to depart Harristown early. It was with some annoyance that she recalled the drive out to Pollaphuca Falls she had promised Ruskin later that day, for she no longer wished to share her most prized beauty spot with him.

Formed from the head of the Liffey and rising from the Wicklow Mountains, the waterfall had been renowned since the eighteenth century and was a sight which Mrs La Touche reserved only for her favourite guests, something she did not for the moment consider Ruskin.

Unable to think of a plausible excuse to defer the excursion, however, she had no alternative but to resign herself to embarking as soon as the children and their tutor had returned to the house in order to change into dry clothing.

Trying to believe herself suddenly indifferent to his charms, Mrs La Touche nonetheless insisted on Ruskin taking the seat beside her in the first open carriage, the groom in front ready to drive the two white ponies who looked hot and irritable even before setting off.

Emily, Rose and Percy had meanwhile taken their places in the second jaunting car, accompanied by Miss Bunnett, and after a pleasant ride of almost ten miles, during which time Ruskin's good humour mellowed any feelings of envy his hostess had recently experienced, the carriages halted, having gone as far as they could, for in order to enjoy the full glory and spectacle of the waterfall visitors were forced to climb the remainder of the way on foot.

There were several paths leading to the summit of Pollaphuca, having been landscaped by an earl in the previous century, and the young La

Touches knew each one by heart. Finding the perils of the rocky precipice exhilarating instead of terrifying like the adults did, before the first groom had even stepped down from the box to assist their mother in alighting Percy had rushed on ahead, encouraging his sisters to do likewise, and leaving Miss Bunnett struggling behind and calling after them in vain.

Ruskin hardly knew what to expect from this much extolled sightseeing expedition, yet he was already focussed on trying to remember each detail of the scenery in order to later exchange it into a more enduring watercolour. Whilst he admired the invention of photography and the many advantages of being able to preserve accurate images for all time, it only made him cling to his own power of memory, firmly believing that there was no substitute for emotions and the way the mind naturally connects people and places through feelings and sensations.

Though he had just started to make his way up the steep promontory, Ruskin pondered thus as he gazed in awe of his lush surroundings. He was surprised to find that, regardless of having scaled the route on countless occasions, Mrs La Touche proved almost as nervous as Miss Bunnett, who not only suffered from vertigo but succumbed to almost any fear. On the other hand, his hostess's hesitation was mainly due to her highly fashionable yet impractical dress, and whenever the path became too narrow she begged the other two to wait for her as she attempted to manoeuvre the hoops of her crinoline, a design which Ruskin viewed as preposterous at the best of times.

Although Ruskin was an expert climber due to his love of Switzerland and the Alps, Rose naturally adopted the role of guide when he reached the spot where she had been awaiting him, and he was thus encouraged to leave her mother and Miss Bunnett in favour of following in Rose's footsteps.

Percy had long since disappeared, having neither the desire nor the patience to lead this erratic group and presuming that their guest would be well mannered enough to escort the ladies to safety. Emily meanwhile, who was at the most difficult and burgeoning period of adolescence and could often be found lost in thought, was happier to fall behind Ruskin and Rose in order to take pleasure in the atmosphere rather than rushing to the top.

Rose displayed her fiercely Celtic streak by selecting the most dangerous, yet most spectacular, course for Ruskin, illustrating both her confidence and agility as she climbed effortlessly over the large rocks which threatened to inhibit their progress, and forcing him to do likewise so as not to be left in her wake.

'This is the *really* treacherous part, but I'll look after you,' she reassured Ruskin, who found her concern endearing and was glad to accept the delicate hand she offered him, for not once did she appear to think of her own vulnerability.

'Rose, you'll not injure yourself trying to impress Mr Ruskin?' Emily called after her, fearing that the pair would soon be out of sight, leaving her with no party at all.

'Don't be absurd, I won't fall and break my neck, if that's what you mean,' she answered obstinately before hastening on.

Emily therefore considered it wise to loiter behind until her mother and Miss Bunnett eventually came upon her, leaving Rose to be the first to introduce her teacher to the waterfall. With Percy still nowhere to be seen and probably in the thick of the surrounding woodland, Rose succeeded in approaching the spectacle just as she had hoped, with Ruskin alone.

Taking his hand firmly, she demanded, 'You must shut your eyes before we go any further,' leading him to the best viewing spot before finally confirming: 'Now you can look.'

Regardless of how many astonishing sights he'd had the opportunity of witnessing during his extensive travels, Ruskin could not fail to let out a gasp on opening his eyes and finding that Irish wonder before him. Known by the locals as Daemon's Hole, at around one hundred and fifty metres in height the cascade foamed furiously into the vortex below and, as the sunlight passed through the trees, a rainbow appeared, like something belonging to some mystical folklore, there and yet not there.

'Well, what do you think of it?' Rose enquired; her voice full of anticipation.

'What do I think? It makes me realise that I spend too long describing things and not enough time looking at them,' Ruskin declared, overwhelmed and still a little breathless from the climb.

'We can look as long as you like,' she assured him.

And he wanted to do just that, although perhaps he would not have found the vision half so momentous had it not been for Rose standing there beside him. Much moved by the experience, he turned to her and declared sincerely, 'How much I value seeing your motherland.'

She smiled proudly before pretending not to have entirely forgiven him for remaining in his room after breakfast: 'Then you'll promise not to do any more work while you're here?'

'I promise,' Ruskin laughed, amused at how she always managed to get her way.

Standing on the craggy precipice and continuing to stare down at the whirlpool, both chose to look on in silence for a moment, and it was then that Rosie suddenly placed her hand in his. It was something she had done many times before, yet never quite in that manner, and Ruskin felt strangely unable to disengage himself from her hold, knowing as he did how fleeting this silent communion would be.

Possessively wanting to share the experience with him and him alone, Rose was gratified by how much he delighted in the scene and occasionally allowed herself furtive sidelong glances in order to revel in his expression of wonder at the continuous and majestic spectacle below.

Yet she remained conscious that all too soon the others would come upon them and spoil everything, nor was she able to hide her annoyance when they did. Emily was the first to arrive and observed not only that their hands had been entwined but that Ruskin pulled away as soon as he heard someone approaching.

Ever intuitive, her sister also saw that Rose lost all interest in the fall when her mother and Miss Bunnett appeared and sought to disguise her feelings of irritation by merrily asking Ruskin to find some clever way of describing the fall. Rose was relieved when Emily suggested they all go in search of a suitable picnic spot, and she volunteered to look for Percy in the undergrowth, thus giving herself a moment to quell her selfishness and chastise herself for her ungodliness.

Selecting a quiet field, not far from where the carriages had originally terminated, the coachmen unloaded the blankets and food hampers, politely refusing any assistance from Ruskin who had forgotten all usual customs in such a setting.

Unlike her pious and frugal husband, Mrs La Touche was extravagant in her tastes, especially whenever he was not present, and had organised a lavish high tea complete with cold meats, game pies, platters of fruit, cakes, wine and champagne. The children were happy enough to dine on cake and the cook's lemonade, as would Ruskin have been had not Mrs La Touche forced a champagne flute into his hand and chinked her glass against his coquettishly.

'The true secret of happiness would be to bolt one's gates, lie on the grass all day, take care not to eat too much dinner, and buy as many Turners as one could afford,' he offered, as though drunk on the atmosphere.

'How happy you're making us,' she complimented, no longer wanting to punish him for his earlier neglect but rather seeking to win him over. 'I don't know what we shall do when you go home.'

He flinched at her gushing, afraid of saying a word, afraid of *not* saying a word, afraid of offending her, and still more afraid of giving her pleasure. 'I doubt anything could disturb the tranquillity here. Things will continue much as they ever did,' he replied, and longing to cool her ardour killed it temporarily by adding, 'only I would like to see Rosie learn Greek.'

Mrs La Touche, irritated at her daughter always being Ruskin's chosen subject, returned, 'As you know full well, Rose will do anything you advise. She would even learn Arabic if you suggested it,' she asserted resentfully.

'She has always been a conscientious student,' Ruskin extolled.

'Sometimes I think you quite prefer her company to mine,' Mrs La Touche said, laughing insincerely and making Ruskin feel uncomfortable at being seated so close to her on the rug. Annoyed on observing his unease, she decided to intimidate him. 'My husband is beginning to find your influence a little disconcerting.'

'In what way?' he questioned defensively, perceiving not only that the lady regretted her earlier tribute but that, due to him not having returned it, she now wished to attack and challenge him.

'As you know, he is an extremely religious man and is wary of anyone who is *not*,' she explained, a hint of a threat in her intonation.

'Is not my creed my own concern?' Ruskin responded indignantly.

'Of course, it only saddens me that you find so much trouble with it,' she answered, displaying false concern.

'I sincerely wish I did not,' he assured her, although he remained inwardly resentful at being cross-questioned by his hostess in this manner. 'My mother fed me daily doses of the Bible as soon as I could read, and despite my loss of faith its teachings have stayed with me.'

'If its moral values remain, perhaps everything else is recoverable?' Mrs La Touche ventured persuasively.

'I very much doubt it,' Ruskin respectfully denied; 'you might sooner get lightning out of incense smoke than true action or passion out of your modern English religion. No, I looked for another world and found that there is only *this*, and sometimes I think that is quite enough,' he said, motioning with his hand to the sublime landscape surrounding them.

'Nothing will ever convince me that anyone but He could have created it,' Mrs La Touche contended.

'I don't so much question there being *a* God, but rather the validity of the Bible, which is as hard to disbelieve as it is to accept,' Ruskin explained. 'The more I investigate it, as I might any other history, the more difficulties I find with it and the less ground for belief.'

'Perhaps it is the *way* you choose to interpret it,' the lady challenged.

'People always say that to atheists, yet is it not fearful to think how God has allowed all who have sought him in the most earnest way to be blinded? Puritan, monk, Brahmin, Churchman and Turk are all merely names for different madnesses and ignorances. Surely what matters most is not which religion a man claims, but how honourably he chooses to conduct himself.'

'You speak convincingly, yet why can you not see that it is *He* who has bestowed such power?' Mrs La Touche asked, not realising how much she insulted her guest by adopting such an inappropriate familiarity. 'Nothing will get me right, save getting *you* right. When you were making a bridge with the children earlier, I thought to myself that if you were holding onto a straw and I to a plank, I would leave my plank, Mr Ruskin, and catch at *your* straw.'

It was a proclamation Ruskin thought ludicrous and he rebuffed it accordingly: 'I hope I don't need anyone to get me right, and trust that all who know me well will vouch for the fact that I carry on my life just as if the Bible *were* true.'

Ruskin longed to be back in the security and solace of his own room, working at anything that might enable him to clear his mind of the lady of the house. He would have found the remainder of the afternoon almost intolerable had it not been for the youngsters coming to his rescue and asking him to play cricket, entirely innocent of the difficult conversation they were interrupting.

When he eventually returned to his chamber he heaved a weary sigh of relief on being able to lock Mrs La Touche out, amusing himself by conjuring up the nickname of "Lacerta", due to her lizard-like ways, for the purposes of writing an unfavourable diary entry.

He was baffled by how quickly the lady's tone had changed, one moment badgering him about his beliefs, the next making wild declarations suggestive of a passion he most certainly did not return. Nevertheless, in an attempt to humour rather than please her, he agreed to participate in the family's prayers that evening, fully convinced that his soul was not, and never could be, immortal.

THE DEPARTURE

THE FOLLOWING TWO DAYS WERE BATHED IN GLORIOUS sunshine, scented with freshly cut lawns, and spent with Ruskin enjoying yet more games with the young La Touches, who never wore themselves out, so keenly did they lap up the excitement afforded by his visit.

He obliged them in being a reliable comrade, whether the three wished to play croquet or charged him with being the search party in a game of hide and seek in the garden, when he was amused to notice that Rose always ensured that she was the first to be found, or the first to be caught if he was chosen as "it" in blind man's buff.

Mrs La Touche, partially screened by a parasol, would sit looking on, smiling her usual disingenuous smile as she watched their play. Her husband never participated in their activities but sometimes Ruskin would look up and observe La Touche standing at an upstairs window of the house, though he would disappear whenever anyone discerned him in the shadows, only to make a sombre reappearance at dinner.

Ruskin was pleased that Rose cleverly engineered that the largest portion of his remaining time was solely devoted to her and her beloved St Bernard dog, Bruno, whom they would take for long walks, which included visits to the cottagers, for she was proud to introduce everyone she knew to the esteemed guest, of whom she was far more in awe than any prince.

It made his heart glad to see her, with a daisy chain in her hair, so at ease among the poor, for not only had she the full run of every dwelling but was regularly invited to dine or sup with them, so warmly did they appreciate her presence. Yes, Rosie was the exception to every foolish rule and custom man ever invented.

He wondered if her parents realised how intimate she had become with the labourers and their families and sincerely hoped that they would never interfere with something so obviously pure in intention.

'I read to the elderly or offer assistance when someone is ill,' she explained as they walked home through the fields with Bruno, illustrating all the goodness he had ever believed her capable of and making him all the more determined to impart his own values to her when she was old enough to understand them fully.

'I take it you mean the Bible?' Ruskin asked sceptically.

'Yes, it was Papa's suggestion,' Rose nodded.

'Help them certainly, but don't talk religious sentiment or preach to them, you little monkey,' he advised, tweaking her nose fondly. 'They are probably, without in the least knowing it, fifty times more Christian than you.'

'Nowadays I visit the cottagers mainly to talk,' she confessed candidly. 'My father would probably be annoyed.'

'Your company gives them pleasure, what can be wrong in that?'

'I always try to please Papa, yet sometimes I feel that I must ignore my own thoughts in doing so,' she reflected sadly. 'I love my father, but he would have me believe his word rather than any other. *Yours* for example.'

'Mine?' Ruskin asked warily.

'Yes, because you have turned away from God, and I trust your judgement on other things, he thinks I will do the same with religion,' she confided, as though desperate to express her fear of their friendship being hindered or sabotaged.

'I never discuss God with you, nor would I,' he refuted, halting in his tracks and placing a hand on Rose's shoulder in order to emphasise his earnestness, 'so you can put his mind at rest.'

'I already have,' she cheered, worried that she had offended him. 'He seems quite fond of you. As much as he is of anyone.'

'You are kind to tell me all this, for I fear that he can never understand me. I do not blame him, for he can't *make* himself like me, and perhaps he would only like me less if he tried.'

Rose did not reply to this but occupied herself by gathering wild flowers as they walked. Ruskin noticed that she was unusually solemn as they neared the house, however, and taking the long path through the woods in twilight she lowered her head, her slight figure like that of a small white statue.

'You will think of me often when you are gone?' she asked abruptly.

He smiled. 'Of course, I always do.'

Rose was only half content with this answer and, wanting to have greater confirmation of his affection, persisted, 'And will you return to Harristown soon?'

'Certainly, but why should you think of that now?

'I should be so much happier today if only I knew that I am going to be happy *another* day – if this day is only a piece of happiness, not the whole of it.'

'Poor child,' he replied, his voice full of sympathy.

Like a radiance, she walked through the dark wood, henceforth bright from simply knowing that such a creature was in it.

'I want you to think of me as a little rose who tries to be worthy of the golden sunshine,' she remarked sentimentally. 'I began writing a fable for you, about a lonely flower in a woodland who has no heart to be happy because she feels that she is of no use to anyone.'

'Did you?' Ruskin asked, bemused yet sensing that this was Rosie's imaginative way of revealing her innermost thoughts to him. 'And what happened to the flower?'

'One day she looked up and began to feel her heart grow larger as she saw the glittering sunlight and the deep blue sky beyond the trees, and the sunshine suddenly said, "I do not think you too small to look upon."'

Rose stopped short, for her eyes were brimming over with tears and she was unable to continue, nor did Ruskin press her. They both knew that it was likely to be the last time that they would be fully alone together before he left for London, and so they chose not to say anything more but instead dwelt silently on their intangible bond and their mutual reluctance at being forced to part. There was a quiet, steady confidence between them and he trusted that even opposing beliefs and paternal loyalties would not be enough to make her turn away from him.

The sun was in hiding on the morning of Ruskin's departure and he awoke heavy-hearted, only to descend the stairs and see Rose peering mischievously behind the drawing room door like the young imp she was, eager to speak to him and having obviously devised some new plan.

Tiptoeing over to where he stood, she indicated the secretive nature of her mission by placing her forefinger to her mouth and whispering, 'A friend of Mama's has arranged a surprise dinner in your honour,' and, knowing full well that he loathed grand society events, she went on in her most persuasive manner, 'but I *hope* you will say that you would rather dine with us downstairs?'

He guessed that the 'us' referred to her siblings and replied reasonably, 'As much as I would like to dine with the three of you, I couldn't well disappoint your parents if their acquaintance has gone to such trouble on my account.'

'They can hardly refuse your parting wish,' Rose continued urgently, fearing that her mother would catch her plotting, and unaware that she displayed her immaturity by always exhibiting petulance whenever she did not get her way.

Thanks to her forewarning, however, Ruskin did decide to respectfully excuse himself from the county dinner, for he had no wish to be paraded like an exhibit in a carnival, declaring to Mr and Mrs La Touche over breakfast, 'I am strange and inferior in all society ways and, if it would be of no great inconvenience to you both, I would like to spend my last evening dining with the children in the servants' hall, for they have set their hearts upon hosting their own banquet and I am not inclined to thwart them.'

Mrs La Touche considered this a most uncouth suggestion, yet knew that she couldn't well force him to attend the reception, nor attempt to dissuade him too strongly before her husband who already had little patience with their guest being fawned over with elaborate soirées, especially as Ruskin was himself embarrassed whenever any fuss was made over his celebrity.

He pretended not to notice his hostess's frustration when she replied, 'I dare say we cannot change your mind if you are quite fixed on such an arrangement, although I have it on good authority that our friend's reception was to rival the homecoming of the Prodigal Son.' Saying which, Mrs La Touche turned to her husband and added spitefully, '*This is the first time one of our guests has ever thrown us over for a supper downstairs.*'

Percy was chasing Rose and Emily around the long oak table in the servants' hall when Ruskin, hoping to surprise them, crept in via the narrow back staircase that evening. It had been quite a relief not to have to dress for dinner, as was the prospect of not having to make conversation with a roomful of people he would never see, or want to see, again – the very reason he had long ago decided not to become a politician.

'You escaped!' Rose announced, delighted that her plan to steal Ruskin away from her mother had worked with surprising ease.

'Yes, I have overthrown your parents,' he laughed, in truth rather ashamed at himself for having appeared so ungrateful to his hosts. Selfish motivations had prevailed, however, for he did not want to miss a moment of Rose's company.

Taking hold of his arm, she wasted no time in ushering him to the head of the table and insisted bossily, 'You and Emily have precedence and must take the head and foot, while Percy and I will take the *quatrefoil.*'

'Righto!' Ruskin agreed, taking his seat and tucking his napkin into his collar comically as the cook entered the room and began laying out a hand-raised pie, salad and triangles of impossibly thin-sliced bread and butter, one of her teatime specialities.

'The game,' Rose announced on settling herself and adopting a ridiculously plummy accent which had the desired effect of making the others laugh, 'is to behave superbly, display impeccable manners and refer to one another as lords and ladies the entire evening. For example, would you care for the salt, Lady Emily?'

'No thank you, would you?' her sister answered, passing the cruet set with a comical flourish.

'What say you to chess after dinner, Lord Ruskin?' Percy asked with a mouthful of food which he gulped down before adding, 'Over port,' prompting the girls to break into fits of giggles.

Ruskin already knew that he should remember the evening as the undoubted highlight of his holiday, and that being such it was inevitably going to pass too soon. The four of them later sang duets, as many as he liked, while Emily played, as skilfully as she could, the out of tune upright piano in the corner which the old butler was known to play once a year at Christmas.

This was followed by two games of chess with Rose and Percy against him, though they purposely distracted him by whispering possible strategies and arguing over them so as to make him forget his own.

The pair had almost grasped victory when Ruskin looked up to see Crawley standing in the doorway. Knowing this to mean that Mr and Mrs La Touche had returned from their friend's grand dinner and that it was time for him to depart, he sighed, which the children took as a sign of his frustration in losing the game.

'Check,' Percy informed him proudly.

'You have me cornered,' Ruskin admitted, glad to see the brother and sister win and only feigning annoyance in order to satisfy them. 'I'm only sorry that I won't have the opportunity of trying to redeem myself, for it's time for me to leave.'

Percy, Rose and Emily groaned on realising that the evening had slipped away without their noticing, and the three looked thoroughly depressed as they prepared to follow Ruskin upstairs to bid him adieu, all the while vehemently tugging his coat sleeves and urging him to visit Harristown again soon.

Their parents meanwhile waited in the uninviting entrance hall, impatient to bid their guest farewell in order that they might retire to their respective chambers. John La Touche stood stiffly with his hands behind his back, while his wife perched restlessly on the edge of an ornate gilt chair a little distance away, their chill manner towards each other illustrating the strain which had built up between them over many years and had only increased since their acquaintanceship with Ruskin.

'I trust you won't be repeating the invitation?' John La Touche questioned his wife abruptly.

'No, I think perhaps you're right, the friendship *would* be better kept in London,' she answered as nonchalantly as she could.

'Friendship?' he scoffed, before asserting violently, 'John Ruskin is no friend of mine, nor ever will be.'

She had long suspected that the two men would never see eye to eye and, having struggled to identify any mutual interest other than Rose, who only appeared to promote a strange kind of rivalry in her husband, was dejected to admit that the past few days, far from uniting them, merely illustrated the impossibility of any fellowship arising in future.

After exchanging a few brief words of polite assurances to Ruskin, namely that they were delighted that he had visited them and that they looked forward to seeing him in London in the autumn, the husband and wife accompanied him to the waiting carriage, as did their children despite it being long past the hour of their bedtime.

The three forlorn faces peering into his carriage window were in marked contrast to the excited ones he had seen on the night of his arrival, and he was greatly moved by their reluctance to part with him.

As their parents joined them in crowding around the carriage, Ruskin perceived that they did not look half so sad to see him go, however, and that La Touche looked especially relieved to be waving him goodbye as the coachman signalled to the horses.

Ruskin tried to dismiss such thoughts as symptoms of his own paranoia and insecurity, yet he could not stop the multitude of other feelings which came over him as he drove away. The saddest one of all was the thought of not seeing Rosie again for months, during which time she was bound to change again. Did he want to keep her from growing up? Of course he did.

In Rose the true and glorious sense of the miracle of human love had been revealed to him, and in the exaltation of her beauty and innocence, the world, which he had until then sought by its own light alone, seemed a newly-revealed and strangely celestial place whenever he was near her.

It was his intention to pause in order to see friends on his way back to Denmark Hill, yet he knew, with every mile he traversed, that he would only be able to think of Ireland, nor could he prevent slumping into his old depression on returning to his parental home. He would live for just one person and struggle under the weight of being unable to express such devotion, yet to all who knew him this pain would be but poorly concealed.

HYSTERIA

E MILY, HAVING BEEN STRUCK BY THE CLOSENESS BETWEEN Rose and Ruskin, was not surprised to witness her sister's spirits decline sharply in the days following his departure, or that she threw herself into her studies with an increased vigour which verged on the unhealthy.

Having been advised by Ruskin that she should learn the Greek alphabet, Rose set herself the task of committing it to memory in one sitting and reported jubilantly in her next letter to him that, having successfully mastered it in just three hours, she had already begun studying Greek verbs.

By the time Ruskin received this missive, which had been jointly composed by Mrs La Touche, much to his irritation, he had once more travelled to France and was then residing in the small town of Bonneville in the Swiss Alps.

Entirely insensible of his mother and father's despair at his inability to settle to life with them at Denmark Hill, he had not been home from

Ireland a week before setting off again, trusting that the distance might help him escape the shadow of dissatisfaction which his love for Rose had cast over his life.

Although his parents talked of joining him in Switzerland, he was relieved when his mother's injured hip was still not recovered enough for her to travel, longing as he did for the freedom which breaking away from them afforded. When alone he could please himself by forgoing dinner in order to spend an entire evening writing Rosie a letter, or simply re-reading one of hers as often as he pleased until his eyelids grew heavy and her sweet words merged into a dream.

But whilst he initially revelled in this solitude, Ruskin found that he grew weary of his own company and began to sense something ominous ahead, a feeling inspired by a series of disturbing nightmares in which all the clocks inside Harristown, and there were a great many, stopped on the stroke of midnight, when their faces would turn mysteriously black.

Fearful lest it should be one of his old fits of madness, he was increasingly sure that this sense of foreboding was intuitive and warned of some danger about to happen to Rosie. With a dread that never left him, he waited to see if he could perceive any clue from her letters and went about day to day in a restless state of agitation that could not be soothed by any occupation he turned to.

Rose was meanwhile continually distracted by having to await Ruskin's delayed communications from abroad; and however much his letters initially cheered her, she too could not shake off the gloom which had enshrouded her ever since the night when she had waved him goodbye.

All her usual amiability had vanished and instead she was only a girl who carried out her studies obsessively, with no interest in idle games. The long summer days were fading fast, as were the happy memories of Ruskin's visit.

Rose's vitality was dissipated along with it, for she had no inclination to even walk Bruno that first chill week of October, a state of mind Mrs La Touche noted with concern as her daughter lolled about in the drawing room each day, reading avidly, with Bruno at her feet. She would barely even acknowledge anyone who entered the room, and would say, 'I missed that, what was it you said?' without the slightest interest if it did not concern Ruskin and the latest instalment of his adventures.

Rose devoted herself utterly to the lessons he had set before going away and nothing would draw her from the determination to complete them all and thereby impress her tutor by the time he returned from Switzerland. Knowing that her mind and imagination, not simply her pretty features, were the attributes he most admired and wished to nurture, she thus sought to expand her capacity as far as she could through tireless exertion and study far beyond the breadth of other girls her age.

Mrs La Touche, whilst impressed to see that her daughter's outlook had changed from that of a capricious girl who loved horses and dogs far more than art or books, could not help thinking how out of character such studiousness seemed and considered with cynicism Rose's motivation in disciplining herself so extremely in order to learn all that her ambitious teacher desired.

It was a cold morning, yet Rose had not dressed appropriately and shivered as she walked lethargically downstairs, wishing that she had worn her shawl but too weary to go back. Regardless of it being the draughtiest spot in the house, she settled herself in the window seat in the hall and waited for the mail boy whom she hoped would bring Ruskin's reply to her last letter.

Attempting to content herself by reading a Mrs Gaskell novel, she was so preoccupied and disappointed at there being no sign of the post that she hardly managed to take in a paragraph, nor did she acknowledge Emily when her sister entered wearing a full riding habit.

'Are you taking Swallow out today?' Emily asked.

'No, not today.'

'You're not feeling unwell?' she questioned in concern.

'No, of course not,' Rose replied defensively, 'I'm just a little tired.'

'Are you missing Mr Ruskin?' she teased, before realising that she shouldn't have, for it caused her youngest sibling to blush and look cross.

'How can I be, when he writes to me so very often?' she denied unconvincingly.

'Letters aren't quite the same as *seeing* someone,' Emily ventured, before considering it wise to change the subject. She cautioned kindly, 'You must have worn yourself out these past weeks with studying. I'm sure Mr Ruskin didn't intend for you to apply yourself quite so enthusiastically.'

'He knows that I am capable of much more than…' Yet Rose did not finish her sentence and, having turned increasingly pale as she was speaking, wavered unsteadily as she went to stand up, falling before Emily on the hard stone floor.

A footman who had witnessed this rushed to assist and, carrying Rose into the drawing room, placed her carefully on a sofa. Emily ordered him to alert her mother who was in the garden, while she remained by her sister's side and attempted in vain to revive her by tapping her hand lightly.

Rushing to her daughter's side and insisting that she be put to bed immediately, it was not long before Mrs La Touche began to rage against Ruskin. Putting Rose's incapacity wholly down to her recent fervour in studying Greek, she apportioned him with the full blame for having set a curriculum so far removed from that which she had originally called upon him to devise.

'Your father warned me that Rose's admiration of him should be extinguished,' she vented to Emily, 'but still I saw no harm in it. What shall I tell him now?'

'It's impossible for any of us to judge whether that is the cause,' she attempted to pacify, 'or if her earlier illness is simply making a reappearance.'

Neither she nor her mother dared suggest to La Touche that Rose had succumbed to some form of lovesickness or hysteria, and whilst the illness mystified everyone, including the most highly respected physicians who travelled from Dublin to attend on the patient, they finally concurred with Mrs La Touche's public stance that her daughter had simply over-taxed her brain, and strictly forbade her to study further until such time as she was fully recovered – for recover she would, they reassured the parents.

***

Enthused at holding so much influence over Rose, just as Ruskin was preparing to send her a letter encouraging her to examine the words "Life" and "Death" from Greek onwards, he received a lengthy account of this strange turn of events from Mrs La Touche, who followed by cautioning him against writing to her daughter on any serious topic.

Explaining the nature of Rose's symptoms, which had continued to alter following her initial inertia, she elaborated:

"She seems perfectly well every day until about five o'clock, when her countenance undergoes a dramatic change and she is no longer able to occupy herself in any way. Very often, at bedtime there is a slight return of the attack, when even her consciousness is partially impaired. For the time being rest is the only suggested cure, and therefore Rose is forbidden to write to you or exert herself in any way, with the exception of occasionally being allowed to sign her name below mine..."

Whilst concerned and puzzled as to the irregular nature of the child's illness, Mrs La Touche's tone prompted Ruskin to think that she took a sinister pleasure in controlling her daughter's correspondence with him, nor did he take kindly to the word "forbidden", as though he should be some kind of disease to be got rid of.

Meanwhile, Ruskin considered it to be an odd irony that Rose's illness gave her mother a welcome justification for increasing the regularity of her own letters to him, for they almost doubled in frequency over the following weeks, something he should not have minded had they solely discussed his dear one.

Although they were always written with the pretence of sending some news as to the patient's progress, he disliked how hastily Mrs La Touche moved onto other, far less worthy subjects, not least herself, the moment she had finished with her perfunctory display of motherly devotion.

Ruskin was unusually glad to find his father dining alone one evening shortly after returning to Denmark Hill, feeling sure that John James would give him measured counsel as to Rosie's illness, however much he might not like his opinion.

Thus, with clenched jaw, Ruskin took up the seat beside him, and his father soon noticed that he was brooding over something and wished to be prompted. Initially unsympathetic, John James eventually rested his knife and fork and urged impatiently, 'Out with it, man! If you're going to make me suffer your gloomy countenance at least have the courtesy to tell me *why* you're wearing it.'

'Rose was taken ill soon after I left Harristown,' Ruskin confessed.

'Is there a connection between the two events?' his father enquired pointedly, wondering when his son would heed his warnings. 'Have I not long since foretold that problems would arise from your association with that family?'

'I assure you, Father, Rose's illness has nothing to do with any regard she has for me,' Ruskin strongly denied, before rising in restlessness and stalking the length of the room, one hand placed on his lower back. 'She likes me to make a pet of her, it's true,' he went on, 'yet it causes her no trouble when I go away.'

'What, then, do you attribute it to?' John James quizzed sceptically, looking at his son from under his untrimmed white eyebrows.

'Her mother blames me for suggesting she learn Greek. Rose didn't say anything at the time, but as soon as I was gone she set to work, and perhaps it was too much for her.'

'Rot!' his father rebutted, rising to replenish his glass of wine and pour one for Ruskin. 'If you really believed that you wouldn't look so harassed.'

However vexed and frustrated John James was that his son never took his advice, he could hardly fail to pity him whilst in such obvious distress, for the affection between father and son, though often tested and rarely expressed, remained boundless. Before returning to his seat he placed his hand on his son's shoulder with reluctant but deep sympathy, a sign of tenderness that Ruskin had long since given up hoping for and therefore appreciated all the more.

His father considered the situation for a few moments before venturing, 'I see that you have your heart set upon her,' raising his finger to silence Ruskin when he opened his mouth ready to interject, for John James would have no interruption and went on forcefully, 'there is no use trying to convince me otherwise. I also know that you would love Rose just the same, a woman or a girl, but as you cannot make her any older or yourself any younger you are cursed with having to decide whether to wait an agonising wait or walk away from this dire situation while your reputation is still intact.'

'I can't do *that*,' he answered simply, too weary to keep up the pretence his father had long since seen through. 'Nor did you ever think of renouncing my mother despite having to endure many years of patience,' he continued, believing they finally had some common ground.

'It was entirely different for us,' John James disputed; 'we were both adults and were prevented from marrying due to inadequate finances. In your case, you must defer courtship until Rose is of sufficient maturity and age to discover what it is *she* wants.'

Ruskin took a gulp of wine in order to stall for time, for his father's statement, however much he acknowledged the truth of it, struck a painful chord and made him feel as ashamed as Adam.

'I feel as though I were being accused of something,' he eventually replied.

'It may not be easy for you to understand, but I am offering you guidance not censure. Others certainly won't view the relationship between you and Rose as innocently as *I*,' John James expounded, shaking his head. 'My concern is to protect your good name, which will be irrevocably tarnished if you persist with this infatuation, for infatuation I will call it until you come to me when she is full grown and then tell me you love her. Therefore, it seems to me that the best course would be to *try* to put her out of your mind.'

'And you claim to understand me?' Ruskin railed, examining his father's lined face, so earnest in its expression.

'Better than you imagine, for what good will this friendship do anyone as it is?' John James challenged.

'I cannot say, I only know that I am perhaps one of the most unhappy men in the world right now,' Ruskin finally admitted. 'You don't know the purgatory of having always to hide my feelings, even though my love is entirely pure and *will* survive the years that I must endure until I can declare it. Until then, I am restricted to using terms of endearment in a childish way for fear that my words will be misconstrued if they are said in seriousness.' He paused before asking his father solemnly, 'Isn't it strange to think that very soon she'll be fourteen and too old to make a pet of, yet still not old enough to pledge myself to?'

John James thought he saw his son brush a tear away as he lifted his glass and drained the final dregs. And without saying anything further, Ruskin left the room, leaving his father to reflect on their exchange, with no solution in sight other than to hope that his son would resolve to break off all contact with the La Touches before his respectability sustained a calamitous injury.

Margaret, who had struggled to regain her former strength following her hip accident, was meanwhile disgruntled that her son appeared to have limited tolerance with her increasing infirmity, and when Ruskin sought her out the following afternoon she identified it as the natural inclination of a child to go in search of one parent when ill-pleased with the other, for such had been his habit since boyhood.

She was resting in the drawing room, her feet propped up on a footstool, when Ruskin sought her out, being in need of an audience who would satisfy rather than challenge his own inclination regarding Rose. Yet so unimpressed was Margaret that he failed to greet her kindly or enquire after her health before he commenced his rant that she was unsympathetic from the off, for he immediately removed a letter from his breast pocket which he prepared to read aloud.

'"How are you today?" might be a nicer opening,' she scolded him, before swallowing a medicine which Anne had just brought in.

'Yes, you're right, forgive me,' he said, leaning over and kissing her cheek penitently when once the old cantankerous domestic had finally withdrawn, for Anne always lingered as long as she justifiably could in the hope of eliciting some gossip which she might share with the servants downstairs.

'Is there any news of Rose?' Margaret enquired indulgently, for she knew that he could think of nothing other than the note in his hand which she presumed hailed from Ireland. 'How fondly I recall the La Touche girls playing in our garden. I long for such youthful company again, especially now that you are so seldom home.'

'The doctors have forbidden her to study and ordered her to rest,' Ruskin proceeded, ignoring his mother's gibe at his persistent absence, 'so I suggested that she take up cookery when she is well enough.'

'She'll like that,' his mother concurred, whilst frowning at her son who continued to scan the letter without looking at her, so absorbed was he when any new report of Rose's progress arrived, though he could not disguise his irritation at no longer having any direct communication with her.

'You and your father were up late last night,' Margaret broached; 'I hope nothing he said will cause you to travel abroad again?' For she anticipated that he might already be making plans to go away and grieved that John James had exhausted his forbearance.

'I intend to depart for Switzerland again next week, but it has nothing to do with anything my father said to me,' Ruskin refuted.

He lied, for his father recognised feelings in him he had not been ready to own, and which, in being forced to admit, had only made him feel more divided as to how he proceeded with the La Touches.

'You must do as you see fit,' she huffed, turning her face away.

Despite knowing that he was driving nails into his mother's heart and into his father's coffin, Ruskin left for the Continent once more, yet something told him as he did so that he was only putting off to some future day the realisation of his father's words.

SWITZERLAND XI

Mrs La Touche continued to keep Ruskin regularly updated as to her daughter's health and informed him, a few weeks after what she described as Rose's first "brain attack", that her daughter had begun to cook the moment she was well enough. "She has made a cake and wishes so much that you were here to eat it", the letter, with only Rosie's name written in pencil below her own, read temptingly.

As he made his way to Switzerland with Crawley, recollections of Harristown persistently took his mind away from the reading he had intended to occupy himself with, and the changing views from the window of the train carriage were constantly interspersed with visions of Rose, some remembered and others prophetic.

The wondrous Swiss landscape, with everywhere the eternal mountains he craved and the infinitude of Alpine snow stretching before him, provided a suitably majestic frame for his memories of Rosie: standing in Denmark Hill's orchard bathed in sunlight; bravely climbing to the summit of Pollaphuca Falls; or simply sketching beside the schoolroom hearth with a kitten on her lap.

Most of all, he smiled to himself on recalling Rose playing croquet with Emily and urging him to leave his work, for she had the most bewildering characteristics of audaciousness, innocence and precocity he had ever encountered. He could not name one quality he preferred to another, for she was a perfect example of all that was worthy of man's admiration.

Rather than simply surmise how Rose would evolve into womanhood, his imagination painted just such a picture, transforming her into an elegant young lady who looked taller and more statuesque in long dresses, yet worryingly fragile. He was relieved to still recognise his old Rose, however, for in these strangely elaborate daydreams her face retained all the angelic qualities he cherished so: her hands remained dainty and she continued to style her hair neatly pinned back, enhancing her graceful neck and slender shoulders.

From these vivid imaginings, all his fears, resulting from a dread of no longer being able to pen her childish verses or refer to her by any nicknames (when she would be thought too grown up to have a tutor at all), fell away like leaves, for he knew that he would always love her.

A strange contentment passed over him that first night at Lucerne; and setting any former sadnesses aside, he amused himself by dining in his quaint, shuttered room, belonging to an ancient, beamed coaching inn known to him of old, where he had requested a view overlooking the Reuss and the covered Chapel Bridge with its tall, red-roofed water tower. His mind would not let him alone long enough to eat, however, for poetry, humble and filled with sentiment, sprang into his mind as effortlessly as the river flowed through the city, making no attempt to conceal his longing to be near his dear one and relieving him of emotions too distracting to keep silent within his breast.

Even in private he was apt to disguise all this in a childish tone which allowed him to use terms of endearment he would soon be forced to refrain from, and he delighted in the innocence of such a language which contained more devotion than any love letter he had ever composed.

"Rosie Posie, Rosie rare,
Rocks, & woods, & clouds, and air
Are all the colour of my pet:
And yet, & yet, & yet, & yet
She is not here – but, where?"

Satisfied with the first verse, Ruskin, alerted by the sound of the town hall clock chiming, leant out of the open window and observed how beautifully the moonlight was reflected on the still sapphire-coloured river, prompting him to wonder, like many a lover before him, what his dear one was doing at that moment and when their paths should cross again. His love for Rose was written on the arched sky; it looked out from every star; it was the poetry of nature and that which uplifted the spirit within him.

"Rosie pet, and Rosie, puss,
See, the moonlight's on the Reuss:
O'er the Alps the clouds lie loose,
Tossed about in silver tangles…

Tower and steeple, chiming sadly
Say (or else I hear them badly)
'Good night, Liffey; bad night, Reuss
Good night, Rosie, Posie, Puss.'"

Acknowledging that he would have to pass many years in limbo, Ruskin was emboldened to go in search of some contentment as a bachelor and, desiring complete parental freedom for the first time in his life, spent the majority of his remaining time in Switzerland corresponding with the Commune of Bonneville about purchasing the whole of the top of the Brezon, the summit of the mountain above Bonneville, where he hoped to build a traditional Swiss house with commanding views towards Geneva, with Jura in the distance and the Salève mountain range to the left.

Persuading Crawley to climb four thousand feet to see the site of his proposed hermitage, which he had already impulsively agreed to acquire from the local authorities, regardless of the impracticalities that would make the scheme all but impossible, Ruskin stood with his hands on his hips scanning one of the grandest ranges of jagged blue mountain he knew in Savoy and proudly declared, 'This is to be my new home.'

'Whatever do you mean?'

He illustrated the size and scale of his ideal dwelling by raising and expanding his arms like an over-imaginative child. 'I want to live in a beautiful, yet unobtrusive Savoy cottage, the finest piece of architecture I have ever had the felicity of contemplating.'

Judging his master's state of mind to be irrational at the very least, Crawley blinked and replied inadequately, 'Really?'

'Yes, for such abodes always suggest a gentle, pure and pastoral life. From such a dwelling I shall be able to see the distant Alpine villages for miles around and the valley in which they sit. Both are overwhelmingly lovely in winter, encompassed in white ripples of drifted snow, just like the foam from a steamer on the sea.'

Taking the architectural plans he had wasted no time in commissioning, Ruskin pulled them from a tin tube and, unravelling them, crouched down on a patch of grass and spread them flat before holding the sheets in place with a few rocks.

Revealing an archetypal Swiss chalet that might have featured in a fairy-tale – two storeys high with charming wooden shutters all the way around that would open onto the most spectacular views – he continued, 'Although I have always been in awe of the scenery of the Alps, it is the picturesque and humble dwellings that lie in their midst I most appreciate and long to retreat to now that my own life has become too much to bear.'

'It will certainly be remote,' Crawley agreed, dumbfounded by the proposition to such an extent that he could only laugh at its folly. 'If you ask your friends for dinner it will be a nice walk home for them, while any unexpected visitors, arriving at an isolated chalet, might not come again.'

'I'm not sure they would come anyhow. But aside from that?' Ruskin prompted impatiently, eager to hear some words of encouragement and enthusiasm.

'You are nothing if not a visionary,' his servant replied anxiously, unable to comprehend the complexity and ambition of building such a house in such an unsuitable location.

'I think it would be foolish to build a mere wooden chalet in which I should be afraid of fire, especially as I should often want large fires,' his master continued, ever more enthused by the various aspects of design, 'therefore, I mean to build a small stone house which will keep anything I want there in perfect safety and will not be likely to be blown away by the north wind.'

'Being several thousand feet from the plain there is no water supply, merely a waste of barren rock with pasturage for a few goats to graze in summer,' Crawley observed, looking down the sloping cliff face, 'and however will you construct such a place with no road on which to transport the materials, never mind the daily expense of getting anything to eat?'

Crawley's attempts to rationalise were in vain, however, for Ruskin had an answer for everything, albeit entirely nonsensical.

'Water is neither here nor there!' he dismissed casually. 'I shall construct a dam to collect snow, and I can get donkeys to carry up the building materials,' he insisted, snatching the plans away in irritation.

'But surely it would take you a whole year just to transport them?' his valet persisted.

'There is nothing that can't be overcome. Don't you see that however many obstacles may be in my way I *must* find a home of my own?' Ruskin asked almost pleadingly. 'Somewhere I can go to escape the world, and not just a cottage in Wales with a pony and my own cabbages.'

'And far be it from me to deter you, only I think this idea might prove more a test than a solution,' Crawley concluded.

His evaluation was further supported when Ruskin went on to share his plans with his parents, who were equally horrified and raised yet more questions. Though inclined to put creative vision before domestic practicalities, and believing that his parents had thwarted him in all the earnest fire of passion and life, after one objection on top of another even Ruskin had to admit that his plan was somewhat fantastical and must culminate in his unwilling abandonment.

'Though I have no intention of returning to London in any hurry, I have quite given up all thoughts of a house in Switzerland,' he announced to Crawley a few weeks later when they were out gathering juniper branches to sketch, 'even if doing so indicates a certain hopelessness. It vexes me how much this news will please my parents, for they never wanted the scheme to succeed.'

His tone betrayed his bitter disappointment, and whilst it was akin to that of a child deprived of a much longed-for present, or the fruit of the Herne Hill orchard he was always forbidden, Crawley pitied his master for not managing to break free of his ties to Denmark Hill, binding him like quicksand whenever he was there, and he felt guilty for having assisted Margaret and John James in bringing an end to their son's beautiful, though outlandish, dream.

Ruskin's one consolation was that by early December Rose had made a promising recovery and, corresponding with him directly, sent him vivid accounts of her cats, her new love of cookery and Emily's piano playing, which, as in all the sweetest music, had a tinge of sadness in every note, as if she too were mourning the passing of youth.

Rose meanwhile grew resentful that her mother continued to supervise her every word and limited the number of letters she could send to Ruskin, believing not that she cared to prevent her overtaxing herself but simply wanted the larger share of correspondence.

> *"Dearest St C,*
>
> *Though you have not returned my last visit, (you haven't had time), I am coming again, for it takes such a long time to get an answer, and I won't wait. My last letter was all about cats; this one won't be, for one reason why I write is because I want to yowl to someone about having to go to London soon. I don't think I'd ever go if I could do what I liked –*

unless you were there. I am sitting at the table by the window where you drew the poplars by the river when you were here, and Emily is playing Schubert's 'Die Klage' while I write, and it's very – ah. I don't know why, but going away gets worse and worse, and this year it's terrible."

The morning prior to the La Touches' annual removal to London, Rose waited in the hall for the post, as had become her custom. She had been there for what seemed like an interminable period, yet she was determined to delay going out riding until she had successfully identified Ruskin's handwriting among that morning's bundle of letters.

Leaning over the butler anxiously after he had snatched the mail directly from the post boy, she grew frustrated when he appeared to be in no particular hurry to sort through them and proceeded to scan each one tediously before setting them down on the salver. As soon as Rose caught a glimpse of Ruskin's familiar scrawl addressed to herself, she beamed with happiness, however, and snatching it out of the old servant's grasp regarded him with a disrespectful sneer.

'Tell Mama I shan't be back in time for luncheon,' she called to him whilst marching out of the house, so impatient was she to go in search of a hiding place where she could read Ruskin's words away from the prying eyes of her mother.

It was a frosty December morning and the ice had only just melted outside, yet Rose hardly felt the cold. Seeing her mother approaching, she hastily mounted Emily's horse, Swallow, and took hold of the reins.

'I don't want you to overdo it, Rose,' her mother rushed over to urge.

'The doctor recommended fresh air,' she responded impertinently.

At a loss to know how to prevent her from going, Mrs La Touche merely sighed and answered, 'You must get your stubbornness from your father.'

'I should think I get it from *you*,' her daughter retorted provocatively before nudging the horse with her heels, forcing her mother to let her pass, and breaking into a quick pace.

Mrs La Touche could only look on exasperated, for Rose never rested when she could be active. A competent rider for her years, even though she would have preferred to ride like a boy rather than always side-saddle, she enjoyed vigorous exercise and found that it gave her more confidence generally, while her mother believed it only made her daughter unduly reckless and harder to discipline.

Steering the animal hard and fast as if in rebellion of maternal control, Rose pushed Swallow as furiously as he would go and thrashed the air with the crop until she felt the exhilaration she always experienced when faced with the dangers of riding at high speed.

Gripping the reins until her hands became clammy and began to blister the soft skin of her palms, she closed her eyes as the horse approached a fence she knew was too ambitious for it, yet which she nevertheless forced the animal to take with the fearlessness only the very young or the inherently wild possess.

Displaying considerable strength despite her frail appearance, Rose delighted in her own daring and mastery of the animal, yet could not deny the sense of relief she felt when she was delivered safely on the other side.

Realising that the stallion was tired and that she had been foolhardy in bullying him so, she commanded him to slow down, only Swallow, being much confused at this, began to buck and kick his heels violently, thus forcing his young mistress to turn back and forgo unbuttoning the brown leather saddlebag in which she had locked Ruskin's precious letter away.

'Stupid beast,' she complained, her cheeks burning from both the thrill of jumping and her annoyance at her mother and Swallow for thwarting the peace she had sought to enjoy Ruskin's communication.

After several minutes and much persuasion she finally encouraged the temperamental creature to turn around and retrace his steps, albeit at a much slower pace, so exhausted was he from his efforts.

Being careful to transfer the letter to the pocket of her dress before alighting, she intended to read it as soon as she was installed in her partially private chamber, for she dared not lock the door or her mother would guess that she was keeping a secret.

Whilst Mrs La Touche had always taken the liberty of reading Ruskin's letters to her daughter, as Rose grew older she wished to guard them from being pored over and analysed by the person who least understood their confidential language, nor did she divulge to her mother the countless responses she passed to Mrs Casey to post for her.

"Dearest St Crumpet,

I got your letter just as I was going out riding, so I could only give it one peep, and then I tucked it into my riding-habit pocket and pinned it down, so that it could be talking to me while I was riding. I had to shut up my mouth so tight when I met Mama, for she would have taken it and read it if I'd told her and it wouldn't have gone on riding with me. As it was, we ran rather a chance of me, and pocket, and letter, and all, going over — for Swallow (that's Emily's horse, which I always ride now) was in such tremendous spirits about having your handwriting on his back that he took to kicking and jumping in such a way that I felt like I was riding a great wave, so you may imagine I could not spare a hand to unpin my dear pocket and had to wait in patience till Swallow had done 'flying — flying south' and we were safely home again."

Rose's temperament was not so very different from her mother's, though she would have been loath to admit it, for she longed to know the content of her mama's correspondence with Ruskin as much as vice versa, being suspicious that her childish faults and immature mischiefs were unfairly recounted in order that her mother might show herself in a better light.

Where Mrs La Touche had always related her daughter's idiosyncrasies in good humour rather than in complaint, Rose became increasingly mistrustful and keen to oversee the way in which she was being portrayed to the one whose approval she sought above and beyond her own parents.

An argument ensued when Mrs La Touche made the mistake of adding, in her Christmas message to Ruskin, that her daughter sent her "best love", to which he replied directly to Rose saying that she might as well have sent him her compliments, there being neither "best" nor "worst" in love.

"It was Mama's invention, that, about my best love — I never sent a bit of it. I hardly ever send a message if I can help it, for I like to say it myself. When did I ever send you my 'best love'? As you say, one's love isn't best or worst, and, if you please, if you've got my love already how am I to send it? No, I only write to remind you of it and to wish you a Merry Christmas."

The charm of this explanation prompted Ruskin to feel guilty for having caused Rose anxiety, yet her words also greatly pleased him when he was at his loneliest and most forlorn in Lucerne, having selfishly ignored the pleas of his parents to return to Denmark Hill for Christmas. Worse still, he afterwards reproached himself, it was quite likely to be the last the three of them would ever know together. How dreadfully he took his mother and father for granted!

Regret being a futile emotion, Ruskin tried to content himself by working, but looking out for a Rosie letter often prevented the concentration he needed. On receiving her reminder of love he could not help but question what kind she intended to proclaim; for whilst it could not yet qualify as being of a romantic sort, he was confident that her meaning was much more than friendship.

It was easy to be tricked into false interpretation, however, for he perceived that his passion naturally increased upon receipt of such flirtations and he looked for any encouragement which offered him hope for the future, even though his ordinary judgement would not allow him to entertain this seriously.

Rose's words of affection spoke more intently to Ruskin than any he had known, and he had been offered much love in his life, both sought and unsought. Pondering on her terms of endearment caused him to idle away whole days simply lost in thought. Isolated and self-pitying, that Christmas Eve he spent several mindless hours throwing stones at icicles in a ravine, like a frustrated, lovelorn adolescent might hurl a brick at a glass and china shop.

How little he could have imagined, sitting in his home corner yearning for a glance of hill snow, that he should be as thoroughly out of humour as ever after a monotonous day in London, perhaps more so. Vanity of vanities! He knew that he should remember that day thereafter and be mad with himself.

Shunning Crawley's companionship by way of punishing himself, the loneliness was very great and any temporary peace he felt from the solitude was as if he had buried himself in a tuft of grass on a battlefield wet with blood, for the cry of the earth was in his ears and there was no quietening it.

Ruskin saw the foolishness of this self-imposed exile, but still he preferred to meander around the desolate Alpine streets, never having felt more out of place. Almost all the residents were installed in their warm and comfortable homes for the festivities, or out carol singing in the neighbouring hills and valleys, on the summit of which the clouds melted into an icy mist and created a mysterious, yet magical, veil over the scene.

There was no sky quite as empyrean as the one he witnessed in Switzerland, nor any air as cleansing as the Alpine kind which he inhaled deep into his lungs over and again as if it were restorative enough to purify the sins of all God's children.

Sensing that a snowstorm was imminent, Ruskin entered a small church in the hope of not only taking shelter and warming himself but of finding some spiritual guidance. Seating himself in one of the incommodious wooden pews, he stared up at the large picture of Christ for several minutes and wondered what to make of the fellow, portrayed in that instance as particularly scrawny and helpless, with a face too full of his own pain to care much about anyone else's.

Though he might get all his sins forgiven for the asking, he supposed he was rather the better for them. He found himself praying, not because he had any faith left but because it would have been nice to find some. Having once believed that he knew well enough how one ought to live, it was a surprise to find his entire world upside down and with no thought within him that did not, in some measure, belong to Rose.

Ultimately, he was too proud to go to God or Christ for assistance, and instead it was to his dear old journal, his single non-judgemental confidant, to whom he poured out his heart that night, knowing all the while that the answer lay within himself if he could only fathom its meaning:

> *"The love of Rose is a religion to me, having gone through life with nothing to love. I love my parents no more than the sun and the moon, only I should be annoyed and puzzled if either of them went out. Still less do I love God, not that I have any quarrel with him."*

The glorious sun cast her healing hands upon Lucerne that Christmas Day morning, confirming Ruskin's opinion that the finest Swiss summer was nothing compared to that of its winter scenery when the weather was fine.

Mount Pilatus looked as if it was entirely constructed of frosted silver, like Geneva filigree work, while beyond the Alps stood serene, lighted by golden rays which cast long purple shadows.

It seemed significant that his first sight of them had been when he was Rose's present age, for they were his first revelation of the full beauty of the earth and the opening page of all the volumes he would go on to dedicate his pen.

Hopeful that painting a watercolour might distract him, Ruskin sketched and painted until his hands grew numb from the cold; yet it was the myriad thoughts of Rosie, and his parents alone at Denmark Hill, and not fear of frostbite, that prevented his dedication to the task and made him pack his things away and give up.

During this introspection, he realised the great danger in becoming overly reliant on his relationship with his favourite pupil, with whom he had a connection that was still impossible to make any real sense of.

Far from their long separations lessening the strength of his attachment, there was something reassuring in the distance between them, though he did have a tendency to exaggerate every possible meaning contained within her letters.

The first note he received after Christmas was from Mrs La Touche and surely confirmed that he was not imagining everything, however, for it contained a peculiar account of a dialogue between herself and Rose which she thought would amuse him, though it simply succeeded in highlighting the lady's rivalry with her daughter whilst lending credence to his own interpretation of Rose's affection.

Mrs L.	*Rosie, don't you wish Mr Ruskin would come home?*
Rosie.	*Yes, indeed I do. How tiresome of him.*
Mrs L.	*Do you think he wants us at all?*
Rosie.	*Well, perhaps he does. I think he wants to see me, Mama.*
Mrs L.	*And doesn't he want to see me?*
Rosie.	*Well... you know... well... Mama, I think he likes your letters quite as much as yourself, and you write so very often – and I can't write often. So he must want to see me.*

Attempting to decipher the workings of Rose's heart was like trying to find the clues to a labyrinth – he was continually lost. Was it simply a happy delusion to think that she might one day love him as he desired? Either way, he couldn't help but feel encouraged by this intriguing scene and chose to frequently reflect upon it until such time as he could discover the depth of her attachment from her own lips.

In a separate letter, Rose described a dream she'd had featuring them both, but more than anything she wanted to tell him how strongly she felt that their thoughts had crossed that Christmas Day, prompting Ruskin to clutch the paper for sheer joy on it being revealed that they had both simultaneously noticed how brightly Venus had shone that night – she from her bedroom window and he from his modest Swiss inn.

Whilst pondering on the symbolism of the evening star, the brightest light of all and the guide of the wise man, she had prayed that he might be guided by it too:

"You needn't tell me that you have not forgotten me, yet I can't help saying that I was looking for a letter. I wanted so much to know what you were doing and thinking this Christmas Day. I have always told you that I can see some things quite plain and I have been living in Switzerland with you all week. Am I not there with you still?"

The greatest Christmas gift he had ever received, Ruskin folded the letter carefully and decided to carry it with him ever afterwards, wrapped in gold leaf, tucked inside his waistcoat, close to his heart, thus granting him the pleasure of being able to re-read his favourite passage whenever he liked.

Crawley often wondered if Ruskin was secretly glad that the house-building exercise had come to nothing, for his master had no wish to remain in Switzerland after receiving Rosie's star letter and instead decided to return to London in order to see the La Touches who had recently arrived in the city and were, save John La Touche, eager for him to come back.

Ruskin had planned to make his way home slowly from Basel, yet the prospect of seeing Rose within a matter of days compelled him to hasten his journey, packing up his things with a giddy urgency which Crawley soon realised was entirely driven by the promised reunion with his favourite pupil.

Far from harbouring any resentment about the failure to make a new life for himself abroad, Rose's fourteenth birthday on the third of January meant that Ruskin put all his energies into returning to London in time to wish her Happy Birthday; for contrary to what he had so recently managed to convince himself, when once he was *certain* of seeing her, letters were no longer a satisfactory means of communication.

He was not able to sleep or think properly knowing that she was there waiting for him, and although he knew that he was only setting himself up for another fit of depression following her return to Ireland come the spring, just the promise of seeing her face and talking with her seemed a fair exchange.

Too impatient to await Crawley's assistance, Ruskin thus began rushing to and fro across the hotel room, grabbing armfuls of clothes from the wardrobe and chest of drawers and hurling them into the trunk with little care as to their state when they arrived at their destination, much to the surprise of his valet who, notwithstanding being used to his master's habit of altering travel arrangements at the last moment, particularly during his bouts of melancholia, had never witnessed him so frantic or eager to be gone.

Suddenly feeling ashamed that Rose and not his parents had been able to persuade him to hurry back, in the midst of the chaos of packing Ruskin somehow found time to dedicate half an hour to writing his father a brief letter explaining his decision to return sooner than he had led him to expect, although he did not belittle John James's intuition by trying to disguise his true motivation.

"*I am sorry to have stayed here as long as I have, but I have had several things to make up my mind about very seriously, and under circumstances of some ambiguousness. What my conduct should be towards the La Touches was the chief of these, and that depended on my finding out, if possible, whether Rosie is what you think her, an entirely simple child, or whether she is what I think her.*"

DAMP AND MILDEW

IT WAS ON STEPPING THROUGH THE DOOR OF DENMARK HILL on New Year's Day that Ruskin realised how much he had dreaded returning to the parental oppression from which he had long sought, and failed, to release himself. Perhaps he had simply been away too often, he reasoned, yet it *was* undoubtedly the last place he felt at home, and his heart sank within his breast as he went in search of his parents.

To make matters worse, he discovered that John James had succumbed to an agonising urinary disease in his absence which caused him to be irritable and short-tempered, and Ruskin to wish himself anywhere but near him.

Far from feeling sympathetic on witnessing what he imagined was his father's final decline, he was only angry with himself for not having been a more dutiful son and at there not being enough time or patience on either side to rectify the way things stood between them.

Sensing both parents' unspoken animosity towards him as a result of his long absence, as he could not change it Ruskin merely sought to avoid them by confining himself to his study for the majority of each day, drawing or studying Latin and Greek, and being only too glad when the Turner bequest demanded his presence, or invitations from the La Touches called him away when he ought to have been concentrating on his next book, a work his father was not yet too feeble to undermine or condemn with his usual sourness.

Everything was utterly dreary, even the walk into town which he had formerly found so pleasant had been ruined due to all the fields thereabouts having been built upon, and as if mirroring his own mental deterioration he was alarmed to discover, during a visit to the National Gallery, that they had stored some of Turner's drawings in the basement, causing them to become stained with mildew.

Deeply dejected that his words in praise of Turner had gone such a short way, and that he had not managed to inspire others to appreciate the painter to the degree he had sought, out of loyalty to his old friend Ruskin set about restoring the pictures, unconscious of any hurt he inflicted on prioritising this over spending time with his sick father.

Traipsing to the National Gallery daily in the hope of salvaging the drawings from blight, the insufferable environment of Denmark Hill made Ruskin even more surly with the curators.

Throwing up his hands he fumed, 'I'm done with the whole business after this! If you don't take more responsibility from now on you must take the mildew off yourselves, or leave it on if you like. It really is unimaginable ingratitude that the greatest artist of our generation entrusted you with his life's works on the premise that you would *display* them, not for you to leave them rotting out of sight.'

The heartbreaking neglect was all the more distressing due to Ruskin having previously taken great pains, on being appointed one of the executors of Turner's will, to sort through and index the many drawings and sketches which the artist had bequeathed to the nation.

Along with two incompetent assistants, he had worked all day and often far into the night for many weeks, determined to preserve the legacy which, within just a few years, the gallery had not only failed to exhibit in a new wing, which Turner himself had left sufficient funds for, but were treating much of his old friend's works with the utmost derision by not storing them correctly.

The sight of the damage was often enough to cause Ruskin to weep and rage simultaneously, and he was convinced that he should have gone mad were it not for his quiet afternoons spent with Rose. They were all that sustained him, for she always knew exactly how to soothe and prevent him from feeling completely crestfallen.

He felt better just leaving the gallery and strolling to the La Touche residence with the promise of seeing his Irish Rose, particularly as she was often alone due to Emily, almost eighteen, being out with Mrs La Touche in preparation for her coming-out ball. The fresh air, what little there was of it, and simply being with her was bound to do him good, for whenever he complained of a headache or some other half-fancied malady she would laugh them away.

'You only come to see me because I pet you when you tell me your ailments,' Rose teased, greeting him in the drawing room with a kiss on the cheek. 'I'm not in the least convinced that you have a headache at all.'

'And I don't think you really want me a bit and care more for your cats,' Ruskin returned, sulking playfully.

Rose smiled and, taking Ruskin's arm, led him into the garden which, long and narrow, was in great contrast to the almost never-ending expanse that was her usual setting at Harristown.

'It's too cold to be in the garden today,' he protested, buttoning up his great coat and shivering theatrically as the wind shook the barren branches of the apple tree against the house until they almost snapped against the window panes.

'Hopefully the breeze will carry away your bad humour, for you're in a yowling mood today,' she asserted.

'Yowling?'

'Yes, just like a dog outside a shut door with its nose in the air!'

Rose had the ability to talk to him candidly, yet with humour enough that whatever she said never caused him any offence. Wearing a heavy velvet dress of midnight blue, with a fine lace collar, it was unusually feminine and grown-up compared with the peasant-like attire she typically wore in Ireland. Wrapping a grey woollen cape around her shoulders for warmth, he was glad when she nestled close to him, as if she regarded him as her best friend in the whole world. He had never had one and what a nice sensation it was.

Just as he had long ago observed how the bright summer sun fell upon pretty Rosie at Harristown, Ruskin now noticed how the rays of the low January sunlight alighted upon her to wondrous effect. This angelic beauty on earth was indeed a thing to behold, he marvelled – the strands of gold in her hair in harmony with the rosy tones that were symbolic of her Celtic fire. No, on this occasion he didn't mind how much she had altered since last he had seen her, for the change was always golden.

Although still frail from past illness, she was eluding girlhood with all the charm and allure she had been able to claim as a young child, in honour of which he took to calling her "Bouton", a fine replacement for her outgrown nickname of Rosie Posie.

'It's true, I must be very difficult to live with,' he sighed as they took a seat in an arbour covered with ivy at the end of the garden. 'I sometimes find the days very long and the nights even longer. First I had to witness the Austrians' war with Venice, careless as to whether they caused irrecoverable damage to the city, and now I find that Turner's bequest was no more prized by the National Gallery than a pauper's belongings by a workhouse. Meanwhile, the Queen has lost her husband—'

'Poor Victoria, they say she will never recover from the grief,' Rose interjected girlishly, always happier to talk about romance or chivalry than bequests and wars.

'Prince Albert was one of the few men who could be counted upon to act on the side of right,' Ruskin continued, 'something we could do with as we get ourselves ever more embroiled in the uprising in America.'

Frowning perplexedly she tapped his arm lightly and asked, '*Why* are we?'

'There is nothing, including fighting on the side of slavery, that England will not do in order to protect her cotton trade,' Ruskin explained bitterly. 'It's a wonder we don't have our own civil war to contend with, for we treat our mill workers no better than slaves. I do believe that I shall live to see the ruin of everything good and great in the world.'

'"Man goeth about to devour me, he is daily fighting and troubling me", she declared, reciting one of her favourite psalms with great dignity; '"mine enemies are daily in hand to swallow me up, for they be many that fight against me. Nevertheless, though I am sometimes afraid, yet put I my trust in *Thee.*"'

'What a devout little thing you are, Posie,' he responded, as much touched by the sentiment as if he were still a believer and quite forgetting his promise to forgo using her old pet name.

'It is far nicer to be good than bad,' she affirmed.

'Nicer perhaps, but isn't it more *enjoyable* to be naughty?' he teased.

Rose did not smile, but proceeded seriously,'I can distinctly remember feeling naughty when I was about two or three years old,' she confessed.'I used to get angry and pinch Percy and Emily and would rather destroy a thing than give it to *them.*'

'I never knew the challenge of having to share anything,' Ruskin remarked lightly.'I dare say that is why I remain entirely selfish.'

'You are the kindest and most generous man alive! My first governess taught me not to be badly behaved when I was about four years old, and when Bun came she began teaching me, not only not to be naughty but *why* not. I became more conscientious and the thought that a thing was right always seemed well worth doing. Fighting against *wrong* was more difficult though, for I never felt a thing to be bad until I had done it, and an impertinent answer would slip out of my mouth before a thought.'

Ruskin shook his head. 'In these times it is seen as wilfulness for a child, particularly a girl, to have their own views, when we should be encouraging it.'

'I used to be punished strictly and then my remorse was great, although I used to think that the punishment was hard, considering how thoughtless the fault was. This galled my sense of justice and, mingled with extreme sorrow for the fault, used to make me very miserable. I think, if people had known how I felt things, I should not have been punished so hard, but I'm sure I *was* a very provoking child.'

'I can't understand it when your own mother used to complain to me of just the same, and once encouraged your single-mindedness.'

Rose allowed the conversation to lie there, for she did not wish to speak ill of her mother and, having nothing nice to say, remained silent, something which Ruskin perceived and admired. This indication of a more mature self-control developing in Rose was both captivating and inspirational when he considered his own capriciousness and often juvenile behaviour at home.

As usual, Rose, with all her unexpected insight, had distracted him from his earlier irritants and succeeded in pacifying, at least for a time, all his gripes, along with curing the headache he had arrived with, lulled as he was by her virtuous, saintly view of the world and confidences that were precious in their rarity and emblematic of her trust.

Observing that Rose was shivering despite her protests to the contrary, Ruskin encouraged her to return inside and warm herself by the drawing room fire, for he was keen to spend an hour or so trying to sketch her and he couldn't very well do that in the garden without acquiring frostbite or having his work blown out of his hand.

'You will make me pretty?' Rose pleaded coquettishly when she had settled herself on a footstool by the hearth.

'You *are* pretty,' he answered with annoyance, looking up from his paper.

'But I'm at an unfair advantage,' she complained, 'for my portraiture skills aren't good enough for me to sketch *you*.'

'That *is* a relief; my portraits are either scandalously flattering or harsh enough to be caricatures in *Punch*.'

But Rose wasn't satisfied with this retort and asked persuasively, 'Won't you give me a photograph instead?'

'Photograph indeed! You shan't have anything of the kind,' he tutted, shaking his head and chuckling.

'Whyever not? Don't you like your face?'

'No, frankly I don't. I can't conceive *why* I'm so ugly, but I *am* ugly, the sun says so.'

Aghast at the violence of his insecurity, Rose demanded, 'You don't mean it?'

'Indeed. I judge my face as I would anyone else's and consider it bad in colour and form.'

'That's ridiculous,' she argued.

'Well, I'm glad to know that other people can tolerate it if they are used to it.'

'I like it very well,' she reassured, with such feeling that he almost blushed and could not catch her eye for a full minute for fear that she would observe how much the compliment meant to him.

Partly due to Rose being unable to stay still or remain silent, and partly because he found it impossible to concentrate on the sketch after this exchange, he failed to achieve anywhere near as lifelike a result as he desired.

'You're harder to draw than any Swiss sunset!' he announced, tearing up the attempt in favour of trying again another day.

'How vexing you are!' Rose chastised. 'After all my pains to sit patiently for you, you tear it up! It's a waste of the whole afternoon.'

'Not the *whole* afternoon,' Ruskin responded guiltily, looking down at the fragments of her poorly outlined face and concealing the papers behind his back in shame. 'Will you let me make amends by taking you to the British Museum where Sir Richard Owen is to lecture on natural history?'

'That will go some way to my forgiveness, but not *all*.'

'What will it take?' Ruskin asked theatrically, clutching his breast, his hands still bulging with the torn paper.

'A photograph.'

'Professor, please allow me to present my talented pupil, Miss Rose La Touche,' Ruskin announced with pride following Sir Richard Owen's talk, nudging Rose, who was uncharacteristically intimidated at being introduced, to step forward. 'I have it on good authority that she is also distantly and curiously connected with the lower order of monkeys and is an expert tree climber.'

'Really? Has she had *you* climbing trees, Mr Ruskin?' Owen asked mirthfully, prompting his new friend to stifle a giggle with her white-gloved hand.

'Not yet, but she *will* keep trying!'

After similar pleasantries Ruskin offered Rose a tour of the Round Reading Room and delighted in seeing her walk amongst books containing some of the greatest thoughts ever committed to paper, though she was more in awe of the magnificent domed ceiling, which she tilted her whole body back to look upon.

Conscious of it not being an appropriate place to converse, they wandered at leisure, with Ruskin occasionally pausing to leaf through a volume or point something out to her. After a period of quiet contemplation, allowing him to study the way in which she absorbed every detail of her surroundings, he noticed a troubled expression come over her face.

Turning to him she whispered, 'You won't really go and live in Switzerland?'

But before he could answer they passed a stern-looking old man with white hair and spectacles, who, seated at a desk just ahead of them, scowled at Rose for having drawn his attention away from the large reference book before him.

She took no notice of his displeasure and continued addressing Ruskin in hushed tones, 'Stones and glaciers are cold friends and... I would miss you terribly.'

Observing that the old gentleman was much surprised on hearing Rose say such a thing, Ruskin judged it best to steer her into another area of the library, all the while smiling tenderly at her concern.

'I enjoy travelling and it's essential for my work, but I don't believe that I shall *live* abroad now,' he reassured kindly. 'But tell me, why does a wild Irish girl spend her time thinking of an ageing art critic?'

Abashed at his directness, she picked out a book in order to delay her reply, eventually laughing to herself on realising that she had inadvertently selected a book on mathematics. Deeming it foolish to continue the pretence of being able to understand it, for her tuition had not ventured into the logical, she replaced it carefully and pointed to the door in order to find somewhere they could talk more freely.

As soon as they stepped outside she took a deep breath and, looking earnestly at him, confessed, 'I can't help but think of you, and I never think of you as old.'

'Thank you!' Ruskin returned lightly, flattered yet unsure how best to respond.

He quickly saw that he had misjudged her, however, and that Rose had intended her words to be taken with less brevity, for she began walking ahead of him to show her irritation and that she had meant her words to prompt an altogether different reaction.

Altering his tone to one of sincere friendship as he attempted to keep pace with her, he went on, 'You will soon be in Ireland, so can hardly mind *where* I am.'

She stopped short. 'I expect you'll think I'm being selfish again, but Emily will soon be married, leaving me quite alone at Harristown, and it would be so much nicer to think of you being in London rather than always abroad.'

'What does it matter what city I write to you from?'

'You are often home before I get your letters. Besides, what about your poor father?' Rose ventured persuasively. 'How can you go away so often when he relies on you more than ever?'

Ruskin looked into the distance when it came to attempting to justify his actions. 'I know my father is sick, but I cannot stay much longer or I should also fall ill, which would only make *him* worse. He has more pleasure when I am able to write him a cheerful letter than generally when I'm there, for we disagree about the entire universe.'

'Why do you quarrel so?' she asked innocently.

'If he loved me less and believed in me more, we should get on,' he confided regretfully. 'Instead, his whole life is bound up in me, yet he thinks me a fool.'

Rose, taking hold of his forearms and pressing them that he should look her full in the face, remonstrated with a force he had never seen, 'John James is only ambitious on your account *because* he has such a high opinion of you.'

'His form of affection galls me like hot iron,' he said, shaking his head, 'so that I'm always in a state of subdued fury whenever I'm home, which dries the marrow out of my bones.'

Convinced that Ruskin would one day regret judging his father so harshly, she persisted, 'He would sacrifice his life for you.'

But he was not ready to dispense with his outpouring of resentment and responded finally, 'Yet he wants me to sacrifice *mine* in return.'

Ruskin saw how much he disappointed Rose by saying such a thing and found himself reflecting on her words later that evening when he came upon his father seated in his usual chair in the drawing room, reading his newspaper by the fire. The day when he would be his own master was to come earlier than he had expected, yet he and his father's opposing views seemed destined to remain unreconciled.

Their way of living together had degenerated into avoiding addressing one another whenever possible, and so it was when Ruskin took the seat opposite, both men stubbornly refusing to greet one another and persisting in an unbroken silence for many minutes, interrupted only by the father, who sighed hopelessly.

Stony-faced, John James eventually peered over his newspaper, though he refused to be the first party to speak. Vexed that Ruskin did not initiate dialogue, he could read no longer and so folded the newspaper neatly and lit a pipe. Resting his head against his high-backed chair, he winced with the pain he wished to ignore for as long as he reasonably could before retiring to bed, for every night he wondered if he should ever rise again.

Commending himself for being the first to concede, Ruskin rose from his seat and leant over his father. 'Is there anything I can do for you?'

But John James ignored any reference to the state of his health and asked abruptly, 'Do you dine at home today?'

'No, Father, I've been invited to Rose's birthday tea.'

'Oh really? And how old is she now?' the old man goaded.

'Fourteen.'

'Well, I only hope you'll be in a better humour for *her*.' And he shook his head and tutted bitterly.

'It will please you to be relieved of my company,' Ruskin returned, more obnoxiously than he had intended.

'Perhaps it shall, for there's too much of a don't-careishness about you, a sort of nought is everything and everything is nought,' he remarked, gesturing with his pipe dismissively.

'Do you wonder when it is *everything* to me to try and save the Turner drawings?'

But John James, incredulous that his son appeared to be more concerned about the National Gallery's neglect than his own well-being, huffed, 'Why should it be *your* responsibility?'

'I was not *expecting* to stumble across them mildewing,' Ruskin answered impatiently. 'What would you have me do other than attempt to save them? I can't very well leave them to rot.'

'I don't say they shouldn't be saved,' John James agreed, 'I simply wonder why the gallery doesn't do it, having itself caused the damage.'

'I'm the only one who knows *how*.'

'You flatter yourself,' his father dismissed, clamping his teeth down on his pipe in annoyance. 'They would do a lot more if you didn't do it for them, free of charge.'

'Doubtless you're right, for they well know how it kills me to see any work of Turner's come to harm,' Ruskin admitted, shaking his head in disgust. 'Why he ever entrusted his property to *them* Lord knows. They don't value his works so much as the expanse of dead brick wall housing them, and they keep his most valuable drawings in the cellar covered by an old sheet of tarpaulin.'

'You talk of them not valuing Turner, whilst *you* are entirely careless of your own time. Imagine what you might achieve in a day if you weren't constantly dividing it between mildewing drawings and the La Touches.'

Feeling as taunted as a boy being lectured about his schooling, but no longer forced to sit beside his father to await the certain flow of criticisms that would be sure to come his way, he took himself off to his study where he remained until the relief of being able to leave Denmark Hill and set off to see Rose came around.

Having carefully wrapped Rosie's sacred present in pretty pink paper and ribbon, Ruskin clutched it under his arm and set off with the first smile he had managed to produce all day. Imagining her reaction on opening it, her pleasure followed by her demure gratitude, made every step weightless. There was so much felicity to be found in such devotion.

He soon discovered on entering the crowded Curzon Street drawing room that she was much too distracted to think only of *his* present, however, and he was put out to find her being fawned over by cousins and friends, most of whom he had never seen before.

Forced to stand to one side and await her notice, he nonetheless forgave the oversight the moment she turned around and beckoned him to her side, for she smiled as though happiest of all to see *him*.

Though he was relieved to find Mr La Touche absent, Ruskin nevertheless felt some trepidation on such a large gathering scrutinising him as he approached the birthday girl, his stomach turning over like a skittish adolescent as he approached and, kissing her cheek, wished her the happiest of all birthdays.

Holding out the precious illuminated thirteenth-century psalter, after she had torn off the paper excitedly, he explained, 'I selected this as the only gift worthy of you, for its hand-coloured illustrations are as immaculate as if angels in heaven had painted them.'

Immediately turning to the flyleaf, Rose read aloud the inscription to the crowd that had gathered around them, '"Posie, with St C's love",' as though she cared more for that than the book itself.

Thanking him sincerely and looking through the volume with admiration, he was sorry to see how easily she put it down when someone called to her from across the room. Going to mark her place in the psalter with a scrap of torn newspaper, Ruskin had urged her not to, before considering how his patronising words might embarrass her.

'You might leave off scolding me *today*,' she responded, half in jest and half in petulance, and she glided off, leaving him to repent.

It was pointless trying to upbraid Rose, he reflected, as she made merry with the entire room before deigning to converse with him again; she was just as human as the next girl and, he observed with a bitterness resulting from exasperated worship, her advancing years had so far failed to arrest a great many of her childish habits. Regardless, he found all her faults as endearing as her charms and always scolded her fully expecting his chides to soon be forgotten.

'I should not have admonished you earlier,' he offered when Rose had finished opening her last present and the other guests had gone away. 'It is yours to do with as you please.'

'You were right to stop me using newspaper to save my place earlier,' she conceded. 'I would have been so sorry to have spoiled such a beautiful book.' And she picked up the volume and stroked the cover self-deprecatingly. 'I wish I wasn't so hot-headed and careless.'

'People are always the same, you can't alter natures,' he smiled in reconciliation, 'nor can I alter myself, so I shall have to try to make the best of myself. Here, I created you a makeshift bookmark,' he ventured on Rose sitting down beside him, and offering her a frayed piece of his blue necktie she carefully placed it inside the opening page of the psalter, never to remove it.

Ruskin was grateful that she had favoured him again, for it was like the sun making an appearance at the end of a long grey winter. Now was *his* time and they might just as easily be sitting in a garden alone for all he noticed anyone else, least of all her society-loving mother who had been too occupied even for him that afternoon and was just then dashing to and fro ordering the servants to clear away the chaos of half-eaten birthday cake and wrapping paper.

'Birthdays are not subjects of regret but sources of resolution to one as young as you,' he mused tenderly. 'By the time you are my age I trust that *you* will have been more useful than I have, for I find it painful to look back on any happiness that has been profitless.'

'Isn't being happy enough in itself?' Rose enquired innocently.

'I'm not sure that it is,' he denied, 'rather, I begin to think that a life more laboriously spent is far more gladdening in retrospect.'

'If it hadn't been for your teaching I would have preferred play to lessons, but now I take as much enjoyment from studying as I do in games. Perhaps even more.'

'You are turning into quite the bluestocking! Come to Denmark Hill for tea tomorrow; I would like to introduce you to some friends of mine.'

***

Rose was intrigued by Ruskin's great literary comrades Jane and Thomas Carlyle for, besides their inelegant, bohemian appearance, they were unlike any married persons she had ever met: the small, raven-haired wife being equal to her white-whiskered husband in intelligence and outspokenness, whilst it was difficult to judge which of the two was the most domineering.

Observing without daring to participate in the initial drawing room exchange, never had she witnessed Ruskin so reverent of anyone as Thomas, nor so willing to listen to his views on all manner of subjects, uttered as though his opinions were as reliable as the oracle of Apollo. Having no children other than a Maltese dog, whom Jane dandled on her lap as fondly as a new mother, Rose perceived that the couple lived solely for their work, with an intimate circle who appreciated and shared their eccentricities, as did Ruskin.

'It is strange to me that you have chosen to spend the afternoon with two cantankerous Scotch women when you could be out shopping for your sister's wedding,' the broad-toned Jane remarked on Ruskin ushering her upright, dour-looking husband into his study in order to discuss more philosophical matters.

Rose, blushing at the boldness of her new acquaintance, pronounced, 'I'd far rather be here.'

'Weddings can be a dull business, not least the courtship beforehand. My husband took four years to woo me by correspondence,' she announced proudly, tucking a stray black hair behind her ear.

Rose, without the least sign of impertinence, gasped in surprise. 'Gosh, so long as that?'

'Anyone who knows my husband will tell you that he is not a man to give up, even though I told him positively that I could not fall in love and that matrimony would interfere shockingly with my plans. Are your mother and father pleased with your sister's match?'

'I think so,' Rose replied cautiously, perceiving that the lady meant to draw her.

'Note that I did not ask whether *she* is satisfied,' she laughed, stroking her lapdog who yapped whenever his mistress's voice rose in her enthusiasm. 'Oh, to be a fashionable wife! I am grateful never to have been anything of the kind and pictured for myself a far higher destiny. But will it ever be more than a picture? As for you, I suppose your parents already have someone in mind?'

'Fie! It was only Rosie's fourteenth birthday yesterday,' Margaret interrupted, throwing up her knitting needles in mirth.

'Forgive me,' Jane retracted, 'Miss La Touche's maturity led me to think her much older.'

'I have no intention of marrying,' the young lady offered assertively. 'Like you, I have ambitions of another kind.'

'Pray tell me more,' she encouraged, much taken with Ruskin's wild rose whose slender frame and delicate features seemed a distraction from her passionate inner self.

'I hope to publish my poetry.'

'You become more entrancing by the minute! I'm so glad that you are determined never to do what is expected of you. Conformity is death. It is odd what notions people have of the scantiness of a woman's resources,' she declaimed, flushed as she voiced the topic dearest to her heart. 'The philosopher who used to thank the gods he was born a man and not a woman must have had more sense than the generality of his calling. Our fate is truly deplorable, is it not?'

'How so?' her young friend encouraged, hanging on her every word.

'Why, as soon as a poor girl takes that decisive step called "coming out" she is exposed to a host of vexatious men who know nothing, the great object of her existence being to get a rich husband and a fine house and give dinners. Really it is unjust! We are apparently the weakest portion of humankind, yet what I would give to be Prime Minister! Even your son thinks women ought to remain by the hearth while men fight our battles,' she goaded Margaret, who sighed exasperatedly and neatened her ball of wool without looking up. 'How little he comprehends his muse's independent spirit. Though you have already failed in one regard, Miss La Touche.'

'I have?' Rose asked anxiously.

'Why, a girl as slight as you should never be made to wear a corset!' Jane cried, touching her infinitely cinched-in waist. 'The very notion!'

'They are very uncomfortable,' she smiled. 'How I envy you not wearing one.'

'No whalebone was ever strong enough to reign me in!'

'Don't listen to her,' Margaret chimed in kindly, 'Mrs Carlyle is an awful tease and makes herself out to be much wilder than she really is.'

'It's true, I *am* a terrible woman,' the lady assured. 'They call me "sweet" and "gentle", and some even go to the length of calling me "endearing", and I laugh in my sleeve and think, *Lord! If you but realised what a brimstone of a creature I am behind all this beautiful amiability!* My husband can vouch for it.'

'What, may I ask, inspired you to marry?' Rose finally plucked up the courage to question, thrilled by Jane's outlandish beliefs which seemed to be at odds with the respectability of her situation.

'Though I was resistant to marryings and givings in marriage, it seemed as if our destinies were long to be intermingled, that we might walk side by side through many bright scenes and assist one another in many a noble purpose. We both have a thousand faults and are full of obstinacy, yet we are true-hearted people and trust in one another, never fearing the tricks of fortune or tempests that fall to us. We live through this earthly pilgrimage united: one heart, one soul, one fortune. When shall the world know my husband's worth as I do? God will reward him for what he has been to me.'

Contrary to Ruskin's fears that Rose might find Jane intimidating, she was much impressed by the lady's outpouring of emotion after her initial display of acerbity, and was eager to tell him so the moment the Carlyles departed for their Chelsea residence.

'I hope she didn't frighten you,' he asked warily.

'Not in the slightest, I long to see her again.'

'So you are firm friends?'

'I am no match for her intelligence,' his pet admitted with a grown-up air that made him smile, 'though it was invigorating to meet a woman reticent of all social affectations,' she enthused. 'Mrs Carlyle is the most liberated person I have ever known. I do hope *I* shall be like her.'

'I'm glad you admire her, but I wouldn't want you to be *quite* the same,' Ruskin laughed, pinching her chin fondly. 'Nor should your recent birthday encourage you to wish your childhood away; the trials of adulthood will come soon enough.'

Using his father's poor health as the excuse, Ruskin gladly abandoned his own birthday feast a month later, for it was a celebration he no longer felt inclined to observe. Turning forty-three, middle age hung over him as gloomily as a raincloud threatening to spoil a landscape painter's unfinished canvas, the passing years only serving to highlight his inadequacies as a son, friend, lover and husband. With a failed marriage behind him and a fascination for a girl almost thirty years his junior, it was better not to contemplate either the present or the future.

When the La Touches returned to Ireland in April, he became as impossible to be around as his father, and, too distracted to continue editing a paper he had been commissioned to write for *Fraser's Magazine*, was indignant that neither of his parents appeared to understand how difficult it had been for him to say goodbye to Rose.

'What am I to do now that she's gone to horrible Ireland?' he complained to his mother, who was lying horizontal on the sofa. 'I wonder what she's doing now... Probably gathering anemones in the wood or catching crayfish in the Liffey.'

'What good does it do to imagine *what* she's about? We live by faith, not by sight,' Margaret sermonised, her mouth contorted in disapproval.

'You think that I should be quite merry, but I haven't had one happy hour since they took the child away. All my work has been wrecked, all my usefulness taken from me.' And he slapped his unfinished article down on the table beside her.

'I do wish you wouldn't be so dramatic, John, your father would have a fit if he could hear you,' Margaret censured, attending to her knitting before going on. 'Your work has not been spoiled, far from it, you throw yourself into it all the more when Rose isn't in London.'

'I go *on*, certainly, but I take no delight in doing so. My father has *you* by his side and is therefore constantly fuelled with inspiration and courage in all that he does, while the only sustenance *I* have is to think what Rose might be doing at such and such a time. I dare say I will end up an entirely solitary old man, loved by no-one.'

XIII

THE OFFER

THE FACT THAT RUSKIN HAD MADE GREAT PROGRESS WITH his work in Rose's absence did not accord with his perpetual cries of woe, and Margaret was peeved to witness how quickly he changed his tune about "horrible Ireland" a few weeks later, when he received a letter from Mrs La Touche offering him a cottage on the Harristown estate that he might use whenever he wanted:

> "A spot for you to write prolifically and draw on the beauty and tranquillity of your surroundings. I trust that I don't have to persuade you too ardently, for you have already seen the landscape we are fortunate enough to call home and know how much we should all delight (particularly Rose) in your presence beside us on the estate."

Astonished, but pleasantly so, the suggestion caused a restlessness and excitement he could not contain as he informed his mother of the news, though she was far from thrilled and listened to another of her son's changes in attitude with an elevated eyebrow, aware that this elation would also pass. If he could just find a way of moderating his feelings and the ensuing histrionics which fatigued her so.

'Located just beside the river and outside their park wall, yet in sight of the blue hills, it promises a tranquillity I've long been searching for,' he enthused, 'so I've written to thank them for their offer and say that I'll go whenever I want peace and kindness.'

Margaret sat forward in irritation. 'Do you mean to infer that you do not get peace and kindness here?'

'Of course I'm only truly happy at Denmark Hill, but there is always so much to distract me from my work now that father is unwell.'

'And I suppose Rose is never a distraction?' the old woman sniffed rhetorically, returning her attention to the woollen sock she was darning for her husband, a custom she had kept up throughout their lengthy marriage, taking pride in the menial tasks of wifehood, regardless of there being no need for her to do so.

Despite the cool easterly breeze, it was the first warm weather Harristown had seen that year, the Liffey glistening just as it had during Ruskin's visit almost two years before, when he had made the prediction that little would change when once he had returned to London.

Mrs La Touche occupied her favourite seat under a parasol as she watched Rose and Emily playing on the lawn with Bruno, but although she had a smile on her lips, which any casual observer would have taken to emanate from her pleasure at the sight, those who knew her well would have recognised her unease following the approach of her husband. Without acknowledging her, Maria grew increasingly anxious when he took Emily to one side and began conversing with her intently, for she believed she knew on what subject he wished to interrogate her.

Growing increasingly agitated the longer the conversation continued, she debated with herself whether it was best to remain nonchalant or think of some way to interrupt them, not least because Emily looked more and more awkward upon answering him, twisting her hands and looking into the middle distance as she always did when she feared giving a response the other party might not hear favourably.

Rose meanwhile continued to play ball with Bruno, entirely oblivious as to her mother's quandary or the fact that her father was engaged in a serious discussion with Emily about Mr Ruskin, for he had singled out his eldest daughter as the only one who would answer him honestly, and without undue bias.

His eldest daughter, whom he flattered himself by believing to be most like him, had satisfied him as much as her conscience would allow, but before La Touche sent her on her way he looked up and saw his wife's piercing gaze fixed upon them, causing him to abruptly halt speaking and march up the garden towards her, his face turning red in anger.

'Emily has just informed me that *we* have promised Mr Ruskin a cottage on the estate. Is that so?' he bullied, taking his wife's arm and ensuring that his grasp was firm enough to convey his displeasure.

'I merely said that it would be good for the children if they were to see more of him,' Mrs La Touche replied, flustered.

'For the children? It strikes me that *they* would be the last to benefit from the arrangement,' he dismissed.

'What you insinuate is ludicrous!' Mrs La Touche defended, whilst being careful to speak quietly. 'Has anything given you cause to distrust him?'

'It is not *his* motives I question,' her husband returned, aiming his suspicions entirely at his wife who now shifted guiltily. 'If the offer has already been made, and I hear from Emily that is has, you must write to him immediately, withdrawing it.'

'That's absurd, it would make us look ridiculous,' she argued.

'It will make *you* look ridiculous,' La Touche denied, 'something which bothers me very little.'

'I fail to understand what I have ever done to provoke such treatment,' she whimpered, though with little hope of arousing his sympathy.

'I will not have you causing talk on the estate!' he shouted, so violently that she jumped. Realising that he had raised his voice enough to alert Emily and Rose to their quarrel, however, he moderated his tone. 'When a woman decides to take a lover the *least* she can do is to use some discretion.'

Saying nothing more, nor giving any opportunity for responding, he left his wife to not merely reflect upon his command but act accordingly. Nor did it take her more than a few moments to reach the difficult conclusion that she must compose the letter he ordered, regardless of the humiliation she would suffer or the confusion it would inevitably cause Ruskin.

Mrs La Touche rose unsteadily and, with her face hectically flushed, hurried feebly towards the house, regretful of not having consulted her husband in the first instance, for perhaps, she considered with a pang, she might have persuaded him if only she had approached him openly about her intention.

She paused for a moment once seated at her ornate French writing desk in the drawing room, overlooking the lawn where Rose continued to sport with her sister and dog in ignorance, for she struggled to think of a suitable reason to give Ruskin. After tearing up several drafts, she could devise no plausible excuse that would justify this retraction, nor could she help her tone sounding strangely officious and as though her husband had been standing over her dictating every word.

A short time later, being curious as to why her mother had gone inside without saying anything, Rose entered and skipped over to her while she was composing one of several drafts to Ruskin, her face pensive and her brow furrowed.

In an especially good humour on having won a game of croquet, Rose leant over and wound a curl of her mother's hair around her finger affectionately, unintentionally startling her. Engrossed in the task, Mrs La Touche was agitated to find her youngest daughter peering over her shoulder and smudged the ink.

'Blast!' she cried, foreseeing Rose's anger at the withdrawal of the cottage.

'Are you writing to ask Mr Ruskin when he is coming to stay?'

'I'm writing to tell him that we must withdraw our offer,' her mother answered matter-of-factly, continuing to write by way of avoiding looking at her daughter's face.

'But why? You can't, he'll be so disappointed!' Rose assailed, her eyes filling with tears of sympathy and anguish.

'It cannot be, our neighbours would never understand it,' Mrs La Touche answered firmly.

She had no wish to embroil herself in another argument; and although she heard Rose choking back the kind of tears that make it hard to breathe, she proceeded with her letter as soon as her daughter had rushed from the room, her hardened expression that of the deepest mortification.

Her husband strode into the drawing room shortly afterwards and, violently snatching away the note she had just finished, instructed her to address the envelope while he read it carefully.

Finally satisfied that there could be no misunderstanding, La Touche nodded at his wife for having done her duty, though he would not dream of exiting the room without the brutal retraction in his hand.

Rose, still breathless from crying, ran into the garden in search of her old, familiar hiding place, the bough of a large oak overlooking the river, not thinking of her own misfortune but rather how grievously Ruskin would react to such a turnabout.

Having witnessed her father talking with Emily, it became clear to her that *he* had opposed the plan in order to punish her mother for harbouring an admiration for her tutor, something she knew was much talked about within their circles.

Yet it did seem unfair that *she* would lose Ruskin's company as a result, and she allowed herself the indulgence of cursing her mother over and again as she climbed further out of reach, the arms of the tree being as strong and comforting as any person.

DUKES AND PAUPERS

O F ALL MEN, RUSKIN WAS CONTENT TO STAY IN THE SELF-containment familiar to him since childhood, for having been a solitary boy he did not seek acquaintances in manhood out of any particular necessity and struggled to find comrades intelligent or sensitive enough to suit him, nor ones unafraid to criticise or challenge his views.

Whilst he could be sociable when he chose, Ruskin was rarely long enough in any man's company to firmly attach himself to them and was as content to look to his work for fulfilment, as in the days of his youth, when it chanced that few, if any, kindred spirits had crossed his path.

If once he had affections as warm as the next person, partly from evil chance and partly from foolish misplacing of them, they were tumbled down and broken into pieces. He considered it the greatest misfortune of his life that his relations, cousins and so forth, were people with whom he had no sympathy and that circumstances somehow or another kept him out of the way of those with whom he could have made friends, so that he had no friendships and no loves.

Having found it all too easy to collect admirers and dependants as his name grew in stature, it was only on reaching middle age that he was at last able to identify and avoid the sycophants who were a natural consequence of his fame and fortune.

Inherently trusting his own instinct, he believed that an aristocrat was as likely to court his acquaintance for their own benefit as a road sweeper, and so approached new faces with enough scepticism to form a clear judgement within a matter of minutes, whilst remaining open-minded enough to acknowledge true allies regardless of their social standing or finances.

He therefore heartily welcomed the recent friendship of the self-taught artist Edward Burne-Jones and his pretty young wife Georgiana, a couple with whom he shared a natural affinity due to their relentless and valiant pursuance of art. Particularly admiring them for continuing their life's work despite an ongoing battle to stave off abject poverty, more than anything Ruskin lauded their natural openness and integrity, for whenever they flattered him he knew that they did so in all sincerity.

When he began visiting Burne-Jones's studio on Red Lion Square near Chancery Lane, it offered the artist the first real hope of receiving the public's full attention, while Ruskin was likewise pleased that his reputation still granted him the power to benefit his new friend; knowing, without being egotistical, that a mere word of praise from him could shape the career of even the most obscure painter.

It became Ruskin's habit to call on Burne-Jones unannounced a couple of times per week, though the artist seemed taken aback to find him on his doorstep late one evening, clutching a bottle of his father's wine in one hand and a joint of ham, supplied from one of the Denmark Hill pigs, in the other.

'You look like you need fattening up!' his guest announced, thrusting the ham into the bewildered painter's arms and marching in without waiting to be invited.

Being both extremely proud and earnest, Ned was not always gracious at accepting gifts or anything that might be veiled as charity, however, and looking down at the joint uneasily he stroked his beard and said, 'You know I wouldn't accept this from anyone but you?'

'Glad to hear it, I don't give my ham to all and sundry; *this* is a prized piece of pork and you should savour it accordingly.' And he removed his coat without any formality and began uncorking the wine with a corkscrew he niftily produced from his pocket.

Burne-Jones responded with his characteristic booming laugh, for the lightness of Ruskin's manner and his refusal to place his friends under any obligation (save the occasional repayment in paintings) made it impossible to be proud for long.

Moved by such generosity, he declared, 'You are much more than everything people say about you.'

'I should hope so, as people do not always say kind things about me,' Ruskin replied drolly, taking a seat, 'even the ones who *like* my books.'

'That's because no-one half understands you, rather you leave all your critics grovelling on the earth,' Ned teased, accepting the glass of wine his companion offered and settling down opposite.

Surprised to see that his guest did not find his remark in the least amusing, he observed Ruskin look into the middle distance as if pondering the truth of it, before responding, 'Perhaps *I* am at fault for not saying things clearly enough, either in life or on the page. I must learn to say all I have to say in the fewest possible words, or my readers will be sure to skip them. After all, it matters very little whether people think I am a good writer. I have reached an age when I need my words not only to be comprehended but *heeded*.'

'And they *shall* be, I have every faith,' Ned cheered emphatically, whilst his friend's anxieties prompted him to scan the several unfinished canvases he was relying upon to pay the rent.

Though he had not yet reached his thirtieth year, the artist's brow was lined from almost constant fear of destitution, his long chestnut beard had already begun to whiten and his expression was serious even when he meant to be humorous.

'You are more confident about that than *I*,' Ruskin responded gloomily.

'It's good to know that even *you* are cursed with doubt,' Ned sighed, remembering his precarious circumstances. 'Yet your self-effacement only illustrates my point, for you *are* much better than even your books, which happen to be the best books in the world. You're so good and kind, yet you never care for any display of gratitude, hence why you're one of the few men I genuinely delight in raising my glass to,' he extolled, doing just that.

'Thank you, but I must beg you not to flatter me,' he demurred, laughing gently before tasting his father's Bordeaux with lip-pursing approval. 'As you say, I am one of those rare people who loathes praise even more than derision, for the one extreme is likely to be as unjustified as the other. I am nearly sick of being loved, as of being hated, for my lovers understand me as little as my haters. I would prefer to be disliked by a man who *somewhat* understood me than loved by a man who understood nothing of me.'

'You must forgive me for my admiration, for having gone from being just a man who once wrote to you and got an answer by return of post I think myself extremely fortunate that I should be at liberty to correspond with you, let alone drink with you,' Ned confessed.

'I consider you an equal and a friend and will have no more of this nonsense,' Ruskin responded with humility. 'You have no doubt heard a great many people saying I am very bad, and perhaps you have been disposed lately to think me very good. I am neither the one nor the other. I am very self-indulgent, very proud, very obstinate and *very* resentful. On the other side, I am very upright, I never betray a trust, never wilfully do an unkind thing and never, in little or large matters, depreciate another that I might raise myself. Now,' he said, his face lightening and his lips breaking into a beaming smile, 'I've been meaning to ask if you and Georgie would be in favour of accompanying me on a trip to France and Italy?'

'You'd really want *us* to go with you?'

'I should not have asked otherwise,' his companion assured.

'We should be delighted, but funds are rather tight just now,' Ned excused, looking down in embarrassment.

'That's a yes then, for you shall both be my guests, nay, my children!' Ruskin bellowed. 'Nor do I want any thanks. If you wish to do something for me you can paint me a nice picture of a view we will share together.'

'I shall do so *gladly*, and so will my wife. Georgie has as much talent as I, yet since our little son came along she has been rather exiled and lives behind closed doors. A change of scene is just what she needs and going abroad with *you* will be like seeing the world anew.'

'I trust travelling abroad will expand both your horizons, for however can an artist paint to his full potential without having first seen some of the world?' said Ruskin, inflamed by the prospect of introducing his friend to the cities far removed from London or Burne-Jones's birthplace of Birmingham.

'In my ignorance,' Ned apologised, 'I have always considered a picture to be a beautiful romantic dream of something that never was and never will be, in a light better than any light that ever shone, in a land no-one can define, or remember, only desire.'

'Then I will undertake to show you landscapes and sunsets beyond your wildest imaginings.'

Ruskin extended the invitation knowing Ned and his wife to be the complete opposite of his father's notion of suitable companions, for John James not only expressed a dislike of most of his acquaintances but believed Edward Burne-Jones to be at the very bottom of the pile and so vastly inferior to his son that he often grew apoplectic whenever his name was mentioned.

John James having refused all his appeals to give the artist financial assistance, Ruskin cared not whether funding the trip out of his own pocket would provoke his disapproval, for he firmly despised such pomposity and enjoyed informing him of the scheme the moment he returned home.

'It seems a hard saying, but it is a right one that one's friends should be neither much richer nor much poorer than one's self,' his father began. 'You are unfortunate in the choice of people you take it into your head to be interested in, for the wealth of the La Touches is to be as much regretted as the poverty of men like Burne-Jones whom you can hardly *fail* to make friends with,' his father scorned, stroking his whiskers impatiently. 'Even the most dim-witted painter wouldn't discourage your friendship, not from any genuine love of you but purely for what you might be able to do for them. Where is Millais now, for instance?'

'It seems to me that you were only ever content when I was associating with gentry at Oxford,' Ruskin reproached angrily, rising from his seat in exasperation and determined that John James would never again interfere with his choice of friend. 'Men who had no feelings except those of brutes, filled their drawers with pictures of naked bawds, walked with their harlots down country lanes, and swore, diced and drank whilst *knowing* nothing and caring for *nothing* other than the names of racehorses.'

'I saw Oxford as a means of elevating you to the best possible vantage point in society, which it *did*,' John James defended. 'How could I have guessed that such noblemen would behave thus?'

'It was precisely because I did not like to disillusion you that I held my tongue, for their conversation at the dinner table would have made prostitutes blush and villains rebuke them. They were men who, if they could, might have robbed me of all my money at the gambling table,' Ruskin went on, increasingly fired up. 'One night they even broke into my rooms and smashed up most of my furniture by way of entertainment, but that didn't stop them coming back the next evening to partake of your wine and make a joke of drinking my health.'

'Such pranks are to be expected at university, you just never had the humour for it,' the old man dismissed with a wave of his hand. Pausing to gather his thoughts for fear of losing the argument, he reclined in his armchair and sipped the company port as if the mention of liquor had reminded him that he was neglecting his glass. 'Besides, I don't much care for being lectured to by my own son. Do you not think I have been long enough in the world to know how it works?'

But Ruskin was hot on his tail and looked his father full in the face. 'Yet you *still* try all you can to withdraw me from the company of men like Burne-Jones, who is not only a genius but is as pure as an archangel and cares for me like a brother.'

'Pray, might I remind you that two wrong ideas do not a *right* one make,' John James retaliated, 'for it seems to me that neither type of association is deserving of you. Isn't there anyone in between a duke and a pauper?'

'Such snobbery has surely destroyed your power of judging noble character, and I declare that, for the first time in my life, I am truly ashamed of you,' Ruskin denounced.

'Have Burne-Jones as your companion if you must, if you're so in need of a friend that you're prepared to pay for one,' his father returned, his shoulders rising in defiance. 'As for any appeals to me for charity, they will surely fall on deaf ears. It is peremptorily not my business to look after other people's sorrow; I have enough of my own.'

THE GLORY OF BEING

A S Ruskin and the Burne-Joneses travelled by railway to Folkestone that May, he took the opportunity of observing Georgiana more closely, whom he found a singular-looking creature with dark hair, wide blue eyes and long lashes. Her small frame and girlish, unaffected manner meanwhile led him to underestimate her intellect as equally diminutive, an error soon corrected.

'Ned, where is the photograph of little Phil?' she asked, already feeling the natural pangs of a new mother as she was carried farther and farther away from the infant, emotions she believed Ruskin would find idiotic due to having several times stated his dislike of babies.

'He doesn't look so very different from every other baby in the world,' he sneered, looking over Ned's shoulder when the image of the child was produced in readiness of Georgie's maternal fawning.

'I never said he did, the only thing that distinguishes him is the fact that he's *ours*,' she defended, snatching the picture away and tucking it inside the book she was reading, an action which offered her the chance to stare at it devotedly whenever another pang came on, something that happened with frequency.

Notwithstanding the fact that she was as good and sweet as could be, Ruskin was soon impressed by Georgie's deep understanding of his works during conversation, and he saw that she possessed an intuitive sense of beauty which often aided Ned in his choice of composition and setting.

Deeply romantic, she had married for love rather than riches and remained uncomplaining no matter how much she struggled to manage the household on the small allowance her husband's occupation afforded. Ruskin found her indefatigable faith in Ned's work touching, not least because she disregarded her own talent in order to support *his*. Meanwhile, he perceived with some concern that Ned was as confident of Georgie's devotion as a child is of their parents' and therefore did not question or cherish her love but appreciated her loyalty indifferently, as if she had been gifted to him by God.

As Ruskin and Georgie walked along the beach at Boulogne that first grey afternoon after leaving England, he looped his arm through hers, as was his habit with those he wished to be close to.

'While I intend this to be an instructive holiday for you both, you shall have to be careful not to look at too many pictures when we visit the Louvre,' he began, jovially, 'for *that* can be as damaging as a roomful of bad ones.'

'I dare say you're right,' she laughed, honoured to have been taken under his wing; 'Ned and I shall be guided by you.'

'We will make copies of two or three of the best, for it is far better to study a couple in infinite detail than glance at twenty before luncheon.'

'You want *me* to make copies also?' Georgie asked, in trepidation of having Ruskin scrutinise her efforts.

'Why yes, I am almost *more* intrigued to see yours than Ned's, for you seem to prefer to keep your work under lock and key. Had it not been for my bullying I should never have guessed what you were capable of.'

'I barely have time to draw these days,' she excused, 'what with looking after baby and helping Ned.'

'You have time *now!*' And Ruskin stretched out his arms to illustrate the vastness of the opportunity. 'Though there's nothing prettier or more wifely than watching you cut your husband's drawings on the woodblock,' he admonished, 'I can't understand why you do not want more for *yourself.*'

'I had no idea what the profession of an artist *meant* before I married,' she confessed, shying away from giving him a direct answer, 'I merely desired to be among those who painted pictures.'

'You are not merely *among* them, you are one of them if you would only stand up to be counted,' Ruskin disputed passionately.

Georgie blushed, not used to such attention. 'I suppose you think it's pathetic how we women long to keep pace with men, and how gladly they keep us by them until their pace quickens and we fall behind!'

'The fact that you chose Ned proves the power of your perception, but although it's admirable that you glory in his work you must not forget your own abilities. Art is in need of a woman's view of the world, not just a man's.'

'I never knew that you were a supporter of the emancipation of women,' she goaded, surprised by his encouragement.

'Bah! I'm not, or rather it depends what you mean by the term,' he refuted with typical drollness; 'so far from wishing to give the vote to women, I would willingly take it away from most *men.*'

They shared the joke for several minutes, for she understood Ruskin well enough to know that his wild statements were intended to provoke thought rather than be considered categorical representations of his own, often contradictory, opinions.

Georgie could see why Ned found Ruskin's companionship so engrossing, yet she observed that his carefree manner changed when her husband joined them a short time later, when he became melancholy of a sudden, having hoped to exchange further confidences with her, not least on the subject that was closest to his heart.

'I see you two are as thick as thieves,' Ned jested, putting his arm around his wife's waist and thereby ruining all possibility of further intimacy between her and Ruskin.

Georgie wondered if their "Papa" was embarrassed to see them embrace, or even jealous, for after looking uncomfortable he suddenly quickened his pace and left them, unmindful of the oncoming rain.

Sensing his desire to be alone, the couple made no attempt to catch up with him, but instead looked on in pity as he strode towards the shore where the tide was far out, his solitary figure the very emblem of loneliness as he approached the water's edge and left the great stretch of wet sand behind him, his imprints as transient as life itself.

Having been raised in a strict Methodist household, quite removed from artistic circles, Georgie felt herself to be in the presence of a new religion whenever she was near Ruskin, for he led her and Ned as determinedly as a wise man pursuing a star and, despite being sad at being parted from her son, wherever Ruskin beckoned her she was compelled to follow.

Their knowledgeable guide was equally invigorated by the prospect of acting as the couple's mentor and remained in fine spirits when they arrived in Paris for the first leg of their journey, displaying a boundless knowledge of the Louvre and introducing the couple to opera, though he insisted upon leaving at the interval of Wagner's 'Die Meistersinger' in favour of dining back at their opulent base, the Hôtel Meurice, the gilded interiors of which were akin to a French palace and caused both Ned and Georgie to cower in the shadow of their host who amazed them by displaying such confidence and ease on requesting a table.

'Of all the clumsy, blundering, boggling, baboon-blooded stuff I ever saw on a human stage, that beats everything,' Ruskin fumed on taking a seat in the dining room and unfolding his napkin, thus peeving the waiter who considered the taking away of his duty an affront.

'I take it you don't care for Wagner?' Ned chaffed.

'Of all the affected, sapless, soulless, beginningless, endless, topless, bottomless, topsiturviest, tuneless and doggerel noise I ever endured, *that* was the deadliest. I never was so relieved, so far as I can remember in my life, by the stopping of any sound, not excepting railway whistles.'

As for the fine French cuisine presented to them, course after course, Ruskin was of a more favourable opinion, whilst relishing the myriad expressions of his guests who had never tasted such food before.

'They are most delicious!' Ned declared in astonishment on eating a frog's leg.

'It's against my better judgement to eat such a thing, but I have to agree with you,' Georgie giggled, setting off her husband's booming laugh and Ruskin's more discreet chuckle. The three combined garnered the disapproval of the severe-looking maître d' who, with slicked back, heavily-pomaded hair, ridiculed them under his breath and vociferously whenever he went to give orders to the chef. Such people did not belong in his restaurant.

'Here we are, surrounded by opulence and polite society, yet put a good meal in front of any of us and we automatically become barbarians,' Ruskin observed mirthfully, tucking into his food with uncommon gusto.

However vulgar he considered the mural-decorated dining room, styled in the fashion of the Salon de la Paix at the Château de Versailles, it provided a supremely entertaining backdrop when in the company of two such innocents, whom he felt impelled to take fully into his confidence and draw very close to him.

Ned's face appeared to melt into its smile like a piece of sugar candy, though it just as quickly evolved into a frown and, lowering his voice, he nudged his host in concern. 'I can't imagine what a meal like this must *cost*. More than one of my canvases, I expect?'

'Yes, it's an outrage when you think of it,' his friend conceded, 'but then there's nothing some people would not sacrifice for a well-cooked turbot.'

'I trust *my* clients will be able to afford *both*,' Ned responded with unusual optimism, taking a gulp of wine and breaking into another booming laugh which caused the buttoned-up waiting staff to mutter to one another with hauteur.

Without allowing Ned and Georgie to notice, Ruskin glared at the attendants severely on witnessing their air of condescension towards his companions; and having successfully prompted them to scurry off, he remarked comically, 'You do realise that the waiters are puzzled as to whether you are my son or Georgie is my daughter? I never knew I looked so old!'

'*Dear* Papa,' Georgie said, smiling fondly and raising her glass, 'no children could be better cared for than *we*.' And the three toasted and made merry until the early hours of the morning, with their host regaling them with tales of his previous adventures abroad and plans of everything he had earmarked to show them along the way.

Just as the party were beginning to settle into the stride of holiday-goers, heady on the city's intoxicating mix of fine art, culture and exquisite food, Ruskin received a strangely formal letter from Mrs La Touche stating that she and her husband reluctantly revoked their invitation of the cottage.

Charging into Ned and Georgie's adjoining room in his eagerness for sympathy, something which was always forthcoming, Ruskin hardly seemed to notice that the pair were still dressing, in his haste to relate this latest calamity.

'Mrs La Touche says she must abandon the idea of giving me the cottage because their neighbours would never understand it,' he announced in disbelief.

'That is probably true enough,' Ned responded reasonably, continuing to button his shirt regardless of the intrusion.

'She didn't care two straws for their opinion before!' Ruskin erupted.

'Perhaps the lady had not passed the idea by her husband when she asked you?'

'Most likely, but I shall have a fine quarrel with Rosie, for I don't think she has fought half hard enough for me,' he complained, keen to lay blame somewhere.

'You're too harsh on the child, there was probably no changing things,' Georgie, who was seated buckling her shoe, tried to placate.

'Yes, she's right,' Ned chimed in, laying an encouraging hand on his friend's shoulder.

'She would have walked past the cottage every day on her way to the village,' Ruskin went on mournfully, 'and now I don't know *when* I shall get to see her.'

'All the sooner if you're gracious in your reply,' Georgie suggested, creasing her forehead sceptically.

'I hardly know *what* I shall write, only it will be hard for me to conceal my indignation. I don't know when I have *been* so vexed.'

Just as John La Touche had calculated, his wife's recantation placed an irrecoverable barrier between Ruskin and Harristown, not to mention obliterating his good humour for the remainder of his time in Paris.

From then on no thought entered his head that was not in some way bound up with the La Touches, while Ned and Georgie were so alarmed by their host's desperation that they began to think they should be forced to turn back for England.

The couple were surprised at the change in Ruskin's attitude, for having begun by treating them like *his* children, he suddenly became theirs, in need of reassurance and comfort in equal measure.

Ruskin tried in vain to banish vexatious thoughts of Ireland as they continued on to Dijon and Switzerland; but not even playing tour guide to the Burne-Joneses, and introducing them to the charming vistas and Swiss inns that were so familiar to him, helped to ease the pain.

Though the couple were often aware that their beloved companion's thoughts were drawn to an altogether different landscape, their holiday was nonetheless settled and tranquil, with both men taking it in turns to row Georgie across the green-tinged lake of Lucerne one day, putting the world to rights as they did so and heatedly debating everything from the latest scientific discoveries to the advancement of animal life.

'My wife never believes me when I tell her that there was a time when huge white cockroaches ruled the earth!' Ned exclaimed, laughing and lifting up his oar in enthusiasm.

Georgie meanwhile looked anxious lest her husband's antics would upset the boat, and proclaimed, 'If I end up in the lake you'll wish they still were!' much to the amusement of Ruskin who, during that brief moment, quite forgot his troubles.

Ever astonished by their host's magnanimous hospitality as they journeyed across Europe, Ned and Georgie both felt far more at ease away from large, ostentatious city hotels and preferred residing at clean unpretentious inns with scrubbed bare-boarded floors and heavenly views of the surrounding valleys, along with copious servings of local specialities such as *truite au bleu* for dinner, a trout so fresh that its skin turned blue as it cooked.

Ruskin's energetic routine not only ensured that he had little time to dwell on personal matters but that they all made the most of their environment. After breakfasting together around seven, when the lake could be seen in glorious stillness, the three would sketch outdoors until luncheon and take a long brisk walk to some new place afterwards, pausing to admire the scenery whenever they liked, although Georgie often found herself almost as distracted as Ruskin and could think only of her baby back in England.

Standing at her husband's elbow as he sketched the view she pleaded softly, 'Ned, won't you draw little Phil for me?' A request which their host collapsed into fits of laughter on overhearing.

'What funny things mothers are,' Ruskin asserted, teasing rather than chiding, 'always seeing everything through a mist of baby. I take you to see the best ravine in Mont Pilatus and nothing will serve you but to get Ned to draw your son back home!'

'You're right, it's foolish of me,' Georgie admitted, hanging her head in shame.

'No, no, go on, Ned, do as your wife bids or we shan't have a moment's peace.' And he settled himself upon the grass and made notes of the flowers growing there while his friend made a suitably handsome portrait of the boy.

This was followed by a lie-down, a change of clothes and a light supper upon returning to the inn after sunset, while come the evening the three huddled by the hearth as Ruskin read aloud extracts from his favourite novels and recited romantic poetry, recognising as he did so that every word and phrase reminded him of his own suffering.

'"He knew whose gentle hand was at the latch, before the door had given her to his eyes", he read from his favourite Keats volume, "and from her chamber-window he would catch, her beauty farther than the falcon spies; and constant as her vespers would he watch, because her face was turn'd to the same skies; and with sick longing all the night outwear, to hear her morning-step upon the stair."'

'"Isabella" was always one of my favourites too,' Georgie remarked, so moved by Ruskin's poignant recital that her eyes glistened.

'I outwear the night with longing, but what good does it do me?' he complained, reclining his head on the wing of the armchair. 'It certainly never helped *me* write sonnets about lovelorn heroes and heroines. My first love, Adèle, the daughter of my father's business partner, laughed in my face when she read my boyish tributes.'

'Cruel!' Georgie cried, trying to encourage Ruskin to make light of his reverie.

'It was a long time ago,' he went on just as woefully; 'I don't suppose she knew the hurt she caused. I called on her and her husband when we were in Paris and she's even prettier than I remember, besides being far happier than I ever could have made her. Now the fair-haired girl to whom I have given my heart can love no-one else but me, yet not me completely.'

Georgie preferred to remain behind sketching when the two men went hiking on Pilatus the following morning, Ruskin having encouraged her to spend every waking hour practising her art during these precious days when she had no household or infant to devote her attention to, though her maternal heart was so full of love and longing that she often gave in to the temptation to peep at Ned's drawing of Phil.

Meanwhile, Ruskin found himself unusually exhausted after less than an hour's climb and, upon pausing to rest upon a rock, lamented, 'Men ought to be severely exercised and disciplined in daily life, they should learn to live on stone beds and eat black soup, but they should never have their hearts broken. A noble heart, once broken, never mends. The best you can do is plaster over the cracks.'

'We are not merely *men*, we are artists,' his companion responded, laughing at his comrade, 'and as such we would not get on half so well were it not for a little nagging heartache over some woman or other.'

'You sound like my mother, but Rose isn't merely an *infatuation*,' he rejected, rising and taking up his stick, 'she's my first and last waking thought and I should be a far *better* man if only I could win her.'

'Forgive me, I did not mean to offend,' Ned apologised, also rising.

'Of course not, *you* with your wife and child and friends cannot understand what a drain of energy just living day to day is with no such source of happiness. You, who possesses everything I desire, have never known the sorrow of blind love, nor do you appear to realise what joy lies at your feet.'

He consented unhesitatingly, 'I know that there is enough love between Georgie and me to last out a long life if it is given us, but it's also true that the minute *I* have something I begin to grow tired of it.'

'Have you?' Ruskin asked, so distressed at having anticipated his friend's thoughts that he began walking on.

'You misunderstand me if you think I am going to complain about my wife,' Ned denied, exerting himself to stay by his side; 'she's entirely faultless.'

'Perhaps *that's* what you weary of,' Ruskin challenged, halting and regarding him intently. 'Rose is anything but. Do not overlook the great gift you have been given, Ned, simply because you long for excitement. It is overrated, I assure you. The path of a good woman is strewn with flowers, but they rise *behind* her steps, not before them.'

Although Georgie had persuaded Ruskin to wait a while before communicating with Rose, he was hardly any calmer when he came to doing so. Reproaching her with the full force of his displeasure, he catalogued the many ways in which the withdrawal of the cottage had impacted on his health so as to discover how much she felt his misery.

Her resulting silence over the following weeks only exacerbated his dejection, however, while Rose worried herself into a state as she struggled to think of some way to appease him or make him understand how much she sympathised.

Only one thing pacified him, and that was receiving a tender note from his beloved, penned in her favourite tree without the knowledge of her parents. Filled with soothing words, it expressed what he most wanted to hear, namely that she too was suffering as a result of her mother's broken promise.

Ned and Georgie were breakfasting on their balcony when Ruskin rushed to find them in order to share Rose's words, nor did he think to pass any courtesies, such as enquiring after their sleep.

'Rosie says she's sorry that I'm so ill,' he began, his voice filled with emotion.

'Are you?' Ned asked in surprise, unable, after so many weeks of such melodrama, to avoid a touch of friendly sarcasm.

Ruskin, much affronted, reminded them, 'You must have *seen* how lethargic and restless I have been?'

'Of course we have,' Georgie conceded, nudging her husband who was unwisely preparing to contradict this. She well knew that their host's particular kind of hypochondria was not likely to be alleviated by disbelief.

'What does she say?' Ned asked, giving way to his wife's sensitivity and being curious to know what Rose had said to transform Ruskin's day into one of joy.

'"If I could say anything, do anything, *write* anything that would cheer you, or comfort you, or make things softer to you, would not I do it?" he read. "But what can I do?"'

Much affected, Ruskin's eyes, hollowed from anxiety and sleeplessness, became moist on staring at the couple in anticipation of their reaction, and taking hold of Ned's arm he declared, much like a starving man who has just been given some nourishment, 'So you see, she really *does* care for me after all.'

Ruskin was much cheered on hearing from Rose, and as he, Ned and Georgie journeyed from Lucerne, crossing the St Gotthard Pass into Italy, they chattered away like old school friends, making hurried sketches of the myriad impressive views they didn't have the chance to study accurately but would finish from memory.

The spiritual power of the air, the rocks, the waters – to be in the midst of it and rejoice and wonder at it. It was impossible to think of exhaustion when travelling amidst such scenery, and as evening fell their energies were greatly lifted upon reaching, as if through a gateway, the wonderful plain with its swift, wide river quenching their spirits as it rushed beside them, while the mountain ranges were so large and numerous that they did duty as if mere hills.

After resting as peacefully as babes that night, they started again the following morning in unfailing sunshine and arrived at the Italian side, where the road cut through the eternal snows that were soon left behind as they descended into the promised land; the three hurled onwards by the rattling coach, pulled by horses which burned as hot as the tips of the mountains were glacier, even on the warmest of summer days.

The leading horses were unfastened and sent to the rear, while the other two flew along with the carriage, though sometimes the zigzag of the road became so sharp as to make the rear horses hesitant on looking down from the turn above.

'That one looks as though he needs but a sign to jump into my lap!' Georgie declared on turning around. But as she and the two men laughed together, her smile faded and she realised how homesick she was for England and her child, and how grateful she was to be on the final leg of the journey. 'Though there will never be any experience so sweet to look back upon as this journey with *you*,' she addressed Ruskin, 'part of me is almost as reluctant to go on as the horse.'

Perceiving Georgie to be in need of comfort, and that her husband was not forthcoming in offering the affection she required, he nestled her to his breast and declared, 'What a nice thing you are! I shall be sorry to part from you, but there is no greater force than nature and the love of a mother for her child. *I*, on the other hand, have no such ties and will therefore stay on a while longer. It takes a great deal, when I am in the Alps, to make me wish myself anywhere else, least of all London.' And he stared out of the carriage window distractedly as they progressed through the most sublime of all Italian landscapes, anxious not to talk further lest he should miss a moment.

After a period of silence, Georgie, considering the wonder of motherhood and her own guilt at leaving her son behind, recalled the themes of Margaret Ruskin's last letter, which as usual Ruskin had read aloud, and asked boldly, 'Isn't your mother expecting you home in time to celebrate her birthday?'

'Yes, and I expect you think I am selfish and heartless for disappointing her, but I heard that the La Touches will be in town and I have no desire to see them,' Ruskin explained, more in pompous justification than apology.

Georgie's skin prickled at the uncharacteristic brutality of his tone, for her affinity with Margaret's situation ran high whenever she thought of her own son, with whom she was shortly to be reunited. 'Mothers forgive their children everything, so I hear.'

'So you *do* think I'm heartless?' he flinched.

'No, I can understand your not wanting to see the La Touches, but surely you might keep out of their way?'

He shook his head emphatically. 'Just being in the same city as them would be enough to drive me insane.'

'You don't still blame Rose for the cottage plan going wrong?'

'Not at all, I realise there was nothing she could have said or done to prevent her parents from abandoning it, I simply can't face any more goodbyes just now, even if the consequence of staying away is to upset my parents.'

'And they surely will be,' she cautioned.

'Yes, I shall be bombarded with a stream of letters from both Mother and Father appealing me to return, but they will plead in vain, for my stubbornness is too great to be undone by feelings of remorse.'

Ruskin may have believed his conviction to be impenetrable, but his conscience was not so, and following Ned and Georgie's departure come September he found himself plunged headlong into guilt-ridden distress, borne out of pity for his parents and himself, while any peace he had hoped to come by was sacrificed upon the altar of regret.

He had gone abroad to find refuge, as if being away from familiar places could blot his feelings out, but when the La Touches ended by cancelling their visit to London due to Rose falling ill again he blamed himself for inflicting sorrow on Margaret and John James in order to avoid his own. How different things might have been if only they had understood him better.

THE VIGIL

ROSE LAY SICK, YET WITH NO PHYSICIAN BRAVE OR WISE enough to offer a diagnosis, let alone a cure, she worsened over a matter of days, her symptoms as baffling and inexplicable to the medical profession as her previous illnesses had been. They each simply muttered, shook their heads and agreed on one point: her condition seemed much graver than ever before.

The family were warned to prepare for the worst, and by early October even John James felt compelled to write to Ruskin, who was still abroad, suggesting that he might visit Rose in Ireland at once, but his son replied forlornly:

> "It can do her no good to see me, knowing as I do that such a visit is not welcomed by her father and would therefore only cause the child more distress. I am not sure I believe that Rosie has overworked her brain this time, but rather her heart, as I have mine..."

Her mother and father were meanwhile forced to talk in whispers whenever they entered her bedchamber, so greatly did Rose complain of a severe pain in her head on there being any sound, nor was she able to tolerate daylight and was troubled by any chink in the curtains despite her eyes remaining closed.

Mrs La Touche kept vigil for several weeks as her child lay quite still and silent in the darkness, fluctuating between blaming herself for always admonishing Rose's strange ways, her husband for encouraging their daughter to follow his own religious mania, and Ruskin for what she considered his unhealthy devotion to her.

Either way, the illness coincided with both the unfortunate business about the cottage and the over-excitement prompted by Rose's first Holy Communion, which her mother selected as the most appropriate reason to offer acquaintances who enquired after her daughter's health.

Weary from both the despair and tedium of keeping watch, Mrs La Touche wrote to Ruskin:

"I am sorry to say Rose has been taken seriously ill with one of her mysterious brain attacks – more persistent than any former ones. At present she cannot bear a gleam of light or a whisper, nor can she admit any of us except one at a time, for her brain is so terribly sensitive that all impressions give pain. I am afraid that she has thought herself into this illness, and I attribute it partly to the strong wish and excitement on being admitted to her first Communion last Sunday. Although not confirmed, she was making herself unhappy at being the only one excluded, and her desire was finally granted, yet I am sure she thought and felt too much about it all."

Rose's fair hair, spread out on the pillow, no longer glistened like strands of gold in the rays of the early autumn sun as once it had in the garden of Denmark Hill, but instead the sunshine fell unheeded upon her window as she continued to slip in and out of consciousness, feverish and racked by pain as her mother remained dutifully stationed in the armchair beside the bed, unable to hold her daughter's hand or stroke her forehead without causing her to moan.

Mrs La Touche turned sharply on her husband entering the room, for she had no concept of time or even the day of the week.

Touching her shoulder gently in an uncharacteristically kind gesture, he whispered, 'Maria, the doctor wishes to examine her.'

'He will talk softly?' she replied anxiously, rising.

Waiting to one side, they looked on as the doctor, the latest in a long line of experts who had visited Harristown, struggled to assess Rose's condition, for even the simplest of tests, such as taking her pulse or getting her to lean forward so that he might listen to her chest, caused her to writhe and wail deliriously, as if anyone merely touching her skin was torture to her.

When the physician had completed as thorough an examination as he reasonably could under such constraints, he sighed and indicated that he wished to address Mr and Mrs La Touche outside the chamber, for he had never seen a case to compare with it and remained deeply troubled as to whether the girl's symptoms were the result of a physical or psychological disorder.

'What did you find?' Mrs La Touche lost no time in asking.

'I was unable to find anything wrong with her,' he answered apologetically. 'Your daughter has a slight temperature, that is all. She complains of pain, yet there are no outward signs to explain it.'

'I nurse her day and night, and you tell me it cannot be explained? She might be dying!' the lady argued, frantic to find an answer and raising her voice enough to be hushed by her husband who placed a reassuring hand upon her shoulder.

'There's no question of her being extremely ill,' the doctor responded calmly, 'but I cannot treat her until I discover the *cause*.'

'We don't doubt your competence, you understand,' La Touche interjected, fearful that the man would withdraw his services, 'my wife is simply overwrought.'

'Please do not speak for me,' she interjected, before bluntly informing the specialist, '*I* doubt it and will call for a second opinion.'

'I thought I was the third,' he retorted bombastically.

Having no answer to this, the lady returned to her habitual post beside her daughter, while her husband invited the man to take some refreshment in an unsuccessful attempt to pacify him.

Life at Harristown was unavoidably disrupted by Rose's illness – from the servants, who could think and talk of nothing other than the girl lying upstairs, to their master's appalling neglect of his duties on the estate.

And thus things continued for a further few weeks, by which time the leaves on the trees outside the sickroom had almost completely fallen away and the family were resigned to being unable to save Rose. It was beyond inconceivable, therefore, when one day she opened her eyes and felt almost completely well again.

Though the drawn curtains made it impossible for her to gauge the hour, the slightest opening revealed enough for her to make out the sky, and thrilled by the idea of taking a closer look, yet not realising how long she had been confined to bed or how much strength she had lost, she pulled back the bedclothes, anxious to look upon the garden as a newly released prisoner might rush to see his home after many years' absence.

Rose would likely have fallen due to the deterioration and weakness of her limbs if a maid had not entered just as she was attempting to sit on the edge of the bed, and who, throwing up her hands in astonishment, rushed to support her as she tried and failed to stand.

'Good grief!' the maid cried, after helping the patient back into bed.

Reclining on her pillow, Rose begged, 'Will you open the curtains?'

'Why yes, miss, if you're sure you're feeling up to it? Your parents did give me strict orders not to.'

'I feel much better today,' she reassured, pointing towards the window impatiently and smiling in her old persuasive manner.

Her attendant finally succumbed, and Rose was surprised to find how long it took her to grow accustomed to the light, which initially blinded her and caused her to squint and blink rapidly. When she opened her eyes a second time, however, all the glories of a misty Irish autumn were revealed to her, the dear old Liffey enshrouded in a faint gauze-like haze which made her long to be outside.

Grateful for the sight but already exhausted from her earlier exertion, she rested her head and asked, 'How long have I been unwell?'

'You've been poorly for many weeks,' the maid answered pitifully.

'Are you new?'

'You don't remember me? I've been here since you were small. Well, it's no wonder everything seems strange, you've just woken from a deep sleep,' the young woman reassured.

'Isn't life strange?' Rose remarked lethargically.

Drawn to touch her hair, which had been cut to the length of her chin during the worst point of her fever, when her hair had been matted from days of writhing, she picked up a hand mirror from the bedside cabinet only to find herself staring back at a girl she no longer recognised.

'I should go and fetch your mother and father, they've been so worried about you,' the maid ventured on seeing that Rose was upset, and she bobbed politely on her way out, bursting at the prospect of relaying the news the entire household had abandoned all hope of.

Mrs La Touche was the first to go to Rose and wept upon finding her making another attempt to stand, for it was like coming upon a miracle. Overcome with relief she embraced her daughter fervently, yet no affection was returned and Rose kept her arms firmly by her sides.

Autumn had finally given way to a vigorous winter when, a fortnight after Rose had first attempted to stand, Mrs La Touche informed Ruskin of the unexpected change in her daughter's illness, oblivious as to how her correspondent had struggled to endure a day with no word and conceited enough to believe that his concern was largely in tribute to *her*.

Although an implicit rivalry had long existed between mother and daughter, the lady was glad to imagine Ruskin's jubilation when reading of Rose's miraculous progress.

Clutching the sacred letter to his breast in relief and thankfulness, an emotion he was only able to express in the sanctuary of his study, Ruskin got down on his knees and prayed to God in grateful tribute, begging

Him never again to torment him with the prospect of losing Rose. He then re-read Mrs La Touche's report continuously for several minutes before fully believing that he wasn't simply hallucinating:

"*Dear Mr Ruskin,*

The most wonderful change has come and Rose is getting quite well by degrees, although she has had a really dreadful illness, so long and full of strange changes. The only thing that never changed was her faith in God and her mother which was wonderful to behold.

In my long watching I often thought of you, for there were what the doctors called "psychical phenomena" that you would have understood better than anyone. Being with her was like a revelation, for there was a sort of clairvoyance, both of spiritual and earthly things, that was startling.

For the first fortnight of her convalescence she was able to tell beforehand every little thing that would befall her through the day and always said that she was guided in everything. The doctors were perfectly amazed and actually yielded against their judgement in allowing her to follow this "guidance", which never once erred, and I do believe it – whatever it was – spared her much suffering and "treatment", although she has become frightfully emaciated after four weeks in bed.

From a state of weakness so great that she could not sit up in bed, she suddenly, after one night's sleep, awoke perfectly strong in body but with an infant's mind and playfulness and an entire oblivion of all acquired knowledge and of every person and thing not known to her eleven years ago.

She eventually grew out of this, however, and it was lovely to watch her growth, a beautiful ideal infancy and childhood lived through in a matter of days. She told me, in the prescience that was given to her beforehand, exactly how all this would be and named the day and hour in which her full strength would return.

She spoke with such authority, and all along said that she would recover perfectly from this illness, body, mind and all, but that the mind would be the last to recover. I was both pitied and laughed at for believing her, but everything has come true and she is well, except for a slight weakness in her brain which makes it painful for her to have any thought or idea suggested to her in words – unless she asks for it – nor can she see people and either read or be read to..."

Bewildered as he was by the circumstances surrounding her recovery, and not altogether sure whether to believe the description Mrs La Touche had furnished him with, Ruskin hardly cared how long Rosie took to mend so long as she was living.

As soon as she was well enough, her mother passed on Ruskin's messages of love, unsuspecting that it was the thing she most longed to hear, for whatever else was confused in Rose's mind her memories of her teacher remained quite clear.

Her first letter to him confirmed the lingering effects of her condition, and he was grieved to find her initial attempts short and dull, as if all her old vivacity and wit had been obliterated by so long a period of unconsciousness.

Ruskin wished that his mother could have nursed Rosie instead of her own clever mama in Ireland, for he suspected that her health would have been far better managed if she hadn't always been forced to listen to a constant stream of religious talk from her parents, who were more at odds than ever over their different faiths following her illness. Whilst God drew the La Touches together in some ways, especially in times of crisis, in others He almost always succeeded in pulling them apart.

AN HONEST MERCHANT XVII

RUSKIN MAY HAVE FIERCELY DENIED THAT THERE HAD BEEN a formal falling-out between him and the La Touches since their withdrawal of the cottage, but he was much relieved when they invited him to one of their soirées when next they were in London, for Rosie's sake above all – for how should he ever see her if he was no longer in her mother's favour?

Though Rose was not yet well enough to travel to England, he trusted she soon would be, and therefore put all his efforts into making himself amenable to her parents, loathing his insincerity as he did so. The walk to the La Touches' house on Curzon Street had not changed, yet everything was somehow altered.

Fearing that Ruskin had succumbed to second thoughts about attending when he was the last guest to arrive, Mrs La Touche made an elaborate display of welcoming him when finally he made an appearance, having urged her husband to be a gracious and hospitable host after promising that he would never be invited to Harristown again.

'There is someone I would like you to meet,' the lady in shimmering green taffeta announced eagerly, sweeping Ruskin away from her husband when she saw how awkwardly the two men conversed and perceived the conversation to be drying up.

'Who? I pray it won't be anyone profuse in compliments of my work, for I am in no humour for polite exchanges.'

'George MacDonald, of whom you are sure to have heard?'

'Yes, it would be impossible to go out in society, even a little, and *not* hear of him,' Ruskin admitted, reluctantly moving through a crowded set of rooms, his assertive hostess leading him onwards in complacent disregard of his protestations.

'Having been turned out of his pulpit for being unorthodox, Mr MacDonald's lectures in London have been a veritable beacon to me since my anxieties over Rose,' she explained, 'and therefore I not only intend to fund his next pamphlet but would renounce dinner parties altogether and become entirely saintly if only my friends would let me,' on which Mrs La Touche laughed away to herself. When Ruskin did not join her, she continued seriously, 'He is also very eager to meet you, although thinks that he will shock you.'

'Very little shocks me nowadays,' he contradicted good-humouredly as they approached a tall man, with a long and lustrous dark beard, who was talking with his wife in a particularly warm and tender manner.

'I'm *so* glad, for it's my strongest wish that you and he will become fast friends,' Mrs La Touche went on presumptuously. 'I don't think anyone is capable of understanding you as well as he can, and you'll find that you can talk to him about anything you like, even Rosie.'

Ruskin didn't have the chance to work out exactly what Mrs La Touche meant to imply, for they were already encroaching on the MacDonalds' tête-à-tête, an interruption which neither spouse seemed to mind. Beaming graciously as Ruskin approached and their hostess took command of the introductions, George and Louisa's extraordinary compatibility struck their new acquaintance before anything else, for they hardly needed words to convey their every thought and impression.

Though Ruskin had long been familiar with MacDonald's writings, he never would have imagined the singular-looking Scotchman standing before him, his scarlet-coloured silk cravat adding to the rather daring splendour which made all those meeting him for the first time involuntarily smile.

Within a few minutes of Mrs La Touche wafting away with Mrs MacDonald on the pretence of introducing her to some other guests, the men discovered many things in common, not least that MacDonald's novel, *David Elginbrod*, had been inspired by the founder of the Working Men's College, F. D. Maurice, a work on which Ruskin was keen to offer his compliments, albeit not unreservedly.

'I enjoyed it a great deal, for it is full of noble sentiment, though I will say *one* thing,' he qualified, resting his hand on his hip matter-of-factly: 'it's nonsense about everybody turning good, for no-one ever *turns* good who isn't.'

'I am deeply gratified that you spared the time to study my book so deeply,' MacDonald replied affably, his rich Scottish brogue reassuringly honest and direct, 'but I meant to convey my belief that there is good in all of us if only we would realise it.'

'How might one do that?' Ruskin asked sceptically.

'There is this difference between some human beings and others, in the one case a continuous dying, in the other a continuous resurrection. Every night that folds us up in darkness is a death, and yet if you have ever seen the first of the dawn you will know that the world is full of resurrections,' he extolled. 'The day rises out of the night like a being that has burst its tomb and escaped into life.'

'Poppycock!' his companion dismissed.

'And you a philosopher, Mr Ruskin! But then I have always thought philosophy merely homesickness. You may think me overly sentimental, yet if there be any music in my reader I would gladly awaken it,' the Scotsman reasoned. 'The best thing I can do, next to rousing his or her conscience, is not merely to give them things to think about but to stir qualities they already possess and make them see that they are there.'

'Perhaps it's just that I can't find any such value in myself, being a pagan,' Ruskin responded bitterly.

'It sounds as though being a "pagan", as you call it, torments you,' he suggested, resting his forefinger on his hairy chin.

'It does. It would be much easier if I could be a member of your congregation and kneel at the altar twice on Sundays.'

'I don't judge you for *not* being able to. People must believe what they can, and those who believe more must not be hard upon those who believe less. You doubt because you love truth. I only hope you can trust in me practically, whether you do theologically or not,' MacDonald encouraged. 'You can never afford me a greater privilege than by letting me help you.'

'Help me?' Ruskin repeated, startled by both the boldness of the man and his proclamation.

'Yes, I want to help you grow as beautiful as God meant you to be when He first thought of you,' he replied simply.

Despite having been irritated that Mrs La Touche thought she knew what would be best for him, or whom it would benefit him to know, Ruskin could not deny that MacDonald, unlike Spurgeon, was a hugely inspirational man, though he did not share his religious convictions.

Remaining extremely human in spite of his spirituality, the most convincing thing about him was not only his goodness but his blind faith in the goodness of everyone he met, a belief which had the strange effect of encouraging them to be better and live their lives more selflessly.

He felt that simply knowing MacDonald would help him to find peace, something he reflected on as he walked home, along with the many questions of faith they had debated throughout the evening.

It was long past midnight when Ruskin returned to Denmark Hill, where he was surprised to find his father still sitting by the drawing room fire, straining to edit the business letter he had spent all evening composing.

Obviously exhausted, he noticed that John James's habitual glass of sherry remained untouched, and he was greatly saddened to see him so clearly failing – a shadow of the man he had revered, with some trepidation, as a boy.

'I hope you did not stay up on my account?' Ruskin enquired kindly, resting his hand upon his father's shoulder, for MacDonald's own sensibilities had already affected him enough to make him more patient with his father.

'No, no, I only wanted to show you the letter I wrote to that blasted merchant,' he replied, unusually keen to receive his son's approval before finally deciding whether or not to dispatch it on the morrow.

Seeing that John James was exhibiting his usual stubbornness and would not retire until he had given his opinion, Ruskin took the letter his father was holding out, only to be immediately struck by the illegibility of the handwriting.

'Why don't we discuss it in the morning? It's very late,' he suggested, stooping to offer his father his arm.

But John James loathed accepting assistance from anyone, least of all his son whom he still sought to be an example to, and thus he waved him away impatiently. 'I won't trouble you if you are in a hurry to be away.'

Seeing that he would not yield, Ruskin took the seat opposite and read the document carefully, though he was too wary of uttering the impossibility of it being seen by eyes other than his own and realised that the only way he might persuade his father to retire for the night was to praise the letter.

It surprised him how much this act of generosity gave him pleasure, and he found himself unspeakably moved when John James struggled to rise from his chair and began walking feebly towards the door, all the while clutching the indecipherable missive in his hand as proudly as if it carried a royal seal.

Breakfasting with his mother the following morning, Ruskin observed that his father was unusually late in rising, something which struck him as odd in light of his pains to ensure the early discharge of the business agreement he had penned the night before.

Pausing from reading his newspaper again several moments later, unable to stop the seed of worry from growing into the worst kind of imaginings, he referred first to his watch and then to his father's empty chair and felt a sudden pang.

'Has father not been down this morning?' he asked his mother, wondering if perhaps he had already departed for the office.

'No, he's been dressing this past hour,' she replied, shaking her head at her husband's change of habit. 'I don't know what's got into him. He never used to be so late to bed and late in rising. He is quite out of sorts.'

'He's the kind of man who, if he feels unwell, would run up and down the stairs just to make sure that his heart is still working.' A drollery which gave rise to the deepest foreboding.

Without enlightening his mother as to his unease, Ruskin rose and rushed upstairs to find the bathroom door locked.

'Father?' he called. But after knocking and shouting several times without receiving any response, it became clear that John James had been struck down with illness.

Charging Anne, the first servant to become alerted to the commotion, to fetch the key, Ruskin's hand trembled as he unlocked the door, and all his worst fears were confirmed upon opening it: his father, naked and barely conscious on the bathroom floor, was still clasping a shaving brush covered in soap and had cut his face in several places. Bleeding and shivering from the shock, not even the injury stirred him from the stupor that had befallen him.

'I'll be ready presently,' his father attempted to utter, his speech severely impaired.

With the assistance of Crawley, whom Ruskin asked Anne to call for, the two men carried John James to bed, where it was strange to see him finally take rest.

His mother was naturally distraught on seeing her husband thus reduced and, though eighty-one and increasingly immobile due to severe arthritis, she installed herself in the chair beside his bed with the devotion she had spent a lifetime exerting. Praying for his recovery, she muttered to herself over and again at the sad state of things, stroking John James's forehead fondly at regular intervals and knitting whenever he drifted off to sleep in order to distract herself from dwelling on what the next hours would bring.

By nightfall and after much difficulty, Ruskin finally convinced her to go and sleep in another chamber, thereby easing her burden for a short time and giving himself the opportunity of holding his father in his arms one last time.

As he kept the lone vigil, he was surprised to find how much light was thrown on all the occasions, numberless, on which he might have given his father pleasure by the mere expression of love, yet never did.

He mourned the gratification he had failed to give him in the past, just as he would mourn anything in the future that would have rejoiced him, and it was only when Ruskin recalled MacDonald's words that he stopped chastising himself, for what good did it do to think of his faults, still less his father's?

Instead, he contemplated John James's infinite devotion to him and how much he should miss his candid advice when he no longer had it – resulting in all past transgressions, on both sides, to crumble away.

Although his father's loyal heart went on beating under his hand until the early hours of the morning, to all intents and purposes it had already stopped. It was after falling into a sound, peaceful sleep beside him that Ruskin awoke to find that his father was finally at rest; his ashen countenance kingly in its repose, with hands that would toil no more folded in resignation of having lived labouring under the conviction that every dawn was as the beginning of life and every setting sun its close.

On fetching his mother, trembling with confusion and disbelief, Ruskin found that his own grief gave way entirely to hers, not because he felt too little but because he felt too much.

Having always loathed funerals and the obligatory mourning period which pervaded every aspect of daily life, from attire to stationery, Ruskin decided to bury his father in the simplest manner possible, whilst urging his mother to abstain from wearing the dreaded widow's cap and instead break the sombreness of the occasion by adopting the fine diamond and emerald brooch John James had gifted her many years ago but which she had never worn due to an abhorrence of extravagance.

Longing to nurse his sorrow undisturbed, Ruskin meanwhile resented the constant stream of people calling at Denmark Hill over the subsequent days, from poor relations, clergymen and undertakers, to lawyers and the staff of Ruskin, Telford and Domecq, who thoughtlessly thrust contracts needing to be signed before his nose as if he would automatically take charge and know precisely what to do.

He loathed being at the helm, for the matters he needed to attend to had seemingly tripled within a day and he was in no humour for any of it. His principle anxiety remained his mother, who had long ago withdrawn from society in favour of becoming her husband's sole companion and was therefore entirely at a loss without him.

Yet despite being more grief-stricken than at any time in her life, Margaret bore her sorrow with unspeakable sweetness, dignity and strength of character, respectfully accepting the decisions her son made as the new head of the family, however difficult she found it not to challenge him out of sheer force of habit.

In the end there was nothing she would have altered about the simple ceremony of that mild March morning, for Ruskin ensured that John James's funeral was attended by only close family or those who had known him well.

He was glad that his young cousin, a pretty, good-natured girl by the name of Joan Agnew, who had frizzy hair and a complexion like a rose, was there to talk to his mother and offer her a sympathetic ear when he would just have been awkward whenever she cried, or said and done the wrong thing.

Joan had an unsophisticated manner, yet she was never shy in company and happily offered to assist the infirm Margaret as they walked to the graveside where Ruskin read aloud the epitaph he had commissioned:

"Here rests from the day's well sustained burden,
John James Ruskin,
born in Edinburgh, May 18th, 1775.
He died in his home in London, March 2nd, 1864.
He was an entirely honest merchant,
and his memory is, to all who keep it, dear and helpful.
His son, whom he loved to the uttermost
and taught to speak truth, says this of him."

Margaret took an immediate liking to her niece, who comforted her when the coffin was lowered into the ground, for Joan seemed to dispel much of the gloom in simply being present, inspiring Ruskin with the notion of inviting her to stay on at Denmark Hill for a period, thus providing his mother with some much-needed company and help in running a household which boasted servants as old as she.

Although he had only met Joan briefly before, and had never spent long enough in her presence to remember her distinctly, he soon guessed what an integral part of Denmark Hill she would become, just from witnessing the affinity the two women shared, the single comfort amongst all the sadness.

'How strange the house feels without him,' Margaret declared sadly when once she was installed in her low chair by the fire during the informal reception.

'We know what a wrench it is for you, Mother,' Ruskin interjected, 'but Cousin Joan has agreed to stay until you are feeling stronger.'

Margaret looked much relieved at this and patted her niece's hand fondly. 'I'm grateful to you.' Then, wanting to make her feel particularly welcome, went on, 'Now, tell me what you like best to eat and you shall have it.'

'That's very kind of you, Mrs Ruskin, but I should be happy to have the same as you,' she replied modestly.

'You're embarrassing her, Mother,' Ruskin laughed.

'Not a bit. Don't hesitate, Joanna, say what you'd really like,' she persisted, wishing so much to make her feel at home, 'starting with luncheon tomorrow.'

Taking a moment to think, the young woman confessed hesitantly, 'Well, I do like cold mutton and oysters,' to which Ruskin chuckled, for it was impossible not to find his young cousin's honesty charming.

'Then cold mutton and oysters it shall be!' Margaret replied warmly.

The month of Joan's visit passed swiftly, with Ruskin noting that her presence entirely altered the atmosphere that had once made him desperate to travel abroad. She had a playful sense of humour that made his mother forget her melancholy, and he began to dread the day when she would have to return home to her uncle.

This reluctant farewell was foremost in Ruskin's mind when he entered the drawing room one afternoon and observed the gladdening sight of Joan walking arm in arm with his mother in the garden, the old woman's mobility having considerably improved with the help and encouragement of her ever-patient niece.

Although he could not hear what they were discussing, he saw Joan halt and turn to address his mother sombrely, which prompted him to continue looking on, for he feared that she was announcing her departure.

'Mrs Ruskin, I had better go home to my uncle soon,' Joan broached anxiously, for she was fearful of causing her aunt any further upset.

Margaret looked at the girl steadily and, touching her cheek, asked with concern, 'Are you unhappy here, child?'

'Oh no! The days have flown by, only my invitation was for a month and I thought—' she began.

'Never let me hear you say anything again about going,' the old woman interrupted; 'as long as you are happy here, stay.'

Comprehending the meaning as if he had been listening to their conversation instead of merely looking on, Ruskin watched his cousin embrace his mother warmly, her eyes filling with tears in happiness and gratitude, for no-one could have guessed her overwhelming relief at not having to return to her uncle, whom she despised with good reason.

'But I must speak frankly, child,' Margaret continued. 'I don't like you calling me "Mrs Ruskin". Will you call me Auntie?'

Joan nodded and laughed with her aunt, who was clutching her hand as ardently as a child, for she had inspired the old woman to display more tenderness in those few weeks than Ruskin had experienced in a lifetime. Age and dependency had softened the matriarch used to dominating, and thus she appreciated the kindness and affection that once she had expected so vigorously that it had been withheld.

And so it was that Joan ended by remaining at Denmark Hill and Ruskin becoming her guardian, Margaret having grown as fond of her as any daughter. Abandoning all plans to live abroad once and for all, Ruskin was delighted that his mother would benefit from a permanent companion, enabling him to travel whenever his work demanded.

Although Joan was not an intellectual and did not pretend to enjoy learning about geology or the great variety of things he considered himself expert in, fortunately she had a remarkable aptitude for housekeeping and in no time at all relieved his mother of the burden of managing a staff which she had long been too elderly and infirm to manage herself.

Extraordinary for an eighteen-year-old, Ruskin watched in amazement as Joan reorganised the servants and imposed orders with a quiet grace, yet forcible determination, which he greatly respected in so young a woman. It also amused him to observe that Joan was perhaps the only person in the world *not* in awe of Margaret, nor too intimidated to assert herself if once a disagreement arose. She ran the house with an altogether different style of leadership, being greatly dismayed at how many servants were equal to their mistress in score years and had subsequently had their duties gradually lightened with no-one to take them over.

When one night at dinner Joan asked her aunt what one female servant, who hovered about without seeming to have any particular role, *did*, Margaret replied matter-of-factly, 'Why, *she* puts out the dessert.'

Despite having inherited a considerable independent fortune of £157,000, pictures worth at least £10,000, and property in the form of houses and land, for the next two years Ruskin found himself strangely content to remain at Denmark Hill, Joan having made the environment altogether more pleasant than it would otherwise have been, and reminiscent of the brightest days of his childhood.

It became his habit to spend each morning studying at the British Museum, while his mother and cousin would entertain themselves in the garden when the weather was fine, or take tea by the fireside when it was not, with Ruskin delighting the women by reading passages from *Cranford* after dinner, adding colour to the work by adopting silly voices for each character.

Whereas in the past he would have been denied his mother's permission to invite a friend to dinner, now Joan acted as mediator and somehow always got her to agree; for whilst Margaret had initially declared that her son had the right to do as he saw fit now that he was master, she would soon have slipped into her former dogmatic ways, offering forth her opinions with no restraint and declaring her son a fool before his guests, had it not been for her niece's calming influence.

Acquaintances of Ruskin who visited Denmark Hill in the months and years following John James's death varied in their opinion of his mother, some believing her to be impossible, while others regarded her as a queenly figure who was to be much pitied on losing her beloved companion of almost fifty years. As with all families, the Ruskin household was never entirely what it seemed from the outside, nor as black as the son sometimes painted it.

PART TWO

XVIII

WILD ROSE

From the bright November morning on which Rose had first risen feeling better, it took a further year for her to be fully herself again, and even then many thought that she was never quite the girl they had known before.

On turning seventeen she was transformed into a striking adolescent, albeit one who seemed to stand warily on the verge of adulthood. A slender, fair creature who mirrored the beauty of her surroundings, her pale skin and rosy cheeks were coupled with a fragility that emphasised her distinctly ethereal presence, as did her deep spirituality, convincing all who met Rose that she belonged more to the next world than the present.

Just as she had prophesied, her mind had been the last to recover, but even when it seemed to be restored her way of thinking proved out of kilter with other girls her age, for it scared rather than excited her to look to the future, and during her long period of convalescence she became perplexed and troubled to observe that her former way of life wasn't only changing but leaving her quite behind.

This fact was harshly reinforced when her parents announced that Emily was to marry Major the Hon. Bernard Ward of the 32nd Light Infantry, a fine and gallant young man who was utterly unconscious that he would be depriving Rose of her closest confidant, nor did he suspect that this was why his future sister-in-law was so often absent when he called to discuss preparations for the wedding.

Having concentrated all her energy on getting well, Rose felt entirely unprepared for this new epoch of grown-up life and longed to hide herself away in the security and familiarity of childhood, even at the cost of being a slave to her mother's love of society and her father's religion.

It was unthinkable that Emily should not always live with her at Harristown, yet she dared not express these feelings for fear of being thought envious or ungracious. Instead, she tried as best she could to conceal her resentment of the forthcoming union and her revulsion of her mother's enthusiasm, and when she wept she did so alone.

It was an unconscious display when she exhibited her bitterness towards her sister's betrothed the day before the wedding, an event which contributed tenfold to her tears of self-pity.

Having been protective of the last few moments of Emily being just her sister and not Mrs Ward, she had thoughtlessly offended Bernard when he tried to join them on a turn about the garden, saying something about three being a crowd and suggesting he take Bruno for a walk instead. Realising how unkindly she had spoken when he walked off looking deeply hurt, her time with Emily was deservedly ruined when her sister ended by going after him.

Despite later apologising to Bernard and having the argument erased by his chivalrous, 'Think nothing of it,' Rose hardly slept for thinking he disliked her. She spent the morning of the wedding bathing her red eyes and blotchy tear-stained face just as the bride did in the neighbouring room for happier reasons, though hers too were tinged with a sisterly reluctance at having to leave her dearest Rose behind.

It was only when both women heard a commotion downstairs that they forgot the high emotions and foolish words that had been prompted by the significance of the occasion and, both rushing to the landing, found that Percy, a handsome young man of nineteen years, had arrived to offer a much needed distraction.

Expelled from Harrow, after much deliberation John La Touche had come to the ill-founded conclusion that travel would be the most expedient way to further his son's learning and moderate his capriciousness, and it was with this in mind that he had duly sent Percy abroad on an extensive grand tour.

Not exactly designed to be a punishment for his poor record at school, neither was Percy intended to derive personal enjoyment from it besides that of purely academic gratification. With an itinerary supplied by Ruskin which he found wearisome, and a tutor forever watching his every move, it was inevitable that the exotic cities he visited, including Egypt as the climax, were not as vivid or transforming as Percy had been led to expect.

His father's idea of a grand tour was certainly not the kind so many of his comrades had so colourfully described, and he was greatly disappointed at receiving fewer liberties and freedoms than the constraints placed upon him at Harrow. Impatient with his tutor, who sent almost daily reports to his mother and father as to how their son was conducting himself, Percy found himself more stifled than at either school or Harristown.

Thankful that Emily's wedding had granted him a reason to return for a short interlude, he was just as mischievous as ever, something illustrated by the pet monkey he had brought home to plague the household and make his sisters laugh.

'This is your wedding present!' he called up to Emily, who, having been in the midst of preparing, wore a dressing robe and a crown of orange blossom as she leant over the banisters and giggled at the sight of the impish creature in her brother's arms which was amusing itself by fiddling with his long, dark hair.

'Oh, Percy, you'll never change!' she replied, nevertheless delighted to see him.

'No, I don't suppose I will,' he returned theatrically, knowing that his siblings always found it impossible to remain vexed with him.

Unable to contain her delight on being reunited, Rose rushed downstairs half-dressed and with her hair looking wilder and more chaotically matted than if she had been out in the fields with Bruno.

Skipping down the cold stone steps barefoot in her eagerness to embrace him, Percy lifted Rose off her feet when she reached the penultimate step; her arms locked around his neck until she nearly fell, half-screaming, half-laughing on noticing that his pet monkey was attempting to climb the slippery marble columns of the entrance hall.

Emily, who had remained on the landing, looked down fondly on her siblings who grew more and more alike in spirit, but after joining them in their hilarity she suddenly dashed into her chamber on catching sight of her mother passing through the hall with the groom's family whom she was escorting to their suite of rooms in the opposite wing.

Embarrassed on coming upon the chaos, Mrs La Touche declared to her guests with intentional vigour, 'Percy may not be my sort of boy, Mrs Ward, but he is *my* boy,' to which her son raised his eyebrows comically and tried to restrain himself from further laughter. 'As for Rose, you'll see that she grows wilder than ever.'

After attending to the groom's parents, Mrs La Touche dedicated herself to the challenge of dressing Rose who, despite being the sole bridesmaid, desisted any overly flamboyant or formal styles of dress.

Eventually conceding to a pink silk gown embroidered delicately with pink and white rosebuds, selected by her mother as the most complimentary to both her complexion and the wedding flowers, she cringed as each button fastened her into the conformity of a society to which she did not belong.

Wearing her hair neatly pinned at the nape of her neck, as was her custom, Rose had no interest in how she looked and, making a point of never once looking at herself in the glass, viewed any form of vanity or unnecessary adornment as a means of distancing herself from Christ.

No matter what great pains Mrs La Touche had taken, she could not make her daughter carry herself with any grace, yet consoled herself with the thought that Rose would always be thought beautiful regardless of her relaxed deportment, informality of manner and obliviousness of all proper decorum.

In fact, most of the guests were drawn to look upon the younger sister far more than the bride as the two glided down the aisle; Rose possessing a radiance and angelic aura that made her sibling's beauty merely secondary in the eyes of others.

As Rose stood in the family pew, looking on forlornly as Emily dedicated herself to the unfamiliar man who would shortly be pronounced her husband, her mind drifted away from the ceremony and she contemplated whether or not *she* would ever utter the same vows – and if so, to whom.

She would soon be eighteen and already her mother had begun to suggest that she might shortly follow her sister in marriage, yet the idea seemed too frightening to imagine and so she tried to focus on the final chapter of the service, sealed with a kiss that signified no obvious love or affinity between the couple but which would nevertheless result in Rose being the only sibling to remain at Harristown.

Like a tragic heroine, Rose became a wild, lonely being following Emily's departure and hardly knew how she would have borne her sister's absence were it not for the companionship of Bruno, with whom she spent the greater portion of each day outdoors and who followed close beside her wherever she went, not least when she took it into her head to call on the cottagers unannounced, day or eve.

Rose related such scenes in her regular letters to Ruskin, and although he no longer found her descriptions dull, as he had during her slow recuperation, they were far more solemn than the colourful reports she had once furnished him with:

> "I go about among our poor people here and come back to my own idle life of comfort in despair sometimes. For it seems to me that they lead a life so much nearer to Christ's than mine, and I go jingling off in my carriage with a sadder heartache than any of them could know. How I long to be more on an equality with them."

Mrs La Touche, who had never felt at home with the tenants, meanwhile chided Rose in vain for her over-familiarity. Whilst she had once declared the custom charming when her daughter was still in short petticoats, she thought it preposterous now that she was practically a young lady with a position to uphold.

This did not deter Rose from continuing to run in and out of the labourers' cabins like a breeze of wind, however, nor from being mixed up with every village bother. When one cottager christened their child "Rose" in her honour, Mrs La Touche could ill conceal her disapproval and groaned whenever the infant was mentioned, not least when she heard from a tenant that her own Rose had taken her infant namesake for a drive to the neighbouring town in her humble pony and trap, a quaint country vehicle which attracted much attention due to being no different than those used by the field labourers.

Though no-one could have denied that Mrs La Touche had been a devoted nurse throughout her daughter's illness, her subsequent passage from adolescence into womanhood greatly tested their relationship, and it seemed to Rose that she fell foul of her mother's approval all the more when Emily was no longer there to shield her or plead on her behalf.

Meanwhile it was easy to take the cloudless summer days for granted when they had continued unchecked for a fortnight, and so it was as Rose, bareheaded and wearing the plainest of dresses and a well-worn pair of boots, made her way across a motionless field of corn one slumberously hot afternoon in August.

Her delicate forehead and cheeks, beginning to scorch, betrayed that she had forgotten to bring her bonnet, while the wicker basket she carried, filled to the brim with plump blackberries gathered from the hedgerows, along with her stained fingertips and mouth, revealed that not everything she had foraged had succeeded in making the final harvest.

Throwing a stick for Bruno, Rose smiled with pleasure when the dog obediently returned it, and as they approached a cluster of workers' cottages on the edge of the field she spotted Mrs Casey, who watched her grow up with interest. Sitting on a stool outside her door, the old woman paused from scraping her son's boots in order to wave to her young friend.

'Good afternoon, Mrs Casey!' Rose called in response, choosing to make her otherwise soft Irish accent more pronounced and handing her the basket of blackberries as a gift.

After they had spent an hour talking and praying together, the young woman kissed her farewell with as much regard as a relative, continuing on her familiar round of the poorest cottagers out of sheer affection rather than duty.

Although many struggled to put food on the table, they would have given Rose their last crust of bread, so little did they consider her as belonging to a superior class. They saw the division between them as merely circumstantial and harboured no grudge towards her because of it; rather, they all judged her to be more at home with the likes of them than her own family, and she had several times confessed that it was so.

Oblivious of the time, the fact that the sky was threatening rain, or that she was wearing neither hat nor coat but only a thin cotton gown, it took until the clouds overhead were as black as soot for Rose to finally grow concerned at the change and that she was at risk of being drenched.

Yet still she chose not to return home, for it had become her habit to avoid dinner, so impossible did she find it to look upon her own family's sumptuous repast after observing a mother on their own estate nourishing her children on barely more than bread and water.

Rose's starvation was a recurring topic with her mother, who continued to plead with her to abandon such senseless martyrdom despite none of her entreaties ever being heeded. Initially fearing lest her appeals would make her daughter more determined to act out of spite, as Mrs La Touche observed Rose grow increasingly slender so she vented her frustration by arguing instead of gently coaxing as she knew she ought, outbursts which only encouraged her child's obstinacy.

The grandeur of life at Harristown, however much her father boasted of the frugality of the household, was not compatible with Rose's Christian beliefs, thus forcing her, as she grew older, to participate less and less in her parents' society events and dinners, making her feel increasingly like a visitor who was forced to respect their hosts' customs whilst trying to avoid them.

Her mind had been turned to such thoughts when the summer rain, heavy and persistent, finally arrived, yet she continued to walk for several miles regardless, only to eventually look down at her dress and see that it was inches deep in mud.

'Mama is going to be cross!' Rose declared to Bruno, who didn't much like being outside either and whined accordingly. 'My dress is spoilt and I'm late for dinner again.'

Her mother had only just noticed the change of weather, however, having gone in search of her daughter. Happening to pass a housemaid on the stairs, she frowned upon enquiring, 'Is Rose not home yet?'

'I believe she's still out walking, ma'am,' the maid replied timidly, averting her eyes from the hard gaze of her mistress whom all the younger members of staff were generally intimidated by.

'Will she never be a civilised being?' Mrs La Touche responded rhetorically, before proceeding to the drawing room.

She was more annoyed at her daughter's disobedience than anxious for her return, for she anticipated Rose turning up as she always did, soaked through and insincerely apologetic for having inconvenienced the household. Dinner, Mrs La Touche decided, was not to be served one moment later than the usual time, with or without Rose, nor was her husband to be alerted as to their daughter's absence until then.

As her mother viewed the storm from the comfort of her palatial drawing room, Rose waded through the sodden grass and heather, pausing to look about her and realising that she had completely lost her way.

Putting her hand to her forehead in despair, she trudged on, oblivious that she was getting further and further from home as she did so, yet believing that if she stopped and began to bemoan her error she might well have to spend the night outdoors or, even worse, endure her parents sending the servants to search for her.

As the darkness advanced and she grew weary, Rose was forced to admit that she could proceed no further and must shelter under a tree with Bruno until the storm subsided, finding solace in his loving licks whilst praying for the rain to stop.

Resting her eyes in exhaustion, when she opened them a few minutes later and peered through the dripping branches she felt like her prayer had been answered. Joe, a young shepherd, was advancing with a lantern as he made his way home from tending to the animals, and, swallowing her pride, Rose called out to him desperately.

'Are you lost, miss?' he asked, straining to make out the figure and finally recognising Rose.

'Very,' she replied, embarrassed at not knowing her own land better.

'You shouldn't be out on such a night as this,' Joe scolded as a fork of lightning illuminated the horizon.

'Will you show me the way?' she asked, not wanting a fuss yet unnerved by the ensuing thunder.

'I can't do that, I will return you safely home,' he insisted, removing his coat and draping it around her damp shoulders.

Thanking him for his kindness, she walked on by Joe's side, with him helping her over the roughest places and taking pride in exhibiting such heroism. Travelling in the direction of the storm, Rose shuddered when the lantern fell upon a petrified tree, and she clung to the shepherd as a deafening clap of thunder broke overhead, the sky a blaze of electricity which seemed to represent a biblical-like punishment, with bolts that grew more frequent as they went.

Captivated by his companion's alarm, Joe laughed to himself and marvelled aloud, 'Whatever will your family think when they see you with a dirty lad like me?'

'I dare say Mama will be too busy scolding me for being so wayward to notice anything else,' Rose reassured, ever more anxious the closer they came to the house.

Unaware of the time, her parents had long since finished dining when Rose finally identified the distant lights of Harristown, and her mother and father were indeed incensed as she stood upon the threshold with Joe. Although Mrs La Touche managed to contain her anger in the boy's presence, Rose braced herself for her wrath as soon as they were alone.

'You can't think what care this boy has taken of me,' her daughter explained, placing her hand on her small knight's shoulder, 'and he has so far to go home.'

'It was very good of you to escort Rose,' Mrs La Touche admitted graciously, too ungenerous to suggest their coachman drive him.

'It was an honour,' Joe assured, remembering to remove his cap.

'Please take some refreshment downstairs before you go,' the lady suggested reluctantly.

'I'm much obliged to you, ma'am, but my own family will be wondering where I've got to,' he declined respectfully, surprised by the echo of his voice and how this emphasised his common accent.

Mortified on catching a glimpse of his muddy face in the large gilt-framed mirror, he had long been curious to see inside the house that loomed large on the estate and thus gazed in wonder at the high ceiling and grand furnishings so removed from his own dwelling.

'I can't imagine how you are ever to be made a modern young lady of,' Mrs La Touche despaired to Rose when Joe had gone on his way. 'You are out from dawn 'til dark, let the weather be what it might, and it's apparently quite useless to expect you to observe any restraint or social custom, or to wear any raiment that would not suit a peasant. You do not one single thing that other girls do.'

'Did it ever occur to you that perhaps I don't want to *be* like other girls?' Rose returned provokingly.

Mrs La Touche, who more than ever longed for the exclusive society which only London afforded her, ensured that she regularly kept in touch with those with whom she intended to exchange calls upon her return to Mayfair, the expectation of which being all that sustained her during the tedious months in Ireland.

Greatly satisfied on seeing her eldest daughter married, she turned her attention to presenting Rose at court before the Queen, ignoring her youngest's unpreparedness and dread of formal occasions along with the unwanted attention it would thrust upon her.

For a child who had shown so much early promise, Rose had taken a strange and wayward course since her illness, yet Ruskin relished Mrs

La Touche's tales of her daughter's adventures and in turn confided to George MacDonald:

> *"I can't love anybody except my mouse-pet in Ireland, who nibbles me to the very sick death with weariness to see her and sends me bits of flowers as if they were just as good as her own self. She's just like a wild fawn and likes me well enough – about as much as a nice squirrel would – while she makes me hate everybody else and is the only living thing in the world I care for. I shall hardly be able to bear it when she gets too old to be made a pet of, which is infinitely ridiculous."*

It was mid-December when the La Touches arrived in the capital and Ruskin was finally reunited with Rose, the girl he had not set eyes on for three long years and could scarcely contain his joy on being able to look upon as much as he liked.

Whilst he had been apprehensive of her approaching eighteenth birthday and what this would mean, he was gratified to find Rose equally resistant to becoming a debutante, proving that his teachings had not been entirely in vain.

Observing with disgust how Mrs La Touche had sought to mould her daughter in her own image, and after being desirous of furnishing Rose with a good education now wanted to showcase her as she might a valuable work of art sent off to auction, Ruskin was inspired to write a book entirely devoted to young females, offering guidance on how they ought to be raised and educated.

Rose was naturally much delighted on discovering that she was the secret subject behind his latest work, and she smiled with pride as Ruskin read aloud an extract containing a poorly veiled criticism of her mother, to whom he was sincerely grateful for not having joined her daughter on her first visit to Denmark Hill in ever so long, "'You may chisel a boy into shape as you would a rock, or hammer him into it, if he be of a better kind, as you would a piece of bronze,'" he read, pausing to look directly at Rose, "'but you *cannot* hammer a girl into anything. She grows as a flower does.'"

Closing the recently published volume entitled *Sesame and Lilies* solemnly, he presented the book to her with a full heart, for words were his only means of paying her adequate tribute.

It seemed somewhere between eternity and yesterday that Rose had last visited them, so at home did she appear beside his hearth with Margaret and Joan, who were still dressed in mourning and were much cheered by her visit.

Ruskin still found it difficult to regard Rose as a woman, however, for so many of her girlish characteristics continued to make an appearance, not least when, after regaling them with one of her latest verses, which she was pleased to recite as opposed to enclosing within a letter, Rose announced that she had no inclination to marry and would far rather devote her life to literature.

'I have decided to become a poet,' she declared seriously, causing Ruskin to look much taken aback, for despite thinking her poetry feeble he had complimented her on her latest attempt by way of humouring her and without realising how seriously she would take his praise.

Thinking it best to dispel her disillusion lest she continue to embarrass herself before others, he therefore teased gently, 'Oh really? I too thought I was a born poet, before I believed myself a born artist, and now I find that I am neither.'

'You do not think I possess enough talent?' Rose retaliated, her face flushing in humiliation on believing him to be mocking her inadequacies.

Ruskin could have cut his own tongue out when he saw her eyes fill with tears of wounded pride, for it was never his intention to crush so naive and harmless an aspiration, least of all one which he had inadvertently encouraged.

'Life being very short, and quiet hours few, we ought to waste none of them in writing valueless poems,' she went on, for distorting his words was the highest insult she could pay him, although by so doing she revealed her intimate knowledge of *Sesame and Lilies*.

'That was cruel of me, I did not mean to dissuade you,' Ruskin tried to appease, secretly pleased that she was familiar enough with his latest writings so as to be able to quote them, inaccurately or otherwise, 'I simply think that it is not always a question of deciding what we *want* to become, but rather trying to discover what occupation we were truly intended for.'

'And what might that be?' Rose asked resentfully, causing Margaret to rise unsteadily and take Joan's arm, for the old woman was canny enough to know when to take her leave and allow the pair to thrash out their differences alone.

Ruskin admired Rose's incredible force of will and how her cheeks burned with defiance when she folded her arms and refused to look at him. How much he should have liked to tell her exactly what he thought her true calling was, but as he could not he remained humbly apologetic for the rest of the afternoon. They had never quarrelled like it before and it gave him his first real insight into just how much she had changed.

'Come now, Rosie Posie,' he tried to disarm her, 'don't blame me for wanting more for you than to spend your life rhyming couplets. Isn't it enough to be my muse?'

Rose smiled reluctantly, unfolded her arms and shook her head stubbornly as she always used to do. It was as jarring and conspicuous for him to call her "Rosie Posie" as it would have been for her to call him "St Crumpet", and her avoidance of addressing him by any name or title was just another poignant reminder that their old ways were lost forever.

Ruskin was satisfied in taking tea with Rose most afternoons and avoided quarrelling with her as carefully and daintily as she poured his tea over the silver strainer and offered him a biscuit.

Pondering on whether or not he should declare his love for her before she was fêted by men more charming and handsome than himself (the natural anguish of a middle-aged man with a passion for a beautiful young woman), he was almost fearful to think of her in a wifely way lest he should tarnish her sacredness, nor did he dare consider the full reality of changing the nature of their relationship.

As he had proclaimed within his latest volume, marriage was the seal which marked a vowed transition of temporary into untiring service, and fitful into eternal love. How gladly he would devote himself to her happiness to the end of his days if only she would allow him.

In order to gather approval from those around him, Ruskin set about introducing Rose to the few close friends he possessed, including the Burne-Joneses who immediately warmed to her and finally began to comprehend his devotion. He was also delighted to observe a close connection develop between Rose and Joan, who being just two years older than his former pupil meant they shared much in common.

His own fondness for his cousin encouraged Ruskin to confide in her his secret hopes of marrying Rose, and whilst Joan was not in the least surprised, due to Margaret having already relayed the depth of his attachment, he felt reassured on talking the matter over frankly with a woman so near in age to his love, grateful to receive measured advice as to how best to proceed with his suit.

Nevertheless, on the eve of Rose's birthday he wavered between giving a name to his attachment or remaining a humble bystander to her life, for what could he offer a girl, nay woman, so many years his junior? Only his heart, possessions and philosophies, for what they were worth.

He soon concluded that he could never be satisfied in seeing her marry another without at least *trying* to win her. If Rose was to bid him leave her, then he would do so without further petition, he reasoned, but *she* alone had the power to banish him.

Spending many paradisiacal hours conversing on all manner of subjects as they walked beside the little stream nestled among the laurels of Denmark Hill, perhaps, he surmised, they were the happiest times ever to be. He attempted and failed to fathom her feelings towards *him* and remained entirely unsure of his ground when he awoke from a half-sleep early on the morning of Rose's coming of age.

The dawn was grey and ominous, encouraging him to stay in bed for several minutes despite being fully awake and restless, still undecided about the declaration he knew he must make and troubling over how he might manage a few moments alone with Rose that evening, having invited her and her mother to dine at Denmark Hill.

No matter how many times he rehearsed his painstakingly worded speech, instead of gaining in confidence he became increasingly crippled with nerves, the like of which he had never experienced, not even when addressing hundreds of men.

Nor had this debilitating hysteria entirely left him when he looked out of the drawing room window just after seven o'clock that evening and saw the La Touche carriage approaching the house.

Thankfully, Rose, whose temper had a tendency of abruptly switching between gravity and light-heartedness, seemed very happy when she arrived and, on Ruskin welcoming her and her mother in the entrance hall, she asked him coquettishly, 'How do you like my new bonnet?'

'Very much,' he responded jovially, as he helped her remove her cape, greatly relieved to find her in such high spirits, 'you look like a milliner's 'prentice out for a holiday!'

'Percy bought it for me in Paris,' she continued, untying the large bow and fleetingly admiring herself in the hall mirror, something he had never witnessed her do before.

Is her mother beginning to influence her at last? he thought to himself. *Or was Rose's saintliness only a ruse all along?*

After Margaret and Joan had kissed Rose and wished her Happy Birthday they proceeded to the dining room where the ladies of the house had placed a large vase of pink roses in the centre of the table in tribute to the honoured guest, though she was more occupied in ensuring that Ruskin took the seat beside her.

Rose had always teased her tutor playfully, but now that she was older her familiarity made the others feel strangely uncomfortable, for she spent the majority of the evening talking almost exclusively to Ruskin, much to the annoyance of Mrs La Touche who resented the fact that her daughter always monopolised their host.

While the four of them feasted on the fare which Joan and Margaret had spent such care in selecting, Ruskin noticed that Rose hardly touched her food and only occasionally sipped the champagne which Crawley kept topping up, causing him to grow pleasantly intoxicated as he sat gazing at her while she babbled on about the London society her mother intended her to rule.

'How did Rosie enjoy being presented to the Queen?' Margaret enquired of Mrs La Touche, who was full of stories of her daughter's first season in London.

'Not in the least, it was an ordeal just styling her hair, never mind getting her to stand still!' she replied, feigning exasperation, before boasting, 'Rose doesn't realise how similar she is to me, for I never realised how much others admired me when I was young. Once, when I was quite a little child, I was picked up and kissed by a nice elderly lady and gentleman at a party, only to discover afterwards that they were the old king and queen!'

At this, and being careful not to be observed, Rose nudged her knee against Ruskin's by way of illustrating her embarrassment at her mother's theatricality. He was meanwhile vexed that Mrs La Touche referred to her daughter as though she had nothing more in her head than a doll. It was strange to see that, despite her eagerness to launch Rose in society, she was even more disinclined than he to accept that her daughter was a woman with the right to voice her own opinions.

Ruskin could barely refrain from sneering at how Mrs La Touche remained entirely unconscious of mirroring her own mother, the Countess of Desart, whose controlling behaviour she had so often bemoaned, or that her own imperious ways were simply encouraging Rose to shun the course she expected her to follow.

'Rosie is a real beauty,' Margaret continued in an attempt to avoid a topic which only drew attention to the strain between mother and daughter, 'and yet she is as sweet as ever.'

'Perhaps one day she will show you that she is not always a sweetness,' Mrs La Touche contradicted, without considering how malicious this statement sounded. She soon realised her mistake on Margaret looking shocked, however, and attempted to pretend that she had spoken in jest, 'Or if she is, it's the sweetness of the wild fruit or the thorn-guarded flower, and so best.'

Unsurprised, yet nonetheless hurt at this attack, Rose turned to Ruskin and observed, 'Mama once told me that she named me Rose because I was born in the depth of winter and brightened the gloomy days, yet she doesn't think so anymore.'

'You still brighten every one of *mine*,' Ruskin whispered, hoping that she would interpret the compliment as romantically as he intended it.

Margaret, who was fast running out of conversation with Mrs La Touche and longed for Ruskin and Rose to join in, enquired, 'I hear that Emily is married now?'

'Yes, at least one of my daughters has proved her worth,' the lady replied, laughing falsely without expecting anyone to participate, 'but Rose misses the companionship dreadfully. That's why she talks about nothing but cats.'

'There are worse things, I suppose,' Joan interjected.

Ruskin, though he had one ear on Mrs La Touche's malevolent remarks, could hardly help conversing largely with Rosie, for as soon as he would ask her mother a question out of politeness the younger woman would divert his attention away or attempt to make him laugh. To no avail, Mrs La Touche raised her eyebrows and screwed up her mouth on the pair excluding the rest of the party from their jokes and became suspicious that they were mocking her.

'Your mother must think me frightfully ill-mannered talking to you and nobody else,' Ruskin whispered to Rose.

'I like you to talk only to me, and as it's my birthday supper you should do what *I* want,' she argued, her rosy countenance showing the little champagne she had tasted but was unaccustomed to.

A short time later Crawley re-entered the room with a tall birthday cake displaying eighteen shining candles, the heralding of a new and bright era Ruskin hoped. After singing with gusto, the gathering applauded Rose for blowing them out on the first attempt and they each kissed her.

'Many happy returns,' Joan beamed.

'I hope you will always have everything you wish for, dearest Rosie,' Margaret offered, pressing her hand fondly, yet all the while weighing up whether her son would ever secure her as a bride and deciding that it was distinctly unlikely.

'I penned a rather clumsily worded poem to commemorate the occasion,' Ruskin announced, rising to his feet yet stooping as if in humility. Addressing Rose directly, he cleared his throat nervously and began, "'Ah, sweet lady, child no more, take thy crown and take thy pride, golden from the great sea shore, now the sands of measuring glide. Thrice they count the noted hour. Thrice to changing spirits given. Once to life and once to power. Last, to judgement, light of heaven. Put away thy childish things, and take thy sceptre, dove-like, mild. They must on earth be more than kings, who would in heaven be as child."'

Only he could know the full heartbreak and poignancy contained within each sentiment and, raising his glass to Rose, which the others joined him in doing, he struggled to shake off the melancholy which befell him following this tender recital.

After dinner, on his mother, Joan and Mrs La Touche retiring to the drawing room, he succeeded in persuading Rose to take a look at his latest Burne-Jones paintings in the library. He hardly knew how he should have managed to be alone with her if she had been disinclined, or if her mother had insisted on joining them, and as Ruskin opened the door and stepped across the threshold after Rose he fairly gasped on imagining the life that seemed just within reach.

'It's such a shame that your father isn't here to celebrate with us,' Rose said earnestly on seeing John James's leather wing armchair. But Ruskin's heart sank on this reminder and, closing the door, he approached her cautiously, for she continued to stand beside his father's old worn seat, resting her arm on the back of the chair and reflecting solemnly on the many things that had irrecoverably altered in the past few years.

'It was a sudden illness, but he would have preferred it that way,' he answered vaguely, not in the mindset to discuss John James, whom he knew would not have approved of his intentions concerning Rose.

'Yes, I know you're right,' she agreed. Then, as if trying to ease the pain of Ruskin's loss and her own loneliness following the marriage of her sister, she pressed his arm kindly before turning away.

'Whilst I wish my father were here now, you don't know what this day means to *me*,' he ventured, confident that she understood his meaning whether she wanted to acknowledge it or not.

'I'm so pleased that your cousin Joan has come to live with you,' Rose went on, pretending to look at Ruskin's newly acquired paintings and sensing that he was preparing to say something that she was not sure she wanted to hear. 'Mrs Ruskin is so glad of her company.'

'My mother is nearly blind and can hardly walk, yet she believes *she* takes care of Joan rather than the other way around,' Ruskin amused her by observing. After hesitating for a moment, he went on, 'What a terribly Irish girl you have become.'

'I suppose I have, but you hate change of any kind, least of all in me,' Rose said, turning to face him and blushing on realising how intently he was regarding her.

'Can you blame me when I only grow older and you more beautiful every day?' he flattered, as ardently and timidly as a youth addressing his first sweetheart.

'I care nothing for all that, I just want to make you proud of me,' she returned sincerely.

'If you knew what immense pride I have in my heart just to see you standing before me, well again, you would not say such things,' Ruskin went on, his eyes becoming moist as he cupped her delicate face in his hands.

Moving away and averting her eyes from his fixed gaze, she teased, 'Have you had too much wine, St Crumpet?' for it was always her tendency to make light of things when she felt uncomfortable.

'Please don't call me that!' he responded rashly, regretting his words just as quickly. 'I'm sorry, Rose, I didn't mean it.'

'You wouldn't have said so otherwise. What would you have me call you?' she asked, confused at the sudden awkwardness between them.

'Anything you like. Most of all I'd like you to call me "husband",' Ruskin suddenly blurted out, hearing someone in the corridor and fearing that her mother would interrupt them before he'd finished. 'Don't you see that I love you, Rose? *Love*, that word which represents the most constant and vital part of being and has never been consecrated on my lips with such meaning. Won't you marry me?'

It was far from the declaration he had perfected in his mind over the past days, yet the footing of their former friendship was irredeemable and the ensuing pause seemed to lay open the years of agonising and waiting which he had, until then, endured silently.

Rose, leaning against the wall of bookshelves as if unsteady from the shock, searched in vain for a response, yet Ruskin, not being able to withstand the ambiguity, could wait no longer and went on, 'I don't ask you to say that you feel the same way. It isn't love that I need, I simply want leave to love *you* and for you to be happy in *being* loved.'

'I don't understand, how can you love me?' Rose asked, her thoughts a dizzying combination of perplexity and bashfulness on having inspired such feelings.

'You're the only living thing in the world I really *do* care for,' Ruskin explained, as though laying his heart at her feet and urging her to tread lightly.

'Don't say that,' Rose pleaded, unwilling to bear such a heavy responsibility and walking about the room as if it would help her think more clearly.

'You were unaware of my feelings?' he asked, having long believed that she possessed an instinctive understanding of his attachment.

'I always thought that you looked on me as a friend,' she denied, unintentionally trampling on his hopes that she might express *some* word of reciprocation.

Dejected, Ruskin took up John James's old chair, whereupon, putting a hand to his brow for a moment, he persevered, 'I trust you will always be that, but do you think you could ever be more?'

'I hardly know,' she answered, still bewildered that they were even speaking about such things.

'Can you say that you feel nothing for me besides?' Ruskin ventured, desperate for any crumb of encouragement.

'No, I cannot say that, and yet I cannot answer you now,' Rose answered firmly. Then, pausing as if trying to find a way of appeasing him, she went on boldly, 'Will you wait until I am of age and ask me again?'

'In three years' time?' he questioned, dreading the prospect of having to wait a moment longer for her answer. 'Do you know how old I will be then?'

'Yes, fifty,' she answered resolutely.

'I will do whatever you ask providing you're not angry with me, Rose,' Ruskin agreed reluctantly, 'and that you don't think I have spoken wrongly.'

'You have only said what is in your heart, I could never blame you for that,' she reassured, standing before him and allowing him to take up her hand and place the gentlest, most adoring of kisses upon it.

'Even if nothing can ever be as it was between us?' he queried apologetically.

'It's true, I hardly know how to think of you now that you want me to be your wife,' Rose admitted.

'What is it *you* want?' Ruskin persisted.

'One cannot always do what one wants,' she explained sadly, already anticipating her mother and father's reaction.

'You intend to inform your parents?' he asked, guessing that Rose was keen for the conversation to end so that she might return to her mother's side.

'I think I ought,' she confessed.

'And I of all people would never ask you to betray or deceive them,' he allowed, 'but you understand why I did not approach them first?'

'Yes, it is brave of you to have spoken at all,' Rose commended whilst moving towards the door.

'Bravery or madness?' Ruskin prompted.

'A little of both,' she weighed up, resting her hand upon the handle impatiently, yet delighting him with the flicker of a smile, 'although I have always found that the less we speak of our intentions the more chance there is of realising them.'

'Surely blurting out all that is in one's head and heart is better than silence?' he continued apprehensively. 'What will you do if they forbid you to see me or write to me?'

'I suppose *I* must decide what my life is to be, not they,' Rose said uncertainly, with her back to him. Then, glancing over her shoulder, she added, 'That is why I beg that you wait until I am twenty-one.'

'I can wait for as long as there is hope. At all events, the *possibility* of hope. Your parents will want you to consider other suitors of course, only at least promise me that you won't engage yourself without telling me first,' he pleaded, standing behind her and placing his hand on hers to keep her from turning the door handle until he was satisfied that he had conveyed his feelings. 'There is a quiet trust between us which can never be broken except by *your* bidding.'

Some strange sensation, a symptom of their intangible bond, held Rose there for longer than she intended, and whilst she made no answer Ruskin found that he did not expect or desire one after all. He removed his hand so that she might leave him, though it was like watching Persephone pass into the Underworld and he wanted so much to make her stay.

It was impossible for Rose, whose colour had drained from her countenance, to think of anything other than the recent conversation when she rejoined the women in the drawing room, and she knew that she but poorly concealed her distraction, especially when Ruskin remained in the library for a considerable time afterwards.

Inevitably, her mother sensed Rose's disturbance and questioned her on the way home without attempting to disguise her curiosity. 'Did you enjoy yourself this evening?'

'Very much,' she replied unconvincingly, continuing to look out of the carriage window in order to avoid scrutiny, for although Rose intended to confess what had really occurred, first she needed to consider her own feelings, whilst taking a certain amount of pleasure in keeping a secret that was sure to inflict a bitter blow to her mother's high self-regard.

'You were a long time with Mr Ruskin after dinner,' Mrs La Touche observed pointedly.

'Was I?'

'I hope he didn't bore you with too much talk about his new paintings?' She persisted, determined that Rose should reveal what was troubling her, and having guessed that Ruskin had simply sought an excuse to talk with her daughter alone. 'The rest of us had almost given you up for lost.'

'Oh, you know how he is, he just wanted to show off and extract as many compliments as I would pay,' she replied casually. 'As it happens though, I admire Burne-Jones greatly and am so pleased that Mr Ruskin is helping him.' In light of what had just occurred, it felt inappropriate to refer to her new suitor so formally, causing Rose to stammer when it came to uttering his title.

Attempting to exhaust her mother's interest by describing at length the paintings she had most admired, Mrs La Touche realised that Rose was determined not to admit what was really on her mind and decided to let the matter rest until the morrow, only praying that the revelation would not be what she dreaded most, something so preposterous as to be quickly dismissed.

Before fully leaving the subject alone, however, she could not bring herself to let it lie without expressing her main complaint. 'I wonder why he didn't invite *me* to see the Burne-Joneses.'

THE SEVERANCE

ROSE DID NOT ATTEMPT SLEEP FOR RECKONING ON THE events of the previous evening, fearing her parents' reaction to Ruskin's proposal yet believing that keeping it from them would only worsen their attitude when eventually they learned of it, for they would surely find her deception even greater than that of which they would accuse him.

Thus, the next morning, Rose asked her mother and father into the drawing room and revealed Ruskin's pledge, declaring her own confusion along with her inclination not to refuse him.

'You don't mean to say that you would even *consider* marrying him?' her mother cried, rising in agony.

She gave no answer to this, for just as she predicted, whilst her father had never liked Ruskin and found the idea of her marrying an atheist abhorrent, her mother's sudden revulsion proved the keenest of all, albeit for reasons she was unable to voice.

Mrs La Touche was careful to disguise any sign of jealousy before her husband, however, and successfully convinced him that her horror of

Ruskin's declaration was solely the result of a natural motherly concern for her youngest daughter whom he had, so she raged, flagrantly preyed upon from a position of trust.

Rose's defence that Ruskin had never behaved in any way that was not entirely proper and that his respect for both her and her parents had prompted him to wait before uttering his hopes of marriage were swept aside in the ensuing whirlwind of bitterness.

Vindictively seeking to discredit Ruskin as a suitor, no rumour that she had ever heard in reference to him was too base or ludicrous for Mrs La Touche to repeat to Rose and her husband in the hours that followed, nor did she spare her daughter from listening to the most malicious gossip that had been in circulation during the period of Ruskin's annulment of marriage, an episode of his life which, until then, Rose had known nothing.

'Whilst you were confined to the nursery,' her mother scorned, 'the abandonment of Ruskin by his wife was a scandal which even overshadowed news of the Crimean War! You have no comprehension how much public interest and speculation the case generated.'

'If you believed all the evil that had been spoken of him, why ever did you invite him to tutor me?' Rose asked, dumbfounded by this sudden change.

'That is a pertinent question, you must admit,' her father chimed in.

'I naturally sought the best tuition for you, and as talk of Ruskin's past had long since abated, and he was again lauded in society when I sought his help, I couldn't see the relevance of it.'

'But it *is* relevant now?' Rose despised, recognising that her mother would never have chosen to enlighten her about the scandal had she not wished to quash any possibility of a union between her and Ruskin.

Ruskin had little concept of the crisis he had caused and still naively hoped that Rose's parents might look on the match favourably, in light of his status and fame, not to mention the devotion and loyalty he had already demonstrated towards their family.

'I have been, albeit reluctantly, granted leave to continue in the shadow of our old ways,' he remarked to Joan over breakfast a few days after proposing, having received an off-hand reply from Mrs La Touche in response to his application to take Rose to the opera at Covent Garden.

'She's probably finding it difficult to adjust to the idea of you as a suitor,' Joan tried to hearten.

'Yes, I suppose it's too early to expect more,' he agreed, always cheered on talking with his cousin, 'but how could she lose Rose less than by giving her to me?'

'Perhaps it's not her daughter that she most dreads losing,' his cousin teased, before colouring with embarrassment on realising the impropriety of such a suggestion. Enquiring, 'Which opera are you seeing?' in the attempt to move away from the subject, Joan rose without waiting for a reply and began attending to Margaret who had been occupying herself with her letters, occasionally looking up in order to offer her companions a foreboding expression.

'Mendelssohn's *Elijah*. It's not the most romantic of operas I must admit,' Ruskin answered, nervous at the prospect of seeing Rose for the first time since his declaration and trying to foresee how her manner towards him might be altered.

However gaily he set off for the opera house, having allowed Joan to convince him that all would be well, there was no sign of Rose in the foyer and come curtain up still she had not appeared. Thus Ruskin found himself seated, nay trapped, in the middle of a central row of the stalls.

Conscious of becoming a tragic figure with an empty seat beside him, he removed his watch from his waistcoat, discovered that the performance was running late by two minutes and sighed before replacing it, deeply annoyed with himself for not having insisted upon collecting Rose in his own carriage.

Turning around to survey the crowded auditorium, he thought for a moment that he saw her, but in reality there was only a fussily-dressed young woman making her way down the aisle on the arm of a gentleman whom he took to be either her beau or her husband. They made a handsome young couple regardless, Ruskin admitted with a pang as the pair took up the seats to his left and whispered to one another with an intimacy he had never known.

All the lights in the theatre, save for the stage lamps, were then dimmed and the audience fell silent in response to the first stirrings of the overture. Although he was far from anticipating the performance, Ruskin felt that he had no alternative but to remain, frequently glancing at Rose's empty seat in an otherwise full house.

Deeply distracted, just as the orchestra got fully underway he opened the small box he had been holding all the while and stared at the ruby ring contained within it, which, even in the darkness, blazed like fire.

On sensing that his female neighbour was observing him, Ruskin swiftly shut the box and tucked it away in his pocket. It was all too painful and humiliating, as was having to endure the grimly religious opera which he had only chosen in order to please the devout Rose.

What kind of Christianity permits her to treat me so? he raged inwardly, the opera failing to draw his attention away from his own wretchedness and unrest.

Hurt and increasingly angry, he found it impossible to exert any concentration or interest in either the music or the drama being acted out, and so, as soon as the interval arrived, Ruskin pushed inelegantly past the lackadaisical crowds and dashed out into the cold night air, desperately miserable and unsure whether this signalled the end of his relations with Rose.

Is this her merciless way of refusing me, or did her parents simply forbid her to accompany me? he asked himself on commencing the many miles home, trying to make sense of the past few days and hours and reproaching himself for having laid himself open to such uncertainty.

Rose was meanwhile forced to tolerate a small, yet opulent dinner party her parents were hosting, which they had insisted she attend in favour of joining Ruskin.

That she was blameless in disappointing him did not ease her conscience; and as her mother had engineered that it was too late for any note of apology to reach Ruskin in time, Rose's only way of retaliating was by being disagreeable company and refusing to engage in conversation. If her parents *would* insist on her presence she was determined to make the most of the opportunity to embarrass them.

'I must apologise for our daughter this evening, for I perceive that she is fixed on being tiresome,' John La Touche announced as the four guests entered the dining room and took their seats. 'Rose is put out because we wouldn't allow her to go to the opera this evening,' he went on pompously, 'but I'm beginning to wish we had,' to which, encouraged by their host, the entire table broke into a strained, uneasy laughter.

Rose neither liked nor respected any of the assembled company enough to mind their ridicule or disapproval, and she was only grateful that her father's bullying made her more in synergy with how she imagined Ruskin would be feeling. Picturing him waiting patiently for her until the final call before the performance, she suspected that this would not be the last occasion on which his faith in her would be challenged, through no fault of her own.

Everything around her faded into a blur of indignation as the butler made a circuit of the table with the claret jug, yet by the time he reached her she was so highly strung that, whilst in the process of trying to refuse the wine, she accidentally toppled over the glass, causing the ruby liquid to spill onto the crisp ivory tablecloth and onto her own ivory satin gown.

The esteemed company, much surprised to hear La Touche chastising his daughter in their presence, were startled to observe this error and assumed that it was simply her impudent reaction to his earlier rebuke.

'What the devil's got into you?' La Touche shouted bombastically as Rose made for the door with tears streaming down her face.

Uncomfortable, yet secretly thrilled by such unexpected entertainment, the guests discreetly averted their eyes from their host – and the stained tablecloth, which the butler was proceeding to disguise as best he could with napkins – and continued to enjoy the sumptuous repast just as if such episodes were commonplace.

Ruskin, perplexed and wounded by Rose's poor treatment of him, might have taken comfort from the fact that she too was suffering an almost equal degree of mortification, also inflicted by her parents.

As he was making the lonely walk home, Rose entered her bedroom and violently tore off the spoiled silk evening gown she had been instructed to wear. Flinging herself face down on the bed, she sobbed uncontrollably, her body still resembling that of a girl due to past illness and perpetual starvation.

Never had such black despair struck her, along with an overwhelming feeling of guilt on failing to provide Ruskin with any explanation as to her absence, and she prayed that he would have enough trust in her to recognise that such cruelty would never have been her own design.

Locking the door and ignoring her mother's many attempts to speak with her, Rose made certain that her written apology to Ruskin, which she toiled over during another sleepless night, was delivered by one of the servants early the next morning.

Rather than apportion the blame to her parents, however, she provided him with a feeble excuse of having felt unwell, for she feared making the relationship between himself and her parents any worse. Instead, she hoped to make amends for his suffering by inviting him out shopping with her the next day, regardless of how opposed her mother and father would be to her seeing him alone.

Ruskin, caring too much for Rose to bear a rift, forgave her instantly upon receipt of the letter, although he still looked tired and careworn when she met him, as if his dilemma of the previous few months had only increased and he felt torn over what his conduct towards her should be.

In turn, he soon perceived that her old carefree manner had entirely changed towards him, despite her making a concerted effort not to show it, for Rose's avoidance of even the most harmless and customary physical contact, such as refusing to take his arm when first they met, insulted him deeply and made him lose his temper.

'I've ordinary etiquette right to give it,' he argued, persisting in holding out his arm.

'Let's not quarrel in the street,' Rose returned, finally placing her hand on his sleeve due to passers-by, who recognised Ruskin, having begun to stare.

'What am I to do if you won't allow me to court you *or* befriend you?' he asked pitifully, at a loss to know why she had beckoned him at all.

'Can't we, just for today, continue in our old manner?' Rose suggested, finally taking his arm, though doing so felt peculiar.

'I should like that,' he nodded. 'Shall we go to the British Museum?'

Continuing to meet for the remainder of Rose's time in London, exploring galleries and taking tea together, although their former closeness was impaired by the revelation foremost in their minds, she would have been reluctant to relinquish the opportunity to discover if they might really be suited for a future life together.

Whenever he looked at her intently she only felt embarrassment, however, and the change that had come about was simply too great to allow her to analyse her own feelings with any real confidence, not least because her mother attributed her consideration of Ruskin's proposal to a mere enjoyment of flattery.

Dismissing her mother's words as hollow and vindictive, Rose was sorry for having wasted the occasions on which she might have better examined her regard towards Ruskin, and she wondered if different kinds of love often became indistinguishable when one had known the person a great many years.

On the morning of her departure for Ireland she crept downstairs early enough to avoid alerting the household as to her movements. Already wearing a cape and bonnet, she opened the front door as quietly as possible and stole out into the sleepy Mayfair street, daringly unaccompanied and with her heart racing in exhilaration.

Entering the room of the National Gallery in which she had arranged to meet Ruskin, Rose found him waiting although they had only just opened, while his failure to notice her granted a welcome moment to observe her former tutor as he stood before a Botticelli painting, his head hung low due to fearing that he would again be relegated to his own company. Knowing that her return to Ireland was imminent, he depressed himself by imagining how long it might be before they saw each other again, months in which her parents would be able to turn her against him.

Approaching silently, Rose touched his shoulder softly, on which he turned to her in surprise. 'I didn't think you were coming,' he confessed, noticeably relieved.

'Of course, I wouldn't have gone without saying goodbye,' she assured, annoyed that he continued to recall, and judge her on, the opera incident.

Ruskin looked lost yet comforted at being able to see her face a last time. 'Do your parents imagine that separating us will be enough?' he asked as they moved onto another painting, although neither of them displayed the least interest in their surroundings.

'Perhaps, or by throwing enough suitors at me that I will be sure to prefer one of them,' she replied, whilst remaining ambiguous as to whether she spoke in jest or earnest.

'And will you?' Ruskin questioned seriously.

'They haven't succeeded so far, and it hasn't been from the want of trying,' Rose answered, smiling in the attempt to make his grave demeanour crumble. 'They can prevent me seeing you and writing to you, but they can't stop me thinking of you.'

Like women who, dreaming of motherhood, observe babies around every corner, so too did Ruskin notice perfect young couples, illuminated by the first flush of love and boasting the radiant smiles of the untroubled. One such pair attempted to view the painting he and Rose were standing distractedly before, causing them to move on and take a seat on the hard leather bench positioned in the centre of the gallery.

Ruskin could restrain his ardour no longer and boldly seized Rose's hand, unsure if she would accept the gesture. Far from her natural instinct telling her to recoil, instead she felt as disinclined to remove her hand as she had been to refuse his proposal, and permitted this first romantic contact to continue for several minutes unchecked.

Despite the seemingly insupportable age difference, there was a deep and mutual emotional connection between them she could not deny and which this slight, yet significant touch only confirmed. However fleeting the moment was, due to neither of them feeling entirely comfortable on acting thus in a public environment, the progression of their relationship was nonetheless irreversible.

'I ought to speak to your father,' Ruskin declared, hoping that Rose, who was already preparing to leave him, would agree.

'You can try but I don't think he'll discuss it,' she advised.

'Still, I feel it's right that I should *try* before you leave London,' he insisted nobly on seeing her out.

'Very well,' she finally conceded, kissing his cheek fondly and disappearing into the crowded street, her presence casting a pleasant shadow over his day.

As Rose had forewarned, Ruskin's subsequent meeting with John La Touche was anything but cordial, with both men positioned at either end of a long mahogany dining table which made conversing on any serious or intimate topic almost impossible.

When his host remarked formally, 'It was a good idea of yours to luncheon together, you and I have never really had a chance to talk properly, or at least not since your visit to Harristown all those years ago.'

'No, we haven't,' he replied, wondering how he would maintain such a stilted exchange and whether La Touche meant to draw attention to the fact that he had not been invited to Harristown since the withdrawal of the cottage.

'I hear a great deal about you from my wife and children of course,' he went on, unable or unwilling to disguise his insincerity, 'and I read a little of your book on education, *Sesame and Lilies.*'

'Oh really?' Ruskin was encouraged, interested to hear La Touche's opinion of it, especially as he had never previously mentioned reading any of his works.

'Yes, it was very pretty,' he observed brutally, succeeding in what was undoubtedly a calculated insult and which led to an uncomfortable pause.

Realising that it was La Touche's desire to avoid the subject of Rose entirely, and unable to stand the futility of the meeting any longer, Ruskin asserted himself, 'If I may speak plainly, the main reason for my visit today was to determine your wishes regarding my conduct towards Rose.'

La Touche took his time before responding coolly, 'My dear friend, let us not spoil a perfectly pleasant meal by bothering ourselves about *that*,' looking down at his plate in order to avoid Ruskin's gaze.

Then, after he considered enough time had elapsed for him to attempt a change of subject, he went on in a tone a banker might use towards his clerk, 'I know what I wanted to ask you, what do you think of Stuart Mill supporting women's suffrage?'

Ruskin was irritated beyond belief at La Touche blocking his earnest desire to explain his addresses towards Rose, for her father had made it plain that he was far from taking him seriously as a potential suitor; not only had he refused to be drawn into a potentially antagonistic debate on the matter but he clearly dismissed Ruskin's proposal as so preposterous that it was not even worthy of acknowledgement.

As Rose was legally unable to go against her parents for another three years, Ruskin at once saw his error in having revealed his hand so early and that it would be more than enough time for the La Touches to browbeat their daughter into obeying their wishes.

He therefore felt that he had no alternative but to bite his tongue and attempt to make himself as likeable as possible to the man he still hoped to one day call his father-in-law; and so he humoured his host by engaging in a wide range of political topics, whilst always being careful to only venture his opinion when he had first established La Touche's immovable viewpoint.

The luncheon also revealed that the family intended to invite Joan to return with them to Ireland for a holiday, infuriating Ruskin all the more and filling him with a jealousy that was in marked contrast to his typically warm and generous nature. He claimed Harristown as Darwin claimed the Galápagos and resented anyone within his circle sojourning there when he was effectively outlawed.

Awaiting him on his return home was a further and altogether more crushing blow: a letter from Rose containing proof of the chasm which her parents were determined to put between them.

Reading "I am forbidden by my father and mother to write to you or receive a letter," he assumed this was a response to her disobedience in arranging private meetings with him prior to her departure, though he could only speculate as to whether her father's personal dislike of him had prompted it.

Worst of all was Rose's request to have Joan travel with her back to Ireland. 'They take Rose away and now they want Joanna!' Ruskin raged to his mother and cousin in the drawing room, clutching the paper until his fist ached and raising his voice regardless of his cousin standing by.

'Me?' Joan exclaimed, anxious that she had caused him to be angry with her.

'The father makes no bones of detesting me, while the mother is jealous of the daughter and has pulled us sharply asunder,' he continued; 'they're just inviting you to Harristown as a means of punishing *me*.'

'Perhaps Rose merely wants to show me her home,' she defended, her eyes beginning to fill with tears, 'but I shan't go if it will cause you distress, Cousin John,' she accepted meekly.

'Of course you must,' Margaret insisted, turning to her son and demanding firmly, 'and you would be as bad as they if you were to prevent her friendship with Rose when once you instigated it.'

'I wouldn't dream of *preventing* her or locking her in her room, I simply want her to know the pain she will cause me,' he went on immaturely, stamping his feet in protest of anyone else partaking of the pleasure he was forbidden.

'I might deliver any messages you might have for Rose now that she's prevented from writing,' Joan ventured.

'John would be exceedingly grateful,' his mother replied kindly.

Feeling guilty for having taken out his frustrations on his cousin, Ruskin finally composed himself.

'Yes, indeed I would. Forgive me losing temper, dearest Joan, all this is bringing out the worst in me.' Saying which, he embraced her by way of begging her pardon, for he treasured Joan as much as if she were his own sister and loathed the La Touches for causing conflict between them.

He was grieved that his cousin had unwittingly become a pawn in his broken friendship with the La Touches, and despite perceiving the hypocrisy of asking her to deliver messages to Rose which he could not relay by any other means he saw no alternative.

There was no denying that Joan was probably the only person capable of extracting a clear understanding of Rose's heart, and so, having started out furious that she had been invited to Harristown when he was prohibited any means of communication, Ruskin ended by seeing the invitation as a blessing he was powerless to refuse.

'You alone hold it in your power to find out for me whether Rosie is acting only in childish love and pity, or whether there is any real feeling on her side. That is, deep enough to justify me in persevering against the absolute device of both her parents.'

JOAN'S HOLIDAY

THE SUN SHONE GAILY ON JOAN'S FIRST HOLIDAY OUTSIDE England and it was warmer and drier than most Aprils, something which only heightened her favourable impression of Harristown, the largest house she had ever stepped foot inside.

Initially struggling to comprehend the scale of the property, not least the expansive estate it presided over, when she finally adapted to the customs of such an impressive household the days began to pass faster than she wished, with trips to nearby beauty spots followed by grand evening dinners and balls, the like of which she had only read about in the romantic novels she was always careful to hide from her guardian.

One benefit of never thinking herself pretty or important enough for anyone to look at her, save fleetingly or out of courtesy, was that the La Touches thought her modest and well mannered, thus allowing her to gain in confidence, a fortunate result of the invisibility she perceived her lack of station afforded.

Relishing standing on the sidelines, glimpsing a world very much outside her own, never daring to think that she could ever be one of those dancing, twirling figures in silk before her, Joan was soon taken under the wing of Mrs La Touche who was keen to thrust her forward the more she shunned the limelight.

The fair Rose, who still missed her sister Emily, was meanwhile extremely grateful for her young friend's companionship. Linking arms with her one Sunday after church as they made a circuit of the croquet garden, they chatted away happily as Percy, who had taken an immediate liking to Joan, frolicked and played ball with Bruno on the pristinely manicured lawn, all clipped and fuzzy in readiness of carefree summer games and garden parties.

'How nice it is to have a friend here!' Rose hailed as she squeezed Joan's arm. 'I have been quite alone since my sister's departure, and Mama and I never see one another if we can help it.'

'What about Percy?'

'He's the light of my life but so seldom here. You shouldn't have met him at all if he hadn't been expelled from Harrow last year.'

'Expelled?'

'Yes, though it doesn't appear to have caused him any unrest or shame,' Rose continued humorously. 'After struggling with any subject remotely scholarly, he was banished after five terms, much to the humiliation of Mother and Father. Just think, if he had remained at school he would never have got to know *you*, a circumstance which offers a possible redemption for all his past misdemeanours if only he can see it.'

'Whatever do you mean?' Joan demurred. 'I'm quite sure that I shouldn't want to be his saviour.' A statement that did nothing to convince her friend, who had vague plans for the two of them to fall in love and marry.

Joan had never met a young man quite like Percy, while he, having recently returned from the final phase of a purgatorial grand tour, was just discovering the attributes of the fairer sex, though he contemplated asking for her hand in marriage with no more thought than trying to win a prize he never seriously considered claiming.

Initially relieved to be home and out of the clutches of his ever-surveying tutor, Percy was already weary of Harristown by the spring and keen to be reunited with his friends in London. He therefore found the amenable Joan both a pleasant diversion and a means of practising his most winning coquetry.

Having several times caught her eye as she was conversing with his sister in the garden, he finally plucked up the courage to rush up to her and plant a kiss on her cheek, causing her to blush as profusely as one of the early flowering rhododendrons, while Rose broke into hysterics at Percy's incredible arrogance.

Even he was unusually embarrassed when his sister's laughter highlighted the inappropriateness of his behaviour, and he resolved to leave the women to their talk, purposely hurling Bruno's ball a good way off so that he might follow the dog, who obediently charged after it.

'Would you accept him if he asked you?' Rose enquired skittishly when Percy was safely out of earshot, as ambivalent of normal conventions as her brother.

'I should never have considered such an idea before today!' Joan denied unconvincingly. 'I know my station in life and have no aspirations to change it.'

'How I should love you to become my sister,' she ventured, without wholeheartedly believing such an outcome likely. 'I know Percy better than anyone, and I can see how taken he is. He's still a foolish boy in many ways, and a long way from being a man, but even he isn't immune to recognising what a good and loving wife you would make.'

'If he *did* make such a declaration,' Joan pondered, warming to the idea, 'I would have to talk it over with my Cousin John. After all, he is my guardian,' she qualified, feeling that she must try to calm her friend's eagerness.

Rose's smile faded instantly. 'He would hate the idea, for he disparages Percy and adores you. I can't say I blame him, for you deserve better than my naughty brother. It's only selfishness that makes me want you to marry.'

Joan did not dwell upon Ruskin's low opinion of Percy, for she enjoyed thinking of herself as a bride and all that this entailed, choosing to counter his probable reaction by predicting that it would be unduly influenced by the opposition he had received from the La Touches regarding his own pledge.

'As I always say, Percy isn't *bad*,' Rose went on comically, fearing to put Joan off the match, 'he just isn't very good either!'

Both women laughed together for several minutes and were still trying to compose themselves when Bruno reappeared without Percy and rolled on the lawn before them, covering himself in grass.

'I wish you could be happy,' Joan ventured, hoping for Ruskin's sake that Rose might open up to her, for she had remained strangely silent whenever there was any reference to him.

'It's hard to imagine being so when Mama grows colder towards me every day. I just shut up because everything I do and say she misunderstands. It seems I must refrain from being me and learn to bear living utterly alone. I shouldn't mind her disagreeing with me in everything if only she seemed to love me. It's not that I *want* to grow hard, but that I must or else *feel* and be unhappy. You see, she says that it is all nonsense,' she finally confided, 'that my love for your cousin is no more than a child's.'

'Surely only you can decide that,' Joan replied gravely, pitying both Rose's quandary and her guardian's unavoidable pain.

'I loved him as a child and love him still,' she tried to explain, illustrating her confusion and anxiety. 'I keep wondering if I said anything that would make him hope too much.' Pausing a while to reflect, aware that anything she said might be repeated, she asked almost guiltily, 'Does he still hope?'

'Very much,' her friend answered sadly.

'I told him that I will answer him in three years, but I cannot tell him what the answer will be; I would not if I could. All I can say is that I care for him very much now with my child heart or woman heart, whichever some might call it, and whatever the end is I know that I shall care for him *always*.'

'Three years is a long time,' Joan said, wondering how Rose's feelings for Ruskin would ever translate into an adult relationship.

'Long enough to know what is right. But he needn't want to discover my thoughts towards him so often, for it isn't likely that I shall stop caring for him. I mean, it isn't *possible*, and nothing will make me answer him sooner.

He doesn't realise how my mother punishes me with her disapproval of me, and it is very hard to live without the love and sanction of those one needs it from the most. I thought she had forgiven me, but it is worse than I ever thought, for it's not only regarding *him*,' Rose still recoiled from using Ruskin's name, 'but in everything that she looks at me so wrongly.'

Joan's faith in a union between the pair wavered as a consequence of this talk and she hardly knew how to prepare Ruskin for a forsaking that might take Rose years to make decisively. Perhaps, so she concluded, her guardian would prefer to live in ignorance with *some* hope, than be at once enlightened as to his failure.

During the second half of her visit Joan received a letter from her cousin asking if she would like to be included in the party of friends who were about to embark with him on a lengthy journey to Switzerland: Sir Walter and Lady Trevelyan, their niece Constance Hilliard, always known by the nickname of 'Connie', who had recently been to stay with them at Denmark Hill, along with Ruskin's valet Crawley and the Trevelyans' servant, Emma, who would be treated on almost an equal footing.

Without questioning whether she would have received the invitation had she not been holidaying at Harristown, Joan was overcome with joy at the prospect of seeing the sights Ruskin had so often described to her, and thus she replied immediately, declaring her gratitude and how deeply honoured she was to be thought of. Always a person who saw good in others before considering any underhand motives, it only occurred to her when she was bidding the La Touches farewell that her cousin was surely only too happy to be hastening her departure.

Joan quickly dismissed any such misgivings, however, and instead reasoned that Ruskin would never have been able to take her, his young female ward, to Europe without at least one chaperone, and had no doubt arranged this select group expressly to make her feel comfortable. Besides, she couldn't deny that she was more than a little relieved to be going away before she embroiled herself any further with Percy, for how could she fully judge his character until they were apart?

***

The blustery squall awaiting Joan as she disembarked the Holyhead ferry reflected the cool welcome she received from Ruskin, who was waiting for her, the rain lashing his face putting him in an even worse temper than the thought of hearing about Rose second-hand.

He forgave himself for his irascibility, and trusted that Joan would also, for was it not natural that he should resent the idea of anyone knowing Rose's intentions or feelings before he?

Joan noticed him frowning crossly as she tramped down the gangway and, carrying a small case, she tried in vain to stop her cape from flapping about fiercely. After embracing her with unusual formality Ruskin unburdened her of the luggage and, without saying anything by way of greeting, led the way to the waiting train.

Initially affronted by this unwelcoming greeting, Joan became bemused as to her cousin's display of petulance, for it was not until the locomotive taking them to London was in motion that he enquired gruffly, 'How was your holiday?'

'They were very kind to me,' she replied, careful not to seem too enthusiastic in light of his ill humour and guarding her secret with a conscience already pricked with guilt.

'What news is there of Rose?' Ruskin eventually asked, although he found the indignity of doing so akin to a dog sitting at his master's feet begging for scraps.

Joan, sighing out of exasperation, urged, 'Please don't press me for it now, dear,' trying to defer disappointing him for as long as she reasonably could, for she dreaded the long journey and the interrogation she would be forced to suffer if he did not like one detail of what she relayed.

'If you only knew how desperate I am for the sight of her!' Ruskin returned fractiously. 'Or how unbearable it is to be forced to wait three years for her answer. Every day is twenty-four hours and each one takes some life out of my soul.'

'Counting will only make it worse,' Joan cautioned.

He shook his head violently in protest. 'You can't know how long even one hour feels when waiting for such a thing.'

'I understand,' she said, pressing his arm sympathetically, 'but what use are snatches of information passed through a third party?'

'You say that now, but half the reason you convinced me to let you go was by promising to help me,' he reminded her.

Joan, torn between her old loyalty to her cousin and her new allegiance to the La Touches, conceded defeat. 'Rose says that, in time, she is bound to know what is best,' she uttered gently, grieved to see the effect her going to Ireland had had upon Ruskin.

'It's not that I doubt her constancy, although I haven't any right to expect any I suppose, or that I don't trust her to fulfil her promise, for I have tried her since she was a child, I just can't see what waiting can achieve other than to make my heart grow cold and my hair turn grey.'

Calling on the Carlyles prior to leaving London, Ruskin was distraught when their maid, answering the door weeping, informed him that Jane had died that very morning when riding in her carriage; the bouquet of flowers he held in his arms proving an unexpected symbol of mourning.

Struggling to comprehend that he would never again know the company of that most unique lady, when it came to departing for Switzerland he declared gloomily, 'Tie up the knocker, say I'm sick, I'm dead,' as the door of Denmark Hill closed behind them.

Joan would have liked to have succumbed to childish exuberance at the prospect of travelling abroad had she not considered that such behaviour would be disrespectful to her cousin, who tormented himself by trying to guess the number of months dividing him from another glimpse of Rose.

Seeing Paris for the first time was not the gaiety and glamour Joan had foreseen on cutting short her Irish holiday, and Ruskin's despondency only increased when Lady Trevelyan fell ill and was confined to bed for several days, prompting her cousin to rage, 'I'm beginning to think Mrs La Touche has put some kind of curse on me.'

While Sir Walter stayed behind at the hotel to nurse his wife, Joan was grateful for the auburn-haired Connie's unshakeable sweetness and vivacity, and the pair amused themselves by frequenting the most fashionable boutiques and tea houses.

Ruskin would meanwhile take himself off to the Louvre broodingly, where he would spend hours on end making studies of favourite works. At other times he was charged with keeping the two ladies occupied with visits to museums, galleries and churches, a duty he was reluctant to perform but ended by relishing due to his companions' youthful enthusiasm for everything they looked upon. Thus prevented from dwelling absolutely on Jane Carlyle, Lady Trevelyan and Rose, his wit and affectionate nature slowly made a return.

Having arranged a day trip to Chartres Cathedral, he insisted upon taking the seat opposite the two young ladies so as to better observe their mutual enchantment as they drove round by St Cloud and Sèvres. For him, every bend of the Seine conjured up images from Turner's studio, while the blossom on the trees beside the river seemed to mirror the high spirits and responsiveness of Joan and Connie to everything they witnessed, putting him in mind of his own early rapture in travel.

The exhaustive itinerary Ruskin had originally designed for the group had been estimated to take around six weeks to complete, yet in light of Lady Trevelyan's fragile health he suggested they abandon visiting Venice entirely, an idea the patient herself vehemently opposed.

'I won't hear of it, John,' Lady Trevelyan contested emphatically when she was well enough to receive visitors. 'How could *you* of all people deny me the chance of seeing Venice?'

'Very well, Pauline, I see that you are more determined than any of us to make haste, so far be it from me to caution you against it.'

'Quite so,' she said, smiling in satisfaction. 'You've said it yourself, there is nothing more restorative than noble landscapes and good company. I shall be as right as rain again the moment I reach Switzerland.'

And indeed, everyone noticed a distinct improvement in both Pauline's health and Ruskin's temperament on reaching the Alps, for he felt a great sense of relief and elation that she felt strong enough to continue, whilst being continually buoyed by Joan's joyous reaction to everything they stopped to admire en route, especially when she fell under the spell of the charming Swiss towns and mountains, along with the theatres and shops to which he introduced her as though they were his oldest friends, not one of whom he had ever lost his affection for despite their age and familiarity.

235

'It's so good to see a revival in your spirits,' Joan complimented one afternoon as they went from shop to shop in search of a present for Margaret. She flattered herself that she had been partly responsible for the turnabout, for trying to improve the psyche of those she loved gave her the greatest satisfaction.

Despite Ruskin's tendency towards introversion when he was downcast, he fully accepted that travelling with friends was his only way of finding any fulfilment in the months following his proposal.

'Yes, I'm very glad that you and the others are here with me. I couldn't wish for anything more,' he went on gaily, before adding, 'other than for Rose to be here with us.'

'Of course, we all wish that,' she agreed.

As he guided Joan through the glorious Swiss valleys, savouring the chance to display his great knowledge of the region, she began to pity his inability to stop hankering after her friend back in Ireland. Although his intellect had always set him apart from most other mortals, his burning love was blunting his ability to take undiluted pleasure in his surroundings, and wherever he was his mind would always revert back to imagining what *she* was doing and thinking.

Joan was overcome with awe on first glimpsing Lake Brienz, not least when she discovered that her cousin had ensured she have a view of the lake from her chamber, so beautiful in first light that she left her curtains open on going to bed so that she might awaken naturally, to the sun alighting on the rippling water.

Residing at the Hotel of the Giessbach on Lake Brienz, the by now high-spirited party befriended the landlord and his two comely daughters, the elder of whom, Marie, had already been made a widow despite being only eighteen years old.

It was she who was responsible for the housekeeping of the inn and for attending to her father's guests, qualities that put Ruskin in mind of Joan's effortless and stalwart running of Denmark Hill, which he was all too liable to take for granted.

Marie showed fortitude in many other ways besides, being forced to wait upon ill-bred and vulgar male guests who would flirt with her outrageously when drunk. Ruskin observed with admiration how refined and composed her bearing remained regardless of the customer or however late into the night they demanded she serve them, though it was not surprising that she showed a particular fondness for their own well-mannered group.

They were always happy in her company due to her regaling them with the traditional Swiss folk songs she had known since childhood, and when accompanying them on walks in the area close to the hotel, if her duties permitted a rest, she took great trouble to explain the folklore surrounding Alpine flowers.

As a result Ruskin developed a keen interest in learning more of this mystical language, particularly any romantic symbolism he hoped to one day share with Rose, often stopping beside the flowers he especially liked and enquiring of Marie the meaning of the species so that he might record it in his notebook.

'There is more fellowship here than any place I have ever known,' he declared to Joan one evening after Marie had served another hearty meal washed down with his favourite beverage, a pint of champagne.

'How lucky, then, that it's my first time outside our own isles,' she cried, tempted to broach the subject of Percy but deciding against it for fear of disturbing her cousin's equilibrium when it had only just been restored.

'I shall never go away again without inviting you to come with me,' he promised, raising his tankard jovially. 'I don't dare to imagine what would have become of us at Denmark Hill without your guiding influence and careful nurturing.'

'It isn't all one-sided, you and Mrs Ruskin have taken the greatest care of *me*, while anything I can try to lessen *your* burden I shall always vow to do.'

'You're a good girl, Joan; don't blame me for being fiercely annoyed when any man ever tries to take you away from us,' he laughed sentimentally, little realising the nerve he had struck or how Joan blushed at the thought of revealing Percy as her suitor. 'I must force myself into the habit of living alone one of these days, for you're sure to be married to somebody before I know where I am.'

It seemed in the way of things that neither Ruskin's nor the rest of the group's jollity was destined to last, and what had turned into a tour filled with merry-making ended with the unhappiest of all circumstances.

Soon too weak to paint or write as she usually did with such energy, it became clear that the return of Pauline Trevelyan's strength had been a temporary blessing and that her health was in serious decline.

So bravely concealing the immense pain she had been enduring for many months, it was a tremendous shock to her husband and friends when doctors revealed the lady to be suffering from an incurable tumour.

Science was not advanced enough to allow the specialist to say from whence the cancer had originated, only that the mass had grown too large to be removed without killing the patient in the process.

Not knowing if she had weeks or days to live, Pauline surpassed even Joan and Marie in Ruskin's estimation of a courageous woman for, despite her great fortitude and determination to survive, by the time the party reached Neuchâtel they all knew that she would never return to England.

Empathising with her husband more than he could express, Ruskin took it upon himself to comfort him as he kept vigil beside his wife's bed, not disillusioned enough to pray for her recovery, only for her suffering to end.

'I'm quite helpless, but I'm nonetheless grateful that you want me to stay,' he began on taking up the seat beside Sir Walter. 'I never thought you cared for my company.'

'Oh really? You are a sensitive creature, John Ruskin. I perceive that nine times out of ten you never realise how much people love and admire you. Pauline and I have always esteemed you above anyone else,' he replied sincerely and with a voice full of emotion on the mention of his wife, who on hearing her name struggled to open her eyes and smile in concurrence.

Though the two men continued to sit in silence for many hours hence, they occasionally looked to one another in acknowledgement and mutual grief at the deterioration they were witnessing.

Golden rays, emanating from the joyous Swiss sunrise, fell on Pauline's cold face when Ruskin finally left her side the following morning, his dear friend having journeyed to a place where neither he nor her husband would join her for many a year, yet which they would both strive towards all the more knowing that she was there.

Joan, who had voluntarily stationed herself outside Pauline's chamber in expectancy of news, had succumbed to dozing and jolted to her feet on hearing the door open. Standing before her cousin she regarded him with a face full of kindness and sorrow.

'My poor Joanie, I never intended to bring you away to see *this*,' he apologised, before breaking down unrestrainedly.

'I'm glad that I'm here,' she insisted, encouraging him to rest his head on her shoulder awhile.

After composing himself as best he could, Ruskin continued to offer Sir Walter solidarity in what was to prove the most desolate hour of his life, whilst feeling supremely guilty for ever having envied the obvious affection between the couple, whose harmonious marriage it caused him tortures of pain to see prematurely end and made him question the merit and meaning of human existence.

There was an inherent need in almost all mortals to find a partner, so he reflected into the night, yet only a small percentage were so compatible and unified as to leave the survivor shaken to their core on being left behind. Sir Walter *was* such an example and, having been nineteen years his wife's senior, had never expected to see her pass before him. It was all so fathomless and distorted.

Ruskin felt the agony of Pauline's death all the more due to still grieving for Jane Carlyle, and he began to experience sudden periods of faintness and a paralysing, though temporary, inability to function. He could never predict when these strange episodes would occur, but when they did it felt like a deep, impenetrable fog descending, enveloping his mind, misting up his eyes and preventing him from conversing intelligibly with anyone.

Unable to continue in whatever occupation he was engaged, if he happened to be out of doors painting Joan would simply have to pack up his materials and take him inside until the attack subsided.

Fearful that he was either going blind, mad, or both, Ruskin duly sought medical advice, but the doctor only concluded that the recent emotional strain he had been under had brought on the phenomenon and that it would almost certainly vanish as spontaneously as it had begun.

'You say that it will definitely pass and I'll be well again?' he reiterated uncertainly following a painstaking examination.

'Yes,' the young man answered, smiling kindly, 'I'm sure that, very soon, you'll start to see a marked improvement in your symptoms.'

'I've had rather a bad time of it,' Ruskin confessed, 'what with death and the north wind, but I'm embarrassed at making such a spectacle of myself when *I'm* not the one who has lost his wife.'

'Every man has his own way of handling tragedy,' the physician sympathised, having lost his own wife a few years before.

'My way doesn't seem to be very successful,' his patient complained.

As Ruskin chastised himself for not being as emotionally robust as either of the husbands whom his dear friends had left companionless, he received Thomas Carlyle's response to the letter of condolence he had written whilst travelling across France:

"Your kind words from Dijon were welcome to me, thanks. I did not doubt your sympathy in what has come; but it is better that I see it laid before me.

You are yourself very unhappy, as I too well discern — heavy-laden, obstructed and dispirited; but you have a great work still ahead, and you will gradually have to gird yourself up against the heat of the day, which is coming on, as the night too is coming. Think valiantly of these things.

I find it more tolerable to gaze steadily in silence on the blackness of the abyss that has suddenly opened round me and swallowed up my poor little world. Day by day the stroke that has fallen, like a thunderbolt out of skies all blue, becomes more immeasurable to me, my life all laid in ruins, and the one light of it gone out.

And yet there is an inexpressible beauty, and an even epic greatness, known only to God and me, in the life of my victorious little darling whom I shall see no more. Silence about all that, every word I speak or write of it seems to desecrate it...

Come and see me when you get home, come oftener and see me, and speak more frankly to me, for I am very true to your higher interests and you. There is a noble fire in you, and your morality aims, with a wonderful folly sometimes, at the very stars."

Grieved to have been absent when his friend most needed him, Ruskin went to Cheyne Walk immediately he arrived in London, and from there travelled onwards to Lothian with Carlyle, where Jane had been placed beside her father in the churchyard of Haddington.

He found his earthly master much altered upon their reunion, for Jane's death had not only made the home they had shared together a spiritless shell, devoid of all debate and laughter, but Carlyle an altogether different man, without purpose or inspiration other than to weep beside his darling's grave.

Gaunt, shaggy and looking very old with an abundance of ill-brushed white hair, Carlyle was broken, though he delighted in talking of Jane to the one friend who understood her best.

'She was the most contemptuous, warm-hearted, lofty-minded, half-devil, half-angel of a woman that ever ruled over the heart of a man and I am destitute without her,' he declared as they sped north.

Ruskin was glad to keep him company before waiting at the church gate, observing the great man stooping as he wound his way to his wife's resting place, as though bowed down by the weight of his loss.

Proceeding, like a shadow, to the spot by the ruined wall of the old cathedral where Jane had asked to be, Carlyle stood awhile in the grass before kneeling by the tombstone, then leant over and kissed the ground again and again as if praying to join her.

It was a long time before he rose and wandered to the gate where Ruskin was waiting, and making no attempt to conceal the breadth of emotion he underwent said, 'Life, a little gleam of time between two eternities!'

'Dear friend,' Ruskin replied, 'I feel as if I am one of those who has a right to grieve with you, though, as compared with yours, my grief must take a secondary place.'

Taking his turn at Jane's grave and placing flowers thereon, only to recall the harrowing day when he had learned of her sudden death, Ruskin read the dedication by her husband in humble wonder of the marriage he had been privileged to witness.

"In her bright existence, she had more sorrows than are common; but also a soft invincibility, a clearness of discernment and a noble loyalty of heart, which are rare. For forty years, she was the true and ever loving helpmate of her husband; and by act and word unweariedly forwarded him, as none else could, in all of worthy that he did or attempted. She died at London, 21st April 1866; suddenly snatched away from him, and the light of his life as if gone out."

PERCY LA TOUCHE

Observing Carlyle and Sir Walter's devotion to their wives, coupled with their bereavement, Joan was encouraged to question Percy's advances more circumspectly. Thus she decided to inform Ruskin of her attachment to Rose's brother only if he should formally request her hand, providing that it was with the knowledge and approval of his parents.

She was young, yet wise enough to realise that being so meant that she was all too easily flattered, whilst her good nature made her liable to believe others were as upstanding and principled as herself. Her guardian's dim view of Percy was ever in her mind whenever he praised the bravery of Carlyle and Sir Walter, and she spent the duration of the return journey to London questioning whether the attentions of her own high-born gentleman would inevitably fade before the summer was out.

Joan's anxieties were not misplaced, for Percy had barely thought of her following their parting due to pursuing his other passions, namely drinking with his peers or playing sport, and it sickened Rose to observe that the only games her brother participated in that did not involve killing animals were cricket and baccarat, though he showed little talent for either and grew as frustrated at being a poor batsman as when he lost money at the card table, which was frequently. A young man who lived for pleasure regardless of how his behaviour might impact his or his family's reputation, he was content to revel in trivial pastimes and shirked the tedium of hard work.

John and Maria La Touche were extremely downhearted to perceive no improvement in their son upon his return home from Europe; and despite him approaching the landmark coming of age, they realised that Percy remained glaringly ill-equipped to go into the family's struggling banking business, for his temptation to gamble with other people's money would surely be too great for him to resist, yet with far more serious consequences than a day at the races.

Unaware that the La Touches viewed Percy's character as unfavourably as Ruskin and would not contemplate him marrying until he had illustrated a deal more maturity, when Joan received a further invitation to visit Harristown in August she naively misinterpreted the request as their way of encouraging his courtship of her, a thought which considerably inflated her hopes. Nor could Ruskin's wildly jealous reaction diminish her enthusiasm.

'I'm of a mind to go to Ireland right now and lie down at their gate, let Rosie's parents do what they like with me,' he proclaimed, pacing the length of the drawing room in agitation. 'I would gladly make terms for just an hour's look at her and no talk. How could they fail to let me see her?'

Joan, all too aware how eagerly Ruskin would await her letters while she was at Harristown, was careful not to provide too much commentary on Rose, or place any undue emphasis on her thoughts concerning him, for fear that he would misconstrue the slightest goodwill as encouragement.

When Rose one day asked her to include a flower for Ruskin within a letter, believing that this fell within the boundaries of her parents' restrictions on communicating with him, Joan did so without guessing the near frenzy of joy that it would spark upon its delivery.

As her cousin's despair suddenly turned to elation and he spent the next few days analysing the potential symbolism of the ambiguous gift, Mrs La Touche was meanwhile devising a strategy to challenge any ideas Ruskin might have of one day winning Rose. Sending colourful reports of her daughter via their mutual acquaintance, Mrs Cowper-Temple, whom she guessed Ruskin would have appealed to for support and any news she chanced to come by, she wrote:

"Old Rose is flourishing, although her two best friends are people whom she cannot invite to sit with her indoors – one of them a dog and the other her horse. She is more than ever devoted to her big dog Bruno, whom we all call her husband, and so far it has not appeared that she will ever have any other – but who can tell?"

Rose's habits had become increasingly eccentric following the birth of Emily's first child, named Florence Rose in her honour, for much as she adored her niece she found it strange to think of herself ever being a wife and mother, something which prompted her to become more rebellious in spirit. Although she was glad of Joan's visit coinciding with the excitement of the new baby, her presence only sought to remind her of Ruskin's proposal and the promise she had made.

Nor could Joan ever witness Rose holding the newborn in her arms without thinking how hard it was to imagine her in such a pose with Ruskin's child, largely because she was still so young in manner herself. This, coupled with Mrs La Touche's determination that she would sooner see Rose a spinster than grant Ruskin her approval, made Joan apprehend the day when her cousin would finally be given his answer.

Joan observed that Mrs La Touche, having once barely spoken of anything *but* Ruskin, hardly spoke of him at all, much to her husband's relief, while if she did ever refer to her old friend it was generally to mutter something unpleasant as to his abiding influence over Rose. This hostility only drew Joan's attention to the self-inflicted pain Maria endured as a result of expelling Ruskin from their lives, for since the lady's first meeting with him she had felt that no-one could enrich her existence half so much as he.

Mrs La Touche, at a loss to fill the void which Ruskin's treachery had created, persevered with her jealously and anger, yet was strangely anxious lest Joan would think that she was being too harsh on him. Thus she decided to raise the subject of Ruskin's alienation on finding her guest alone in the drawing room shortly after her arrival.

'I hope you understand why I cannot allow Rose and your cousin to meet just now?' she asked, taking up the seat on the sofa beside Joan.

Surprised at the subject being raised, she answered perplexedly, 'I'm not sure that I do.'

'It is so very unfortunate that it has come to this,' Mrs La Touche sighed, 'for I'm quite sure poor Mr Ruskin would give anything in the world for Rose to mean less to him. Were it not for that, he might be so happy with us.'

'Whilst I'm sure he longs for things to be as they were between you, I do not believe my cousin would ever *regret* the love he feels for Rose,' Joan contradicted pertinently, certain that Ruskin would want her to defend the infallibility of his feelings.

'He might go on *loving* her, but you must help him to understand that any idea of him ever marrying her can never be,' she asserted, patting her guest's hand.

These sentiments did not endear Mrs La Touche to Joan, though her bond with Rose only strengthened over the course of the next few weeks, as did her attachment to Percy when once they had passed a shaky start with many misunderstandings.

Joan set aside the fact that all who knew him judged him to be a fickle youth with no aptitude for marriage, for she believed that he genuinely admired her. Indeed, a man with so little backbone himself was naturally attracted to her own strength of character, and he regarded her with awe whenever she spoke her mind freely, regardless of whether or not her opinion would please her hosts.

For once, Percy's age and inexperience did not prevent him from pursuing a pure and unselfish affection, and he considered the tenderness he bore towards Joan as his first step towards manhood.

Embarrassed at not having corresponded with her as he had promised to do during their months of separation, and having sensed her displeasure on her arrival, he saw all too easily how his usual arrogance would lose such a girl. Thus he shadowed her for the duration of her visit and pledged in all sincerity to be a more constant lover when next she went away.

On the day of Joan's departure Mrs La Touche observed to Rose, 'We shall all miss her dreadfully, but I perceive that Percy will miss her most.'

XXII

DELUSIONS

Though the rain fell hard against Ruskin's study window, he was undisturbed by it and continued poring over his latest manuscript, only looking up when Joan entered without knocking and crept towards him.

Placing her hand upon his arm tenderly, he regarded her solemn face perplexedly, for he hated to be disturbed when he was working and guessed that she was about to deliver some bad news regarding Rose.

Turning around he said simply, 'Well?'

'The La Touches are coming to London,' Joan announced as softly as she could.

'What you mean is – *you* will see Rose but I will not,' he retorted before taking up a sheet of writing paper and scribbling furiously.

'What are you doing?' she asked in alarm lest his reaction should exacerbate the situation, whilst empathising that it was not just the wait for Rose's answer which continued to cause him such mental anguish, but being forbidden by her parents to write to her or see her.

'I'm writing to her father,' he responded without looking up or halting what he was doing. 'If he wants me to plead like a common beggar then I shall do so.'

On finishing the draft he handed it to her and she saw at once that it only amounted to a feebly penned sentence: "For Christ's sake – that I might see her face."

'You can't send that,' Joan concluded, tearing it in half with her usual decisiveness and tucking the torn pieces into the pocket of her apron.

Ruskin, who always spoke in the most dramatic language whenever on the subject of Rose and his unquenchable passion for her, shrugged in agreement before going on, 'All I get is a word or two from a letter she is allowed to write to *you*,' he appealed; 'can anything be worse than being shut out in the cold? I wish to God that I had waited until Rose was of age before raising the subject of marriage; my impetuosity has cost me dear. I suppose the end will be just as it should, that she will be a good girl and do as her parents bid.'

Joan did not wonder that her cousin grew increasingly distracted when the family arrived in the city, nor could she help but feel guilty and duplicitous for seeing Rose almost daily.

Furnishing him with news of her health and humour, not to mention detailed accounts of their outings together, she perceived that these second-hand reports were more a curse than a comfort due to being time which he felt had been stolen from him.

'*I* may not be thought fit company for the La Touches or their daughter, yet I have to sacrifice your presence whenever they demand it,' Ruskin complained testily to Joan as she was preparing to depart Denmark Hill one morning, 'not to mention being forced to welcome Percy if he decides to drop by – an insult too much.'

'I think it rather noble of him to continue to call on us,' Joan denied, unsure as to whether Ruskin was suspicious and was therefore trying to draw her. Still she could not bring herself to reveal her attachment to Percy, nor her secret hopes that he would soon formally ask for her hand in marriage.

'What a lark! Fairy Rosie's brother calling here two days running to see minerals and the like. Who would have thought *he* would have been interested in such things? I sometimes wonder if he doesn't just want to look on the strange fossil I have become in being cast aside.'

In truth it never occurred to Ruskin that there could be any romantic motive behind Percy's visits to Denmark Hill, so occupied was he with venting his annoyance at the La Touches and viewing it as highly hypocritical that they permitted one of their children to visit him whilst forbidding Rose any contact whatsoever.

The La Touches had been installed in their Mayfair residence for almost two weeks when Ruskin gazed at the distance fixedly on approaching Westminster Bridge, entirely lost in harrowing thoughts of loneliness and rejection.

As he observed the traffic on crossing the road, he noticed three women riding in an open carriage, with one member of the party immediately striking him as being of Rose's build and age, her face pale with rosy cheeks, and her hair, the colour of hay, curled at the nape of her neck.

Allowing his heart to leap at the possibility of looking on her and conversing with her, no matter if it was entirely by chance, he thought perhaps even her mother might take pity on him and allow him to speak with her for a few moments if once she saw how desperate he was.

Filled with such terrific dreams of a reunion, Ruskin was determined not to lose sight of the carriage and, breaking into a run in order to keep up, he followed the vehicle for more than a quarter of a mile, the exercise invigorating rather than tiring him and a seemingly boundless supply of energy flowing through him.

It was only when the progress of the carriage was interrupted by several dairy carts blocking the road that Ruskin was granted the opportunity to catch his breath and look more closely at the women seated in the carriage. However, as he approached them jubilantly he discovered that the three ladies were entirely unknown to him and that he had been labouring under a blind, nay lunatic, misapprehension.

Aware that his appearance must be that of a man possessed by the most extreme delusions, both parties regarded each other in utter surprise as Ruskin rested his arm on the frame of the vehicle momentarily and appealed to the women, 'Forgive me, I mistook this young lady for a friend.'

Never had he known more degradation than on finding before him a plain, rather stupid-looking girl whom he considered it an insult to liken in any way to Rose. He could barely look at the stranger who was regarding him searchingly.

'Is *this* how you greet your friends?' she at last enquired, prompting her companions to snigger at his expense.

Mortified, Ruskin stood aside as the carriage, no longer held up by the traffic, moved away and the women muttered to themselves in delight at such an irregular scene having taken place during their morning ride.

'We shall have to change our route in order to prevent such an occurrence happening again,' declared the eldest, a plump, matronly woman who, despite claiming to detest such public embarrassment, could hardly conceal her enjoyment of a scene that would fuel her tea party gossip for weeks to come.

Meanwhile, the lady whom Ruskin had mistaken for Rose was motivated by curiosity to turn around and observe him one last time, still more than a little piqued that the attention had not been intended for her.

'He does look a pathetic figure standing dumb beside the thoroughfare,' she announced to her companions, 'yet I can't help but wonder what kind of young woman would prompt a man not far short of fifty to become so frantic in his attempt to see her.'

'Count yourself lucky that it isn't *you* he was after,' the elder lady cautioned, sniffing with middle-class disdain.

Breaking out of the abstraction he had succumbed to at the start of his journey, Ruskin retraced his steps over the bridge and paused awhile to contemplate the foreboding-looking river, his fathomless despair increasingly distorting his view of the world and everything in it.

***

Seated in his father's old armchair by the drawing room fire, his arms folded crossly, Ruskin had gladly succumbed to a bout of influenza in the few days following the carriage incident and was grateful to have the excuse not to work or suffer social engagements.

Breaking into a fit of coughing as Joan entered the room, dressed in readiness of going out, he spluttered, 'Enjoy yourself,' as disingenuously as he could manage before closing his eyes in weary meditation.

'Should I call for the doctor?' Joan asked with uncharacteristic detachment, aware that her cousin was in a particularly difficult mood yet determined not to rise to his provocations.

'It's just a cold, there's no need to concern yourself,' he went on martyr-like, succeeding in making her feel guilty for going out with Rose and leaving him alone.

Joan, well used to treating Ruskin as though he were a demanding infant, pretended to take his reassurance as genuine, however, and after kissing him on the cheek made a swift exit before he could say anything else to deter her from going.

The La Touche carriage was waiting on the driveway and Ruskin, whose inquisitiveness got the better of him, was prompted to hobble over to the window in the hope of catching a glimpse of Rose. It was sheer torment to think of her being just yards away, he inwardly raged, for was it not the ultimate cruelty to place herself so close by when her old place beside the hearth stood empty in anticipation of her return?

Questioning whether she had stationed herself before his door to provoke him or convey her own longing to see him, he was forced to withdraw his gaze when Joan appeared outside, for as if sensing his presence she noticed him standing looking out. Raising her hand as if intending to wave him goodbye, she appeared to change her mind on reflecting how painful the situation was, and hurrying towards the carriage ensured they were soon on their way.

Retreating to his seat with slumped shoulders as the carriage wheels were set in motion, Ruskin did not observe the dandyish Percy, dressed in a fine grey suit with a white rose in his buttonhole, alight, swaggering up the path, conceitedly swinging the silver-topped cane he had purchased with gambling winnings during a recent sojourn in Italy.

Contrary to Rose's prediction, her brother's feelings towards Joan had not lessened, and Percy had returned more determined than ever to woo her friend, confident that, knowing how fond his parents were of her, he could eventually gain their approval should he first manage to persuade her guardian to agree.

As Ruskin settled down to read a book on botany in an attempt to take his mind away from the pleasant evening he imagined Rose and Joan to be enjoying, he heard someone at the door and for a moment imagined that Rose, feeling remorseful at having treated him so badly, had returned in order to see and comfort him.

He pictured his dear one entering the room; and though he was ill-attired to receive her, nothing would have prevented him from welcoming her. However embarrassed that she should find him so unkempt due to his malady, his delight at the prospect of seeing her after so long an interval convinced him to dispense with any social proprieties or etiquette.

Straining to listen to the voices now conversing in the hallway, after what felt like an interminable period Crawley entered and announced, 'There's a Mr La Touche to see you.'

'Show him in,' Ruskin replied, utterly taken aback and suddenly imagining that Rose's father desired an interview.

Nor could he conceal his dismay when Percy stepped jauntily into the room, grinning like a schoolboy in a tuck shop. Bowing and offering Ruskin his hand respectfully, the young man blushed upon realising that his host was bemused by his flamboyant attire. Without rising to his feet to greet him, he merely settled back into his wing armchair and sighed as if he had aged several decades in a few minutes.

'I do apologise, Mr Ruskin, I hope you weren't expecting my father?'

'I was hardly *expecting* either of you,' he returned, bewildered as to what possible motive Percy might have to pay such frequent calls.

Joan and Rose were thrilled by the colourful Japanese jugglers and fire-eaters at the Crystal Palace, a blaze of theatrics and vivid costumes, yet the thought of Ruskin prevented them from being able to fully enjoy the spectacle, for their hearts sank at having left him behind. Laughing and nudging one another in wonder, their smiles were fleeting and false, a pretence of pleasure neither kept up long enough to convince the other.

Sad not to have seen Ruskin, Rose soon sensed that Joan's mind also gravitated to Denmark Hill owing to Percy's meeting with her guardian and teased, 'Do you suppose your guardian will allow you to marry my botheringest of brothers?' as they made their way home after the performance.

She sighed hopelessly. 'I wouldn't wonder if Percy doesn't have the courage to ask after all, my cousin so has a habit of going off on a tangent about his watercolours and the like.'

It was well after midnight when the La Touche carriage dropped Joan home; and with no lights shining from inside, the coachman escorted her to the front door where Crawley assisted her with a lamp for bed as she removed her bonnet and cape.

Believing Ruskin would have long since retired to bed due to his illness, she yawned from exasperation at having to wait until the next day to hear his verdict regarding Percy, only to jolt upon spying her cousin observing her in the shadows of the landing.

'Joan, you'll be tired but can I trouble you for a moment?' Ruskin asked, not venturing downstairs but indicating that she was to follow him, too infuriated to allow the evening's revelation to remain unaddressed.

Rarely having heard his tone so imperious, she compliantly trailed into his study, noticing when she entered and stood before Ruskin that his cold appeared to be considerably worse and that he was trying to disguise that he was shivering with fever.

'I suppose you know that Percy La Touche called on me whilst you were out?' Ruskin began crossly.

'Oh,' Joan replied, biting her bottom lip anxiously.

'Initially I thought he had come to see the minerals again, but then I realised that he had a wholly different agenda.' Observing that Joan already assumed that he found Percy an unsuitable match for her, he continued in a softer manner, 'I'm not angry with you, Joan, only sorry that you weren't able to tell me about the liaison yourself.'

'I never *wanted* to keep anything from you,' she pleaded, 'it was only because I wasn't sure if anything would come of it.'

'The fact that you were so doubtful should tell you something,' he propounded. 'I would have thought you considered me friend enough to have sought my counsel, for as your guardian I feel that it's my duty to inform you that Percy is a fool – has been since I first knew him. If anything, my view of him has only worsened over the years for, whilst one expects a certain amount of arrogance in a youth, a *man* so wrapped up in himself makes a very small parcel.'

'I believe there is good in him,' Joan contended.

'Choosing you as his wife is perhaps his first expression of it,' Ruskin allowed, before pausing for a moment in order to take stock of this unexpected crisis, yet another involving the La Touches. How strange that his cousin should also have chosen to become bound to that family. 'You know it's quite impossible for me to believe that anybody will care for you as much as we do here at Denmark Hill?'

'I don't doubt it,' Joan agreed.

'Do you really think you could be happy with him?' he asked, genuinely wanting to do what was best, even against his instinct.

'Yes,' she answered simply.

'I'm no tyrant, so if you really think you *could* I have no intention of preventing you,' he finally granted, shaking his head despondently.

'Thank you,' she answered gratefully, the tears which she had managed to hold back thus far rising to the surface and streaming down her face. Too overcome to talk, she embraced him with the hesitation of one who suspects that they are acting in error.

'You oughtn't come so close lest I give you this fearful cold,' he shooed, embarrassed to show her how grieved he was at the prospect of her leaving them.

'I don't care,' she answered obstinately.

'You soon will when you aren't in the least attractive to your groom,' he laughed, patting her head fondly. 'In case things go wrong for us, we should lay plans for getting a little house in the country with a pretty garden, for I'm not convinced we two are cut out for marriage.'

'That will be their loss,' she declared, managing a smile.

They bade one another goodnight tenderly and on the best of terms, though Ruskin hardly slept for considering the consequences of this new development, fearing that Joan's union with Percy was unsafe until it was with the blessing of the La Touches.

However much John and Maria thought Joan to be a pleasant, amiable companion and friend to Rose, people of their class would almost certainly view her social status as too far below their son's to countenance such a union, he surmised.

Whilst he accepted that his own outlook had become distorted by their renunciation, he perceived that his ward was almost equally affected with the poor judgement that comes with passionate love, and it was his strong paternal feeling that made him dread her being hurt far more than any injury the La Touches could inflict upon *him*.

ROSE AS SAINT

KNOWING NOTHING OF PERCY'S PROPOSAL TO JOAN, MARIA La Touche was still absorbed with keeping Rose from the clutches of her former tutor, naively believing that her daughter might be distracted from thinking about Ruskin altogether if only a younger, more attractive suitor might be found with whom, by the laws of nature, she would be bound to fall in love.

Alas, any hope she had of achieving this relied upon parading Rose, against her will, around London's relentless social circuit, something which proved an incalculable challenge and fuelled an already tense atmosphere whenever the subject was raised.

Scornful of the Mayfair balls her family were regularly invited to attend, Rose made her mother impatient whenever she pleaded ill health as an excuse not to go, declaring that she felt too weak to sit long enough to have her hair curled or wear a corset, for Mrs La Touche knew well enough that her quiet constancy towards Ruskin, coupled with her religious fervour, had made her scorn such vain pursuits.

The only consolation during this especially glittering season, attended by dignitaries and royalty, was that Joan, not possessing any fashionable gowns, made her daughter look considerably less plain.

For the second time in a week Mrs La Touche had invited her to accompany them to one such event, knowing this was her only way of persuading Rose to go; yet as Ruskin was still suffering with a worsening head cold, Joan was more than ever reluctant to leave the helpless residents of Denmark Hill to their own devices for another evening.

Ensuring that Margaret, now more or less permanently confined to her room, had everything she needed to make her comfortable, whilst Joan did not care for such gatherings she was grateful for the temporary respite from her duties, something she would never have owned to her guardian, who took her attentions for granted out of habit rather than any lack of appreciation.

'Rose shouldn't be able to enjoy herself when I'm suffering so much,' Ruskin complained, supping the broth Joan had placed on the desk.

'I won't hear a word when you're still sitting there working,' she retaliated, resting a hand on her hip in her lovable matron-like stance.

'I'm sorry, Joan, I don't really want to spoil your fun or hers, it's only that I dread them finding her a husband.'

'I've told you before, she loathes society and would do anything to avoid it. I've never seen her so much as look at another.'

'One glimpse of my beautiful Rose and they'll never let her away,' Ruskin rejoined, mopping his mouth with a napkin.

'The bond you share isn't to be forgotten in the course of a few parties,' she reassured frankly, sitting on the edge of his desk.

'Who knows how easily her head might be turned?'

'You wouldn't love her if she was as capricious as you make out,' she challenged, rising and collecting his empty bowl.

'I know,' he acknowledged, 'but if they *can* bring about a marriage, it will hurt far more if it comes after a year or two of silence than if they had let her be to me what she always was,' Ruskin went on, pressing Joan's arm pitifully. 'Can't they be generous enough to admit that she might care for me a *little?*'

'They must, or else why stop your correspondence?' she consoled.

'Her mother is foolish to interrupt our letters or our meetings,' he fumed, bringing his hand down on the desk forcefully, 'for Rose is not likely, any more than I, to alter her mind *because* of a forced separation, whereas if we had been allowed to continue as we used to, I would have treated them wholly fair and her just as she wants, as my child-friend should she have preferred it. Perhaps Rose *would* have been more inclined to consider another man if our separation had not been taking up all her thoughts.'

Joan was relieved that she did not have to respond, due to Crawley entering and announcing that the La Touche carriage had arrived.

'Please don't stay up for me,' she requested; 'and don't work too hard,' she insisted, kissing her guardian on the forehead before closing the door behind her.

As Joan was fetching her bonnet and cape, Ruskin and Rose simultaneously noticed a shower of meteors overhead, he from his study window and she from the coach that was once more stationary outside his house but which he could not bear to look upon again.

White, green and golden shooting stars burst forth, radiating light in quick succession. Almost before Rose had time to lean her head out of the carriage window, there was another and yet another darting across the heavens, making her wonder if Ruskin too was observing the spectacle and would feel less alone knowing that she was sharing such a vision.

Wondrous, luminous beams continued to fall and cast their transitory blaze, each standing out sharply against the night sky, yet it was a sight all the more mystical to Rose for being in the same spot as Ruskin at that very moment – a beacon of hope she reflected on long after the phenomenon had ceased.

Joan, having known nothing of exuberant social events prior to her acquaintance with the La Touches, was astonished to enter a ballroom featuring floor-length gilt mirrors for the first time, offering no mercy to those like herself who were dissatisfied with their appearance, and prompting her to avoid catching a glimpse of her own image as best she could by focussing her attention on the ever multiplying sight of those better dressed or more attractive.

Although she had become accustomed to hiding her awe of lavish surroundings, as Joan tiptoed beside the ethereal Rose that evening she thought she had never seen such a grand venue, the windows draped with yards of silk, much like the dresses of the fine ladies passing by, while numerous chandeliers glittered below a ceiling painted with plump cherubs, as smug and well fed as the lords beneath dancing waltzes and mirroring them as so many heavenly beings.

Rose, on the other hand, found such displays of extravagance obnoxious and ached to be near Ruskin on hearing from Joan that his cold was worse. Looking every inch the Irish girl he always teasingly declared her to be, the peppermint-coloured silk she wore brought out the copper tones of her hair, making her the most striking young woman in the room.

Unaware of the attention she provoked, Rose stood demurely beside her parents and Joan, dreading the prospect of being noticed or asked to dance, and longed to tear up her dance card in order to avoid such a fate. Yet the more she concentrated on blending into the background the more she sparked curiosity, and after less than half an hour Rose *was* very much noticed by all the young bachelors in attendance.

Looking down at her feet and fidgeting as soon as she observed a handsome young man threading his way through the crowd towards her, she wanted to hide or be anywhere other than amongst the best people in society, all of whom she had no desire to know. This kind of courtship was no better than being a poor fox in a hunt, vainly running through the woods to escape his pursuers without any real chance of survival.

Rose was determined not to be ensnared, however, and as her mother bestowed her most radiant smile upon the gentleman, titled and priggish, approaching them, she did the opposite and showed herself worse than ill-mannered – downright rude.

After bowing formally and introducing himself, egotistically interpreting Rose's manner as bashfulness, he kissed her gloved hand and asked for the next dance, causing her to grimace and well up with obstinate tears.

'Oh, please don't ask me, ask Joan,' Rose responded, nudging her friend to step forward. 'Do dance with the young man,' she commanded.

'He didn't ask *me*,' Joan replied, mortified at being suggested as a stand-in and not willing to be her friend's second despite sympathising with her plight.

'Don't be so impolite, Rose,' Mrs La Touche intercepted, perceiving how insulted the stranger was to have brought about an argument between the two women, neither of whom, to his great astonishment, wished to dance with him.

Regretful at having inadvertently made the young man feel undesirable, although suspecting that such rejection would probably do him some good, Rose reluctantly handed Joan her silk purse and declared, 'Very well,' as she took his arm and stomped inelegantly across the floor.

Nothing could bring Rose to enjoy herself, and so distracted was she by thoughts of Ruskin that she frequently lost the rhythm and forgot the simplest of steps, almost causing them to collide with another couple. When the dance was finally at an end she made no attempt to disguise her relief and, after curtseying formally, marched back to her disgruntled mother and father.

'How can you suffer such vulgarity?' Rose attacked her mother, unmindful of who could overhear. 'It's appalling the way girls are paraded from one ball to the next in the hope of finding a husband. As I'm not looking for one, I don't know why we're even here.'

'Hush!' her mother returned, flushing in embarrassment at her inability to control her wilful daughter.

'People are looking,' her father added, equally powerless.

'*Let* them look. I only speak now because it's the only time you'll ever listen to me,' Rose decried, her words the culmination of long-suppressed resentment. 'If you won't allow me to make my own choice, then I shan't marry at all.'

'If your choice is John Ruskin then your father and I will never allow it,' her mother countered in a fierce whisper.

'You seemed to like him well enough in the past.'

'How dare you speak to me in this manner,' Mrs La Touche raged, struggling to keep her voice down. 'She's hysterical,' she added to her husband, who was unable to countenance such a public outburst between his two women and was painfully aware that they were drawing considerable attention.

'You always say that whenever I disagree with you,' Rose continued.

'He's too old for you,' Mrs La Touche stated dogmatically; 'he could never make you happy.'

'I'm not happy *now*. He's ill and I'm out dancing. What would God think of that?'

Due to the argument getting increasingly heated, their gracious host judged it best to advance and try to intervene – a tall, serious-looking man who managed to dispel some of the family's tension by exhibiting a kind and unassuming manner, characteristics Rose immediately found winning in such an imposing environment.

'I trust you are enjoying yourselves?' the duke asked disarmingly, directing the question to Rose, whom, frail and outnumbered, he perceived to be the most in need of support.

'Rose's friend is unwell,' Mr La Touche asserted, too apprehensive of his daughter's response to leave her to answer, not least as several inquisitive guests had gathered around to observe the scene more closely. They had become, La Touche realised with a shudder, a spectacle to be peered at and talked about.

'What a kind girl,' the duke rejoined, clasping his hands together; 'is there something I can do to help?'

'Might a prayer be said?' Rose asked, not giving her father another opportunity to silence her.

The duke, taken aback at such a request, yet finding her beauty and character unusually enchanting, replied, 'I don't see why not. We're all God-fearing here despite our apparent frivolities. I'll ask the musicians to pause for a moment.'

'That is out of the question, we can't ask you to interrupt the evening,' Mrs La Touche discouraged vehemently, dying at the prospect of the entertainment being halted in order for Rose to hold a spontaneous prayer meeting. Once she gained a reputation for obsessive religiosity it would be harder than ever to find a suitor.

'It's no trouble,' he dismissed, 'I consider your daughter a most remarkable young woman and it would be my pleasure to grant such a selfless wish.'

'He wouldn't think it nearly so wonderful if he realised for whom the prayer was intended,' Mrs La Touche muttered to her husband as their host proceeded to make his way towards the conductor.

Mrs La Touche would have fled from the room had it not been for her husband preventing her by squeezing her arm firmly, encouraging her to play out the role of a proud parent delighted to observe the power of Rose's devoutness.

The duke wasted no time in fulfilling his promise and, having ascended the orchestra platform, stopped the musicians without further ado, much to the confusion of those in the midst of dancing.

Encouraging Rose to join him upon the stage, she did so timidly as he launched into an explanation: 'Ladies and gentlemen, forgive me for interrupting your evening, but I trust you will sympathise when I explain that this young woman is in great distress for a sick friend.'

Saying which, the duke kissed Rose on the cheek reverently and for once she didn't feel in the least afraid of the startled audience before her, so possessed was she by faith and the power of prayer to redeem and heal.

'Would you all oblige me by saying a prayer?' she asked, her slight, girlish voice only discernible due to the silence that had fallen.

While some looked to one another in bewilderment, eventually each and every guest murmured their consent and obeyed the request by kneeling and putting their hands together as they listened to Rose's angelic wish that her friend's health be restored as a result of their efforts.

Far from doing so simply out of respect to their host, many belonged to the burgeoning circle of evangelicals who regularly attended prayer meetings in the upper-class drawing rooms of Mayfair and St James's during the London season, and they thought this occurrence contributed rather than detracted from the evening.

Entirely oblivious to such an act being carried out in his name, the growing fashion for spontaneous religious observances was extremely distasteful to Ruskin. Therefore, it was no small irony that he was the object of Rose's attempt at a miracle, something he would have denounced had he been present, whilst criticising the La Touches for indoctrinating their daughter to believe the Bible's teachings too literally.

Having ignored her request not to wait up, Joan returned to Denmark Hill to find Ruskin in the drawing room, lying prostrate on the sofa and coughing violently. Continuing to recline as his cousin began her account of the ball, he listened with disbelief and annoyance as she began relating Rose's grand gesture.

'She made the entire room pray for you,' she went on, expecting her guardian to be overjoyed at such a clear expression of love.

But Ruskin was too concerned for Rose's sanity than to be won over by any feelings of flattery; and raising his hand to his forehead in exasperation of all that had been said and done in ignorant conviction, he plumped up the cushions he had been resting on and sat bolt upright in readiness of decrying such wanton histrionics.

'I cannot understand how a girl of her intelligence can believe that her faith gives her the wherewithal to restore my health,' he began, prompting Joan to take the seat opposite. 'Far from being pleased, don't you see that *no-one* should encourage her in this? If everyone convinces her that she's a saint, things will go from bad to worse. Has she changed *so* very much since I last saw her?'

'Yes, I suppose she has,' Joan answered sadly; 'she seems very confused at present and thinks God alone can help her find the answer to all that's troubling her.'

'This is religion in its most corrupted state,' Ruskin observed with sorrow. 'Rose is wasting her greatest powers by dedicating herself to a grievous and fruitless meditation of the Bible, for she's bitterly mistaken and has much to learn if she believes she can solve the problems of the universe simply by following its lessons. If I were permitted to speak with her, perhaps I could make her see that she is far more likely to unravel life's mysteries by understanding herself.'

The third day of January saw Rose turn nineteen, an event which prompted Ruskin to calculate and note in his diary how many hundreds of days were still to be endured until he discovered her answer. Ever since proposing, the year had dragged, and yet the closer he nudged to the day of reckoning the more his torment increased.

The bitter cold and the chill wind that fairly froze his face whenever he walked into town suited his temperament, for he had never felt his dream to be more hopeless than on hearing rumours that his darling had a firm admirer who was, by all accounts, both young and eligible.

Knowing well enough that her mother was not above planting such gossip simply in order to wound him, he nonetheless waited with trepidation to see if anything would come of it, recalling his father's words that he was powerless to make Rose any older or himself any younger.

Rose, as if having heard Ruskin's suggestion that she should set about understanding herself before trying to fathom God, had meanwhile commenced an autobiography, for despite not having many years to draw upon she hoped that such an occupation would soothe her melancholy on returning to Ireland, her health worsening just after her birthday on recalling that Ruskin still had two years of waiting to discover if she would consent to be his wife.

It was a burden that lived with her almost constantly until William La Touche, her father's sole surviving brother, fell seriously ill a week later, thus taking her thoughts away from Ruskin's proposal for a time and causing her to pray night and day for her adored uncle's recovery.

Although Rose recognised that he was failing and that her mother and father had utterly given up on the prospect of saving him, *she* continued to hope, couldn't help it. Convinced that certain actions of hers could change the outcome of things, on one of her walks she took it into her head to pick a primrose and bring it home as a symbol of her belief in God's mercy.

Carrying the flower safely through the woods and fields, cupped in her hand and shielded from the slightest breeze within her riding jacket, she stepped cautiously as she went, protecting it from the slightest disturbance. But as she approached the house Rose came across one of their terriers mauling a hedgehog and, losing all concentration, dropped the flower without thinking in order to rescue the poor defenceless animal who had rolled itself into a prickly ball in feeble defence.

Only after chasing the vicious dog away and having the satisfaction of seeing the hedgehog crawl free, did she remember the primrose, and was overcome with emotion on realising her carelessness. Sitting on the ground she cried like a child as she placed the one remaining leaf in her palm.

'Stupid girl,' she chastised herself.

What she had intended to be miraculous had become a bad omen, something that was confirmed when her uncle died the following morning before sunrise.

Her confidence in her ability to alter events had been woefully misplaced, and so she mounted the primrose leaf on the page of her diary that marked her uncle's passing to remind herself of her own stupidity and the infallibility of God's will.

The leaf came to embody all her failings, and so restless was she the night before the funeral that, dressing by moon and starlight, she crept downstairs to the library, books being her only solace when her mind was thus disquieted.

There, expecting to be alone, she found her father, also too grief-stricken to sleep and pacing the boards waiting for the morning. Both relieved to have an unexpected friend, they kept each other company by the fire until daybreak, when the undertakers would arrive and take their beloved William away.

La Touche asked, 'Shall we pray together?' and Rose saw that, for the first time in her life, his eyes glistened in the darkness with sorrow.

'Yes, Father,' she replied softly.

And so they knelt beside the hearth with their hands clasped in prayer for many minutes, their differences set aside as they each revisited their most vivid memories of the man who would lighten the darkness of Harristown no more.

'We have had a heavy loss and must seek guidance,' he said, eventually breaking the silence, rising to his feet and leaning against the back of an armchair as though weakened by grief.

'Yes, Father,' Rose agreed, standing before him as he reflected and wondering if she had ever felt so close to him as at that harrowing moment, which perhaps God had chosen to bring them together.

'Your uncle was a man with a very rare nature, having more heart than intellect, he would not mind my saying, for he had next to no education, yet loved and helped every creature that came near him.'

Though she knew herself to be foolish in thinking so, these words prompted Rose to recall the rescued hedgehog and believe that she had acted rightly after all, for she had been following the intuition which her uncle's example had sparked within her.

'Yes, from now on I will always try to remember him whenever I have an opportunity to do some good,' she answered solemnly, taking up her father's Bible and selecting a psalm to read.

When Rose and her father were finally summoned, after hours of shared contemplation, the dimly lit hall was full of men, each wearing black from head to toe, starkly contrasted by a white scarf. Rose was wary of approaching this ominous-looking group, but her father led her on and the men parted respectfully.

With his arms behind his back and his face stony, he exchanged hushed words with several of the men, which, though she could not make out, caused her to shudder at the finality of that morning.

The front door was opened and the undertakers, mourners and pallbearers went on ahead, six carrying her uncle's heavy, brass-fitted coffin on their shoulders and a further six close behind so as to change places with them when they could bear no more.

They went on carefully and deliberately through the snow which had fallen heavily in the night, making the route to church treacherous for the pallbearers, for they feared slipping on the ice.

Their every step, slow and precise, made Rose reflect upon the difference to that snowy day when she had played gaily with Emily and Ruskin in Hyde Park, never having known grief or how to comprehend God's purpose in taking loved ones away.

Beside her father, Rose followed the coffin, their heads hung low while the rest of the household walked close behind in respectful silence, and she was sorry that her mother's faith meant that she could not join them. More than anything, her feet were so cold that she longed to speed up, an idea she reproached herself for. Rose could not stop shivering or her teeth from chattering, however, and she only hoped her father could not hear them as they continued along the interminable route.

Struck by the silence of the procession, the only discernible sound was the tramp of feet through the soft, powdery snow and a voice now and then as the men quietly changed bearers. Their sombre black attire mirrored a solitary crow flying overhead, their white scarves the blindingly bright snow thawing in the sunshine, and she was impressed by the haunting beauty of the scene, not least because it was the first time she had ever witnessed the funeral of a close relation. It was all like a dream, only it seemed to teach far more about life than death.

It was a relief to find that the pathway to the church had been cleared, and when they reached the entrance, using the boot scraper to remove the snow clinging to their boots, the kindly old clergyman, Mr Hare, made the sign of the cross and greeted them with the words, 'I am the resurrection and the life,' so natural and beautiful to Rose, who had held them in her heart the entire way and continued to do so throughout the service.

With the weather worsening and a foot of snow falling over the course of the next two days, Rose was forced to spend her time indoors and occupy herself as best she might. She found a wounded robin in the hall which she nursed back to strength and, when a crowd of five gaunt, starved-looking ruffians came to the door begging for food and firewood, she feared them not but went out and spoke to them compassionately.

'We can get no work, miss,' the boldest of the men began, stepping forward and stooping humbly, 'and we all have wives and children.'

'Tell me what it is that you need and I will do my best to supply it,' Rose offered, much grieved for the obvious deprivations that had prompted these men to stand before her.

'Firing and food are very dear,' the man admitted, his lips trembling with the humiliation of having to speak for them all.

'Stay here a moment,' she told them, and after being gone for several minutes returned with a full purse. 'Here, distribute it evenly amongst you. I wish you and your families well. If you go to the servants' entrance our cook will see to it that you have nourishment and the footmen will provide you with fuel.'

All the men removed their hats like gentlemen and said, 'God bless you!' before going on their way, moved as they were by kindness which was given freely and unhesitatingly, with no desire for thanks or gratitude.

As was her wont, her mother later scolded her for not only assisting the men but for having given them enough to make them come again, yet Rose could not countenance such heartlessness and reproved her mother's lack of charity with Christ's words, 'I was hungered and ye gave me no meat.'

No matter how much good she carried out, Rose still felt guilty for having disobeyed her parents by writing to Ruskin in secret during her uncle's illness, nor could she help doing so again in the days following his death, when she looked for his sympathy and related the events of the primrose and funeral, for only he would understand her childish ways and her habit of drawing significance out of the most common occurrences. She included some hymn-like verses which he appreciated for their sentiment rather than their composition.

> "I am tired and fain would rest
> Close my weary eyes in sleep
> Father, let thy angels keep
> Watch and guard around my nest.

Have I grieved Thee Lord this day
Turn not from me, Lord, thy face –
Wash thou all my sins away
Through my Saviour's blood and grace."

Ruskin was pleased that his words of kindness and reassurance appeared to give Rose comfort as she wrestled with grief for the first time, although when the La Touches visited London the following month he was still forbidden to see her.

He never could grow used to the idea of being within four or five miles of their house without being able to look upon her face, and would happily have waited with the night beggars in the street just to watch her pass had it not been for his awful pride. Instead, he determined to avoid walking near her door for fear that Rose would see the desperation etched upon his face.

THE LAND OF POETS

XXIV

P ATIENTLY OCCUPYING HIMSELF ALL WINTER AT DENMARK
Hill by studying mineralogy and botany, Ruskin took himself off
to Keswick in the Lake District when summer arrived, for Joan
had departed for Harristown again and he was forced to curb his envy of
croquet on the lawn, trips to Pollaphuca Falls and the generous picnics
she would be blessed with, not least the long walks and conversations
with Rose beside the river. How distant his own time there seemed.

Not desiring to put too much distance between himself and the Irish
Sea, yet refusing to waste his days pondering on how his cousin might be
occupying herself with the La Touches, Ruskin soon satisfied his desire
for quiet meditative afternoons by taking to Lake Skiddaw alone, not
even inviting Crawley, with whom he had travelled, to join him.

On fine days, when the grass was dry, he would lie down and gaze
upon his surroundings: the ground herbage of buttercup or hawkweed
mixed among the blades, while the hills, occupied with grazing sheep,
were so lovely that he thought he would never want to cease looking at

them, nor the fleeces of clouds overhead, which, though he tried to draw and understand how they went, wouldn't stay still!

Recalling his boyish verse dedicated to that beauty spot, he was pleased to find that the observations he had made at nine years of age still held true.

"Skiddaw, upon thy heights the sun shines bright,
But only for a moment; then gives place
Unto a playful cloud which on thy brow
Sports wantonly, then floats away in air..."

As was his habit, he had chosen to lodge in a modest coaching inn offering clean accommodation and simple local fare, a fine base from which to explore the haunts of his childhood, where each place conjured up glorious, long-forgotten memories and gave him the desire to one day settle amidst such wondrous landscape, akin to heaven after London.

He did not stay long courting daydreams, however, for there was more pleasure to be had outdoors walking amongst scenery which offered an unparalleled sense of peace and freedom and instantly brought out in Ruskin a childish pleasure in simply observing the infinite detail of everything around him, from the animals in their natural environment to the rolling clouds overhead.

Allowing himself to imagine Rose beside him, her hand in his, while he traversed the land that meant so much to him, the joy of the delusion prompted him to sing a little to himself. It mattered not if it threatened rain, rather the damp air heightened the freshness of the season and the vibrant colours of the verdant trees and valleys. There was beauty in the very stillness of the weather, even in the absence of sunshine, when all was quiet and calm under the grey sky.

After resting for a while on the highest shoulder of a hill under Mount Skiddaw's summit, where the perfect calm of the air was akin to being in a room, Ruskin observed vast volumes of white clouds foaming from the west towards him. Undeterred, he rose and went along the stately ridge towards Skiddaw's peak, where he hammered and poked about for quartz. After a time, however, two people, an elderly English gentleman and his wife, came upon him and forced him to pause.

Hearing that they were both panting due to having descended in a great hurry on seeing the mass of approaching cloud, Ruskin looked upon them kindly, despite being partially annoyed at the disturbance to his solitude.

'Shall we be lost in the fog?' the old gent asked fretfully.

'No, there's no fear of that,' he replied confidently, pointing with his stick, 'the path is plain enough and you'll soon be out of the cloud if you keep on.'

'Oh, what a relief! We are no great walkers, you see,' he explained needlessly, for Ruskin had already observed the lady's inadequate boots.

'Well, aren't *you* coming? You're not going to stop up here all night I hope?' the homely lady asked as she prepared to set off.

'No, not quite,' Ruskin laughed, 'but I've my compass in my pocket, so I don't much care what happens to me.'

And so the pair trotted off as fast as their legs would carry them, rejoicing at having survived a calamitous fate, while he continued with his mineralogy, looking up occasionally to see that the dense cloud had filled all the western valley, including the desolate moors.

The motionless air, and the fact that the weather deterred any other walkers from setting out that day, only added to the sense of serenity, and so Ruskin took the opportunity to kneel, clasp his hands together and pray, both for his union with Rose, and Joan and Percy's, which appeared to be in as much jeopardy as his own.

Praying seemed to have a much more intense meaning up there, so feeble did he feel his own person to be against such a mighty backdrop, and when the rays of the July sun eventually decided to pierce the parting clouds they appeared like some sort of revelation, granting him the clearest vision yet of his love and giving him the fortitude he needed to trust in her own judgement.

'What a fool love makes of man,' he muttered as he prepared to hammer some more rock, cursing as he did so at all the hours and labour he had wasted in pining for Rose.

Exhausted from tension-releasing hammering, Ruskin attempted a faithful likeness of the mountain ranges before him, finding nothing equal to quiet drawing for occupying the whole mind.

Languidly, but not idly, he began sketching out the scene before him, and as he drew so did his languor pass away. The beautiful lines insisted on being traced, and more and more beautiful they became as each vale and mountain rose out of the rest and took its place upon the paper. With wonder increasing every instant, he saw that they composed themselves, by finer laws than any known of man.

When the light grew too poor to continue he sauntered down as leisurely as he had ascended, reaching the inn with time to change before an unrefined, yet delicious dinner, consumed with an appetite heartier than he had known for aeons.

After an equally good night's slumber he awoke to find that an envelope had been slipped under his door: a note with just Rose's name written in pencil and a pressed dog rose, which he took as an emblem of constancy and proof that their thoughts had crossed again.

'God *has* given her to me,' he declared to himself aloud, running his hand along the paper so recently touched by hers, 'and except by His word of Love or Death we cannot be kept asunder.'

Immensely grateful for the communication, no matter how slight its content, it encouraged him to attend church that Sunday, not having done so since that desolate Christmas in Switzerland when he was cursed with harbouring in silence his intentions concerning Rose.

Striding into the nave as the bells rang out in summons, Ruskin went partly to please himself and partly to please Rosie, for though he could not write to tell her of his attendance it was enough to know how happy she would be to see him there, as would his mother.

Convinced that Rose had asked God to teach and guide him, this notion seemed to do him good. Even the psalm spoke to him directly, not least the words, 'From the end of the earth I will cry unto thee, when my heart is overwhelmed: lead me to the rock that is higher than I, for thou hast been a shelter for me, and a strong tower from the enemy.'

His love for Rose made him want to carry out her every wish but, while he found himself praising the Bible's greatest morals and teachings, he loathed clergymen and the way they imparted lessons.

Not for the first time, Ruskin felt drawn to reassess his faith without entirely reaffirming it, an act that was nonetheless coupled with a private expression of devotion that stayed with him for many days afterwards. He recognised all too well, however, that he was a fickle subject and wanted unfair reparation for his loyalty.

Compulsively, he could not stop looking for signs that meant God would finally reward his patience as a lover, and he was almost too afraid to give Him up for fear that losing Rose forever would be the punishment.

Seeing a mass of yellow roses in full bloom as he left the churchyard gladdened him and, with half the three-year waiting period elapsed, he was beginning to allow Hope to enter his breast, the jacket pocket of which contained two of Rose's most treasured letters between two sheets of gold, more sacred to him than any psalm.

He felt much better on being away from London, getting regular exercise and rest, and trusted that he should not fall into the state he had succumbed to that winter, grievous to himself and stupid to everybody.

As usual whenever he was away from home, Ruskin wrote daily letters to his mother and Joan, recording his ambitious walking expeditions and his rediscovered appetite for salmon, muffins, lamb, claret and Irish whiskey, along with the vague intention of one day purchasing a property in the area.

After two months of residing in peaceful Cumberland he felt truly buoyed, having persuaded himself that, despite receiving only a flower in the post as proof, his situation regarding Rose was markedly improved.

But Doubt, his old enemy, was never far away, and by penetrating his subconscious as he slept had a habit of turning his brightest dreams black. Early on the morning he was due to depart Keswick, before the late August sun was fully risen over the inn, he dreamt that Rose was seated all alone in a rowing boat on Lake Coniston, yet her face looked pained when she saw him standing on the shore, and she continued to row away despite him calling out to her.

These visions were his only way of seeing Rose and he was grateful for them, though trying to understand the meaning of them proved as difficult as trying to go back to sleep in order to be with her again.

He was fortunate in that the second dream also contained Rose, and water, although he was not sure why he associated her with that other than remembering her beside the dear old Liffey flowing through Harristown, or Pollaphuca Falls where her handholding gesture had led him to think that he was not alone in feeling that they *were*, after all, drawn to one another.

In his latter dream, they were holidaying, newly-wed, on the shore of the calmest of Swiss lakes and were about to go swimming, yet Rose became fearful of the water as soon as she jumped in, prompting him to hoist her onto his back and swim with the pleasant sensation of her trustingly holding onto his shoulders and their bodies merging with the cool water.

THE BOUNDER

PUTTING ASIDE HIS OWN ROMANTIC ASPIRATIONS, RUSKIN made a short diversion before returning to London in order to call on Joan's family and inform them of her forthcoming marriage to Percy, unaware that she had meanwhile begun to experience grave reservations on witnessing her fiancé's coming of age celebrations.

Percy marked this momentous occasion by a display of immaturity and vice that were revealed to Joan in the most startling manner, with both he and his feckless school acquaintances jockeying one another to consume copious quantities of alcohol over many hours – not for pleasure or the sake of merriment, but merely to settle a bet as to which of them possessed the strongest constitution.

Having chosen to spend the day of his twenty-first birthday not with his fiancée but the same caddish chums with whom he regularly went to Punchestown races, he gambled recklessly with his allowance and birthday money and drank in commiseration rather than celebration, uproariously bewailing his bad luck after each race.

After a day of considerable losses, Percy's remaining hope was a bay horse running in the final stakes, on which he had decided to risk his last pound. Exhilarated at the great chance he had taken, he waved his arm and betting slip furiously as the runners and riders shot from the starting post and the entire grandstand roared with anticipation.

Conscious of the substantial winnings dependent upon the outcome, Percy leapt in the air as the bay made a charge for the lead, clenching his fists and laughing in the belief that he would recoup his previous miscalculations in one fell swoop.

'If this horse doesn't win my father will never allow me to marry Joan,' he shouted to his comrades as beads of sweat clung to his forehead. 'He says I already have enough debts without a wife adding to them.'

'I wouldn't be so very sore about *that*,' replied one of the men, causing the group to laugh raucously.

Despite having only met her for the first time earlier that day, his old Harrow associates enjoyed nothing better than to tease him about the young woman whom, they had all assessed as they might a racehorse, was not nearly pretty or well-bred enough to marry Percy La Touche.

'You never *did* have much of an eye for pedigree,' another chimed in as their friend's horse miraculously maintained the lead with less than a furlong to go.

Nor did Percy take it upon himself to defend Joan, being too much distracted by the race, for it was to decide where he and his friends would go on next.

'Hush now, let me watch this,' was all he could utter as the nearing sound of hooves and cut-up turf was drowned by the cheers of the crowd spurring on their own horse.

Though it did not win the race, or recompense Percy for all that he had wagered at the meeting, the bay managed to secure a place finish and thus saved him from being forced to return home early; he and his compatriots viewing bankruptcy as a temporary inconvenience due to their fathers, after a little grumbling, being just as accommodating at paying off their son's creditors as were the fathers of the disreputable fellows whom Ruskin had avoided when he was a student at Oxford.

Wasting no time in calling for champagne, the man of the hour shared it around glibly as his companions toasted both to his partial success and his maturity, their host having no intention of remaining sober on account of Joan, who was just then preparing for the ball that was to be held in his honour that evening, in full expectation of their engagement being officially announced.

Even Mrs La Touche embraced her warmly as she was changing into a gown which Rose had gifted her, intending to convey that she had come around to the idea of her son marrying someone for love rather than riches. She could not deny that Joan would be a much needed calming influence.

'You look quite beautiful, Joan,' she admitted, holding her hands and stepping back to admire the transformation she flattered herself for having wrought. If Percy must marry someone so socially inferior then at least she would have the amusement of turning her into a lady whom no-one would suspect had originated from such humble beginnings.

Joan, perceiving her future mother-in-law's pleasure, felt uneasy, for she wanted to be loved and respected by the family as she was rather than for how easily she might be altered and moulded to their own ways.

It was several hours after the ladies had prepared for the ball before Percy made an appearance, managing to make it to his chamber without being noticed though he was too intoxicated to maintain his balance. Crashing into a table and toppling over a vase, he swore as he realised that this would alert the household as to his presence and sorry condition.

Still clutching a half-empty bottle of champagne from which he imbibed directly, causing the liquor to trickle down his chin and waistcoat unchecked, he slumped into the nearest armchair and began to drop off.

Struggling to open his eyelids more than a fraction when his father entered, Percy could see enough to recognise that his pater's face was full of fury, not least when he made a vain attempt to stop his words merging together in shamelessly poor excuses.

'I had a spot of luck today,' he slurred cheerfully to La Touche who, decked out in evening dress, became increasingly discomposed as he regarded his son's half undone necktie and muddy boots.

'I'm delighted to hear that, but I doubt if it will be nearly enough to repay your debts,' his father returned, anxious as to how the reception could possibly go ahead with his son in that condition.

'When I'm married I shall give up my vices like a God-fearing man like you,' Percy replied, rising to light a cigar.

'Don't expect an allowance from me. If you marry Joan you can take her into the gutter with you. That said, your mother and I care enough for her to hope that she sees what you really are before it comes to that.'

'I don't suppose two men could be more different than you and I, could they?' his son murmured forlornly as he undressed, puffing on a cigar and staggering like a drunkard as he removed his breeches.

Mindful of the worrisome responsibilities and cares that came with running Harristown, Percy made no attempt to disguise his dread of such a burden, something which reinforced his determination to enjoy his bachelorhood for as long as he reasonably could, whilst making him want to shy away from the enormity of marriage, which, in his current mode, seemed far too serious a step for someone as young and energetic as he.

Percy, with the negativity that alcohol always produced in him, had begun to hope that his libertine antics would cause Joan to retract, thus saving him the bother of having to let her down.

'You think I've acted too rashly?' he goaded his father, only too keen for him to forbid him to proceed with the marriage.

'You always do, you're as unpredictable as one of those horses you like wasting money on,' La Touche chastised, 'but on this occasion you're not only injuring yourself. Characterful and good as Joan is, she will never be able to control you, and not even you want to run wild *all* the time.'

Joan, despite feeling nauseous with unease at the fact that Percy had made no appearance, stood smiling falsely as she stood in line beside Mr and Mrs La Touche to greet the guests and excuse their son's absence as diplomatically as they could. The humiliation choked her even more than they, and she berated herself for having been gullible enough to believe that Percy had ever meant to change his ways.

Even her daydreams had turned from golden to Gothic, and she pictured arriving at church on the day of the wedding, dressed in a simple ivory gown adorned with orange blossoms, only for a messenger to bar her entrance just as Ruskin offered her his arm and prepared to give her away. The telegram, informing her that Percy was not going to marry her, caused her legs to give way beneath her, and she leant upon her ever-faithful guardian for support.

A reverie tinged with too much reality; upon receiving no explanation or apology from Percy as to his failure to appear at the ball intended to announce their betrothal, Joan recognised that she ought to be noble enough to break away from *him*, and thus left Harristown the next day as crushed as if the imagined scene had actually occurred.

Within three months of Joan returning to the familiar faces and customs of Denmark Hill, she began to feel tremendously relieved at having discovered Percy's true character, her aunt and cousin reiterating the good fortune of her escape and praising her courage in abandoning the disastrous course before it was too late to retrace her steps.

Nor did the dissolution between Joan and Percy come as any surprise to Rose, who had recognised all along that her brother had been concealing the worst of his nature. While she was almost as disappointed as Joan at their not becoming sisters-in-law, she believed that her friend would find a far worthier suitor when once the pain of first love had subsided. Rose nonetheless greatly pitied her for having to inform Ruskin of yet another doomed La Touche match, for didn't she believe that their own was just as ill-fated?

With no likelihood of ever being permitted to invite Joan to Harristown again, Rose was bitterly lonely and longed for the three people she loved at Denmark Hill but had no hope of seeing. She was in the process of describing such feelings to Ruskin by letter one night when her mother entered her chamber in order to bid her goodnight, thereby discovering their secret correspondence.

'I'm sorry, Mother, I know it was wrong and I'll burn it at once,' Rose assured her, tearing the paper and throwing it onto the fire in order to illustrate her sincerity.

'Either way,' Mrs La Touche shrugged, 'there'll never be any affection between us now that you have deceived me,' she informed her daughter calmly before turning to leave.

'I never meant to hurt you. Won't you let me explain?' she pleaded, reaching for her mother's arm and gasping in agitation.

Conscious of her command over her daughter whenever she threatened to withdraw friendship, she continued, 'I merely wonder how you can encourage such a man when, if he had any honour at all, he would never ask you to betray your own mother.'

'You mustn't blame him, it's all *my* fault,' Rose protested, but her mother had already walked away, slamming the door behind her and leaving her daughter with no-one save her beloved Bruno, who slept in his customary spot at the foot of the bed, whining in empathy when his mistress cried.

XXVI
HOPELESS LOVE

ONSPICUOUSLY UNSHAVEN AND DISHEVELLED, RUSKIN stood by the French doors of the drawing room contemplating the melancholy of New Year as he looked out on the bright snow-covered garden of Denmark Hill with a heart full of longing.

Every year dissatisfied with what he had done the last, the dawn of that January, with a calendar of blank, empty days he must fill, brought only sadness with it, as winter followed winter and another year of hopeless love was lost to him. He found no comfort in home or work, and whenever he complained to his mother or Joan they seemed to have grown too used to his constant lamentations to take notice.

Other men in his place might have considered marrying the dear, unchallenging Joan, he pondered, as he turned around and regarded her seated faithfully beside his mother who was lying on the sofa, contentedly mending one of his nightshirts and smiling at him when she noticed him observing her.

She was more devoted than he might have expected from the best of wives, yet the nature of their bond had always been apparent and there was no use trying to change it for the sake of convenience or because they both craved marriage.

Rather, their love was all the more unshakeable and precious for not containing any shred of romance and was the one steady beacon in an otherwise mystifying and tortuous world filled with broken promises and unrealised joy.

Remaining at the door, Ruskin was staring fixedly at the snow-blanketed lawn and orchard, far away in thought, when Joan called out to him, 'John?'

Answering distantly and without turning, he murmured a woe-begone, 'Yes?' as if nothing could break him out of his angst.

'You seem preoccupied, is something troubling you?'

'Do you know what day this is?' he asked, turning abruptly, as if he had been disturbed from sleep with a jolt.

Though she knew full well what the day signified she was reluctant to own it lest it sparked a tirade of angst, but finally said, 'Yes, the third of January.'

'Rose's twentieth birthday,' he nodded seriously, 'meaning that I'm only one year from knowing her answer.'

'I don't suppose she has forgotten,' she reassured.

'You say that, but she promised to write at Christmas and I've heard nothing.'

'Christmas is a busy time,' Joan dismissed.

'Too busy to think of *me*. I lay my life in her hands and she throws it to the dogs,' he said, pressing his palm against the glass of the door and regarding how his hands were beginning to look like an old man's.

After pausing for a moment he removed one of Rose's letters from the breast pocket of his frock coat and turned it over, thinking how much he needed another. 'It was the worst Christmas I ever passed and she has cursed the day forever to me.'

'Please, John,' interjected Margaret, who, rarely making an appearance downstairs, saw it as her duty to upbraid her son when she heard him making irreligious statements in a fit of temper.

'Forgive me, Mother,' he apologised meekly, 'but such fatal bitterness possesses me, a combination of poisoned love, distrust and scorn.'

'Joan and I are both well used to your gripes, yet we've never heard you talk in *quite* such a way,' his mother observed with consternation.

Having waited for a letter from Rose in vain for several weeks, Ruskin found himself at the peak of despair and was even beginning to contemplate suicide as a means of ending his misery.

'I'm not sure that I have ever been so miserable. I can understand how men come to sacrifice the greatest thing they ever receive.'

'I hope you don't mean that,' she interrupted violently.

Desperate to make his mother and Joan understand the depth of his anguish, he continued, 'I feel as though any love or tenderness is dead in me apart from the affection *she* generates. I can't work out if any chance I had of happiness has been destroyed or simply never was. My faculties have been irrevocably injured,' Ruskin persisted, prompting Margaret to nudge Joan in concern, 'but it is not the mere crippling of my means that I regret, it is the crippling of my temper and the waste of my time.'

Though he paced the room in agitation, his cousin was too accustomed to his dramatic declarations to react apart from to raise her eyes from her sewing momentarily, on which she observed that he did indeed look extremely haggard and tormented.

Her own heartbreak over Percy made her understand his emotions all too well, though she was tired of her cousin's need to express his innermost thoughts and feelings ad infinitum, annoyed that he never considered her own pain and always believed himself to be the sole sufferer in the household.

'Don't you *see*, both of you, I cannot command my thoughts except in a broken way?' he continued, frustrated at not hearing the words of sympathy he was used to.

'If you had stayed true to the Church perhaps you would not suffer so deeply,' his mother criticised.

'You talk as if it were nothing less than my duty.'

'It *is* how you were raised,' Margaret reminded sternly.

'My duty is to believe nothing but what I know to be fact, and to expect nothing but what I've been used to. If it were possible for me to go to God, which alas it is not, I would say to him, "Why have you been teasing me like this, you wicked man? You show me all the toys in the cupboard, but the very one I want you won't let me have." Everything is dead as I look out of my fitfully lighted window into the garden, the leaves tumbling over each other onto the lawn, the fallen sticks from the rooks' nest, the twisted straws out of the stable yard.'

Saying which, and giving his mother no opportunity for expressing her abhorrence of such melodrama, Ruskin opened the doors and, letting a momentary blast of cold air into the room, stepped into the garden.

Roaming around in a circle, first cantering then breaking into a run, he became so giddy and wild-looking that the women inside hardly knew what to do. Margaret was too old and infirm to get to her feet but Joan did so in her stead and looked on in bewilderment as, wearing neither hat nor coat, Ruskin rubbed his hands together whilst pacing the garden.

He had just enough hold on reality to know that he no longer saw the world as Joan and his mother did. To him the lawn and trees looked enchantingly beautiful, covered as they were in a dense white quilt akin to an illustration in a fairy tale, prompting him to begin laughing excitedly like a child, believing himself back in Hyde Park making merry in the snow with Emily and Rose.

How pretty they both look in their fur-trimmed bonnets and warm cloaks and mittens, he thought. *If only they would never grow up!*

Scooping up handfuls of the white powdery substance, just like confectioner's sugar, he hurled one after the other into the air, delighted at how a mass of the stuff could so easily be dispersed, and which, upon tasting, he found rather nice, if strangely cold.

Joan continued to watch dumbfounded as her cousin collapsed in a heap on the soft white ground, giggling uncontrollably due to being convinced that the two girls were trying to make a snowman out of him.

It was all too amusing that he couldn't understand why Joan wouldn't join them when he waved at her to come out. How was it that she preferred to remain inside with his mother and miss all the fun? She was even beginning to look cross, nor could he fathom the reason for her looking so much older than her friend Rose.

As if living in a happy, deluded Elysium from which he never wanted to be disturbed, Ruskin would have stayed in the garden with the girls forever, despite noticing that his fingers were badly frostbitten. Other than that, he hardly minded the cold and only felt refreshed and cleansed the longer he stayed out in it.

Recognising that her cousin was hallucinating, Joan was fearful to interrupt him lest he should grow angry, and thus continued to observe him from indoors until it began to grow dark and she could leave him no longer. When the maid came in to light the room, seeing that another flurry of snow was beginning to fall, she finally gave in and ordered the girl to call for the doctor.

'What if they want to take him away?' his mother asked.

'I'll see to it that he's kept here,' Joan reassured, pressing her aunt's shoulder kindly.

When once the thin, white-haired Doctor Acland arrived, one of Ruskin's oldest compatriots and a rare friend from his lonely student days at Oxford, he encouraged him to go inside and upstairs, where he lay delirious and unable to work for several uncertain weeks. Nor was the sympathetic physician confident in being able to offer Margaret or Joan any indication as to how long this state of mental and physical incapacity was likely to last.

'It's as bad a case of brain fever as I have ever witnessed,' he frowned.

'Madness, you mean?' Joan asked boldly, her characteristic Scottish directness amusing rather than insulting to her cousin's gentle friend.

'He is mentally exhausted,' he nodded, as diplomatically as he could, 'therefore rest and loving kindness is the only thing I can prescribe.'

'He will get plenty of both,' she assured, standing tall with matronly pride.

Joan, who could do nothing but hope and pray that he would soon recover his senses, thereby shut herself away with Ruskin and committed all her energy into caring for him and trying to restore his ability to reason away the visions that were plaguing him.

For fear that word would get out that John Ruskin was mad, Joan prevented all his friends and associates from calling at the house, furnishing them with only the vaguest of explanations as to his sudden reclusiveness and claiming that, being in the midst of the most wonderful inspiration, he could not tear himself away from his writing to see anyone.

The nights were the worst of all, for the feverish black dreams Ruskin suffered came with the most frightening premonitions of not only his own future but Rose's. Woven with mythical symbols and perplexing warnings, sometimes Rose was Rose, while at other times an altogether different girl whispered in his ear, until he knew not whether he awoke in darkness or in his own coffin.

THE MYSTERIES OF LIFE

ROSE, HAVING BELIEVED THAT IT WAS BETTER NOT TO contact Ruskin at Christmas in light of the tension it would inevitably cause between herself and her mother, remained oblivious as to the pain she had thus transferred to him by breaking her promise.

Though the harshness of winter and the mental torments Ruskin endured as a consequence eventually passed away, he never entirely shook off the unconquerable depression which hung over him like the sword of Damocles.

By late spring the visions and dreams with which he had been tormented passed away and he found himself able to work again, relieved to have the solace of new projects. Only one thing disturbed his peace at Denmark Hill and that, he well knew, was motivated by selfishness – for didn't others have the right to find happiness even if he could not?

He considered whether the outcome would have been different if he had accepted the invitation to the Richmonds' that mild April, but though he was recovered he was still in no humour to watch one of their ludicrous home theatricals. Therefore he insisted upon Joan going alone, for they knew the family well enough for her not to require a chaperone.

'The carriage will collect you at eleven,' he informed her curtly, immovable at his desk as Joan planted a sisterly kiss upon his cheek. '*Try not to enjoy yourself too much,*' he goaded, a remark tinged with enough self-pity to make her feel guilty for leaving him behind.

'I'll do my best,' she half-smiled, moving to the door; and provoking, 'I'll give them your regards, shall I?'

'Bah!' he laughed, waving her away and returning his attention to the notes he had been making.

The Richmonds' well-appointed red-brick townhouse in Marylebone was already ablaze with laughter and mirth when Joan alighted from the carriage, and she soon forgot any awkwardness at being unescorted when the society portrait painter George Richmond and his wife welcomed her heartily at the door.

She took pleasure in being received by such esteemed company, for despite her love of Denmark Hill, and the fulfilment she had gained from her role there, she was a young woman keen to see something outside her own domain, not least because the acquaintances she had established thanks to her guardian were more worldly than most.

Due to Ruskin having hosted a great many important personages, Joan never found herself timid or at a loss for words at such gatherings, nor did it ever take her very long to make friends, by virtue of her obvious good nature and modest confidence.

Shortly after taking a seat in the drawing room in readiness of the play, a young man approached her and asked disarmingly, 'I say, would you object to my taking the place beside you? You look far too nice to be left all alone.'

'Not at all,' Joan beamed, delighted by the young man's ease of manner.

'Thank you. It's Miss Agnew, I believe?'

'Yes, that's right,' she answered, surprised that he should know, for she considered herself by far the most insignificant person in the room.

'I'm Arthur Severn,' he said, and they shook hands merrily.

'I know that name from my guardian, Mr Severn. Aren't you the son of the painter Joseph Severn, the great friend of Keats?'

'Quite so. It's my ambition to be just *half* as renowned as my father.'

'You paint also?'

'Yes, only not nearly so well,' he confessed, hanging his head a little.

'Who says so?' Joan challenged.

'It's generally agreed.'

'You should allow me to judge for myself,' she encouraged.

Just then their talk was interrupted, for the evening's amiable host placed a hand on Joan's shoulder and enquired of her, 'Would you do us the honour of singing until the curtain goes up? I recall what a lovely voice you have and we should all so like to hear you.'

'With pleasure,' she consented, leaving Arthur torn between disappointment that their interlude had ended for the time being, and a natural curiosity to witness Joan perform before so intimidating an audience.

He observed with some interest that she did not blush or demur at Richmond's flattery like others her age might have done, rather she received the request and compliment as a truly unconceited young woman, while her simple dress and frizzy hair was further testament to her lack of vanity.

Joan wasted no time in selecting some music and taking a seat at the piano, for she was always as happy to entertain as others were to hear her, possessing a natural gift for judging exactly the right atmosphere to create.

Correctly assessing that the present mood was light-hearted, her playing was as assured as her voice was pure, while her Scottish accent and intonations were rich with personality as she sang the popular "Nelly Bly" to the appreciative gathering, not least the fair-haired Arthur who was captivated by his new acquaintance's natural charm and artlessness.

He wondered if she might look his way, and fancied that she did so fleetingly as she sang, 'listen, love to me, I'll sing for you and play for you, a dulcet melody,' although he concluded that as Joan was so far from being a flirtatious girl it was hard to tell whether her friendliness towards him carried any significance. This only fuelled Arthur's interest and he was determined to find out where she lived and how he might manage another encounter with her.

Arthur introduced Joan to his pretty sister Mary following her performance, which they both profusely complimented, and all three settled down to watch the play together, laughing and applauding the comedy in unison.

In the interval they decided to brave the crush for refreshments and successfully tackled the crowd flocking towards the supper table by walking three-pronged, fork-like, in search of ices.

All too soon the curtain fell and the party was over, and Arthur was sorry that Joan's carriage was announced so promptly at eleven.

'Might I take you and Mary home?' she asked, as reluctant as the siblings to part yet still not displaying any hint of coquettishness or overfamiliarity.

'Only if it's not out of your way,' his sister chimed in before Arthur had a chance to decline in modest gentlemanly fashion. 'Whereabouts do you live?'

'On Denmark Hill,' was the answer, and suddenly all became clear.

'Oh indeed! Do you know Mr Ruskin?' he enquired, thrilled at the possibility of having a mutual association.

'I live with Mr Ruskin and his mother; they are my cousin and aunt.'

'How splendid!' Arthur declared more enthusiastically than he had intended. 'Perhaps I can call on you, and Mr Ruskin might give me some artistic criticism. I certainly could do with some advice as to the correct way to paint clouds.'

Joan nodded. 'I'm sure he would be glad to help.'

'I would be grateful. I expect there will be much for me to learn.'

'You mustn't take offence if my cousin is too brutal with his opinions.' And she smiled reassuringly, allowing Arthur to see how sensitive she was to his insecurities.

'It will be worth any insult just to renew our acquaintance,' he uttered, in order to illustrate that his true desire to call was not for any professional reason.

***

Sure enough, he soon found an opportunity to call at Denmark Hill, though he had to overcome a great deal of trepidation at Ruskin passing judgement upon him, not only as an artist but as, so he quickly perceived, a potential suitor for Joan.

Ruskin's own romantic failures made him all the more reluctant to see others make love before him, and he wasted no time in showing his guest that he had discerned the real motive of his visit and was unimpressed by his thinly veiled pretence of seeking artistic advice or patronage.

Arthur, who knew himself to be no match for Ruskin's intellect, was left floundering on several occasions when his host, showing him to his study crammed with Turner watercolours, asked him to relate his preferred technique or his opinion on this or that of his contemporaries.

'Meeting you makes me suddenly conscious of my age,' Ruskin confessed, pointing to a foreboding-looking sketch of The Vatican he had made decades before, 'for I recall meeting your father more than five and twenty years ago in Rome. He didn't much care for callers, least of all a young man as forthright as I was then, yet I was determined to go along, and my good mother and father somehow helped to convince him I was worth knowing. That said, I don't believe he ever trusted my theories on art, nor do I suppose he does now.'

'He thinks very highly of you,' Arthur denied.

'Surely not enough to suggest his son follow *my* principles over his own?'

Conscious that Joan would think him a booby if he did not hold firm, he answered, 'My father follows his path and *I* follow mine, as all artists must.'

'That is very true, though who knows *where* we will be led? I certainly could not have guessed that I would ever meet and discuss art with Joseph Severn's son,' Ruskin ventured kindly. 'Strangest of all is that it was not any connection I have with *him* that brought you to my door, but rather a certain young lady whom I rather unwisely sent to the Richmonds' unaccompanied.'

'Why unwisely?' Arthur replied guardedly, being easily offended and oversensitive in the company of such a man.

'Come now, I am more than twice your age and twice as shrewd,' his host laughed, holding his waist theatrically. 'Why do you young men never think it would benefit you to speak frankly once in a while?'

The young man was beginning to perspire, for he sensed that he was being backed into a corner and knew not how to withdraw. 'I call this a rather abrupt way to address a guest.'

'If you really *must* deny it, tell me why you have never called here before now?' Ruskin interrogated, taking a seat at his desk.

'It never occurred to me that you would welcome me before Miss Agnew said otherwise. I think perhaps she was mistaken,' he huffed.

'Joanna has a right to invite whomsoever she likes here, she doesn't require *my* approval.'

'I should like it all the same,' Arthur pleaded, 'for I confess that I would like to court your ward if you are agreeable.'

'Agreeable?'

'Why yes, I can see that you aren't merely Miss Agnew's guardian but her closest confidant and adviser. So you had best tell me now, sir, if you refuse your permission to my suit.'

'I don't say I *refuse* it,' Ruskin uttered authoritatively, 'but I do *withhold* it until I am confident of your character. Joanna is all too easy to treat ill, so the onus is on me to ensure that those soliciting her regard and affection are wholly worthy of it. Were I your father I should say you were quite wrong to think of marriage yet and that you might get a better wife than Joanna, albeit not a more loving or devoted one, but a stronger, shrewder, more serviceable one.'

'Pray what, in your opinion, constitutes a *serviceable* wife?' Arthur interrupted, flabbergasted at such a statement and recalling the many rumours he had heard surrounding Ruskin's own marriage and subsequent annulment.

His host was not to be sidetracked, however. 'The very same qualities that make for a serviceable husband. I also think I can get a better one for her, and I mean to do so.'

'Perhaps we should conclude our discussion for today, Mr Ruskin, for it sounds as if you have already decided my fate,' the young man challenged boldly, moving to go.

'On the contrary, if I thought there was no chance of my being convinced of your suitability I would advise you at once to keep out of her way,' he laughed, though his undertone was unmistakeably serious. 'I will certainly not give you Joanna unless you prove yourself, not only able to make her happy but happier than anyone else I can find, and this will not take a short time. In the meantime both of you shall use your eyes and intellects as best you can, to see whether you can find someone else fitter for you.'

'I assure you, *I* shall not,' Arthur replied adamantly, his cheeks turning pink with irritation.

'You are both too young to appreciate the value of patience,' Ruskin urged, 'but if you are truly meant for one another there *will* come a time when you shall thank me for insisting you proceed cautiously.'

Despite being overwrought by this assassination, Arthur, who was fidgeting nervously with a button on his jacket pocket, proclaimed nobly, 'If you assure me that I have a chance with Miss Agnew then I shall be only too glad to wait.'

An enthusiastic response which succeeded in satisfying Ruskin and prompted him to become amiable. After all, it was no good alienating the young man in case he should become a fixture.

'Then let us leave it at that,' he pacified, 'and I can return to showing you my watercolours,' upon which he rose from his seat and escorted his guest to the drawing room to join the ladies.

Inviting Arthur to take tea with them, Ruskin entertained everyone with many amusing accounts of artists within their mutual acquaintance, observing as he did so the pleasure Joan took from his kind attentions to her beau, for she beamed whilst singing a Scottish folk ballad duet with him on the piano and looked away when Arthur applauded heartily.

The rest of the afternoon passed so merrily that he almost forgot the tensions of his earlier conversation with Ruskin, not least when, upon his departure, his host shook him warmly by the hand and urged him to call again soon.

Far from being wholly dejected when he went away, he was quite won over by Miss Agnew's eccentric guardian and rather respected his directness and sincere wish to protect Joan from heartache. Arthur was more than willing to prove himself, yet he could only wonder how long it would be before Ruskin was fully satisfied.

It was with some foreboding that Ruskin accepted the invitation to lecture in Dublin towards the middle of May, for though it was just a small part of a wider tour, that city above all others would surely prove the greatest test to his newly restored composure.

He would enter the concert hall of the Exhibition Palace with trepidation lest a member of the La Touche family, perhaps even Rose, was present to hear him without his knowledge; and instead of worrying about what he should say, he was more concerned with how changed he would appear to the one he hoped to marry. Being gripped by nerves was something unfamiliar and especially off-putting when he most wanted to impress, even if Rose only got to hear of his magnificent performance second-hand.

He tried and failed to banish such concerns as he prepared in his dressing room, thumbing through his notes listlessly as Crawley brushed his frock coat, for the audience was already waiting. The largest venue in Dublin, Ruskin's fame as an orator had enticed men and women to journey from miles around to hear him, nor did they particularly care as to the topic on which he would speak.

'How many are out there?' Ruskin enquired, unsure if knowing the number would boost his self-confidence or merely exacerbate his anxiety.

'A good two thousand, I'd say,' Crawley answered matter-of-factly, for it was nothing unusual for his master to address many more.

'Whyever did I choose to come here? I fear my voice will fail me for heaviness of heart,' he confessed, gulping down a glass of water.

The hurried rap on the door came before Ruskin was ready and, expecting it to be the concert hall manager with his cue to go on stage, he turned around in order to hide his apprehension. He was therefore surprised when a messenger entered with a parcel addressed to him, which Crawley took receipt of.

'I recognise *that* handwriting,' the valet observed with a sneer, before passing it to his master, who promptly untied it, revealing a spectacular cluster of Erba della Madonna in full bloom.

'It must be from Rose,' Ruskin exclaimed with joy; 'it was always my favourite plant at Harristown. So she *does* still think of her old friend,' he mused, continuing to study the gift.

Crawley, who had long been resentful towards Rose for the damage she had wrought on Ruskin's health, had no time to offer a pertinent response, for the stage manager entered without knocking and enquired, 'Ready, are we?', his face scarlet due to having just witnessed the electrifying atmosphere in the hall.

'Give us a few minutes,' Crawley ventured on seeing that his master was still too distracted by the ambiguous communication.

'Right you are, but make sure it's no more; it's like a pack of hungry wolves out there.' And even his chuckle seemed to carry his Irish accent, as he retreated, slamming the door as abruptly as he had opened it.

Whilst Ruskin was initially thrilled to receive such a token from Rose, a clear sign that she was thinking of him and wished him success, his elation soon turned to despondency when once the manager had gone.

'How far will her disobedience to her parents extend?' he questioned, looking up at Crawley wistfully. 'For she *is* disobedient in not casting me off altogether. If only she could resolve to do so and stay firm then perhaps neither of us would be so miserable.'

After considering the beautiful, yet confusing symbol before him in silence a while longer, unmindful of delaying the lecture, Ruskin eventually got to his feet determined to put all thoughts of Rose to one side and concentrate on the message he had journeyed so far to convey.

Following Crawley through the dark network of backstage corridors, he repeatedly muttered to himself the line he intended to open with, yet the enormous crowd waiting for him made him doubt himself.

The crowd began to nudge and whisper as he entered and made his way to the lectern, illuminated by unflattering gaslight, while each man and woman stared expectantly as he grasped his notes with sweaty hands, attempting in vain to compose himself and quiet his roaring heart. He could not recall ever being struck down by such apprehension, but then he had never given such an address in Ireland before.

Relieved to observe from their dress and general demeanour that most of his new disciples belonged to the lower order, he would at least benefit from their unfamiliarity with the usual protocol, for the fact that the majority had never attended a lecture in their lives made them more likely to be open to his outlandish ways.

Having subscribed to a talk entitled "The Mystery of Life and its Arts", a theme Ruskin deliberately intended to intrigue, most of those gathered were entirely at a loss to know what this might refer to, nor did they try to second guess. Having heard that Ruskin's talks were highly energetic and theatrical, and that he often erred from his initial subject in order to theorise on a great many political questions or the failings of modern society, they simply wanted to witness the orator for themselves and perhaps improve their understanding of a world in which they reigned insignificant.

Ruskin's mouth was parched with trepidation, yet taking a sip of the water placed before him made no improvement save for allowing him to stall for more time. He could not prevaricate any longer, however, and sensing that his audience would soon lose patience and interest he took one last look at the crowd, all of whom were silently yet noticeably urging him to begin.

The one person he yearned to see and could not find was Rose, yet just as he was about to give up searching and begin his speech he spotted her, or thought he did so, to the far left of the stalls. He couldn't be sure as there was a woman's hat obscuring his view and driving him wild with desire to know if it was really her.

Quite oblivious to anyone thinking his behaviour odd, he craned his head, first this way and then that, to catch a glimpse of a pair of blue-grey eyes full of sorrow, a braid of golden hair pinned back and the frugal weather-worn clothing her mother always chided her for going out in.

Although he wanted it to be Rose, he soon realised that the prospect of her watching him would make him lose all control, and after mumbling a hoarse 'Forgive me', Ruskin dashed from the stage and ran back to his dressing room, much to Crawley's consternation, who followed in his wake, along with the stage manager who had the surprise of the door being slammed in his face.

It took a great deal of reassurance and encouragement from Crawley to persuade Ruskin back onto the stage that day, so convinced was he that Rose was in the audience, a thought which terrified and struck him dumb.

Nonetheless, it was the suggestion that she would be more disappointed in him were he not to go ahead that convinced Ruskin to again venture onto the platform, and Crawley was astonished to observe his master's ability to fully compose himself within a few minutes, so at ease with the topic he finally decided upon that he never so much as glanced at his notes.

Careful not to look in the direction of where he believed Rose to be seated, Ruskin cleared his throat and began, 'What do you think that a man, any man, candidly and earnestly looking into his own heart will find there? He will find, I think, selfishness and an instinct for choosing his own good rather anyone else's. After all, the first reason for all wars, and for the necessity of national defences, is that the majority of persons, high and low, are *thieves*, and in their hearts greedy of their neighbours' goods, land and fame.'

The confident, authoritative opening impressed all those present, especially after such a shaky beginning, for Ruskin spoke not with any sign of pomp or arrogance but with a conviction which inflamed them with as much passion for the subject as he; conveying, through a well-timed and impeccably worded delivery, a feeling of a common goal. Pacing the stage slowly and deliberately, his hands behind his back, he spoke as if he were addressing friends at dinner.

'Do we not do great injustice to Judas in thinking him wicked above all common wickedness?' he asked, scratching his forehead as if genuinely perplexed. 'He was only a common money-lover, and like all common money-lovers did not understand Christ, could not make out the merit or meaning of him. Yet, when he found that he would be killed he was horror-struck, threw his money away instantly and hanged himself.'

Pausing in order to heighten the drama and give his audience time to reflect, he concluded, 'How many of our present money-seekers would have the grace to hang themselves whoever was killed?'

Ruskin predicted that his listeners would gasp on hearing this, and so they did. Some fidgeted uncomfortably in their seats and many appeared visibly horrified at the mere suggestion of Judas being acquitted of blame, while others nodded their heads in agreement, including Rose, whom he noticed smiling with pride on witnessing his influence over those around her. He did a double take but there was no doubt this time: it *was* Rose; he had a clear view of her seated in the front of the stalls, and this, coupled with her looking altogether different from earlier, forced him to admit that his first sighting had been no more than a mirage.

Having arrived late, Rose knew nothing of Ruskin's earlier desertion, and she was delighted to behold the full force of her old teacher's charisma and prophet-like magnetism, a power which increased tenfold on him recognising and exchanging a glance with her, for to know that she was there willing him on made him keener than ever to impart his most important philosophies.

'Although your days are numbered, and the following darkness is sure,' he went on, shrugging his shoulders comically and taking a moment to allow a ripple of laughter and sniggering, 'is it necessary that you should share the degradation of the brute simply because you are condemned to its mortality? Or that you must live the life of the moth and the worm by virtue of the fact that you are bound to companion them in the dust?'

Ruskin stopped abruptly and, standing at the edge of the stage, looked fixedly at the auditorium as if wanting to direct this question to each and every person. 'No! Even though our lives be as a vapour that appeareth for a time and then vanisheth away, let us do the work of men for as long as we bear their form, and as we snatch our narrow portion of time out of eternity let us also snatch our narrow inheritance of passion out of immortality. Whether you are devout or no, a believer or an unbeliever with no heaven to look for, is *that* any reason for selfishness or that you should remain ignorant of this wonderful and infinite earth which is firmly within your possession?'

Ruskin, nigh approaching the age of fifty, uttered these words as a man looking back on his own forsaken hopes and shattered faith with a firm resolve not to be resigned to failure, viewing the life before him as illuminated by a sunshine that was fast fading and only serving to highlight the fragility of life.

This speech was, as always, entirely unscripted, yet he felt a desire to be unusually candid with his audience and make a frank disclosure. 'Mortality is just as much a mystery to me as it is to *you*, nor have I managed to find any theory which offers a satisfactory explanation as to the purpose of any of us being here. Therefore, do not look to *me* for all the answers, for you see before you a man searching in the dark just as much as you.'

With his shoulders slumped, he shook his head slowly from side to side and continued to stalk the stage before eventually stopping in his tracks. Looking up with a wry smile on his lips, he declared, 'That said, I may have made *some* observations which may be of use to you. For example, do you believe that there is just *one* day of judgement?' he posed, keen to keep challenging his eager listeners who, utterly absorbed, were nonetheless wondering where Ruskin's tangent would take them next. 'Why, is not *every* day a day of judgement? Think you that judgement waits until the doors of the grave are opened? Fie! It waits at the doors of your houses, my friends, it waits at the corners of your streets! We are in the midst of judgement. The insects we crush under our feet are judging us. The moments we fret away are our judges, the elements that feed us judge as they minister, the pleasures that deceive us judge as they indulge.'

It was a bold finale and a sentiment that was enthusiastically received, most of all by a young woman who was hearing Ruskin speak publicly for the first time, without the knowledge or consent of her parents. How much Rose would have liked to have stayed and congratulated him, not only on for being able to inspire so many but irrevocably change their outlook on life in such a short time.

She would have done so had not she believed that doing so would be a much greater betrayal than simply listening to Ruskin as a stranger might, and therefore she gathered up her coat and left the hall long before the crowd had finished applauding him, rehearsing in her mind as she made her way back to Harristown a convincing tale to explain her absence.

The memory of Ruskin's Dublin lecture lived on in Rose's memory; and despite regarding it as sinful to deceive her mother and father, she was immeasurably glad to have witnessed his remarkable capacity for reaching out to those of all classes and faiths.

She should never have understood how wise Ruskin appeared to others had not she witnessed his power as a lecturer with her own eyes and ears, his poetical way of talking enforcing his most idealistic hope for a fairer society made up of right-minded men and women who would each carry out some good in the world.

She too shared his opinion that people should live simply and be content with what they had; it only seemed ironic that her own discontentment stemmed from thinking herself too blessed and undeserving of the worldly goods bestowed on her.

Warmly welcomed to Dublin and fêted by the local dignitaries for the duration of his stay, Ruskin could not bring himself to depart Ireland without once looking on Harristown, and thus he devised a plan to take the train to Sallins and walk along the edge of the La Touche estate on the off-chance of catching a glimpse of Rose in the sunlight, satisfied in just looking on his love, an other-worldly heroine, whom separation had elevated into a divine and celestial being he revered too much to beseech her notice.

Contrary to his hopes that the Erba della Madonna signified Rose's intention to claim her independence on coming of age, the guilt of attending his lecture prompted her to write to him a few days later:

"As you know, I am forbidden by my father and mother to communicate with you, nor will I disobey them from now on, but first I wanted you to know that this has been a happy month to me – enough to throw a light over all the rest of the year, however veiled with cloud that may be."

Alas, her note put paid to Ruskin's scheme of walking along the perimeter of her homeland, and foreseeing that his presence would cause her great distress if he was discovered he decided instead to climb a portion of the Wicklow Hills that he might look down over the estate where Rose and Bruno roamed each day.

It was not the glorious afternoon he had anticipated on setting out, but rather by the time he arrived the sky was grey and threatening rain, contributing to his low mood as he surveyed the endless plains towards Harristown, where once he had been welcome.

He did not care for being lionised by the rest of the country while Rose's parents still shunned him, and after an hour of studying the landscape, so inextricably a part of her being, he realised his mistake in wanting to look upon it.

Retracing his steps and boarding the first ferry departing Dublin, he knew that he should never be able to set foot in Ireland again if things continued thus, a thought that would have been all the more certain if he had known how tirelessly Lacerta was working to cut him off forever.

XXVIII

EFFIE

I F Ruskin was considered temperamental by all who knew him, nothing ever riled him so much as when he returned home in early June to find that Mrs La Touche had been corresponding with his former wife for the several weeks he had been absent.

The letter from his and Mrs La Touche's mutual friend, Mrs Cowper, informing him of the treachery, was waiting on his desk among a stack of other seemingly more pressing communications, trampling on any illusions he had previously harboured of persuading the La Touches to reassess his pledge towards Rose more favourably.

As the full horror of the intrigue unravelled, too advanced for him to curtail, he found himself reliving the last days of his marriage, along with all the animosity he had felt on discovering his wife's deceit, causing him to curse and bring his fist down on the desk by way of venting his anger towards both her and Rose's mother.

Rushing downstairs in order to implore Joan to give her advice, he came across his cousin and mother taking tea in the flower garden, as gay and serene as he was demented – oblivious, on seeing him approach, as to the whirlwind that would throw their quiet Sunday into disarray.

Too feverish to pass any courtesies, he stormed without hesitation, 'Mrs La Touche has been communicating with my former wife!' still clutching the letter laced with poison. 'Did she ask my leave?!'

'Whyever would she do such a thing?' Joan enquired innocently, having heard only a vague account of his marriage.

'Clearly with the intention of blackening my name, but is there *nothing* she won't do to achieve it?' he castigated, surprising even Joan with his rage. 'Her jealousy of Rose is so great that she has sought to break all possibility of an engagement by any means in her power, even if it should bring her daughter, utterly holy and pure, into contact with those who will only speak evil of me.'

'But how can Effie dare to lay the blame at your feet, when it was *she* who abandoned you?' she persisted naively.

'She always accused me of being responsible, nor did I ever stoop to deny half her lies,' he affirmed, kicking the gravel. 'Her version of events is precisely what Mrs La Touche wants to hear, so I am dammed either way. It is all a device to make any love Rosie might have for me perish in the most pitiable way. By the time they have done with her she is sure to despise me.'

'Effie might not have spoken against you,' Margaret tried to hearten her son, so clearly crestfallen at the revelation. 'She's been remarried for years with a family of her own whom she wishes to protect from further scandal; why should she begrudge you happiness now?'

'It is in her nature. She hates as only those who have injured *can* hate,' Ruskin rebuffed. 'The thought of Rose being influenced by her words is unthinkable,' he went on, reeling as to the best way of countering her inevitable aspersions. 'Should I write to Mrs La Touche with my own account? Or at the very least plead with Rose not to believe whatever has been said against me?'

'If you do approach her, you would be wise to do so cautiously rather than in haste,' his mother interjected before Joan could put forth her own opinion. 'Who knows *what* the poor girl has had put into her head, or if she is inclined to believe it. Rushing to defend yourself without knowing the nature of the so-called misrepresentations Effie has made will only make you look *more* culpable.'

Ruskin hardly needed to read Effie's narrative of their marriage to know how she would have presented the tale to Mrs La Touche, nor was he surprised to find that the fourteen years since their annulment had done nothing to lessen her resentment.

He was not wholly unsympathetic that she had been banished from all noble company as a result of their very public parting, for London society had judged her as severely as a fallen woman, whilst his own reputation had hardly been tarnished, allowing him to continue circulating amongst the highest personages when she was expelled forever.

In recent days he had been inclined to view their parting more generously, considering that they had both been victims of an ill-matched union, even if it was impossible to sympathise with Effie fully when he recalled the means of betrayal she had adopted in order to free herself from their irreconcilable alliance.

Despite this, Ruskin had never borne her ill when hearing of her subsequent marriage and children, and would have remained gracious and congenial had it not been for her own provocative desire for vengeance. He only wished that he could reason with her and halt the destruction that would never satisfy so deep-rooted a grievance, but it was too late to beg for mercy, the story of their division had been spun, with Rose poring over Effie's letters, he knew not how many, line by line and word by ghastly word.

In the attempt to tarnish her former husband's character as brutally as she could, Effie had described the most personal details of their life together, declaring to Mrs La Touche that Ruskin was quite unnatural and utterly incapable of making a woman happy, without explaining the full circumstances that had made her reach such a conclusion.

"I think if your daughter went through with marrying him her health would give way after a time and she would receive the same treatment as I. It is very painful for me to write all this and to be obliged to recollect all those years of distress and suffering, of which I nearly died. My nervous system was so shaken by the experience of living with him that I will never entirely recover, yet I hope there is still time to save Rose."

Effie claimed that she made these defamatory statements against Ruskin reluctantly yet out of necessity, for she shared Mrs La Touche's concerns for her daughter and raised the question as to the legality of her former husband remarrying. As their own marriage had remained unconsummated before being annulled on the grounds of his incurable impotency, how could he be entitled to enter into another union?

"I confess I dread the possibility of my first marriage being resurrected in law if Ruskin should be able to prove himself to be other than impotent, for example if he should father a child with Rose. Although admittedly I possess a limited knowledge of the law, I hope you will understand my anxiety and forgive my raising such an indelicate subject, lest such a proof would thereby make my subsequent marriage void and each of my eight children illegitimate."

Having ignored her second husband, who had advised her to leave the matter well alone, it was concern over her own children and not Rose that mainly prompted Effie to join Mrs La Touche's quest to ruin Ruskin's hopes of taking another bride.

Effie begged her equally desperate correspondent to seek legal counsel forthwith, whilst urging her to pity the emotional turmoil she had endured since the annulment, for not only had she lived through a horrendously public scandal, resulting in her becoming a social outcast, but now she faced the uncertainty of whether her children's prospects were to be ruined should they be branded misbegotten.

"The whole thing is impossible," Effie declared, *"and I trust that Rose will consider the implications and search her conscience most carefully. Should the banns of my marriage to Ruskin be revived, thus injuring my own family, I would have no compunction in publicising the decree of impotency against my former husband."*

This vehement protest not only gave Mrs La Touche all the ammunition she desired when it came to battling with her daughter to discontinue any thoughts of Ruskin as a suitor, but, as requested, she immediately sought the advice of her solicitor in the hope of confirming this unforeseen complication and being able to lay one final and insurmountable barrier between the pair.

Rose was heartbroken when her mother, interrupting her treetop solitude one afternoon, threw Effie's letters on the ground and insisted that she read the sickening contents for herself, quoting her correspondent's choicest accusations when she perceived that her daughter was not judging her own words as seriously.

'You must see that I was right all along to protect you from this man?' Mrs La Touche urged when her daughter, who had climbed down, began to walk away, leaving the letters, saturated with the worst kind of vindictiveness, where they lay at her mother's feet.

Pursued until she finally agreed to read them, though Rose recognised that Effie's words were probably not to be trusted, and that her mother would stop at nothing to break her fortitude, she was so shocked and disgusted by the disclosures that she broke down upon her mother's shoulder and agreed to give up all idea of becoming Ruskin's wife.

Rose's anguish was doubled in one stroke a few days later when they received the horrific news that Emily had died at sea whilst making a voyage from Mauritius with her husband.

The irreplaceable loss of her sister's love and friendship following on from Ruskin's expulsion was the worst of all possible bereavements, and Rose conjectured whether it was God's way of punishing her for a lack of loyalty towards Ruskin, or her past disobedience towards her parents.

Her mother meanwhile exacerbated her pain by crying all day as she drifted from room to room like a phantom, muttering over and over, 'My sweet, fair, gentle Emily, the child who never caused me a moment's unrest.'

IN SEARCH OF PEACE

RUSKIN WAS STRUCK WITH THE DEEPEST GRIEF WHEN HE discovered sweet Emily's demise, and out of respect and sympathy for Rose laid aside the subject of Effie until she herself raised it.

The senselessness of Emily's death put matters into stark perspective, and he journeyed to Abbeville in Northern France towards the end of August with a heavy, questioning heart, a place he always longed to be whenever he needed peace of mind.

A lovely old town, immaculately kept, lying amidst tall groves of aspen poplars beside the Somme, it benefited Ruskin by not being too far from his mother, who had sharply deteriorated in health in recent months.

The warm weather and pure air meanwhile made him glad to be out of doors and allowed him to devote himself to sketching the landscape or hiking through the chalk hills, then gloriously carpeted with bluebells, a flower which always reminded him of his homeland in spring.

Irritated that lovesickness had caused him to largely waste the past few years, he attempted to put his poor, suffering Rose as much from his thoughts as he could, feeling almost untrue to her when he began to feel quite himself again.

Even his modest appetite improved, and he delighted in writing his mother and Joan vivid accounts, not only of his daily activities but the hearty fare he enjoyed at the Bull's Head Inn where he was residing: from cutlets, fowl and roast pigeon, to Neufchâtel cheese at every meal.

He had discovered the Bull on climbing the tower of Saint-Vulfran Cathedral during the first few days of his sojourn, surprised and amused to find that it was not a typical inn as its name belied but a turreted château boasting a handsome courtyard, thus prompting him to transfer from the Hotel de France where he had initially taken rooms *"like a true Briton"*, so he joked to the ladies of Denmark Hill in his next letter.

Ever afterwards referring to his new abode as the "Hotel of Beef-Head", it was this kind of jocular anecdote which reassured Joan that her cousin's spirits had been much revived by the trip, and she warily allowed herself to hope that such blitheness would continue when he returned home.

Sleeping more deeply than he had in years, it became Ruskin's habit to awaken shortly after sunrise and, on being quite refreshed, open his window wide and inhale deeply before settling down to complete any letters he had not managed to finish the previous night.

The habitual exercise of corresponding sustained him in good temper and bad, though it was unusual to find that he had no inclination for self-pity, and he smiled to himself on realising that for once his missives were not filled with misery or complaint and might instead bring pleasure to the recipient.

After dressing he would stroll along the ramparts, where the morning mists created a dreamlike effect among the trees, and leaning against the dramatically high red wall in quiet contemplation of his surroundings he would remain there until hunger inspired him to return to the inn for a breakfast of rolls and tea which, regardless of its simplicity, he would partake of ravenously in anticipation of many hours' walking.

Although Abbeville was comfortingly familiar to him, he had never taken the trouble to study the unique characteristics of each valley so carefully before, nor the extreme rural poverty which had gradually befallen the inhabitants over the past twenty years and was now pitifully obvious from the disorder and neglect of the cottages he passed just outside the centre of the town.

Rather than look on helpless, Ruskin felt obliged to pen an essay on the unemployment crisis afflicting the neighbourhood, giving him far more energy than mere sketching, especially when it came to trying to understand the causes and potential remedies of the hardship affecting so many in the community.

A subject he derived much gratification in researching, it was on being invited to join a committee run by local businessmen that he began to observe the full impact this scourge was having on the lives of the Abbevillois citizens.

Faces that had once smiled back at him wore a saddened expression, while girls who had looked kind formerly had become cold, hard women – the absence of any charm being directly related to their menfolk no longer having any work to fulfil or occupy them.

Identifying the need of the townspeople for help and a clear example of how to lead a simple yet useful life, Ruskin began by recalling the sanguine plans and idealistic visions he'd had of old for establishing a colony whereby he and his friends might get things into a bright, working order before gradually expanding their field of work for the general good of the town.

This proved a deal harder to carry out than he had been prepared for, however, and without achieving nearly so much as he intended the days merged into weeks just as they had whilst holidaying in the Lake District the previous summer. He was nevertheless delighted to be asked for his advice and, taking pleasure in making new acquaintances, began to wonder whether he was, after all, destined to live a solitary life.

He had been stationed in Abbeville a little over a month when, taking his usual morning walk across the hills, he was reminded of the expansive views he had once enjoyed at Harristown – the green valleys drinking up the sun.

Resting awhile, to his utter amazement it occurred to him that he was happier than he had been all those years ago in Ireland, for the love he

312

carried in his heart for Rose might add colour to all he saw and did if only he lived in the present and freed himself of the irrational pain of trying to second guess the future. It was like breaking a piece of flint and aided him to see that, though he had nothing save his work to take pride in, no wife or child for companionship, he was content in his own company and to accomplish work which required the abundant liberty at his disposal.

The serenity of Abbeville made Ruskin glad rather than resentful at the prospect of returning to London when the time finally came, a sensation he found singular indeed when, for years past, he had mourned that he could not stay abroad all his life.

He arrived at Denmark Hill determined to put his energy and focus into his next book rather than winning Rose, no longer sure that it was within his power to make her happy, so insurmountable seemed the lies that had been spoken against him and the religiosity with which she had been indoctrinated.

Weary of being judged, yet conscious that his defence had never been loud or vehement enough, as a man who understood and accepted his own failings, he was increasingly reluctant to be compared with Christ. If they were ever to know joy then Rose must have enough conviction to stand firm against the warnings of her parents, Effie and those preached from the Bible.

A typically abrupt note from George MacDonald heralded his return to England, who, having just heard of Effie's correspondence with Mrs La Touche, posed the question no-one else was brave enough to ask: "Was it true that you were incapable?"

The thought that Rose, as pure as the Virgin, was being confronted with his ignominy, appalled and mortified him, yet however much he shied away from addressing these questions, and was loath to leave the path of resignation he had so recently adopted, he knew from MacDonald's own frank outpouring of curiosity the great importance of doing so just as soon as she would grant him an audience.

CONFESSION

ONLY SIX MONTHS AWAY FROM ARRIVING AT HER TWENTY-first birthday, Rose appeared much altered following the loss of her sister, nor could Ruskin conceal his surprise on seeing her step so feebly towards him through St James's Park.

This venue he had suggested due to the recent spell of warm weather and its equidistance between Denmark Hill and the La Touche residence on Curzon Street, although he regarded it as strange that their only chance of a private conversation was in such a public place.

After exchanging an awkward greeting, made so due to the long interval since their last encounter, coupled with Effie's pernicious meddling, they began to relax into something like their old manner as they made a circuit of the lake and felt the rays of the warm, soothing sun upon their heads.

Taking up one of the benches positioned on the perimeter of the lake when Rose tired, they remained silent as a fair-haired young boy of about four or five years, dressed in a sailor suit, trailed his hand in the water under the supervision of his nanny.

Occasionally allowing himself a sidelong glance at Rose, it struck Ruskin how markedly different she seemed, though he could not work out exactly *how*, nor whether it was more her physical appearance or the slight coolness of her demeanour. Aside from being more solemn, her face had visibly aged since last they had set eyes on one another, though it enhanced rather than detracted from her graceful beauty.

The longer he regarded her the more he became wary of mentioning what was foremost in his mind, however, and whilst her entrancing face seemed to invite openness her obvious unease did not. It was impossible to broach the subject of his past without the risk of her walking away, and he held onto those few moments of silence with the possessiveness of one already condemned, all too aware of the poignancy of being forced to look upon a scene that made them both question their own regard for one another.

The nanny, a young woman with a comely face, pushed a pram close beside them, never taking her eyes from the boy, who set his toy sailing boat on the water and gurgled with delight as it journeyed to the other side of the lake, dazzlingly pretty in the sunlight.

Ruskin wondered if the scene made Rose think about Emily's motherless child, or motherhood in general, and when the nanny went off in the direction of the little boy and the boat he was encouraged to speak the words that had brought him there.

'I have waited for almost three years to hear your answer,' he began, uncertain of how Rose would respond to so abrupt an opening. 'Will you consent to be my wife?' he asked earnestly, taking up her hand.

Rose hesitated before looking away and uttering the words he dreaded above all others, 'I can't.'

Unable to accept this without trying to fully understand her reasoning, as no explanation was forthcoming he could only try to incite an argument that might change the course of his fate.

'Tell me why your parents are so against me?' he pleaded, wishing that she would look at him instead of staring blankly at the water. 'Because I'm a pagan and you're a Christian, you're young and I'm old?'

'We *all* wish you had faith, but that isn't the reason, nor is it because of your age, as you know full well. You will outlive *me* anyhow,' Rose replied, crossing her arms defensively.

'Don't say that.'

'It's true, we both know it so why be afraid to speak of it?' she retorted. 'I'm only twenty, yet I feel as if I have lived longer than anyone.'

'I know my marriage to Effie concerns your mother,' Ruskin went on, 'and I will answer any questions you or she may have honestly and frankly, however much it may turn you against me.'

'You must resent my having discovered your past,' Rose provoked, trying to hide the jealousy she felt towards his first wife, for she could hardly comprehend that Ruskin had once professed love for another when he had convinced her that she was all to him.

'No, I only loathe you hearing one side of it. Cannot you see the wrong in listening to reports of my words without hearing them for yourself? As it is, you have formed an opinion of how I lived with my former wife simply by reading an evil account written by *her*,' he reproached, shaking his head. '"Heaven has no rage like love to hatred turned, nor hell a fury like a woman scorned". Even your mother must realise that there is more to a marriage, especially a *bad* marriage, than just one party's view of it.'

'I wasn't naive enough to believe *all* that Effie said in her letters, but it did make me question something,' she conceded hesitantly.

'Go on, ask me anything you like,' he encouraged, hoping to be offered the chance to redeem himself.

'Would you want our marriage to be as your first?' Rose asked timidly.

'Of course not,' he vigorously denied, relieved that she had finally made reference to the grounds on which his marriage had been annulled.

Rose unfolded her arms and regarded him questioningly.

Misunderstanding her meaning and rushing to convince her that his current protestations of love were incomparable to any affection he had felt towards his former wife, he went on rapturously in the hope of illustrating his passionate nature. 'The love I have for *you* has made me see

316

how little I ever cared for Effie. I should never have married her, for a man should choose his wife as he does his destiny.'

'Why *did* you, then?' she tested.

'I married like a fool,' Ruskin confessed, 'because her face pleased me and I was in need of a companion due to being overworked and despondent. She married me for my money and position, breaking her faith to a poor young lover so I later discovered.'

Rose reflected for a time, unable to find any way to express her own feelings when they were no more than a tangle of confused thoughts and imaginings planted there by her mother.

'Perhaps I was not clear when I asked if you should want our marriage to be the same,' she faltered, 'for I meant the *way* in which you lived.'

'You refer to my union with Effie never being consummated?' he tackled with a forthrightness which disarmed her.

'Yes,' she answered bashfully, recoiling at discussing the most intimate detail of his marriage, yet wanting to know what might be asked of her should she consent to become his wife. Contrary to most young women's expectations of marriage, Rose was entirely opposed to losing her virginity, so devoutly did she wish to observe her faith.

'Don't be embarrassed, you have things you wish to know, that's only natural,' he reassured, 'but the simple answer is that I want *our* union to be different in every way. Does that answer your question?'

'Yes, I suppose it does,' she agreed, disconcerted by his earnest affirmation of desire.

Ruskin got to his feet and, offering his arm, guided her along the path beside the lake, although they were both too distracted to enjoy the fine weather or the setting.

'As time went on the more I dreaded having children by Effie,' he continued, 'although I felt it was my duty to make her my wife whenever she wished.'

'And *did* she wish it?'

'No, fortunately she dreaded rather than desired it, although I dare say she thought me a very poor husband,' he granted, sighing.

'Still, you must have been very sorry when she left,' Rose ventured, with more sympathy than before.

'Perhaps it is shameful of me, but my sorrows were of quite another kind. For example, Turner's death was worse to me, a hundredfold, than any domestic calamity. You see, I have always believed that I have work to do which cannot be carried out by any other hand, and which no vexation ought to interrupt. I'm afraid there is something wrong in this, but so it is, and that is why I recognise how different my feelings are for *you*. Now it is only the thought of making myself more worthy of you that makes me continue.'

'You talk of being worthy of me, yet Mama says that you should never have offered marriage to any woman in light of the annulment grounds,' Rose reprimanded, halting suddenly and turning to face him in an accusatory stance that took him by surprise.

'I was wholly free to pledge myself to you, as I am now. Any doubt just stems from Effie's ludicrous and selfish fear that our marriage will be resurrected should I go on to have children, for she always knew that the basis of our legal separation was an outright fabrication and that I might easily have proven the accusation of impotency completely false had I chosen to do so.'

'The very idea of *how* is impure and sinful,' Rose censured, flushing in girlish innocence.

'Forgive me for any impropriety,' he apologised, 'but this was never destined to be an easy discussion. It is vital that we understand one another, however. Won't you believe in me enough to accept the darkness as well as the light? Though I am no saint, you have my assurance that I have been saved from sin and am utterly deserving of you,' he urged, taking hold of her hand as she attempted to break away. 'You must know that I have done you no wrong from the hour we met to this instant? No man living could have loved you more purely than *I*, and if you come to me you will find me all that you once thought.'

'People are always the same, you've often said so, and therefore you can't alter your nature however corrupted it might be,' she rejected. 'I grow so confused by what you say to me and all others say *of* you.'

A deep animosity towards those who had tried to tarnish the bond between them challenged his composure, yet, determined that she should recall the man she once trusted unconditionally, he touched her angelic face gently and uttered softly, 'Trust not *me* but your own heart, for there is nothing, legal or otherwise, to hinder our marriage if only you would consent to it.'

Quite certain of her mind and heart, Rose turned and wept but would make no reply, leaving him as unsure as before.

'Do not cast away this great love unless in *sure* knowledge of some fatal obstacle,' he begged, 'for I have loved, honoured, laboured, wept and borne every form of insult for you, and all these limitlessly. Will you turn away from me now, Rose?'

PART THREE

BOWERSWELL

A DECADE BEFORE RUSKIN FIRST BECAME ACQUAINTED with the La Touche family he had stood before a Scottish minister repeating, with little conviction, the marriage vows that were intended to bind him for life – the howling Perthshire wind rapping the window as if in protest.

Though his vixen-haired young bride, Euphemia Chalmers Gray, was generally admired and considered a great prize, he discovered that fixing oneself to another before God was a peculiar sensation he was eager to conclude, nor did she seem any more pleased by the event when he lifted her veil and placed a tentative kiss upon her cupid-bow lips.

Despite having known Effie all her life, the idea of growing old alongside her became a formidable prospect the moment they were pronounced man and wife. There was no point in regret, however, and having realised the enormity of such a step too late Ruskin thus adopted the strictest resolve to make the best of things.

The cool way in which the couple were congratulated was influenced by the bride and groom's own despondence, while the unhappy circumstance that brought about the Grays' long association with the Ruskins was much discussed in whispered snatches by the select few who were present to witness the joining of these two Scotch families.

Superstition still carried much weight in that remote corner of the country and, although they said what was expected of guests towards newly wedded persons, they shook their heads when they went away, convinced that the gruesome accident which had resulted in drawing the pair together boded ill.

Effie's father, George Gray, a solicitor by trade, had first become acquainted with John James Ruskin on acquiring Bowerswell Villa, the Perthshire home of his father, John Thomas Ruskin, who had sliced his throat with a razor so as to escape his creditors.

Margaret, John Thomas's niece, despite being overwrought on coming across so horrific a scene, attempted in vain to stem her uncle's bleeding with her skirts as, bathed in blood, he spluttered and choked for air, regardless of his earlier inclination to be gone.

The wound being too severe to repair, yet not deep enough to extinguish him at once, meant that both she and John James were forced to look on as he died a slow and painful death lasting three days, distraught to witness the excruciating final hours of a man who had managed his demise as badly as he had his life and finances.

United in grief and the scandal which inevitably engulfed them, Margaret soon afterwards married John James, the old man's only son, to whom she had been engaged for nine years whilst he struggled to save enough money to support her, the son being as conscientious with money as the father had been reckless.

Confident that she had chosen a man who would always take care of her, Margaret made one condition on becoming his wife and, declaring the house cursed due to the horrors she had witnessed there, refused to step foot inside Bowerswell again, thus persuading her new husband to put it up for sale.

Removing to London, where John James meant to make his fortune by importing sherry, a trade he had been apprenticed in, they resolved never to speak of the troubles they had endured together and became as devoted to one another as if they had both survived shipwreck.

Having sold Bowerswell to the Grays, a young couple almost as ambitious as they, it chanced that Effie was given life in the very room in which John Thomas had chosen to quit *his* only a short time before; a beginning Margaret and John James could have no idea would have any bearing on their own lives or that of their son.

John Thomas's death continued to cause the couple distress and hardship for many a year, as by ending his life prematurely he had unwittingly placed a great financial burden on his son, who thenceforth toiled, not only to keep himself and Margaret but to clear his father's debts and uphold the family name.

Partly out of necessity and partly through learning from his father's mistakes, John James became an astute and confident businessman, always keeping in mind how John Thomas, who had owned a small grocery business, had gradually fallen into debt due to an ineptitude for figures and a generosity of spirit.

More magnificent in his expenditure than mindful of his family or expenses, not to mention indiscriminate and boundless in his hospitalities, John James often recalled how his father's numerous guests would arrive at their door, only for him to have to enquire their name.

Despite Bowerswell always being associated with John Thomas's violent deed, John James and Margaret remained on good terms with the Gray family and, though they would not be persuaded to visit them in Perthshire, were happy to welcome them whenever they found themselves in London.

Not having heeded her own prophecy concerning Bowerswell, Margaret deeply regretted ever having encouraged the Grays' friendship when their only son, John Ruskin, reached thirty and, having achieved some success as a writer and art critic, announced his intention to marry the Grays' beautiful nineteen-year-old eldest daughter Effie.

He had become attached to Effie after a brotherly fashion and, finding that her pleasant society could refresh him and make him happy, thought that she would be all that he desired in a wife. Due to Ruskin's limited experience of women, and being unpractised in judging their faces except on canvas, however, he wrongly believed that Effie loved him. Still less did he understand the indefinable affinity that made for a successful marriage; his own parents, blessed with the strongest of partnerships, having been his only example.

Assuming that the same good fortune would befall *him*, he dismissed his mother's opinion that Effie's connection with Bowerswell and John Thomas's grim history was a portent of evil and that this alone was a strong enough reason to avoid forging a union with her. Decrying such warnings as the stuff of old wives' tales, he argued that there were too few marriageable young women within his sphere of acquaintance to allow him to be so choosy.

'I understand that your ordeal has made you wary of me linking myself with the place,' he sympathised with his mother on walking home from church one Sunday, 'but if I am too particular about my wife I will assuredly get a bad one,' attempting to win her round with a smile and his most persuasive tone.

'I beg that you will make yourself easy and do anything you feel would be most conducive to your own happiness,' his father interjected kindly on observing that Margaret intended to continue protesting. 'Whether you were to choose a wife from Paris or Perth, from small fortune or great, your mama and I should never be satisfied but by seeing you happy, isn't that the case, my dear?' John James prompted.

'I know my son well enough to recognise that *this* won't make him so,' Margaret denied stubbornly, causing the men to look to one another in exasperation. 'I don't go in for romance but *reason*.'

'It doesn't seem very reasonable to me that you think Effie unsuitable simply because she had the mischance to be born at Bowerswell,' Ruskin countered, walking on ahead and leaving his parents, arm in arm, to argue for the duration of the way home.

After days of similar cajolement on behalf of Ruskin and his father, Margaret finally made a pretence of relinquishing her long-held superstitions and granted her reluctant approval, realising that nothing would deter her son from proceeding with the match. She nonetheless tormented John James by expressing her supreme dissatisfaction whenever they were alone, or during the nights when she found herself unable to sleep for turning the matter over.

'It has long been my opinion that John's enjoyment and usefulness would be infinitely greater if he were to marry, yet I always felt sure that when he decided to do so it would be to a woman who had proved herself worthy of him,' she explained sorrowfully. 'Effie Gray is certainly *not* what I had in mind.'

'You always thought her charming before,' her husband reminded, still half asleep and refusing to sit up simply to go over it all again.

On this Margaret placed her handkerchief to her nose before declaring in her most acerbic tone, 'Yes, charming as a friend, never as a wife! Not only does she not possess the qualities and gifts necessary for such a mind as John's, she is nothing short of *provincial*.'

'It is academic regardless, and I am disposed to let matters take their course,' John James concluded, reluctantly sitting up and lighting a candle on finding himself wide awake long before dawn. 'It is *his* choice and we must respect it.'

'We should never have invited Effie to stay with us, for she is the very girl I always said was most to be feared,' she chastised herself.

'In that case, perhaps we should take responsibility for throwing them together. I imagine it would be difficult for any young man to regard Effie with complete indifference,' her husband confessed.

'A long engagement would surely have changed his mind,' Margaret conjectured; 'as it is, the ceremony is to take place in no time at all and on the very spot your father—!'

Leaving her sentence unfinished, John James shuddered to recall that the ceremony was to be conducted on the very spot where his father had succumbed to the greatest despair a man can ever know.

'It *is* strange that they should have elected to marry there,' he concurred, pausing awhile to reflect.

Margaret shook her head soberly before going on. 'Well, nothing shall persuade *me* to attend. I vowed never to return to Bowerswell, and no man, not even my son, will succeed in getting me to break it.'

Not wanting the Grays to suppose that his wife's absence was in any way a snub, John James left his bed jaded a few hours later in order to pen a sincere apology to the bride and her parents, describing to Mr Gray the degree of apprehension in which Margaret regarded Bowerswell, without thinking it appropriate to refer to the precise cause.

"*You expect Mrs Ruskin and I should come to Perth and nothing can be more reasonable – I at once acknowledge that we ought to come, but with Mrs Ruskin's feelings and prejudices as they are I scarcely dare contend. For my own part, I am sincerely desirous of coming, but on the best consideration I can give the subject I have decided to keep away.*"

XXXII THE WEDDING

RUSKIN, THOUGH DISAPPOINTED THAT HIS PARENTS WOULD not join him on such an important event in his life, made the arduous journey by rail and coach to Bowerswell with no other companion save his valet, complacent in his steadfastness and with no thought that his mother's forebodings would partly be realised on the eve of his marriage.

Flabbergasted when Effie's father took him aside and revealed that he was a ruined man and in fear of being declared bankrupt due to an ill-advised speculation on the railways, Ruskin foresaw his mother's condemnation for having embroiled himself in such a mess.

This bad investment had resulted in Gray losing a considerable fortune, some thousands of pounds, yet he did not reveal this with the burden of shame Ruskin expected, but rather explained his catastrophic downfall to the man who would imminently marry his eldest daughter in sheepish reluctance and a begging bowl tucked behind his back.

Gray's study was a confused mass of papers illustrative of his recent

329

panic, though running a hand through his thinning mane of white hair as nonchalantly as he might have announced a poor weather forecast for the morrow, the unfortunate speculator uttered with a smile, 'In fact, I've lost almost everything I possess in the world.'

As if history were repeating itself in remarkable symmetry, with Bowerswell's masters destined to become victims of crippling debt, Gray was forced to admit that his reduced capital meant that he would no longer be able to honour the bridal dowry agreed upon, a matter of little concern to Ruskin who was more anxious as to Effie's motivation in accepting his proposal, it being strange to him that the full extent of her father's losses had been concealed from him until this moment.

From having always believed the family to be plain, straightforward people, the groom now questioned whether they were not in fact a designing family and had encouraged Effie to accept him in order to save them from destitution.

It was a startling knock to Ruskin's unscathed ego, but after pondering on the situation in his chamber, and whether or not he would be foolhardy to proceed, he concluded that Effie was too pure of heart ever to be coerced into such a mercenary scheme and decided to continue with the arrangements, though his mother's presentiments were ever at the back of his mind, casting their shadow.

Before the ceremony Ruskin took the opportunity of seeking a further confidential talk with Gray in his study in order to bluntly inform his soon-to-be father-in-law that he should have no delusions that *he* would be able to settle his debts or reimburse him for his losses.

'I myself am entirely at the mercy of my own father, financially speaking,' Ruskin began candidly, preferring to stand while his host remained seated, tapping his hand on the desk impatiently, 'nor do I imagine that you would wish me to disclose your situation by appealing for his assistance?'

'Certainly not,' Gray answered, flushed with embarrassment on realising that he was being manoeuvred into a position from which he could not later retreat.

Due to not being at all confident that Ruskin would go through with marrying Effie if he so much as gave an inkling that he might afterwards apply to him for relief, Gray saw that there was no alternative but to deny the possibility most vehemently, assuring the young man as to his sincerity in desiring him to join their family, completely unmotivated by his straitened circumstances.

'That is what I thought you would say, knowing you to be a man of pride and honour,' the younger man responded with a touch of cynicism, 'and I trust you appreciate the same qualities in *me*. Many men would have had no compunction in asking to be released from this betrothal, even at such a late stage in the proceedings as this.'

'Yes, you are very good,' Gray replied through gritted teeth. 'I trust you did not think that I was petitioning either you or John James? I merely wanted to tender my apologies for not having the wherewithal to bestow upon my daughter that which was originally promised.'

'Do not feel badly on account of *that*,' Ruskin dismissed, avoiding his opponent's disappointed eye; 'rest assured that Effie shall want for nothing.' Then, with the intention of bringing their exchange to an end, he referred to his shining pocket watch and exclaimed, 'Gosh, I must go and prepare,' offering his hand courteously but without the respect he had once felt towards Gray.

Whatever he had said to the contrary, Ruskin did in fact regard it as far too late to flee, however much he might have been tempted to do so had the knowledge of Gray's ruin been imparted to him sooner. Nonetheless, he at least felt a degree of relief at having set out his own stall, leaving Effie's father with no doubt as to the hopelessness of benefiting from the alliance, save that of having one less child to clothe and feed.

The uncomfortable discussion with Gray, coupled with Margaret and John James's absence, added an undeniable sense of doom to the ensuing marriage service, turning the groom's attitude towards his future from that of anticipation to dread.

As if in sympathy with his feelings, the day was dismal and made for as Gothic-looking a scene as if it had been drawn directly from a Walter Scott novel. Even at the best of times, Bowerswell, situated across the

River Tay, was an ugly, modern property of grey stone and did not boast an especially pleasing aspect to visitors, surrounded as it was by a bleak bog-like landscape. Yet on such a wild day, and with no decoration in the house to mark the festivities due to the family's depleted means, it was a depressing occasion for both the couple and the small number of guests.

The two grim-looking coachmen who brought the handful of visitors, mainly consisting the Grays' closest neighbours, turned the collars of their coats up in order to keep out the rain and wind as they waited impatiently for the completion of the formalities, for the housekeeper had restricted refreshments to the point where visiting servants were now forced to go hungry, something both men griped about endlessly given such weather.

The guests inside the uncharitable-looking drawing room were meanwhile dressed in dark, heavy woollens more appropriate for a funeral than an April wedding, nor were their expressions any cheerier than if they had been paying their respects to one departed as the equally dour minister of Kinnoull began the matrimonial service.

So lacking in romance was the day that the bride, as prickly as a thistle, bit the inside of her mouth in order to check her tears whenever not called upon to say vows, feeling herself to be a sacrifice on the altar and dwelling sorrowfully on the sweetheart she had thrown over in order to fulfil her duty to her ill-plighted father.

Following a sombre wedding breakfast devoid of merry-making, the couple retired for the night filled with apprehension on greeting one another alone as husband and wife.

No passion inspired either of them, while Effie was especially nervous due to no-one having provided her with a detailed account of the duties of married persons to each other, leaving her with only the vaguest notion as to relations of the closest union.

Although the house had been rebuilt during Effie's infancy, the large wood-panelled chamber to which the couple withdrew might have been famous for the ghostly presence of John Thomas, such was the chill owing to Mrs Gray having ceased lighting fires in the bedrooms in order to save on fuel.

The cold was merely another example of the embarrassment Effie endured as a result of the paltriness of the occasion, and she felt herself to be at a supreme disadvantage on becoming Ruskin's wife, imagining that he would take delight in relating all her family's inadequacies to his parents upon their return to London.

Removing her unfashionable ivory wedding ensemble, borrowed from her mother, in the adjoining dressing room, Effie slipped into bed wearing a simple cotton lawn nightgown and pulled the sheets and blankets up to her chin, her wavy auburn hair spread out on the pillow.

Shivering as she fumbled to remove her nightgown beneath the covers, she wished that she had taken more wine at the breakfast, supplied by John James with his compliments, increasingly nervous as each drum of her heart counted down the moments to when Ruskin would transform her from a girl into a woman.

Bracing herself as she lay back on the pillow, she observed her husband of only a few hours pointlessly rubbing his hands over the unlit hearth as if to show his annoyance at the inhospitable accommodation.

Ignoring Mrs Gray's restrictions, and more concerned for his own comfort than the thought of keeping his bride waiting, Ruskin proceeded to build and light the fire, encouraging the flames with the help of bellows.

Satisfied with his achievement, he stood warming himself before removing his clothing, nor was there any sense of urgency when he did so. Without acknowledging the woman he was to spend the rest of his life with, he might just as easily have been settling down for the night as he always had, alone except for a good book.

Placing each garment on the chair before donning a nightshirt, he climbed into bed without looking at Effie or addressing her, nor did he make any indication that he intended to touch her, keeping his body a safe distance from hers and promptly closing his eyes.

When Effie turned towards him after a few moments, however, she saw that he was fully awake and that his face showed all the trepidation he was doubtless internalising, though he seemed to be working up to something unpleasant rather than pleasurable.

Knowing nothing of the niceties of wooing, Ruskin sat up abruptly and, folding back the sheets, prompted his bride to let out a slight gasp. Undeterred by her surprise and obvious self-consciousness he peered at her pale skin for what felt like an eternity, and she suspected that he was judging her as he would a painting.

Nor did he appear to approve of the woman who lay before him, his own wife. As if having witnessed an ill-conceived work or something abhorrent about her person, he covered her nakedness as abruptly as he had revealed it and left the bed without so much as uttering a word in explanation, spending the remainder of the night on the uncomfortable wooden bench before the fire.

THE FAIR MAID OF PERTH

AFTER DRESSING CLUMSILY, WITH TURNED BACKS AND averted eyes, Effie and Ruskin set off on a brief honeymoon tour of the Highlands the following morning, the bride observing an increasing awkwardness between them which prompted her to initiate conversation with the most unlikely, and in her husband's opinion inappropriate, people at every place they paused, for she could think of no other way to ease the tension that had existed since the previous night.

Whilst both parties realised after just a few days that they were irrevocably ill-suited, neither of them wished to acknowledge the grave mistake they had made, with Ruskin trying to remain hopeful that they might adapt to one another's ways in time and that their former sibling-like affection would carry them through. It was the fear that it would *not* which prompted his peculiar pretence of joviality as they travelled north, but which was so uncharacteristic as to only add to the strain.

Oblivious that Effie saw through this affectation, Ruskin thought her to be in equally good spirits as they went from Killin to Finlarig, especially when she appeared much delighted by the company of their wise old Scotch guide who invited the newly-weds into his cottage and offered them fruit cake, cheese and whisky, something she appeared to relish the novelty of.

Writing to John James from the Tarbert Inn, Ruskin expressed his bemusement of such scenes, though his father detected a note of annoyance within accounts which, to his mind, arrived far too frequently at Denmark Hill to suggest married bliss:

> "Effie courts strangers as much as I seek to avoid them, and talks to everybody she can make stand still, everywhere and anywhere. I did not leave her to herself for ten minutes at Kenmore, but when I came back I found her inside the Turnpike engaged in confidential conversation with the Turnpike woman and a gentleman smoking. Then at Killin, she got over an old man who showed us Finlarig until she got into his cottage, and before I knew what she was about she was sitting at the fire drinking the old man's health with whisky. We met some people on the road today, as we were walking, whom she addressed as if she had known them thirty years — and if I hadn't remonstrated, a little farther on, she would have been quite thick with a party of tinkers, not to speak of various terriers and shepherds' dogs, and a lamb she must have on her lap in the carriage."

Qualities which Ruskin had previously found charming and quaint in Effie during their courtship were rapidly becoming tedious in a wife, not least because he found her love of gossiping with strangers alien and uncouth and wondered how this would transfer to London.

Openly comparing her with his mother, he also regarded it as odd that a country girl should become so easily exhausted after walking no more than a mile, something extremely troublesome to one such as he, well used to covering in excess of a dozen miles a day without any fatigue.

Once again Effie complained of feeling tired during the journey south to Keswick, so instead of suggesting that she join him in hiking Ruskin urged her to sit and rest while he rowed them up and down Derwent Water. This concession meant that he expected her to be fully recovered by the next day and insisted that she join him in an excursion to the top of the two thousand feet high Cawsey Pike, compromisingly allowing her to climb most of the way on a white pony.

Ruskin was not able to be so accommodating when it came to the three thousand feet high Skiddaw a few days later, however, and he informed his wife matter-of-factly that she must draw on all her strength in order to reach the summit.

'I hate to be the bearer of bad news, but you will have to cover most of the way on foot,' he stated on arriving at the base of the mountain, causing Effie's brow to furrow on assessing the steep, rugged and barren ground that lay before her.

As was typical for the Lakes at practically any time of year, the weather deteriorated rapidly the further the couple ascended, with a torrent of rain commencing only minutes after they first set out to scale Skiddaw, thus making Effie's dress heavier and more cumbersome as she tackled the incline, whinging as she went.

Ruskin, on the other hand, was eager to reach the summit before the views far into Scotland were obscured by the low-lying cloud and therefore had little patience with Effie trailing behind him.

'I observe that your physical strength is chiefly confined to dancing,' he remarked sardonically, making no adjustment to his regular brisk pace.

'It is true that, whilst I admire the landscape roundabout, I do not find *this* an enjoyable pastime,' she retorted breathlessly, hitching up her skirts and proceeding over the uneven path at a snail's pace.

Ruskin was irked to find that, as he had anticipated, the wide-reaching views were entirely obscured by the clouds on arriving at the mountain top, thus making him determine that Effie's handicap should not prevent *him* from seeing the scenery in full on future expeditions.

Ever afterwards he took the precaution of carrying a portable camp seat wherever they ventured, which he would demand his weary wife sit down upon until he deigned to come back for her a few hours later, pointing at the stool as if instructing a disobedient sheepdog.

'You will no doubt ask me what I found interesting enough to keep me away all this time?' Ruskin asked cheerily upon rejoining his wife, keen to boast of the discoveries she had missed.

'I shan't,' Effie replied disinterestedly, pretending to be intent upon the novel with which she had occupied herself in his absence, and believing herself fully justified in acting churlishly due to her husband having given no consideration as to the boredom or chill she would experience on having to wait for him in the drizzle.

'You are vexed at me for leaving you behind,' Ruskin observed, 'but you shan't get an apology out of me, for I must go on with my work regardless of whether or not you are able to keep up.'

'And pray, what work have you accomplished by scaling mountains?' Effie sneered, folding up the camp seat and handing it to him in vexation.

The sky, electric violet with rosy ripples, framed the sunset and suggested a turn in the weather, yet Effie's mood remained stony throughout the long walk back to the inn and far into the honeymoon, for though they took the same road they walked apart, both heavy-hearted at the reality of marriage, a journey so recently commenced but already so much harder to navigate than either had imagined.

Day after day Ruskin thought himself extremely tolerant of *her* rather than the other way around, whilst priding himself on possessing a great deal of equanimity when Effie persuaded him to pass a further fortnight at her parents' house prior to travelling to London where they were to live.

Whilst at Bowerswell she and her mother endured a time of much suffering and anxiety on seeing Mr Gray in abject difficulty as to the mismanagement of his assets, causing Ruskin to become suspicious as to whether they were all trying to play upon his generosity with their pitiful outpourings of emotion.

As the womenfolk consoled one another and wept unrestrainedly in the drawing room, he avoided them by occupying himself outdoors, sketching or taking long walks regardless of either the hour or the weather. He was grateful to be unreachable when out wandering on the moors and, for once, returning to London could not come soon enough.

It never occurred to him that Effie and his in-laws might think him insensitive when he, one evening over dinner, described to Mr and Mrs Gray the palatial Mayfair residence which John James had generously leased for three years as a wedding gift, rapturously cataloguing all manner of improvements that were being done to enhance their comfort, until his bride kicked him forcefully under the table.

By the end of April Ruskin had developed almost as equal a hatred of Bowerswell as his own mother, and it struck him that, however much he longed to relate the business of the Grays' railway embarrassment to his parents upon returning to Denmark Hill, he would have to remain silent in order to prevent them from questioning his judgement in marrying Effie, fearful that they might treat her with condescension and even more distrust were they to hear of her father's calamity.

Forced to make up his wife's missing dowry out of his own small income, he felt the deceit most sorely and suspected that his shrewd father would soon come to discover the intrigue.

XXXIV

MRS RUSKIN

DESPITE LOATHING TRAIN TRAVEL AND THE BURGEONING stations that went with them, Ruskin was never more delighted to find himself at King's Cross than when he returned from honeymoon, far from jubilant on marching his bride through the crowds.

As the new house was not quite prepared, he was glad of the excuse to accept his parents' offer to spend a short interval with them at Denmark Hill, for he had missed their company as much as Effie claimed to long for her parents the moment she was gone from Bowerswell.

It was by way of welcoming his new daughter-in-law that John James personally greeted the couple at the station and insisted upon driving them home in the newly painted family carriage, though he was dismayed to notice that neither exuded the glow expected from newly-weds and gibed, 'Cheer up, the pair of you!'

As they drew up outside the house, both Ruskin and Effie were astonished to find all the servants standing in a line ready to greet them, the gardener stepping forward to present the bride with a large bouquet of geraniums, myrtle, orange blossom and heather of the most delicate kind, all tied with white satin ribbon.

Margaret, who stood on the front steps with her arms outstretched ready to embrace her son, was meanwhile dressed conspicuously in her best gown of brown satin adorned with black fringing, reminiscent of curtain trimmings, a costume she had not had the opportunity of exhibiting for a good many years, nor expected to again.

She had even hired a small German band to play a wedding march in tribute to the new Mrs Ruskin; but while her son was overcome by the enthusiastic welcome, Effie cynically put the display down to her mother-in-law's pang of conscience at not having attended the wedding, an oversight she was not inclined to forgive.

'I've never seen you look so well,' Margaret lied to Ruskin, before turning to Effie and saying almost bossily, 'and I hope *you* will be quite a daughter to me.'

When the couple had thanked the servants for their good wishes, the old woman escorted them inside and proudly revealed the redecorated suite of rooms located on the top floor of the house which they were to have sole use of for the entirety of their stay.

'It's only right that you should have as much privacy as we can offer,' she insisted.

Yet it soon transpired that Margaret expected her son's presence downstairs just as much as formerly and was severely put out when he announced during dinner that he intended to pay morning calls and accept whatever evening invitations Effie should see fit to attend by way of introducing her to society.

'My wife is naturally excited by the prospect of being promenaded before London's most illustrious gentlefolk,' be began, 'which means we may cause some disruption to the quiet ways of Denmark Hill.'

'The servants won't stay up late,' Margaret sniffed, 'so you will have to let yourselves in.'

'Just so. I shall book tickets to the opera at Covent Garden.' Ruskin nudged Effie and, with a certain wryness at the corner of his lips, enquired, 'Would you prefer to go twice to the stalls or once to a box?'

'Oh, the stalls if it should afford us the pleasure of going again!' Effie replied giddily, while Margaret observed that it was the first time her daughter-in-law had smiled since arriving.

'Yes, but that's no good, you won't be *seen* in the stalls,' John James interjected light-heartedly, whilst being no less serious about the point he had raised, 'nor would you have a sufficiently good view of the Queen, and surely *that's* more amusing than any opera.'

'Oh, Father,' Ruskin sighed, 'the practice of keeping up appearances in society is a mere struggle of the vain with the vain.' A remark he aimed not only at John James but his new wife, whom he perceived would relish the whirl of London events with equal shallowness.

Effie settled herself into the carriage with her husband long after midnight, breathless from her first London ball and ready to furnish him with a detailed account of her impressions.

Rolling her eyes, she scorned, 'Did you *see* how fat and trollopy the duchess looked?'

But Ruskin, not being in the least interested, 'hmmed' rather than have to endure the tedium of her commentary, prompting her to think up something bound to provoke a reaction.

Giggling into her white glove, she observed, 'She looks like the kind of woman who breaks wind in her sleep!'

'Effie!' he rebuked. 'Am I to take you out in society only for you to ridicule it?'

Without replying she turned her attention to the ladies and gentlemen pouring out of the mansion, every one of them decked and jewelled as richly as Christmas trees. Smugly wrapping her fur cape around her shoulders as the crowd searched for their coachmen in the damp evening air, it mattered little to her that their own carriage was blocked by countless others, only too content was she to observe the exclusive world to which she not only belonged but was determined to dazzle.

'I think we were quite the smartest couple there,' Ruskin offered, joining her in peering out of the window, 'and I notice how everyone always gazes at *you.*'

'Do they?' she demurred without the slightest hint of a blush, unsure whether he meant to criticise or compliment her for attracting attention. 'I wouldn't expect the great John Ruskin to notice such things.'

He realised that this was not the time to venture his opinion that the current female fashions were overly ornate, for he observed that Effie was justifiably conceited as to her appearance, her new gown consisting of four skirts of white glacé silk which had shimmered like silver in the candlelight, while the flowers in her hair complemented both the wreath of blossoms embroidered onto the edge of the dress and the posy she had held sweetly throughout the evening.

'I can hardly avoid noticing that my pretty wife was quite the handsomest lady there,' he answered proudly. 'I often think to myself, "Yes, you may look as much as you please, for she is mine now, all mine."'

'Well, *almost* yours,' Effie denied, giggling coquettishly, and without giving a thought as to whether he might take exception to the remark, being both heady from the wine and still naive enough to believe her beauty to be so irresistible as to eventually spark passion even from him.

Effie only suspected that her comment of the previous night had caused Ruskin offence when he underwent an abrupt change in temperament, his boastful good humour coming to an abrupt end the following day when he proclaimed himself tired of accompanying her on the endless social engagements she was intent upon.

'I no longer wish to spend my days in leaving cards, nor my nights in leaning against the walls of drawing rooms,' he announced to Effie and his parents over breakfast.

The young Mrs Ruskin, thinking her husband to be having no more than a tantrum, cried, 'Why so? I thought you enjoyed yourself last night.'

'Such distractions do incalculable harm to my ability to concentrate on my work,' he complained with finality, 'and I perceive this to be the reason I'm finding so much difficulty with my current manuscript.'

'I thought you were getting on very well,' John James interrupted, having been set upon his son embracing a more public life now that he had a wife to ease his misanthropy.

'Not as well as I should like,' he denied, exasperated by his father's interference, 'whilst being frequently out late has induced a head cold. I don't know what is the matter with me, but people seem to give me a chill that makes me feel both uncertain and incapable of purpose. Proofing the second volume of *Modern Painters* is a serious task and therefore I mustn't be disrupted under any circumstance.'

'What am *I* to do?' Effie exclaimed, causing her mother and father-in-law to exchange a knowing glance which inflamed her further.

She, in turn, stared daggers at Margaret, who smiled away to herself whilst the argument continued, ill-concealing her delight at the prospect of having her son at home of an evening.

'You must please yourself by attending as many parties as you like, providing that you do not mind going without me,' Ruskin appeased, with no thought as to propriety.

'Very well, so I shall,' she huffed and rose in order to prepare herself for a round of morning calls.

Ruskin generously allowed his wife to go about unaccompanied, little foreseeing that his mother would insist upon waiting up for Effie whenever she stayed out late, often until the early hours of the morning; a gesture motivated, not by any concern for her daughter-in-law's well-being, but solely in order to shame her for what she considered immodesty in venturing into society unescorted by her husband.

Disappointed that the two women were increasingly at odds with one another, which no attempts of his to mediate ever settled for very long, Ruskin soon felt himself to be a chess piece that his wife and mother were fighting to control.

Urging his mother to be more forgiving of his young bride's carefree ways, and *her* to be more considerate of her hostess's old-fashioned habits, he was ultimately inclined to empathise with the elder and not the younger Mrs Ruskin, thus inadvertently estranging Effie and prompting her to despise the customs of the household and cease making any effort to keep the peace.

With all cordiality between the womenfolk impaired by wilfulness, even when Effie acted thoughtlessly Margaret accused her of purposely seeking to disrupt Denmark Hill with her haphazard comings and goings, not least when she took to being late for meals, a transgression not to be tolerated.

'Tardy again, and on a Sunday too!' she erupted at John James and Ruskin when Anne had finished serving, tutting and raising her eyebrows in reference to Effie's empty chair.

'Thank you, Anne, that will be all,' John James dismissed, knowing how the servant enjoyed gloating over anything that annoyed her mistress.

'Mightn't we begin?' Ruskin asked his mother, longingly surveying the roast lamb dripping with gravy.

'And allow Effie to make *us* look ill-mannered? No, thank you!' Margaret declared, her cutlery remaining as untouched as the dinner that would soon be cold.

'I will speak to her, Mother,' he conceded, 'for she does not realise her offence, coming from such a large family. Effie has so many siblings younger that they all eat at different times.'

'I have no interest in what is customary in the Gray household,' Margaret responded sharply, 'for I expect her to observe *our* practices for as long as she is a guest here.'

'She is hardly a guest, she is my wife,' he corrected.

This remark raised the old woman's hackles further and prompted her to sit forward. 'Do you even know where your *wife* is?'

Ruskin shifted at his own remissness. 'She said that she might pay a call on a friend after church.'

'An equally graceless thing to do on the Sabbath,' his mother griped. 'Effie seems to associate Sundays more with dressing up and parading her new wardrobe than participating in any devotion.'

When the three had sat sufficiently long as to observe the steam from the gravy fully evaporate and the roast potatoes lose their crispness, the younger Mrs Ruskin finally made an appearance.

'Oh, I hope you didn't wait for me?' Effie asked on seating herself beside her husband, thinking the Ruskins ridiculous for having refrained from so delicious-looking a repast. Laughing as she took up her plate and heartily helped herself to the cold meat and vegetables, she admitted without any sign of remorse, 'I quite lost track of the time!'

'John will need to buy you a watch,' Margaret answered provokingly as she regarded the ruined meal she no longer had any stomach for.

'There's no need, I have a watch already,' Effie assured her mother-in-law in quick-witted retaliation.

'Perhaps you should use it, then.'

'I think even if I did you and I would always keep different times,' Effie returned facetiously as Ruskin and his father, not wishing to be drawn into the argument, remained silent, their eyes downcast.

The atmosphere between the two women, far from improving with time, grew increasingly strained when Margaret insisted that she and John James would join the young couple on a week-long visit to the picturesque city of Salisbury, where Ruskin meant to gather material for his next work, *The Seven Lamps of Architecture*.

Now so easily reachable due to the ever-expanding railway Ruskin always complained about but never minded availing himself of, it was anything but a jolly countryside excursion from the off, with Effie irked at having to put up with the old couple trailing after them when they had been married so short a time and were already forced to endure residing alongside them at Denmark Hill.

Things got considerably worse when Ruskin developed another head cold after three days, having been studying the Gothic cathedral in minute detail in wet weather, giving his mother the excuse of being able to fuss over him and assert her authority over Effie.

Insisting that he stay indoors after dinner when he did not improve, the ever-devoted Margaret persuaded her son to take a blue pill and remain in bed at the cramped, incommodious White Hart Inn for the remainder of the week. Thus Effie was thrown together with her bossy in-laws, who dictated every hour of the day with their tedious sightseeing itineraries and early mealtimes designed to ensure they were early to bed and early in rising.

Holding the neurotic Margaret largely responsible for ruining the holiday, Effie returned to Denmark Hill to find the old woman even more cantankerous towards her than usual, continually ushering her away whenever she approached her husband's sickroom, which had been set up on the floor below, and bellowing, 'He is best left alone!'

Margaret naturally excluded herself from this rule and, forgetting that there was another better placed to care for her son, adopted the role of head nurse, determined that he be laid up with more pillows and coverlets than required and insisting that the patient remain there until such time as she was completely satisfied that he had fully recovered.

Content to read, or have his mother read to him, Ruskin became a pathetic figure in Effie's eyes and only confirmed her long-held belief that he enjoyed being overindulged and lay there more for rest and attention than from illness.

On the first day of him being up and about he appeared to forget all about his cough whenever no-one mentioned it, yet would suffer a vigorous bout of wheezing whenever either of his parents enquired how it was. Surprised not to receive similar kindness from Effie, he wrongly believed that complaining would spark such a response.

'My cold is not yet away,' he whined on finding her alone upstairs studying new dress patterns.

'I think it *would* go away if only your mother would let you alone,' she replied curtly; 'she is always fussing so, not to mention concocting all kinds of remedies which doubtless do more harm than good.'

'Having successfully managed my health this past thirty years I don't suppose there is any reason why she should stop now,' he defended, blowing his nose needlessly.

'I can't see that her advice and pandering improves anything that would not right itself,' Effie retorted, slapping her pattern book down on her lap in impatience. 'Do you imagine that when you are well she insists that you shouldn't go out after dinner because she really fears you catching a cold or because she prefers you to stay at home with her?'

'You are not so fond of my mother as you used to be,' Ruskin admonished, unable to endure Effie challenging his mother's hierarchy.

'Rather, since our marriage, I perceive her manner has quite changed towards *me*,' she defended, 'for I know that she would have preferred you to marry an altogether different sort of woman.'

'Why must the female sex always be afflicted with competitiveness as well as paranoia?' Ruskin dismissed.

'You know I speak the truth. Before you were promised to me, she took pleasure in describing the girl she hoped you would marry, saying, "If my John gets *her* he *will* have a treasure, for she is very elegant and high-bred."'

'How well I know it, but you mustn't yourself trouble about that,' he laughed, 'I barely met the lady in question more than half a dozen times and my mother never even set eyes on her! Besides, she would still think I could have done better if I had married royalty.'

Ruskin was alarmed and disgusted to hear his mother criticised in such a brutal manner, and it was partly due to having grown weary of constantly having to reconcile the two women over petty quarrels, coupled with the belief that a warmer climate would improve his health, that made him resolve to take his wife to Normandy as soon as he was strong enough to travel.

Fixed upon remaining abroad until their new Mayfair residence was declared ready, for months if necessary, he trusted that distance would be enough to heal the rift between the younger and elder Mrs Ruskin.

THE VIRGIN WIFE

Enthused upon the subject of his next book, Ruskin made no allowances for the trip to France being the first occasion on which he had taken Effie overseas. He was intent upon a vigorous study of cathedrals that would mean rising at six o'clock each morning and working until late in the evening with as much regularity as if he were a lone traveller.

Discussing his plans with an excitement he never displayed towards her, by the time they reached their destination Effie was sick of every building she was yet to set eyes upon. Smiling in admiration and gushing her approval, she could not help but feel disconnected to both her husband and her surroundings; and though she tried to take comfort in being away from Denmark Hill and look for some pleasure across the Channel, one place seemed as dreary as the other with such a single-minded companion.

Nothing, not even the pretty town squares, surrounded on all sides by red-brick buildings flourishing French flags, cheered her or convinced her that this would be a place of enjoyment.

'There is an unalloyed pleasure in arriving here on a fine summer's day. After Salisbury I find Abbeville possesses such a luscious richness,' Ruskin affirmed on alighting from the carriage outside their hotel and looking about him with his hand on his hip. 'It is so exquisitely picturesque that I feel as if I have never really *seen* it before now.'

Despite addressing her, he gazed upon his new surroundings as if she wasn't there, until, startled that Effie failed to concur, he turned and interrogated, 'What is *your* first impression?'

Hardly thinking that he had any genuine interest in her opinion and fearful of him judging her ignorant, she answered hesitantly, 'I don't think I have ever seen anywhere quite so charming,' with a tone that belied her listlessness at having spent the past few hours in a coach with a man whom she considered dull beyond belief.

Acknowledging the sentiment by shrugging his shoulders haughtily, he declared, 'I shall know more about these buildings than any French architect before I am finished. In fact, I think I will rush down the street to take a look at Saint-Vulfran before the sun is off its towers.' Saying which he planted an unfeeling kiss on her cheek and presumed, 'I expect you will want to rest after the journey?'

Relieved to escape her husband's incessant hyperbole, Effie hardly minded making her own way inside, yet on announcing herself at the reception she perceived that the staff thought it untoward for a lady to arrive unaccompanied and thus proceeded to look her up and down quizzically whilst enquiring after "Monsieur Ruskin".

Cross with her husband for putting her in such a position, without it occurring to her that this was contradictory in light of how frequently she chose to go into London society without him, Effie's command of French soon put paid to the rudeness and disrespect of the hotelier's wife and she insisted on being shown to her quarters.

Though Ruskin had chosen the best room solely for its panoramic views rather than any romantic inclination, Effie was suitably impressed when once she looked out of the window, yet soon became grieved at being deprived of seeing the town on foot and irritated by her husband's childlike, selfish eagerness to explore his surroundings without having to play guide.

He meanwhile experienced no remorse at delaying Effie's first full glimpse of Abbeville, for he felt that he should have been just as damned for insisting on his wife's company after so long a journey as for failing to invite her. Knowing how contrary she could be, he had not the patience to adapt his preferences to her changeable mood and accordingly sought to please himself.

Spending the following days devoting himself to the flamboyant Gothic church of Saint-Vulfran, with its otherworldly ivory stone turrets and towers rising proudly over the bustling town, he found that he possessed an energy that flew in the face of his recent ill health and the extreme August heat, though he anticipated the onset of severe physical exhaustion if he did not rein in his frenzy.

Nevertheless, he did not pause long enough to concern himself that his po-faced wife, after just two days of dragging behind him as he sketched countless buildings and hearing detailed explanations as to the architectural evolution of the town, announced that she would rather remain behind at the hotel.

Although Effie felt herself to be sacrificing a great deal by burying herself away, not least the joy of feeling the warm sun on her face after so many cold, miserable days in Perthshire, she tried to console herself by being able to live entirely on another plane to her husband with the aid of her treasured volumes of Dumas.

Breaking up the long hours of reading, and easing the inevitable headaches which resulted from barely lifting her eyes from the text, she would take tea and sandwiches in her room, not daring to go downstairs to the parlour for fear that she should attract the sympathy of the English ladies who sat gossiping and would invite her to join them, motivated not by kindness but by their fascination in her famous husband.

It did not take long for her to tire of this self-imposed reclusion, however, and having grown in confidence on being so often left to her own devices in London she gave in to her overwhelming curiosity to explore Abbeville, thrilled by the reckless pleasure of forgetting to inform the hotel when she intended to return and leaving behind her map and guidebook.

Effie was blinded by the sunlight and beauty on first venturing outside, not only of the town but of the inhabitants sheltered within the boundary of the cosseting, high red-brick wall.

Everywhere she turned there seemed to be people more blessed than herself: from a handsome Russian couple strolling arm in arm, more interested in one another than the landmarks they encountered, to the humblest of families who sold their wares in the square on market day and were as unconscious of their own contentment as she was aware of her dissatisfaction.

The dawning awareness of her deep unhappiness made Effie desire solitude again, but just as she was about to retrace her steps she observed a fair young woman selling vegetables from a cart, and a little golden-haired child beside her who was amusing himself by playing with a heap of onions as she proceeded to bargain with the locals.

Something about the scene made her pause awhile and continue to study the two, especially when the young woman, having taken no notice of the boy for some time, eventually turned on her heels only to discover that he had been making a game of rolling the onions into the gutter.

Good-humouredly, but with her cheeks flushing pink out of exasperation, Effie easily translated the scolding she gave to the child in her native language, 'Fetch them at once, you little onion robber!', words combined with gestures expressing the deepest maternal love.

Effie, who was still as much a virgin as on the morning she had adorned her wedding gown, found it hard to bear the envy which this pretty tableau gave rise to, for she hardly knew if such a blessing would ever befall *her*, and she sat down on a nearby bench and reflected on her own pitiable state and the months of marriage, passed in a surreality unlike anything she had ever known.

As she lay beside Ruskin that night, she allowed herself to imagine what it might be like to have him touch her with romantic instead of platonic affection, thoughts she well knew were the symptom of rejection rather than lust.

After lying awake, channelling the resentment she felt towards him and distressing herself by comparing her marriage to those of wives with loving husbands, she eventually fell asleep only to rise and dress the next morning as if their way of life were natural.

Her pride was still too great to confess her situation to her mother, with whom she corresponded most days, nor did she feel it appropriate, in light of her father's financial worries, to complain of her own circumstances when she appeared to be living lavishly and with more liberty than most women of her acquaintance were ever likely to attain.

Trying to look on the many advantages of her marriage, and being no more keen to consummate their union than her husband, Effie checked her tears and wrote cheerful accounts of all she saw and did, disguising, with the most vivid descriptions, a woman yearning for home and her mother's embrace.

XXXVI DEFERMENT

NOT EVEN THE CLOSEST OR MOST OBSERVANT OF RUSKIN'S friends could have guessed how he chose to live with his wife, a circumstance which not even he, with his dizzyingly frenetic workload, could ignore indefinitely.

Aware that he had so far failed in fulfilling his matrimonial duties, he requested that Effie join him in serious conversation shortly after their return from France, their new Mayfair drawing room providing an austere backdrop as he calmly suggested, 'I propose that we defer uniting as man and wife for a further six months.'

His wife, taken off guard, repeated, 'Six months?'

With so many reasons as to why the performance of this duty should be postponed, in an attempt to quell the disappointment he imagined she would suffer by remaining his wife in name and not in fact, he held the back of her chair and explained, 'It would be nigh on impossible to have children when I require you to accompany me across Europe. You are little help as it is, but imagine how much *less* you would be if you were straddled with a wailing infant?'

Effie, too overwhelmed by the insult to answer at once, turned to face her husband, greatly doubting that his crusade of art and architecture was the true reason for his reluctance. She had long since concluded that his lack of physicality could be for no other reason than a lack of desire, something he doubtless judged it too cruel or embarrassing to admit.

Far from any tenderness having developed between them, the more Ruskin saw of Effie the more he dreaded any intimacy. He only hoped that she felt the same and regarded him with a total absence of covetousness. She certainly had never *seemed* averse to delaying matters, he mused, yet when she remained silent he became unsure and decided to elaborate, thereby twisting the knife still further.

'Whilst you have my heart,' he stumbled, 'I think it would be doing you a grave dishonour if, when I exhibit my feelings for you, they do not seem intense or worthy enough.'

'Are you saying that you don't consider yourself fit to become my husband unless your regard for me much alters?' Effie confronted, deeply wounded by Ruskin's feeble attempt to address his insufficient passion.

'Yes, I suppose I am,' he assented, 'nor will you be fit to be *my* wife unless you also love me *exceedingly*, and I am not yet convinced that you do, although you have often proclaimed that it is so.'

'Perhaps that is a result of only being permitted to *describe* my feelings rather than display them,' Effie replied, tears of humiliation rising up.

'I didn't mean to imply that you were not sincere in your protestations,' Ruskin denied, 'but if we are content as we are there is no need to change things. I feel that God has given you to me and, as He gives no imperfect gifts, He will surely also grant me the power to make your heart joyful one day.'

'One day?' she challenged, suspicious of such obscurity and determined to know precisely what he had in mind.

'Yes, perhaps six months *is* too soon,' he replied with urgency, seeing her query as merely an opportunity for negotiating an even longer stay of execution. 'It might be best to delay our union until you are twenty-five, when I am certain to feel more equipped to settle down to family life.'

'Five years from hence?' Effie asked in horror, the tears rolling down her face on foreseeing the best years of her youth slipping away in chaste servitude to a man she had begun to despise.

'Unless of course you believe that your health suffers from the way in which we live, in which case you must tell me so at once,' he urged weakly, moving to place his hand on her shoulder, a gesture she avoided by rising.

Stepping forwards, he offered her a handkerchief, and insisted, 'You should dry your eyes and bathe your face with cold water if you still wish to dine out this evening.' For he deemed it wise to bring the conference to a close and leave her to quell her distress.

Although she had not seemed pleased with the outcome of the discussion, Ruskin was greatly relieved in having initiated a postponement, for being unconvinced that Effie possessed romantic feelings for him he was only baffled that she should argue against continuing as they were, nor could he empathise with the neglect such an arrangement induced her to feel.

For his own part, he had no difficulty in living thus and viewed the time of her twenty-fifth birthday with dread rather than anticipation, choosing to put the milestone to the back of his mind as some far-off penance that it was not worth troubling himself about.

The early months of marriage had been trying for Ruskin and Effie in equal measure, yet his confessed lovelessness sparked the beginning of a more fractured household, with Effie constantly sullen and depressed. Having begrudgingly accompanied her to evening receptions in the first few weeks following their return from France, Ruskin was afterwards to be found at their address on Park Street less and less due to wishing to avoid his wife's ill temper.

Effie meanwhile saw not a little irony in her situation, for despite being emotionally starved she never wanted for material things, such as sumptuous new dresses and jewels, and found herself living in a residence overlooking the manicured gardens of Grosvenor House belonging to the Marquess of Westminster.

Yet even such an estimable dwelling had considerable drawbacks, for Effie found such a large, imposing property, six storeys high, isolating without the necessary friends or acquaintances to entertain. With Ruskin devoting the majority of each day to his book, her opportunities for establishing a social presence were few, thereby forcing her to suffer running a household to no purpose, possessing neither children nor a husband who had any inclination to favour her with his presence.

Effie had never been apart from her family and beloved siblings for any lengthy period before and, whilst she accepted it as inevitable that she should experience homesickness, this malady was heightened by long periods of solitude, something her husband failed to comprehend, proceeding much as he had when a bachelor.

It became clear to Ruskin that he was sorely ill-equipped to share his life with this emotionally-charged young woman, nor did he think it his duty to bother himself about Effie's state of mind or aid her in making her way in society.

Likewise, she could not understand how her husband could be so close to his own parents without being able to understand her plight in losing *hers*; rather he saw this wrench as a woman's lot upon marrying and believed consoling her through her difficulty would be to encourage it.

If Effie had initially tried to hide her grievances, by degrees she saw no reason to conceal the wretchedness that worsened by the hour, bitter that Ruskin, having identified the absence of anything for her to devote her love or attention to, failed to grant her the blessing of motherhood, a petition he dismissed by declaring her emotional state too unstable for raising a child.

'Your current behaviour, so far from persuading me to start a family, encourages me that I am right to reject the very notion,' he stormed, responding to another quarrel his wife provoked on retiring for the night to separate chambers. 'If you are too empty-headed to either occupy or content yourself, however will you prove as a mother?'

Ruskin withdrew himself more fully from Effie's presence after this exchange and would drive out to Denmark Hill to work in his study, where he had left all his books and papers behind, spending the night in his old room after dining with his parents as if he had no other obligation.

Whilst Margaret and John James were pleased not to have lost their son's company, even they began to view the regularity of his visits to Denmark Hill as concerning, as was his grim account of married life.

'My wife must dissolve the ties that bind her to her former home in order to be more entirely *mine*,' Ruskin mused to his mother and father over dinner.

'Should you not do likewise in order to be more entirely hers?' John James suggested, raising his eyebrows. 'You appear to see more of us than you do of Effie.'

'I would, only she is always moping and languishing whenever I am there, or rather whenever she is not at a party, occasions when she is miraculously restored to her former equilibrium,' he derided.

'It sounds as though she is in need of the diversion,' his father rejoined, still eating his dessert with relish, 'and that you could be kinder to one who has endured so dramatic an alteration of lifestyle.'

'I am not *unkind* to her and never scold her,' Ruskin reassured, 'I am simply indifferent. I have come to the conclusion that it is best if I make my own way and let her make hers, for it seems my only hope of having any peace is to let her do as she likes.'

'Unlike you and your mother who have always talked against her,' his father defended, causing Margaret to flinch, 'I can't see anything so very wrong in Effie caring for parties and the like. I for one would be delighted if she could entice you to appear in society more and confess I *am* disappointed that you always seem to find some excuse for declining invitations.'

'My work can hardly be called an excuse,' his son protested, 'and I don't think it necessary to accept every invitation one gets from the sort of people *you* mean. They think twice as much of you if you *don't* go, and ask again all the sooner.'

'That may be so, but not only is it ungentlemanly of you to leave your wife so much alone and allow her to go out unaccompanied, it is also doing *me* a disservice, for I especially found you the property on Park Street to better enable you to be among your own distinguished set and entertain them accordingly.' Here the old man, already intoxicated, lifted his glass and found that he had drained the last of its contents and that of the decanter before him.

'You know that I have always detested such a "set", Ruskin responded scornfully, 'along with the so-called "season". If I asked you for forty thousand pounds to spend in giving dinners I could have it at once, but you would not give me ten thousand to buy all the existing watercolours of Turner.'

'I would be more inclined to give you money for Turners if you occasionally humoured *my* whims,' John James grunted.

'What a nice thing it was at six years old to be told everything you were to do and be whipped if you did not do it!' his son disparaged.

'Fie!' Margaret gasped. 'Whipped? Apparently your father and I did not whip you, nor tumble you down the stairs nearly enough, judging from the impudence you exhibit towards us.'

'Yes, I am the result of the fondest, faithfullest, most devoted, most mistaken parents that ever a child was blessed with, or ruined by. But on the subject of placing myself in society, or hosting the imbecile elite, you must let me be very firm,' he said, folding his arms to show his inflexibility, 'for if I do not believe in their religion, disdain their politics and cannot return their affection, however shall I talk to them?'

'I've never seen you struggle in conversation before,' his father taunted.

Ruskin, rising from his seat and making his parents think that he was going to leave them, opened another bottle of wine and poured out a measure for himself and John James, Margaret never partaking of wine or liquor despite the impressive quantities which furnished their cellar.

'You claim that it is ungallant of me not to escort Effie places,' Ruskin continued more reasonably on returning to his seat, 'but she is far better suited to socialising than I, who am shown to my best advantage when I remain in print.'

'But surely you wish to engage with men of a similar intellect?' John James objected. 'And alas *they* can only be found in high places, however much you detest them. I urge you to cultivate those with influence solely that your work might not be overlooked; when you like to put up with wine merchants you may dine here.'

'I hope I am not being banished,' Ruskin jested, before deciding to change the subject in order to avoid being preached to. 'Talking of merchants, Effie asks if you could see your way to helping her brother George secure a position as a clerk through one of your associates.'

'Did she indeed?' he retorted, draining his glass. 'The very effrontery of such a suggestion!'

'It's not such a great favour, is it? Seeing as you're so fond of your daughter-in-law,' he reminded, winking at his mother.

John James did not appreciate the humour, however, and grew increasingly flustered as he searched for an excuse.

'I couldn't very well countenance her brother being a *clerk* if I am ever to succeed in getting the two of you accepted by the *beau monde*. It simply wouldn't do to be seen about with a relation in so lowly a position.'

'That seems a little harsh,' Ruskin interrupted, saddened that the claims made upon his father every day had made him look on the worst side of philanthropy.

'Perhaps, but there it is. You'll have to tell Effie that, whilst I'm sure her intentions are well meaning, her brother's future cannot be any concern of mine, and shouldn't be any of *hers* now that she has a position to uphold. I will gladly write to the young man explaining my reasons if she should wish it.'

Furious when she heard of John James's refusal to help her brother, Effie resolved to draw Ruskin away from his mother and father whom he continued to defer to whenever he sought advice, overruling her opinion should it contrast with theirs.

Having avowed a deep attachment to the elder Ruskins before her marriage, their influence over her husband had soured all affection to such a degree that Ruskin sought to keep them apart whenever possible, blaming Effie for the rift rather than acknowledging his own part in bringing about the animosity.

Effie, isolated in their Mayfair residence with no callers to distract her, schemed to escape the torture of her loneliness, concluding that if only she could persuade her husband to break away from the authoritative atmosphere of Denmark Hill they might have a chance of happiness.

But Ruskin, guessing her device when she expressed her desire that they should relocate to Scotland, would hardly countenance leaving his mother and father in favour of joining hers.

'What you really want is for me to be anywhere but near my parents,' he accused on one of the rare evenings they dined together.

'I merely want us to make a home of our own,' she denied, gently trying to win him around.

'If you haven't succeeded in creating a home in London why should it be any different *there*? I can only look upon this house as I should a lodging,' he reproached, 'and I expect I would feel the same wherever we lived.'

'That is more a result of your perpetual absence than my housekeeping,' Effie contended aggressively. 'If this place feels like an hotel then it is because you treat it as such, regardless of any attempts of mine to make you comfortable.'

'I might be induced to stay if I didn't have a wife who was always glum and restless.'

'I will not apologise for being miserable when you are entirely responsible for it,' she defended, too angry to weep.

Ruskin placed his napkin to one side and reflected stoically, 'Are we not equally accountable for the peculiar way in which we live? I accept that my feelings of homelessness are not wholly your fault, yet whatever the reason I *am* an anchor-less man at present.'

Effie's first winter in London was far from the dizzying round of society balls she had imagined upon marrying so illustrious and well-connected a man, nor was she inclined to accept the many invitations they received as depression steadily gained and caused her confidence to decline. She no longer took pride in her appearance or any interest in new dress fashions, for not even the admiration of all society could replace the matrimonial love so woefully lacking.

By December Ruskin was bewildered to notice that Effie was unusually indifferent to society events she would have been thrilled to attend previously, whilst her countenance was permanently sullen.

'If you had not been unwell of late I would ascribe your current mood to some kind of disease of the brain,' he remarked on returning home one evening to find her face blotchy from sobbing when she should have been dressing for dinner with his parents.

'I am too unwell to see anyone tonight,' Effie pleaded, burying her head in her hands.

'Just as you like, but you'll have to write my mother a note of apology,' he replied, relieved that they would not be forced to spend the evening together, let alone endure the predictably silent journey.

Reluctant to call out a physician on suspecting that his wife's symptoms of lethargy emanated from a nervous rather than a physical disorder, his only solution was to repair to the sanctuary of Denmark Hill alone, complaining to his parents that he had been greatly deceived in his wife's character, though his mother would have the satisfaction of being proved right in her early judgement.

'It seems my wife is hardly saner than Mrs Rochester,' he lamented, collapsing in an armchair beside his parents, 'for her recent unsociability is worse than when she was trying to cajole me into going out every night.'

'Oughtn't you to be home if she is in such a state?' John James muttered, taking a dim view of his son's remissness.

'Do not think me hard-hearted, Father,' he defended, sitting up. 'Far from dreading being alone as she once used, Effie abhors my presence to such a degree that she is often overcome by sudden fits of rage and bouts of weeping verging on the hysteric whenever forced to endure *my* presence. Indeed, I invited her to join us this evening, but she refused.'

Ruskin considered himself lenient when it came to his wife's avoidance of his parents, yet insisted upon Effie spending Christmas at Denmark Hill, a great sacrifice to a woman so desperate to see her own family.

Appalled at her husband's perpetual neglect and exhausted by the elder Ruskins' authority, Effie had no aptitude to pay them any courtesy and therefore left the three of them downstairs and retired to her chamber upon her arrival, passing the time in writing to her mother.

In a further attempt to extricate herself from joining the family downstairs for the umpteenth-course festive meal, she declared herself to be suffering from influenza, a condition his mother dismissed on entering her bedchamber without invitation.

'Why are you not dressed?' Margaret asked in astonishment on finding Effie prostrate on the bed in her nightdress. 'We have been waiting for you this past half hour.'

'I'm not fit to sit at table so intend to take my meal here,' she explained woefully, rubbing her head.

'You'll do nothing of the sort,' the old woman scoffed, placing the palm of her hand upon her daughter-in-law's forehead; 'there is no sign of fever and if you were really ill you wouldn't want any dinner, sent up or otherwise. No, you are quite well enough to join us downstairs,' she asserted, 'and I ask you kindly *not* to keep us all any longer; the servants are also waiting to dine and they have just as much right to mark Christmas Day.'

Saying which, she stormed out of the room as tempestuously as she had entered it, leaving Effie to cry into her pillow in anger and self-pity and long for the kindness of her own dear mother.

Nevertheless, being fearful of Margaret's wrath, she forced herself to dress and appeared in the dining room a short time later looking much dishevelled, startling the Ruskins' guest of honour, a widowed physician by the name of Dr Grant, by her woebegone appearance.

'I fear we cause your poor wife much agitation in requesting her company this night,' the doctor observed to Ruskin when Effie remained silent and refused all food as if to score a point with her mother-in-law.

'My wife has been out of sorts for some time now, only as we do not know what ails her we are at a loss as to know what treatment to pursue,' he replied without showing the least concern.

'You needn't discuss me as though I were not present,' Effie chided, succeeding in embarrassing him before their guest.

The repast lasted several hours, over the course of which time Dr Grant observed that the young woman looked increasingly pale and had broken into a cold, clammy sweat. Rising as the party was about to retire to the drawing room, the doctor approached Effie, who had remained slumped in her chair, and quietly studied her features, shaking his head.

'Your wife is presenting all the signs of oncoming pyrexia,' he confirmed, addressing Ruskin adamantly. 'Assist me in removing Mrs Ruskin to her quarters immediately. We must attempt to minimise the fever as much as possible.'

Ruskin, who had been convinced by his mother that Effie was afflicted with hypochondria and not any genuine illness, looked much taken aback at this revelation, though he promptly came to his senses and offered the doctor his assistance.

John James and Margaret meanwhile crowded around the patient, surprised when the two men supported Effie on either side and proceeded into the hall and upstairs.

'Do you really think this is necessary?' the matriarch asked crossly on seeing her carefully arranged dinner party break up.

'In my professional experience, yes,' the physician replied emphatically as he continued to usher Effie.

Margaret made no attempt to hide how put out she was that Dr Grant had ordered her daughter-in-law to bed on one of the most important religious dates, insisting that she remain there for at least several days or until she was strong enough to return to Park Street, for it was just like Effie to upset all her plans.

Further exasperated when the patient would take no other nourishment besides beef tea and refused the medicines she judged to be the most effective curatives for influenza after a lifetime of nursing John James and her son, the old woman fumed whenever her remedies were left untouched.

'What are these messes?' Effie questioned sceptically, looking into the glass containing a murky substance. 'I wouldn't be in the least surprised if you were trying to poison me.'

'It's a trusted family recipe of Shepherd's Ipecacuanha and coltsfoot, you ungrateful girl!' Margaret huffed, the lace on her cap trembling when she turned her face to the heavens in rage. 'Accusing me of trying to murder you must be one of the *more* unfortunate symptoms of your condition, yet perhaps it shows that you're returning to your former health and character.'

'I am well enough to perceive that whilst you are only too encouraging of John remaining in bed when *he* is unwell, you cannot wait to be rid of me,' saying which, Effie rolled over and faced the other way, leaving the old woman to retreat with the unwanted potion.

A few hours later Margaret returned, not with potions but with pills, regarded with equal suspicion by her daughter-in-law, who sat up a little in order to handle them.

'Before you refuse them, these are the famed Dr Walshman's tablets to be taken once a day for influenza and coughs,' the old woman offered. 'They are infallible.'

In truth Margaret barely knew any more as to their contents than Effie, who finally submitted and swallowed them, ignorant that she was dosing herself with an emetic powerful enough to cause vomiting for the remainder of the day, something she succumbed to in between cursing her mother-in-law whom she vowed never to accept another curative from as long as she lived.

On completing his manuscript in the spring, Ruskin was eager to escape London and refresh his mind by seeing the Alps, anticipating with some relief that his wife would still be too weak to join him and his parents on the extensive tour they planned to make largely by carriage.

Fortunately, Effie seemed pleased rather than disappointed at the prospect of being left behind and was keen to recuperate with her family at Bowerswell rather than be at the mercy of his mother's advice a moment longer.

'I am much grieved that you won't be joining us in Chamonix,' Ruskin assured her the day before she was to depart for Perth, a pretence he felt obliged to keep up for the sake of civility.

Reclining upon the drawing room sofa quietly reading, she did not look up from the page when she replied contemptuously, 'Don't mind leaving *me*, your parents may take as much enjoyment in your company as they please, for I could hardly see any less of you than I do already.'

'As you intend to leave for Perth, I consider that *you* are as much leaving *me*,' Ruskin asserted vigorously, 'nor would you wish to join us even if you were well enough, having long determined never to make friends with my mother.'

'You always *will* take her part over mine,' she scorned, her eyes glinting with disgust as she lifted her eyes and looked him up and down. 'I don't believe she ever wanted a daughter-in-law, let alone one who answers her back, and is never more delighted than when she has you entirely to herself.'

Ruskin, refusing to be drawn into an attack on his mother, remarked, 'It wasn't as if you weren't invited.'

'On a tour which all three of you designed to be far too challenging after my illness?'

He flinched at the truthfulness of the statement. 'That's nonsense when you always said you would return to Perthshire in the spring. Everyone finds *your* going away far more astonishing than my departure, for husbands can't be tied to their wives constantly.'

'Lord knows, you never are to me. I suppose you think it's my duty to always sacrifice my own wishes for yours?'

'I don't consider it unreasonable to have once hoped that you might be interested in my accomplishments,' Ruskin chided, unconsciously displaying his most selfish qualities. 'At the very least you might have sought to give me no unnecessary anxiety so that I should better be able to carry out my vocation.'

'And what of *my* calling, having neither children nor a home that you consider worthy of remaining in more than a few hours at any time? It's little wonder that my health suffers.'

London seemed blissfully far off as Ruskin commenced the long fruitful days in the tranquil Swiss valleys, and he often forgot, or chose to forget, that he was no longer just a young bachelor touring Europe with his parents, climbing and sketching the familiar mountains for which he felt an admiration quite beyond anything he could ever bestow on Effie, who was too human and full of faults to love absolutely.

Sometimes it seemed almost like a dream that he had a wife, and he considered how he might have prevented their wrong-footing if only he could have lived through that first bridal night again. It was much more pleasurable to imagine himself free than trouble himself about his life in England, however, a sensation that would end abruptly whenever he remembered the obligation of having to write to Effie.

Hardly knowing the best tone to adopt, he forced himself to compose flowery tributes such as he had written so effortlessly during his courtship, but which had a habit of drifting into perfunctory reports of his daily activities with no reference to the reader. They were, he was the first to acknowledge, rather like they had been copied from his journal and revealed the truth of his emotions far more overtly than if he had declared his detachment.

Having devoted his life to learning, and knowing next to nothing of romance, he believed that a husband ought to address his wife in more the manner of a parent than a lover, and thus, after ludicrously poetic openings, he bombarded Effie with well-meaning suggestions on how she should occupy herself in his absence, urging her, as if the matter lay fully within her control, to get well in time for his return.

Effie had meanwhile almost completely regained her composure on returning to Bowerswell, nor did she wait long to seize the opportunity of confiding in her mother the reality of her marriage.

'Child, I can hardly say how shocked I am to learn how you live. That you still remain in your maiden state is unimaginable after so long a time, especially with a young woman as beautiful as you,' Mrs Gray observed incredulously. 'Whatever does your husband say about it?'

'John explains it away as if it were common.'

'No wonder your nerves suffer so,' her mother muttered, embracing her daughter with all the tenderness she had sought. 'You must see Dr Simpson in Edinburgh. They say he is the finest ladies' physician and perhaps *he* can persuade your husband to do his duty by you.'

'However would he do that?'

'By convincing him that your health is being impaired, it goes without saying.' Her mother nodded confidently, as though there was nothing under the sun that she could not remedy.

'You are very good, Mother, but I'm not sure I care to have my husband ordered to do that which he clearly finds repugnant. Don't you see?' Effie explained, choking back sobs of relief and humiliation. 'He is likely to be most aggrieved that I have spoken to you of our most intimate relations, let alone if I solicit medical advice without his knowledge.'

'The very fact that there is an entire *absence* of intimacy justifies both your divulgence and your pursuance of a professional opinion that will see the matter resolved, one way or the other.'

Persuaded to consult the physician in order to ascertain the effects of such neglect, Effie found the rotund, genial Simpson to be a skilled gynaecologist with an unusually courteous bedside manner, noting her concerns and symptoms with consternation and sympathy as she looked to her mother for encouragement and reassurance.

As Mrs Gray had foreseen, he regarded his patient's situation as singular after over a year of wedlock and agreed that Effie's persistent ill health would almost certainly improve were her husband to consummate the marriage and grant her the gift of motherhood.

'Though,' Simpson concluded with a sigh, 'I'm doubtful that *my* opinion will prompt so dramatic a turnabout in Mrs Ruskin's marital relations,' a verdict that caused Effie to weep and take her mother's hand.

Indeed, Dr Simpson's medical report inspired anger in Ruskin rather than shame; and after overcoming the initial dismay of receiving such an admonishment from a third party, he was mortified to think of the Grays passing judgement upon him.

Above all, however, it was the idea of joining with his wife and her carrying his child which tormented Ruskin and gave him many a restless night afterwards, yet he knew that he could not ignore the stratagem Effie's parents had devised against him; and under the greatest pressure he wrote to Mr Gray with a detailed explanation as to why he could not countenance such a course of action, even in the hope of improving his wife's health.

"I think it well that you should know my feelings respecting Effie's illness, as this knowledge may better direct your influence over her. I have no fault to find with her; if I had it would not be to her father that I should complain. I am simply sorry for the suffering that she has undergone and desirous that you should understand in what way your advice may prevent its recurrence. If she had not been seriously ill I should have had fault to find with her – but the state of her feelings I ascribe simply to bodily weaknesses; that is to say – and this is a serious and distressing admission – to a nervous disease affecting the brain.'

XXXVII

THE STONES OF VENICE

RUSKIN SUPPOSED THAT MR GRAY HAD ENCOURAGED HIS daughter to reflect solemnly on her recent conduct following his letter, for on reuniting with Effie at Park Street after the summer he found her health and general mood improved and that her visit to Scotland had done much to alleviate her tendency towards ill humour.

Though he would sooner have pulled out his own teeth than draw reference to the doctor's report, he nonetheless remarked, 'You look much better,' when she greeted him at the door with unusual gladness.

Presenting her with a posy and kissing her cheek as he might a distant relation, her appealingly homely plaid dress made him recall the bonny lass he had courted, and he wondered at the changes their marriage had wrought. Nine months of separation would, he hoped, enable him to see her anew.

'What pretty flowers,' she smiled, holding them to her nose. 'Now that I am stronger, I hope we shall be better friends,' she ventured.

Taking his hand and leading him to the drawing room in her most alluring manner, he was confused by such a wifely display and wary that it might be some kind of ploy designed by his in-laws.

'Likewise, my dear,' he responded awkwardly.

She did not seem to notice his coolness, however, and sat him down in all seriousness, making him dread what she was about to say.

'When I was in Scotland I spent much time reading the books you suggested, and I thought, on you saying that you plan to make Venice the subject of your next work, you might take me with you,' Effie suggested tentatively. 'I have always longed to see it.'

'And I have always longed to show it to you,' he responded sincerely, buoyed by the change in his wife's attitude. 'It is only the recent unrest in Europe that has prevented me.'

'Then we shall go?' she asked, much thrilled and taking up his hand.

'Yes, my pet, let us set off as soon as it can be arranged!' Ruskin agreed jubilantly, relieved that, having set aside their differences, Effie meant to make amends for her appalling selfishness by considering how best to make *him* happy.

She meanwhile hoped that Venice might inspire a more tender side of her husband's nature and naively imagined that it was the prospect of introducing her to his most beloved city that made him frantic with joy, and not the Gothic architecture he meant to extol.

Approaching foreign travel more for the purpose of pleasure than education, very soon she became disenchanted by the idea of Venice, for with Ruskin as her guide it would be no more than a living museum with so many historic details to learn and commit to memory.

Even before they embarked he lectured her as though she were a child, officiously pointing out all manner of things 'she ought to consider' before-hand, from preparing herself physically by taking long walks, to tackling yet another reading list he had furnished her with in order to advance her limited knowledge of Venice's history and improve her conversation over dinner.

Worst of all, he urged Effie to commission her seamstress not to design the most glamorous, but the most practical, of dresses for travelling, when she had envisaged an opulence quite superior to that of London or Paris and had clung to the idea of being fêted by an altogether more exclusive kind of society.

'So as to be quite clear when you order your new clothes,' he elaborated soberly on finalising plans, 'you must insist upon only the plainest and most simply made dresses, of stuffs that will not crush, nor spoil, nor be bulky in a carriage or a boat.'

'But surely I will need grander gowns for the receptions and balls?' Effie questioned petulantly, having already earmarked the prettiest new silks and lace collars.

'One or two dresses will suffice, but choose muted colours that won't stand out or be remembered, so as to get as much wear out of them as possible,' Ruskin dismissed.

Thus, within just a few weeks of rejoining her husband at Park Street, Effie realised that no matter how hard she endeavoured to please him by compromising or even sacrificing her own desires, their views and tastes were too diametrically opposed to ever be simultaneously gratified. Ruskin, so she observed despondently, approached their forthcoming continental excursion not as a belated honeymoon but more a working holiday, with merely the addition of a wife whom he could teach and instruct should he have the time or inclination.

The faintest whisper of a moon peeked behind the Gallerie dell'Accademia as the subdued winter sunlight fell serenely on the humbler terracotta rooftops, a twilight hour which cast Venice's otherworldly spell long after her visitors had departed and would look on her no more.

Effie reflected on this as she proceeded down the Grand Canal in a gondola with her husband, a couch of rest like no other, and yet there was a melancholia about the city in the sea that she had not expected. The seaweed clinging to the marble palaces made her feel more ensnared, while the ebbing and flowing of the turquoise water lulled her into a false state of resignation rather than happiness.

Ruskin had meanwhile never been more elated, though her presence had no bearing on his pleasure she well knew, enraging her and causing her stomach to knot each time he declared it.

Looking up from his sketchpad momentarily, he hailed, 'Thank God I am here! It is the paradise of cities and there is sun enough to make half the sanities of the earth lunatic, striking its pure flashes of light against the azure water.'

Effie was numb to his fine words, however, and making no reply conjured up her own descriptions as she floated along as hopeless as Ophelia.

They had reached the city in mid-November and would remain throughout the winter when the centre would be far less populated due to the inclemency of the weather, thereby affording Ruskin more freedom to make a meticulous study of the architecture he intended to describe in his next work.

Much deserted by tourists, Venice's inhabitants were also greatly reduced in number due to the recent Austrian bombardment, with many Italians having fled prior to the arrival of the now occupying army.

Irrelevant of any political opinion, Ruskin had been most anxious for the fighting to stop due to Venice's buildings and art being endangered when she had stood alone against the might of the Austrian Empire, prompting him to seize the temporary calm resulting from the occupation and record all that could so easily have been lost.

Although his mother and father had expressed unease about their son journeying to a city with such unrest, nothing could persuade him to postpone his visit a second time, for he viewed the Austrians as not merely the latest in a long line of Venice's temporary owners but ones capable of spoiling the city's most precious relics forever, with no hope of accurately describing them afterwards.

Venting to his wife as they passed under the Rialto, Ruskin pointed furiously to the landmarks that had been jeopardised. 'Did the finest architects and stonemasons create only to have their work wrecked by armies brandishing weaponry or sending balloons into the sky in order to drop explosives?'

Having arrived to find the railway completely destroyed, in his dread of finding what other damage the Austrians had caused Ruskin began to think that none of his previous work would be as important if he should succeed in capturing a true account of Venice on the page.

All the past loves he had been cherishing seemed frivolous in comparison, for this was not the time for watching the clouds or dreaming about quiet waters; there was more serious work to be done. It was a time for endurance rather than meditation, for ambition and courageousness rather than happiness.

Having once believed himself born to conceive what he could not execute, recommend what he could not obtain, and mourn what he could not save, he was made frantic by the power at his fingertips and overwhelmed by the realisation that he alone had the capability of composing a faithful account of Venice for all eternity, so beautiful that the world should not only understand and appreciate her marvels better, but lament her loss all the more if once she fell.

Ruskin might just as well have been riding in the gondola alone for all he considered the wife he was seated opposite, for his mind was entirely taken up with the enormous challenge he had set himself. Nor did he perceive her annoyance and malevolent screwed-up eyes as the gondolier steered them pass the Ca' d'Oro, his face radiant as he attempted to take in any detail he might have missed on last looking.

Here was a city of marble, nay, a golden city paved with emerald, for truly it seemed that every pinnacle and turret glowed in the amber sunset. A wonderful piece of world. Rather, *itself* a world.

It was his habit to devote a considerable amount of time to sketching and note-taking whilst gliding along the main canals and the city's narrower passages in a gondola, believing that this slow mode of transport allowed him to gain an entirely different perspective from that achieved on foot.

Guiding his pencil carefully rather than hurriedly, he traced the outlines of each and every intricately arched Gothic palace, as delicate as lace and as awe-inspiring as heaven itself, peering in wonder regardless of how many times he had seen the same sights, for every journey upon the water revealed something new, from the most ornate churches and bridges to the humblest of slum dwellings where even the peasant washing lines seemed to enhance the colour of the stone. Whether tarnished or restored, *all* was now endangered by the present political unrest and therefore of equal merit when it came to documenting.

'I should like to draw everything stone by stone,' Ruskin cried, 'eat Venice up into my mind, touch by touch.'

'You'll be hard pressed to do that in five months,' said Effie, sitting forward to examine her husband's painstakingly detailed sketch, barely covering a third of the paper. 'Haven't you always said that even if one spent a lifetime here, there would still be more to discover?'

Ruskin regarded his wife sternly for failing to respond to his enterprise with any degree of understanding, amazed by her disinterestedness in the beauty surrounding her and her ingratitude on having been given the opportunity of witnessing so many jewels.

Displaying the irritation of a schoolboy on receiving neither praise nor encouragement, he returned his full attention to replicating the scene and was occupying himself thus when the gondolier distracted him by humming a popular opera tune.

'Stop that, will you? *Silenzio!*' he insisted, turning around and glaring at the Italian. 'If we want opera we shall go to the proper place, Teatro La Fenice!'

Settling down to draw only when he was satisfied that peace and quiet had been restored, Ruskin reminded himself aloud, '*This* is one of the downsides to such an antiquated and inconvenient mode of transport,' prompting Effie, who had been flirting with the gondolier, to stifle a laugh.

Before arriving in Italy, she had only read about such dark and swarthy men and was pleased to discover that the Italians were all that everyone said about them, being far more forward and flirtatious than any she had encountered in London or Perthshire.

The attentions she received were often the highlight of otherwise tedious days escorting her husband as he studied buildings or waiting with his art materials when he sought permission to climb a bell tower, for either Ruskin was too occupied to notice that young men blew her kisses or threw flowers at her feet, or did not care.

Though Effie thought Venice the most exquisite place she had ever seen, with skies and sunsets of the most heavenly shades, and a sea so fresh and calm and green, she refused to show her admiration and took a warped delight in infuriating Ruskin with her impenetrable nonchalance, scorning his labours and throwing cold water on all his discoveries.

Bored after the shortest period of intense sightseeing with her husband, she thought, *If every day is to be as dull, I would prefer to drown myself in the Grand Canal,* tempted to share the joke with her mother in Scotland, but fearful lest Ruskin should discover her sentiments and think she was being hysterical again.

Effie was musing on these frustrations when the gondolier had winked at her, rolling his eyes to heaven by way of showing her that he considered it a waste to see such a handsome young woman straddled with such a sober, exacting husband, who appeared to have no interest in anything other than Venice's buildings, something the Italian had become increasingly indifferent to in light of his occupation.

Effie had asked her husband to bring her to Venice on being desirous of a change of scene, believing that a continental adventure would do her health good, yet she saw that being with him when he was fixated upon work was more tiring than remaining at home.

In turn, she felt that her presence was more of an encumbrance than a help, for she often grew weary and had to disrupt his day by asking him to escort her back to their apartment at the Hotel Danieli, which fashionable accommodation he had selected solely on account of the sublime views over the Grand Canal.

Regardless of the beauty around every corner, there was only so much admiration of Venice's great landmarks Effie could find it within herself to conceive, and she considered how much *more* appreciative she might have been if she had visited the city as a mere tourist. Seven months of marriage might have been seven years for all the hope she had of sparking any passion in her husband; and while the elder Ruskins referred to their current sojourn as a "honeymoon", it was a term that tinged the trip with hurtful irony and disappointment.

Having initially made an effort to aid Ruskin in his fastidious analysis of the city, when Effie saw what his daily schedule entailed, and that there was not the slightest element of any romance to the itinerary so carefully arranged, she began making excuses in order to stay behind at the Danieli, anything being preferable to viewing the interior of another church or watching her husband scale a building he wished to measure for posterity.

'I lament you not joining me,' Ruskin feigned on Effie begging to return to their rooms one rainy evening in December, the cold and mist not preventing the daily performance of the Austrian military band, numbering some sixty men, who blasted their national tunes in the centre of St Mark's as if to reinforce their rule.

'It will be much better if we follow our different occupations and never interfere with one another and are always happy,' she reassured him as they arrived at the door of their apartment.

'Perhaps you're right,' he agreed; adding perfunctorily, 'I won't come in!' before hurrying away in his eagerness to make the most of the final portion of the day.

This arrangement more than suited Ruskin, who was always able to concentrate on a prodigious workload but felt that he achieved much more when left alone. Disconcerted that his wife did not share his obsession for Gothic, having felt sure that his teaching would inspire such feelings, it was a relief when Effie graciously withdrew and allowed him the liberty of working uninhibited.

Rising early each morning, Ruskin would meander to one of the low wharfs at the extremity of a canal, with steps on each side down to the water, fancying for an instant that it had become black with stagnation. Another glance undeceived him, for it was covered with the black boats of Venice, lined up in readiness of gracious voyages on tranquil waters, distance and speed being of no consequence.

Entering one of them, as if to see if they were real, Ruskin glided away, the water yielding continually beneath the boat and letting her sink into soft vacancy, the lagoon stretching to the horizon.

The water was clearer than any he had seen lately, of pale green; the banks only two or three feet above it, of mud and rank grass, with here and there a stunted tree, moving past the casement of the gondola as though they belonged to a painted scene.

Stroke by stroke, he counted the plunges of the oar, each heaving up the side of the boat slightly as her silver beak shot forward. He lost patience and extricated himself from the cushions, the sea air blowing keenly by as he stood leaning on the roof of the floating cell.

Ordering the gondola to be lashed to the stern of a fishing boat, allowing him to sail as the wind served, within or outside the Lido, he sketched Venice as she glimmered and dazzled, beckoning and luring sailors and merchants far beyond her islands.

Returning only to the Danieli at six o'clock in the evening for the *table d'hôte*, which he sampled more for sustenance than indulgence, Ruskin knew no remorse on being so often apart from Effie; on the contrary, he believed that *she* should have felt it her duty to share the burden of his undertakings, whilst offering praise, contributing ideas and taking pleasure in helping him gather information for the book that would, so he trusted, prove his greatest literary contribution to the world.

Although he made every effort to be kind when she expressed exhaustion, Ruskin was irritated to notice that Effie always seemed to revive from her petulant fatigues whenever they were due to attend a reception or some other kind of entertainment, something he put down to her considerable vanity.

Their residence, an opulent, balconied suite of rooms with high ceilings, marquetry flooring, oriental rugs, crystal chandeliers, antiques and oil paintings, was reluctantly being financed by John James on his son having insisted that it was the only suitable accommodation.

Such lavishness demanded they keep servants and maintain a pseudo-aristocratic lifestyle, which in turn granted the couple entry into the highest society in Venice, including the *Austriacanti* nobility whom Effie became transfixed by on attending balls where the ladies literally blazed with diamonds, the encrusted chokers around their necks making them look as rigid as china dolls.

Ruskin observed with some alarm that his wife not only competed against the women in her new set, but courted attention from soldiers wherever she went, not least from the Austrian officers of the occupying forces, who took little or no notice of *his* presence or the fact that she was obviously married.

Although he was not fluent in German like his wife, he nevertheless realised that the officers' compliments flowed as easily as the champagne, and that Effie, still being an impressionable young woman who had seen little of the world, was growing heady on both.

In contrast, Ruskin was only gratified by those who complimented him on his work and therefore considered it pitiably shallow that Effie should be so easily charmed and taken in by every man who flirted with her or praised her appearance.

When she was not repeating every compliment she received, she delighted in relating her opinion on the nobility she encountered, scornfully detailing their failings.

'I don't think the Princess of Mecklenburg-Schwerin so very grand,' she began disparagingly after meeting her outside the Basilica of St Mark's, 'and she walks very badly with enormous long steps. I should think her fine-looking were it not for her bonnet completely spoiling her face, its blue velvet casing being truly frightful. The other day she wore a splendid black cloak trimmed with fine sables reaching from her neck to her ankles, but the same dreadful bonnet!'

The fact that her husband never commented or joined in did nothing to dissuade Effie from making such hollow observations, while he resolved that allowing her to ramble on was easier than trying to contradict her or appeal to her intelligence.

She was, so Ruskin was ashamed to admit, never happier than when comparing herself with other, more noble personages, a weakness and immaturity in her character he despised and which made him bitterly regret having allowed her presence to taint the city he loved above all others.

XXXVIII
PAULIZZA

T HE EXCLUSIVE WORLD TO WHICH RUSKIN HAD unconsciously subscribed had no relevance to the work he had embarked upon, but rather detracted from his idealistic view of the city. Unlike his wife, he marvelled not at uniformed soldiers or bejewelled ladies but at palaces, churches and paintings that spoke of Venice's golden age.

A ball attended by only the most elite members of this faction and held in the most magnificent palazzo overlooking the lagoon, confirmed Ruskin's error in having established such a position in Venice, not least when Effie held court to several officers, much to his embarrassment and the amusement of their hosts.

Not having heeded his stipulations regarding travelling attire, Effie had gone ahead and ordered several of the most fashionable evening gowns, all tailored in a daring style of which he did not approve. Wearing her particular favourite, a low-cut dark green silk taffeta trimmed with lace, she succeeded in setting off her pale skin and auburn hair, ensuring that she remained the focus of attention all evening.

Taking up the centre of a red velvet conversation seat, Effie motioned her fan provocatively as two soldiers, dressed in striking military tunics, stood on either side of her, vying for her favour. Conversing under the pretence of improving her knowledge of their language, the men encouraged Effie to pronounce inappropriate words and phrases which, on her uttering in a broad Scottish accent with seeming ignorance, prompted them to hold their sides and rock with laughter.

'I don't think Effie has any more serious faults than pure conceit and cold-heartedness,' whispered the evening's mousy-haired hostess to the ladies encircling her, all of whom were eager to exchange views on the young wife of the famous John Ruskin.

'Yes, she really is *close* to being a charming creature,' chimed in another, 'but though she *is* pretty and exquisitely dressed, an extraordinary beauty she is *not*.'

'I for one can't blame her for going in search of some diversion in light of whom she is married to,' added a gaunt woman who unashamedly craned her neck to observe Ruskin. 'He is the strangest being I ever saw and, despite having a compelling voice and speech, as well as charm of manner, must be the most unlikely lover imaginable.'

'Not to mention the most unsociable of husbands!' interjected a hawkish-looking middle-aged woman with a feather poking out of her hairpiece. 'By all accounts, he has been quite intent upon his work since he arrived, cutting everyone in the street and hardly ever returning calls.'

'Unless urged by his wife,' the hostess confirmed, much to the hilarity of the others. 'Is it not strange that Ruskin professes to be such a connoisseur of beauty, yet is seemingly unappreciative of his wife's attractiveness? I suspect that his annoyance at her coquetry has more to do with her diverting attention away from *him* rather than any jealousy towards the soldiers at whom she flutters her eyelashes.'

The irritation they supposed Ruskin to be feeling was largely imagined, for he was determined to ignore Effie's immodest behaviour by discussing his latest work with Rawdon Brown, a serious, grey-moustached middle-aged scholar he had recognised standing by the fireside. Knowing of

Brown's mutual love for the city, he sought conversation in order to take his mind away from his wife's vain pursuits.

'I have lived here for over fifteen years, yet I never wake in the morning without thanking God for allowing me to pass another day in Venice,' Brown proclaimed, trying to prompt some equally enthusiastic speech from Ruskin, whom he thought unusually forlorn.

'I too have found nothing in all Italy comparable to Venice, nay the world,' he agreed. 'It is insulted by comparison with any city of earth or water. If they knock down Venice I shall give up all architectural studies and keep to the Alps,' he vowed, fired up by the pleasure of conversing with someone who shared his passion; 'they can't knock down the Matterhorn.'

Though he believed that the worst thing he could do would be to rescue her, over the course of the evening Ruskin's attention was repeatedly drawn to his wife and the Austrian officer who remained by her side, for he could observe them in the mirror above the fireplace. Nor could the other guests avoid noticing that Effie had failed to circulate with the other women, so flattered did she appear by the attention she received from the dashing Charles Paulizza.

Aged thirty-eight, Paulizza was first lieutenant of the artillery and considered incredibly brave, remarkably intelligent and strikingly handsome. Fair with expressive eyes, he possessed a fine clear complexion and a long dark moustache which, when coupled with the grey, scarlet-lined cape draped on his left shoulder, and an array of medals prominently displayed on the right breast of his tunic, made him by far the most distinguished-looking man in the room.

A strategic military mastermind, the young soldier had successfully directed the final aerial bombardment of the city with the ingenious use of air balloons, which, although extremely precarious, had proved instrumental in the Austrian capture of the city and meant that he was tipped to make a swift career advancement.

Effie had discovered not only what feats of bravery had earned him each medal but that Paulizza also held much wider interests than those commonly associated with military men, being both a poet and a pianist and speaking five or six languages.

Any stranger observing the pair speaking in German might have been forgiven for assuming that *he* and not Ruskin was her new husband, so at ease did they both seem in one another's company.

'You are, in effect, still a bride,' he remarked on Effie relating what had brought her to Venice, for she had begun to feel deceitful in having taken so long to enlighten him as to her circumstances.

'More like the Bride of Lammermoor,' she laughed.

'How do you find married life?' he asked wryly.

'John and I are as happy as two people can be,' Effie answered unconvincingly, looking over to where her husband stood with dissatisfaction.

'You certainly look radiant,' Paulizza complimented, 'though I oughtn't have spent so long in talking with a woman on her wedding tour,' he apologised good-humouredly.

'I wouldn't call it *that*,' Effie scoffed; 'I barely see my husband due to his work. As he says himself, he has no heart nor eyes for anything but stone.'

'I should not care to look at buildings when I could look at *you*,' he eulogised, 'but I can see that you are adept at amusing yourself in your husband's absence,' he teased, insinuating that she had used him for just such a purpose.

'Rather *you* are adept at amusing *me*, and having initially believed myself entirely on the side of the Italians and in firm opposition to this Austrian rule I find that I am quite converted.'

Ruskin accidentally drew Brown's attention to the intimate scene between his wife and Paulizza by asking his companion to repeat what he had been saying.

Apologising profusely for his remissness, he explained frankly, 'Forgive me, but operas, balls and drawing rooms have become nuisances to me. I go out to them as if I were passing time in prison, and whenever anyone talks to me I answer them wondering all the while whether there is anyone coming to take them away. I do not refer to *your* company, you understand.'

'I sympathise with your plight, for it's a pity that your pretty young wife does not feel the same,' the academic laughed, peering at Effie over his wine glass as she threw her head back in laughter at something Paulizza whispered in her ear.

'These gatherings are her only chance of finding amusement,' Ruskin admitted sadly, 'for she is generally very patient with me despite often being forced to wait for hours as I clamber over rooftops scrutinising buildings.'

'A woman willing to make such a sacrifice must either be very loving or very virtuous,' Brown replied darkly.

'You say that as if my wife must be either one or the other, when I can assure you that she is *both*,' Ruskin demanded.

'I don't doubt it,' Brown reassured disingenuously, waving his hand as if to retract his insult.

'I have told Effie that she can choose between accompanying me and being fatigued, or staying behind and being bored, which she naturally thinks best now that I have well and truly tired her out.'

Beginning to feel that the entire room was mocking him, and that he had been misguided in believing that Effie would be a wife who would improve rather than tarnish his reputation, Ruskin was irked by the judgemental way in which Brown was regarding him and felt a fool for not having journeyed to Venice alone.

Not only did he resent having to attend parties almost every night, hours he could so easily have put to better use, he saw that the ever-evolving Venetian society was a dangerous environment for so suggestible a woman as Effie, previously uninitiated into this exuberant type of culture in which flirtations were not always harmless.

The colourful whirl of cosmopolitan fashions, extravagant balls and confident European men was the opposite of everything Effie had known in Perthshire, something which justified Ruskin's conviction that she acted from naivety rather than design, nor did he harbour any real fears that the intoxicating atmosphere might seduce her into making a moral slip.

Crawley, who had travelled with the couple and witnessed their growing discordance, was not so convinced by Effie's guilelessness and took it upon himself to observe her at close quarters out of loyalty to his master, particularly when the lady remained indoors in preference to accompanying her husband on his daily rounds of the city.

As Crawley anticipated, she soon grew weary of this self-imposed confinement and, being desirous of discovering a different side of Venice from that which Ruskin wished to show her, began going out alone without his knowledge.

Unaware that Crawley was following her at a well-judged distance, Effie enjoyed navigating the intricate maze of paths and bridges which added to the intrigue of her adventures, nor was it long before she acquired a local's knowledge of the streets and canals she was initially baffled by, gaining confidence in speaking Italian as a result of being forced to ask directions from strangers.

To ensure that she avoided an accidental meeting with her husband, who would doubtless have put paid to such unseemly escapades, Effie made a habit of enquiring over breakfast which building or area he intended to spend the day studying, thus bypassing the route she thought him most likely to take.

She was equally careful to return to their apartment long before he was expected for dinner, the only period when they were obliged to endure one another's company but which she minded far less now that she had forged her own independence and formed her own impression of the city.

Ruskin meanwhile continued to excite the liveliest curiosity from members of their acquaintance, who could not decide if his eccentric behaviour was the result of madness or genius.

He remained oblivious as to the debate he inadvertently provoked, however, for nothing could interrupt the mighty task he was set upon, nor would it have concerned him how they mocked him behind his back whenever they chanced to see him with a black cloth over his head taking daguerreotypes, climbing about the capitals with measuring devices, unmindful of the dust and cobwebs, or lying stretched out on the floor of St Mark's near the altar, drawing the alabaster columns and surrounded by an audience of idlers.

Without her husband suspecting that it was so, Effie was just as much stupefied by the mystical nature of Venice, so captivating did she find the fragile palazzos, elaborate stone bridges, lagoons and gondolas, not to mention the harbour, where trade and industry had sparked the city's soaring rise to power and was not merely symbolic of mercenary gain but was the pathway to exotic and far-off lands from which its people had drawn artistic and cultural inspiration for over a thousand years.

Whether purchasing lace from a starving beggar or making the acquaintance of two Dominican friars, the more familiar Effie became with her environment the more she became convinced that she saw a side to Venice her husband could never fully comprehend, regardless of how much energy he exerted in studying her glorious monuments.

She made this judgement as a result of Ruskin never revealing his true sensibilities to her, thus underestimating his intuitive feeling for the city and allowing herself to imagine that she exceeded his understanding of its infinite layers by touring the lowliest quarters during her covert meanderings to the outer-lying and most impoverished suburbs.

The Austrians having conquered the Republic of San Marco just three months prior to their arrival, Effie observed with horror that a great many of the poorer Venetians were on the verge of starvation and were destined to fall to their new rulers despite their fortitude in remaining.

Proceeding through the slums without realising that she endangered herself by exploring districts in the grip of cholera, she witnessed the families of many fishermen living like animals, with women and children huddled together in one room without an article of furniture, feeding on any scraps of food they could find discarded in the streets.

One old woman, with tears of desperation in her eyes as she cowered in a doorway, begged Effie to buy the point lace she was selling at any price, something she readily agreed to, knowing that the like of such fine work would be worth double in London.

Effie was amused when the careworn old woman, whose sons had left her on being conscripted, took up her hands and pressed and kissed them in pantomime fashion, making a sign of the cross and imparting a thousand blessings when once she had exchanged her last possession worth bartering for the eighteen golden Napoleons. Tucking her purchase away, it gave Effie great pleasure to have made the poor creature so happy, and to think what the lace was really worth.

For months, as the Austrians continued to deny all reports of cholera, so too did Effie persist with her secretive explorations, though any feelings of liberation she had first experienced developed into a damning paranoia which almost threatened to ruin her pleasure. She no longer rambled but walked hurriedly, listening for the footsteps of the traitorous Crawley whom she supposed meant to report her movements to Ruskin.

Although Effie was not mistaken in believing this, it was out of concern for her safety rather than her reputation which motivated Crawley to continue his pursuit, reasoning that, for as long as he saw no evidence of any form of betrayal, he would remain silent.

No matter what the country, the favourite diversion of servants during a moment of leisure was partaking in talk regarding their employers, and Crawley was already aware that a great deal of speculation surrounded his mistress's lack of propriety, something he feared had the potential to find its way back to London and the elder Ruskins.

Whilst Effie had become well versed in thwarting her husband, she could hardly fail to come across others during such expeditions, ladies who were shocked to see her going about without her husband or any chaperone, and would make her blush with their interrogations. If they also happened to observe Crawley in her wake, even more suspicious did they find it, although he tried to make it seem as though he was escorting his mistress and had merely fallen behind.

It was raining heavily on the mild spring afternoon that Effie first came face to face with Paulizza, an event she had long since given up hoping for. He was equally surprised to see her unaccompanied, nor did he hide his felicity on finding himself at liberty to exchange words he could not say in company or in the presence of her husband.

Her heart never failed to quicken on the sight of him, nor could she avoid noticing the many striking dissimilarities between Paulizza and

Ruskin, something which made her increasingly bitter at having married a man who had done nothing to ease the plight of her parents, who were no better off as a result of the union.

After offering a short greeting in German, Paulizza, conscious of inadvertently compromising Effie's reputation should she be seen conversing with him, enquired, 'How do you come to be walking *here*?'

'That's a charming way to address me,' she teased in English.

'I did not mean that I am not pleased to see you, only that I fear for your well-being. You know that there is cholera in this quarter?'

'No, I did not,' Effie replied anxiously. 'There is always gossip flying about.'

'You must make haste and leave this place at once,' he urged.

'I shall,' she agreed, affected by his concern, which was more earnest than she might have expected from their brief acquaintance.

On going to leave, he caught her by the sleeve and uttered in a whisper, 'Will I see you at the reception tomorrow night?'

'If I can persuade my husband to go,' she answered doubtfully.

'I very much hope so,' Paulizza encouraged, prompting her to smile.

Looking over his shoulder to ensure that they remained unobserved, and finding himself unable to resist the temptation which lay at his feet, he kissed her and found that Effie succumbed to his ardour.

He just as suddenly remembered himself, however; and chiding himself for having taken advantage of her solitude, muttered, 'Forgive me', before leaving her.

Dazed by the encounter and the sensation of being desired, though Effie knew herself to be inexperienced in love and recognised that she was vulnerable as a result of the great disillusionment of her marriage, she reasoned away her responsiveness to Paulizza, considering it an honour to receive attentions from such a man, tributes her own husband had never paid her, even on the day of their betrothal.

Sheltering under a bridge in order to regain her composure, she closed her eyes and listened to the faint echo of Paulizza's steps and the rain merging with the lagoon, before winding her way home, entirely preoccupied with the soldier's image and the thought that it could not be altogether wrong to dream of another when her own husband had no inclination to make her his own.

Effie was dismayed when Crawley showed Paulizza into the drawing room the following afternoon and she blushed tellingly when he kissed her hand formally and dismissed the valet.

'Where is your husband?' he asked, taking up the seat beside her.

'He's been shut in his room ever since dawn and I suppose he intends to remain there all day so as not to be disturbed,' Effie offered with a sigh. 'He even asked for breakfast to be brought to him.'

'Have you seen him at all?' Paulizza asked, astonished by Ruskin's carelessness.

'Only once for a very short time. He had his stove heated to such a degree that when I went to see what had become of him I could not remain a moment, though he said I could stay if I liked,' she laughed, encouraging the soldier to do likewise. 'Did you much want to see him?' she queried archly. 'I will happily fetch him from his furnace if you wish.'

'No, I wouldn't dream of distracting him when he is so engrossed,' the soldier replied seriously, 'especially as I am here for entirely selfish and frivolous reasons, for I simply wanted to know if I was sure of seeing you tonight? Both of you,' he stammered.

'I never can tell until the last minute,' Effie answered exasperatedly, lifting her shoulders and tilting her head; 'as you know, my husband does so hate parties.'

Paulizza lowered his voice and spoke in German. 'If I had gone tonight and you had stayed away, I should have imagined that it was because you were affronted by my actions yesterday.'

'Affronted? Of course not, but we can't discuss that,' she whispered in his native tongue.

'Perhaps I have made another error,' he began, rising to depart.

'No, don't go,' she insisted, standing before him and taking his hand persuasively. Deciding it best to continue loudly in English, she remarked lightly, 'It's coming up to ball season and I do so want to waltz! Won't you practise with me?'

'Now?' Paulizza asked, much surprised.

'Yes, why not? We only need to move a few things out of the way,' she insisted, dragging a table to one side and encouraging him to help her roll up the rug.

Boldly placing the soldier's hand on her hip, Effie hummed a waltz by Chopin as they began gliding about the room, as elegantly as two dancers ever did in a ballroom.

The moments flew as fast as their feet, nor did she pause before indicating a change of dance. A polka this time, fast and energetic, found them colliding with the furniture, yet neither wished to stop and continued laughing, not missing a beat and displaying their skill by adeptly maintaining a pace much hampered by the confines of a drawing room crowded with ornaments.

The sound of their steps, despite being delicate and well-timed, alerted Ruskin as he worked in silence down the corridor, however, and he stood unnoticed in the doorway for several moments until his vigorous applause succeeded in distracting them.

'Bravo!' he cried in high spirits, which unnerved rather than encouraged the pair, who broke their hold and looked embarrassed.

'Thank you. I do hope we didn't disrupt your work,' the solider apologised breathlessly.

'Far from it, I am not for dancing but that was very fine indeed. Have you been here long?' Ruskin asked, shaking Paulizza warmly by the hand.

'Not long, I merely dropped by to make sure that I would see you both this evening.'

'You should have called me,' he turned to Effie; 'I am much in need of some pleasant company to divert me from my work,' the insensitivity of which caused her to look to Paulizza knowingly.

'I should be going on my way,' the Austrian offered in a courtly manner, 'but I am most grateful to your wife for the dancing practice.'

'It doesn't appear that either of you were in need of it,' Ruskin beamed, holding Effie's waist with a possessiveness she despised.

***

When Paulizza had taken his leave, Ruskin having agreed to escort her to the ball, Effie sat quite still in her chamber before dressing and reflected on her fascination for the soldier, persuading herself that it was no more than a harmless flirtation, yet revealing her captivation by writing a lengthy account of him to her mother.

Mrs Gray was shocked to discover that her daughter took more interest in relating the young man's attributes than describing her famed surroundings, and thus replied by return of post offering words of caution and asking Effie to promise faithfully that her actions were not attracting notoriety, a warning her daughter resisted.

Effie flinched on Ruskin entering the salon as she was composing her defence one afternoon before Christmas, and seeing her jolt only piqued his curiosity to know why she was so guarded.

Peering over her shoulder so as to observe whom she was addressing, he became suspicious when she tucked the letter into the drawer of the desk and folded her hands upon it, visibly annoyed by the interruption.

'Are you writing to your mother again?'

'Why *again?*' she snapped, embracing her shawl. 'Aren't you always writing to yours?'

Without making it clear whether he spoke in jest or asperity, he remarked, 'It seems you write a deal more than I. So many in fact that I shall have to start calling you Mrs Scratch, for your pen is always scraping back and forth across the paper.'

'What rubbish.'

'I don't suppose you have anything good to say of *me* in your reports?'

'I hardly mention you,' she replied curtly, intending to wound him.

He shrugged casually. 'Then they must be very dull letters indeed, for most people consider me a most curious specimen of humanity.'

Saying which Ruskin sloped off to his study, though the disturbance had the odd effect of making his wife tear up the letter she had previously composed and write another, more dutiful, example referring to him in gushing terms.

"My Dear Mama,

Thank you for your letter of advice. I assure you I very much value
it and act upon it. I am so peculiarly situated, for as most men think
I live quite alone I am more exposed to their attentions, but I assure
you that I stop anything which might be hurtful to my reputation and
I only encourage the most perfect propriety.

Besides, I never could love anybody in the world but John, who
removes me from any desire to coquetry, which he declares I possess
very highly. I tell him every word Paulizza says to me and tell the
latter so too, so that they perfectly understand each other…"

But like all unworldly children, Effie soon forgot her mother's advice and,
shortly after receiving her parent's protestation, complained to Paulizza of
a sore throat one evening at a grand dinner and unthinkingly permitted
him to place his hands on her neck, much to the consternation of the
other guests.

'I too suffer, having sustained a wound to the head some time ago,' the
soldier related bravely whilst making his assessment of Effie. 'Sometimes I
arise in the morning without being able to see my hand in front of my face.'
And he rubbed his brow comically in order to make light of symptoms
which increasingly troubled him.

'Gracious, have you sought the opinion of a doctor?' she enquired
anxiously.

'Oh no, I've received much worse injuries than this,' Paulizza boasted,
'and anyway, we're evaluating *your* health tonight, not mine.'

'It sounds as though we oughtn't to be.'

Taking up her delicate wrist, he held it between his thumb and
forefinger and declared solemnly, 'Your pulse seems steady, but I don't
think it's telling me the true story of your heart,' a diagnosis which caused
Effie to colour deeply and withdraw from his touch, though she observed
that her husband continued his conversation oblivious as to the attention
they had aroused.

Imagining that anything she did in Venice would have no bearing on
her reputation back in England, she was not inclined to resist waltzing with

Paulizza several times later that evening when her husband encouraged him to do so.

It was impossible for Effie to walk down the crimson-carpeted stairs leading to the ballroom on Paulizza's arm without feeling very distinguished, the mirror and gilt room brilliant in the glow of the candlelight emanating from rows upon rows of crystal chandeliers, so heavy as to defy gravity.

As Paulizza took her hand and led her into the middle of the floor, two dozen men in every imaginable Austrian uniform of Cavalry and Infantry bowed to their dance partners on the striking up of the orchestra, and she wondered how she came to be a part of such a set.

'You won't forget me when you return to London?' Paulizza whispered in her ear after a few bars, words which made her light-headed when coupled with being spun around the room.

'Of course we won't,' she replied diplomatically.

'I meant *you*,' he emphasised, looking her full in the face until she almost forgot her steps and should have collided with another couple had it not been for the soldier steering her so confidently, his reassuring, guiding hand firm on her waist.

'I shan't forget,' she answered simply after a pause, this being the most that she could venture when her husband was looking on.

She could not guess what was passing through Ruskin's mind as he regarded them each time they passed by, yet the thought dissolved in the eyes of Paulizza who smiled at her so admiringly as to encourage the same from her. Nor did her gaiety diminish for the rest of the evening and long after she reluctantly departed with her husband.

Being so caught up in the excitement of dancing with Paulizza, Effie could not stop herself from writing a further ill-judged letter home on returning to their apartment just after midnight, referring to the soldier as her favourite physician and dance partner, with romantic undertones that caused her mother to fear imminent disaster.

Mrs Gray wrote by return of post, but suspected that it would not reach her daughter nearly fast enough, expressing the greatest concern over her acquaintance with the Austrian and suggesting that Ruskin might be intentionally compromising her in the hope of bringing about a separation, a form of manipulation which had not occurred to Effie.

Immediately denouncing such aspersions and defending her husband's absolute trust, these dark suppositions nevertheless prompted Effie to be more guarded when meeting Paulizza in future, a coolness which caused the soldier much confusion and misery.

Whereas Effie had found her husband's company vaguely tolerable in the early days of their marriage, the more he became engrossed in his work the more she loathed being near him.

Going to great lengths to avoid any hindrance to his workload, and preferring not to converse with her over dinner, Ruskin was so absorbed with the volume on Tintoretto he was reading that he did not notice Effie break down on being forced to sit in silence.

Seated at the opposite end of the banquet-size dining table, he paused only to turn a page or take a bite of his roast fowl, and was therefore startled on looking up to discover that his wife was quietly weeping, her food untouched before her.

'Has something distressed you?' he questioned, entirely unsuspecting that he was the cause of her upset and hoping that her tale would not be a long one, due to being desirous of returning to his book.

Finding it impossible to curtail her emotions any longer, Effie pushed her plate away and took a gasp of breath, her sobs inhibiting speech.

'I'm sick of being ignored!' she complained, no longer able to hold herself back from issuing forth a list of his faults.

'I wonder whether you think a husband is a thing to be fastened to his wife's waist like a pincushion, only to be taken about with her wherever she chooses to go. You don't seem to appreciate that I have important work to do,' Ruskin defended haughtily, snapping his book shut. 'You knew *that* before you married me, and rather than criticise me for it you ought to make yourself of service to me.'

'I'm not one of your protégés,' she argued.

'But you are my wife and as such I naturally hoped that you would be led to examine the beauty of Venice so that our joint sympathies would grant us *both* pleasure,' Ruskin countered. 'As you do not pay attention to anything I show you, however, you are naturally forced to pass many irksome and tedious hours alone, for I don't see why I should feel obliged to give up my studies in order to nanny you.'

'I never suspected that you married me simply in order to further my education,' Effie responded bitterly, brushing away a tear, 'or that you wanted a wife in *name* alone.'

'As you exhibit such a vehement disliking of me it would be nothing short of sinful to enter into a proper union with you,' Ruskin observed calmly. 'I wouldn't love *me* either if I were you, yet I see that there is someone you *do* care for.'

'Have you charged Crawley with spying on me?' Effie demanded, not realising that the very question betrayed her guilt.

'It's common knowledge that you're a flirt,' Ruskin stated matter-of-factly, folding his napkin.

'You show me no affection; this city is the only thing you worship,' she returned, bringing her fist down on the table and already feeling an overwhelming sense of relief at this outpouring, from which there could be no return and no regret.

'How can you think only of yourself?' Ruskin asked, frowning and shaking his head in disbelief. 'I am working against time, for my book shall be a monument to Venice when nothing else remains. God has lent us the earth for our life and it is a great entail. It belongs as much to those who are to come after us and we have no right, by anything that we do or neglect, to deprive them of that which was in our power to bequeath. And yet these very walls are crumbling before our eyes, dissolving as surely as a sugar lump in a teacup.'

'Is not our marriage in the same predicament?' Effie fumed, rising from the table and storming out in a temper she had never yet revealed to Ruskin but which had been stored up ever since the failure of their wedding night.

Whilst Effie had no more physical yearning for Ruskin than he towards her, this did not prevent her from feeling the pain of such indifference and rejection. Attention, admiration and flattery from others was the natural substitute to a beautiful young woman ignored by her husband, and she forgave herself liberally for feeding upon such satiates.

A MARRIAGE DISSOLVING

NTERMINABLE GREY SKIES AND TORRENTIAL STORMS MADE
Venice's inhabitants weary and claustrophobic, for there were only
so many balls to divert their attention from all they could not enjoy
during the day.

It poured with rain, such as is only seen in Venice: a deluge which merged
with the lagoon, flooded the streets and made the squares almost impassable
on foot. Nonetheless, Ruskin and Effie ventured towards the port in readiness
of the steamer that was to take her away, having agreed that she would return
to England while he remained behind in order to complete his research.

A great many other passengers were preparing to board; but unlike
the fond farewells Effie witnessed, she moved away when Ruskin
attempted to kiss her. Flushed with silent rage, she had no illusions as
to his complacency regarding her departure and therefore rebuffed any
disingenuous display.

'It's vital for my work that I should stay,' he justified, trying in vain to
make their parting less awkward. 'Crawley will look after you.'

But Effie refused to answer him and perceived Crawley's embarrassment on being in the presence of a couple so clearly at odds. The moment she arrived back in London could hardly come soon enough, nor was it clear how long they could continue to live together when once her husband returned.

Effie, holding her bonnet, the ribbons of which flapped wildly in the squall, refused to speak or look at Ruskin, prompting him to bid her adieu with the merest tilt of his hat. Opening his umbrella on walking away from the port, he was a pathetic figure, so she thought, as shadowy and isolated as Venice in a thunderstorm.

She watched him go, praying for the sight of another, craning her neck to see if Paulizza, in his striking uniform, would make an appearance; she was desperate at the prospect of leaving the city without expressing her sorrow in parting from the one person who had been glad of her company.

A few moments before the boat was due to launch, she flushed on observing the soldier in his bright tunic, while he, no longer worried about social graces or the fact that Crawley was looking on, embraced Effie fervently on reaching her, tenderly kissing her cheeks in the most passionate, yet noble lament.

Too appreciative of this display of affection to mind the impropriety, she was so moved by his emotional outpouring as to be almost thankful when he had gone; so great was his distress that she could not help but cry with him and ever afterwards compare this strong, brave man, so overwhelmed with grief, to her cold husband who expressed far less attachment to her than the buildings he would continue to devote himself to in her absence.

It was impossible for Crawley to observe these doomed young lovers without experiencing a degree of pity at life pulling them asunder, and he considered it as well to remain silent about the scene he had witnessed in light of the uncertainty of the pair ever meeting again. Out of indignation at Effie's deception towards his master, however, he remained officious and curt for the duration of the voyage, carrying out his duties with no sign of the sympathy which had been sparked despite his vehement loyalty to Ruskin.

Decidedly melancholic after leaving Effie at the steamer, despite not really being sorry to see her go, Ruskin wasted the day by strolling aimlessly through the main thoroughfares which appeared ghostlike in the enshrouding mist.

Eventually finding himself back at St Mark's Square for no purpose other than to admire the Basilica and shelter from the rain for a time, he lingered in the dark cloisters of the cathedral, where the draught chilled him through and through and the stained-glass windows cast a glow like the blood of kings and queens.

The rain was depressingly relentless as he stood in the entrance looking out at the square, practically devoid of people save for a cluster of middle-class European men sitting idly inside a café sipping strong coffee and smoking cigars, a few locals hurrying home, and a bevy of doves undeterred by the weather, feeding on a handful of crumbs which an impoverished old Italian woman scattered to the winds.

Regardless of the downpour, the Austrian military band blew on their bombastic brass instruments in the centre of the piazza just as they always did; the sounds jarring strangely with the vespers being conducted from inside the cathedral, as if they too were at war. It seemed wrong to Ruskin that the march largely succeeded in drowning out the solemn evening Mass, as if the imposters' desire to enforce their own heritage on the city was uncompromising, no matter whether or not there was anyone to hear them.

Only knots of beggars, ingrained with dirt, listened but paid no attention to these confused melodies as they sheltered beneath various arches, and Ruskin was struck by the tragedy of the poor always having to accept their rulers complacently, much like the weather they endured day in, day out – unprotected save for the half-cover provided by a doorway or passage and as washed up as the city itself.

Ruskin could not put himself in the right frame of mind for carrying out any research, not only due to the rain but to the ennui which had come over him following Effie's flight. Forlorn as he turned away from the imposing beauty of the cathedral, he commenced a circuitous route back to the apartment where his wife would no longer be waiting for him or criticising him for reading while he dined.

It was an odd sensation to have a spouse whom he felt no earthly connection with, and he wondered if he was simply not the type of man to feel a deep affection for another human being. He loved painted angels and sculptures much greater than real women of flesh and blood.

As he walked beside a narrow stretch of canal he came across a pair of Italian lovers sheltering in a doorway, the woman allowing herself to be embraced and kissed by the man without appearing to care if passers-by should see them, prompting Ruskin to question how people could be so free with their feelings.

He had never witnessed such overt sensuality in any country save Italy, something he felt a deep revulsion towards. To his mind the city was a sacred place, and as such people and all their sordid deeds defiled her. Did *he* alone value this unique and holy sanctum, he pondered, hurrying past the couple as fast as he could.

Perhaps Effie had also been subjected to such scenes of carnality during her walks alone, for Crawley had protected her secret to no avail, Ruskin having long suspected that Effie would not have been content to remain indoors for days on end.

Any disappointment in his wife only heightened his supreme grief in Venice's decrepitude as he expertly navigated her narrow streets and bridges, dignified in her decay and left for beholding in the final period of her decline. Merely a ghost upon the sands of the seas, she was so weak, so quiet, so bereft of all but her loveliness, that anyone might well doubt, as they watched her faint reflection in the mirror of the lagoon, which was the city and which the shadow.

This morbidity was not the result of any longing for Effie's company, but only the bleak assessment of his life which their rupture had inevitably hastened, causing him to experience a surge of inspiration as he went, careless of returning to his solitary apartment.

Partly in gratefulness of no longer having to worry about a wife or attend social soirées he had no interest in, his mood gradually lifted and he determined to start the morrow with a new sense of discovery and purpose. The fact that there were no demands upon him was a liberation that made him want to prolong the separation for as long as possible.

Yet Ruskin overestimated his temporary enthusiasm, for the result of so much hard, dry toil and exhaustive analysis, coupled with the unhappy associations of places he had introduced to Effie, meant that he lost Venice's charm before he was done and realised that it would be some time, years perhaps, before his love for this idolised land would flourish once more.

He glided along this canal or that only to look upon the buildings lining them as so many mouldings, windows and doors, with no more of his old devotion than the gondoliers who took their majestic surroundings entirely for granted and laughed at the tourists who swooned and groaned with naive, ignorant appreciation.

Everything appeared infinitely sad, for Venice not only made him anxious as to her potential destruction but his own mortality and the sense that time was running away, a mood which had, he well knew, an unfortunate effect upon his writing.

He grew irritable whenever he perceived that the gondoliers he hired got bored of waiting for him to complete his sketches, when the bells rang as he worked among the steeples, or at the tide going in or out when he least wanted it to. Just as places had the power to shape emotions, so his emotions influenced how he felt about places.

Perhaps he had enjoyed so much of lovely things that they had almost ceased to be lovely. The canals seemed shallower and dirtier than before and he quite lost the childish delight at floating along the lagoon and watching the oars and waves.

Akin to the city's own dissolution, there was no way to stop the increasing sense of hollowness and detachment Ruskin felt towards his environment. The days flew like dust in the wind until, on his mother writing and declaring herself "sickened and sorrowed to see his face again", he was provided with an excuse to flee like a Venetian escaping Austrian rule.

THE SEASON
XL

Having relished being welcomed into the Venetian elite, Effie was determined to play just as prominent a role in London upon returning to Park Street, using Ruskin's absence to reflect carefully upon the state of their marriage and how best to please herself.

Setting feelings of animosity aside, along with any thought of a severance that would see her relegated to Perthshire, she was buoyed by the prospect of seeing as little of her husband as she had in Italy and concluded that not even the most dramatic alteration in his conduct would ever again persuade her to demand either his affection or his companionship, for she needed neither in order to derive satisfaction from life.

To implement this ambition Effie contrived to solicit the support of John James who had long wanted his son to be more visible in society and whom Ruskin perceived had been in cahoots with his wife as soon as they settled down to their first family dinner together at Denmark Hill, his father hardly allowing him to draw breath before expressing his vehement desire that he should take full advantage of his wife's success amongst the nobility of Europe.

Encouraging Ruskin to ingratiate himself into the highest rank, he proclaimed, 'It seems to me that Effie would be far more likely to tolerate the empty days ahead of her, and being so often left to her own devices, if she had some excitement to anticipate, isn't that so, my dear?' exchanging a smile with his daughter-in-law.

'I had rather thought she had enough adventure in Venice,' Ruskin remarked dryly, yet failing to make Effie blush or look down with shame.

Instead, she remained as cool and composed as ever, wryly observing the discussion between the two men as if they were puppets to which she held the strings. Knowing how much her husband loathed being lectured to on the subject of fraternising with those he did not care tuppence worth for, gave her a great deal of satisfaction.

'The more reason not to allow her to grow weary now. As you wrote to me yourself,' John James reminded, 'the Alps will not wrinkle but your wife's cheeks *will*,' winking at Effie by way of proving his advocacy.

Thus Ruskin, propelled by his wife and his father, felt himself duty-bound to escort her to the largest and most exclusive, yet stiffest, dullest and fidgetiest, dinners and receptions in all London, not to mention the pinnacle of being presented to Queen Victoria and Prince Albert at court.

'Well, what does Her Majesty *really* look like?' Margaret asked Ruskin eagerly the day following the presentation, for she shared John James's view that their son's introduction to the royal family was the greatest acknowledgement of his eminence.

'Much younger and prettier than I expected and very like her pictures, even those which are thought to flatter most,' he reported generously, helping himself to a sliver of sponge cake.

'Is that so?'

'She offered her hand very graciously but looked bored, as well she might with a quarter of a mile of people to bow to her. That said, after *us* having to wait over an hour and three-quarters to see *her*, I really think she might have allowed us to look at her for at least a minute.'

'And was Effie well received?' his mother interrogated, determined to extract all the details despite her son's flippancy.

'She got through it unscathed considering what a crush there was. The floor was covered with the ruins of ladies dresses, torn lace and fallen flowers, yet I still heard people say, "What a beautiful dress", which gratified her immensely.'

'I can imagine,' his mother sniffed, taking a sip of tea so as to restrain herself from saying anything further.

Ruskin regarded it as no small irony that whilst his wife and parents regaled in him being the toast of London, he dreaded such extravagance and attention. Judging it a great imposition to have to draw himself away from his Venetian masterpiece, he agreed to attend such soirées only out of courtesy to his mother and father who, having come from humble origins, were much gratified to witness their son's rise in stature.

Being a naturally outgoing young woman, Effie meanwhile thrived whenever in company, and having grown weary of the constraints of her own drawing room was willing to put up with the many disadvantages of being married to a man she did not love in return for being fêted by an echelon of society she was now entirely comfortable within.

Even Ruskin saw that she became more agreeable at home whenever her diary was full, and on witnessing this change John James and Margaret became convinced that this compromise on their son's part would be enough to save the couple from a grievous rift resulting from their blatant incompatibility.

It was not long before his parents were forced to concede that this way of life was at the cost of their son's constitution, however, for it was clear that he found their trivial calendar of balls and dinners intolerable and far from conducive to his writing, which had become stunted.

Whilst Effie was taking a holiday at Bowerswell, Ruskin therefore took the opportunity of confiding in them his unwillingness to continue with the rigmarole of trying to appease everyone by playing a role he felt himself ill equipped for.

'When we married, I expected to change *her* and she expected to change *me*,' he related sorrowfully, 'and because neither of us have succeeded we are both displeased. I think that it may be as difficult for Effie to live *without* society, as it is for me to go *into* it, even though I told her fairly what sort of person I was before I married her. I *am* what I always was.'

Effie returned from Scotland in October, bringing the rain clouds and squalls with her. She had not expected to find her husband at Park Street, let alone contentedly installed in his study and more focussed on work than ever, for he never chose to work anywhere but Denmark Hill when she was home.

'I'm glad to see that you are feeling refreshed from the country air,' Ruskin complimented, resting his pen and rising in order to kiss her cheek, all the brighter for being away from London.

'Yes, but it was so *very* quiet, with hardly any form of entertainment,' she returned giddily; 'I fear Venice and London have quite spoiled me.'

Smiling wryly, he patted her hand in a fatherly manner. 'I expect you can't wait to be back in the thick of it again?'

'Yes, I shall go directly to a ball!'

'I must beg you to refuse all invitations for me,' he urged. 'I will not see anybody when they call on me, nor call on anybody. I am going to do my own work in my own way, in my own room. While *you* should accept as many as you like, and I imagine *that* will be a great many.'

'As you wish,' she replied merrily, removing her bonnet and rubbing her neck which ached after the long journey.

'I'm sure you know enough people by now for me to dispense with following you about carrying the train of your dress,' Ruskin continued disparagingly, 'and I have every confidence in you being able to make even more acquaintances without me in tow.'

Effie raised her eyebrows and smiled. 'It's true that people are generally hospitable whenever they see that I am without my husband,' she berated provokingly, almost tempted to say "a husband".

'It's almost like being a widow, but without the sombreness of having to wear black or refrain from dancing,' Ruskin remarked, leading her upstairs.

'My relatives in Scotland were beginning to think you *had* died,' she agreed, tripping lightly up the stairs in her conceit at always having the last word and little thinking that her husband had another blow ready.

'Whilst you were away,' he began authoritatively, holding open the door to a large second floor bedroom that was never used, 'I took the liberty of arranging a separate chamber for myself, as I am an early riser and neither wish to be disturbed by you coming home late or awaken you when I go out early. It will be my habit to leave for Denmark Hill shortly after breakfast and remain working there until six.'

Content to spend as much time apart from his wife as he reasonably could, come May Day Ruskin took pleasure in listening to the birds of Denmark Hill through the open window of his old study, unmindful of Effie who was attending the opening of Prince Albert's Great Exhibition, John James having procured her a ticket at ludicrous expense.

Effie had grown tremendously in confidence on going about unaccompanied, no longer having to do so covertly as in Venice. Adding to her enjoyment was the fact that such behaviour was in strict opposition to her mother-in-law's dictates, who, after hearing accounts of her activities, demanded that her son put a stop to such freedoms.

Ruskin no longer cared to take notice of his mother's aspersions that this was merely the preamble to a more serious compromise to his wife's reputation, however, for he and Effie had finally established a harmonious way of living together, albeit unconventional.

He could not guess how often his wife's thoughts returned to Venice and Paulizza, nor how hard she found it that her life could be so outwardly dazzling yet so inwardly miserable. Although people were very hospitable and made her out to be a much better person than she really was, she would still rather have been in Venice than crammed into the overcrowded salons of Grosvenor House.

How desperately she longed for another glimpse at the calm and melancholy beauty of the Grand Canal from her palazzo window, or have her uncomfortable London carriage miraculously transformed into a gliding gondola.

Ruskin, who believed himself amenable to all his wife's whims, felt helpless to remedy Effie's gaining discontent, nor could he remain in the same room with her without being forced to suffer an argument.

Coming upon her one afternoon as she was staring absentmindedly out of the drawing room window, he enquired pleasantly, 'What are you looking at, my dear?'

On which her shoulders rose and, turning abruptly as if he had accused her of some wrongdoing, she replied, 'Nothing.'

'What are you *thinking* of, then?' he persisted, still jovially.

'A great many things,' Effie answered, yet more antagonistically.

'Why don't you tell me some of them,' Ruskin went on, perplexed by her obvious vexation.

'I was thinking of operas and excitement, and, and… a great many things,' she snapped, flushing crimson.

'And what conclusions did you come to?' he goaded, amused that even she was no longer satisfied in looking forward to some form of society event come the evening.

'None, because you interrupted me!'

'I shan't do so again,' Ruskin replied bluntly, approaching her that he might survey her in disgust; before adding, 'I often think it remarkable that I once thought you modest, open-hearted and gentle in manner, for no-one, observing your grace and pleasantness outside, would ever believe the kind of attitude you exhibit at home, where your temper turns this house into purgatory.'

Determined not to permit Effie enough time to think of a rebuttal, Ruskin left her to her preciously guarded thoughts, hardly caring what his wife dwelt upon so intently.

She remained by the window until, a short time later, Crawley brought her word that her husband had gone out and would not return for several days, well knowing that there was nothing she loathed so much as being left alone when she was depressed and that she found even *his* company preferable to none at all.

THE BROTHERHOOD

E FFIE MARKED THE DAY OF HER FOURTH WEDDING
anniversary by drawing a black cross in her journal, severe
enough to stain her fingers with ink, for there was no reason to
celebrate her still unconsummated marriage or to think that she would
ever have the family she once desired.

Rather than dwelling further on her situation or giving in to
tears of self-pity, however, she prayed to God to grant her a means of
freeing herself, every day looking for a sign that He had listened to
her plea.

Thus, when Ruskin a short time afterwards became acquainted
with a group of handsome young painters calling themselves The Pre-
Raphaelite Brotherhood, Effie saw this as a possible chance of being
rescued from her desperate unhappiness, not unlike a heroine in one of
their pictures of medieval ladies.

Still too attached to Paulizza to identify her knight at first, she quickly
decried her initial disinterest when her husband first leapt to the defence

of the artists whose work had been brutally attacked within *The Times'* critique of the Royal Academy's Summer Exhibition.

'Read,' Ruskin demanded, thrusting the newspaper into Effie's hand as she lolled on the sofa in the drawing room, struck down with her customary malaise. Pointing to the article and pacing up and down while she scanned it, he smiled upon seeing her tedium change into animation.

'"We can hardly imagine anything more ugly, graceless and unpleasant than Mr Millais's picture of 'Christ in the Carpenter's Shop'. Such a collection of splayed feet, puffed joints and misshapen limbs was assuredly never before made", she read, pausing to laugh. 'I like that, but *you* don't usually find such things amusing.' And she guffawed until her eyes became moist.

Becoming annoyed by her flippancy, Ruskin blustered, 'I intend to challenge the critic who wrote this to reconsider what qualifies a *well-executed* work from a *poor* one. Yes, I mean to put before the public such an argument that will not only redeem these artists' tarnished reputations but mark them, singly and collectively, as the country's most talented young painters.'

'Goodness, aren't they lucky to have *you* fighting their corner,' Effie scoffed, closing her eyes in weariness of her husband's arrogance.

Too inflamed by the prospect of challenging the newspaper to notice his wife's insult, he stood before her and, with one arm behind his back, read aloud his drafted response in full lecturing mode, '"They are endeavouring to paint, with the highest possible degree of completion, what they see in nature, without reference to conventional or established rules, but by no means to imitate the style of any past epoch. Their works are, in finish of drawing and splendour of colour, the best in the Royal Academy and I have great hope that they may become the foundation of a more earnest and able school of art than we have seen for centuries."'

'Is that all?' she yawned affectedly, much amused when he stomped out of the room.

Ruskin was much gratified to receive a heartfelt letter of thanks from the artists the day following the publication of the letter in *The Times*, announcing smugly to his wife over breakfast, 'You see? Some people appreciate my opinion.'

'I dare say they do,' she returned nonchalantly.

'I propose we call on them!'

'Now?' Effie asked, bemused by her husband's keenness to become their champion.

'Yes, right this moment, for I'm extremely keen to find out what sort of men they are, and *you* aren't so very busy,' he observed.

'Very well,' she submitted, rising from the table, 'but I expect you'll only be disappointed when you meet them.'

'Why do you say that?' he said, taking a gulp of tea.

'Well, *The Times*' critic *can't* be so very wrong. I expect you were only being contrary in defending them,' Effie taunted, looking over the letter he held out.

'Thank you, but I think I know how to judge pictures better than either *The Times* or you,' he provoked, snatching the letter.

'Perhaps, but are you so good a judge of people?'

Effie, despite her determination to disagree with her husband about everything under the sun, found that she soon changed her view upon meeting the founder of the brotherhood, John Everett Millais, whose studio was located in his parents' smart, ebony-painted townhouse on Gower Street, a short distance from their own residence.

The young man, with sandy curls and a keen bright eye, shook Ruskin heartily by the hand and declared, 'I thank you most profusely for your support of our philosophy,' on inviting them inside his chaotic den.

'I should not have done so had not I believed you all to be a talent worth championing,' he assured him, half-distracted on wandering around the disorganised studio lined with Millais's unfinished canvases.

Effie was also fascinated by such creativity and how the artist flapped and fussed in the attempt to make them both comfortable, for there was hardly a clean surface amid the paints, brushes and general paraphernalia, least of all a seat to offer.

'You find me at sixes and sevens,' the artist apologised humbly, running his hands through his paint-dappled hair in exasperation of the disorder from which beauty, nonetheless, peeped out from every corner.

'*This* is nothing compared to the disarray of Turner's workroom, I assure you,' Ruskin heartened, examining a canvas with the magnifying glass he withdrew from his pocket.

Despite his guest's graciousness, Millais was conscious of needing to make a good impression if there was any chance of Ruskin becoming his patron, and so he exhaustively set about trying to charm and impress him.

'Both I and the rest of the brotherhood feel that we should have been positively ruined without your support,' he began enthusiastically, 'especially when Dickens lambasted my picture.'

'What does *he* know of such things?' Ruskin quipped good-humouredly. 'If only novelists would stick to writing books, eh?' A sentiment which prompted Millais and Effie to unite in laughter.

She was impressed by the artist's animation upon explaining the inspiration behind his latest subjects, along with his delight when her husband offered to purchase several at the full asking price, enforcing the miraculous turnabout in his fortunes, his boyish expression of surprise and disbelief winning when contrasted with Ruskin's over-confidence.

Wondering all the while how Millais's mother had enough tolerance to relinquish such a substantial portion of her house, Effie remarked, 'Mrs Millais must be your *greatest* patron for having accommodated such an enterprise.'

'My mother is indeed a wonder; it only grieves me that, as yet, the fruits of my labours have failed to make either a favourable impression on the public or a financial improvement to my pocket,' he answered modestly.

Witnessing the obvious pleasure he took in his work, Effie could see that it would be impossible for anyone, least of all a mother, to refuse him anything. She was much struck by this engaging twenty-two-year-old, her husband's junior by a decade and hers by just a year, for he possessed such an infectious energy that she forgot her own joylessness whenever she looked into his face.

411

'You must take courage from my husband's words, Mr Millais,' she cheered, smiling.

'Please, you must both call me John,' the artist urged.

'I too,' Ruskin interjected, turning his attention from sketches he had found lying about carelessly.

'I can't call you *both* John if we are all to become firm friends,' Effie laughed.

'Then call me by my second name, Everett.'

'Very well,' she agreed as he took up his sketchpad and attempted to draw a likeness of her profile.

Effie smiled to observe that Everett's mind was so full of invention that he could hardly keep still for a moment and, not being a man of many words, preferred to sketch ideas rather than converse, his pencil and his paintbrush being his natural way of expressing himself.

Having been hailed as a child prodigy on becoming the youngest student accepted by the Royal Academy, Millais's enthusiasm for art was not represented by flowery rhetoric like her husband but displayed through his work, which informed even the casual observer of his deep understanding and appreciation of both his present environment and those of folklore and legend which he was able to re-imagine with an unharnessed creativity and a palette of vivid colours.

Notwithstanding his immense promise, Millais was still greatly in need of a respected proponent, and therefore Ruskin's approval was all, with the power to not only save him from struggling against the tide for years, but catapult him into being one of the most sought-after artists of the day.

Surprised at how submissively the artist took up any suggestions Ruskin offered, with no sign of the conceit typical of young men, Effie began to question if Millais was merely being sycophantic, finally concluding that she would be even *more* in awe of him if that were the case, so rare was it to meet someone astute enough to employ a strategy when handling her husband.

Even when Millais did voice an opinion contrary to Ruskin's, he did so in such a well-mannered and unassuming tone that his supporter was pleased rather than offended.

'Although I can't boast of being as well read as the rest of the brotherhood,' Millais ventured as the two men stood before a canvas depicting Shakespeare's Ophelia, 'I still can't make out how our hard-edged realism isn't in complete contradiction to all that you formerly declared great in art.'

'My theories are not as inconsistent as you suppose, Everett, for whilst *your* works do not in any way resemble Turner's, you both display an idealistic devotion to nature and seek to present on canvas what you find in reality,' saying which, Ruskin illustrated the point by drawing Effie's attention to an intricately painted leaf. 'To understand me at all you must know this of me, that my opinions are *living* things and are therefore changing continually. Yet they are the changes of a tree, not a cloud.'

Within a few hours, Ruskin had taken the young artist so completely under his wing that he not only commissioned him to paint his portrait, but invited him to return with them to Park Street for a week, an invitation which thrilled Effie, who was keen to extend her acquaintance with Millais and very much hoped that his abundant optimism would change the typically strained atmosphere in the house.

Effie and Ruskin were exceedingly grateful for any outsider who might prevent disagreements simply by being there, whilst, as both husband and wife vied for Millais's favour, they displayed only their best qualities and were never once seen to quarrel.

This in turn led Millais to believe that the pair were quietly content in their own way, although he found it difficult to imagine any young woman entirely suited to living with a man such as Ruskin.

The three got on famously over the course of the next few days, with Effie no longer inclined to rise late or mope around the house as she usually did, Millais succeeding in bringing out her former sense of humour and amiableness, traits which Ruskin had long since ceased to excite.

Effie meanwhile encouraged Ruskin's generous attentions to the artist and, increasingly swept up with further ideas of how he could best help this newly discovered talent, he devised ways in which they might all spend more time together.

'Would you be in favour of accompanying my wife and me to Switzerland this summer?' he suggested as the three of them dined together one evening. 'There is nothing like travel to unharness the skills of an artist.'

'That is very kind of you, but—' Millais began.

'You perhaps think it premature after only a few days' acquaintance,' Ruskin interrupted, fearing a negative answer, 'yet, and I think I can speak for my wife here also, you already feel like an intimate friend whom we have known for many years.'

'Oh yes,' she agreed. 'Do say you'll join us?'

'I only wish I could,' he stammered apologetically, running his hands through his hair uneasily, 'not least because I'm enjoying your company so very much and should greatly like to paint the Alps.'

'Then it's settled,' Ruskin seized; 'let us toast to our adventure!'

'Alas, I must decline your kind invitation,' Millais interjected, raising his hand in order to halt his host's excitement, 'for I have made a prior commitment to spend the summer painting with a friend and he is sensitive enough to never speak to me again if I throw him over.'

'Can you believe it, Holman? I have just spent the entire week with Ruskin and his wife, dining and breakfasting with them each day!' Millais declared to his fellow artist, Holman Hunt, on returning to his Gower Street studio the following week.

'Really?' Hunt replied, frowning in bafflement as he imbibed liquor from a paint-stained teacup. 'I thought Ruskin was famous for being surly and unsociable.'

'Not with me. We're such good friends that he and his wife even wish me to accompany them to Switzerland,' he continued, putting the finishing touches to a work which his benefactor had promised to purchase as soon as the paint was dry.

'I hope you won't leave the rest of us behind when you're more celebrated than we?' Hunt teased, ill concealing how hard done by he felt at being left out.

'I am still trying to convince Ruskin to like my work *more* than Turner's,' Millais scoffed; 'and to illustrate what a loyal pal I am to you, I declined his offer of a holiday, informing him that I've already promised to spend the summer with *you*,' he went on, throwing a paint-splattered cloth at Hunt in jest.

'I'm honoured, but I don't expect you to sacrifice yourself on my behalf,' he demurred rancorously, thrusting the day's paper under his friend's nose. 'I see the first volume of Ruskin's *Stones of Venice* has just been published, yet I doubt if it becomes popular with the larger public, for they are as incapable of understanding it as I am.'

'I don't suppose Ruskin cares one way or the other,' his comrade replied, as familiarly as if he had known the author for many years. 'As he said to me the other day, "Everett, I do not write for fame, or money, or for conscience' sake, but out of *necessity*".'

'Rather like you paint?' Holman Hunt sniggered, referring to his companion's lust for money and celebrity.

Hunt was not alone in predicting poor sales of Ruskin's latest book, merely the first volume out of a tome as magnificent in scale as Venice herself, for John James grew agitated at the prospect of failure in light of the considerable funds he was continuing to lay out in order for his son to complete his research.

As Ruskin's one and only proofreader, adviser and investor, who graciously financed the substantial printing costs whilst allowing his son to claim all the royalties, John James felt himself fully entitled to enquire as to what returns might be expected.

Broaching the subject shortly after the book's publication, he caught his son off guard one evening by raising the blunt question, 'I wonder if you are enough concerned by the obvious lack of demand for the work to discontinue the project?'

'Heavens no! And nor should it shake your confidence. I believe you will like it better when it's finished, Father,' he replied temperately, rising to light his father a pipe. 'At any event it would be foolish to abandon the labour of two whole years now that it is just approaching completion.'

'But the public don't seem to have taken to it,' John James persisted.

'The public?' Ruskin reiterated with contempt. 'I never could write for the *public*. I cannot write anything but what is *in* me and interests me, and I never *have* except under the conviction of a thing's being important, wholly irrespective of the public's thinking so too. My power, such as it is, would be lost the moment I tried to catch people by fine writing. That said, books are divisible into two classes, the books of the hour and the books of all time, and I mean to write the latter not the former.'

His father raised his eyebrows in response and asked, 'Why, then, do people not buy it?'

His son, leaning against the mantle and taking a sip of sherry which allowed him the chance to reflect, went on, 'People should read like they take medicine, by advice and not by advertisement. I never promised them romance, I only promised them *stones*.'

'You did not used to be so sensitive to my critiques,' John James chided, clenching the pipe between his back teeth as an irritable baby might soothe toothache.

'That's true, perhaps I have become so due to my work costing me more labour,' his son admitted with a sigh. '*That* coupled with being nervous as to how my books will be received.'

'Nervous? Just this moment you scorned writing to please anyone! You are a contradiction in terms,' he despaired, rubbing his forehead.

'Although I will not tailor my writing, I would still *like* people to think my works contained some value,' Ruskin argued. 'You think that I have failed and perhaps that is true. The horse fails just at the leap, not as it crosses the ploughed field. But, if it is a good horse, the rider should know it has rightly measured its powers, and that he had better be shaken in his seat a little rather than go altogether.'

'I perceive that you consider yourself a great genius since this latest volume,' his father admonished, lifting the book from the table and flicking through its pages appraisingly, an act which wound up his son to concert pitch.

'I believe I possess genius certainly, something which is quite different from mere cleverness in the way that millions of people are, lawyers, physicians and the like, for *genius* is a superior way of seeing things.'

'Pardon my anxieties, I will not call them fears,' John James reassured. 'You interpret my concern as a desire to recoup the money I have invested, but you are mistaken, for I never lend without the intention of loss. Nor have I any criticism of the work itself, your words are finer than ever, but regardless of the substance or truth it contains it is whether men will care to *read* it that I question, and I do so only because I wish you to achieve the success you deserve.'

'Our interpretation of the word "success" has always greatly differed, Father. For me, it has been worth all the mental and physical exertions I have undergone, the early mornings and the frostbitten fingers acquired whilst scaling cathedrals and palaces, it will probably even cost me my marriage, but I would gladly sacrifice everything over again in order to put my name, and therefore *yours*, to such a book. I only trust that you will agree when you read it in its entirety, and without overly weighing up any debts I have incurred.'

'I had no idea the enterprise meant so much to you,' John James granted, surprisingly moved by his son's display of passion and, for a time at least, remaining silent.

A GREAT LOSS

O NE REASON ALONE CONVINCED EFFIE TO JOURNEY WITH her husband to Venice again, eighteen months after her first expedition to the city, and that was the prospect of seeing Charles Paulizza, whom not even Millais could dispel her fixed impression of, or cast away her longing to see.

Although she was sorry to leave the young artist behind, having been grateful for his spirited company over the past months, Effie did not hesitate to trade him for the soldier's wit, charm and gallantry, nor London society people in favour of more cultivated Europeans.

She had heard reports of the city having become more cosmopolitan than ever thanks to the fashionable Viennese society who had naturally followed when their country became the new governing power of Venice, and Effie whiled away her months in London anticipating countless balls and receptions spent in the company of Paulizza, whom she expected to have been well rewarded for his strategic efforts in capturing the city.

'Venice is more beautiful than ever,' Ruskin announced with less feeling than usual on opening the shutters of the drawing room belonging to the Casa Metzler apartment his father had rented for six months, an expense he took entirely for granted.

But Effie's interest was taken up with the prospect of being reunited with the handsome solider, and she asked as casually as possible, 'Have you heard anything from Paulizza?'

Her husband, who had been standing with his back to her, made a sudden movement on hearing this name, and turning around with a look of foreboding answered hesitantly, 'I was going to tell you, but I didn't want to upset you on the journey, my dear.'

'What is it?' she urged, recalling the many scenarios that had passed through her mind in the months they had been absent: that Paulizza had been billeted elsewhere; that he was engaged or married; or, worst of all, injured. But before she had time to visualise any of these eventualities the words she had *never* contemplated came.

'He died a short time ago.'

'He died?' Effie repeated, crestfallen. 'But how, when the fighting stopped long ago?'

'They say it was an old head wound,' her husband explained as delicately as he could, having been greatly distressed by the news himself.

'Oh God,' she uttered, and Ruskin saw at once that she was far more overcome than he.

He surprised himself by feeling no jealousy at the sight of her grief, despite it being clear that it stemmed from passionate love. Instead he wished to empathise and comfort her; feebly removing a handkerchief from his breast pocket as her eyes overflowed and the shock gave way to intense pain, he approached and rested his hand gently upon her shoulder, powerless to know how he might ease her suffering.

'I too am grieved,' he affirmed, 'for I never knew a nobler person than Charles Paulizza. Brave and kind, he was knightly in courtesy and ready at any instant to lay down his life for his country and emperor,' a tribute which only caused Effie to sob uncontrollably, as did his conclusion: 'At least he went from this earth taking pride in his work.'

Ruskin knew his words to be deeply inadequate, nor did Effie have the strength or inclination to conceal her devastation at the soldier's death, her sorrow being far greater than any she would have endured on the news of her own husband's demise.

He recognised that it was so and accepted her misplaced regard with a courage and honour inspired by the lost soldier whom he blamed no more than she. It was the way of things that his wife had turned to another for feelings he had bestowed on a land of stone and marble palaces, and so he left her to her memories and tears and went back to his city.

It was several days before Effie recovered enough composure to accompany Ruskin anywhere, and when she did she was conscious of her grief-stricken appearance, pale and red-eyed from sleepless nights spent regretting having ever returned to London.

Her desolation piqued her husband's sensibilities, yet made him gentler and more patient than she had ever known, something that worsened her anguish tenfold.

Adopting a black velvet dress with lace collar and cuffs, she often noticed him regarding her in concern, and sometimes, when they were in their box at the opera, he would take her hand and press it as if offering comfort to a friend in mourning.

Yet despite this display of sympathy, Paulizza's passing firmly established Effie's determination to be freed from her loveless marriage. Nor was her courage shaken when her husband learned of Turner's death one cold, bright day in late December, for it seemed strangely fitting that they should both lose the people they most idolised.

Ruskin was walking among the tombs of Isola di San Michele overlooking Murano, the island of glass said to produce vessels so refined as to smash when filled with poison, when the letter from his father told him of the artist's passing, tidings which suddenly permitted him to revere Turner as he might a god and curse those who had ever decried his name.

Death, both her glory and her plague, was never more omnipresent than upon that serene island, with no human companions save for those deceased. The hoarfrost lay untrodden and thick upon the ground, while not a cloud obscured the Alps, and the green waves sighed sadly along the cemetery shore. Sitting for a time among those comfortably installed in their graves, wondering at the futility of going on each day when all present achievements were destined to be forgotten, Ruskin wept.

Having been drawn out of the bustling canals and streets of the main island, the wreaths of the sea mist wove in and out of the gravestones like mourning veils, until the pure, yet thorny air of winter, which fairly took his breath away, awakened the need in him to pack up his things and return to England.

'Is it not curious that I have been working, this past three weeks, in the cemetery that Turner once painted, *and* that I should be in that very place when I learned of his passing?' he mused to Effie over dinner.

A kind of friendship had sprung up between them following Paulizza's death, while the acknowledged failure of their marriage was another kind of bereavement which touched them both and held a light up to their ugliest flaws.

'His death leaves an infinite void,' she sympathised.

Ruskin nodded in agreement, adding resolutely, 'As I was long prepared for his passing I consider it the *world's* misfortune that such a man is out of reach, not my own,' and he raised his glass of wine in honour of his late friend and drained it, much to Effie's surprise. 'How differently all Turner's former critics will regard any paper once touched by his hand, for the sunshine and the sky so speak of him now that their supreme witness is no more.'

'He was a great man,' she agreed.

'And great art is the expression of the *mind* of a great man,' he added.

'I sometimes think that you care more for the paintings than who created them,' Effie observed, struggling to pity a person so guarded against relationship.

'I can't deny it, for to me paintings *are* like people, only considerably easier to understand,' Ruskin admitted. 'A painting doesn't expect anything of you, like people do.'

Effie admired her husband so much more when he gave way to his emotions, and particularly when his parents were not close by, for it was as though he could never truly be himself when they were always badgering and interfering.

If she was ever to find a way out of the strange fortress of marriage it would be easier to detest him, however, and so she bade him goodnight long before he was ready to terminate their discussion, resolving to stamp out all feelings of compassion and determined that she would never return to Venice with Ruskin by her side.

Effie needn't have tried to distance herself from Ruskin, for he withdrew more than ever in the weeks following Turner's death, never confiding in her again or speaking of his own writing as once he did so zealously, with any prevailing harmony between them finally destroyed shortly before they left Venice.

Hearing Effie call frantically from her room the night prior to their departure, Ruskin rushed to her chamber to find her standing by the bed in tears, her jewellery boxes chaotically upturned on the quilt as her maid scoured the room.

'What is the meaning of this?' he asked in dismay.

'My jewels!' Effie screamed, joining the maid in searching every cupboard and crevice. 'Everything has gone, including the pearls, the serpent, the diamond bird and the ruby heart. All except for a few worthless trinkets.'

'Perhaps you simply moved them whilst preparing my wife's luggage?' he calmly suggested to the maid, concerned that his wife might be experiencing another episode of hysteria.

'No, my mistress told me to pack them,' she denied, shaking her head vigorously, afraid of being accused. 'It must be a theft.'

'How disconcerting,' he replied sceptically, 'to think that we have either been burgled or unwittingly invited a criminal into our home.'

'Are you not very cross?' Effie asked, having prepared for a scolding.

'Not in the least, I am pleased that you have been taught a lesson about leaving your jewels about.'

Without seeing any point in participating in the search, Ruskin set about questioning each of the servants before alerting the police, who soon pointed the finger at an English acquaintance of theirs, a Captain Foster who was in the Austrian Service and had called on the couple earlier that day to bid them farewell.

'Unbeknownst to us,' he explained to Effie after the police had carried out a thorough examination of the apartment, 'Foster returned here when we were out, apparently wanting to write me a letter.'

'Did he break in?' she pressed, baffled by her husband's complacency and pacing the drawing room in restlessness.

'There was no need. Mary, knowing him to be a regular guest of ours, admitted him without question, nor did she think to stand over him for the twenty minutes he took to draft a note asking me to send him some razors from London.'

'How strange,' she granted. 'I expect this means that we will have to delay our voyage?'

'Yes,' he nodded, taking up the window seat. 'There may still be *some* hope of recovering the jewels, but I should warn you that it may cost me my life.' A statement he added theatrically, being curious to see whether Effie would flinch at jeopardising his safety if there should be any chance of recouping her most treasured possessions.

'How so?' Effie asked without expressing the least concern.

'If Foster hears that we're accusing him of making off with your diamonds, I dare say, knowing what the fashion is for fighting duels in Venice, I will have to defend my honour. And yours too come to think of it,' Ruskin announced. 'The police have already interrogated me about how intimate you were with him, implying that *that* was how he came to be permitted access to your room.'

'The very idea! How is it that *I* should be humiliated, when a crime has been committed *against* me?' she fumed.

'Do we not both know how unjust life is? We should prepare ourselves for this whole matter being turned against us,' he warned.

Sure enough, after a further few days of a clumsy investigation by the police, and reports of the incident finding their way into the newspapers,

Ruskin received a bullish letter from a representative of Foster asking him to either deny all possibility of his superior's involvement in the crime or face a duel.

'As I foretold,' Ruskin announced, calmly folding the note and handing it to his wife. 'And, as I am neither a good swordsman nor a good shot, I see no alternative but to politely decline duelling in favour of quitting the city immediately. I trust you would rather lose one hundred pounds' worth of jewels than your husband?'

The scandal surrounding their retreat from the city caused Effie considerable distress and embarrassment, yet Ruskin was never successful in cheering her, not least because he was preparing to deliver another disappointment, considerably worse than that of her lost jewels.

On setting off for the Continent all those months before, he had failed to inform her that they were not to set foot inside their house on Park Street upon their return, though he was duty-bound to declare it before they arrived at the door of their new, less dignified address south of the river, a suburban dwelling far removed from the glamorous palazzos of Venice or the elegance of Mayfair.

Effie was predictably appalled when he officiously informed her on reaching London that they were to relocate from their substantial townhouse to a property entirely bereft of any grandeur, and taking him to mean that the move was imminent rather than academic she was outraged upon learning that everything had been arranged during their absence and that they would repair directly to their new abode.

'Do not fly at me, when it is largely your own doing,' Ruskin protested, 'my mother having discovered, on looking over our accounts, that you have been vastly extravagant in your expenditure.'

'*Me* extravagant?' Effie assailed. 'That's rich coming from you who thinks nothing of taking up the grandest apartments when we're abroad. Meanwhile, your parents are always affectionate to my face, yet are sure to speak against me the moment my back is turned.'

'They do not blame you *entirely*,' he retracted, 'for they understand that Park Street involves keeping our own carriage and more servants than the two of us require, but they feel that if we relinquish our well-appointed address we would be able to rein in our outlays.'

"*If*, you say?' Effie interjected, her cheeks burning in temper. 'How can you say "if" when she has already cleared us out of our house without my knowledge!'

'Kindly refrain from referring to my mother as "she",' he chided.

'I owe her only the respect that she has shown towards me. Your mother might complain about the expense of keeping a large house and entertaining important people, but your father was once of the opinion that I should *encourage* you to enter society. I wonder what ever can I do to please them? I expect they even blame *me* for the theft of my jewels.'

'Don't be ridiculous. I don't know how you can rail against them so, when they have never been anything but kind and generous towards you,' Ruskin admonished.

'Kind?' she contested. 'Well they might have been if I had been such a slave as you. You Ruskins all consider yourselves to be perfect people, whilst *I* am to be treated as a fool or a child. This is simply another example of your mother's never-ceasing disappointment that you married *me* instead of Miss Lockhart or some other person of higher rank and greater fortune. It's as though your sole objective in wanting me to accompany you to Venice was to get me out of the way so that you might arrange things between you all.'

Holding her husband just as responsible as her in-laws for the betrayal, whilst Effie did not yet know how to extricate herself from being called a member of their family, she seized this turn of events as a challenge to conclude her role as John Ruskin's wife.

Both seething, the pair did not converse for the remainder of the journey over the Thames, with Effie's anger and tears fighting their own battle as she passed each milestone, for the nearer she came to seeing her new house the more desperate she was.

Despite Effie thinking the small red-brick house at 30 Herne Hill inconceivably unattractive, there was no budging her husband's determination to take it, the property being half a mile from Denmark Hill and just next door to the house where he had lived as a child.

'The only person this place would be fit for is a clerk!' Effie stormed as they stood in the front garden, paved with yellow gravel and planted all round with multi-coloured chrysanthemums. 'You did not consult me because you knew I should never have agreed.'

Crawley meanwhile directed the transfer of the couple's luggage from the carriage, content to avoid the inevitable argument and seeing both sides of it well enough, Effie scowling at the removal of her jewel-less belongings and kicking the gravel.

'As it was a necessary arrangement financially, I could give you no choice in the matter,' Ruskin replied calmly, ushering his wife through the bright green front door and looking over the public rooms, all of which were narrow, gaudily papered and with considerably lower ceilings than their former residence.

'We didn't *have* to live quite so close to your parents,' she disputed, removing her bonnet.

'No, but considering my mother is almost seventy years of age, we might as well be near her as far away and always forced to travel,' he reasoned. 'You are fortunate that I did not agree to us living with them at Denmark Hill, for that is what they originally desired.'

'Ha! You couldn't very well have done that, for they don't know how we *really* live,' Effie countered, 'although it would have given me some amusement to observe your father's reaction to our needing separate quarters. Perhaps he would be disappointed in his son after all.'

'The reason for my suggesting *this* alternative rather than living with them was solely due to you never getting along with my mother,' Ruskin protested, turning his back and continuing into the drawing room.

'It really is the crudest house I have ever seen, both inside and out!' Effie exclaimed on entering the canary-yellow room. 'And it still wreaks of paint,' she sniffed, putting a handkerchief to her nose. 'Part-furnished in the worst possible taste and vulgarity. This isn't a *drawing room*, it's a parlour! How ever did you let your father decide the furnishings?'

'He didn't, he simply gave the builder two thousand pounds, a substantial sum I think you'll agree, to select the furniture and decoration as he saw fit,' Ruskin answered, unable to further defend what had clearly been a grave oversight.

'And *this* from people who accuse *me* of extravagance and boast supreme good taste!' his wife scorned, running her finger along the modern, factory-made wooden mantelpiece.

'I never realised how much Venice had spoilt you,' Ruskin reproached.

'No-one is more of a snob than you, and however much you protest to the contrary I will never believe that you like it here,' she countered, inspecting each element of the upholstery and fittings with disgust.

'I suspect even paradise would be hell if you and I were forced to share it, though admittedly it *will* be a difficult house to invite anyone to, being a numberless, commonplace dwelling, with a gate like everybody's gate, a garden like everybody's garden, and chimneys and windows the same,' he conceded tauntingly.

'I sincerely hope you will *not* invite anyone,' Effie urged, 'for I should be positively ashamed for *my* acquaintances to see this house, nor would it do *your* reputation any favours. *Punch* would declare you a hypocrite of the highest order for leasing such a place,' she scorned, handling the cheap mustard-yellow curtain material with blue fringing. 'Our only saving grace is that no genteel society would *dream* of venturing so far to pay a call.'

'I'm afraid you're right, my dear, most of your old friends will think you quite out of the way now,' he provoked, 'and whilst I am sure *I* shall be very happy and will have enough to do in the neighbourhood, with any disagreeableness only increasing my pleasure whenever I visit the Alps, *you* who always dislike quiet so will doubtless find our hideous furnished house a considerable trial.'

'I *will* be greatly unhappy here, John,' Effie exclaimed petulantly, sinking into one of the armchairs in despair, 'and what's worse than all your scheming is that you don't care if you should make me miserable. I wouldn't be surprised if that wasn't your intention all along.'

'Believe me, it causes me inconceivable pain when you are dissatisfied, for I alone have to live with you. And whilst I admit that a cottage in

Norwood is no elegant thing for a woman of your social ambitions,'
Ruskin granted, 'if you *are* wretched here that will be entirely your fault
and not mine.'

Effie decided that Margaret had conspired to remove them to Herne
Hill in order to restrict her opportunities for socialising and have
more control over her son, yet her subsequent silence and apparent
submission was due to refusing the old woman the satisfaction of
hearing her complaints.

Whilst she refrained from *voicing* her grievances, Effie made her
displeasure obvious from her surliness of manner, though even then her
in-laws never seemed to consider her opinion save when they thought
that her despondency and ill temper might affect their son's work. They
barely noticed that she no longer looked at them directly or they should
have read the loathing she harboured towards them, nor did she speak
unless personally addressed, which was rarely.

Effie detested the old woman for always manipulating her son and
when, on the day they moved into the property, Ruskin informed her
that they were to dine with his parents at Denmark Hill that evening she
raged at the new order of things.

He ensured that they always arrived punctually despite knowing that
his wife considered her in-laws' habitual dining hour of five o'clock both
unfashionable and inconvenient, being loath to spend her evenings by the
fireside listening to John James make droll remarks to his son on reading
the day's newspaper, while Margaret, who was beginning to feel the effects
of age and did not sleep well at night, would drift off in the chair and snore
reverberantly until her husband summoned enough courage to wake her
and insist upon retiring to bed.

'Do you perceive them to be happy?' Margaret enquired of her
husband one night on getting into bed beside him.

'They never appear to have more than a decent affection for each
other,' he answered gruffly, pulling up the sheets, 'John being divided from
Effie by his pictures and writing, and she being more interested in parties
and pretty dresses than his work.'

'You can distinguish more feeling between them than *I* can,' Margaret sneered. 'I think her a selfish miss and very much doubt if she ever had any more feeling for him than a passing acquaintance. She certainly doesn't seem quick to have a family.'

'Perhaps we are guilty of interfering too much, for they must settle their comings and goings between themselves.'

'I wonder if they would speak at all if it weren't for me chivvying John,' she denied.

'They're a deal away from the companionship that you and I have known,' John James granted, kissing his wife's hand tenderly before extinguishing the single tallow candle which had provided just enough light for the couple to undress, pray and observe one another in conversation. 'I only trust that our son may not live out his life without receiving such a blessing.'

Besides the ugly house, there was much for Effie to grind her teeth about, not least the abrupt curtailment of all her previous freedoms due to no longer possessing her own carriage.

Although Margaret made a pretence of allowing her daughter-in-law the use of her own brougham for once-weekly trips into town, she was liable to withdraw the offer at a moment's notice, furnishing her with the feeblest of excuses as to its unavailability.

Intolerant of the routines of Denmark Hill, and feeling herself an outsider to all the Ruskin ways, Effie joined Margaret in knitting beside the hearth, not from any particular interest in the occupation but out of sheer boredom, using the mindless diversion as a means of daydreaming about her next visit to Perthshire, or Paulizza and all that might have been.

The sound of smashing china startled her from such reverie one dull afternoon, and Effie could barely disguise her pleasure when she looked up from her knitting needles to find that Margaret had broken one of her prized ornaments.

'It slipped out of my hand as I was dusting it!' the old woman cried, woefully regarding the fragments at her feet.

'Oh dear. Still, I'm sure it's easily replaced,' Effie consoled sardonically, looking on as Margaret knelt to gather up the pieces.

'Easy to one who thinks that money is no object,' she returned, holding the broken china in her hands.

'If you are referring to the large overdraft you believe *I* am responsible for accruing, I beg you to check the accounts more carefully. If you do, you will see that John spent as much as one hundred and fifty pounds on books in six weeks.'

'A book is a book and a dress is a *dress*,' Margaret retaliated, silencing Effie who continued knitting with her eyes downcast.

She knew not how to vent the animosity she felt boiling up within her other than to send her mother the most unflattering descriptions of the Ruskins and all they did to antagonise her:

"They are strange people and I am free to confess that I do not get fonder of them as I get older. I never heard a word of our new house until it was all settled, and John is all the more obedient for fear that his mother should think he listens too much to what I say."

The two women had long fought for precedence in influencing Ruskin, yet it was only on relocating to Herne Hill that Effie realised how deluded she had been to imagine that he might break away from his mother's control, for it was clear that Margaret's hold over him was unshakeable.

Whilst her husband was content to be dominated by his parents, Effie was assuredly *not*, with every moment spent in their company confirming that the move from Park Street was a catalyst to something far greater.

Setting aside her grief for Paulizza, she passed each day consoling herself with the thought that it was one less she would endure alongside the Ruskins, ready for any opportunity which presented itself to seize a future life away from Denmark Hill and the autocracy of Margaret.

THE ORDER OF RELEASE

MILLAIS WAS DISAPPOINTED TO HEAR THAT EFFIE WOULD no longer be a regular presence at social gatherings following her departure for South London and, anticipating her feelings of isolation, thought he might alleviate her boredom by suggesting that she model for his most important work of the year, "The Order of Release", in which he would portray her as the wife of a Highlander wrongly imprisoned during the Jacobite rising.

On Ruskin fully supporting the idea and soliciting his wife's agreement, the artist duly arrived on the couple's doorstep the following Monday morning armed with canvas, easel, brushes, paints and varnishes, too stunned by his patron's vulgar new residence to offer the usual compliments.

'Oh good, I see you plan to set up right away!' Ruskin greeted Millais warmly, patting him on the back and directing him forthwith to the attic that was to double as the studio. 'It *is* cramped but there is still good light,' he announced on opening the door.

'It will do very well,' the young man thanked, resting his equipment and opening the shutters.

'You are free to use it whenever you choose,' his host went on; 'and should you be too tired to journey back home, my wife can prepare you a room for the night.'

Effie, whom Ruskin forgot to assist on climbing the narrow staircase, was too delighted by the unexpected diversion of Millais's presence to show her irritation and, being flattered by the attention which a mere housewife in a middle-class neighbourhood could hardly expect, was more than willing to sacrifice whole days to the tranquil occupation of sitting or standing in the various postures the artist dictated.

This role she eagerly adopted as soon as her husband, after ordering them both to work hard, jovially bade them farewell on leaving for Denmark Hill, promising to resist the temptation to peep at the canvas before it was complete.

'It strikes me that you are sure to find sitting for a picture a deal more tedious than knitting all day,' the painter observed after several hours had elapsed and the light was beginning to fade.

'Despite the exhaustion and muscle ache, which I assume is the inevitable result of remaining still from morning till dusk, I have enjoyed myself tremendously and can't think how I ever occupied myself before,' she confessed, rubbing her aching neck.

'I only wish all my models were so obliging,' Millais teased, looking up from cleaning his brushes.

'Perhaps *they* have more fulfilling lives,' she replied sorrowfully, wrapping a shawl around her shoulders.

'I hope you don't mind my asking, but did something happen in Venice? It's just that you haven't seemed quite yourself ever since,' he enquired, trying to look preoccupied with tidying away his materials.

'How observant you are. I discovered that a good friend of mine had passed away,' Effie answered forlornly; yet, becoming conscious that Millais would guess that her feelings had been romantic, she quickly changed her tone, 'and then of course there was the theft of my jewels, reports of which followed us to London and appeared in all the newspapers just as if we were the guilty party.'

'Yes, I read about that. It must have been very distressing.'

'I trust *you* did not believe that the thief had access to my bedchamber?' she ventured lightly.

'Alas, I was not privy to such aspersions, but no-one knows better than I how damaging the press can be. You must follow *my* example and surround yourself with people who do not amuse themselves by reading lies over breakfast.'

Effie laughed, cheered by the reassurance. 'You will come again tomorrow?'

'Why certainly, if you're agreeable,' he replied, rolling down his shirt sleeves and adopting his jacket.

'I'm so very glad of your company,' she ventured frankly, 'and in return I want to be as much help to you as I can.'

'It seems an unfair bargain, for *I* benefit both ways.'

'I don't know about that,' she jested as Millais closed the garret door and helped her to descend the stairs, 'I expect the papers will soon report that I'm keeping you locked in my attic!'

This routine, which began with the artist arriving promptly each morning, went on for many weeks and resulted not only in a masterpiece but in the pair falling deeply in love, filling Effie with hope that her Herne Hill existence was drawing to a close.

Ruskin, who was ever dismissive of social conventions, and unsuspecting of his wife's desire to break away, meanwhile scoffed at his mother's concerns when he casually informed her that Millais was visiting Herne Hill in order to paint Effie, an anxiety which increased tenfold when he revealed that the two of them were left unchaperoned all day.

'You mean to say that you continue to work *here*, whilst they are entirely alone *there*? John, what is this inexplicable silliness?' Margaret exclaimed, throwing up her hands. 'I have never *been* so angry with you for being so blind, and I shall have no sympathy if something dreadful happens. Even if it doesn't, it is *bound* to cause talk, and Effie's reputation isn't pure enough to withstand any further slight.'

Ruskin, who simply put his mother's views down to an ongoing hostility, replied indifferently, 'There is no harm in her remaining behind with Millais, she is simply keen to assist him with his work.'

'Well, excuse *me* if I never think of Effie as particularly self-sacrificing,' Margaret sniped, turning to her Bible in order to find some passage on adultery. 'When did she ever help you?'

'Mother, I think you ought to credit me with a little more sense and my wife with a deal more morality,' he protested, slamming his teacup on the table with enough force to upset its contents.

'Precisely how long is this likely to go on?' she persisted, without waiting for her son to respond. 'I foresee that Millais will make slow progress indeed without *you* there to hurry him along.'

'I have no intention of doing any such thing,' Ruskin dismissed

'I certainly see less and less of Effie these days. Why have you allowed her to excuse herself from joining us for dinner?'

'I shall not force her to comply with the routines of Denmark Hill if they do not suit her, we live in the nineteenth century not biblical times.'

Tutting, but finally keeping quiet, Margaret regarded her son's reference to her religiosity in poor taste, yet she was more alarmed that he showed no sign of listening to her appeals, much as he had on first announcing his intention to marry Effie.

What Margaret Ruskin viewed as Effie's haughtiness, Millais admired as his subject's natural poise and grace, and everything Ruskin had ever found displeasing in his wife's personality and temperament the artist was appositely entranced by.

Millais did take the liberty of making fun of his model's considerable grandeur, however, and took to calling her "The Countess" whenever they were alone. In fact, so frequently did he refer to Effie as such that, whenever Ruskin dropped by to see how work was progressing, the painter was forced to check himself, for he well knew that this epithet would reveal volumes.

Millais was equally gratified at how very often Effie used his middle name whenever they were alone, and noticed that she never asked him a question or made a remark without uttering 'Everett'.

Any attraction he had initially felt towards his muse strengthened the more time he spent in her company or studied her features, nor was having to ask her to stay still or refrain from talking any barrier to the intimacy that was quickly established between them, something acknowledged just a week after the commencement of the painting when Effie boldly offered to act as his barber upon noticing that his hair was so long as to prevent him from seeing clearly.

'Now it is *your* turn to sit still, Everett,' she demanded confidently.

Long past caring what her husband might think of such over-familiarity should he have chanced to witness it, after dashing away to get the scissors from her sewing box and a towel which she draped around Millais's shoulders Effie positioned herself firmly behind his chair and began to snip away the excess strands.

'Don't look so apprehensive,' she reassured him, 'I always play coiffeur to my young siblings.'

Thus, wielding the instrument, Ruskin's wife proceeded to tidy the painter's wavy locks until they no longer hindered his vision, though the gentleness of her touch evoked tenderness rather than efficiency and conveyed so much more feeling than any cautious words of affection she might have spoken.

Having only shaken hands with Millais up until that moment, she felt an inevitable thrill on being permitted to run her fingers through his soft, fair hair, nor did his consequent embarrassment deter her from asking to retain a lock.

'I will only agree if it should be in exchange for one of *yours*,' Millais returned, smiling and stroking his head to feel the alteration.

Without answering, Effie loosened the pins which had been holding her hair in place, allowing the tresses to fall to her waist, and cut a lock from the nape which she presented with a winsome look.

This gesture meant that the rest of the day was spent not in the artist devoting his attention to the painting but in sketching his interpretation of the scene, ever to be remembered by them as the first expression of their attachment.

When Effie accompanied Millais downstairs on his departure there seemed an added significance in her familiar question, 'Will I see you tomorrow?'

XLIV

GLENFINLAS

HAVING PROLONGED PAINTING EFFIE FOR AS LONG AS HE reasonably could without arousing suspicion, Millais reluctantly packed up his materials and visited Herne Hill no more regularly than a humble dinner guest, something Ruskin did not encourage due to so frequently spending his evenings with his parents at Denmark Hill.

In the two years since meeting Millais, Ruskin had been impressed by the progress he perceived the artist to have made, attributing much of this improvement to the fact that *he* had been overseeing his work, not to mention the advice he had offered as to each project embarked upon by the Pre-Raphaelite. Nor did Ruskin fail to take credit for having allowed his wife to model for Millais's best work to date.

"The Order of Release", the ironically-named painting in which Effie's earnest face and fulsome figure featured prominently, was exhibited at the Royal Academy to great acclaim, those acquainted with her applauding Millais for having so successfully captured her likeness, whilst speaking in hushed tones as to Ruskin's impropriety in allowing his wife to model

437

and questioning *her* moral character. This conjecture only fuelled interest in the work, however, and when the critics hailed it as "the painting of the year" a policeman had to be employed to guard it from the dense crowds gathering each day to view it, a steady procession forming from the gallery's opening until close.

Despite most visitors displaying a great deal of patience on awaiting their turn, the majority never got a clear sight of the picture when once they reached the front of the queue, forced as they were to contend with so many rows of bonnets belonging to pushy women who elbowed their neighbour and craned their necks to get a better view.

Unbeknownst to Millais, Ruskin and Effie, who were exhilarated by their own part in the notoriety of the painting, not everyone went with the intention of admiring the work; some simply wanted to boast of having seen it, while others were determined to look upon, and ultimately judge, the face of the lady who had caused so much comment.

'Whatever will Ruskin do next,' they hooted, 'allow his wife to go on the stage?'

Yet the man who had caused such a stir by his modernity was entirely unmindful of public opinion, and even had he realised the dim view his peers took of his wife modelling for an artist, something associated with courtesans, would have lambasted them all to eternity with no consciousness of how fate would scorn his trust in his wife and friend.

Having long since commissioned his protégé to paint his portrait, the uproarious response to "The Order of Release" impelled Ruskin to act upon the idea. Thus he fixed upon a scheme whereby he, Effie and Millais would set off for the Highlands on a painting holiday that summer, having settled upon Glenfinlas as the most impressive backdrop to the full-length representation of himself in which he would stand, prophet-like, on rocks before a cascading waterfall, his blue eyes reflected in the torrent, his authority emphasised by a dark frock coat.

'When you say *we*, who will be going altogether?' Holman Hunt asked Millais, who had received countless commissions since his recent success.

'Just myself, Ruskin, Effie and their manservant,' he replied, sketching out his latest canvas.

'I am much intrigued by Ruskin's enduring beneficence towards my comrade in arms, yet the fact that Effie will be the only woman in the party is rather singular,' Holman Hunt ventured, raising his eyebrows comically, 'and could prove troublesome to a man as easily enamoured as yourself.'

'Ruskin doesn't seem to mind her being in the company of men,' Millais defended. 'He positively encouraged her to sit for me, saying that she has just the face for a loyal Scottish wife.'

'I'm not sure her mien comes into it,' Holman Hunt returned, laughing heartily, 'nor do I think *you* can boast much loyalty to your champion if you have been flirting with her as much as I suspect. I always knew his good opinion of you would never last. I'm still surprised that he permitted it; noble *ladies* usually only pose for pictures in which *they* are the chief subject, whilst appearing cold and heartless.'

'Effie isn't either of those things,' Millais refuted, 'though you could hardly blame her if she *was* should you witness Ruskin's lack of affection towards her.'

'I don't doubt it,' Holman Hunt replied, satisfied on revealing his friend's secret, 'nor that *you* have inspired warmer feelings in her to surface judging from these sketches,' he teased, examining one of his friend's portfolios crammed with drawings of the aloof-looking Mrs Ruskin, whom the artist had perfectly captured: from her way of tipping her head back loftily, to her dark, rounded eyebrows which framed her all-knowing eyes.

As bashful as an adolescent, Millais left off sketching and, dashing over to where Holman Hunt stood, snatched away the volume in which so many private encounters had been documented yet were never intended for prying eyes.

Soon after he had set the collection out of reach, Ruskin was announced, forcing Millais to greet his patron sheepishly, and his friend hardly less so due to being privy to matters which blurred the line between gratitude and honour.

'Mr Hunt!' Ruskin enthused, delighted to see the member of the brotherhood he chastised himself for neglecting so sorely. 'I have been meaning to appeal for your help.'

'*My* help?' Hunt asked, bewildered and wanting to do the same.

'Yes, I have recently heard from a very pitiable poor artist who says he is lying in sickness and poverty not far from where you live. If I were to write down his name and address might you enquire into his state?'

'Why, certainly,' he agreed, mortified at having thought only of how Ruskin might help *him*, not to mention greatly embarrassed at knowing how Millais was deceiving the man who had most supported him.

'I am much grieved at having mislaid the letter for some weeks and hope I may yet be in time to be of some service,' Ruskin went on, shaking his head at his own tardiness.

'Does he want money, do you think?' the flame-bearded young man asked sceptically.

'Perhaps, my dear Hunt,' he answered in gentle defiance at being considered weak, 'but a little thought and kindness are often worth more than a great deal of money.'

Taking up a sheet of paper and a pencil lying about on one of Millais's workbenches, Ruskin scribbled down the man's details and thrust them into Hunt's hand with a look of earnest appeal.

'I will try to find out what I can,' he assured.

'I *am* grateful,' Ruskin pledged, pressing his hand to his chest in sincerity. 'I know one can't help everyone, but he seems like someone I might really assist. I feel constantly as if I were living in one great churchyard with people all around me clinging to the edges of open graves and calling for help as they fall back into them, out of sight. What is one to do?'

Effie's twenty-fifth birthday passed with another insufferably dull dinner at Denmark Hill, felicitations which only increased her yearning to leave the Ruskin fold.

Though she had reached the age her husband had once declared as the most suitable to begin a family, it was ignored as if he had never spoken of it and they continued to live as separately as ever, a circumstance which caused her both anger and relief, feelings Millais could only guess at from the way in which she sometimes snapped at Ruskin.

Millais was meanwhile irritated by Hunt's accusation of disloyalty, for he harboured no guilt on encouraging Effie's attentions and judged Ruskin's invitation to holiday in Scotland as too tempting an opportunity to refuse. He therefore replied promptly, stating his anticipation of the journey and asking if his brother William, also an artist, would be permitted to join the party, for he had enough foresight to think he might be glad of an alibi and adviser.

Ruskin, delighted by the prospect of encouraging his protégé to draw nature in greater detail and likeness, unhesitatingly agreed and insisted on the excursion being a lengthy and circuitous one, commencing with an extensive tour of Northumberland prior to reaching Scotland.

Yet Ruskin was disappointed by the artist's lack of enthusiasm for his new surroundings and, before the group had been away many days, observed to Effie as they were walking alone on the plains that Millais did not appear to take to the outdoors and seemed oddly abject, hardly supposing that she knew herself to be the cause of the painter's angst and uncharacteristic emotional state.

'I wish the country agreed with Millais as well as it does with *us*,' he went on, without perceiving how much Effie loathed it when he coupled his own inclinations with hers. 'I wonder what ails him so? He is the most miserable person I have ever seen, one moment all excitement and restlessness, the next depressed, sick and faint as a woman.'

'Perhaps he needs time to adjust,' Effie suggested weakly. 'The country takes some getting used to after London.'

'I expect you're right, or I certainly hope that's the case, for I don't know how *I* shall manage him if he doesn't know how to manage himself.'

'He might get on better without you trying,' she suggested curtly, walking on in order to avoid further discussion.

On reaching Brig o' Turk, Ruskin continued to express concern for his friend's health and remarked to Effie that the artist's appetite also appeared to suffer.

'His eating habits are strange to me,' he declared one morning on Millais going out without any sustenance. 'I always take my meals like clockwork, whereas Everett hardly ever takes breakfast, which, although he sometimes remedies by consuming enormous amounts upon returning in the evening, generally fails to provide his body with enough fuel for his exertions.'

'He seems quite well,' Effie rebuffed, not wanting to promote her husband's analysis of their guest, for even she saw that he *was* behaving eccentrically and swung between lethargy and the most uncontrollable vigour, like a man with St Vitus' dance.

Whenever Millais *did* have energy he painted outdoors all day until his limbs were numb and his back ached, only resting when the light became too poor for him to see either the landscape or the canvas before him. Whilst Ruskin tried to persuade him to take exercise in a regular way, his erratic behaviour continued: running for several miles before settling down to work, or bathing with his brother William in any torrent or stream they came across as if the bracing cold were bound to set him right again.

Finding the idea of group nakedness repulsive, Ruskin avoided such opportunities of comradeship with the Millais brothers in favour of his usual solitary walks. Abandoning the younger members of the party, who appeared to get on very well without him, he rambled and sketched alone, though it was far from the holiday he had intended.

> *"When I came away with Millais,"* he wrote to his father, *"I thought to bring him back a meek and methodical man. I might as well have tried to make a Highland stream read Euclid. He, on the other hand, thought he could make me like Pre-Raphaelitism better than Turner, but he has given it up now. There is a wonderful, wise old proverb —* 'one cannot make a silk purse out of a sow's ear.'"

Despite having identified all the symptoms, it never occurred to Ruskin that the affliction ailing Millais was the age-old complaint of lovesickness, a condition that worsened with every passing day and led him to think the young man's companionship tedious rather than life-affirming.

Conversely, Effie thrived in the presence of Millais and his brother, sewing while the men sketched their surroundings or fished for trout, and whenever the weather changed suddenly, as it invariably did in the Highlands despite it being early July, the three would happily shelter from the rain under a cloak, chatting and laughing like old school friends until the downpour passed.

'Oh, Everett, I admire you for adopting the custom, but I really don't think you should wear a kilt in this weather!' Effie teased, seeing that the garment was soaked through and that he was bravely shivering beside her.

Charmed by his ineffable brother William, she nonetheless showed Everett, with knowing looks and smiles, that she would far rather have him entirely to herself, something she further communicated by not showing any inclination to take up Ruskin's suggestion that they all embark upon a forest trail the following morning.

Having never proved herself a walker with any stamina, there was no need for Effie to insist that her husband spend the time as best pleased him, for he generally did so regardless. Agreeing that Millais should keep his wife company while he made the excursion with William and Crawley, Ruskin inadvertently granted his wife's dearest wish by devising a route that would take the better part of the day.

Rising early in anticipation of being alone with Millais, she prepared a generous hamper to fortify them, with local trout, blackcurrant pudding and cream, besides provisions of tea, Dundee cake and whisky, particularly necessary when the late afternoon air became chill and they required fortification to prolong their time away from the rest of the party.

The couple well knew that the evening back at the cottage would be monopolised by Ruskin's lengthy account of how *he* had passed the day, nor was it the only occasion on which they were granted such pleasant interludes due to his preoccupation with compiling the index of *The Stones of Venice* and writing his forthcoming Edinburgh lectures, leaving Effie and Millais quite at liberty to explore the glades and the glens hand in hand, with the consequence that their desire for one another soon reached fever point.

Having never visited Scotland before, Millais revelled on witnessing such a landscape through Effie's eyes, perceiving how the burden of marriage entirely passed away whenever Ruskin was absent. Whether hopscotching barefoot on rocks across a stream, her boots and stockings laid aside, or walking through the woods bonnet-less, she was transformed into a confident young woman without a care, radiant in the landscape she cherished above all.

Although Millais had no means of expressing his admiration for Effie other than to draw countless sketches or rhapsodise about her beauty in letters to Holman Hunt, his brother, who ensured Ruskin and Crawley were kept out of the way, sensed that the infatuation was bound to be noticed before very long.

'She is the most delightful, unselfish, kind-hearted creature I have ever known,' Millais enthused to William one evening as they stood smoking with their backs to the cottage wall, 'a woman whose acquaintance is a blessing.'

'I don't think her husband finds it so. Most afternoons Ruskin asks me to take up pickaxe, barrow and spade and join him in trying to cut a canal across a bend in the river,' he replied, smirking as they both watched through the window Effie scrubbing the pots and pans. 'Is it not strange that he prefers to leave you two to roam the hills together? Often declaring quite jovially, "How well your brother and my wife get on together!" I ask myself, is this not a very dangerous experiment?'

'As you say, Ruskin's conduct is incomprehensible,' agreed Millais confidentially, 'for his frequent absence seems purposely to put Effie into my arms.'

'Were it not for your integrity, evil consequences would naturally occur,' William reinforced, prompting Millais to become unusually coy and keen to curtail the conversation.

Throwing his cigar on the ground and stamping it out with more violence than was necessary, he returned indoors, leaving his brother to surmise the possible outcome of the sojourn and the detrimental impact it might have on his reputation and career.

When Ruskin unexpectedly came upon Millais and Effie by a brook the following afternoon, he discovered the artist not hard at work on his portrait but painting his wife, posed with a pink foxglove in her hair. However, contrary to Millais's fear lest his patron should think his day would have been better spent otherwise employed, he declared it as fine a work as he had ever conceived.

'I like it very much!' Ruskin complimented enthusiastically, stooping in order to better examine the detail of the flower. 'What will you take for it?'

'I don't think I shall sell this one,' Millais responded casually yet firmly, careful not to show how reluctant he was to part with it.

Unlike Ruskin, who did not desire the work for any reasons of sentiment but merely because he admired the composition and the techniques employed, Millais knew that he would cherish the work for many a day, not least when he was once again parted from Effie and longed to look upon her face.

'I wouldn't dream of depriving you of it if you are really so much pleased with it,' Ruskin assured, martyr-like.

'No, of course you must have it, especially as it is of Effie,' Millais insisted, afraid to appear ungrateful when Ruskin had funded the holiday, though he knew he would later regret such generosity.

'What a good friend you are,' Ruskin thanked, much pleased with the acquisition and patting Millais on the shoulder in a manner which irritated the artist who would sooner destroy the work than see it on the walls of his patron's loveless house.

The party had been travelling for almost a month when they arrived at Glenfinlas, the hallowed Highland setting selected by Ruskin as most worthy of being featured in his portrait – to be duly paid for by John James and exhibited for the admiration of their callers.

Amused that Ruskin considered himself equal to such a mighty setting, Millais was obliged to begin work on the commission whenever the weather permitted, his subject positioning himself upon a rugged piece of ancient rock covered in moss, with the foaming torrent of Finglas Water gushing past that was intended to highlight his love of nature.

'More than anything,' Ruskin declared, looking anxious as to the precariousness of the boulder on which he was balancing, 'this work shall illustrate that no man's reputation or word can ever equal, let alone surpass, the beauty of the natural world.'

'The foam of the current will be something quite new at the Academy,' Effie chimed in, keen to stop her husband from talking of himself.

'Precisely the reason I set the challenge,' he boasted, as if Millais were his student. Turning his head to address him, thereby ruining his pose, he continued, 'The majesty of nature depends upon the force of the human spirit, and if you master the water it'll be one of the finest portraits in a generation.'

Effie made no further comment but merely sighed and returned to her humble sketch of Scottish heather, her artistry having greatly improved under the supervision of one a deal more patient and encouraging than her husband.

Inevitably, Ruskin could not resist making countless other suggestions as to how Millais should approach the composition, causing the artist to grow vexed at being disrupted whilst he was sketching the outline. The only thing that stopped him from throwing down his tools and storming off was Effie, who glanced at him occasionally as if to say, '*Now you understand what I live with.*'

Yet, as Ruskin could not be on both sides of the canvas at once and was constantly urged by Millais to be still and refrain from talking, he became an extremely impatient model. Not content to stand for more than an hour at a time before declaring that he needed a walk to relieve joint stiffness, he thus enabled the artist to draw what he liked, namely Effie adorned with flowers and corn ears, works that would most definitely remain within his possession.

The trials Millais endured over the portrait became the furthest thing from his mind when Ruskin later directed the party to the small schoolmaster's cottage he had rented for a minimal sum.

A single-storey thatched dwelling with only one chimney, a parlour with a small dining table, cooking range and a recess for Crawley to sleep in, besides two tiny bedchambers, it was immediately obvious that such cramped accommodation was inadequate for five people, let alone a man in love with his friend's wife: Ruskin having unwittingly intensified the difficulty Millais faced in living alongside Effie to such a point that he would happily have slept outside under the stars.

Having limited experience of the tortures of passion his brother was experiencing, William never considered the difficulties of this temporary abode, and instead believed himself generous when he insisted on repairing to the nearby New Trossachs Hotel, thereby leaving Ruskin, Millais, Effie and Crawley to enjoy the full camaraderie and novelty of a typical Highland dwelling. Effie alone recognised Millais's brave attempt to conceal his torment when he made countless witticisms following his brother's departure.

'Yes, there are serious downsides to renting a place no bigger than a snuffbox, but there are many benefits too,' he remarked, opening and closing the windows and doors like a man possessed, much to Ruskin's bemusement.'I am able to touch both sides of the room with outstretched arms, open the window, shut the door, and shave all without getting out of bed!'

On each of them preparing their own bed in makeshift fashion after dinner, Ruskin selflessly designated himself and Crawley the parlour whilst allocating Effie and Millais the more comfortable sleeping quarters. Yet, with just a thin partition dividing him from his love, this only caused the artist to lie awake as he struggled to bear the frustrations which such an environment naturally entailed.

By first light he had determined to have nothing more to do with the Ruskins upon returning to London, so much did he loathe having to wrestle with his desire for another man's wife, a resolve which evaporated like Scotch mist when he pulled back the curtain to find not only that Effie had also endured a restless night but that Ruskin was absent and his bed had not been slept in.

'It proved too uncomfortable to sleep in the chair so I ended by walking to the hotel,' Ruskin informed them jovially on entering with William and sitting at the table in readiness of his wife and Crawley preparing breakfast. 'I really must apologise to you all for choosing so unfeasible a lodging!'

A revelation which caused Millais and Effie, who had long since learnt to communicate without needing words, to smile at the thought of having spent the night under the sole chaperonage of Crawley, who happened to sleep deeply and snore loudly.

Millais, desperate to return home, saw no alternative but to confide in William the moment he found him alone, hopeful that his imperturbable brother would be able to offer guidance.

'Having always believed Ruskin's soul to be in the clouds and out of reach of ordinary mortals, I am astonished at his apparently unshakeable trust in his friends.'

'Friends?' William provoked after a brotherly fashion, a gibe Millais chose to ignore.

'Not only is he lax regarding social customs,' he observed, 'but he never seems to consider how this carelessness might impact on Effie's reputation or his own. It is all so unbelievable for a man of his intelligence that I am beginning to wonder if bringing me out here wasn't a scheme on Ruskin's part.'

'If you suspect that he wishes to unburden himself of Effie, you must go forth with decorum and self-control in order to prevent the accomplishment of such a malicious design,' William cautioned. 'Whether you are accurate in your conjecture or not, if *you* do not falter then any such villainous plan will prove impossible.'

Millais sometimes wondered if he was not very wicked in calling into question his host's apparent innocence and enduring goodwill towards him, and asked himself if he wasn't only trying to justify his own disloyalty and deception. Although the cottage was outwardly charming, he realised that the claustrophobia of such a place had only heightened his romantic turmoil and the feeling of tension which resulted from falsely pretending to be Ruskin's comrade.

The following evening, therefore, when Effie had retired to bed and Crawley was busy preparing his master's walking equipment for the morrow, Millais attempted to establish his patron's true agenda by sharing a drink with him at the hotel, eager to ascertain why he so often sought to avoid his wife's company.

'I have long believed that all women ought to depend upon themselves for diversions,' Ruskin answered matter-of-factly, 'and Effie is more than capable of occupying herself. Besides, she is equally indifferent to *my* society, hence my solitary roamings are never truly neglectful, as they might be if my wife missed me when I was gone.'

'I'm sure she feels your absence very much,' Millais felt obliged to offer, colouring as soon as he had uttered the lie.

'Forgive my disagreeing with you, but that simply isn't the case, my friend,' Ruskin denied. 'Every day Effie and I spend together there is less and less sympathy between us, while any feelings of affection she might have once held towards me have long since faded. Doubtless *I* am to blame, but it is long past remedying.'

Feeling exonerated upon Ruskin admitting that his marriage was no more than a sham, Millais was inspired to inform Effie of his feelings the next day, confessing all the admiration she had never received from her husband and prompting her to break down in tears.

Finally granted the opportunity of relating her tale of woe, made all the more pitiful in the pale mist of that Glenfinlas afternoon, a setting which heightened their declaration of love and the ties that bound her to remain virtuous, Effie clung to one who might rescue her from such abject misery and succeeded in presenting herself as faultless.

As Ruskin, William and Crawley had gone climbing, she had no fear of them returning to find her hysterical, and she went forth with her story in the hope that Millais would offer not only consolation but the promise of a new life.

'Not even my own parents know how separately John and I still live,' Effie elaborated, 'and that I shall surely never have a family if I remain with him.'

'You mean...?' Millais hesitated, too embarrassed to utter his presumption aloud.

'Yes, nor is there any likelihood of anything altering between us, for he says that if I am not very wicked then I am at *least* insane and the responsibility of having children by me is too great for him to countenance.'

'*That* is his reasoning for not making you his own?'

'He has alleged various reasons, hatred to children, religious motives, a desire to preserve my beauty, and finally this last year he told me the truth, that he had imagined women were quite different to what he saw *I* was, and that the reason he did not make me his wife was because he was disgusted with my person on our wedding night.'

'I am utterly appalled to learn the wretchedness of your position,' Millais sympathised, embracing her warmly and kissing her forehead. 'How he can expect you to go on like this is beyond all reason.'

'If he had only been *kind* I might have lived and died in my maiden state, but there is no empathy between us whatsoever,' she went on, brushing away tears which continued to fall regardless.

'Uselessly, I think that I should never have accompanied you here nor encouraged our friendship,' Millais apologised, 'for I only seem to have disturbed your existence.'

'Whilst I cannot deny that it *does* cause me pain to imagine the kind of marriage I might have known, your company is a great solace to me and a thousand times more preferable to the solitary and meaningless life I knew before,' she said.

'Do not speak as if you are quite resigned to continuing like this, for surely you will grasp your destiny and release yourself from this hell?' Millais encouraged. 'Not only are you perfectly justified in taking such a step, but you should be compelled to do so. How can he expect to keep you as his wife when he treats you so cruelly?'

Effie coloured with anger. 'I am not sure that he wants to be married any more than I, and perhaps imagines, by leaving us so often alone together, that he will get me into some kind of scrape.'

'I too have wondered that, and if it is true his cowardliness must be without parallel. Yet regardless of his intentions, I am glad that he has afforded us this chance to speak openly; and as we are not guaranteed another, I must say this,' Millais went on, becoming more confident: 'if you are wondering whether I would do all that you could desire of me should you be brave enough to part from him, please allow me to put your mind perfectly at ease.'

Effie experienced a terrific sense of deliverance on hearing that Millais desired her freedom so as to be able to offer marriage, and after further discussion and assurances felt that she had been given a new sense of momentum in trying to free herself from Ruskin.

When the mist became dense in the twilight and the dampness caused Effie to shiver, Millais wrapped a shawl around her shoulders and poured a tot of whisky that they might make a silent yet meaningful toast.

Drying her eyes which had wept, not from mortification but the relief of unburdening herself, Effie rose from the blanket and gathered everything together so as to return to the cottage long before anyone should seek them out.

It was a blind man who did not observe the sympathy between the pair that evening, however, along with their avoidance of Ruskin's eye, an inevitable consequence of declaring their love and deciding upon a strategy which they would spend the remainder of the holiday perfecting. Effie's desertion of her husband being, Millais pronounced to his brother on the morrow, the only fair conclusion to a marriage vow which Ruskin himself had broken.

On the morrow, as if sensing the need to be present, Ruskin suggested accompanying the pair on a sketching expedition a small distance from the cottage, offering him the chance to observe that Effie acted quite differently whenever she was around Millais and appeared as sweet-natured and amiable as in her maiden days when she never displayed anything of her petulant or selfish ways.

Most of all he was struck by her sudden interest in drawing under Millais's tuition and, on observing the considerable pains she took to sketch the Highland scene before them, declared, 'You never care to learn anything *I* teach you.'

'*You* never take any trouble,' she replied, determined to counter his provocations.

Millais felt a knot in his stomach on witnessing the discord between Ruskin and Effie, for they hardly exchanged a word that was not said to provoke argument and ultimately preferred to remain silent rather than risk further cross words before their embarrassed guest. Thus the three continued sketching in quietude until, deciding they needed a new setting, they came to a stream which interrupted their path and forced them to communicate. But whilst Ruskin and Millais leapt across uninhibited, Effie hesitated on the other side of the bank, fearing lest she would fall into the water.

'Go on, woman!' Ruskin cried in annoyance at having to wait.

'I don't think I can cross,' she explained, looking down at her impractical attire.

'Well, you know how to find your way back,' he called, turning and marching on.

Out of sheer vexation, Effie would gladly have carried out this command, yet Millais, who was shocked at such spitefulness, jumped across in order to assist her.

'You see, I am simply an encumbrance to my husband,' she stated bitterly, clinging to his arm.

'I don't think he realises how cruel he can be,' Millais reasoned, astounded that Ruskin could stride on, leaving his wife scrambling on the other side of a brook.

'No, I expect you're right, for how else could he think it acceptable to keep a notebook in which he documents all my defects?' Effie mused rhetorically. 'Alas, I appear to have a whole list of peculiarities and am often likened to the mad woman in *Jane Eyre*.'

'Soon he will have no need of such a record, and I certainly shan't when you are mine,' Millais reassured her, pressing her hand. 'I can't perceive one fault in you, whereas *he* certainly possesses a great many. Poor creature, he really knows nothing about women, for if he did he would see that you're the sweetest of them all.'

'In truth, I am far from perfect, but I expect my husband to love me in spite of my faults,' she expounded tearfully.

They made no attempt to catch up with Ruskin, who had continued to march on with no care as to whether the other two were following, nor did he perceive the symbiotic language the pair exhibited as they conversed arm in arm.

'It's strange that a man so gifted in other respects can be so cold,' Millais remarked as Ruskin stalked into the woodland or knelt to collect botanical samples.

'Cold and brutal,' she railed. 'If I were to suffer the pains of eternal torment, it could not be worse than having to return to Herne Hill with him.'

'Be satisfied in knowing that you will not be forced to abide there much longer. And, by liberating yourself, you will probably be doing John Ruskin a greater service than either you or I can realise.'

The evening before their departure, Millais was plunged into considerable agitation, for he was only too glad to bid Ruskin farewell and all too sorry to part from Effie.

Their last dinner was sheer agony, with toasts aplenty to hail the success of the trip and a celebratory repast he barely touched for nausea, made worse whenever Ruskin praised his friendship, or his brother's knowing glance reminded him of his insincerity.

'Millais is really very ill tonight and has gone early to bed complaining of lethargy and a headache,' Ruskin related to his wife as she was packing. 'I don't know *what* to do with him, and the faintness seems so excessive as to be almost hysterical.'

The artist's inability to contain his feelings had forced him to lie that his emotional state had been brought on by the recent news that Holman Hunt was to go to Syria, prompting his patron to write to his friend in the deepest concern.

> *"Dearest Holman, here is Millais crying on his bed like a child. I had no idea how much he depended upon you. I have no hope of you abandoning the thought of Syria, yet if I had known sooner how much he wanted you I should have at least tried."*

On hearing that such a letter had been sent, Millais was forced to compose another directly, urging his friend to ignore Ruskin's earlier note and assuring him that he would one day explain how such a confusion had arisen, proclaiming, "I wish there were a monastery I could go to. I am beginning to be perfectly sick of life. I have much that I could tell you but cannot in a letter."

Hunt received both communications prior to his departure and required no such explanation, being quite certain that his friend had not heeded his warnings about putting himself in Effie's way.

The events in Scotland would doubtless become the stuff of Pre-Raphaelite legend, so he reflected, placing the final item of clothing in the trunk and closing the lid, counting himself as fortunate that he had never joined the Highland party and that he was leaving behind the resulting hostility for other shores.

INDEFINITELY

ON ENTERING THE CHAOS OF HIS STUDIO MILLAIS realised how entirely his life had changed, or should if Effie went ahead with the plan they had devised: altering, without much contemplation, his situation from that of a young man without any responsibilities to very real ones.

Having never held a brush with the concerns of rent to pay or a wife and children to keep, he wondered how these burdens would affect his creative output, not to mention the artistic ideals he had so ardently forged with the rest of the brotherhood. A whole week spent painting a leaf or flower would become a luxury he simply could not afford, and he saw for the first time that the artistic principles so admired by Ruskin were restricted, if not by class then most definitely by circumstance.

The portrait of Ruskin, despite it being the reason for the pilgrimage to Scotland, remained largely unfinished when the party went their separate ways, Millais having found himself too distracted by Effie and their confession of love, and too resentful of her husband to be remotely inclined to study his features.

How differently he regarded his patron on returning to London! The face he had once considered favourably, focussing only on its best qualities, had become truly repulsive, not least the protruding bottom lip which was a result of Ruskin having been bitten by a dog in childhood.

Millais noticed this blemish all the more when he regarded him following Effie's confession, taking a peculiar pleasure in the scar, nor was he inclined to flatter his subject to the point of ignoring his defects, for he knew them to run much deeper than any minor physical imperfections he might avoid committing to posterity.

Even Ruskin's attractive blue eyes took on a coolness that would be sorely telling of Millais's loathing towards his benefactor if he should paint them now and, when exhibited before the public, might reveal more than he wished to declare. How could eyes that could perceive the intricacies and beauties of the natural world be seemingly blind to all human feeling or the suffering he had caused his own wife?

A young man who knew nothing of love save for the knights and ladies he painted, Millais did not recognise that his infatuation obscured his judgement and allowed him to see only one side of the picture. Unconscious as to how his passion for Effie made him elevate her attributes and regard only the faults of his patron, he could not countenance Ruskin's neglect of the woman he loved, nor comprehend her years of tolerance.

Having given the excuse that ill health prevented him from continuing with the portrait, Millais preferred to withstand all his sitter's persistent queries and moans of disappointment rather than touch it, the god-like figure upon the rocks, who just a short time before had been his saviour, having fallen catastrophically from the pedestal on which he had initially placed him.

'I understand that you are ill and I am truly sorry for it,' Ruskin began sympathetically, calling unannounced at Gower Street shortly after their return from Glenfinlas.

'I am in arrears with your portrait and others besides,' Millais explained forlornly.

'Only imagine how much progress you *might* have made if you had not attempted, in vain, to instruct my wife in painting. As it is,' his commissioner went on with increasing irritation, scrutinising his face upon the canvas without detecting the artist's poorly concealed abhorrence, 'you will have to paint my figure *here* and go back to Scotland to finish the background. A disjointed affair if ever there was one.'

'I had thought to go to Wales in order to finish the waterfall,' Millais mused aloud, dreading the idea of setting foot in Scotland until such time as Effie was his.

'That won't do at all,' Ruskin dismissed firmly, 'Welsh rocks are of quite a different strata.'

Although he considered it impossible, ludicrous even, to feel jealousy towards such a man, Millais remained undecided as to whether he could ever bring himself to complete the work, for the prospect of having to stare at his spineless benefactor day in, day out, was far more terrible than any guilt he harboured at plotting to steal his wife away.

As soon as he had bade Ruskin a pleasant farewell, the insincerity of his reassurances and adieu causing his stomach to knot like so many naval braids, out came the paint-splattered dust sheet to cover the painting and allow him to put off its completion until some future day when Effie might have claimed her freedom.

Out too came his battered hip flask containing single malt, a painful reminder of his recent Highland adventures. A short swig informed him that the contents were running disappointingly low due to frequent application, for although Millais well knew that liquor increased rather than abated his anxiety, and made his thoughts more fuddled and hazy, he dwelt somewhere between a hapless hero and a lovesick adolescent, preparing to assert himself upon Effie's command and wasting countless hours in trying to predict the next epiphany in his romantic history.

Why Ruskin ever thought to marry her without first establishing his desire for her, perplexed and troubled Millais, yet the more he thought it over, the more adamant he was that Effie could, in no way, be culpable on seeking to be released from such a marriage, nor he in seducing a woman so sorely neglected.

Feeling the full weight of responsibility for having encouraged her to desert her husband and home, however, he was determined to prove himself worthy of her faith and trust, convinced, as he succumbed to intoxication, that the love and support of their families would help them endure all the challenges Ruskin and a hypocritical society would doubtless set them.

Effie had meanwhile informed her mother by letter that she had fallen deeply in love with Millais during their time in Scotland, on which Mrs Gray, anxious to avoid rumours, wrote to the artist directly, begging him to exert his full discretion and asking that he cease all communication with her daughter.

Millais, insulted by the request, which seemed to insinuate an impropriety on his behalf, replied audaciously by return:

> *"I should never have written to your daughter had not Ruskin been cognisant to the correspondence and approving of it, or at least not admitting a care in the matter, for it appears that he cares for nothing beyond his mother and father. If I have meddled more than my place would justify it is because I am only anxious to do the best for your daughter. I cannot conceal the truth from you, that Effie passes her days in melancholy and has more to put up with than any woman living…"*

Terrified to consider the implications of her daughter leaving her famed husband and comfortable London address in favour of running away with a young artist, this brief, yet direct communication impressed Mrs Gray, who granted that Effie must decide her own course without fear, shame or interference.

As life sometimes had a habit of dealing even amounts of both good and bad tidings, Millais was meanwhile overwhelmed to discover that he was to be made an Associate of the Royal Academy at the unprecedented age of twenty-four, and thereby wrote again to Mrs Gray assuring her of his reliability and that he would soon have a large enough income to provide for a wife and family should her daughter have enough fortitude to extricate herself from her loveless marriage.

To prove himself in earnest, Millais promised to refrain from corresponding with her daughter, granting that it *was* inappropriate, yet relinquishing any right to do so in a language telling of his respect and devotion. Imploring Effie to write to him as soon as she was able, such a letter he would await indefinitely, for it would signify that her days as Ruskin's bride lay as much behind her as those, when at last she would become *his* beloved wife, were happily within reach.

ABANDONMENT

EFFIE MET THE SIXTH ANNIVERSARY OF HER MARRIAGE IN April the following year with new optimism rather than despair, having besought her parents to obtain the necessary legal advice that would enable her to seek an annulment, her maiden state being her greatest chance of forging a case against her husband.

Although she no longer heard directly from Millais, whenever she saw him out socially or he was invited to Herne Hill she would attempt to exchange a brief word with him in order to reassure him that her plans were well in hand, and that every day she edged closer to realising the long-held dream of him addressing her as plain "Miss Gray".

Having received word that the law was on her side, Effie drew on all her courage by boldly announcing to her husband over dinner one evening her intention to journey to Scotland the next day on the pretext of visiting her family, timed to coincide with his imminent tour of Switzerland with his parents, an excursion she had fortunately not been invited to join.

Relieved at the thought of having the house to himself for a fortnight prior to going abroad, and believing that Effie's regular visits to Bowerswell were vital in maintaining her equanimity, Ruskin was eager to agree to her proposal.

'That's very sudden,' he said, looking up, 'but of course you must go. In as dull a place as this the time must slip by like oil.'

'I wasn't asking your *permission*, you understand?' she rebutted, the day when she would no longer have to seek his approval being within clear sight.

'Nor should you,' he replied calmly. 'It would please me to think of you with company whilst I'm away. Allow me to see you off at King's Cross?' he insisted, rising and withdrawing the train timetable from the bureau.

'If you must,' she sighed.

Scanning the morrow's departure times to Edinburgh, Ruskin meant to persuade her to take an early train and thereby leave him in peace to prepare for his own holiday, little guessing her eagerness to be gone as he thrust the railway guide before her.

'You might take the eight fifteen and be in Perth by dinner,' he suggested, pointing to the timetable. 'I will see that Crawley accompanies you the full way.'

'I don't require him,' Effie asserted aggressively, fearing that this would ruin the plan she had spent so long devising.

'That's as may be, but you know how people are always accusing me of being too lax with decorum,' he teased, putting her reluctance down to her usual obtuseness.

'As you like,' she conceded, rising from the table as proudly and serenely as one of Shakespeare's vixens. 'I shall go and prepare.'

'Is that all you have to say, when we'll be apart for three months?' Ruskin questioned sombrely, touching her arm in a gesture he intended to be romantic but which struck her as paternal and condescending.

'A few months is surely of little consequence to a marriage such as ours,' Effie smiled, closing the door behind her.

***

Crawley observed that Effie appeared pale and weary the next morning, and yet she bustled about the house restlessly, as if anxious not to forget anything. Each time he enquired if he might assist her in any way he was rebuffed sharply and sent away, however, something which made him suspicious that her motivation in going was not all that it seemed.

Intrigued as to Effie's obvious agitation, the valet, whilst intending to keep his head down on reaching the station, could hardly fail to scrutinise the scene when his master and mistress began to exchange cross words on the platform, attracting attention despite the throng of travellers and porters being intent upon their own affairs.

He looked on in bewilderment as Effie raised her voice sharply and pushed away the coin purse Ruskin held out in generosity, an action which prompted him to strain to hear what they were arguing about.

'I have made my plans and it will take a cleverer man than *you*, John Ruskin, to upset them now!' she shouted, slamming the door of the first-class compartment in her husband's face, her hands trembling as she settled herself in the carriage and counted down the moments until the sounding of the whistle.

It occurred to Crawley, as he went to assist the porter in loading Effie's trunks onto the train, what a considerable amount of luggage she was taking for only a few weeks. This, coupled with her rudeness, alerted him to suppose that some scheme of desertion was afoot, though his master remained as unsuspecting and naive as he had shown himself in Venice.

As it was by no means the first occasion on which Effie had embarrassed her husband in public, Ruskin was not unduly discomposed by his wife's discourtesy, nor led to surmise, as he watched the train draw out of the station like a scene in a Russian novel, that it was to take her away forever.

Should he have possessed enough foresight to predict such an outcome, he would have been just as inclined to calmly wave her farewell, for his patience had long ago exceeded its limits and he dreaded Effie's return to London as keenly as he welcomed her departure.

Thus, in the full knowledge and support of her parents and Millais, Effie made her escape that April morning, disembarking at the next station of Hitchin where she delighted in dismissing Crawley brusquely on being joined by her mother and father who seconded that his services were no longer required.

Flushed in her excitement and thrilled by the covert nature of the enterprise, Effie revelled in picturing Ruskin standing alone on the platform unwittingly abandoned, nor could she conceal her jubilation as the train sped northward, taking her further and further away from those whom she now referred to as 'the batch of Ruskins'.

'*This* is the most important event of my life, upon which all my future depends,' she proclaimed, gripping her mother's hand and looking at her father in fixed resolution. 'I am so grateful to have your approval in the course of action I have embarked upon, for already a quiet happiness has settled on my spirit in finally being away from those wicked people.'

'Oh, my darling child, we are confident that *right* will out,' her mother encouraged tenderly, 'and that the rest of your life will be a deal happier than the past half decade.'

'They could hardly be worse,' her daughter smiled, tears of relief surfacing. 'I feel as if I have been reborn and am about to begin my adult life from the beginning.'

'The note I received from Mr Millais before we came away offers *proof* of it,' her mother went on, withdrawing the letter from her pocket and reading it aloud with satisfaction, "'I keep my promise in writing to *you* and not to Effie, and hope that you will allow me to say that when you return to Perth the poor, ill-used Countess, who has been imprisoned for so many years, must return to her former happy life, playing, dancing and drawing, and never for a *moment* permit her thoughts to rest upon the tragic farce in which she has so patiently played a suffering role. It delights me to think that she is to have an "Order of Release" of her own, and the knowledge that she is at this very moment going home has a most beneficial influence upon me."'

Margaret Ruskin had meanwhile discovered and read, with considerable glee, the letter Effie had left behind for her, summarising in the plainest, least remorseful language that she would never return to the ugly house on Herne Hill and that it was her intention to immediately apply for her marriage to be dissolved:

"The law will let you know what I have demanded, and I put it to you to consider what a very great loss, in every point of view, your son's conduct has entailed upon me for these best six years of my life."

Believing Ruskin to be faultless in most everything, Margaret harrumphed, folded Effie's sanctimonious vindication, signed decisively "Euphemia Gray", and placed it in her apron until such time as her son arrived to view the contents for himself.

No more, no less than she would have expected from the daughter-in-law she had ever opposed and disapproved of, Margaret was gratified at the prospect of having her son's undivided attention again, and gloated oblivious of any insensitivity now that her earlier judgement had proved so astute. The woman whom she had long regarded as a self-serving miss would no longer be able to make fools of them all.

Despite reading his wife's letter on returning to Denmark Hill, and Crawley arriving soon after with a vivid account of his abrupt dismissal at Hitchin, Ruskin was nonchalant of the revelation and too convinced of his wife's fragile mental state to believe that Effie acted in all seriousness.

Thinking it no more than a hysterical prank designed to punish him for failing to invite her to Switzerland, it was only when two court officials called as he was dining with his parents and insisted upon seeing him that he finally believed his marriage was at an end.

The gentlemen, who could hardly be called such due to their ill manners and the shabbiness of their appearance, declared themselves to be on urgent business and would not wait for the family to finish their meal, huffing and puffing in the lobby until Crawley could be persuaded to carry forth their request.

Taking just a few minutes to serve a citation on Ruskin, in the presence of his parents who would not countenance leaving the table in the midst of their dinner, the men refused to answer any of the questions directed at them and, turning on their heels, without so much as bidding the family a good evening, departed as boorishly as they had entered.

'So it is done,' Ruskin admitted, scanning the document briefly before continuing with his repast.

A few days later a packet, addressed to Ruskin with no letter enclosed, arrived at Denmark Hill containing Effie's keys, household accounts and her wedding ring, items he quickly banished to the bottom drawer of his desk as if he had never laid eyes on them.

Convinced that he was the victim, regardless of whatever lies Effie would inevitably carry abroad, Ruskin made no hesitation in furnishing his solicitor with a full and honest statement, explaining that he had married in order to have a companion and not for passion's sake. Admitting that his marriage had remained unconsummated, he added that his wife had fully consented to the arrangement and that it was not because of any physical impairment on his part.

'Had she treated me as a kind and devoted wife would have done, doubtless I should have longed to possess her, body and heart,' he justified to the aged family solicitor, who slumped in his chair much taken aback by his client's frankness, 'but Effie was neither kind nor devoted.'

Prendergast frowned and, leaning forward so as to rest the weight of his corpulent person onto his forearms, asked, 'Are you quite sure that there is no way of redeeming the situation? Are you not too much in the throes of anger to make such a decision?'

'It is *inconceivable* that I could ever take that woman to be my wife or welcome the prospect of her bearing my children in light of what has recently passed. Therefore,' he concluded, pausing as if to emphasise the point, 'I have no intention of defending the suit, for *that* might result in being lumbered with her for life.'

His adviser snorted at the vehemence of the response, yet quickly remembering himself suggested measuredly, 'Perhaps the consequences of an annulment have not yet fully dawned on you?'

'On the contrary, when I consider the likelihood of never seeing Effie again, I feel as cheerful as if marriage had never been invented among mankind,' Ruskin boasted.

'But the scandal…' he reminded.

'What care I what people say about me? They can all go to the Devil with their rumours and speculation.'

The man of letters listened to this declaration with no doubt as to its truth, for, notwithstanding that the annulment case was overshadowing news of the Crimean War in the press, he saw only too well that Ruskin would consider it worth any short-lived humiliation to be a free man again, and thus accepted his client's instruction to offer up no defence with an obliging air belying his own feelings towards the female sex.

Whilst Ruskin took on a dissident air publicly, he nonetheless felt the failure of his marriage sorely when it came to relating the details of the solicitor's meeting to his mother and father upon returning home after dining at his club, the old couple having waited up expressly to hear the measures that would be taken to uphold their son's good name before a baying public.

No matter how they reassured him that, however reverently they both viewed the bonds of marriage, he could not be blamed for Effie's conduct, nor leaving the suit unchallenged, his mother's biblical teachings resounded in his ear, as did her countless warnings all those years ago that the bad tidings of Bowerswell would doom his marriage.

Pouring himself and his father an exceptionally large sherry as they talked long past their usual hour of retiring, he announced submissively, 'I shall give up Herne Hill and return home for good if you will have me,' offering himself up like a boy ashamed at having received a poor school report and being threatened with expulsion.

'There will always be a place for you here,' John James affirmed, raising his glass to the son who would ever be his pride and joy, though he did not often express it.

'It's more than I deserve. I don't think I have ever fully appreciated you both until being forsaken by Effie,' he mused penitently, turning to his mother. 'Marrying her was the greatest crime I ever committed.'

'How so?' she asked.

'By acting in opposition to *you*.'

'You are not to reproach yourself, my son,' she dismissed, shaking her head; 'most people were taken in by her, *I* just wasn't as easily hoodwinked.'

'I still cannot make out what made her act thus,' he pondered aloud. 'Was I really such a terrible husband?'

'*Some* people you can never please,' Margaret sneered.

On rising in order to bid his parents goodnight, Ruskin dutifully shook his father by the hand and kissed his mother's cheek, it being almost miraculous for Margaret to consider that their son was returning to the fold and that their harmonious Denmark Hill existence was to be restored after such irregularity and discord.

In contrast to the re-established peace of his old home, Ruskin found that he could hardly venture outside without being interrogated as to Effie's suit, the tediousness of which challenged his composure and made him eager to go abroad at the first opportunity.

In response to many of Ruskin's oldest male acquaintances claiming to find it strange that he could have abstained from a woman so attractive, he admitted to finding Effie's face beautiful before going on to qualify this to three bewildered men seated at his table in the Athenaeum Club.

'To experience ardour for a woman I hope that I am not fickle enough to consider only her *looks*, for surely her personality must also be agreeable?'

'I'd go for a fine figure over a winning personality any day,' one remarked salaciously, putting Ruskin in mind of the university men he had encountered at Oxford.

'As it happens, Effie's person was *not* formed to excite passion,' he denied, 'although I pride myself on being too honourable to divulge what prevented this from being so. Let us just say that, rightly or wrongly, I had imagined women to be quite different.'

Lest his indiscretion should be the result of Effie's humiliation, he described to those eager for information his feelings of abhorrence rather than elaborating on the precise cause, something which only increased speculation regarding the mystery of the couple's marital relations and fanned the flames of gossip spreading through the city's most affluent drawing rooms like the Great Fire.

Regardless that the majority of Ruskin's circle sympathised with Effie, they did so privately whilst welcoming her deserted husband, whose position as one of the most notable figures in London was elevated tenfold in the wake of his infamy. Indeed, far from being ostracised following the very public failure of his marriage, Ruskin was bemused to receive more invitations than ever he had hitherto, so eagerly did hostesses wish to have the most talked about man in London at their dinner parties.

He had no wish to pique their curiosity further or portray himself as a Byronic figure, and thus he continued to make arrangements to journey to Switzerland with his parents, hopeful that the public's interest would diminish in his absence. Even declining invitations did not prevent him from being tormented by a veritable stream of callers hoping to glean more nuggets of gossip, however, and on the eve of his voyage a female acquaintance, whom he had never exchanged more than a dozen words with, called at Denmark Hill on the pretence of offering her friendship.

'You can be of no use to me at present, except by not disturbing me, nor thinking of me,' Ruskin spurned, offering the lady tea but no sweetmeats. 'I cannot continue to contradict reports of my marriage *ad infinitum*, after all the world must have its day of glory, but rest assured I shall neither be subdued nor materially changed by this matter. No man of real worth can love what is unworthy, enough to be ruined or even permanently hurt by discovering that it is so. Trust me when I say, the worst of my pain is over.'

Ruskin's countless enquiries from Switzerland as to how the picture was progressing and when its completion could be expected nudged Millais to resume work on it, reasoning that as soon as the paint was dry he could send it from his studio never to look on it again.

Disgusted with the way in which society mixed up his name in the affair, Millais reluctantly journeyed to the Highlands in the face of the scandal, not, as some people supposed, to see the unfortunate lady, but simply in order to finish the background of Ruskin's portrait, insisting to his friends that he would never have the bad taste to see Effie whilst the matter was in lawyers' hands.

Ruskin was residing in Lausanne when the decree nisi, returning him to his former bachelorhood, was pronounced a few months later, something he was as relieved as his former wife to receive; so too Millais, who was away painting when he tore open a letter from Mrs Gray hailing her daughter's freedom.

After eight torturous months since last he had met or corresponded with Effie, before the hour was out Millais had composed four rapturous pages describing his great joy on hearing of her liberty and his intention to pack up immediately and return to Gower Street.

"My dear Countess,

I cannot see that there is anything to prevent my writing to you now, so I will wait no longer.

I consider that I have a special right to be amongst the first of your congratulating friends, for no-one has been so keenly interested in the trials you have gone through, or is so happy at this blessed termination.

I had so thoroughly convinced myself of the improbability of ever speaking to you again that I find my brain unable to keep pace with the sudden alteration of affairs, and I am writing this in a state of incredulity.

I was surprised to find your mother's letter upon the breakfast table, for I knew at once what it contained – the best news I have ever received in my life.

This time last year there seemed no more chance of what has happened than that the moon should fall; and now you are Miss Gray again, I feel half frightened at the thought. But how glad I shall be to see you! This is all I can say now, and you must imagine the rest…"

No. 30 Herne Hill was shut up and ready to be leased to a new husband and wife when Ruskin eventually returned to London, the servants having been dismissed and the hideous furniture, which Effie had kicked and knocked about in temper, having been auctioned off at a considerable loss to John James.

Seeing the shell of his former existence made him overwhelmingly gladdened by the thought of removing to his familiar room at Denmark Hill, which in truth only meant sleeping where he had never really stopped living, effortlessly allowing him to resume his contained existence with no-one to distract him from his work or rebuke his attentions to his mother and father.

He little supposed, as he sat for Millais during the finishing touches to his portrait, that the Scottish trip he had so meticulously designed to boost the artist's career had brought about his current situation, or that his young friend was meanwhile waiting patiently to announce his engagement to Effie.

To ease his conscience and pangs of deceitfulness, Millais remained convinced that Ruskin had engineered him to fall in love with his wife, no matter that his patron continued to show the warmest amiability and seemed as innocent of any understanding between himself and Effie than on the day she had left King's Cross.

While all London surmised Millais's treachery, Ruskin defended his protégé vehemently, putting the gossip down to the wildest fabrication and unsuspecting his friend's design to lay low for fear that not waiting a proper period of time to announce his engagement would promote rumours that they had committed adultery.

Effie was meanwhile resigned to never being admitted into the echelons of society that once had lauded her, and merely sought to minimise the damage which the annulment had already caused to her reputation. The thought of returning to London as Mrs Millais was enough to sustain her during her exile, nor did she desire any role but that of a devoted wife and mother.

Whilst she was forced to remain tucked away in Scotland for an indefinite period, Millais found it intolerable whenever Ruskin invited him to dine with his parents at Denmark Hill, the old couple being keen to regale the artist who was painting their son's portrait.

In light of all that had taken place, and that which was still being covertly arranged, Millais considered having to socialise with Ruskin, let alone having to paint him, as one of the most hateful things he ever had to do, considering it ironic that it was for Effie's sake he feigned intimacy with her former husband and benefited from his usefulness by way of recompense for the ill treatment she had endured.

It gave Millais abundant amusement to think how hurt and disappointed Ruskin would be when he discovered his disloyalty, for the man whose hospitality he accepted with the gall of Judas had no experience of true friendship save for his parents. He was provokingly gentle and solitary. There never was such a quiet scoundrel!

Ruskin dispatched Crawley to Gower Street with a case of wine and a note of jubilant praise upon receiving the portrait that December, displaying it to the admiration of all who visited Denmark Hill until it was announced in the newspapers, a little over a year following the annulment, that Effie had married Millais at Bowerswell.

Even more incensed by the betrayal than his son, John James interrupted his breakfast on reading the report and, marching into the drawing room, took down the portrait and ordered Crawley to take it anywhere but where he could see it.

'I shall write to Mr Millais,' his father fumed to Ruskin, 'letting him know that, at best, I shall never let the picture be exhibited, and at *worst* I will obliterate it with a penknife!'

Ruskin, as a faithful preserver of art no matter what the politics or sentiment behind it, saw no alternative but to immediately send the painting in a hansom cab to the safety of Rossetti's studio, though he found himself equally glad that it was gone when he received an audacious letter from Millais ending their friendship and stating that he would have no more to do with him.

'Instead of asking my forgiveness at having deceived me for years,' Ruskin protested, finally showing the emotion of his father, 'or for running off with my wife, he condescends to put an end to our acquaintance, whilst insinuating that I *purposely* contrived to throw Effie into his arms!'

'I hope you will emphatically deny it?' John James insisted.

'I should sooner think of denying an accusation of murder,' he refuted scornfully, tearing the letter to pieces. 'Let those who say I have committed murder *prove* it, and those who believe I have committed it without proof continue to think so. Whilst I have had to learn many bitter lessons, Millais has given me one last example as to the possible extent of human folly and ingratitude.'

'How could he have so readily ranked himself on the side of your enemies and slanderers after all that you have done for him?' his father pondered in disbelief.

'He is blinded by her temporary charm I suppose, yet, if there is any retribution in this life, then there will assuredly be dark hours in the distance for Millais and *she* whom he has chosen. For my own part, as long as I feel, whether erringly or not, that my work is useful in the world, I shall never again devote myself to any woman.'

PART FOUR

THE LAWS OF FREEDOM

TEN YEARS HAD ELAPSED SINCE RUSKIN'S FATEFUL MEETING with Maria La Touche and her daughter, fourteen since the annulment of his marriage, yet those two seemingly unconnected events capsized all possibility of any present equanimity and threw even his own liberty into question.

Tormented by the great mistake he had made, sleepless nights followed as surely as weeks of impenetrable London smog as he looked back upon his short and fruitless partnership with Effie, a chapter of history he could neither undo nor erase but which had the power to upset his entire future.

Having spent the intervening years attempting to put his marriage and all its bitter associations firmly from his mind, his desire to marry Rose meant that he was forced to revisit the past and attempt to justify his failings to those all too eager to condemn him.

Divorce was inevitably scandalous when one of the parties was as famed as he, yet, with only a very few knowing the terms which had unshackled him from Effie, Ruskin was confounded by the impudence of

475

Mrs La Touche in getting hold of a copy of the original judgement and taking it upon herself to consult her solicitor as to its contents.

The only benefit resulting from Mrs La Touche's disgust upon reading of Ruskin's incurable impotency was that it finally extinguished her own ridiculous passion for him, though in the end it was far better to have the lady's admiration than hate: the abhorrence with which Maria pored over the contents of the legal document prompting not only a violent revulsion towards the man she had revered above all others, but the deepest humiliation in ever having befriended him, a feeling which grew into the most bitter and vengeful hostility.

Sorely embarrassed for having once entertained the foolish notion of making Ruskin her lover, where Mrs La Touche had once felt spurned now at least she could attribute his lack of feeling to an unnaturalness or inherent unmanliness. Effie was beautiful in her day, and Maria still considered herself handsome enough to garner attention, but what it was that drew Ruskin to love her daughter she could not understand, Rose's only desire being to devote herself to Christ.

Riddled with jealousy and spite, Maria would stop at nothing until Rose had abandoned all idea of her former teacher, and thus she instructed her solicitor to assert in writing that no clergyman could marry a man whom he knew to be incapable of consummating marriage.

Surprised by the underhandedness of the battle Mrs La Touche was forging against him, Ruskin discovered her stance through third parties, though he strongly doubted that the law would impede him from remarrying when once they had proclaimed him free.

Nevertheless, he felt her accusation of wrongfulness in asking for her daughter's hand most painfully, and it was the hope of exoneration that made him seek to prove the lady wrong in her denouncement.

After receiving countless recommendations from friends, he finally applied to Dr Thomas H. Tristram for his opinion, one of Chancery's most esteemed legal minds, whose experience of civil law was as impressive as the letters following his name, inscribed on a brass plaque outside his foreboding chambers within the Temple, where Ruskin was summoned one dreary afternoon when the wind howled around street corners, blowing up his coat tails and throwing dust into his eyes just as if his enemies also had a hand in the skittish London weather.

Having unsuccessfully battled with his umbrella, he found himself in a foul temper on arriving at Tristram's chambers, a peevishness made worse by having to wait for over an hour. Due to impatience more than arrogance, Ruskin always intensely disliked being kept waiting by anyone, and so he stalked the small, dark, wainscoted ante-room as anxiously as a convict in a dungeon preparing to hear the jury's verdict.

He could not make out if he was more comfortable in sitting or standing and, having tried both postures, failed to distract himself by dipping into the copy of *Bleak House* he found lying about, being in no mood for caricatures of those seeking legal advice or embroiled in a system designed to extract money rather than reach conclusions.

After a considerable interval due to Tristram running late on another case, Ruskin was finally ushered into the snug, cluttered office, nor was he immediately impressed by the doctor, who looked rather debauched, possessing a flabby neck which hung obscenely over his collar as he made notes he might have avoided if only he had paid more attention to his client's initial, yet comprehensive, enquiry.

'My good Mr Ruskin, what is your objective in coming here today?' Tristram asked, turning to a new page and scribbling something thereon.

'Put simply, I wish to remarry,' Ruskin answered.

'And do you believe there is an impediment?'

'Some people have suggested that I may not be entitled to do so due to the grounds on which my first marriage was annulled,' he replied vexatiously, irritated in having to repeat that which he had already explained by letter. *It's little wonder Tristram's appointments run so far behind with preparation such as this*, he thought, emphasising his annoyance with a protracted sigh.

'And what grounds were those?' the lawyer asked, intrigued enough by his client's guardedness to peer at him quizzically.

'Incurable impotency.'

'Ah, I see,' Tristram responded sympathetically. 'A tricky business!'

'I feared you'd say that,' Ruskin rejoined, shifting in his seat.

'Was it, or rather *is* it *true?*'

'My impotence was through choice rather than any physical impairment, but when my wife began annulment proceedings I thought it only fair to agree to it rather than defend myself.'

'Fair?' Tristram repeated, perplexed.

'Yes, as *I* had no desire for her, I supposed she had every right to find a man who *did,*' Ruskin explained reasonably.

'Quite so,' he nodded, jotting something down hurriedly.

'Although I assured my solicitor that I could prove my virility at any time,' his client went on, becoming flustered in the process of trying to get his point across, 'I refrained from doing so lest I should have been forced to remain with Effie.'

'Am I to gather that you now question the validity of the annulment because you *chose* not to offer a defence?' Tristram posed, making a bridge with his hands.

'That, and whether the terms make it impossible for me to marry *now*. You see, the family of the woman I wish to make my wife have been advised that the Church is not permitted to wed a man believed to be impotent. Worse still, they suggest that I would invalidate the annulment of my first marriage were I to father a child, and perhaps even be declared a bigamist.'

'Nonsense!' he disputed firmly. 'The *law* no longer assumes that, just because a marriage remains unconsummated for three years or more, the man is *unable* to perform his duty. A fellow may be impotent with one woman but not with another. As the old adage goes, one man's meat is another man's poison. Is that not so?'

After chortling to himself and looking into the middle distance momentarily, Tristram rose to his feet like a Regency gentleman struggling with gout and began searching among his extensive library of legal volumes, revealing an expansive waistline previously disguised by an even more substantial desk.

Ruskin fairly gasped when the solicitor realised that the reference book he required was on one of the top shelves and, drawing the library steps towards him, made an almighty effort to heave his corpulent body onto the bottom step. Making the wood creak under the strain, he displayed generously proportioned stockinged calves and gold-buckled shoes, which informed his client that he had spent the morning in court and had been too busy to change.

Ever more breathless and unsteady on his feet as he strained to read the spines of several volumes, Ruskin, observing the spectacle in wonder, became concerned lest his adviser should take a fall; his hands firmly clenched on the arms of his chair as he viewed the acrobatics better suited to a man half Tristram's age and size.

'Ahh!' he yelped, becoming severely unbalanced on seeing the book he sought and proceeding to stretch with all his might.

Ruskin, instinctively jumping to his feet, took hold of the steps in order to provide Tristram with a more secure platform, and suggested eagerly, 'Might *I* fetch it for you?'

'No need, *this* is the blighter!' the doctor declared, holding the tome aloft before puffing his way down jovially. 'D'you know, I'm up and down that ladder half a dozen times a day.'

'Gracious,' he remarked wryly, impressed at the carpenter who had constructed such a durable item of furniture.

'Now, let me see,' Tristram muttered, settling himself at his desk and flicking through the pages until he reached the relevant law.

Reading the declaration most carefully, it was several minutes before he spoke or looked up again, leaving Ruskin to feel anxious indeed.

'Well? Do you find anything to prevent my marrying again?' he asked, unable to contain his inquisitiveness.

'As a matter of fact I *don't*,' he granted, smiling serenely and reclining in his chair with the air of a man who has just won a large bet. 'There was a similar case affecting the Earl of Essex in the reign of Elizabeth I.'

'Is that not long out of date?'

'You'll find most English law is out of date,' he scoffed, raising his wiry eyebrows. 'Anyhow, Lady Essex obtained a divorce due to no marital relations taking place between herself and her husband, yet as the earl proclaimed himself impotent *solely* in relation to *her* both parties were declared free to remarry. Nowadays the Civil Divorce Court handles such matters, leaving the Ecclesiastical Court impotent, if you'll pardon the expression. Therefore, for all practical purposes I can't see any reason why *you* are not equally entitled to follow suit.'

A man who could match Ruskin's high opinion of himself pound for pound, Tristram offered his legal interpretation without hesitation; time was money and there were far more pressing matters on his mind, or rather cases that would bear more fruit for his jam-making.

'You don't know what a relief it is to hear you say so,' Ruskin replied jubilantly, the creases of consternation transformed into smiles.

'A satisfactory conclusion to our meeting, is it not?' said the lawyer, clapping his hands and struggling to his feet.

'It *is* indeed,' Ruskin agreed as Tristram opened the door, eager to usher him away.

'I only hope you find your *next* wife more desirable,' he ventured, shaking him warmly by the hand. 'I am recently married myself and can vouch for what a blessing marriage is when you find the right woman.'

'There never were two more different women as the one I am free of and the one I hope to win,' Ruskin mused. 'The former being selfish and designing and the latter as pure as an angel, too innocent to learn the unromantic ways of the law or my calamitous misjudgement.'

'If she is as kind and good as you say, all that will be as nothing,' Tristram assured.

'You have given me hope at least,' he nodded, adding sadly, 'for sometimes it has seemed my destiny never to fall in love when I should have a chance of success.'

The lawyer bade his client farewell blithely, stating that his invoice would be sent on by post, while Ruskin, who'd had few dealings with the profession, should have been content to pay double for such an outcome.

With a musty waiting room of baying customers, Tristram was a hugely likeable fellow despite dispatching clients from his shadowy chambers as hastily as a hangman, and Ruskin hardly noticed his sense of urgency to be rid of him, so elated was he at the thought of there being no legal obstacle to his union with Rose.

Confident that Tristram's stance would destroy the barriers conjured up by his band of adversaries, he entered the street as weightlessly as a man unchained from shackles and considerably more liberated than on the day when he had received the decree stating his independence from Effie.

Rose alone had given him reason to desire such confirmation and, as he made his way home, eager to inform his mother and Joan of the news, he strode like a young man rather than one approaching fifty, his quick, expansive steps illustrative of a new sense of purpose.

MOTHER AND DAUGHTER

A FULL YEAR HAD PASSED SINCE THE CRUSHING NEWS OF
Emily's passing, leaving Harristown bereft and silent; the piano
left untouched, ever reminding them of their loss and the sweet
sounds they would hear no more.

All Rose's charms were as nothing to the poor, dutiful sister whom
her mother grieved over and compared her with in vain. Rather than
cherishing her youngest daughter following the tragic demise of her eldest,
Maria became increasingly severe and hardened, spurning all maternal
kindness in favour of pouring poison onto the head of the child she had
once hailed as a younger version of herself.

Withdrawing from her kin as if she alone suffered, Maria dwelt in
Emily's old room during the initial stage of mourning, weeping until her
eyes ran dry and the loneliness of night showed her the futility of tears.
Expelling Rose from her company during the daylight hours as though
she could not bear to look on her, diatribes against Ruskin secured the
discordance between them and cast out all sympathy.

Although there was nothing in her mother's flights of rage which had not been said countless times before, namely how disloyal and perverse she considered Ruskin for wanting to go from being her daughter's teacher to her husband, she stormed with an increased violence after Emily's death, thereby doubling Rose's grief and making her question why *she* and not her beloved sister remained.

Recollections of that long tranquil summer with Emily and Ruskin left a hollowness in every corner of the house and grounds she wandered listlessly: the woodland where they had played hide and seek amongst the lime trees; the croquet lawn where she had stamped her feet in protest of lessons; or the river over which no bridge would be built for many a day.

The weeks and months went on as if no troubles to come could have any power over her, and yet it was hard to live without the love of those one wanted it most from; the pain was exacerbated by her mother's rejection and taunts, making her long for Ruskin all the more, for he alone could comfort her and restore the joy and gladness of living her mother sought to stifle.

Unable to defend him for fear of worsening the tension which hung over the estate like dense black clouds obscuring the merest ray of sunshine, Rose thought only of those she loved but had no prospect of seeing as she faced the anguish of her sister's death companionless; her one consolation the golden days her mother tried and failed to blight, saving her from the suffocating loneliness that threatened to envelop her, crippling her former spirit and taking away any impetus to escape the walls in which she was incarcerated.

Effie's harrowing account of her life with Ruskin not having had the effect Mrs La Touche desired, the legal implications of any potential marriage became her sole argument when it came to bullying Rose to abandon all thoughts of becoming his second wife, making no attempt to explain these complications in any detail and preferring to leave the whole matter a mystery.

Though Rose no longer trusted her mother and greatly doubted Effie's honesty, constant arguments and her own religiosity eventually challenged her loyalty to Ruskin. Despite early fortitude and steadfastness, with no friend in whom to confide Rose began to buckle under the strain of isolation, judging her dissent and wilfulness as God might do and praying for redemption that she might prove herself to be worthy of His pity.

With no desire other than to perfect herself in the shadow of her sister's memory, it struck Rose cruelly that she would never see her wise, virtuous Emily again, whose face was engraved upon her mind as clearly as her name had been chiselled upon the pure white marble tomb which lay, new and out of place, in the family chapel. Nor was any dedication thereon sufficient to describe the loss she felt when laying flowers for the daughter, sister, wife and mother taken for no reason if not to unite them in sorrow.

'Answer me when I call to you, righteous God,' Rose cried, her face bathed in tears and her hands clasped together. 'Give me relief from my distress. Be merciful to me and hear my prayer. I am surrounded by the darkness of death and grief. I am unsure of my steps, for the path is hidden and unknown and the journey seems endless.'

As Rose was preparing for bed one night her mother startled her by entering unannounced, clutching a blanket as if to excuse the intrusion. Apprehensive of a quarrel, Rose shivered in her thin white cotton nightgown and, resting her comb on the dressing table, stared at her enquiringly in the mirror.

Mrs La Touche, pale and drawn from months of anguish, offered no word of greeting and placed the blanket in the linen chest positioned at the end of the bed as casually as if no breach existed between them, prompting Rose to conjecture that perhaps she was sorry for her behaviour and meant to ask forgiveness.

'I don't want us to quarrel anymore,' she began finally, sitting upon the chest and folding her hands primly.

'Really?' Rose asked tentatively, turning to face her and daring to hope they might be reconciled.

'Sometimes I think I'm turning into my own mother and I hate myself for it,' Mrs La Touche confessed, rubbing her sleep-deprived brow in weariness. 'I hope you know that I never *intend* to be cruel, it's just that sometimes you won't see reason.'

Rose looked to the heavens in exasperation. 'By reason, you mean that I should always defer to *you?*'

'Aren't we always told to honour our parents in the Bible?'

'Why are you so against me marrying, Mother?' she confronted, failing to make her question gentle.

'I'm not against you marrying, it's the *man* you wish to marry I contest,' she dismissed, rising and moving towards the door on perceiving that the path to her daughter's friendship lay strewn with contention.

'You always *used* to hold him in the highest regard,' Rose persisted, for surely the only chance of healing their fractured relationship was to lay everything bare.

'Whilst I always respected Ruskin, I never considered the possibility of him wanting to marry one of my daughters.' And her mother stopped short as if the idea was too repellent. She looked ugly and rancorous in the dim light afforded by the oil lamps, and grew more so as she continued to raise her voice, 'All of Dublin is rife with gossip surrounding his marriage to Effie, and now your name is coupled with *his*.'

But Rose was defiant and showed herself just as quick-witted as the woman she was but a small and seemingly insignificant version of, speaking with a wantonness her mother had never witnessed before. 'And who is to blame for the rumours if not yourself? What do I care if people talk about his affection for me? I am *honoured* to have his regard.'

'How can you even consider him as a suitor when he drove his first wife to despair with neglect and never consummated the marriage for no-one knows *what* strange reason? It is hardly pardonable that he should have offered marriage to any woman upon earth.'

'The circumstances are entirely different. He didn't love Effie, whereas he loves *me* and that's why you hate him now.'

'You think I envy you his love?' she demanded.

'Yes, you wanted him for your own, but it all went wrong,' Rose condemned. 'Having used me in order to get close to him, you finally realised that he would never have visited for any other reason, certainly not to see *you*.'

'How much I cherished you when you were a child, but even the truest affections become bitter when tainted by disappointment.'

Her daughter touched the silver cross around her neck. 'Bitterness is never a part of love, but only proves its imperfection.'

'It's as though Ruskin taught you only to love *him*,' her mother chastised, shaking her head woefully.

'He simply taught me how to think for myself.'

'He's too old for you and that's an end to it,' she concluded emphatically.

'One party must always be older,' Rose observed, rising to her feet as if gaining strength, her openness entirely at odds with her mother's introversion and cynicism.

'Not almost thirty years,' she winced, as if experiencing physical pain; 'the very idea is grotesque.'

'Some people believe that we each have a predestined mate, and if that be true how are we to know how it will present itself? *That* is why he has waited for me all these years,' Rose declared with a pride that could be seen in the very way she held herself.

Mrs La Touche jerked her head in contempt. 'He will wait forever if *I* have anything to do with it. Not everyone shares your romantic view,' she went on scornfully. 'You seem to forget that you were raised before God and to honour your parents by marrying the person *we* select.'

'Is marrying without love a duty *anyone* should impose on someone?' she retorted, shivering a little at her tenacity, for it took tremendous effort to defend herself.

'Your father and I have only ever sought to do right by you, while Ruskin doesn't possess any respect for the judgement of your natural protectors. One's own kin always knows what is *best*.'

'You admit, then, that you would never have chosen my father freely?' Rose asked impertinently.

'I would not change what has been,' Maria denied unconvincingly.

'And what about Emily? My sister married to please you and as a consequence lies dead,' she incriminated without fully comprehending the injury.

'That's a *wicked* thing to say!' Mrs La Touche railed, reaching out and catching a hold of her daughter's arm.

Raising her hand as if going to strike her, she faltered as Rose crouched down and shielded herself with her arms, realising the seriousness and ungodliness of her actions.

Breathing heavily, Maria stopped short and lowered her clenched fist as her daughter remained at her feet, a weak creature whom God would always love and protect. Sighing, defeated by Rose's ability to reduce her to such rage, she saw that this climax only confirmed the jealousy she had earlier denied.

Rising from the floor, Rose, with her back turned, quietly asked her mother to leave, which she did without a word of remorse or apology for having widened the breach she had intended to heal. What did God mean by dividing them?

Alone and at the mercy of self-pity, Rose could think only of how grateful she would be for Emily to talk to just then, and tears fell unchecked before she eventually climbed into bed and sought the solace of prayer and sleep.

She could find no rest, however, and following a night disrupted by tortuous dreams, from which she frequently awoke in distress, Rose went out riding early the next morning in order to avoid seeing her mother, for they were more bitterly opposed than ever, nor were their differences likely to be overcome with more discussion or insincere amends.

Singing hymns as she went by way of comfort, Rose looked for a sign that God found her blameless, yet met with only sadness and pain. Having ridden for no more than a mile, she found a beggar making his way to the village, who, urging her to stop, his face obscured by a low-brimmed cap, raised up his hands as if in gratitude to the heavens that she had crossed his path.

'He must have heard me,' the man said, approaching her desperately.

Alighting from her horse and offering him silver without hesitation, she found that he had no need of money but instead implored her to help him find a doctor, his one eye being swollen and unrecognisable from cancer. Trying not to show her horror, or that her breast swelled with pity, she urged him to wait at Mrs Casey's dwelling whilst she sought help – pain and partial blindness making it impossible for him to venture far.

Settling him beside the old woman's hearth, Rose left knowing that nothing could be done for the man and feeling as guilt-ridden as if she had caused God to smite him herself. How awful it was to be helpless to one so afflicted, she thought, rushing to the village with as much speed as if she could change his fate by will alone.

If this was the sign He had meant for her, it was a cruel and punishing one. 'Eye for eye, tooth for tooth,' recalled Rose, 'and if a man smite the eye of his servant, or the eye of his maid, that it perish; he shall let him go free for his eye's sake.'

THE QUEEN OF THE AIR

ROSE, AFTER LEAVING THE SUFFERING MAN IN THE CARE OF
the local doctor, rode ferociously for over a dozen miles across
country with no aim save that of delaying the inevitable meeting
with her mother: her golden hair streaked with flashes of copper flowing
loose, while her hands blistered as she gripped the reins.

Riding, more than anything else, enabled her to shake off anxieties and
cares, a temporary pleasure removing her from all troubles and allowing
her to take solace in a world outside her own.

She was at one with the beloved landscape she had grown up alongside
and the panting animal beneath her thighs, and the faster they went the
clearer her mind became, taking in only the sights and smells of the forest
where once she had walked beside Ruskin, a solemn child who set too
much store by duty and religion.

As soon as she paused, her thoughts returned to the rift with her
mother, however, and she supposed with angst that her father would be
hearing a false account of the previous evening and that her early departure

would convince him of her guilt, something she no longer possessed any inclination to deny.

Having taken no sustenance since the previous evening, Rose soon grew tired upon the excitable Swallow and barely knew how she would find enough energy to retrace her steps, yet the weather was too pleasant to persuade her to turn back.

Birdsong lured her further into the wood and a hazy light resembling fine gauze wove its way through the tall grey beech trees, falling upon a bed of moist green moss below, which offered itself as an all-embracing couch and lured her to pause awhile.

After securing the horse, who was equally glad to halt, Rose rested her weary body, though her mind would take no respite and continued to present harrowing visions of the sick man who needed a miracle to see the beauties of the world again.

Cushioning her head in her hand, she stared at the pale sky latticed by the branches overhead before removing from her pocket Ruskin's latest book, *The Queen of the Air*, a volume he had managed to send covertly through one of the maid servants.

Filled with mystical ideals and wisdom that made her reflect many times over, she remembered how much she missed his company, and her breast rose and fell with a sigh before she closed it and put it aside.

Resigned to loneliness, she accepted that it was largely her own fault for not seizing a new life away from Harristown, but she had long decided that such an existence was contained within her heart rather than any future reality – her girlish dream of becoming a woman of letters slim comfort now that everything around her was soured.

Mourning her sister, Ruskin and everything beyond reach, she excused her cowardliness by concluding that she had neither the courage nor talent to strike out alone, nor did she choose to go from being a dutiful daughter to the wife of a man who was sure to dominate her. She took a strange kind of pride in her loyalty towards a mother who had cast her aside, for she believed God meant her to remain.

Walking between her favourite pines, their spiky evergreen crosses forebodingly stark against the faint blue above and the slight breeze, the leaves of the deciduous varieties rustled as though they *would* have spoken to her if only they could have, delighting her with their imposing shelter and granting a sense of insignificance which seemed to justify her timidity and longing to linger there long after dusk.

Eventually overcoming her apprehension of confronting her parents and returning home, Rose found her mother and father seated side by side in the drawing room, though she was surprised when they did not look up or regard her when she entered. Without criticising her rebellion as she had imagined, they chose to punish her by keeping a determined silence, though it only made her want to ride out again and never come back.

Rose perceived that her father was annoyed, for he fidgeted with his flame-coloured whiskers whilst pretending to read a Spurgeon paper, not deigning to glance at her no matter how she stared at him. Her mother meanwhile embroidered with a self-satisfied expression that told of the evil she had spoken in her absence.

Dinner was passed in equally grim quietude, with Rose shrinking from both the meal and spending a moment longer in their company than necessary, prompting her to stop short during the customary procession back to the drawing room and, without a word, alight the stairs to bed.

Confounded by their behaviour, and unsure how long her parents were likely to maintain such torture, on the morrow she cowered in her room with a headache rather than attend the family church service, something she knew would displease her father but could not help.

Nothing set that Sunday apart from any other save the omnipresence of ill feeling and a sickening sense that some worse retribution was coming, a presentiment that was confirmed when her father stormed into the drawing room that evening and found her kneeling in prayer.

Rising to her feet on realising from the weight and urgency of his step that he was angry, she supposed him to be cross because she had absented herself from church, yet saw the moment she looked into his face, and from the smart, newly bound book he was clutching, that it was far more serious. Ever boastful of his fiery Irish temper, never had he appeared

491

so wild as when he hurled the book at the floor as if to shock her into submission.

Being well used to his flashes of rage, Rose remained calm as she bent down and scooped up the volume splayed spine up, recognising with foreboding her precious copy of *The Queen of the Air*. At once understanding his meaning, she knew that it would take all her strength to save the forbidden possession from being confiscated, an item she assumed her mother, the hateful agitator, had found in her saddlebag and had passed onto her father in order to incite his enmity.

'Explain!' La Touche demanded.

'Mr Ruskin sent me a copy of his new book; is that so very bad?' she appealed boldly.

'You have deceived me!' he yelled, his perspiring face as red as his whiskers.

'I have never disobeyed you, Father. No *word* has passed between us,' she attempted to appease, despite recognising how resistant he would be to hearing any justification. 'He sent it without enclosing so much as a note, I promise.'

'How can you *countenance* such a book when it mocks the very religion I uphold?' La Touche bellowed.

Using his considerable stature to intimidate, he stood over Rose and held out his hand, for although he had thrown the book at her feet he now desired her to relinquish it as a symbol of her obeisance.

'I'll return it to him, I promise,' she went on, clutching the volume within her tightly folded arms like a young bird trying to protect itself from prey.

La Touche turned and began pacing the room. 'You may keep it if you bring me his letters.'

'You wish to destroy the only thing I have left to me?' Rose pleaded, her eyelids creased with pain, so greatly did the forfeiture wound.

'Get the letters!' La Touche commanded, catching his daughter's arm as she attempted to dash from the room.

Driving his fingernails deep into her delicate skin and squeezing her flesh until the impression of his hand was red and sore upon her arm, it was his loathing towards Ruskin and not the creature in his power that made him persist; but though Rose winced and tears smarted her eyes, she continued to struggle.

Instinctively trusting her own resilience, she wriggled and kicked with such endurance that she eventually managed to wrench herself free, nor was there any question of her trying to run when once she had broken away. Standing resolutely before him, she held her breath as she raised her hand and smacked her father hard across the face with a force which surprised them both.

Stunned more than injured, La Touche staggered against a table, unbelieving that his daughter, once so faithful to him, had responded with such defiance. Regarding her quizzically, certain that she would repent as he touched his stinging cheek, he held out his hand for the book.

The slight, trembling figure before him held firm, however, and recalling all her abuser's wrongs, over so many years, felt no remorse rise up within her, nor did she believe God would judge her for retaliating. Shaking her head as if to reinforce her actions, Rose took a deep breath to calm herself and went from the room, *The Queen of the Air* locked within her grasp.

Ruskin was shocked and dumbfounded when he heard the report of Rose having struck her father, yet, despite being unaware of the precise circumstances which had led her to do so, believed that she would never have acted thus without due cause.

He ached with frustration at his own inability to save her from the warring household in which she lived and at her own blindness in making a martyr of herself. Why would she not go to him when she could never find peace at Harristown?

Rose's saintliness had been corrupted by the religious fanaticism of her father, he pondered, removing her star letter from his breast pocket and running his fingers along the paper his pet had written all those years ago. The girl he had witnessed change into a woman by fits and starts was an increasingly unpredictable and combustible creature, the natural result of belligerent parents who cared more for imposing their views on their daughter than allowing her the freedom to form her own.

Having fallen in love with Rose's beauty and innocence, he was fearful that her difficult transition into maturity had produced a woman far too easily impassioned and devoid of all normal reasoning and judgement: one moment devout and dutiful, wild and wilful the next. How could he compete with her own father or God for her fidelity when she had been raised to worship them, and them alone?

Ruskin was dismayed when he came to hear, via his and Mrs La Touche's mutual friends, vague reports of increasingly fractious events at Harristown, explaining Rose's declining spirits and why she edged closer to the brink of insanity than she ever had before. There was nothing he could do save beg for snatches of information, patched together in his mind until the pattern grew too busy to read, for just as soon as he received one paltry fragment he was desperate for the next that he might stitch and weave his own story, however far from the truth his conjecture verged.

Lying awake, night after night, the very darkness pained him: a void filled with fantastical imaginings and hopelessness in equal measure. Weary of retiring to his solitary room of an evening, he folded back the bedclothes and touched the hallowed space he had reserved for Rose, praying over and again in the impenetrable black silence for God to deliver his wife, companion and friend until he thought his heart would break.

Nor did the morning bring any consolation, with one incident distressing him more than any other. The worst of all possible crimes, Ruskin found himself wringing his hands and cursing her parents as frenziedly as he imagined Rose had when she discovered their betrayal, for what more could be inflicted upon two divided souls? It was a crucifixion as surely as if he had been stripped naked and nailed to the cross until his hands and feet bled.

The day following the conflict between father and daughter, Mrs La Touche, after waiting for Rose to go out, entered her bedroom and commenced a lengthy search for the letters which Ruskin had addressed to her daughter over a period of many years. Frantically opening the drawers in the dressing table and clothes chest, Maria was near to giving up when she discovered, concealed beneath a loose floorboard, several bundles bound with ribbon. Unhesitating, and having made up her mind to inflict the greatest suffering she could think of, Mrs La Touche removed them from their hiding place, carried them away and destroyed them all.

Rose intuitively went to her chamber upon her return and was appalled to discover that her bedroom had been pillaged, nor did she doubt the culprit. Immediately realising that Ruskin's letters had been the motivation behind the plunder, the thief had made no attempt to conceal the burglary, nor had they replaced the floorboard which her eyes fell upon in horror.

Unsure if there was still time to save these most treasured communications, Rose rushed downstairs and charged into the drawing room where she found her parents engaged in heated discussion.

'You took the letters from my room?' she demanded, directing the question at her mother.

'They were doing you no good,' came the matter-of-fact reply, for she was gratified rather than moved by her daughter's distress. 'It is time for you to put Mr Ruskin out of your mind.'

'What have you done with them?' Rose cried, approaching the unlit fireplace and scrambling in the grate without waiting for an answer.

Whilst her mother and father looked to one another in disbelief and embarrassment lest one of the servants should enter, Rose responded not to their protestations and continued to search for the remains of letters containing love which needed no declaration to be known and returned.

'Get up!' La Touche insisted as his daughter continued to examine the dust between her fingers, vainly hoping to salvage the merest fragment.

After several minutes, realising that either the vandalism had not taken place there or that, either way, any remnants had long since been swept away, Rose stopped searching and, sobbing uncontrollably, collapsed with her head on the hearth: her dress, face and hands covered in dust and ash.

This frenzy, rather than provoking her parents' sympathy, vindicated their decision to have her removed from Harristown, for was not her behaviour wholly unacceptable and akin to madness? Indeed, Rose herself felt taunted to the edge of reason and lay before them as devoid of rational thought as any lunatic.

There was little likelihood of her ever marrying, they reasoned, and her moods were increasingly unpredictable, with flashes of mania they were unable to tolerate given their position. It was only a matter of time before she caused them grave public humiliation and therefore they had no alternative but to seek professional assistance.

The wait for the psychiatrist seemed interminable to La Touche, for Rose remained by the fireplace, weeping and thumping her head on the stone hearth as if to soothe her other agony. Maria meanwhile stood guard at the door, deeply ashamed by Rose's conduct yet relieved that the crisis she had engineered had finally brought about a resolution.

When once the doctor's sedative had begun to numb Rose's distress, La Touche lifted his daughter from the floor and, concealing her blackened dress and hands beneath a blanket, carried her to the waiting carriage bound for a sanatorium in Dublin with a reputation for the utmost discretion.

Rose made no sound or movement by way of resistance as her mother helped to place her inside the vehicle, for the opiates were more powerful than any pain, allowing her to forget the cruel world long after her father slammed the carriage door and signalled to the driver.

After returning to the drawing room and setting it to rights, Maria La Touche composed a sharp, decisive note to Ruskin explaining that Rose's health had sharply declined – failing to mention that she was being cared for elsewhere, not from shame but from fear that he might attempt to see her.

> "Mr Ruskin,
>
> Rose is unwell and I beg you to end all correspondence with her. The doctor says it is vain to hope for any progress as long as there is the possibility of renewed agitation. Please understand how painful it is to receive any communication which remotely recalls the idea of you and the outrage you have offered us."

Above all, Ruskin was troubled to find that Mrs La Touche had enclosed Rose's strangely battered copy of *The Queen of the Air*, which he examined for some clue, pondering on whether the lady's obvious disapproval of the gift had resulted in her daughter's latest relapse.

Disturbed at the thought of being in any way to blame, a wave of guilt came over him for having violated the mandate banishing him from Rose's life, yet the more he considered his actions the more he saw nothing wrong in them.

Ruskin found all the reassurance he needed when, shaking the book by its spine, knowing not what prompted him to do so, a flurry of dried rose petals fell out from between the pages, telling him in the sweetest manner that his love had cherished the book, for it was always Rosie's habit to dry flowers in any work she especially liked.

For further encouragement her name was etched on the title page in her gentle hand, along with the date she had completed the book, allowing him to conclude that she may well have understood the secret messages he had scattered throughout the text just for her.

Holding a rose petal between his thumb and finger, symbolic of the fragility of his dear one, he decided to keep the book close by him in case he should ever have the opportunity to present it to her again. Sometimes, when he felt particularly melancholy and lonesome, usually before retiring, he would open it and stare at her name, hoping that one day he might change it to his own.

THE NURSING HOME

THE LONG, STERILE CORRIDOR WOUND ITS WAY AROUND the circular atrium of the sanatorium, blindingly white in the sunlight that flooded through the sash windows as two nurses navigated Rose in a metal bedframe – every shudder of which might have been felt through the thin mattress if only she had been conscious.

Her attendants, usually insusceptible to feelings of empathy, pitied the young woman who, for the past week, had lain sedated with no visitors, and they shrank from tightening the thick brown leather straps encompassing Rose's wasted body, a measure the doctors had taken when she wrestled with them on first awakening.

Not knowing who or what had brought her to such a place, though Rose had raged in vain, her vulnerability and beauty set her aside from other inhabitants, sick in mind and abandoned by relatives years ago, who, abhorrent of the scourge and humiliation of madness, removed them from their family history with shamefaced callousness.

No patient knew pain or distress after a few hours' confinement within those walls, nor did any experience despair like that of first being admitted there, embracing the oblivion offered that they might close their eyes to their surroundings and withdraw from the grotesqueness of a reality as dire as any hell in afterlife.

While Ruskin had undergone his own mental torment since being separated from Rose, her suffering was far greater than he could have comprehended, nor had he any reason to suspect the gravity of her decline or the endlessly blank hours she was forced to endure away from the world, trapped inside her subconscious by annihilative narcotics that would only add to her emotional disturbance when once she was released from their bonds.

Distraught on Mrs La Touche finally confessing that Rose's health had deteriorated to such a degree that she had been hospitalised, though he respected her command that he keep away, he managed to persuade her to allow his former pupil, a young woman by the name of Lily Armstrong, to visit on his behalf and let him know her state.

As a Dubliner and vague acquaintance of Rose's he was convinced that Lily was the best person to act as intermediary, though she barely recognised the Miss La Touche she had met through society events years ago, so woebegone was the patient who drifted off to sleep at intervals or stared at her wantonly as if she had no recollection of her whatsoever.

Duty-bound to furnish Ruskin with an honest account, however distressing he would find it, Lily described her anguish at finding her friend strapped to the bed – her thin, gaunt appearance the result of a sustained diet of opiates replacing any fresh air, exercise or nourishment. Most of all she was impressed by the deep sadness pervading Rose; despite squeezing her hand and trying to ascertain what she thought and felt, Lily could glean nothing and was eventually forced to leave her, unsure how to offer assistance or comfort.

Grieved to hear that Rose was quite alone and hardly ever visited by her parents, Ruskin felt a thousand times more helpless upon discovering the conditions in which she existed, and could only bring himself to reply, 'Yes, dearest Lily, she ought to look sad, and for many a day to come. For all days to come in this world.'

This despondency soon gave way to rage, for he could not countenance that her parents would prefer to see their daughter keep company with the lunatics of the world rather than allow *him* to take her away and care for her. How gladly he would have devoted the rest of his life to nursing her, and how vehemently he resented them for thwarting such noble desire.

Lily's sad tidings heralded the arrival of Christmas, yet there was nothing to make Ruskin welcome the time of man's rejoicing, and he simply muddled on with his collar turned up and his head hung low, a man as abject as could be, with nothing and no-one to reassure him that this too would pass.

When Joan persuaded him to venture to John James's graveside that he might pay his respects to the ally he had only appreciated in death, the night frost had barely had a chance to thaw before dusk restored the glinting coat of ice that beckoned Christmas Eve.

How much he needed his father's counsel and how saddened he was to think of all the advice he had never taken! Yet, in the pale light of the December moon, the recollection of the old man's words urging him to cast Rose aside never seemed more at odds with his sense of loyalty, for wasn't he the only one who might offer her salvation?

That same loyalty was illustrated through the steadfastness of his cousin, conscientiously kneeling beside her uncle's grave pulling up weeds, while he, a lost figure, stood over her ineptly holding a bouquet of flowers, tapping his foot on the ground in impatience, not simply due to the cold but because he still found it impossible to read his father's name upon the headstone without being flooded with a stream of regrets.

Resistant to weighing up all his past faults, to his mind graveyards served no purpose other than to inspire the living to feel guilt or sorrow, for he might just as easily have remembered his father back at home or by traversing a path they had once taken together.

'I'm almost done,' Joan encouraged, aware that her cousin struggled to see the point of visiting the grave as regularly as she insisted upon.

'I'm not complaining. It's good of you to remember my father. I only wish he were in a position to appreciate the attention,' he quipped.

She smiled sadly without deigning to respond and, perceiving that his mind was elsewhere, enquired, 'How is Rose?'

'Not good,' he sighed restlessly, handing her the winter roses which brought some life to the surreality of the cold stone so inadequately marking his pater's existence.

'What news is there?'

'She's in a nursing home in Dublin and barely knows her own name they've got her taking that much poison. How gladly I would change places with her! She'll be twenty-one next January and I have as much hope of hearing the answer she promised as if I had never asked her to marry me.'

Gathering up the weeds she had tugged away with mittened hands, more living than anything else thereabouts, Joan shook her head woefully as she placed the cheerful posy upon the grave, a custom which could only please the living and therefore struck Ruskin as peculiar.

'How is it that her parents aren't caring for her?' she asked pitifully, accepting her cousin's hand as she rose to her feet.

'I know no more than you, but if they won't, why prevent *me*?' he railed, running his hands through his whitening hair.

'Perhaps she's beyond even *your* help,' Joan suggested mournfully.

'I might do as much as anyone. At least at Denmark Hill she'd be surrounded by people who *love* her. You show more feeling and respect towards my dead father than they in relegating her to such a place and never visiting her. I sometimes think her mother would sooner see Rose go from this world than give her to me.'

'Surely not?' Joan protested.

'I wish it were otherwise, but that woman has such fearful pride, and pride is nearly always at the bottom of all great mistakes,' he concluded, giving a final glance to his father's grave.

Instead of simply passing the door of John James's former study when he returned home, Ruskin looked in and sat awhile at the green leather topped desk, recalling how his father's passion for hard work was greater than any man he'd ever known, a deal more than his own, and as long as he remained at Denmark Hill his sire's shadow would loom large, encouraging and chiding him in equal measure.

Weary of the daily struggle to keep going, Ruskin wondered if perhaps he *needed* such a phantom, for he continued working with his father ever whispering in his ear, causing him to experience the desire for immortality that fuels a dying man when he writes knowing that his work will be posthumous. Should Rose's coming of age pass without a word, and it surely would, he could see nothing else to go on for.

Such were his thoughts as he stroked the worn desk leather which bore the markings of his father's pen, and, studying the photograph of himself which John James had always kept within sight as he worked, he wondered what had become of the proud young graduate of Oxford, placing the frame face down that it would taunt him no more.

The following morning, Christmas Day, was all the more burdensome for having sat up late in such tortuous contemplation, and the pleasanter Joan and his mother tried to make the occasion the more he choked upon having to withstand another hour of being forced to smile and dine as if he could simply set aside all concerns of his love in Ireland and what she might be suffering.

Letters from friends had fallen away over the festivities and he had heard nothing about his dear one or whether she was home. If she was, how ever could she bear to look upon her parents after such abandonment? He doubted whether he could have been so forgiving if his own parents had acted thus, though he had surely done *them* more wrong, such as selfishly refusing to return to Denmark Hill from Switzerland the winter that, with the clarity of a glacial stream, he had admitted the love that placed Rose supreme in his affections.

Regardless of the anxieties in his own breast, he nonetheless granted, as he looked to his mother and Joan, that there was nothing like being home and with one's own kin at Christmas, it being the single day of the year when every human soul should put aside their quarrels and live in harmony together. Wherever Rose might be, he hoped that she was loved and cared for.

Ruskin had long since given up the futile exercise of counting down the days until Rose's twenty-first birthday and the fulfilment of her promise in his diary, so that when that chill January day finally dawned he might pass it unobserved. And he should have had it not been for a harrowing dream of frantically wandering the slums of Dublin at night.

Searching for someone, Rose, he was hampered by a fearful gloom and a sense that the stinking alleys, cluttered with detritus of every kind, were becoming increasingly narrow the further he went. It was impossible to avoid the ashes and rags, beer bottles and old shoes, battered pans, smashed crockery, shreds of nameless clothes, door sweepings, floor sweepings, kitchen garbage, back-garden sewage, old iron, rotten timber jagged with rusty nails and every manner of newspaper, advertisement and big-lettered bill festering and flaunting their last publicity in the pits of stinking dust and mortal slime.

The poor stood in their doorways with their arms folded, and instead of begging stared at him with menace as if they knew all too well that no-one would assist them; while the more he ventured into the thick of it, a rambling network of terraces backing onto yet more terraces, the more people gathered to see him, so different was he in appearance from they, nor could anyone understand what this smartly attired gentleman was doing in their midst.

He felt sure that Rose was inside one of the houses, offering charity and comfort, yet he didn't know which one and was too timid to ask for fear of being spat at or lambasted. Though he grew less and less comfortable in such an environment his determination to find Rose was unshakeable and he continued on in the hope that he might see her appear: fearless in the darkness and squalor, dressed hardly better than the poorest inhabitants and carrying a basket filled with provisions, a Bible tucked under her arm.

At last, when he was breathless from walking hurriedly, he reached a brick wall so tall he could neither look over it nor climb it. Frantically looking to left and right, perspiring with panic and stupefaction, he found that there were only more walls, nor could he retrace his steps due to the path behind him having vanished, along with all possibility of seeing Rose.

Stricken with dismay at not being able to find her, he awoke with an almighty start, opening his eyes to find himself sitting bolt upright in bed, gasping for air.

He had no concept of how long he had been dreaming thus, yet his body clock told him that dawn had broken some time ago as he lay awake waiting for the windows to lighten. After a moment, he remembered what the day signified and felt as exhausted as if he really had been running through the streets of Dublin all night to find his love.

Having doubted whether Rose would live to see the day he had been so eager for, he thanked God that she had survived, even if he should never call her his wife. She was no more a woman released of all parental bonds than on the day they had first met, for some ties were too great to overcome by passing a birthday.

The day came and went without a word, thus confirming the futility of having spent the past three years waiting for her answer. Her blank response was as mystifying as life and creation itself, only twice as depressing. He chastised himself for ever having proposed, yet still could not bring himself to relinquish the idea of making her his own until *she* told him that she would never come to him.

DUTY BEFORE SELF

AVING SPENT HIS FORMATIVE YEARS RAILING AGAINST any similarity to his father other than a striking familial appearance, Percy dreaded maturity as much as his school friends anticipated it: displaying abundant arrogance and rebelliousness until age unsettled him to such a degree that he could not find the same pleasure in the dissolute pastimes that once had distracted him from the inevitable burden of Harristown.

The time for boyish excuses was slipping away; where once he had convinced his father that he possessed neither the acumen nor the patience to help manage the estate or enter the bank, La Touche was putting increasing pressure on him to accept his duties.

His parents resented him for vices they attributed to him not having any more purposeful occupations to replace them, and between the tension that existed between Percy and his father, his mother and father over their religious differences, and their joint opposition to Rose and her relationship with Ruskin, he hardly thought he could be blamed for preferring to spend the majority of his time in London, where he accumulated enough gambling debts to prompt unusual humility upon his return.

It was a way of life that could not continue indefinitely on account of the family's depleted finances and, after many heated discussions with his father, he agreed to both engage himself to the daughter of the Earl of Clonmel, a young lady he barely knew, and consider a career in the bank.

Reclining in his father's palatial office, a leg over one arm of the green leather chair in contemptuousness of his surroundings, Percy was sick to the back teeth of La Touche's sermonising and wished himself in London, if only to distinguish himself from the bombastic, rigid man before him.

'You have my agreement to this ludicrous marriage,' he sighed. 'Isn't that concession enough for one day?'

'Concession is simply another word for duty,' La Touche responded indignantly, seated behind his desk as if he were addressing a clerk. He clicked the stiff digits of his fingers impatiently and continued, 'I expect you to honour me as I once had to honour *my* father.'

'Forcing me to enter the bank is to castrate me, to tear out my soul and throw it to the lions!'

'Oddly enough, becoming a man feels *precisely* like that and I have neither the means nor the inclination to allow you to continue an idle, debauched existence.'

Percy rose from his seat and lit a cigar, another of his vices which garnered his father's disapproval, feeling no connection to the place that was to be his new domain. Floor to ceiling oil paintings of his father riding the Kildare hunt perplexed him by their irreligiousness and their reminder of the life his sire had shunned in favour of salvation.

'It's apparent that I should take a step back and let you take control of your own destiny,' La Touche went on, 'for I firmly believe that having a wife and responsibilities will be the making of you.'

'As it was for you?' his son scoffed, intentionally puffing smoke in his father's direction.

'It was only when I found God that I understood and acknowledged my failings, yet not even *I* am naive enough to imagine that *you* will ever accept His guidance.'

'Rose followed you into the light and look where it got her,' Percy challenged, knowing the subject of his sister to be a raw nerve.

'She always had the Devil on her shoulder,' La Touche seethed.

'You mean John Ruskin?' he provoked, taking pleasure in seeing his father's hackles rise.

'For as long as that man continues to influence her she will never get well, nor will she truly be my daughter.'

'You talk as though he corrupted her, whereas he never taught us anything but goodness,' his son denied, shaking his head emphatically. 'If he loves her as he says he does, you may be sure it is with a pure heart.'

'I will not hear another word!' La Touche raged, covering his ears as petulantly as a child. 'How can you defend him when he tries all he can to take her away from us?'

'I would sooner see her with him than where she now lies,' Percy reasoned, 'for I can barely imagine what possessed you to send her to such a place.'

'You're never home long enough to know what Rosie is like to live with,' he dismissed; 'if you were you would see that she *must* be taught to control her wilfulness and trust that her mother and I know what is best.'

'I doubt she will trust either of you again,' Percy returned, an attack partially prompted by shame at not having spent more time with his sister in the days since Emily's death.

He considered himself just as misplaced as Rose and saw only too well how impossible his father was to challenge when once he was set upon a course. Was not he being committed to an institution of another kind?

Unconvinced by his father's attempts to justify his abandonment of Rose, Percy travelled to Dublin again the next day on the pretext of visiting the bank, yet determined to see for himself whether his sister was being sufficiently well cared for just as soon as he had met with the board members he was to join the following month.

The aged bank officials were as pompous and priggish as he had expected, while they regarded him with derision for being gifted a position they had toiled decades to achieve. Caring not to earn their respect, the bank was awash with dissatisfied young clerks going about their business with hunched shoulders belying their long working hours and inadequate pay, and it was they who made Percy blush at the prospect of becoming their superior when he hadn't earned the right. He cowered at the thought of men his own age ridiculing him behind his back for taking up a post he had once so vociferously renounced, the hypocrisy of which reinforced his apprehension of taking up the desk beside his father's and issuing orders.

The ominous-looking red-brick institution housing his sister worsened his attitude towards all that the name of La Touche stood for, and he unwittingly lost his usual swagger as soon as the heavy double doors, reinforced with equally imposing locks, were closed and bolted behind him; a sanatorium presenting itself far more like a prison than a hospital. Perhaps, so Percy considered with alarm, the bank would prove just as difficult to escape.

The malevolent-looking head nurse, with a mop of tightly pinned-back greying hair which made her look all the more severe, scratched his name down in the visitor book and sniffed guardedly as if he had no business there. The smell of disinfectant reeked from floor to ceiling, filling Percy with a growing apprehension and nausea that made him want to heave as he was escorted by a younger, though no more attractive, nurse along one in a network of narrow passages.

'This is one of the longest corridors in Europe,' she boasted, prompting Percy to wonder who went about measuring such things.

Despite his cowardliness and the fact that he grew visibly paler, it was clear from her encouraging smiles and blushes that she considered him prepossessing, something Percy imagined might prove advantageous given the unwelcoming environment in which he found himself.

Disturbed to hear the wails and moans of countless patients as they proceeded, he was under no illusion as to the type of regime his younger sibling was being exposed to. More shocking still was that the inauspiciously long corridor led to a pitch-black, gas-lit circular example, presumably designed to disorientate any patient attempting to break free.

Having no beginning and no end, like one of Dante's circles of hell, any potential escapee would merely find themselves back where they had started. Sixty small cells were positioned around the inner sanctum like a clock-face, while the main structure, despite being relatively newly built, was reminiscent of an impenetrable medieval tower which he supposed few ever left alive or with their sanity improved.

Akin to being buried alive, those within its walls were incarcerated in order to be forgotten, not saved. A system designed to subdue and pacify rather than heal, no visitor brought flowers or went at all if they could help it, and the further Percy ventured the more he recoiled to see the conditions to which his parents had voluntarily subjected his sister.

Barely able to conceal his disgust on the nurse showing him into the starkly furnished room where Rose lay alone, his own resentment towards his father doubled on seeing the whitewashed dungeon that might have been reserved for those who had committed the most heinous crimes, and where isolation was perhaps the only luxury in such a grim, formidable environment.

Aware that being alone with his sister was in breach of hospital protocol, he placed a hand on the nurse's arm and smiled persuasively. 'Could you leave us for a moment?'

Without replying, the woman was glad of a handsome visitor for diversion and returned his smile as she exited, though Percy's disingenuous grin faded as soon as she was away. Edging with trepidation towards the screen concealing Rose's bed, the full horror of his sister's deterioration was revealed in all its ghastliness.

Appalled by the leather straps restraining her, though she possessed not even the strength to sit up in bed, he took hold of Rose's hand and squeezed it with increasing pressure in the hope of arousing her, but it was like trying to bring a drowning man back to life.

Tears smarted his eyes as she struggled to open hers, for the several weeks since she had seen any familiar face might just as well have been months. Incapable of focussing due to the effects of the opiates, despite wanting to stay awake and being so gladdened by the sight of Percy, her lids were too heavy and languid to remain open for more than a few seconds at a time.

So too was her speech impaired, for her mouth merely made incomprehensible sounds Percy could not make out the meaning of, though she tried several times to utter something.

'I'm going to take you away,' he whispered, conscious that he needed to act swiftly if he was to fulfil his promise.

Though Rose made no sign of comprehension or encouragement, and only peered at him blurredly for a moment before drifting into another drugged stupor, Percy realised that it was an occasion for action rather than thought and thus set about unbuckling the leather straps: removing the bedclothes only to be faced with the shock of his sister's emaciated frame, a reality which convinced him that he acted rightly, for surely she never could have survived another week.

Murmuring, 'Wake up, Rose,' as he manoeuvred her to the edge of the bed and draped a blanket around her shoulders, these words finally seemed to spark some life in her.

'Did Father send you?' she slurred.

'Not exactly, no,' he answered, scooping her light, almost fleshless body into his arms and making his way to the door.

Nudging it open a few inches, he checked the corridor anxiously and observed two nurses talking close by. Holding his breath lest they should discover his intention, he kissed Rose's cheek in relief when their chatter grew fainter as they progressed on their rounds and unknowingly granted him an opportunity to rescue his sister and attempt to overturn the damage that had been wrought.

Forced to wait until their voices died away altogether, after taking a gulp of courage Percy entered the passage as stealthily as a wild animal; Rose, worrying weightless, asleep in his arms. He did not pause to deliver any explanation to the nurse who challenged him in the vestibule, nor did he accept her initial refusal to unbolt the front door, instead drawing upon the authority and intimidation he had learnt from his father.

The cool air disturbed Rose's slumber when once they were released, and she shivered uncontrollably as he bundled her into the family carriage waiting outside. He could not pause to make her comfortable, however, for a doctor was descending the front steps and waving his arms in protest, prompting Percy to order the coachman to make haste, although he had no idea where to direct him, nor what friend he might call upon with a sister whose body, mind and soul had been ravaged by his own parents.

Try as he might to quieten and reassure Rose, her agitation and confusion was boundless, and she continued to moan with nausea and alarm as the carriage sped through the bustling city streets, directionless as a ship without a compass.

Percy felt almost as sick at the thought of the repercussions that would ensue as a result of going against his mother and father, for he had acted without considering the consequences, though he should not have chosen a different course if all fury reigned as a result.

In that moment they were as much removed from their old life at Harristown as two street urchins, and they would have been just as much in the gutter had it not been for the remainder of Percy's allowance providing shelter until he masterminded a way of removing his sister from Ireland and any possibility of further persecution.

Every yard distancing Rose from the sanatorium allowed him to take pride in his boldness and for allowing sibling love and humanity to lead him to righteousness. God was not obvious in his method of offering redemption, yet it seemed that all His goodness was channelled through Rose and that He, having led him to save his sister, would surely guide him in the difficult days to come.

The carriage halted outside the Shelbourne Hotel in the chill of twilight and Percy carried Rose inside hastily. Gradually awakening from her delirium, just one glimpse of the lobby told her where she was and granted her a relief like she had never known.

Insensible of the conspicuousness of her appearance, Rose pointed to familiar objects and babbled as Percy reserved a suite of rooms at the reception, rushing her upstairs as soon as he had sent the carriage back to Harristown, making the man swear that he would deny having aided their escape, with no knowledge of their whereabouts.

Inhabiting a series of elegant rooms overlooking St Stephen's Green, Rose was still too numb to appreciate or take comfort from her plush surroundings, content to remain in bed or on the sofa for the next few days as her brother arranged her removal from Ireland without concerning her with the details.

Although her condition considerably improved with the removal of narcotics, Percy nevertheless feared that the effects of memory would linger indefinitely, for she hardly touched her meals, while her conversation swung between nonsense, such as someone sleep-talking, and genius and poetry combined.

Dressed in ill-fitting, ready-made cotton dresses Percy had acquired in a department store, Rose's slight, malnourished figure was manifest, nor did a corset save any purpose other than to support her and disguise the muscle weakness which days of bed rest and starvation had precipitated. Her appearance alone would tell Ruskin all that she had endured, he surmised on observing her looking out of the drawing room window one morning, in wonder of all she had missed and yearning to have the strength to venture outside.

Having prohibited the hotel from revealing their residency to anyone, least of all their parents, Percy trusted that his mother and father would regard the Shelbourne as too obvious a hiding place before turning their attention to London, not that this deterred him from booking the crossing to Holyhead, nor arranging a hotel in Mayfair conveniently placed for the Royal Academy.

The low sun was a blaze of colour as they drew up to the port in a hired cab and a stream of travellers crossed the gang rail to the waiting ferry. Rose witnessed the commotion without anticipating her own departure, for contemplating her new freedoms proved terrifying rather than exhilarating.

Though her clarity of mind was steadily improving and Percy was confident that in half the time again her old character would be restored, even the simplest of tasks were overwhelmingly exhausting and difficult to carry out, least of all the prospect of travel.

Perceiving her reluctance, Percy alighted first and, offering his hand, said simply, 'Come.'

'I don't understand,' she stammered, looking to the ferry in bewilderment.

'Don't let Father do to you what he's determined to do to *me*,' he urged her, pressing her hand warmly. 'You have someone who loves you, who'll protect you, if you'll only allow him.'

Knowing at once to whom he was referring she leant upon his arm and climbed out, embracing him as if there were no other way to express her gratitude, for words were strangers to her and she became tongue-tied if she attempted more than a few at a time.

Across the Irish Sea to Holyhead, Percy travelled with his sister harbouring a silent confidence: hopeful that, with each uneasy current, she edged ever closer to a new beginning. Thankful that circumstances had allowed him to be the catalyst that might break the chains binding Rose to Harristown, he would nobly bear the ramifications in the name of his other sister, of whom he often thought as he stood on deck watching the tumultuous waves that would transport them to England.

Rose meanwhile closed her eyes and imagined Ruskin waiting for her at the door of Denmark Hill with outstretched arms, yet she could not picture herself as anything other than a little girl, while he had become an old man, careworn with years of waiting.

Throughout the crossing she studied her hands, still that of a girl, and became conscious of people remarking on her strange, haggard appearance: her face pale and sad, as though her destiny had been revealed to her without any means of changing it.

BURLINGTON HOUSE

THE SQUALLING JANUARY RAIN FELL ON THE GLISTENING pavements of Mayfair like icy nails, prompting rich and poor alike to huddle in doorways for respite, although the longer they delayed their journey the worse the gusts and downpour became.

Rose, on the contrary, did not mind the weather but was glad of any reason to be out of doors, and continued on, Percy's overcoat around her shoulders and her eyes fixed upon her destination, disdainful of the ceaseless grey sky overhead urging her inside.

Passing through the gates of Burlington House, she sought shelter of another kind, though she could not have said whether she entered the Royal Academy despite the chance of seeing her old friend, or because of such a possibility, and should have been relieved to have gone away without finding him.

Percy had persuaded her to go, yet she had set off without realising how unprepared she was for a reunion – part of her longing to know his sympathy, while a greater side dreaded him witnessing the great change she had undergone in the three years since last they had met.

Leaving her sopping umbrella by the door and smoothing her damp hair, pinned in her customary fashion at the nape of the neck, a style which in adulthood gave her a devout appearance, she trembled upon looking up and seeing him at the top of the stairs discussing a Reynolds with two academicians.

Far from being glad, she only experienced an irresistible desire to flee, and would have done so had not he already noticed her and asked his companions to excuse him. Amazed on catching sight of Rose cowering hesitantly in the lobby, he skipped down the stairs, smiling joyously at his unexpected good fortune.

Ruskin's face fell as he moved to embrace her, however, for he not only observed that she did not look at all well, but that she looked timidly, almost unfavourably on him, and ignoring his gesture of ecstatic reunion stepped as if she were sleepwalking into the first gallery.

'Rose?' he called after her, much to the amusement of the gentlemen whom he had left mid-diatribe on the landing.

Unmindful as to how the scene appeared to his associates, he followed his love and caught at her sleeve, more roughly than he intended, though not so as to justify how much she flinched. Confused by her presence and her hurtful coolness, he could not know the wave of emotion that his touch precipitated or that Rose momentarily imagined herself back at Harristown, struggling to release herself from her father's grasp.

Abruptly moving away from Ruskin, despite not really fearing him, she was wary of allowing him to help her, for she knew how he would want to if once she explained how she came to be there. She could not allow herself to be overwhelmed or controlled again, even if kindness and devotion were the motivation.

Apprehensive as to what should happen when her parents finally discovered her whereabouts, Percy had gravely misjudged her recovery, for her mind was as fragile as glass and she feared that those she loved most would never understand her pain or how the suffering she had endured distanced her from them forever. It mattered not how much

515

Ruskin wished to comfort her and nurse her back to strength, the pride and duty she felt towards her parents and to God remained inherent and forced her to stay mute.

With hardly enough strength to circuit the room she paused awhile before every picture, although she took no interest in the works, something which Ruskin, on observing her at a distance, was surprised to see – her eyes alighting upon each canvas as emotionless as if she had no more understanding or appreciation of art than if they had never met. But what distressed him most was her avoidance of him, for she proceeded to ignore him despite his persistence in trailing after her and looking askance.

It was a cruel meeting after so long a severance, and in the hope of provoking *some* kind of reaction from her he withdrew from his breast pocket the two sheets of gold protecting his favourite letter from her and held it out, grief-stricken.

'I think you lost something?' he asked quietly, for he was beginning to think that this was to be the rupture he had long been dreading.

Rose, without being lured into a discussion, merely shook her head and replied emphatically, 'No,' before moving on to the next picture.

'No?' Ruskin challenged, at a loss to understand her or how to respond.

Her fragility and mournfulness lent her a new and powerful grace, so much that he faltered to know how to approach or address her. Yet before he could question her further she turned, rushed from the room and hurried down the stairs, their few years of separation as seemingly ruinous as if a decade or more had elapsed.

Following her downstairs, he deliberated for a moment, the treasured letter still in his hands, but held himself back from pursuing her further for fear of appearing to harass her. Standing looking on as she crossed the crowded lobby, passed through the main door and stepped into the torrential London rain, as quick and furious as his heart, he raised his hands to his head, scarcely able to believe that she would disappear without so much as a word of greeting, but so it was.

Peering through the rain-dappled glass door as if he were on the other side of the world, he watched Rose lift her skirts to avoid the countless puddles before dashing along, avoiding the umbrellas of passers-by until she was finally swallowed up by the tumultuous Piccadilly thoroughfare, overrun with cabs and omnibuses.

Overcome, Ruskin took a seat in the lobby and, after replacing the letter he had carried in his breast pocket for years hoping for a more tender one to replace it, buried his head in his hands, as baffled and wounded as if she had married another.

It had been a great mistake to see him, Rose decided, relief coming over her when she had walked far enough to be certain that she was alone, closely superseded by guilt at the cruelty she had inflicted upon the one person who was ever faithful to her.

Turning around to see only strangers in her wake, tears began to mingle with the rain as she feebly wove her way back to the hotel, reliving the scene that had been the opposite of what she had intended and questioning how she might have acted or spoken differently.

Chastising herself to such a degree that any feelings of vanity at having the power to snub Ruskin vanished, each step increased her exhaustion and the desire not to reflect on what had just happened, for every thought only ended in lament.

The wind chill assailed her gaunt cheekbones, and having left her umbrella at the Royal Academy in her eagerness to be gone, she was sodden and dishevelled by the time she entered the public lounge of the hotel, though this did not deter her from going in search of her brother whom she found reclining in an armchair by the fire, smoking a cigar.

Percy looked up in surprise on seeing Rose back so early, while her crestfallen expression told him that either Ruskin had not been there or that the meeting had gone badly. He supposed hindsight would make him wish that he had accompanied her.

Anticipating his annoyance, Rose leant against the mantle and braced herself to relate events she did not feel wholly part of and, oblivious of an old couple taking tea in the corner, began wearily, 'I should never have gone,' resting her head on her arms.

'You didn't see him?' Percy prompted.

Rose looked up and, seeing herself in the mantle mirror, understood why others stared at her.

'Yes, I saw him, but that was all,' she stammered.

Percy leant forward in annoyance, resting his cigar. 'You saw him and didn't speak to him?'

'It's been so long, I didn't know what to say,' she pleaded.

'You should have told him what happened to you,' he insisted, jumping to his feet, 'and that you love him.'

Rose broke down at having her ineptitude pointed out so starkly, while Percy, sorry for being too harsh or indelicate, put his arm around her consolingly, much to the interest of the elderly couple who continued to listen intently.

'You *must* tell him before it's too late,' he went on passionately; 'we can't stay here forever and if you don't seize the opportunity you might not have another chance.'

'But what can I *do?*'

'You must change your clothes and go to him, lie down at his feet and ask for mercy if you have to, but for God's sake don't leave him believing that you scorn him when the reverse is true.'

It had been raining mercilessly for several hours by the time Rose reached Denmark Hill in a hansom cab, the rain having turned to sleet and the gloom of evening increasing her apprehension.

Although she had made every effort to compose herself to look presentable, she felt no more at ease on climbing down and making her way up the familiar path than if she had been going to meet God to ask his pardon – her legs as heavy as lead and her heart beating as fast as the coach which had taken her away from the sanatorium. Unbearable regret gnawed at her as she approached the house where she had spent some of the happiest days of her life, and she tugged the bell penitently, both martyr and sinner.

Ruskin, who had also walked home through the torrent, cursed aloud as one who has been spurned too many times and has no inclination for self-restraint. Believing his courtship to finally be at an end, he abhorred

Rose for her ill treatment of him and weighed up whether to compose a letter as harsh as the Day of Judgement so that no doubt might evermore be cast on their relationship.

Sitting in silence by the fireside, he would eat nothing Joan offered him, preferring to fume inwardly whilst trying to decide the choicest words to wound. If only he could make Rose feel a tenth of the pain she had inflicted upon *him*, sentiments his cousin, who refused to leave his side, predicted he would later grieve over and eventually intercepted by coaxing the pen out of his hand.

Joan ached to see his eyes glisten with sorrow and, stooping over his chair, placed her hand over the half-composed letter, saying simply, 'Enough now.'

Looking up from his reverie, he clutched her arm pitiably. 'She bade me wait for her, but in so doing I have learnt the vanity of trust. I am a moderate man, I take wine for the sake of sociability rather than wantonness and eat merely for sustenance, yet I *love* to the point of madness. I gorge myself upon it even when I know it's no good for me.'

'She cannot realise the injury she causes,' Joan soothed.

'Surely one glimpse at my face after all these years must have *shown* her. Rose is an angel and the Devil too. Dearest Joanie,' he pleaded, grasping her hand with the despair of an opium eater, 'keep me from ever seeing her or hearing of her again?'

He made many such declarations that evening, listened to by his most loyal companion who nodded with a tender patience which had been challenged countless times before and doubtless would again, for her cousin's harsh words melted away on his tongue as soon as he heard someone at the door.

Joan witnessed with conflict her cousin's pale blue eyes light up and his lungs breathe in hope in its most life-giving form on hearing the bell ring, recognising that this joy was the most destructive kind of salvation when disappointed.

Sitting forwards in his chair, eager to know whether it really was her, Ruskin suddenly became embarrassed to think how contradictory his actions and words were, right down to his last vow of reticence. Flogging himself for his feebleness, he turned to Joan, who had risen to her feet, and stated adamantly, 'I won't see her.'

But his cousin tutted dismissively, knowing that he would never have the strength to send Rose away should she be standing before him, and setting his words aside as false went to fetch the visitor.

Joan was much disturbed by Rose's appearance on beckoning her inside, for she looked deathly pale and thin, while the gloved hand she held out in order to restore their former acquaintance shook with anxiety lest she would receive a curt reception or Ruskin would refuse to see her.

'Is he very angry with me, Joanie?' she asked contritely, bowing her head and staring at the floor as humbly as once she used to when accused of some wrongdoing.

Her friend could not help but pity Rose and touched her reassuringly on the shoulder. 'He was only sorry not to have spoken with you earlier.'

'I wanted to; you must understand. It's just that I've been out of the world for so long that I find it difficult to converse as I used to. I should hate for him to think me a fool or, worse still, mad.'

'He would never think *that*,' Joan denied firmly, 'but that isn't really why you wouldn't talk to him?'

'I'm so glad to be here,' Rose avoided, smiling tenderly on recalling the day when Ruskin had first welcomed her to Denmark Hill. 'How well I remember the tour your cousin once gave, every room a new treasure of minerals and books, paintings and watercolours,' she enthused wistfully, her recollections vivid enough to transport her.

She stepped forwards and craned her neck in order to view the door to Ruskin's study at the top of the stairs, wondering if he was listening to their conversation and if he would appear.

'You are fortunate, for he rarely puts on such a show nowadays,' Joan remarked, drawing Rose back to the present; 'his friends must take him as they find him.'

'It always feels like such a peaceful house,' she observed, her thoughts momentarily drifting back to Harristown and how contrasting an atmosphere her own home seemed.

'I'm glad to say it *is* so, and Cousin John is the kindest, most generous master anyone could ask for,' Joan responded merrily, 'though he struggles to find contentment.'

Rose responded uneasily, 'I never cease praying for him, no matter how long I am absent, and one day God will surely hear me and give him all the quietude he deserves.'

Joan, though she loved them both, remained fiercely loyal to Ruskin, and replied, 'I hope so,' with a note of annoyance and scepticism that struck the visitor sorely.

'Is he at home?' Rose enquired timidly, sensing that their conversation was exhausted.

'Yes, would you like to see him?'

'Very much,' she nodded tearfully, 'if he will allow it?'

Without responding, Joan placed her hand on the small of Rose's back and ushered her into the drawing room where Ruskin remained torn between wanting to rebuke her on one hand and reiterate his proposal on the other. Joan was meanwhile weary of her role as intermediary and, after making her apologies, left the pair to discuss matters which no letter could have settled.

Ruskin hoped, nay *knew*, that Joan would invite Rose inside and, although he had been determined not to give her an easy time of it or look pleased to see her, her unsettling fragility was such that he didn't have the fortitude to hold onto his resentment. The wait for the two women to stop conversing in the hallway had been agony, only increased by his inability to overhear what they were saying.

When Joan finally showed Rose into the drawing room he observed much which had escaped his notice earlier. The very image of beauty and loveliness despite her obvious ill health, Rose was a girl, and yet not a girl: her height accentuating her emaciation, whilst her bearing told of the wild Rose who once had sported, ridden and climbed over rocks like a young imp. Nobly serene in her decline, her eyes were luminous and kind, with a gentleness that made Ruskin wonder how he could ever doubt her fidelity.

Notwithstanding her glory, he was pained upon observing the dark circles under her eyes and her sunken cheeks, destroying the effervescence he had first admired and which was made all the more apparent in the dimness of candlelight. Yearning to embrace her, he found himself transfixed by her lost expression, unsure whether she intended to appease their earlier meeting or merely reinforce it.

Rose was meanwhile anxious not to be dismissed without having her confession heard, and therefore rushed to speak despite being overwhelmed with agitation on preparing to utter the loving words she had spent the past three years contemplating.

'Forgive me,' she began, her fear passing away on kneeling before him.

'I don't understand,' he said, scrutinising her with wide eyes that conveyed both his desire and his confusion.

Taking up his hands and cupping them within her own, she looked into his face imploringly, her expression wild. 'You must think me cruel, wicked, but if you only knew what my life has been I believe you *would* pity me.'

'I pity us both,' he returned sadly, 'as do all our true friends.'

'I have allowed my desire to be dutiful to God and my parents engulf me, but know that I *will* trust you and that I *do* love you,' Rose proclaimed ardently, much to his astonishment.

'You love me?' he repeated, disbelieving his own ears.

'I have loved you though the shadows that have come between us have made me turn from you, but I love you and shall always, always,' she vowed, kissing his hand as faithfully as Rebecca, wife of Isaac. 'I have wished not to love you,' she continued solemnly, 'yet, as surely as I believe God loves you, I love you *still* and always. Please do not doubt this anymore.'

Stunned at this outpouring of emotion, the stuff of fantasy and not reality, Ruskin kissed her forehead before asking incredulously, 'Can this be true, my pet? Have you *really* spoken the words I have turned grey in longing to hear?'

'Yes!' Rose answered, rising in order to kiss his cheek devotedly.

He felt impelled to kiss her rosebud lips in reciprocation, but as soon as the idea of doing so occurred to him her smile began to fade and she looked forlorn again.

Settling down at his feet and looking away, she continued, 'If there had never been anything but friendship between us how much pain and suffering might have been spared!'

'Think of all the joy lost too,' he denied, 'and all the happiness we will surely know in future, from this day onwards.'

But her manner changed at once on him presuming that she was promising herself to him in marriage, and she rose and stepped away in order to clarify her position. 'My father and mother forbid my writing to you or seeing you and I cannot do so in secret, but if my love is any sunshine to you, take and keep it.'

Baffled at the thought that she might yet go from him, despite her passionate avowal, he perceived that Rose would not grant him the opportunity to reply or challenge her and saw no alternative but to respect her stance with quiet awe.

Stooping to touch his face before walking to the door, a quiet peace came over her, a glimmer of her old self. Content that he would never again mistrust her constancy, she had given him a part of herself; a consolation in his solitary hours.

Though Rose had promised nothing tangible in return for all the years of patient devotion, he could not be dissatisfied with such a resolution, for her words had been enough to transform the worst day of his life into the happiest, and he was too elated to risk losing the ground that had been gained by pressing her further.

DEFIANCE

P ERCY, BITTER THAT HIS OWN HOPES OF LOVE HAD BEEN dashed by his parents, hardly dared imagine that his mission in taking Rose to London would result in her accepting Ruskin's proposal, yet he was nonetheless pleased at the outcome of their meeting and trusted that time and her own maturity would offer up the resolve she needed in order to break free, his sole comfort during the final phase of their journey back to Ireland.

Pondering on the silent revolution he imagined raged within Rose in defiance of their parents, he smiled whenever she looked to him, for he felt obliged to hearten her on observing her fearful expression and the flush of trepidation of what lay ahead, a mere shake of the head informing him that whilst she appreciated his kindness she was not inclined to hear reassurances he did not believe himself.

Acknowledging one another's dread at being again confined within the estate, neither could help being mesmerised by the majestic though barren Irish landscape that bright January twilight, or the little church that had shaped them both unconsciously. Religion and environment were as entwined as the sibling bonds which had led Percy to act against his father, for had he and his sister fled to the other side of the world they could not have escaped the ties of their homeland, as impenetrable as the stone walls in which they had both taken their first breath.

The golden winter sun sinking behind Harristown House heralded their return as they passed through the gates and swept down the seemingly interminable gravelled approach, its very length testament to their achievement in breaking away and their cowardice in going back.

Exchanging a final glance fully expressive of her foreboding, Rose climbed out of the carriage to find her father standing stoically before the line of servants ready to greet her as if nothing was amiss, yet his professed happiness to see her was clouded by everyone else's shock at her fragility, the staff avoiding her gaze in an attempt to hide their compassion and their disgust towards "The Master" whose regime they each had their own reason for despising.

Ignoring him entirely, Rose moved along the row of men and women and enquired after their health, hoping that no-one would ask the same of her and conversing all the more when she saw how the courtesy infuriated her father. She was diverted by how severely he greeted Percy, however, for he bowed submissively only to be rebuffed by La Touche who uttered through gritted teeth, 'You've gone too far.'

Rose accepted with sadness that Percy would never have the courage to disobey him again. All the mistakes he had ever made were as nothing to the betrayal of the past weeks, and he would spend a lifetime trying to make amends for the one good action he had performed in exchange for his own peace. He would marry not for love but duty, and would work every day at a business he had no more heart for than the wife he returned home to each evening.

Perceiving all that she had unwittingly brought about, Rose mourned the loss of her spirited brother just as dearly as her fair Emily, their lives bound together by adversity in the face of duty. But as guilt tried her conscience, hatred towards her parents grew.

Just as she wondered where her mother was, and whether her absence was intended as a statement of hostility, Mrs La Touche exited the house and rushed towards her with arms outstretched, an action Rose would sooner have replaced with honest contempt, so unnatural did it feel to be embraced by the woman she regarded as her greatest adversary.

Rose did not doubt that, had it not been for Percy, she would still be lying alone in Dublin, restrained or dead, and therefore not even her most passionate Christian beliefs could persuade her to forgive. No affection or apology could return her most treasured letters or undo the torment of being incarcerated against her will, nor was there any sign of remorse in her mother's brazen demonstration of love.

'It's wonderful to have you home,' Mrs La Touche gushed, relaxing her hold only to scrutinise her daughter's face and find a stranger staring back at her blankly.

Rose could not, would not reply and proceeded inside as abruptly as La Touche sent the servants about their duties, whispering to one another as they went.

Choosing to keep to her room, everything familiar was tainted by what had been, and she knelt down and wept at the sight of the mended floorboard and all that had been taken from her, far more than words on paper which she had long committed to memory.

Though her ordeal had finally transformed her into a woman, Rose was ever a child before Him and believed God meant her to endure her unhappiness with dignity and quietude. Kneeling with her hands clasped together in desperation, surely He would tell her what her life was to be?

Considering whether to publish her poetry or take up the modest position of governess in a neighbouring family, an idea her parents would undoubtedly scorn and believe she had determined on merely to humiliate them, her existence was as desultory as it had ever been.

Whatever scheme she fixed upon, all her intentions of leaving Harristown became confused by prayer, and the forbearance she possessed in the confines of her room vanished the moment she left it.

One conviction remained unaltered, however – the thought that marrying Ruskin might prove as detrimental as remaining in Ireland – for she questioned whether he could ever regard her as a true equal. Even his most loving guidance and helpful wisdom was bound to undermine her craving for independence, and would she not find herself as subservient to the ways of Denmark Hill as Harristown?

Ruskin, having been left dazed by Rose's loving words, was meanwhile reliant upon snatches of news from friends in order to keep him from the abyss of depression: a sickness that had become a second skin and was all the harder to shake off due to always attaining sympathy from his dear Joanna.

When Mrs Cowper-Temple was good enough to send him an old photograph of his darling, taken at the time of her eighteenth birthday, he looked upon her former self with an adoration blighted with sorrow at having been instrumental in her decline.

She stared, with her luminous, penetrating eyes, not into the photographer's lens but straight into his soul, her fair hair smoothed Madonna-like just as it had been on the day she had pleaded for mercy at his feet, the large cross that was her only ornament a woeful reminder of God's cruelty in dividing them.

No gladness could be found in recalling the girl tarnished by religion and jealousy, he only felt inexpressibly sad to think that neither of them could have guessed what lay ahead when the image was taken, or that her present cares would be chiselled upon her face as permanently as marble. Despite everything, however, Rose's exquisite grace shone through and made him worship her all the more. Recalling their last meeting at Denmark Hill, he remembered her as far more statuesque in person than the girl in the picture and wondered how it was that her torments only increased her enchantments.

Though Rose becomes more rarefied with every trial and disappointment, the same cannot be said of me, he griped, eyeing his own white hair and creased forehead in the looking glass when shaving, his misery punctuated by unusual merriment when he read the letter from George MacDonald that was waiting for him at breakfast.

Contorting his eyebrows and holding his cup aloft as he read, Ruskin discovered with amazement that his beloved was intent upon publishing her poetry, a recent example of which MacDonald had done him the honour of including.

"'We weep for every vanished thing, we call the winter long,'" he read aloud satirically, "'Tis but the harsh before the spring, when all things wake in song.' Bah! She wouldn't sell more than ten copies, and even *they* would have to be purchased by the likes of you and me,' he sneered, passing the letter to Joan and continuing with his boiled egg.

'That isn't very complimentary,' his cousin chided, 'and merely shows how peeved you'd be if Rose became self-sufficient,' saying which she threw a roll at him in sport.

'I protest!' Ruskin denied, brushing away crumbs from the sleeve of his coat. 'If I believed her poetry could do *that* I'd offer to publish them myself. Rose is always scrambling about trying to find her *calling*, whether it's as the bride of Christ or the next Elizabeth Barrett Browning, but tell me what is so very wrong with being a wife? Is not that just as worthy a vocation?'

'For some women perhaps,' she granted, 'but Rose is not, and never has been, a typical example of femininity, nor would you love her if she were.'

'It is hopeless denying it, wise Joanna. What perceptive observations you always make.'

'If only you'd listen to them,' she smiled wryly, rising and ringing for the maid to clear away breakfast.

Days, months, years of listening to her cousin's emotional dilemmas had made Joan bolder with her opinions and frustrations, nor was she beyond hoping that one day she might have her own stresses to contend with, quite aside from those of managing Denmark Hill or trying to allay Ruskin's tribulations.

In reality Rose had no more confidence in her slim volume of sonnets than Ruskin, who was not in the least surprised when MacDonald wrote again soon afterwards announcing that her idea of becoming a poet had been abandoned, yet any relief he experienced was replaced with further exasperation upon learning that the young poetess meant to set aside her own ambitions in favour of channelling those of others.

'A governess!' Ruskin repeated in dismay, thumping his fist upon the table during another tedious breakfast for Joan. Appalled at the thought of associating such a mundane profession with his dear one, he was also deeply hurt that Rose should prefer a life of service to the comfortable, loving home he wished to offer.

'You don't mean it?' Joan returned, equally baffled.

'She's come up with some wild schemes, but *this* is the wildest yet,' he avowed, feigning jollity, for whilst reason told him to dismiss what was bound to be another short-lived fancy, his passion made him regard the idea with dread lest she should prove him and her family wrong out of sheer spite and contrariness.

'I think she would be a good teacher,' Joan defended, 'nor do I see any shame in it. I should have considered the same path if only I had been better educated.'

'But *Rose* is quite another matter,' he deprecated without thinking. 'I can't get over the notion of *her* as a mere governess. Just imagine Rosie being tucked up in a back attic with a party going on downstairs!'

Affronted at being thought socially inferior in her cousin's estimation, Joan dismissed, 'She'll never do it so let's not waste our time discussing it.'

'Part of me wishes she *would*,' Ruskin concluded. 'No-one knows better than I that teaching is far more rewarding than writing second-rate poems, and at least she'd be away from Harristown and all the obnoxious influences that continue to crush her.'

No matter how ludicrous he considered Rose's latest invention, Ruskin saw that it was prompted by ever strained relations with her parents: arguments followed by long silences, and stubborn tempers that did not mellow when harsh winter frosts dissolved with more temperate days. Such disappointments he all too easily recognised on reading her poetry, which, although inadequate and feeble, possessed an honesty and rawness that called out to him and lessened the miles distancing them.

He gathered, from the snatches of information he gleaned here and there from correspondents, that Rose remained at odds with her mother and father, although he could not guess the magnitude of their daily quarrels or that John and Maria begged their daughter to end her self-imposed exile and starvation: acts they believed were purposely designed to increase their disconnection, with the consequence that Rose's already impaired strength deteriorated further and made her striking appearance all the more marked.

As Ruskin lived out the clockwork habits of Denmark Hill which Margaret continued to impose, from the early dining hour to reading aloud a novel upon retiring by the fireside of an evening, Rose did all she could to evade the customs of Harristown, taking her place at the long dining table night after night with no intention of accepting sustenance.

With her eyes tightly closed as her father said grace, she could not help but peep at the butler who was slicing a rib of roast beef, a sight which caused her brother and father to salivate and she to wince.

Withdrawing her prayer-posed hands, she folded them on her lap in bold refusal to so much as touch the shining polished silver or the blood-soaked meat which the rest of the family devoured as ravenously as dogs chasing a fox through the undergrowth, judging them not, though she was too repelled to join them.

Instead, the judgement fell to her, and La Touche grew angry at his daughter's persistent abstinence. Saying nothing, he rested his knife and fork and regarded her intently, daring her to defy him.

'I should like to be excused,' Rose requested, preparing to rise.

'You may not. You will stay until you finish the meal God has provided.'

'Please,' she answered weakly, avoiding his gaze and that of her mother, who looked askance at her.

'Eat, I tell you!' La Touche shouted, slamming his plate down with violence enough to make the gravy spill.

'I'll see that she eats something later,' her mother interjected, for she loathed scenes before the servants.

He was too provoked to be silenced, however, and turning on his wife, asked, 'Does she want to starve to death?' his temper boiling over when he heard his daughter mutter the affirmative. 'What did you say? You know that it is a sin to end your own life?'

'To love is a sin, apparently,' she replied, determined not to buckle.

'To love God is not, to love *that man* is inhuman.'

'You wear me into the ground with your God and sin!' Rose raged, throwing her cutlery onto the floor in remonstrance of his hypocritical preachings.

'You don't know the dangers of trusting to your own judgement,' La Touche went on, his complexion turning puce. 'This love you talk of is a kind of madness.'

'Madness?' Rose challenged, moving her plate closer and taking up the meat with her bare hands as if to mock his own carnivorousness.

Gorging herself barbarically until her cheeks bulged and her fingers were stained with blood, she choked and swallowed down the food until her plate was clean, then, draining the glass of wine before her, refilled it to the brim and drank again, much to her parents' horror and her brother's warped satisfaction.

Yet even Percy's smirk vanished when Rose began to gag and wretch, purging herself before them in so shocking a manner that they each turned their heads away in disgust of the plate now bearing her rejected fare.

Grotesquely triumphant at having achieved this act of absolute defiance, Rose spat one final time before wiping her mouth daintily with her napkin in as obscenely contrasting a gesture as she could muster and, rising from the table with uncharacteristic hauteur, went from the room confident of never again being forced to dine with her parents.

PARALLEL LIVES

SIX MONTHS HAD ELAPSED SINCE ROSE'S PROCLAMATION OF love, rallying, through the dead of winter, every sensibility within Ruskin and causing him to bemoan her interminable absence when he might have been returning tenfold the ardour she had at last declared.

Determined to live on the outside of his emotions as best he could, he was ever conscious that any hopes concerning marriage would override any possibility of work if once he allowed them to control his thoughts entirely. From moment to moment he simply tried to live on and not to think of his love in Ireland. The sun, he well knew, rose and fell not for his benefit, and thus he began to see the world much as his father had – every dawn as the beginning of life, every twilight as its close.

Having existed in a cobweb of fate for so long, he was never more in need of a different axis when Destiny, who was not always unkind, intervened and saw to it that he was given a new purpose beyond his wildest imaginings. Invited to become the first Slade Professor of Fine

Art at Oxford University, a title designed expressly with him in mind, it was an opportunity even the most humble of men might be forgiven for taking pride in.

He leapt at the chance to prove his worth once more, grateful that, although his mother was fading fast and was invariably bedridden, God had not called her to His side before she had the gratification of seeing him achieve the pinnacle of her long-held ambitions. For once he was not opposed to the distinction and, gladdened by the thought of pleasing her, permitted himself a share in her delight.

'You consider my becoming a professor almost as laudable as your once-held dream of my being made an archbishop?' he teased boyishly, chuckling on seeing her cheeks glow with maternal conceit.

'Most certainly!' she declared.

'It's an altogether different kind of calling,' he persisted.

'Yes, but both professions rely upon the teacher *himself* being enlightened,' she returned stoically, folding her hands on the quilt matter-of-factly and pursing her lips. The very lace on her cap shook with the chuckle that rose from her toes to her shoulders, prompting her son to smile at her never-ceasing faith in him.

'I dream lofty dreams certainly,' he admitted, accepting only a portion of the compliment.

'Who knows, perhaps you will end by becoming a Member of Parliament,' she went on, eyes glistening and cheeks glowing as she grew delirious imagining the myriad opportunities that lay in store for him. If Oxford had been the pinnacle of his career yesterday, the Palace of Westminster was the ambition of tomorrow.

'Why is it never enough to be what I *am*, Mother? I don't want to be a Member of Parliament, I have never voted for anybody in my life and never mean to!'

'Fie!' Margaret retaliated, waving away his denial.

'I merely want somebody to nurse me when I'm tired,' he continued in exasperation, 'for Turner's pictures not to fade, to be able to draw clouds and understand how they go. I have long given up trying to make the Italians industrious, the Americans quiet, the Swiss romantic, the Roman

Catholics rational or English politicians honest, and nowadays all I want is to get everyone a dinner who hasn't got one.'

'That is quite enough,' Margaret agreed, closing her eyes primly as she always did when stumped during an argument.

Ruskin seized such opportunities to work and would nod off in the armchair installed beside her bed any time of the day or night, for he preferred to be close to her whilst writing the series of lectures he was tasked with preparing for the following university spring term, the ever-encouraging Margaret ready to listen to extracts from his text and offer him the praise he needed to keep going.

Despite extreme mental exhaustion, his willingness to offer his mother contentment in her final days impelled him to focus on the task at hand and keep his thoughts of Rose at bay, although it was a sacrifice that often provoked much grumbling.

'I *had* thought seven lectures would be a suitable number before I was informed that I should prepare a minimum of twelve,' Ruskin complained in response to her consternation at awakening from a long sleep to find numberless papers strewn about the room.

'Only twelve?' she asked facetiously, shaking her sleepy head. 'It looks like you have enough material for twenty.'

'You've no idea how little I'll be left with after editing, the prospect of which makes me weary, as does the pressure of having a deadline hanging over me, for I have been my own master for too long. Taking orders at my age is no easy thing.'

Flattered at being esteemed by men considerably higher in the academic sphere than himself, the opportunity to teach and shape scholars was a great one. Despite being initially overwhelmed by the volume of work expected of him, Ruskin welcomed no longer having the time to centre his very existence around Rose or worry what would become of him when his mother was no more.

Like that of a priest, his life was no longer his own and would be devoted to education and the ancient temple in which learning was most glorified; Oxford, a golden sanctum where sages and leaders had honed their expertise and refined their philosophies. The honour of being invited into this hallowed place as a teacher of such men prompted Ruskin to forget all his past miseries as a gentleman-commoner and fixate solely on his future role.

A venture which demanded that he keep his new obligations at the forefront of his mind, any vanity initially satisfied by the appointment turned to blistering unease when he discovered that his election to the post had sparked a minor furore among some of the senior university members, of the opinion that he was far too controversial a candidate and would prove wayward in his opinions and teaching methods.

Visiting the university prior to the commencement of term, Ruskin was appalled to find countless dons whispering in corners, all of whom appeared abashed on seeing him and lowered their voices whenever he passed by. Surrounded by those who wished to oust him before he'd begun, he should have accused himself of paranoia had not his suspicions been confirmed by Acland, with whom he shared a quiet drink at the Crown & Thistle in Abingdon, his chosen lodging that first term.

Set in the heart of the bustling market town, the Crown was a characterful timber-framed inn with an uneven cobble courtyard, a thriving bar, and enough coaches and tradesmen to distract any man from the torture of conspiracy and politics.

'I can't deny it, your reappearance among the spires *has* ruffled feathers,' Acland admitted regretfully, staring into his cloudy beer, his hands on his knees.

'Just as I thought,' Ruskin returned, his sigh exposing his supreme disappointment at finding himself unpopular at Oxford for a second time.

'I shouldn't let it worry you. You have defeated greater dissenters than all of *them* put together,' his friend cheered, patting his shoulder like an elder brother might have, for he was keen to see Ruskin seize the challenge of overcoming his objectors.

'Oxford is a beacon of education, but she doesn't much like change,' he remarked sorrowfully, draining his tankard of ale with uncharacteristic thirst. 'I am strangely troubled to have enemies before I have started, yet I am willing to approach my first lecture cautiously and with due reverence to the powers who permitted me such a platform, for it *is* a great credit to influence men who might go on to wield some good in the world. I am therefore determined to avoid saying or doing anything which the university might consider inappropriate.'

'Those like myself, who know your capabilities, are behind you all the way,' Acland buoyed, rising in order to replenish their ale.

But Ruskin interrupted his friend's task by observing, 'I appreciate your confidence but I have to contend with the fact that youths are sent to Oxford, not to be apprenticed to a trade, nor to be advanced in a profession, but rather to be made gentlemen of. *I*, on the other hand, see the purpose of the university quite differently.'

'Of course you do,' the doctor agreed, a knowing smile upon his lips.

'The function of this professorship is to establish both a practical and a critical school of fine art,' Ruskin continued on Acland returning from the bar. 'Practical, so that any man if they choose to draw, may draw *rightly*, and critical, so that they may be directed to such works of art as best reward their study.'

'I can see that this role will bring you much reward and pleasure,' the doctor predicted merrily, his flowing white hair a poignant reminder of their thirty year friendship.

'I well need some; it surely would have given much to my poor father. Ah well,' Ruskin sighed again, resting his chin upon his hand, 'perhaps it may yet give some to the person who has given me my worst pain.'

But Acland was irked by the reference to Rose, whom he regarded as a young temptress. 'There are others besides who are glad to see you here.'

'Thank you, Henry. I hope quietly and patiently to be of very wide use. I am just ripe for it too, for it will allow me to obtain attention, and attention is all that I need to say what is *useful* instead of what is pretty or entertaining. Oxford launched my career so it's only right that she should have the best of me now, even if there are those who would banish me to hell just to silence me. It would certainly be well to stop mewing all day, for I suspect it may be *that* which makes God so angry with me.'

'I should gripe if I had to stay in such a place as this for long,' Acland gibed, shaking his head in reference to their companion drinkers, who laughed uproariously and clutched their overfed stomachs, tight as drums from a seven-day-a-week diet of sour ale and cheap cuts.

'*They* are just about ready for the abattoir,' Ruskin observed as the men guzzled, smoked and blasphemed to their hearts' content, 'yet I confess I am glad of the entertainment which such a place as this provides gratis. A ringside seat here quite takes me out of myself.'

'It certainly *is* a den of iniquity. Are you quite sure you would prefer to lodge here rather than with me?'

'You are very kind, but there are times when I am more at ease at an inn, just like my father during the days of his enterprise,' he explained. 'My parents never *would* spend a night in another person's house, and the older I get the more intolerant I find myself to the concept of trying to adjust to unfamiliar ways. We Ruskins have always been difficult house guests and can only abide visitors because *they* have to adopt our quirks.'

Acland chuckled and returned magnanimously, 'That's as maybe, but you'll always be welcome at my humble abode if the company here gets too unsavoury.'

Requesting a quiet room, positioned a safe distance from the busy rear courtyard and High Street entrance, where the morning traffic sounded long before daylight was established, the Crown & Thistle provided Ruskin with a convivial base despite its unappealing aspect.

The accommodation was basic but clean, nor did he have a demanding or refined appetite, the simple inn fare suiting him well enough. Just as his parents had always detested luxury, he felt drawn to reside at such places whilst working, for they offered a humble familiarity that was altogether lacking in more formal, ostentatious hotels, let alone the stifling atmosphere of the university where one could never feel entirely at ease.

Having dedicated more time to his inaugural lecture as Slade Professor than any he had yet composed, Ruskin awoke early on the February day he was to address his new pupils – his fifty-first birthday by strange coincidence – and was energised by the sight of the jovial landlord in his chequered trousers, along with those characterful tradesmen who stopped to wish him a 'good day' when he set off, relishing the six or seven mile walk to Oxford via Bagley Wood despite the weather being changeable.

Refusing to wear a hat or carry an umbrella, the professor preferred to shelter under a tree should the rain become too tiresome, while the early snowdrops which brushed the tops of his boots announced that spring was nigh and another chapter of his life, perhaps the best, was there for the taking.

On reaching the quaint, picturesque village of Ferry Hinksey, he paused awhile, admiring, as he gazed on the chill horizon, the city's far off domes and spires glistening in the frosted glory of fading winter and impressing him with the enormity of the task ahead.

Having started out with time enough to see the pale morning light over Christ Church and his old friend, Tom Tower, whose faint, ghostly bell sounded in his imagination by way of summons, the sight of the cathedral contributed to his sense of destiny and the belief that Oxford would connect and validate his past and future achievements, for to be entrusted to teach men in whom he would inevitably find his younger self reflected was a juxtaposition like no other.

Though his steps were light, the weight of importance grew heavier the nearer he came to his new place of work, for academic life was a deal more than just imparting knowledge and wisdom; the university revolved around petty politics and futile jealousies that were far beneath the minds of great men.

He had no inclination to encourage insincere associations or practise diplomacy, and merely prayed to be let alone to work in solitude, a conviction which fortified Ruskin as he strode onwards, buoyed by the prospect of his own name, and more importantly his father's, being added to the annals of Oxford's history.

This reverie was broken when a gig, journeying in his direction, pulled up by the roadside and caused him to halt. Driven by the ruddy-faced innkeeper, who first acknowledged Ruskin by tipping his cap, he held the reins firmly and asked, in a broad country dialect, 'Might I take thee yonder, Mr Ruskin?'

'It is very kind of you to stop, but it is my custom to walk,' he replied, unmindful that his woollen trousers and boots were splattered with mud.

'As you like. I shall see thee later, then,' the man returned glibly, preparing to start up again, his trusty grey mare tossing her head impatiently and kicking the dust on the unkempt highway.

Nerves mingled with excitement as the hour of reckoning drew closer, with a flustered Acland arriving at Ruskin's college rooms just after one o'clock to announce that a throng of young students and townsfolk were queuing patiently outside the Oxford Museum in order to hear him.

Like a young man receiving his first dose of fame, Ruskin couldn't help but open the ancient leaded window to see for himself, and sure enough a determined line of men and women were waiting in the street, nor had he any fear of disappointing them, so much effort had he devoted to his maiden speech. Having arrived at perhaps the most momentous occasion of his varied career, this sight gave him a late burst of energy and confidence as he made his final preparations, his father and Rose ever in his mind's eye, urging him on.

Acland was hardly less moved by the turnout when he approached the museum an hour later and attempted to skirt past the droves of graduates, undergraduates, dons, ladies, townspeople and villagers from round about. Several hundred people or more lined the corridor all the way to the main hall, while an excited hum of anticipation sounded on entering the auditorium, where he found many more hundred conversing as they awaited their first glimpse of the new professor.

Assessing that the lecture could not continue as planned when so many would be left disappointed, Acland went away to ponder on whether the event should be postponed to another day, something which might cause uproar given the doggedness of Ruskin's supporters.

After a few hurried discussions with colleagues, however, the doctor was pleased to resolve the dilemma and, returning through a door on the far left of the hall with a broad smile upon his face, exhaustively pushed his way past the teeming crowd to the lectern. Waving his arms about wildly in order to attract the attention of the men and women engrossed in conjecture as to what was causing the delay, he fairly shouted, 'Excuse me!' before being granted the silence which allowed him to continue.

'Ladies and gentlemen,' he went on breathlessly, 'I must apologise for keeping you waiting, but it seems we have greatly underestimated the number of you wishing to hear Mr Ruskin's inaugural lecture. It is very flattering that such crowds of you have flocked to hear him but even *this* room is clearly too small to hold you. Therefore, we have been busy trying to find another venue to accommodate everyone. Would you all kindly make your way to the Sheldonian?'

Those whom he addressed took the request good-naturedly, there being no question of them giving up and going away, they merely shrugged their shoulders cordially and began a makeshift procession to the nearby Sheldonian Theatre; several dons meanwhile remarked to Acland how extraordinary it was to find so many people determined to hear Ruskin speak.

'This is a landmark in the history of Oxford, for professorial lectures are not usually matters of great excitement,' remarked Dean Liddell sourly, 'nor have I ever known the museum to be inadequate.'

'No-one could have anticipated such a response, least of all Ruskin,' Acland agreed, 'yet it's testament to the university's wisdom that they have recognised his popularity and his ability to address the undergraduates as one who once stood in *their* shoes.'

But the dean was unnerved by such adoration, and dismissed, 'I doubt his favour will continue when term begins. This is no more than a compulsive desire to be part of something.'

'I do not expect their regard to wane,' Acland contradicted firmly, suspicious of the dean's disapprobation. 'I watched some students talking with him on his first day and you never saw admiration like it. The young do not always listen to their elders, yet they listen to *him* with a rare and precious openness.'

Whilst news of his appeal, excluding his haughty colleagues, naturally thrilled Ruskin when Acland returned to update him on the change of venue, and that he would now be addressing a much larger audience, he doubted whether he could ever live up to the expectation of so many.

During the interval afforded by the change of locale, he recalled his own average performance as a student and questioned his gall in preparing to bestow his views on art and a great many other things to a new and impressionable generation, a singular change of circumstance.

Ruskin smiled to himself on remembering his father's frustration when he had failed to adjust to university life, something his mother remedied by taking lodgings on the High Street in order to be a reassuring presence. Taking tea with her each day, no matter that his peers mocked him, was something he longed for just then in order to settle his nerves.

It was responsibility rather than insecurity that unsettled him now, however, and he took a deep intake of breath before closing the door to his apartment and setting off to meet his merry band of judges.

Never had the Sheldonian Theatre, which Wren had ambitiously modelled on an example from ancient Rome, hosted a more motley or expectant throng, nor a more appreciative one.

Crammed with all classes, both sexes and varying degrees of intellect, none showed any sign of exhaustion regardless of how long they had been huddled together. Each man or woman was simply thankful to have a place at all, for despite the capaciousness of the eight-sided building there were a deal more who had been turned away.

Wearing a long black gown over his coarsely-woven tweed suit, along with the velvet cap of a gentleman-commoner, Ruskin strode theatrically onto the stage, followed by a snivelling, elderly assistant who bore witness to the proceedings with astounding indifference.

Amused rather than offended by this, Ruskin took a minute to weigh up his wider audience, having always believed that no two were ever alike. Preparing to adjust his tone according to his observations, he also took a moment to exchange recognitions with friends who were present, turning away on feeling the electric pulse of anticipation from the crowd and continuing to set out his books and papers.

Almost three decades of toil had elapsed since he had stood on that very spot ready to recite the poem for which he was awarded the Newdigate Prize, his name unfamiliar to those outside the university or his own small circle. The crowd was manifold greater in number on the present occasion, nor had he ever felt so many watchful and encouraging eyes upon him.

Having laid everything out with his usual precision, Ruskin stood at the front of the stage as though he were standing at the edge of a wide chasm and began with grave dignity, 'There is a destiny now possible to us, the highest set before a nation to be accepted or refused. The England who, seizing every piece of fruitful waste ground she sets foot on and is mistress of half the earth, cannot remain herself a heap of cinders, trampled by contending and miserable crowds. She must yet again become the England she once was, happy, secluded and so pure that in her sky, polluted by no unholy clouds, she may display every star that heaven doth show: her fields, ordered, wide and fair. She must guide the human arts and, gathering divine knowledge, transform manhood from despairing into peace.

'I hope you will agree with me when I say that you could not have had a Turner landscape without a country for him to paint,' he went on, signalling to the assistant who held up a landscape by the painter.

Ensuring that everyone had a chance to view the work, Ruskin directed the man to place the picture on an easel to his left and, taking up a paintbrush and palette, began mixing watercolours, an action which caused the majority of the audience to murmur in wonder.

Before they had a chance to fathom what he was about, the professor frantically covered the glass screening the work with grey paint, thereby creating the impression that the beautiful scene had been blighted by swathes of smoke.

'I was looking over my kitchen garden the other day, and I found it a miserable mass of weeds,' he went on, standing back to admire his handiwork, 'the roses putrefied, the half-ripe strawberries all rotten at the stalk.'

Laying down his paintbrush and palette, Ruskin slowly paced the length of the stage with a casual authority, all the agitation he had felt just moments before dissolving as he noticed his diverse admirers staring up at him, transfixed.

'You will laugh and say that I should replace my gardener,' he remarked drolly, pausing to allow his audience to chuckle, 'but I believe the industrial age is to blame. The powers of nature are being depressed or perverted, together with the spirit of man.'

Perceiving this declaration to garner a mixed reaction, not least from a young man seated three rows back, who piqued his attention by sniggering disrespectfully, Ruskin paused to hear the insult muttered against him.

'Utter rot!' the man declared to his friend. 'The man's deranged. Simply because his walled garden has gone to seed Mr Ruskin thinks we are witnessing the decline of man!'

'Well, if *he's* mad, it's a pity there are not more lunatics in the world,' replied his companion reproachfully, folding his arms and continuing to give his undivided attention to the professor.

Ruskin, accepting that he could not always convince a younger generation to adopt his theories, was no less satisfied at his aptitude to spark debate between the students, a most powerful weapon. Aside from teaching them how to appreciate art, he felt it his duty to challenge his protégés to examine the country in which they were living, and the consequence of human failings, that they might better assert themselves on leaving Oxford.

Pleased rather than offended to observe the two men exchanging words, Ruskin addressed them boldly, 'I am often thought mad, in fact I often think so myself,' he admitted, waiting for the crowd to cease sniggering, 'but never on *this* particular subject.'

'You attribute the ruination of your strawberries to the modern thirst for industry?' the impudent young man confronted.

'I merely use my fruit as an example,' he answered calmly, 'for the damage is potentially much worse than any of us realise. If science might tell me where the weather changes come from I would be grateful, but I suspect I may have found the answer – the storm clouds pouring out of every chimney and factory in the land. They look as if they were made of dead men's souls, and surely they will hurtle us towards oblivion faster than we know.'

Fired up, Ruskin no longer referred to his prepared text and, wishing to be more approachable to his audience, hastily removed his cap and gown to reveal his favoured homespun tweed ensemble.

'Forgive me, but I must rid myself of this ridiculous cap and gown. They were doubtless designed to make you better respect me and hear what I have to say, when in fact they are far likelier to distract you and cause you to ridicule me,' he tutted in frustration, for not even the honour of being asked to wear such a garb could make him see the sense of it.

Letting out a sigh of relief on disposing of them, the costume change revealed a jacket a little too large for him, with an equally ill-fitting double-breasted waistcoat. Adjusting the sleeves of his high-collared shirt and straightening his sky blue necktie with his usual single-mindedness, not only was the usual lecturer's uniform uncomfortable and stiflingly hot when one got into a passion, but Ruskin was convinced that he should have more success in delivering his message if he did so whilst on a level footing with the students.

'I trust that those of you here today who will be directly under my tutelage shall listen to me for reasons other than my university title or wider fame, for in the end I am dedicating my time not for the prestige of belonging to this great place of learning but to ensure that each of you leaves with a firmer idea of your own powers than when you started. To challenge one's mental and emotional capacity is the beginning and end of true education,' he went on, 'and my only desire is to help you further both so that you may go from here with confidence.'

The audience, entirely captivated, showed their approval by smiling receptively as Ruskin muttered, 'I should return to my original thread,' and, striding across the stage, pointed to the picture he had earlier blighted with charcoal paint.

'I have seen strange evil brought upon every scene I best loved or tried to make beloved by others. The light which once flushed those pale summits, with its rose at dawn and purple at sunset, is now umbered and faint. The air, which once inlaid the clefts of all their golden crags with azure, is now defiled with languid coils of smoke, belched from worse than volcanic fires. The light, the air, the waters, all defiled!

'Every breath of air you draw is polluted,' he pronounced. 'This poisonous smoke is blanching the sun and blighting the grass. Nature's harmony is broken as year by year the darkness gains. The puffs of steam, which pass under the wooded hills where I used to walk, moreover signify that some human beings are all going one way in the hastiest manner, and, having fastened themselves to the tail of a manageable breeze, are being blown down to Folkestone!'

His vivid blue eyes, coupled with ever-changing facial expressions, from grave to gay, from excitable to severe, magnetised the audience, each listener convinced that he spoke to them directly and read their soul. Indeed, anyone sensing Ruskin's eyes resting upon them felt as though they *had* a soul.

Overwhelmed with solemn awe, the students and townsfolk remained absolutely still and silent until the conclusion of the lecture, and they no more considered responding to it with a thunderous applause than they should have thought of cheering at the close of a seraph's song, for Ruskin could make the very heavens mute.

Whilst the Slade Professor's series of lectures proved, to many students, an epiphany of their time at Oxford, Ruskin's thoughts, the more comfortable he became in his new role, gradually returned to Rose and the one question to which no amount of hard work and resolve delivered an answer. Would she ever come to him? And *if* not, what could he do to change the destructive course she was intent upon?

Over-analysing his emotions and continually endeavouring to define the limits of insanity, he tormented himself by harbouring revenge and a kind of hatred towards Rose for the turmoil she continued to cause. Resentful that any enjoyment he found in life was always distorted by the state of limbo in which he lived, he wondered if it would not be better to dispel her image from his mind once and for all, though short of being able to remove his brain from his skull, or set fire to his memories, he knew not how this might be achieved.

Granted, it *was* easier working among the spires of Oxford than at Denmark Hill, where from girlhood to womanhood Rose had ingrained each and every crevice with her own perplexing image of beauty, purity and flirtatiousness, yet she remained with him even at the university where she had never yet stepped foot.

No matter how hard he attempted to manipulate his love into hate, bitter thoughts made him think of her almost more than loving ones, for guilt-ridden regrets were added to the pile of admonishments against Rose which he sounded along with his nightly prayers and repented of just as soon as they were uttered.

"My mind is so mixed up with desire for revenge and a kind of hatred which my love is changing into," he confessed to Mrs Cowper-Temple, *"distorting my whole life so that I don't well understand anything, besides feeling a shame and anger at myself which increases day by day and lowers me fatally."*

An unexpected letter from Rose, in response to the repeated chastisements he unwisely sent via Mrs Cowper-Temple, finally brought him to his senses, although any affection he received from his dear one only made the pain greater.

"I do not think it is much use my saying how bitterly untrue some of your letter is. Of one thing I am sure: it is utterly impossible for us to judge each other – you me, or I you. Certainly I cannot know your circumstances or feelings, and every word you write shows that you have not the faintest idea of mine. You are unjust to me, terribly unjust. Cannot you see that it needs a greater faith in me to remain silent when I long to write but fear it may be wrong of me? I am not the little thing that I was and, rather than try to step back into a position I can never hold with you again, I leave you to God, believing that the love I give you is not utterly in vain and not wholly disbelieved by you, who has no Trust."

But it was the fragment of a poem she enclosed that brought him most peace. Despite being as sanctimonious as ever, there was a kindred sympathy that reached out to him and took him by the hand. Did not it prove that their thoughts were as entwined as ever?

"He who hath balm for all our pain
Knows every grief of ours;
We shall not cry to Him in vain
In life's most hopeless hours.
Oh, doubting heart, look up again;
He will revive thy powers."

Exalted by these words and her categorical avowal of allegiance, the maturity of her tone surprised Ruskin and allowed him to conclude his first term at Oxford in better spirits.

Resigning himself to his quiet bachelor existence, he abandoned the anger he had previously felt towards Rose, unable to bring himself to blame her for not challenging her parents with any real conviction and reasoning that the few ties he still held with her were better than none at all. His life, which had been entirely at an end before she entered it, was so much better than it might have been.

PRAETERITA

THE UNIVERSITY TERM PASSED SWIFTLY, THOUGH RUSKIN never took one day of it for granted, nor allowed his students to become complacent when warmer months encouraged them to study outdoors, their manicured quad ever cluttered with art materials and sketches in readiness for the next lecture. His bookended career at Oxford meanwhile taught him that the future was only the past in waiting, though *he* was as contradictory about change as any man.

On the one hand he liked to picture himself with Rose in a home entirely their own, while on the other he was secretly content with the prospect of returning to Denmark Hill, there being much comfort in the staid regularity he had grown accustomed to: the familiar staff, whom in many cases he had known since boyhood, and the companionship and confidence of his kind, dependable Joanie, whose presence he took as much for granted as the stalwart old cedar in the driveway.

It was with great distress that he returned home in March to discover that old Anne Strachan had died, his mother lightening the mood by declaring, 'She always persecuted *me*, but one must hope there are intermediate kinds of places in heaven where people get better.'

Coupled with the chasm which the absence of such a character naturally left within the household, Ruskin was surprised to find Joan less willing to tolerate his usual lamentations concerning Rose, for her mind seemed very much elsewhere, nor could he manoeuvre her focus onto himself even when he made a concerted effort to be in good spirits.

Much to his irritation, the dependable Joanna had not forgotten Arthur during the months he had made the pair wait to consider their potential union, and instead sulked and sighed like a lovesick youth until he had no choice but to accept that she had better be married if he was ever to have a sensible talk with her again.

The couple's affection for one another had been tested long enough, Ruskin was forced to admit, perceiving that the pair drew closer to one another while *he* was an increasingly wearisome guardian to be tolerated rather than respected. There was no denying that running Denmark Hill had turned his cousin into a confident young woman who had developed great shrewdness since her grave miscalculation of Percy La Touche; and after all, he could hardly boast of being any judge of romantic affairs.

He blushed at the hypocrisy of urging Joan to proceed with caution whilst he squandered the best years of his life praying that Rose would finally succumb to his charms, as testing and thankless a pursuit as trying to catch a newly burgeoned butterfly.

'You understand that it's not because Rose has made *me* wait that I ask you to do likewise?' Ruskin asked abruptly one evening when they dined alone, the one advantage of his mother's bedridden state being that they could converse more frankly.

'It isn't?' Joan challenged boldly.

'Do you really think I would derive any pleasure in inflicting the pain *I* have endured?'

'We are not always conscious of our motivations,' she suggested, averting her gaze.

'You are right,' he sighed, 'it is wickedly selfish of me to want you always beside me. If I managed it you would only end by hating me.'

'I would never do *that*, but you must believe me when I say that I will never venture far.'

'Ever dutiful,' Ruskin returned with a cynicism that wounded her deeply in its unfairness.

'Not duty, *choice*,' she denied.

'I don't deserve you, Joanna,' he repented, 'but then there's probably no man alive who *does*.'

'I think Arthur, waiting all these years, has proved his worthiness.'

'Perhaps that's true, and I well know the burden of indefinite longing. You might have done better, but then again you almost did far worse. I only hope that you don't think you *need* to find a husband, for you will always have a home wherever I am, and even if I should get wee Rosie I shall always be the same towards *you*. Time was, when I would not have said so, when Rose would have been all in all to me, but our life together here has become more and more sacred to me.'

'And I, Cousin,' Joan reassured, placing her hand on his arm in a gesture that aimed to heal his insecurities. 'Leaving Denmark Hill, if I ever do, will be as great a wrench.'

'Just not as great as giving Arthur up?'

'I shan't give him up,' Joan answered firmly.

'I have often thought that it is the weakest-minded and hardest-hearted men who desire change, and that because I am neither I live in constant fear of the unknown, even if the alternative course should be of huge benefit to me,' Ruskin confessed.

'You give so much hope and inspiration to your students, yet privately you're as much in need of encouragement as any of them,' she observed, sighing at the irony.

'However much I try,' he lamented, 'I simply can't see any *good* in soon being orphaned,' a word which arrested Joan in its feebleness and prompted her to withdraw her hand, 'or losing Rose, not that she was ever mine. Your marriage will come just when I can least bear it.'

'But bear it you *must*,' Joan declared adamantly, for her compassion was waning and there was nothing for it but to address her guardian as a nanny might admonish a spoilt child.

'In that case,' he smiled, slapping his thigh as if he had been physically jolted out of his self-pity, 'you and Arthur shall have to see about fixing a date.' Removing his diary from his breast pocket, he asked, 'How about April?'

'Next month?' she hesitated, baffled by the change.

'I hope you will do me the honour of allowing me to give you away?'

'Why of course, it is *I* who should be honoured,' Joan exclaimed, blotting a tear with her napkin, for she had not expected her situation to alter so suddenly.

'Pray, after you have discussed the matter over with Arthur tomorrow, allow me to accompany you to the dressmaker. I know how much my mother would have loved to have advised you on your bridal gown, but I trust *I* have better taste.' And he giggled wickedly, causing her to do likewise and thus putting an end to all tension between them.

Reflecting on the days of old when his mother would take a dim view of Bible lessons not learned, Ruskin climbed the stairs to her chamber after dinner with his shoulders slumped, such was his dread of informing her of Joan's engagement.

As he anticipated, her tired, pain-lined face fell when he imparted the news, and he foresaw that the loss of her niece's constant companionship would be sufficient to hasten her journey to meet his father.

'How have you agreed this without consulting me?' she balked, struggling to sit up in the bed, a response Ruskin was well-braced, yet ill-equipped, to answer.

'I am Joan's legal guardian and there is no justification in asking her to wait any longer,' he defended, looking out of the window that he might avoid the old woman's grief-stricken mien. 'They abided by my terms and now I must respect their attachment to one another.'

She would hear no reason, however, and turning pale, she could think only of herself. 'They might have waited until after I was gone. How can Joan think of abandoning me now?'

'You know full well that she will never abandon you. Try to be thankful for all that she has done for you, not judge her harshly because she wishes to have a husband to care for besides. It's the natural way of things.'

'Arthur won't appreciate her as *I* do,' Margaret persisted as Ruskin turned and stood at the foot of the bedstead, resting his weight on the wooden surround as though he were the rationalising parent and she the demanding child refusing to go to sleep at bedtime.

'I don't suppose he will, but that's no reason she should remain a spinster for the rest of her life,' he shrugged. 'Besides, you'll only truly realise her devotion to you when she's gone away.'

'That's a fallacy, John, I have always lauded her kindness to me.'

'Either way,' he huffed, 'I can see that no attempt of mine to jolly you along is going to convince you to content yourself with regular visits from Joan instead of the constant attention you have grown accustomed to.'

'You make it sound as if I have been the only one to profit, when we offered her a home away from that horrid uncle,' she flapped with increasing petulance.

'Don't speak as though she has been in your employment these past years rather than having become the cherished daughter I know her to be.'

'A *daughter* would never have dreamt of leaving me in such a state,' Margaret denounced, illustrating her invalidity with a flourish of her hand upon the quilt.

'I must warn you that you're likely to lose her altogether if you don't grant her your blessing,' Ruskin cautioned, 'and I mean genially not reluctantly. I well remember the sorrow I experienced when you refused to come to *my* wedding.'

'*Indeed*, and look how that turned out,' she defended with an emphatic nod.

Joan meanwhile, anticipating the end of their brief conversation, crept guiltily from her listening post on the other side of the door, for despite being no eavesdropper she desired to know her aunt's true feelings. Nor did she interpret her acerbity as anything other than an outpouring of grief that their quiet, sedate existence was destined to change irrevocably. Moved rather than hurt by her aunt's words, Joan was grateful for the life she had known at Denmark Hill and forgave her freely.

Hurrying along the corridor in fear that her cousin would discover her underhandedness, Joan sought the shelter of her room, not to indulge in sobbing but to pray to God for forgiveness. Gratitude towards her aunt and guardian gave way to intense remorse at being thought selfish; instead of believing the old woman wrong for such possessiveness, Joan determined to prove her faithfulness to the family who had adopted her as their own, even to the detriment of managing her own household and caring for her future husband.

However averse Margaret was to accepting her son's advice, she was too shaken by his warning to ignore it out of hand. Thus she remained mildly stoic and attempted to conceal her devastation at her niece's imminent departure from Denmark Hill as best she could, over-compensating for her meanness of spirit by choosing what she considered to be a most elaborate gift.

A canteen of cutlery or a set of porcelain crockery was not nearly sufficient, she judged, and having spent the following morning pondering on the best way to commemorate her maternal feelings towards the young woman, she invited her niece to converse with her privately in her room: a summons which terrified Joan all the more after overhearing the old woman's initial reaction to her engagement.

Lying low in the bed as if to emphasise her decrepitude, Margaret still retained her stern, matronly air due to her customary lace cap, while her little round spectacles drew Joan's attention, not only to the pointy end of her aunt's nose but to her beady, scrutinising eyes.

'John tells me that you and Arthur are to be married,' she began, her tone bitter rather than encouraging.

'Yes, Aunt,' Joan confirmed apologetically, 'but I don't want you to worry about anything, I will still look after you just as I do now.'

'Don't make promises you can't keep,' Margaret snapped.

'I simply mean that it is not my intention to desert you. Arthur realises that I have responsibilities and that I mean to uphold them.'

'You're a good girl, Joanna,' the old woman admitted with a sigh, withdrawing a cheque from under her pillow and handing it to her officiously, her lips pursed into the semblance of a smile. 'And before you say anything, I don't want thanks,' she insisted staunchly.

Accepting the crisp paper timidly, Joan exclaimed, 'Heavens!' on seeing the considerable sum that was to be transferred to her.

'I may not want you to go, but I do want you to have the best start to married life. John James and I were not so fortunate.'

'You are most generous, Auntie,' she thanked sincerely, leaning over and kissing the cheek which the old woman graciously presented.

'There is a condition attached to this offer,' Margaret went on, raising her finger authoritatively, 'for it is *only* to be spent on furniture, and it must be mahogany.'

'I see,' Joan nodded, disappointed and bemused by this stipulation.

'You'll think me particular, I know, but mahogany never goes out of fashion,' she explained, gesturing to her own heavy bedroom suite which she intended to pass on to her son whether he should care for it or not.

'Mahogany is very nice,' the bride agreed politely, 'but we shan't be needing much furniture.'

Though Joan did not share her benefactor's taste, she saw that there was no dissuading the stern old woman, who remarked with finality, 'Well, you always require more than you think,' before closing her eyes as an indication that she wanted to sleep.

Unmindful of the convention that a bride would typically meet her dressmaker accompanied by another female relation or close friend, Ruskin begged to escort Joan the following afternoon, expressing his opinion as to the most appropriate styles and demanding to be shown only the finest embroidered silks and lace.

Contrary to the bride's modest tastes, he insisted that yards upon yards of fabric be unravelled for his inspection, causing the severe, dark-haired French proprietress to raise her hands in despair and mutter 'Quel désordre!' at the wanton chaos her client was causing, becoming amenable only when she calculated the potential order.

Deflated at having her bridal gown selected without once being asked her own preferences, Joan meanwhile surmised that her guardian could hardly help but imagine Rose in similar circumstances and felt an awkward chill as he draped a swathe of silk around her shoulders and, tilting his head to this side and that, considered how it suited her complexion and figure.

'But, Cousin, I don't require anything nearly so extravagant; it's only a small affair not Westminster Abbey,' she appealed.

'You have waited long enough to be a bride,' Ruskin dismissed, oblivious of her discomfort and proceeding to select a fine Italian lace veil which the dressmaker, smiling falsely, arranged by securing a costume tiara on Joan's head.

'I *was* once,' she replied curtly, recalling the humiliation of being jilted by Percy, though her anguish was concealed by the tragicomic bridal vestige, 'but it was not to be.'

'Quite,' he agreed, ashamed at having overlooked her former suffering yet determined not to let the memory interfere with the present festivities, 'therefore all the more to celebrate now.'

'I suppose so,' she consented when her cousin finally lifted the veil.

Why ever is the young lady's guardian customising the gown to suit his own taste? the French matron wondered. *A veil at her age!* she thought, noting down the measurements and preparing the invoice.

Joan, well used to Ruskin's unconscious insensitivity and overbearing ways, upbraided herself for her ingratitude and ended by accepting his beneficence humbly, hoping that by allowing him enthusiastic control she might erase the embarrassment of her earlier jilting. Even if her cousin had little respect for Arthur, at least his affection was a hundredfold greater than her former fiancé.

Thoroughly satisfied with his morning, it never occurred to Ruskin to enquire if Joan was pleased with the gown he had commissioned, not expecting anyone to question his artistic vision or rebuff his bounteousness, and thus he settled into the carriage beside the bride-to-be with the demeanour he had often worn after persuading his father to purchase a new Turner.

If Ruskin initially felt his concession to Joan a noble sacrifice, he soon wallowed in her delight at the prospect of becoming Arthur's wife and resolved to be as generous towards her as if they shared the same parentage. Admiring her diplomacy regarding his mother's gift of mahogany furniture, yet suspecting there was something still more useful that could be bestowed upon the couple prior to their wedding day, he longed to shower upon his cousin an endowment far beyond mere silk, or wardrobes and chests of drawers.

It gladdened him to adopt a paternal role with one as sweet and appreciative as Joan, and he found pleasure in the uncommonly radiant March sunshine falling on London, despite the last wave of dead leaves lying damp on the pavements after the previous night's rainfall. The bare yet budding trees offered hope though no shelter from the bluster which, regardless of the cloudless sky, continued to make its presence felt: a scene representing the tense atmosphere of Joan's imminent departure from Denmark Hill and her guardian's confused emotions.

The thought of the wedding nonetheless brought spring a little closer, and Ruskin was glad that the torrents had ceased that he might give Joan a favourable impression of his cherished old home. Without indicating that they would be going on somewhere, he took a close interest in her natural intrigue when the carriage drew up on Herne Hill outside the semi-detached, three-storey property which united his fondest memories of youth and had been purchased leasehold by John James prior to his death.

Richly set with old evergreens, No. 28 was one of four houses sitting proudly atop the summit; and although there was nothing exceptional about the architecture, the position offered remarkable views of London and its environs, from the commanding dome of St Paul's to the elegant sailing boats gliding along the Thames at Greenwich.

Harrow was conspicuously visible to the north and the imposing fortifications of Windsor Castle stood proudly to the west, while at the base of the slope were huddled the rural villages of Walworth and Dulwich, lending the setting an idyllic charm not yet infringed upon by the bubbling cauldron of the ever-expanding capital.

'It may not be the pristine Eden my mother left behind, yet the lilac and laburnum still greet visitors at the front gate when the time comes,' he announced, smiling tenderly whilst leading the way to the black-gloss-painted front door. 'And the apple and magnolias will likewise show their merry blossom come May,' he continued, ushering Joan to the garden at the rear of the house.

'It's very charming,' she complimented, perceiving the sentimental importance her guardian attached to the place.

'Belonging to the richly wooded North Surrey Downs, the stretch of country round about is fed by two glistening streams, the Wandle and the Effra,' Ruskin continued, 'inexpressibly dear to me since childhood. I will ever walk around this garden imagining myself four years old, working on my Latin beside my mother as she pruned the roses and quizzed me on my lessons.'

'So much more inspiring than a schoolroom,' Joan observed cheerfully, albeit the garden was far from the paradise her cousin described.

'The fruit trees were always heavy with fruit each year but, just like Eden, all was forbidden to me.'

'How so?' she enquired, considering his upbringing privileged compared with her own.

'Having practically no companions besides my mother, I led a very small, conceited sort of life and believed *I* occupied the central point of the universe. A dangerous misconception that perhaps I still maintain as a result of such an unorthodox youth.'

'None of us can see the purpose of the world other than to please ourselves when we are young,' she dismissed kindly, his sudden gloominess a reflection on his long-held sadness at being forced to leave his childhood haven.

'You're right. Like all homes, they are only life-giving when we venture from them and look up at the horizon, yet wherever I go I never find anywhere that equals my recollections of this heaven, this *praeterita*. If I ever do I will buy it instantly.'

'I really ought to be getting back to see about your mother's medicine,' Joan reminded, sensing that her guardian's wildly reminiscent mood was destined to lead to melancholy.

'Never mind about that, she'll get someone to attend to her or woe betide them. This is far more pressing, for I want to see if you like it here.'

'I like it very well,' she nodded, 'although it saddens me that you have more affection for *this* house than your own.'

'A mansion and staff do not a happy man make, or at least only a foolish and blinded one. I have always seen Denmark Hill as my parents' home rather than mine, for I should never have chosen it, nor would I ever have found contentment there had not you joined us.'

'You flatter me, but even if it is partly true I am glad to have brought you comfort,' Joan accepted reluctantly. 'In turn, you must take glory for bringing about my fulfilment these past years.'

'Not a bit. You are more worldly than all of us and should be happy wherever you are, so long as you are loved. Arthur is a fortunate man to have won such a wife.' And he wound his finger around one of her stray curls with sibling-like tenderness.

Unwilling to abandon his reverie before showing Joan the inside of the empty, long-neglected dwelling, he navigated her around rooms which his vivid memories allowed his imagination to recreate: every corner crowded with his parents' possessions and astir with the bustle of their old life.

After pausing to daydream thus, he turned to Joan and went on, 'That brings me to the point of our visit. Would you and Arthur wish to live here?'

'It is well out of *our* humble means,' she balked, having no aspirations other than a small cottage or terrace.

'I did not ask if you could afford it, I asked if you should desire it.' And he swept up the staircase and into the master bedroom in order to show her the best viewpoint.

'Who could not?' she conceded.

'Then you shall have it,' he declared, clapping his hands. 'I shall sign the lease over to you upon your wedding day.'

'It is too much, Cousin,' Joan demurred, trailing behind him as reluctantly as once she had confessed that her favourite meal was cold mutton and oysters.

'On the contrary, it's a mere *token* of appreciation for all that you have done for us. While Arthur shows little ambition of achieving more than a sufficient income for a wife and family,' he couldn't help but gibe,

'*I* have riches I know not what to do with, including property I have no inclination to grow wealthier from.'

'But perhaps that isn't what your father intended,' Joan considered, abashed and wary to accept on her fiancé's behalf.

'I upbraided him for abandoning this place when our finances warranted keeping a larger establishment, and so I can think of nothing more appropriate than to see you and Arthur begin your life together here. It's an ideal residence for a young married couple and plenty large enough for a family,' he encouraged.

'It's more than we could ever have dreamed of,' she thanked, pressing his hand.

'It's far from perfect, but knowing what a supremely good home-maker you are I don't doubt that you can soon set it to rights,' he affirmed, laying his palm against a wall exhibiting signs of damp.

'We shall be forever indebted to you,' Joan said as she followed him downstairs whilst he made a brief list of improvements that were needed.

'Let us have no talk of debt; it's a gift not a loan,' Ruskin insisted, locking the front door and handing her the key as casually as if he were gifting her a book. 'I will be only too glad to think of you nearby.'

'You will visit us often?' she urged.

'Very often, or at least for as long as I stay at Denmark Hill,' he speculated as they made their way to the gate.

Incredulous at such an idea, she stopped short, breathless at trying to guess his full scheme. 'Are you planning to leave?'

'I suspect I shall be *forced* to depart shortly. You of all people will understand how unthinkable it is for me to remain at Denmark Hill without the lady of the house.'

'Of course,' Joan acknowledged woefully. 'In that case, won't you come and live with us here?'

'Gracious no, this house wasn't attached with a prerequisite of having *me* as resident lodger,' he laughed. 'You should settle down with Arthur and I must make a nest of my own for once.'

'I can't bear to think of you being alone.' And she took Ruskin's arm as helplessly as a child.

'My work at the university prevents any feelings of loneliness, I assure you, although, after I sell Denmark Hill I *would* be grateful if I could have use of the attic to work and sleep whenever I'm in London?'

Margaret, having only just recovered from the shock of Joan marrying, was appalled to learn that Ruskin had bestowed Herne Hill as a wedding gift, not because she minded the idea of her niece having a respectable home but that it caused her own present to pale into insignificance.

'You've outdone my mahogany furniture and no mistake,' the old woman seethed, a reaction her son, being prepared for, shrugged at.

'No, Mother, I have merely given them *need* of it,' he responded drolly. 'Without a roof of their own your furniture would have been neither use nor ornament.'

'You always have to play the chivalrous knight; it was the same when you gave our Turners away.'

Choosing to ignore the latter comment, he threw down a further gauntlet believing the debate to be heated yet not entirely serious, 'You've said yourself that Joanna can never have enough for your liking, but only if *you* endow it. Surely it should bring you pleasure to think of not only Joan and Arthur occupying our old home but a happy brood of children whom I shall play doting godfather to? The prospect has given *me* quite a new lease of life.'

'To account for the lease you've given away?' Margaret grumbled. 'It matters very little to me *where* they will live, for at eighty-nine years of age I am not likely to leave this room other than in a coffin.'

'I expect you'll be wanting one of solid mahogany?' he mocked.

His mother, letting out a sufficiently loud tut in dumbfounded protest, removed her spectacles and looked daggers. '*That* would be sacrilegious.'

'How so?' Ruskin persisted.

'It would be a tremendous waste and God would *hardly* approve of such show. All I need is a simple vessel when I am laid to rest,' she informed martyr-like, adding pitifully, 'and some days the end can't come soon enough.'

'Very well,' he laughed, drawing a notebook and pencil from his breast pocket and taking up the seat beside the bed, 'but today let us discuss preparations for Joan's wedding and not your funeral.'

'Why consult me? No doubt *I* will be quite left out, being stuck up here,' she whimpered, straightening her cap.

'We will ensure that you are very much a part of the occasion,' he contradicted, smiling wryly as he scribbled. 'I have spoken with Joan and Arthur and they are in agreement that the wedding breakfast should be given downstairs for expressly that reason.'

'Really?' Margaret beamed, her spirits instantly reviving on having been considered.

'Yes, you will have the same meal sent up and receive as many callers as you desire,' he settled, envisaging the comicality of the scene.

The couple were relieved by the sharp turnabout in Ruskin's attitude to their marriage, and he cut a merry figure on their wedding day in April, presiding over the occasion as guest of honour, host and a kind of father-of-the-bride combined.

Having travelled down from the Crown & Thistle Inn early that morning, his new bright blue stock made him look surprisingly youthful, as did the light grey trousers and frock coat which verged on the fashionable, while the pink rosebud in his buttonhole meant that he could almost have been mistaken for the groom.

Ruskin passed the day as gaily as if he had been promised a lifetime of love and companionship himself; so effervescent and charming was he throughout the ceremony and wedding breakfast that when it came to giving a speech praising Joan and welcoming Arthur to the family, he was applauded by the guests more enthusiastically than after the bride and groom were first pronounced husband and wife.

Margaret meanwhile remained in bed with a steady stream of guests climbing the stairs to pay their respects, all of whom she received like a horizontal, yet no less regal, Queen Victoria. Ruskin surmised that his mother enjoyed the occasion far more than if she had been downstairs, all too easily forgotten in her old seat by the fire, although he was not surprised to find her weeping when the last guest had departed.

When the festivities were over and the crumbs of the cake lay stale, mother and son united in selfish mourning, with Ruskin dwelling upon the sordid fact that his innocent Joanna would share a bed with a man for the first time – a thought he had, up until then, successfully banished from his mind in the whirlwind of the wedding arrangements.

Repulsed by all that marriage encompassed, and recalling his own miserable wedding night when he had shivered by the unlit hearth not so much from cold as from aversion, he was thoroughly ashamed at his own hypocrisy in appearing gay while internally he recoiled from celebrating an occasion that would change his cousin into a mere ordinary woman.

Unconsciously hoping to preserve Joan's purity for as long as possible, Ruskin had organised for the newly-weds to begin their honeymoon with the Reverend William Kingsley of South Kilvington in Yorkshire, a fellow he vaguely knew due to the gentleman's great knowledge of Turner, and whom he had persuaded to host the couple during their tour of the county where some of Joan's relatives resided.

Contrary to what Ruskin anticipated, however, it chanced that the reverend was an extremely cordial and liberal-minded host who left the couple to themselves by and large and delighted in toasting them with a generous supply of wine, holy or otherwise, whenever they dined together. In fact, Kingsley enjoyed the presence of the newly-weds so much that he invited them to extend their stay, thus upsetting Ruskin's plans for them to join him in Derbyshire.

Realising that it was unlikely that Joan had remained a virgin after holidaying at the vicarage for almost two months, he cursed Kingsley privately and wrote to Joan in baby talk, upbraiding her for being too busy to write to him every day. Despairing at finding himself alone with his mother for the first time in his life, without Joanna to lighten the atmosphere and inject humour, every hour he spent keeping the invalid company was begrudged by the minute.

"Me mifs oo so mut," he began woefully; *"me not no fot to do. Me very sulky and seepy. Me had a long walk, found frillery flowers, but it's all no use now you're not here. Very ill, no etties yesterday, no etties today."*

'Well, what does the old gent have to say for himself?' Arthur enquired derisively whilst enjoying another hearty Yorkshire breakfast.

Before Joan could reply, the Reverend Kingsley looked up from his eggs and chuckled, for his limited acquaintance of Ruskin led him to believe that he would almost certainly be overprotective of his pretty young ward.

'I dare say he is feeling sorry for himself now that you are gone,' he remarked with raised eyebrows.

The bride, too embarrassed to read her cousin's childish passage aloud, blushed and found herself paraphrasing the note with a great deal of imagination: 'He's as active as ever, walking and trying to keep his mother entertained.'

'You surprise me,' her husband admitted, 'I expected him to be making himself sick waiting for your return to London.'

Despite thinking herself well equipped to handle Ruskin's melodramas, Joan fell into the trap of writing daily accounts of her Yorkshire escapades in order to pacify him: reassuring her cousin and aunt of her dependability by answering humdrum questions regarding any day-to-day household strife which occurred in her absence.

Repeatedly uttering that her recently altered marital status would have no bearing on their closeness, she thus agreed to joining Ruskin at Matlock just as soon as she and Arthur had parted from the hospitable Reverend Kingsley, a phase of their honeymoon far from anticipated by her new husband.

STORM CLOUDS
AND CLEAR SKIES

Joan's marriage prompted Ruskin to brood all the more on his own romantic failures, and despite relishing his established routine at Oxford, encouraged by the response of his students, this was not enough to pull him back from the severest depression he had ever known.

His head spun with overwork and, having continued writing at a prolific rate whilst devoting himself to his professorial duties, it was only when he paused for the summer in Matlock that he knew himself to be suffering from physical and mental exhaustion: turning his mind inside out with inflammatory scrutiny as he waited to meet Joan and Arthur, who were bound to injure him with their newly-wedded elation.

Careless that his mother would feel his absence more than ever with her beloved niece gone, he was drowning in self-pity too much to reproach himself, his sole thought that of his own state of mind and how he might restore his unease by distancing himself from Denmark Hill and the demands he could never satisfy.

Overlooking the crystalline Derwent Water, Ruskin took rooms at the New Bath Hotel where he had resided with his parents as a boy: a serene spot which, affording countless geological and mineralogical pursuits, had first inspired his love of the natural world.

A passion he had expressed by writing poetry of all he saw and felt, he re-read the boyish verses his father had treasured on sitting by the water's edge, feeling that he had a soul, like his boy's soul, once again: the wondrous naivety and enthusiasm of his younger self making up for any lack of literary talent and allowing him to relive those first impressions so nurtured by his parents.

> "Now Derwent Water come! – a looking-glass
> Wherein reflected are the mountain's heights,
> As in a mirror, framed in rocks and woods;
> So upon thee there is a seeming mount,
> A seeming tree, a seeming rivulet.
> All upon thee are painted by a hand
> Which not a critic can well criticise…
>
> Thy polished surface is a boy at play
> Who labours at the snow to make a man,
> And when he's made it, knocks it down again;
> As when thou'st made a picture thou dost play
> At tearing it to pieces. Trees do first
> Tremble, as if a monstrous heart of oak
> Were but an aspen leaf; and then as if
> It were a cobweb in the tempest's blow."

There being no-one to hear him, Ruskin recited his father's favourite verse, which, having made him blush in early manhood, now struck him with pride. That his nine-year-old self could have pondered so maturely on themes he still dwelt on, with no resolution, in the declining years of middle-age, was something to treasure rather than deride.

The poignancy of looking upon the same sight so many years on filled Ruskin with sentimentality, for he knew every stone and tree upon the shore, the colour of every shallow and the clear deep of every pool. Nor was there any pleasure akin to the childish one of seeing boats float upon the still water of the glassy Derwent.

A place almost too beautiful to live in, he was relieved to find the pretty village barely changed, where practically every essential trade was accounted for with well-presented family-run stores. He took in the familiar streets as if walking through a dream, the only difference being that the "sons" proudly referred to on almost all the shop signs had long since taken over as the main proprietors in the decades since he first promenaded the high street with his mother and father.

Admiring the simplicity of such an existence, one he hoped to share with Rosie before long, he imagined her running a tea store, her once pale face rosy and glad from greeting customers, while her hearth-side conversation, filled with all the local gossip and tittle-tattle, would cheer his evenings after hours spent philosophising about matters he was safely removed from.

Professionally, he reflected, his ambitions were very great, yet romantically they were exquisitely humble: a quiet, rural home, no larger than necessary, was all he wanted, with wide-stretching views of an England destined to give way to a growing, needy population. More than anything, he desired a mind free from anxiety and bitter longing, with Rosie for wife and companion always.

The Derwent ever called to him and, finding himself back where he started, he stared into the gently rippling water which created rainbows in the rays of the sun, recalling the first momentous event in his life: that of being taken to the brow of the cliffs where he had experienced the indescribable rapture of being allowed to explore a cave.

He was certain, on looking back, that his cosseted existence at Herne Hill had increased his wonder at Derwent tenfold as a boy, and made that corner of England the one he most longed to rediscover whenever he found himself fighting another fit of gloom.

As the hills became obscured in a curtain of cloud, he thought of Joan's departure from Denmark Hill and was both desperate to be reunited with her and fearsome upon conjecturing how the honeymoon might have altered her, for she would not be the young woman who went away.

Although he had no definite idea of the changes he expected to find in her manner and bearing, Ruskin was nonetheless convinced that it would be obvious to the most casual observer that Joan was a wife and not a maiden, with all the spoiling this entailed.

Perhaps she would have a more dignified deportment or stance than formerly, a righteous tilt of the chin, a telling glow about her cheeks. She would seem more womanly because she would *be* more womanly, he surmised, preparing to ignore the indications which turned his stomach as much as thinking of his own conception.

How strange it was to consider that he and not Joan remained a virgin: a celibacy once chosen and now painfully endured. A childless, wifeless-man was he, bound by all the have-nots of life, while Joan would bear children he would be forced to watch grow up, living out a family life vicariously, as devoted and beloved as any uncle or godfather but undeniably removed from the sanctity and joys of fatherhood.

Rose, whom he revered as Dante adored Beatrice, was an ever more distant figure, hardly more than a figment of his memory, whose pretty features gradually became obscured with each passing week and month. Nor was this lack of clarity improved by staring at the old sketches or daguerreotypes he always travelled with.

Having heard from Mrs Cowper-Temple that Rosie was ill at Harristown again, contemplating whether or not to send her his good wishes drove him insane with uncertainty. Work which should have been his life's blood lost so much of its significance, for he craved the merest glimpse of her as once his pen had coveted notice and immortality.

As a bride she would surely be a vision of purity and loveliness; he could see it in the reflection of the clouds upon the water, a glorious mirage in its transience. He shied away from the prospect of leading her to sin, however, for had he not been taught that the act of procreation was a bestial, low thing? A lesson he would gladly seek to overcome if he should be granted the chance to make her his own.

Despite crediting himself with being a passionate man, the possibility of becoming a groom again was terrifying to one who had refused to consummate his first marriage and now prayed for a second opportunity. His mother, Joan and Rose were foremost in his peculiarly superstitious and idolatry principles regarding women, for how could there be anything more contradictory than wanting Saint Rosie for wife?

Good and not evil had brought him into the world, he reminded himself when trying to imagine a wedding night that might be a blessing and not a scourge upon his soul, for how could his expression of love for Rose be anything but noble? A consecration of mutual faithfulness, he would become just a man again in the act of casting off his riches, fame and past. Naked as he was born, in the dignity of dedicating himself to another he would find enlightenment such as had never dawned.

Ruskin awoke to the most terrific thunderstorm just before three: the thunder rolling incessantly like railway luggage trains, the air one loathsome mass of sultry and foul fog when he looked out of his window to observe the display which sent waves of electricity throughout the entire building.

Anxious voices in the corridor told him that his fellow guests had been disturbed by the rumpus, though rather than trying to flee the commotion he marvelled at the spectacle and, opening his window, leant on the ledge that he might see how it played out: flash after flash lighting up the horizon and illuminating the hills with blindingly magnificent white bolts. Scarcely raining, the lightning was not forked or zigzag but rippled quivering streaks, lasting on the eye half a second with grand artillery peals following – not rattling crashes or irregular cracklings but effectively delivered volleys.

Lasting an hour then passing away, the storm lent the day a strange atmosphere, as if a skirmish had taken place, and the inhabitants of the town were relieved when their enemies proceeded onto another town.

He, in turn, became morbidly desirous to meet old ghosts ahead of his reunion with the newly-weds and set out just after seven in order to revisit some of his favoured childhood haunts.

Age, like time itself, was only a perception or a measure of physical change, for didn't he feel the same excitements and fears of youth as he took the helm of a rowing boat in the bewitching grey light?

The silky water lapped the boat like a sweet caress, luring him on, yet coupled with stupor from lack of sleep he became so mesmerised by his surroundings that he could not fathom how to get back. Unable to pull his thoughts away from the whirlpool of reminiscences that did him no good, he was struck with too many nostalgic visions to focus on the shore or take up the oars with any strength.

He could not say how he came to be standing in his chamber hours later. Alone for what could have been either an eternity or just a few moments, paralysed by this peculiar state of mind, he was not sure if he had been sickening for something all along, or if breathing in the moist air had prompted him to catch a chill, but the spell would not be broken though he wrung his hands in protest.

Stalking the room as woefully as if he were an innocent man imprisoned in the Tower of London, pulling his hair and crying the cries of one who has been exiled and abandoned by everyone known to him, his mind had become a vile, stinking cell from which he could not escape and where he was destined to see out the rest of his days alone and unloved.

Gripped by psychosis, he lived through every hour in a blur of hallucinations past and imagined, with no-one to draw him out of the unreality, no God to whom he might pray. He hardly knew what he was being punished for, he was only conscious of having been dealt the harshest of sentences with no hope of reprieve.

Even if he had been handed the keys he would have chosen to remain, however, for there was solace in finally being away from the judgement of the world, before whom he was always having to keep his wits. Sanity, or the need to convince others of it, was an exhausting business he had grown too weary to contemplate. Far easier to let madness wash over him like the soothing, rippling waters of the lake outside his window.

When Joan and Arthur alighted from their coach that evening, Ruskin was confined to bed, delirious and muttering insensibly. Within a further few hours he circuited the low-ceilinged room wearing only his undergarments, burning with a high fever and swearing at the top of his voice in a manner quite out of character.

In his usual clear voice and exquisite tone, he raved and swore with no care as to the shock or offence he might cause Joan; a torrent of words modulated betwixt sweet tenderness and the fierceness of a chained eagle, short disconnected sentences with no decipherable meaning.

'Did you expect to see me?' Joan asked.

'Yes, I thought you of all people would come,' he replied pathetically, resting quietly for a time as if reassured by her presence.

Very soon, however, his fears and anxieties rose up again and he beat his chest and clasped his cousin's hands as if to urge her to save him from the most terrible fate. Powerfully impressed that he was about to be seized by the Devil and that he must remain awake for him, he removed his breeches and marched up and down stark naked, wondering at the non-appearance of the visitor.

'There are so many strange creatures in this castle!' he fretted, his arms flailing wildly in the hope of staving them off.

'We are not in a castle,' Joan denied, questioning whether her recent flight from Denmark Hill had sparked this mental decline.

As if oblivious to her response, he pointed at the window. 'There!'

'What is it?'

Manoeuvring her in front of the casement, he opened it and leant out, his torso startlingly slender and pale in the moonlight.

'There's a wolf running beside the lake, don't you *see*?' Ruskin pointed.

'Yes, so there is,' she agreed, perceiving the pointlessness of contradicting him.

When dawn arrived he looked out again to make sure that the feeble blue light really was the heralding of day, yet as he did so a black cat sprang out from behind the free-standing mirror, a creature Ruskin took to be the Devil himself, and he promptly threw himself upon him with all his might and main. He had triumphed!

In fact, the cat, with a piercing meow and erect tail, evaded the strange figure hurling itself at him, and dashing from the room left his incensed pursuer face down on the floor with arms outstretched. Breathing heavily from his exertion as Joan looked on helplessly, Ruskin's imaginary evils had become horribly real, but how to stop the aberration?

Eventually worn out from watching and waiting, his body benumbed with the bitter cold of fever, he staggered to his feet and collapsed upon the bed. Shivering, exhausted, drenched in perspiration and panting with dehydration, though he refused the merest sip of water to quench his parched lips, he fell back and drifted into a kind of half-sleep.

No respite did he find, however, and assaulted with the most vivid nightmares he writhed like one possessed and yelled in agony until, after many hours, he at last fell silent and peaceful, Joan remaining by his side, as fearful of the Devil as he.

Sitting bolt upright upon awakening, she was relieved to find him restored by sleep, although she soon observed that one delusion had merely been replaced by another.

Clutching her hand ecstatically, he beamed, 'My dearest Joanie, isn't it marvellous news?'

'What?'

'What?! You ask me that when Rosie and I just got married! After all! Such a surprise! Bruno's out of his wits with joy, but then so am I!' And he laughed to himself as he fell back upon the pillow and continued his happy dream.

Joan could not make out if her cousin was either gravely ill or had succumbed to the worst kind of insanity; and whilst Arthur was inclined to believe the latter, she consoled herself with the fact that real physical symptoms coexisted with the mania.

'The fever cannot be denied,' she objected, 'nor his quickening pulse.'

'I am no doctor,' he shrugged.

Having little patience for Ruskin at the best of times, and being suspicious that this was merely a ploy to ensnare Joan into caring for him, Arthur made himself scarce while his wife, frantic with worry, kept vigil in case he should deteriorate or awaken and think himself alone again.

Attempting in vain to bring the fever down by laying cold towels upon his forehead, or encouraging him to drink iced water and milk, Joan despaired at his unwillingness to take anything.

'Take a *little*,' she urged after another interval.

'Give me brandy, Goddammit!' Ruskin shouted, unable to lie still for trembling, his limbs convulsing in excruciating spates.

'That will hardly help things,' Joan insisted.

'Well, bring me buttered toast and cold roast beef, then,' he demanded. 'Why does everyone always deny me the things I *know* will do me the most good?'

In another twelve hours Ruskin, too weak to stand, drifted in and out of consciousness, plagued by a vile taste in his mouth and hallucinations with no beginning or end.

He saw the Devil in the form of a Venetian gondolier with red eyes, and a religious ceremony in St Mark's characterised by priests and women dressed entirely in black, their forebodingly forlorn faces barely visible behind heavy lace veils.

But the third vision was the worst of all: a chambermaid filled his bathtub with serpents as the deadliest writhed under his door and rose up like a cobra with vicious eyes, and breasts like the Medusa's.

When he refused to get into the tub, the satanic creatures pursued him, following him into another room until he found a marble bust upon a table and hurled it at them. This was enough to kill the fiercest but not the smaller ones which fastened onto his neck like hissing leeches.

Joan knew not the reason for her cousin's repeated calls for help, yet her own fears that his condition was worsening beyond remedy were reiterated by the local doctor whom she had begged to visit first thing.

'Bloodletting is the best thing for it,' the large, pompous physician advised when outside the chamber, quite defeated by the patient's symptoms yet keen to collect his fee.

'*That* ancient custom? It's nothing short of barbaric,' she disputed.

'It has saved many of my patients before now, I can assure you.'

'My cousin is surely done for if *that's* your only idea of a cure.'

Stunned by her boldness, he raised his shoulders. 'I have been bloodletting throughout my career of over twenty-five years.'

'And with what success?' Joan challenged, intentionally unclear as to whether she referred to that practice or his overall history.

'It's often a last resort,' he quivered, irritated that a woman should call into question his judgement or reputation.

'Well, it won't be *mine*.' Saying which she descended the stairs and, ushering the doctor to the lobby, dismissed him with her customarily firm handshake and unapologetic curtness.

Wishing that she had listened to her initial thought of telegramming Doctor Acland, the competent young woman wasted not a moment in rectifying her mistake: explaining the urgency of her cousin's condition in very few words and requesting that he board the first express train to Matlock, regardless of it not being scheduled to stop there.

The passengers looked askance at their fellow travellers as the locomotive screamed to a halt and their cushioned rears were tipped from the well-upholstered first-class seats, forcing them to hold onto their nearest and dearest or clutch any carriage fitting to hand.

There had been no alternative other than to pull the alarm cord, Acland reasoned, jumping onto the railway platform: as sprightly as a man half his age yet twice as wily, his flowing white hair lending him a gravitas he trusted would prove useful in such circumstances.

After coughing his way through the billowing smoke, he explained to the angry guard that he was a doctor assisting in a medical emergency and, handing him his card by way of evidence, was easily excused due to his courteous bearing and the many letters after his name.

Whilst the plan could be deemed a success, Acland thought himself too old for such schoolboy adventures as he made haste to the New Bath Hotel as quickly as the gig he boarded outside the station would carry him, necessity and the longevity of his friendship with Ruskin overcoming all obstacles.

Considering his loyalty to the professor far greater than his many university commitments, he was horrified to find Ruskin far worse than he had expected: ranting and raving like an over-enthusiastic street preacher.

Overwhelmed to see his old friend, Ruskin gripped Acland's hand and pleaded, 'I'm so grateful to see you. I know not whether I am ill, mad, or *both*, but for God's sake discover whatever it is so that my cure might commence. Just look how my hand shakes.'

'I will do my utmost,' he assured, breaking away from his grasp that he might begin his examination. 'How long has he been like this?' he addressed Joan, who looked on anxiously, her arms wrapped about her waist in self-comfort.

'A few days. I tried to get him dressed but he can't even stand.'

'I'm sure you've done all you could. Would you leave us for a moment?'

With Joan gone, the doctor continued his careful assessment, though he was soon interrupted by the patient, who, desperate for a diagnosis, reached for his arm again and tugged it frantically.

'I fear my mind will destroy my body,' he whimpered. 'Tell me I won't be incarcerated as a lunatic?'

'No, I shouldn't have thought so,' Acland replied lightly. 'What symptoms especially concern you? How do you sleep?'

'I can sleep well and long, the difficulty is in the waking; and I have the most disturbing dreams, the Devil and Rosie all mixed up together.'

'Anything else?' the doctor prompted.

'I have the oddest craving for pepper and mustard.'

'I confess I have never come across *that*,' he chuckled, trying to alleviate the patient's agitation.

'The shadow of Death is in my midst, and yet I know that I'm not ready. How everything bears down on me though!' Ruskin shouted, perplexed by the variety of his ailments.

'My good man, that's because you shoulder too many worries; you must learn to let life take its course,' he insisted, patting his hand.

'How can I when I'm assailed by such harrowing visions? And always Rose to worry about.'

'At least try to stop brooding.'

'I do *try*. I found myself staring at a bowl of grapes for three hours the other day,' Ruskin confessed. 'So many act without a thought while I can't seem to do a single thing without over-analysing to the verge of lunacy. *Am* I mad, do you think?' he asked, creasing his forehead, already clammy with apprehension. 'However does a madman *know* himself to be mad?'

'You are experiencing some kind of inflammatory fever, but that's not to say it hasn't been brought on by mental anxiety and overwork,' the doctor replied calmly, sitting down on the bed.

'Will it pass?'

'I expect so, although I can't say *when*. I will stay and attend to you for a few days, by which time you'll hopefully be out of danger.'

'I am in danger, then?' Ruskin repeated.

His friend bowed his head. 'I can't deny it.'

'And with no hope of Rosie at my bedside,' he tutted, looking into the distance. 'It's not her fault that she's not here, she's ill herself. I wrote telling her to get well and she promised she would.'

'As I said earlier, you must not dwell on things if you are to get better, nor do I want you to relapse in a couple of months. To *stay* well I suggest you give up anything that causes you disquiet.'

'If you mean Rose, I am surely a dying man, for I can no more give her up than the earth can exist without sunlight.'

Sensing that he was becoming increasingly agitated, Acland urged, 'Let us talk no more today, you need rest,' and turned to go.

Despite feeling ghastly, Ruskin should have liked to have spent more time in the doctor's company, for he was afraid of being alone with thoughts he was incapable of reining in. It was nevertheless a weight off him knowing that Acland was present and keeping watch, so much so that he was encouraged to believe that a turning point was in sight, for his friend's thoughtful and tender care possessed far more curative powers than any medicine.

It was a week before Ruskin eluded the fever, several before he could haul himself out of bed, yet he made steady progress under Acland and Joan's calming influence and was only sorry that his recovery meant that his companions would be certain to go away.

'How are we today?' the doctor enquired, relieved to find his patient out of bed and taking breakfast by the window one bright morning.

'Better,' he nodded, though his unshaven beard and sunken eyes showed his recent ordeal. 'I can do everything but walk. I just *can't* get any steadiness on my feet, despite giving up the brandy and water.'

'Quite right,' Acland laughed, trying to estimate the degree of Ruskin's recovery. 'I don't suppose that was aiding your balance.'

'I have only just come to myself, if this *be* myself and not the one who lives in a dream,' Ruskin returned earnestly. 'I know how thoroughly ill I have been. I've not been so near the dark gates since I was a child, but I also know, better than anybody else could, how strong the last fibres and coils of anchor were, and though I clearly recognised the danger I should have been much surprised to have found myself dying.'

'Thank God you are safe now,' his friend heartened, taking up the neighbouring seat, 'though you'll need to take a holiday when you are well enough to travel, and I don't mean for you to exert yourself in any way. Go to the place you were happiest and pause awhile.'

Ruskin beamed at the very idea. 'I fancy I should truly get well if I could float on Coniston Water!'

'By float, I trust you mean to use a vessel?' Acland ventured.

'Perhaps that *would* be preferable in light of my present health,' he conceded casually, carrying on with his boiled egg and hot buttered toast.

'Glad to hear it, though I shouldn't have put anything past you.'

'I may be as enchanted by the Lakes as I was when I was a boy, but nowadays I prefer to stay dry,' the professor assured humorously.

When Acland's amusement had passed he touched Ruskin's arm and announced, 'I'm afraid I must break up our jollity by announcing my departure.'

'Ah,' he sighed forlornly. 'Are you to go imminently?'

'Yes, this very evening. I am relieved to say that other patients are more in need of me.'

'You think I can get on without you?'

'Just fine, but I don't want to see you back in Oxford before you have carried out my orders by fully recuperating.' The doctor smiled fondly. 'Coniston, wasn't it?'

'Indeed, I shall float my senses away – that's if I can be said to have any remaining.'

LVII
BRANTWOOD

B Y THE END OF SUMMER THE DAYS OF BEING AN INVALID were safely behind Ruskin, with Joan and Arthur, who journeyed with him to Denmark Hill, observing that the illness had brought with it a welcome change in his attitude and temperament. His conversation was genial rather than despondent and he was more pleased with life in general.

'What are you about?' Joan enquired of her cousin who was seated in the shade, interrupting her gardening to observe him scribbling on countless pieces of paper and becoming frustrated with the result.

'I'm trying to write some autographs for my admirers but it's like trying to forge my own signature,' he chuckled.

'It will come, don't be so impatient.'

'I'm not accustomed to sitting still for so long, Joanna, yet your knowledge of my inner thoughts means that I am always at rest.' And he pushed away the papers and regarded her intently. 'I hope you know how I value you, whatever I say or don't say?'

'You and I have never needed words to understand one another,' she replied, moved at this outpouring.

'I'm glad you feel that too. Few women in this world can ever have had more influence for good, or used it more constantly. If *you* had not stood by me I believe I should have gone down.'

'I won't have it,' she denied, removing her gardening gloves and taking up the seat beside him.

'It's true, you gave me breath and life enough to hold on until the wave passed,' he went on. 'As it is, I have clearer sight and purpose than I ever had before. These weeks have made me acknowledge the things I used not to value, and I have decided to revert to my old way of discovering beauty where no-one else can. Instead of growling at the countryside being polluted, I mean to see that there is still much to be admired.'

'There really is,' she agreed, looking about her.

'I expect this state of mind, and being in Coniston again, will inspire my forthcoming lectures, for I want to teach my students that it is impossible to be a true artist until they can successfully mirror nature. The artist's skill does not emanate from a love of *art*, but of mountains and seas, clouds and rocks, valleys and streams!' Ruskin enthused, throwing open his arms in unabashed enthusiasm.

While it pleased Joan that her cousin could again consider his future work, she regarded such extreme fluctuations of mood as a worrying thing, for he was either wildly happy or desperately sad, with hardly any middle ground.

'Do you think this excitement might be more than you are ready for?' she suggested timidly as they took a seat in the arbour he forever associated with Rose.

'Acland told me to go to the place that makes me glad and that's precisely what I shall do. But it's not only the idea of this holiday that fills me with delight, for I have received the most extraordinary sign that I must go there permanently.'

'How so?' Joan asked, aghast that he should think of making any momentous decision when his mind had not regained its equilibrium.

'Here,' he said impatiently, handing her a letter which she began to scan with confusion. 'Only yesterday I received this pleasant and unexpected note from an old acquaintance of mine, a poet and engraver by the name of Linton, who is emigrating to America and wishes to sell his Cumbrian house, Brantwood, without delay.'

'And you plan to look it over when you're there, with a view to purchasing it?' she enquired with consternation. It was all too sudden and she very much wished that Acland was there to rationalise with him.

'No, I intend to view the house as the owner.'

'Whatever do you mean?' she jolted.

Snatching the letter out of her hand and holding it aloft, he explained passionately, 'I see this as a fateful command and therefore I have replied to Linton agreeing to pay the asking price.'

Horrified, Joan raised her hand to her forehead and exclaimed, 'Without so much as *seeing* the house first?'

'What difference does that make?' Ruskin dismissed. 'I know precisely where it is situated, and if there is anything I don't like about the property I can either knock it down or alter it to suit myself.'

'When will you go?' she asked, flustered. 'I should go with you.'

Annoyed at her discouragement and her offer of nannying him, he snapped, 'No, that won't do. As soon as I am in possession of the keys I shall travel up with Crawley, for I need a companion who won't try to dissuade me or judge me.'

'You're mistaken if you think *I* judge you, I simply remind you of the lack of reason which so recently affected you.'

'What good has reason ever done me?' he shrugged defiantly before marching inside and ordering Crawley to begin packing.

He might have been inheriting a kingdom, so eagerly did Ruskin anticipate viewing his own sacred land, for it was not the house but the setting of Brantwood that most appealed to him. And it was easy to imagine, that first golden September day, what could be made of the countless acres of garden facing west, the air perfectly calm and the sunlight pure as it alighted on the grass through the thickets.

Incredibly steep and consisting of copse, moorland and rock, he relied upon his walking stick to maintain his balance over the uneven ground and winding paths, yet even as he scrambled he could not stop from lifting his head to look at the tranquil Coniston Water just ahead.

Following glen or shore as his eye glanced or his heart guided, a happy nightingale singing as much as he could in every moment, only when Ruskin's energy was depleted from having to beat a path through the dense ferns did he follow the path back to the house: a dilapidated cream-washed two-storey lodging hardly bigger than a cottage with as haphazard a layout as the sloping gardens that wound their way to the water's edge.

'Here I am, thank God, to all intents and purposes quite well again,' he declared to Crawley who had been waiting for his master outside the entrance of the property. 'It is wonderful to me that I should have gone so heartily mad, but I was within an ace of the grave and I realise that I must change my way of living.'

'I can see that the *views* are very fine, sir,' his servant observed after a brief scrutiny of the ground floor, 'but as for the house you must possess more imagination than I.'

Yet nothing could sway Ruskin from his determination to love Brantwood and persuade his companion to do likewise, with each idiosyncrasy only adding to his conviction.

'The eccentricities of it accord perfectly with my own,' he approved, finding enchantment in every room, 'for what is the purpose of a dwelling other than to give shelter and provide its inhabitants with pleasure when looking out of the window?'

'I should have thought you would consider the aesthetics of the architecture just as vital,' Crawley observed, weighing up his master's contradictions with bemusement.

'The older I get the more ugly houses appeal to me, for they are like stray dogs in need of patient owners willing to tame them.'

The valet chuckled but became grave when he saw the rotten timbers above his head. 'Do you really need the challenge after everything you've been through?'

'It's the very thing to save me,' Ruskin continued sincerely. 'I should like to live here, Crawley, even though it's damp and smoky chimneyed. I don't care if it isn't the prettiest or grandest house I have ever seen, and in reality as much will have to be done to it as if it were only a shell of bricks and mortar, but there are rocks, streams, fresh air and, for the first time in my life, the possibility of the *home* I have always sought.'

'I too can see that,' Crawley at last conceded.

'The delight of meeting the first light here! Of breathing in the morning air and gathering up one's spirit upon awakening from the darkness and dreaming! Hearing bird, breeze and billow, and going forth with the limitless energy of creation. This place will offer me the independence of which I have always been deprived,' he went on, walking into a small, unassuming ground-floor room with a breathtaking panorama of the lake that made him forget the failings of the interior.

'But surely many a house could have offered you *those* things,' his cautious adviser suggested.

'Perhaps, but there is plenty besides that draws me to Brantwood, for whilst I am not sightless to its many shortcomings, this place possesses the finest views in Cumberland or Lancashire, not to mention a spectacular sunset visible from this room, which I intend to make my study.' And he opened a window and urged Crawley to look to the horizon, speckled with pink clouds.

'It will indeed be a change from Denmark Hill.'

'Sometimes change is the very thing that's needed. We should all of us consider the present as the only available time and act accordingly. How pleasant it will be to pause and look out over the lake to the Old Man of Coniston every day.'

'Who am I to dissuade you from something you're clearly so set upon?' Crawley sighed with resignation, for he had spent too many years by Ruskin's side to imagine that anything he might say would influence his master. 'At least it doesn't have so many logistical obstacles as the plans in Switzerland you once considered.'

This gibe, far from offending Ruskin, prompted him to smile graciously in acknowledgement of his previous error of judgement, though he did not wish to lose confidence in that which he had set his heart on.

Leading the way outside, he directed Crawley to his favourite part of the garden: not facing the lake as the servant expected, but in the opposite direction. Drawing his attention to an opening in the woodland, a glade which had been left entirely to its own devices for many years, Ruskin pointed to a waterfall making its way down the hillside: a miniature version of the one he remembered so fondly in Ireland.

'Here we will have *light* instead of the darkness and clear air in exchange for the foul stench and smog of London,' he asserted, looking at the sun as it peeped mischievously through the trees, 'not to mention an abundance of land in which to cultivate flowers and provisions for our table all year round. In the country every morning of the year brings with it a new aspect of springing or fading nature; a new duty to be fulfilled upon earth, and a new promise or warning in heaven. No day is without its innocent hope, its special prudence, its kindly gift and its sublime danger. As country dwellers we shall live an innocent life governed by the seasons: the divine laws of a seed-time that cannot be recalled, a harvest which cannot be hastened and a winter in which no man can work. And then there'll be the neighbours round about and the great sense of community and place. Won't you be glad to leave your life in the city for all *this?*'

'I can't very well leave Mrs Ruskin,' Crawley rejected strongly.

'It is *she* who will soon be leaving us,' his master dismissed sorrowfully, 'and when that day dawns I hope I can convince you to make a new home with me here. To go on living at Denmark Hill isn't something I could easily stand, and therefore it's vital that I find somewhere of my own before the time comes. Regardless of my age, it still seems unimaginable that I shall soon be parentless. It makes one feel as vulnerable as an abandoned child left on a doorstep.'

The autumn slumbered and awoke to the most intemperate of winters as Joan nursed Margaret in her final days, prompted not by martyrdom but by the deepest affection, for they had been one another's closest companions for so many years that the younger woman would have been lost had it not been for the husband she went home to each night.

Ruskin was adamant that his cousin should feel no obligation to housekeep for him when his mother was no longer in need of her ministration and, recognising that Joan's role of nursemaid was soon to be ended, insisted that her extensive duties at Denmark Hill should be replaced with the more rewarding responsibilities of wife and motherhood, for he sensed that Arthur resented every hour she spent away from their own hearth.

Despite being keen to stamp his mark upon his new residence before the winter set in, Ruskin recognised that his place was in London and thereby sacrificed whole weeks at Brantwood in order to be at his mother's bedside, informing her of the world outside her chamber, or slumped in an armchair reading his work to her, never mind that she could barely stay awake long enough to hear more than a few paragraphs.

Once so formidable, though she slept more than she was awake he fancied that she always knew of his presence and took comfort from it. He regarded the woeful deterioration of her faculties, declining to the grave, as the worst possible death to witness and, much as he longed to flee to Coniston, knew that he could not venture too far from Denmark Hill in case she should pass before he had bidden her a last farewell.

After all the mistakes he had made when John James was on his deathbed, he tried to be the son he had always intended yet failed to be. Feeling a pang whenever she murmured his father's name, he shared her eagerness to end the penance and loneliness of old age, along with her anticipation of being reunited with her husband. Whatever his own struggles with faith and marriage, it was a fitting conclusion to their unshakeable partnership.

Gradually fading into a sleep lasting three weeks, Ruskin was reconciled to his mother never awakening, when, in the first week of December, she took her last breath just after he had uttered an evening prayer. Taking up her cold hand and kissing it, the humble gold wedding ring which he placed to his lips seemed utterly symbolic of her devotion and constancy to John James even after death. Any tears that he shed were, he admitted, solely for himself.

After an initial outpouring of grief, Ruskin studied his mother's face and observed how remarkably young and pretty she looked, as if the release from the great burden of life had restored her to the girl his father had so tirelessly courted.

The scythe and tooth of time had proved itself both scytheless and toothless, for it was human failure which gnawed like the worm and consumed like the flame. He had never felt more alone than in those few moments beside his mother's body, and yet all he could think of was Rose and how enraged he should be if *she* ever left him.

When Joan, who had been keeping vigil outside, entered the room, one look at her cousin told her that the wait was over.

'My poor Joanna,' he offered, rising to comfort her, for he considered her own pain a deal greater than his own.

The bagpipes began their melancholy dirge as Ruskin prepared to lay his mother's body beside his father's in the family plot at the churchyard in Shirley: twenty or so mourners shocked to see, upon gathering around the graveside, that the coffin had been painted sky blue.

Ruskin observed their disapproval with mirth as the vessel was carried along the path by the pallbearers, for he had spent the past few days painting it in scorn of funerals, along with the dark, foreboding trappings that went with them.

Bracing himself to engage in small talk with the distant relatives and acquaintances who had once enjoyed his mother's hospitality and wished to bid her a dignified farewell, the two people he was most glad to see were Ned and Georgie Burne-Jones, whom he embraced warmly.

'Dear friends,' he greeted.

'You have been much in our thoughts,' Georgie offered, her face showing the stresses of marriage despite her attire displaying a considerable rise in living.

'My parents were not always as kind and respectful to you as they should have been,' Ruskin stammered, his voice broken with emotion, 'and your being here certainly shows their error.'

'We harbour no ill-feeling,' Georgie insisted; 'on the contrary, we both admired your mother and father's spirit.'

'But we are here to support *you*,' Ned elaborated. 'We can never return the great friendship you have shown us, yet want you to know how much we care for you.'

'I have never doubted it, but it is a great comfort to have you with me on this day. You both know how I despise funerals,' he muttered as the coffin was lowered into the ground.

'So do I,' Georgie agreed, squeezing his arm tenderly.

Joan, standing by her guardian's side, was the first to scatter the allotted handful of earth over her aunt's resting place, her hand trembling upon looking down into the dark chasm which appeared more a gateway to hell than heaven. Passing the duty onto her cousin without being able to look him in the face, she sympathised with his abhorrence of such grotesque customs.

'This scene horrifies me,' he vented, shaking his head resentfully. 'If it were you or Rosie I was burying I should pitch gravel in everyone's faces,' he declared, indicating with a sneer his derision of the majority of attendants whom he had reluctantly invited to share in his grief.

Surprised at the indelicacy and violence of the comment, Joan failed to stifle a nervous laugh, while the stern faces looking back at her from the other side of the grave judged her ill for finding amusement during the sombre proceeding.

On the monument Margaret would now share with her husband, Ruskin read aloud the inscription he had commissioned, '"Here, beside my father's body, I have laid my mother's, nor was dearer earth, nor purer life recorded in heaven."'

'Amen,' the mourners uttered in unison, closing their eyes without knowing one ounce of his sorrow.

'Everyone, save the Burne-Joneses, were appalled at the coffin, but I know she would have liked it,' Ruskin observed to Joan as they walked from the graveside arm in arm, Arthur remaining behind to talk with Ned and Georgie.

Joan smiled in acquiescence. 'Yes, it would have reminded her of one of Mr Turner's skies.'

As they passed through the lychgate Ruskin paused and took one last look at his mother's new home, declaring, 'This is where she longed to be, not to be near my father, not expecting to be so high in heaven, content if she might only see his face again.'

'She surely will,' Joan ventured, knowing his views on immortality yet feeling that his mother's passing had affected his previously held opinion.

'They are together at least,' he replied, taking the seat beside her in the carriage bearing his father's crest.

'And that is *everything*,' his cousin sighed contentedly.

Drawing a blanket over his lap, for the occasion made him feel the cold and long to be back indoors again, Ruskin dreaded the prospect of seeing his mother's former place by the fire or her empty bedchamber with its stripped sheets.

'I fancied I knew pretty well how I should feel at the end,' he confessed, 'yet I'm more surprised by the new look of things than after the sun set for my poor father, for I am much worse off now.'

'In what way?'

'Because I never loved my mother. I was deeply grateful to her, imperfectly dutiful to her, but I did not *love* her. Love does not always follow relationship, for it is not a matter of blood but spirit.'

Shocked at such a statement, Joan contended, 'You might not think so at this moment, for death has a way of detaching us from emotion in order to protect us, but your feelings *will* return and you'll end by cherishing the memory of them both.'

He offered no contradiction, nor did he intend to say anything more as they journeyed back to Denmark Hill in order to host the spectres for luncheon, until, pulling up outside the house, an overwhelming desire to explain his feelings made him cry out, 'Oh, don't you see, all that I had of love was given to one person and thrown to the kites and crows? Now I will have to get on without any.'

Just as Joan had predicted, when the numbness of his grief wore off in the New Year, Ruskin became pitiably depressed and decided to sell Denmark Hill, a house too filled with poignant reminders of his parents: from his father's old study to his mother's beloved mahogany bed, where she had held court for what seemed like a century.

After voicing his desire to be independent and free of his parents for so long, Ruskin, at the age of fifty-three, realised that he found it impossible to be entirely alone and was anything but content in his own company. Despite having travelled abroad all his life, there was no adventure or enjoyment in such solitude, and the last night he spent at Denmark Hill was the worst he ever endured.

Extinguishing the lights and locking the shutters of the drawing room, he recalled the many visitors and gatherings the room had witnessed, from Turner and the Carlyles to the La Touche girls dancing in and out of the sun-bathed garden. Memories, particularly happy ones, were far more dreadful than real ghosts, he decided, for they were impossible to escape wherever you went.

He could not bring himself to do away with all associations of his old home, however, and choosing to transport the majority of the prized furniture to Brantwood at great expense, he designed his new drawing room to feel familiar to both him and the friends who visited.

Preferring to spend three times the price commissioning the London upholsterer his father had used for old acquaintance' sake rather than the convenient Coniston tradesman, he imagined how pleased his parents would have been on finding that he had upheld their taste.

Taken off guard by how much he missed them, he felt not so much the loss of their presence but the infinitude of the love they had given him, love which he had taken entirely for granted, as all children do, and that no other person living could ever equal.

'No-one knows what loneliness means while they have father and mother,' he mused to Joan as he unpacked in his new study. 'I thought I did, and lamented the absence of those I thought were more to me, yet now, if I could call and be answered by the one voice I desired, it would be my father's.'

He was utterly miserable after all the recent changes, and adding to his woes was the realisation that he had been waiting for an agonising six years since first proposing to Rose, nor was there any end in sight. Like a migrating swallow who is lost from the flight, he knew he must leave

Denmark Hill forever, and go without fear: a thought which made him recall George MacDonald's words of encouragement, "You must learn to be strong in the dark as well as in the day, or you will always be only half brave."

He wondered if he was foolish in having believed that Brantwood would bring him the peace he sought, or fill the lonely days he dreaded on finding himself hurtling towards old age. Having spent a lifetime rebelling against his parents' possessiveness, he finally understood their past grievance whenever he had challenged them or sought his own dominion, for he suffered just the same now that Joan no longer needed him.

Purchasing Brantwood without so much as setting foot in it had been an act of frenzy and desperation, though he remained convinced that it would turn out to be the best decision he ever made: a blank canvas for him to transform as he saw fit. No longer having to return to Denmark Hill to visit his sick mother, or apply to his father to fund anything, he would revel in pleasing himself. And he could well afford to, for in Margaret's short but succinct last will and testament she had left everything she possessed to her son.

No-one could deny the many benefits of being able to lead an entirely independent life, yet he felt his substantial wealth to be more a burden than a blessing and would have preferred to have inherited just enough to live comfortably without having to fret about sharing the remainder. With no wife or children, he could be as beneficent as he chose, although he would gladly have exchanged this circumstance for the demands of a family of his own.

With no prospect of either marrying or becoming a father, he was not long in his new home before acknowledging that he would happily have sacrificed everything, his dreams of Coniston included, in return for winding back the clock and living with his parents at Denmark Hill, where, his mother and father seated either side of the hearth of an evening, or presiding at the head and foot of the dining table, he would appreciate all he had once despised.

Recognising that it was his nature to always strive for the unattainable, he tried to find fulfilment at Brantwood where he might: taking nails and a hammer and hanging a dozen Turner watercolours above his small, narrow bed, while with a spade and the assistance of his loyal gardener David Downs he began turning his lakeside wilderness into his own version of Elysium.

Labouring alongside Downs, who did the majority of the rough work, Ruskin dug countless holes, irrigating and assisting with clearing paths through the woodland until, drenched with sweat, he thought his back would snap in two and he was forced to lean upon his spade for fear of never being able to straighten up again.

'There can be no sensation more powerful than that of tilling your own soil,' he hailed, inspecting his mud-encrusted hands and dirty fingernails with pride.

'Though it is not my land, I am glad to be here,' Downs allowed, scanning the corner of England it was his privilege to inhabit and tend.

'It is just as much yours as it is mine. The most important task,' Ruskin went on optimistically, 'will be creating our own harbour, for I intend to sail to Coniston every day and get to know my neighbours.'

'Whatever you say,' Downs sighed wearily, mopping his brow.

'Have a little imagination, man! The harbour *will* be built and we shall keep a bounteous kitchen garden,' the professor proclaimed excitably, 'with plentiful supplies of fresh strawberries, and cream from the farm on the hillside. When we are done clearing these blasted paths, we shall plant masses of narcissi to remind us of Switzerland in springtime and abundant rose bushes to remind me of my love in summertime, and just as I did in my youth, I will lie down on the lawn and draw each blade of grass, each one an infinite picture and possession.'

THE GENTLE PRINCE

THE SERENITY AND CALM WATERS OF LAKE CONISTON worked their magic on Ruskin who, by the commencement of the first term at Oxford the following year, exhibited abundant energy and amiability, as if a piece of Brantwood went with him wherever he ventured.

Transformed into the most tolerant and agreeable man in society, he finally succumbed to taking rooms at Corpus Christi: a spacious first floor apartment with views of Christ Church meadow and the distant Isis, located not two hundred yards from the old college chambers he had inhabited thirty-five years before as a student.

Very soon the rooms resembled a museum-cum-gallery filled to the rafters with Ruskin's priceless objects which he was pleased to share with his students and those who called on him, while whenever he was absent he entrusted his keys to another Corpus don, who had permission to show the contents to interested visitors. Most came, not so much to see his collection of precious stones, Turners and Titians, but to listen to the professor and engage in conversation that left far more of an impression than any of his treasures.

More inclined to accept invitations and join in the vibrant dinner party debates he had previously abstained from in favour of solitary evenings at the Crown & Thistle, Ruskin was full of questions and grateful for any new information on a variety of subjects of which he considered himself to possess an inferior knowledge, listening deferentially to others however pompously they laid down the law, yet drawing all to listen to *him* whenever he uttered so much as a word.

His voice was thought most winning and his language simply perfect, for instead of tumbling out his sentences like so many portmanteaux, bags, rugs and hat boxes from an open railway carriage, like other dons set upon prevarication rather than poetry, he seemed to delight in building up sentences so as to make each deliverance a work of art, with a message that would live on in the minds of his listeners.

Never changing his tone during a disagreement, when Dean Liddell challenged his varying opinion regarding religion one night during dinner in the historic Tudor Hall, Ruskin merely leant forward and smiled, offering up his confession to the dean with no sign of remorse.

'Some of my hearers may have heard it stated of me that I am rather apt to contradict myself. I hope I am *exceedingly* apt to do so.'

'Our students rely on *us* to provide answers,' the dean disputed.

'Oh, you and your answers!' Ruskin pooh-poohed. 'I'm perfectly overwhelmed under the quantity of things which must be kept in mind, like a juggler's balls in the air.'

'If you liken yourself to a juggler, Professor Ruskin, then it goes without saying that you consider the university to be no better than a big top,' he swiped, causing the entire table to erupt with laughter and strain to hear more of the skirmish.

'I never met with any question yet, of any importance, which did not need, for the right solution of it, at least one positive and one negative answer, like an equation of the second degree,' he contradicted, conscious of his ability to easily outwit his counterpart.

'The second degree, you say?' Dean Liddell scoffed.

'Indeed. Most matters of any consequence are three or four-sided, or polygonal; the trotting round a polygon is severe work for people anyway stiff in their opinions.' Here Ruskin rolled his shoulders as if to unloosen any tension. 'For myself, I am never satisfied that I have handled a subject properly until I have contradicted myself at least three times, but *once* must do for this evening.'

However much Ruskin remained a controversial figure among the dons, many being deeply regretful of having championed his election to the post of Slade Professor, his popularity among the undergraduates showed no signs of waning; rather his name was more revered than the historic men, kings and saints whose ancient colleges bore their noble heraldry.

'You are to be maintained all your life by the labour of other men,' Ruskin opened his first lecture that term, careless that a member of the royal family was present and likely to take offence at the sentiment. 'You will have to make shoes for nobody, but someone will have to make a great many for *you*. You will have to dig ground for nobody, but someone will have to dig through every summer's hot day for *you*. You will build houses and make clothes for no-one, but many a rough hand must knead clay, and many an elbow be crooked to stitch, just to keep that body of yours warm and fine. You do not merely employ these people, you *tread* upon them. It cannot be helped, you have your place and they have theirs, but see that you tread as lightly as possible and on as *few* as possible. What food, clothes and lodging you honestly need, for your health and peace, you may righteously take, but see that you take the plainest you can serve yourself with, that you waste or wear nothing vainly, and that you employ no man in furnishing you with any useless luxury. England at this time is a mere heap of agonising human maggots, scrambling and sprawling over each other for any manner of rotten eatable thing they can bite off. It should not be condoned for a well-educated, intelligent or brave man to make money the chief object of his thoughts, just as it would be sickening for him to make his dinner the principal object of them. All healthily minded people like making money, *ought* to like it, and to enjoy the sensation of winning it, but the main object of their lives should not be money but something *better* than money.'

Far from being embarrassed by these words, they struck a chord with Queen Victoria's fourth and last son, Prince Leopold, who, having just become an undergraduate of law, planned to attend all Ruskin's deliverances and eagerly sought his company and instruction.

The prince's slim frame belied a life of illness, yet his mind was as strong as his body was weak, his large, deep-set eyes part-lion, part-spectre. Unafraid to know or speak his own mind, the young man was ready to hear the professor's unique viewpoint first-hand, convinced that he was just the man to mould him.

Inviting Ruskin to dine at his well-appointed residence at the northern end of St Giles, Wykeham House, the prince insisted that the professor be seated beside him as guest of honour and encouraged him to stay on when the others departed that they might get better acquainted over a game of chess, a pastime for which both men, neither being athletic, shared a lifelong passion.

'I am ever thankful to escape my work to play chess,' Ruskin remarked, rubbing his hands together in anticipation of trying out a new strategy. 'I enjoy it to the point of its becoming a tempting waste of time, very difficult to resist. Pleasant play truly, is it not marvellous to sit calculating and analysing for twelve hours, tire each other into near apoplexy or idiocy and end in a draw or a victory by an odd pawn? Whilst I have no claims to be ranked among players, any more than among painters properly so-called, I delight in the game almost as much as I do drawing.'

'I too,' agreed the prince, rotating the gold signet ring on his left pinky as he prepared to make his opening move; 'it is the only battle one can be satisfied in fighting with neither argument nor violence.'

'Are you prone to quarrel?' the professor asked wryly.

'Only with my mother,' the young man confessed.

'Treason,' Ruskin tutted mirthfully, for he perceived that they shared the same droll sense of humour and that the prince would not easily be offended by his Scotch frankness. 'I sometimes think my own, who passed away recently, fancied that *she* was the queen and I her loyal subject, yet her absence is all the greater now that she is no longer here to command or restrict me. Liberty is truly bewildering when one has waited a lifetime for it.'

The professor admired the gentle prince, who, cursed with haemophilia and epilepsy, never complained of his ailments but only that which he had been prevented from experiencing as a result. Prohibited from joining the army or navy like his brothers, it chanced that Leopold was more suited to academia than militia and possessed a keen instinct for learning, with every intention of dedicating himself to Oxford as Napoleon had the sea, though he was vexed that royal protocol demanded his degree must be gifted rather than earned.

'Christ Church is my first taste of it, and *I* like it a great deal,' Leopold assured, positioning his knight decisively but hastily. 'It's only regrettable that I am not permitted to experience student life in full, for there's no enjoyment in lodging in a grand house away from one's friends, nor pride in an honorary degree.'

'Nonsense, I can see that you are as intellectually equipped as any man and could just as easily graduate under you own steam were it necessary.'

The prince leant forward confidentially. 'But don't you see the shame in it *not* being? It's as if I were only offered a place due to my rank rather than merit.'

'I should be grateful if I were you,' Ruskin advised sagely, removing his opponent's bishop and grinning teasingly at having taken advantage of His Royal Highness's lapse of concentration.

Unusually, Leopold was too caught up in the conversation to mind about losing and paused to consider the professor's sentiment rather than his next move.

'Without meaning to be quarrelsome after earlier proclaiming myself generally good-natured,' the young man contradicted, 'I don't in the least believe that *you* would have accepted such a pass.'

'That's where you are mistaken, my father paid handsomely for my place as a gentleman-commoner. University is about far more than the grade you get at the end of it,' Ruskin asserted vigorously, 'therefore I don't see what the bother is about.'

Floundering at the game, the prince made another foolhardy move before looking his opponent in the eye and asking incredulously, 'But getting in with a helping hand isn't the same as not taking final examinations. You can honestly say that you would never have sat yours if you'd had a choice in the matter?'

'Absolutely!' Ruskin declared, jumping back in his seat for emphasis. 'Let us just say they were not my strong suit.'

This admission caused Leopold to roar with laughter and clutch his silk waistcoat for several moments, dumbfounded that a don should be so dismissive of the system he was supposed to champion. When his gaiety finally subsided, he took a nip of brandy, smoothed his heavily pomaded wavy hair and toppled his king to resign both the game and the debate, thus securing their mutual understanding and friendship.

'You're a mighty adversary,' he conceded, shaking the victor graciously by the hand.

'I have triumphed in that you have shown me the manner of English youth and good sense, for we both of us live far externally to the college quadrangle, whether physically or no,' the professor reflected seriously. 'I was always quite out of place amongst the hunting, shooting and fishing set in my undergraduate days, while the dons were even more peculiar than I'm regarded today. A certain Dr Buckland used to fill his house with stuffed hyenas and crocodiles whilst boasting of having served most of the animal kingdom, cooked, at his table. It was there that I was introduced to Charles Darwin. You are well to be out of the way of such types as Buckland. I only wish you and I had been contemporaries. As it is, I hope I can assist you in fathoming what benefits there are to reap here at Oxford, so long as you remember that *none* of them are accolades.'

The prince enjoyed many such convivial evenings in the professor's company, a much looked forward to diversion amidst a tireless daily timetable of activities carefully co-ordinated by his tutor, the courtier Sir Robert Collins, who had accompanied him from Windsor.

Collins in turn welcomed Ruskin's patronage of his pupil, having the highest regard for him both personally and professionally, though he had been too long within the walls of the establishment not to be wary of a man so remiss of royal customs, a dubiousness furthered when Leopold, confined to bed following an epileptic episode, invited the professor to Windsor Castle for tuition and companionship.

'I was sorry I wasn't able to welcome you last night,' Collins began on coming across Ruskin carrying a parcel of books in the Queen's private apartments the morning after his arrival.

'It's entirely my own fault for turning up so late,' he apologised.

'How does your accommodation suit?'

'If I'm entirely honest, I expected to have a room with a view, if the room was *ever* so little,' the guest complained fastidiously. 'Instead, I've got a great big one looking into the castle yard that makes me feel exactly as if have been sent to the county jail. This castle surely serves to keep its inhabitants in rather than aggressors *out*.'

'I'm sorry to hear how unsuitable you find it,' the courtier responded abruptly, his smile concealing the offence he felt on behalf of the royal household. 'Would you like us to relocate you?'

'It wouldn't be worth the trouble,' Ruskin rejected, too single-minded to watch his words. 'I expect one room is much like another here. Forgive me,' he added, 'I'm horribly sulky this morning due to lack of sleep. I'm honoured to have been invited here, naturally, but I can't imagine calling such a place as this *home*. However did the prince turn out to be such a charming young man?'

'I'd like to think *my* instruction has played some part,' Collins blustered, puffing out his chest.

'I'm sure it has, but why must he always be shielded so?' the professor challenged. 'He greatly resents being held back.'

'It is not only his position but his *health* that makes his life necessarily restrictive,' the courtier defended, his arms behind his back and his manner as rigid as the castle boundaries. 'Leopold's condition is more perilous than either he or you realise.'

'Judging from the way he talks of all things eternal, I suspect he's more aware of his mortality than you suppose,' he observed solemnly, pausing to address Collins face to face. 'This would explain his desire to seize every opportunity to *live*.'

'That is all very well, but he must not be overworked to the point of hastening the inevitable,' the courtier warned. 'The Queen is adamant that her son's time at Oxford should in no way overtax him. In fact Her Majesty was not at all convinced that he should go, and I would hate for you or I to feel responsible should anything unforeseen occur.'

'I may not be a medical man,' Ruskin asserted, inclined to rebel against what he considered a preposterous caution, 'but I know enough to be sure that scholarly work can't cause any adverse effects in epilepsy or haemophilia, short of me knocking the prince on the head with a book.'

'Quite so,' Collins agreed, flustered.

'Now, will you take me to him?' Ruskin asked charmingly.

Although he had no particular interest in the monarchy, Ruskin was extremely fond of the studious, thoughtful young man who had been made in the mould of his father, Prince Albert, and was equally passionate on the subjects of art, architecture and education.

'You do me a great service by visiting,' Leopold began on Ruskin entering his dim chamber, shrouded from the daylight by densely lined curtains. 'I was beginning to go mad locked away.'

'I can well imagine,' Ruskin commiserated, shocked to see how underweight the prince appeared lying on his couch.

'It's all nonsense my being confined here,' the young man protested, lighting a cheroot, despite his mother's prohibition of tobacco on royal premises. 'They think it will calm me down and make me reflect upon the workload I have taken on, but instead I'm only more determined to get back to Oxford and continue my studies.'

'I empathise, having battled many periods of ill health, both in my youth and more recently,' he commiserated in a rallying rather than despondent fashion. 'Nowadays it's my mind rather than my body that tends to let me down, yet work is all that keeps me going. Which reminds me, here are some books of mine, though they will almost certainly add to your boredom rather than alleviate it.'

Placing the parcel on a table without desiring thanks, the professor unintentionally illustrated his mental instability by becoming momentarily distracted. Curious to see the prince's view, he peeped behind the curtain and harrumphed on glimpsing the formal garden that was a vast improvement on his own imposing yard outlook, albeit concealed behind swathes of damask.

'Until I marry I shall never be able to live as I truly desire,' Leopold griped, oblivious to Ruskin's interrupted train of thought.

'Do you have anyone in mind?' he asked, taking up the seat beside the prince without waiting to be offered it.

'Not yet; there are some nice girls at Oxford,' the prince observed, offering Ruskin a cheroot from a silver box engraved with the royal coat of arms which the professor refused with a courteous waving away. 'Dean Liddell's daughters, for example, but neither of them would "do",' he bantered. 'In the end it doesn't really matter *who* I marry; practically anyone would suit me just to be free of my mother.'

'I never heard of a man believing marriage would help them *gain* freedom,' Ruskin laughed. 'I know *I* did not.'

'Most men do not have *my* mother,' Leopold ventured. 'I can't imagine there being a woman alive quite as demanding. She still bemoans giving birth to me! Never stops going on about how beastly it was and how I nearly killed her. Sometimes I wish I had.'

'And then you would be answerable to your brother, a fate far worse,' Ruskin denied.

'Yes, I suppose you're right,' he conceded, stubbing out his cheroot and lighting another. 'My brothers all consider me half a man because I can't go into the army.'

'Doubtless your father would have refuted that,' his companion cheered, rising to look at the paintings lining the room.

'How I wish he were here now! Thank God I have you to advise me,' he smiled sincerely.

'You don't need an adviser,' he returned, bowing his head humbly, for he not only related to Leopold's longing for his father's counsel but saw how their relationship mirrored his esteem for Turner, their divide in age and experience benefiting them both.

'*Much* that you say dwells on my mind; and as you know, I have a great deal of time to think,' Leopold extolled, indicating his disdain of his surroundings with a flourish.

'I had no conception that you saw so far into things or into *me*,' the professor returned. 'When I consider the quantity of my wise talking, which has passed in one ear of the world and out at the other, without making the smallest impression upon it, I am often tempted, for the rest of my life, to speak no more.'

'Don't do that while *I'm* alive,' the prince exclaimed, raising his hand in protest, 'it's my ambition to go from this earth with just an ounce of your wisdom.'

Very soon Ruskin realised that his young protégée could have as positive an effect over his life as vice versa, not least when Prince Leopold defended his plans to create a new Oxford drawing school, for what was the point of theorising about art without teaching it practically?

By making the prince a trustee, the university hierarchy opposed to the project were forced to abjure their resistance, while Leopold was delighted that his name had given credence to such a beneficent scheme, readily agreeing when Ruskin asked him to officially open the school and speak a few words in celebration of its foundation.

So roused was the prince upon the subject that any nerves which naturally arose at the thought of making his first public address were overtaken by sheer enthusiasm and pride at having helped such a project reach fruition, nor was he deterred by the torrential downpour which threatened to spoil the gaiety of the occasion.

'In John Ruskin we see a man in whom all the gifts of refinement and genius meet,' he commenced, addressing those assembled outside the University Galleries, home to the new Ruskin School of Art, 'who does not grudge giving his best to all in teaching and sympathy, and intends to give future artists the power whereby they may gain the full measure of instruction and happiness from this wonderful world in which rich and poor alike gaze.'

Ignorant that the speech was not concluded, Dean Liddell, who was eager to escape the rain which had turned from a drizzle into a deluge, handed the prince the scissors whereby to cut the official ribbon, only for Leopold to smile politely and continue with his presentation.

'As Mr Ruskin says, "None of us can ever love art until we love what she mirrors *better*", words which not only brought a smile to the prince's lips but improved his projection and delivery. '"What we create on canvas does not rest on the love of art, but mountains and seas, clouds and streams. Fine art is that in which the hand, the head and the heart of man go together." Would that I could adequately express the exquisite grace and tact with which Professor Ruskin puts his pupils at ease, or the skill with which he succeeds in inducing even the shyest among us to take part in his discussions. For my own part, I am blessed, not only to know and receive his tutorship but to call him "friend".'

Saying which, the prince paused for a moment and, opening a well-thumbed book, recited from it with a command and dignity that took the sceptical Dean Liddell entirely by surprise.

'"To be taught to read, what is the use of that, if you know not whether *what* you read is true or false?" he quoted with mesmerising vigour. '"To be taught to write or to speak, what is the use of speaking if you have nothing to *say*? To be taught to think, nay, what is the use of being able to think if you have nothing to think *of*? But to be taught to *see* is to gain word and thought at once; it is poetry, prophecy and religion."'

Closing the book solemnly, Leopold looked up to judge whether his audience of dons and undergraduates concurred with the sentiment, only to be met with rapturous applause.

'What make you of that?' Collins nudged Ruskin as the prince finally cut the ribbon and ushered the group inside.

'I can't deny I'm deeply moved,' he returned as they followed in his Royal Highness's wake, Collins pausing to study a series of art prints which the professor had donated to the museum, including several by his old friend Turner.

'It must be strange to hear one's own words recited?' the courtier enquired. 'Very beautiful in themselves.'

'I never knew ought like it,' Ruskin shook his head. 'Leopold is so full of good that he convinces me that not *all* my ideas are bad.'

LIX
BROADLANDS

RATHER THAN ACCEPT THE PASSING OF TIME AS A DROWNING man succumbs to the pull of the tide, Ruskin felt himself reborn at Oxford, nor did he allow Great Tom to chime on the close of any day without having first seized it as a new opportunity to challenge his students and university superiors with his radical approach to teaching.

The dean and chancellor, the very towers and steeples, were girded against the might of Ruskin: an eccentric, crow-like figure, flapping and blustering about old corridors in his black gown and mortarboard between lectures. Imbuing the college with his unparalleled spirit and dedication, none who passed him failed to be impressed by his tireless enthusiasm, tenfold greater than many men half his age, and even those who mocked him behind his back went away the more industrious for having witnessed the Slade Professor on his rounds.

Finding himself unable to heed Acland's warning about brooding or burning himself out, his vigour would not be quelled, nor was any action taken without Rose for inspiration. How glad he should have been to know that his successes, including the lauded school of art now bearing his name and implementing his long-held techniques and principles, were recounted to his love through mutual friends, acquaintances whom she also asked to summarise his lectures that she might pore over them in her solitary hours.

Others had meanwhile informed her of the professor's dangerous period of illness at Matlock following Joan's marriage, old Mrs Ruskin's death, and the purchase of Brantwood, which Rose longed to see and tried to picture as she went to her sister's grave each morning: the only meaningful purpose she had for leaving her room since burying Bruno beneath the favourite tree that once she had climbed.

She was so thankful her former teacher's life had been spared that he might continue to do good in the world, whilst his new home would grant him a place to rest and reflect when he was not required at Oxford, the learned city she imagined through information gleaned from old tomes in the Harristown library, which, despite their age, provided a wealth of accurate detail and allowed her to imagine herself beside him.

Rose envied Ruskin's new peaceful lakeshore abode, coupled with the high-minded debates he enjoyed with his intellectual kindred at Oxford, for she had long since avoided all society as a means of punishing her parents, and although she was still loved amongst the cottagers she could not help but recognise how limited their shared interests were as she grew older and more insular.

She had nothing to do all day but what she liked – hour after hour with no occupation, work or amusement besides that which she managed to find for herself. Reading, and seeing one or two poor people, was the most each day yielded, though traversing the estate was not the same without Bruno as her devoted companion. It seemed that the very things her nature, spirit and soul needed she could not have.

Like a mare trained to become a racecourse yet constrained within a small paddock, Rose saw her education as having served no purpose other than to make her eternally restless. She felt ungrateful and unchristian for harbouring such resentment and prayed for forgiveness in the sanctity of the chill family chapel where she wandered like a spirit among the tombs of her sister and uncle, wondering when she would join them.

When the temperate midsummer coincided with Rose discovering that Ruskin had embarked on an extensive tour of the Continent with Joan and Arthur, she was moved to accept the Cowper-Temples' invitation to stay with them at their estate in Hampshire, no warmth or sunshine alleviating the cold disconnection she felt towards her own home and parents.

A white Palladian-style mansion with an extensive Capability Brown parkland sloping down to the river, despite Broadlands being a showy property with grandiose columns far superior to even Harristown, it possessed a unique atmosphere due to the Cowper-Temples' free-spirited and unceremonious hospitality.

Inspired by an environment which seemed to encourage shared confidences, Rose was thrilled to find George MacDonald also visiting, one of the few people she could rely on to assess her present situation and Ruskin's likely perspective. Thus she seized the opportunity of asking his assistance when he invited her to walk with him that first morning, the English summer suspended behind the clouds like her own happiness.

'On a clear day you can see the Isle of Wight,' MacDonald remarked optimistically, pointing to the grey horizon with his walking stick, for he too had altered in the years since their last meeting, something which increased rather than lessened her self-consciousness.

Perceiving that she had no interest in the view, he turned and regarded Rose as one watches the sunrise. Though she was a mere shadow of the girl God had intended her to be, her face was enchantingly fair, with eyes like the night sky, each with a star dissolved in the blue.

Looking down at her feet, she began hesitantly, 'I can't say how glad I am to find you here.'

'I too,' he replied, his Scotch accent lyrically reminiscent of Ruskin's own Celtic lilt, the voice she most longed to hear.

'It seems to me that you could help me, and I think you *would* help me if you could,' she went on, 'for I am in need of honest counsel.'

'I hoped you would say that,' he encouraged gently, guessing from her frequent requests for news about Ruskin what was foremost on her mind.

'Does God ever put one in a position whereby it is impossible to do His will and equally impossible to either alter the situation or escape from it?'

'He tests us constantly,' MacDonald nodded, taking a slight yet humble bow and putting his hands together in prayer.

'But is it wrong not to accept with perfect contentment the circumstances decided by His providence?' Rose asked, raising a hand to her forehead in confusion.

'He does not always make the course we must take clear to us,' her quiet confidant offered, pointing at the clouds overhead as if they too were of God's design.

'I've been tossed to and fro frightfully, God knows,' she continued. 'Heart and desires, head and judgement, *my* interpretation of right and my parents' all pulling in different directions.'

'We live in constant strife, a strife between the flesh and the spirit,' he acknowledged, stroking his dense greying beard musingly, 'but past tears are present strength and sometimes the best way to manage pain is to dare it to do its worst, to let it gnaw at your heart until you find that you still have a residue of life it cannot kill. You will never arrive at an understanding of God so long as you cannot see the good that often comes as a result of pain, nor must you forget the bond between you and your parents, no matter how great your differences may seem.'

'Please do not think me unloving, it is so hard to be thought so at home,' she urged, sobs beginning to tighten her chest.

'I think *you* unloving?' MacDonald denied vigorously. 'Your heart is an inexhaustible fountain of love. You love everything you see! And all love, believe me, will one day meet with its return.'

'The other day I sat down at my mother's feet, laying my head on her knee and aching to rest my heart there too, but she said that I was a baby instead of a young woman of twenty-four and, though I tried to draw closer and she *tried* to understand, the end was a wakeful night for both of us,' she confessed frankly.

It was liberating to reveal her innermost feelings to MacDonald after holding them back for so long, for he was the easiest of confessors, being not only highly sensible and pragmatic but thoroughly patient and kind.

'We are all anxious to be understood, and it is very hard not to be, yet *I* see much change in you,' he assured; 'you write and speak to me with the thoughts and feelings of a woman, not a child.'

'My parents always regard maturity as wilfulness. They can't comprehend why I feel so constrained by their way of life, but I go about our poor people and come back to my own idle comfort in despair, for it seems that *their* lives are much more like Christ's than my own,' she explained, brushing away a tear. 'I go jingling off in the carriage with my ponies and bells with a sadder heart than anyone could know, for I want to be more on an equality with them, serve them, help them, learn from them. My mother and father think I have only to take some medicines to be quite myself again and marry someone after their own ideas.'

MacDonald was relieved that Rose had finally made reference to marriage and, though he rested his gaze upon the lake out of respect for the delicate nature of their conversation, he was nonetheless curious enough to say to his companion, 'You must resent not being able to make your own choice?'

Looking down at her bare hands, she assented dolefully, 'I do not believe I shall ever marry, but if only I might have kept the affection of the one who has brought such pain and suffering among so many hearts.'

'You refer to our friend John Ruskin?'

'Yes,' she acknowledged with a tender half-smile, 'what I would give for him to have remained just that.'

'Do you consider him more?' he pressed gently, fearful of making Rose close up, yet anticipating her need to divulge all that troubled her.

'A *great* deal more,' she replied, blushing virginally, 'but what does it mean if you love someone with your whole heart, only never think of them in a certain way? A wifely sense.'

'What you describe is love in its purest form,' he answered, noticing how she clutched the silver crucifix around her neck as though she already repented of having spoken, 'and I'm sure he would be glad to receive any you would give.'

Rose, too timid to refer to Ruskin by his Christian name, looked away. 'Do you really think the professor would be happy with me just as I am?'

'Yes, I do,' he affirmed strongly.

She bit her bottom lip. 'I can't understand it.'

'It is by loving, and not by *being* loved, that one can come nearest the soul of another,' he declared. 'You love not this and that about each other, but each the *very* other, a love as essential to reality, to truth, to religion, as the love of God. Where such love is, let differences be what they may, you two must, by and by, be thoroughly one. God only knows how grandly, how passionately, yet how calmly and divinely you might, may, *shall* love each other.'

'You are so wise, whatever would I do without you to talk to?'

'Shouldn't you be speaking with him?' MacDonald suggested.

'He's abroad,' she answered dejectedly.

'I'm sure he would return if you would agree to see him.'

The idea confounded her and she took a seat upon the grass overlooking the lake, though no amount of meditating on the best course seemed to provide the answer. In contrast, the low-lying morning clouds were melting away, revealing the full glory of the estate and a vista looking out to sea and distant shores.

Wrapping her arms around her knees, she despaired, 'I haven't the least conviction in my own judgement.'

MacDonald, who suffered from arthritis, used his stick to lower himself to the shaded patch of ground beside his young friend and, regarding her troubled face, asked, 'You still believe in God's grace bringing good out of our sorrowful human tangles?'

'Yes,' she nodded piously, convinced that he would never lead her to do wrong, 'I try to keep faith and be brave, but sometimes I'm overcome with hopelessness.'

'To try *is* to be brave,' MacDonald smiled consolingly, taking up her hand and pressing it. 'There is no harm in being afraid, the only harm is in doing what Fear tells you. Fear is not your master and neither should

Doubt be! Doubt may be a poor encouragement to do something but it is a bad reason for doing nothing.'

'I do miss the professor very much,' she admitted tearfully, 'and whenever I think of him it is with *such* an ache.'

'Nothing can equal the mere presence of one whom we love utterly.' And he sighed at the juxtaposition between the beauty of the day and his friend's suffering.

'Will you please write and ask him to come home?'

'I should be glad to,' he agreed, buoyed on hearing the word "home" and gratified that Rose had entrusted him with what would undoubtedly prove a difficult mediation with a far from guaranteed outcome. Trust, so he had always believed, was the greatest compliment another human being could pay towards another.

'Then don't delay or I might change my mind,' she teased, laughing so as to change the tone they had adopted, though she quickly fell solemn again. 'How will our story end?'

'Oh, no story really ever ends,' he asserted, rising and shielding his eyes from the sun, 'and I think I know why.'

Saying which, he strolled towards the shining lake, leaving Rose to muse on all he had said. The pollen-scented air reminded her of Harristown: the butterflies and dragonflies whispering to her as they skirted the long grass. Picking a daisy and twirling it between her fingers, she discarded it with a furrowed brow, for whichever way she turned the path seemed wrought with questions to which she had no definitive answer; the restorative, enchanted kingdom of Broadlands was hardly more than an illusion destined to fade with the passing of summer.

The balmy afternoon turned to dusk, twilight to night, as MacDonald considered the best words to use on taking up his pen to Ruskin. Unmindful of the responsibility he thereby shouldered, nor the blame Rose might place at his feet were he to misjudge the tone of the communication, he acted as if God directed him, and in so doing neither dwelt nor disputed His plan.

Torn between the urgency of bringing Ruskin to England before

Rose fled, yet feeling the need to tread carefully, he nonetheless wrote in his typically forthright style, presenting his young friend as a heroine who, recognising her error in casting her lover aside, now repented. Made frantic by her fault, she wished to throw all guilt away by looking into his eyes, saying, 'I did it and wish I had not, and I am sorry for having done it.'

It was no simple matter to explain the suddenness of Rose's command and implore Ruskin to abandon his holiday, and, as MacDonald anticipated, one note quickly turned into a series, with his perplexed correspondent firing a stream of questions to which he could not possibly know the answers.

Reporting that the La Touches were already asking Rose to return and that she only lingered in the hope of spending a few days alone with him, Ruskin's holiday was wholly disturbed by this unlooked-for occurrence, nor could he shut out the shadows of doubt. Exasperated by years of unpredictability, and having received no direct word from Rose requesting his presence, past experience taught him that he should be deeply reluctant to agree to what was probably just another of her impetuous demands and would surely result in humiliation and despair.

Though it was baffling to think that he had no other friend besides MacDonald whose opinion was worth anything to Rose, the possibility of seeing his love allowed Ruskin's imagination to take flight and made him incapable of rejecting the chance. Might she be planning to accept him after all?

He had been embarrassed too many times before, however, and thus he telegrammed MacDonald, who had all but given up hope of arranging a reunion, to guarantee that his journey would not be for nothing. "I WILL NOT MOVE UNLESS IN THE CERTAINTY OF SEEING HER"

The go-between wasted no time in replying in the affirmative, expressing his relief that Ruskin was preparing to depart Venice, for there were outstanding matters between them which would prove too delicate for Rose to commit to pen and paper, nor would one be able to decipher her meaning when once it had been veiled within the restraints of propriety and modesty.

***

'Still nothing?' Rose whispered in MacDonald's ear as he led her into dinner a week after her arrival.

'On the contrary, your prayer has been answered,' he beamed, taking the seat beside her. 'The professor is making his way back directly.'

'Oh, Mr MacDonald!' she exclaimed, stopping short when their fellow diners looked askance.

Having been subdued for days whilst she awaited news, the staring faces, though not unkind, made Rose flush, caught as she was between excitement and trepidation at the prospect of an imminent meeting with her suitor. Her smile faded and she would not touch the meal before her but sipped only water, MacDonald perceiving the slight tremble of her hand whenever she moved the glass to her lips.

Sensing her natural anxieties now that the reunion was confirmed, MacDonald nonetheless became anxious that she might bolt before Ruskin arrived and advised her quietly, yet sternly, 'I urge that you put your parents off after all my pains.'

'Perhaps I am making a mistake by not going home,' she speculated, mortified by her indecision.

'Now that you have committed yourself to remaining, put any such notions aside and focus on keeping your word to *me*. Would it not be just as bad to go now that I have assured a certain other that you will stay?'

Looking up with eyes in which the heavens and all their mysteries were reflected, she implored, 'Wait with me?'

'I should only be in the way. As soon as you take one look at each other, all will be well,' he reassured, patting her hand whilst avoiding the enquiring glance of Georgiana Cowper-Temple, who saw that something was afoot and wished to learn more.

'You say that when so much has changed?' Rose pressed.

'Nothing has altered your feelings, least of all time, which only serves to prove what some have tried to *disprove*. His face will always be the one on which changes come without your seeing them, or rather you will still see him the same, despite all the shadows which the years have gathered upon it.'

***

MacDonald never failed to give Rose confidence with his enlightened views, and therefore the wait for Ruskin to reach Broadlands was a lonely one when once he had gone, prompting her to consider the various outcomes of her stay in Hampshire as helplessly as though her fate lay in a hand of cards, to be dealt in her favour or no. Could she bring herself to reject the professor and lose their friendship irrecoverably, or at last agree to marry him without fully understanding what such a step would mean?

Urged by MacDonald to vent all her concerns when once Ruskin was before her, with no sleep and barely any sustenance to help her think more rationally or allay her worries, the pressure she put upon herself to give the answer so long overdue destroyed all possibility of looking forward to the professor's arrival, her conscience worn down by the thought of causing Ruskin further injury.

Wearing a simple gown of pale blue silk which made her look pretty rather than beautiful, devout rather than fashionable, Rose stood restlessly beside the fireplace in the morning room, aware that every passing moment was one less opportunity for deliberating.

Scanning the prized paintings and ornaments without absorbing anything, she began to feel faint the more she tried to prepare what to say, the one object her eyes were repeatedly drawn to that of the ornate French mantel clock adorned with a gilt bronze of Venus depicting "Love".

Catching sight of herself in the Rococo oval mirror which showed the truth however lavish its casing, she winced on observing her gaunt face and the dark circles under her eyes conveying the sleeplessness of her uncertainty. Touching her pale cheeks, she wondered if MacDonald's sermon about lovers being blind to change in one another were true. Would her suitor even recognise the fair Irish girl he once desired? Ashamed for asking herself this, she knew it was vain to court the admiration of one who had suffered for so many years by her own design.

It seemed as though she had been languishing against the mantle for an age when the drawing room door finally opened and Ruskin, flushed from hurrying, entered and removed his hat formally. He was altered, yes, but not half so much as she, for his face and sandy hair were remarkably youthful, as was his energetic bearing.

Momentarily reminded of their first encounter and having stood so boldly before him as a child, ready to learn all that he was willing to impart, she considered his countenance just as winning as when he had handed her the rosebud to sketch, an item which, unbeknownst to him, remained one of her most sacred possessions, the more so for not having been discovered by her mother and destroyed along with his letters. Her earliest memory was nonetheless painful due to all that had come to pass subsequently, heightened when she perceived his consternation at her slight figure and his hesitation in approaching her.

Without knowing Rose to be overcome with insecurities, Ruskin stood motionless, trying to preserve the vision of his dear one and lock it away, for he had not seen her in so many years that his eyes, having mourned the absence, were dazed by the woman standing before him, ready, so he trusted, to become his wife.

'Why is it that you only know how much you miss a thing when it is before you again?' Ruskin stammered.

'The same reason that you only realise that you love someone when you try to stop,' she answered, beginning to approach him. 'And I did *try*,' she added, as if making an admittance of guilt.

'Let me look after you, Rose,' he begged.

'There is nothing to be done,' she insisted, turning her head so that he was able to admire the familiar curve of her chin, the nape of her neck and a delicate curl of baby hair peeping out from beneath her neat chignon.

'I thought, when you asked MacDonald to send for me, that you had decided to be mine,' he chided, his voice full of disappointment as he halted in the centre of the room.

'Perhaps I should have married you a long time ago,' she answered regretfully, moving towards him and holding out her hand, 'but I cannot marry you now.'

'You *cannot?*' he balked, brushing her away. 'You brought me here to tell me that?'

'I was not certain of my answer when I asked Mr MacDonald to send for you, but now I realise that it can never be and want to tell you *why*.'

'I desire no explanation,' he turned, unable to help sounding bitter.

Still she pursued him, though he would not look at her. 'I hope nothing he said caused you to misinterpret my desire to see you?'

'Do not fear exciting any vain hopes after this, you have broken my heart much too thoroughly for any such weeds to grow in the rifts, though I think you ought not to allow yourself to be made a tool of torture to me.'

'I see the ways in which, at different times, I have hurt you and I am truly sorry for it,' Rose offered. 'I have every cause to trust in your affection, and you hardly any to trust in mine. I should have told you how futile your love for me was at the very beginning, but each time I tried, in the months and years hence, I could never bring myself to banish your regard for me. It was selfish and unmerciful of me.'

Dreading his response and afraid lest his anger would rise up against her, she gazed out onto the garden that he might not witness the emotion she wished to conceal.

Instead he only sighed and said, 'There's no question of forgiveness or of my pleading, but you can't forbid my loving *you*. Whatever I can do for you I will.'

'Can't you resign yourself to letting me go on my way? You have so many things to give you joy and strength: your work, your friends, your powers of thought and appreciation. You do not lose much by losing me.'

'I lose *everything*,' he denied vigorously.

'You can't grieve over something you've never had,' she scorned, though her eyes smarted.

'That's the worst grief of *all*. "Love, it is a wrathful place,"' he declared, reciting *Roman de la Rose*, '"a free acquittance, without release. A pain, also it is joyous, and cruelty, right piteous."'

Ruskin almost pitied her more than himself, however, for he knew that she made the sacrifice against her will. Finally moving towards Rose as though she were an injured animal, he saw the agony she endured in casting him away and touched her face devotedly.

Accepting this act of kindness and appeasement, she rested her head upon his breast and allowed him to feel how her own harboured a remorse she could barely contain.

'God cannot have meant nothing but pain to grow out of the strange link of love that still unites us to one another,' Rose surmised.

'I believe our feelings are as clear a sign that there *is* a God as I have ever witnessed,' Ruskin replied emphatically, the gentle kiss he bestowed upon her forehead a symbol of the ardour he longed to express but was obliged to rein in.

Seeking an interview with Georgiana Cowper-Temple, who was eager to know if Ruskin's meeting with Rose had proved successful, he found her alone in her private sitting room before dinner, half reclining on a button-back sofa and sewing distractedly, for her mind was almost always occupied with the affairs of her guests.

'I was wondering when you'd come and say hello,' she smiled warmly, offering her hand to be kissed.

Though her shiny dark hair was styled for dinner, she had not changed out of her plain day dress in anticipation of their interview. Considered a handsome woman, Georgiana's lack of coquetry prevented society gossip despite her possessing a dozen or more male friends, for all looked on her as a pious confidant, ready with sympathy and clear judgement. She was simply an angel on earth, Ruskin considered, and though her husband was less radiantly such, even he was no less so in fact.

Adopting a maternal role towards friends following the misfortune of childlessness, Georgiana took consolation in her bond with Ruskin and others who depended upon her, for in the act of listening and advising she herself found fulfilment.

'How can I ever thank you for bringing us together?' Ruskin began, taking a seat at the end of the sofa. 'All yours and MacDonald's doing.'

'We want so much for you both to find happiness,' she professed.

'I do not believe that any creature out of heaven has been so much loved as I love that child,' he uttered, shaking his head.

'I know it, but you must take care of your own feelings too,' Georgiana cautioned sagely.

'The greatest thing is finding how noble she still is, for she is *worth* all the worship.'

'How quickly we all forget heartache when we receive just a moment of tenderness,' his confidant observed adroitly before turning silent. Knowing that her friend wanted no advice but only to voice his ecstasy, she awaited Ruskin's next tribute with a pitiful sigh, alarmed that he could find no perspective other than his own, distorted to suit himself.

'She was so good and so grave, and so gay and so terribly lovely, and so merciless, and so kind, and so ineffable,' Ruskin rhapsodised, not choosing to dwell on Rose's refusal on having convinced himself that he could change her mind by the end of the week. 'Did you ever see anything *half* so lovely?'

'She is indeed a rare girl,' Georgiana replied hesitantly without lifting her eyes from the embroidery.

Far from being affronted, she was a woman of unqualified generosity and humanity who took pride in offering her friends a refuge away from prying eyes and interference. Her only qualm was a dread of being blamed for the turmoil that was bound to arise if Ruskin was forsaken.

'I'm very fond of Rose, yet she is as changeable as a breeze-blown spring flower,' she reminded. 'One day this, the next day that. I'm not referring to her love for you, but what she decides to do about it.'

'Rosie has no need for shame, in anything that she has done or thought, in even what she has *not* done, for *she* isn't in the true sense to blame, her mother only. Apparently she wishes me to be lover and friend no more, speaking as fearlessly as a woman in Shakespeare, as the purest women are always able to do.'

'Perhaps it is better when you are both living in separate worlds?' Georgiana ventured.

'Never,' he denied vehemently, rising and pacing the room. 'The idea of Rose being gone from this one is just beginning to dawn on me, and the more unjust and pointless I believe our separation has been. All I know is that she is still happy to be with me when she allows herself to be so.

Find me a soul she would rather be with and I will gladly withdraw into the night.'

The following morning was entirely calm and clear, the mist from the river at rest among the trees with a rosy light on its folds of blue. A landscape befitting the romantic poets, Ruskin's hopes were elevated just imagining what the next few hours might bring.

He was grateful that his room overlooked the gardens where shortly he and Rose would commune, the immaculate lawns of which led to ancient woodlands originating long before the house was built in the eighteenth century, the only cool place to stroll in the heat of the day.

It was already quite warm though only nine o'clock, and fully intending to squeeze every last drop of sunshine from his precious time with Rose among the Hampshire countryside, Ruskin sent a servant to take her a quickly penned note, enquiring if she had slept well and if she would take tea with him out on the terrace.

She did not answer but simply appeared downstairs looking ethereal in a simple gown of white muslin, reminiscent of styles he remembered her having worn during that treasured summer at Harristown.

Appearing refreshed and gentle towards him as she poured his tea, *Perhaps*, he surmised, *she too is determined to find peace here.*

Broadlands, where friends had brought them together, was a glorious backdrop for long afternoon walks hand in hand, he reflected as they sat in silence like a couple who had spent a lifetime together.

Inseparable, they would have as many perfect summer days as Rose would permit, full of quiet laughter and tenderness, though the dreaded time of her departure was ever on his mind, threatening like an August thunderstorm to break up their contentment.

Perceiving that, despite her apparent serenity, Rose's mind was still fraught with guilt at having deceived her parents in order to be alone with him, Ruskin hoped that the bravery of the action might be the first step towards his love asserting her desire to be his, regardless of what she had already said to the contrary.

Having cautioned her husband and the other guests to leave Ruskin and Rose to their own devices, Georgiana was delighted to look out of her bedroom window and see the pair walking down to the river arm in arm, for she had long prophesied that Broadlands would be their common ground and the foundation of their future happiness if only they should seize it.

Ruskin walked with the vitality of a young man, equipped with a rug and a picnic he knew all too well that Rose would refuse to take anything from. Helping his love into a little rowing boat moored by the lake for pleasure seekers, he noticed how unsteadily she leant upon his arm and became fatigued after the slightest exertion, a decline it pained his soul to witness whenever he considered the girl she had been, always ready to run into mischief or play boisterous games.

Attentively placing a blanket over her lap when she shivered despite the warmth of the day, he asked, 'Do you feel unwell?'

'Not *unwell*, just like an old worn-out instrument in need of new strings,' she replied wearily. 'Even on a beautiful day such as this I find it hard to take pleasure from it. I've been waiting for my end for so long that I don't remember how to *live*.'

Her companion was visibly unsettled by this pronouncement, for he felt sad and helpless on doubting the possibility of being able to restore her to health. All that he could do was to protect and nurture her for as long as she allowed him.

'You're just at the beginning of life,' he dismissed, hoping to lift her spirits; 'imagine how *I* feel on exceeding half a century!'

'How gladly I would end my quarter,' she responded woefully. 'For what *is* life? To me it is merely a waiting time until eternal rest, when no troubles can have any power over me. The days go on, yet it seems as though I am far nearer the end of my journey than the beginning.'

'For one who loves God, you throw away his greatest gift far too easily,' he rebuked.

'You misunderstand me,' she denied, sitting up a little. 'I am grateful for my life, I merely wonder why He made it impossible for me to truly enjoy it. I am very tired and can only look forward sorrowfully. Though

617

I may live for ten or twenty years more, each hour makes me ache with eagerness to be gone.'

'It pains me to hear you say so,' he said, shaking his head sorrowfully.

'I'm sorry for putting another cloud in the sky,' she apologised plaintively. 'I have such a knack for spoiling things, don't I?'

'I too have known days when I wished to be no more, and it's akin to wrestling with the Devil, the sunshine and warmth increasing my malaise worse than the wind and the rain. And yet I have tried to carry on and remind myself that it's my duty to make the most of this short existence, if only on behalf of those who went before me or will come after.'

Rose leant forward with interest and in so doing forgot her fatigue for a moment. 'Whatever do you mean?'

'Distant views always make me think of my father in his grave, and the mystery of mortality becomes perpetually more terrific as I get older. Not because I'm not moved *enough* by it but because I'm not trying hard enough to do right. Surely the only thing to be done by any of us is to be kind and cheerful always?'

The professor's words entirely suited her frame of mind, although she did not respond. Lifting the oars again, he began to row gently, the water refreshing in the increasingly hot sunshine and the sensation of gliding granting her a momentary respite from pain.

Ruskin, basking in her beauty, wondered if Rose had ever appeared more enchanting as, leaning over the side of the boat and dipping her hand into the water, she peered at her reflection pensively.

'"On either side the river lie long fields of barley and of rye, that clothe the wold and meet the sky; and thro' the field the road runs by to many-tower'd Camelot. The yellow-leaved waterlily, the green-sheathed daffodilly, tremble in the water chilly, round about Shalott",' he recited tenderly, steering the boat towards a shady bank.

'Yes, I suppose this *is* our Camelot,' Rose agreed, struck by the similarities to her own predicament. Looking up at the clear blue sky, disrobed of all morning cloud, she allowed a tear to roll down her cheek unchecked. '"It was the closing of the day: she loos'd the chain, and down she lay; the broad stream bore her far away, The Lady of Shalott."'

Rose's glory was all the more devastating because of the tragedy drawing her away into the other world beyond his reach, and yet Ruskin's experience of despair told him that it was futile to try to lure her back.

Regarding one another intently, he concluded that it was not sadness that made her continue crying but the realisation that they were living out a dream that would end all too soon.

Taking up her hand and pressing it firmly, he declared, 'You do know that you make me as happy as it is possible for a woman to make a man?'

'I have caused you nothing but anguish,' she replied, frustrated that his adoration continued despite her neglect and ill treatment.

'Better all the hurt than to have gone through life without knowing *this*,' he assured. 'From a little girl to now, you have taught me to smile when I didn't want to smile, work when I didn't believe in work, to *live* when there was no reason for living.'

'At least *some* good has come of my existence, then,' Rose replied caustically, for her weakness and lethargy meant that she grew irritated by his passion and vivacity.

Sensing that she was loathe to hear romantic adulation, Ruskin changed to an altogether less serious tack in the hope of cheering her. 'Though I've known some really nice girls in my time, who wouldn't have been nearly so hard on me as you, none of *them* had a slim waist and a straight nose quite to my fancy.'

Laughing and wrinkling her nose at the flattery she was nonetheless pleased to hear, he recognised that his love was waning in the heat of the day and moored the boat downriver, where a glade of drooping willow trees screened them from the blistering midday sun. Here he encouraged her to take a glass of lemonade and recline against him as he read a passage of *Sesame and Lilies*, although there was not one sentence she did not know by heart.

'What chapter would you like next?'

'Of Queens' Gardens,' she answered unhesitatingly.

'The true nature of home?'

She propped herself up on her elbows and recited, 'Yes, "Home, it is a place of peace, of shelter. In so far as it is not this, it is not home." You see? I know it all perfectly.'

'"And wherever a true wife comes,"' Ruskin went on, smiling though the sentiment choked him, '"this home is always round her. The stars only may be over her head; the glow-worm in the night cold grass may be the only fire at her foot: but home is yet wherever she is; and for a noble woman it stretches far round her, better than ceiled with cedar, or painted with vermilion, shedding its quiet light far, for those who else were homeless."'

'Did you write it for me?'

'Of course.' And his heart fluttered like a lovestruck youth as Rose touched his cheek with her delicate hand.

Pausing to regain his self-assurance, Ruskin continued to read and, lulled by the soft tones he imparted to the text, the warm air and the lapping of the water against the boat, Rose began to doze.

Waiting until she was fast asleep before putting the book away, as he looked down on her fair eyelashes and her chest rising and falling peacefully with each breath, he lost all reality and his mind began to dance with the vision of Rose returning to Brantwood, the home he longed to share with her above all. He and Joan might look after her and nurse her back to strength and, at last removed from her parents' dogmatism, she would flourish once more.

So wonderful was this idea to him, Rose in what would be *their* house, woodland and garden, that he could barely wait until she awoke to tell her of his vision. He wanted to describe every detail of Brantwood, including all the improvements he would make, such as an octagonal turret with lattice-leaded windows he would add to the master bedroom so that the awe-inspiring view of Coniston Water would delight them every morn.

'There is no light so breathtaking as when the day first reveals the lake and its quiet shores,' he extolled when once she had awoken, his eyes shining as he described every detail.

'I wish I could see it, for I can well imagine you there,' she returned, careful not to say anything he might interpret as her acquiescence to fulfil his dream.

'I hope you *shall*,' he replied emphatically.

Yet rising and taking a seat in the boat, she avoided his request pointedly. 'Will Joan and Arthur live with you?'

'Who is to say?' Ruskin shrugged, unloosing the boat from its moorings and taking up the helm. 'I shan't ask them, they must come only if they desire it. Meanwhile, I shall live quite alone save for my pets as companions.'

'Animals are one thing but they're not the same as having someone to converse with,' she argued against herself.

'Yes, you're right,' he laughed, unbuttoning his cuff and displaying superficial scars on his right arm. 'I've got a cat, but she scratches, while my dog, a shepherd's, won't do anything wrong and is more dull than I am myself.'

'I don't like the thought of you being lonely,' she remarked sweetly; '*I* know how much solitude can blight a life.'

'Everyone used to call Bruno your husband,' Ruskin recalled with the intention of raising the topic of marriage, though he knew how gravely he erred in doing so.

Rose regarded him forlornly. 'He died last summer, so I suppose that makes me a widow.'

The unintentional blunder made him lose his footing, and when she concluded by announcing matter-of-factly, 'My father and mother want me to return soon and I feel I ought to obey them,' the last hope of changing her mind was obliterated.

Rose was sorry to have tainted the day by the mention of her departure, something she had only raised in order to keep talk of marriage at bay but which cast a shadow over the rest of the afternoon.

To show him that she did not *want* to go away, she invited Ruskin to talk with her a while longer after he assisted her in climbing the stairs to her chamber, for she could barely reach the top without pausing several times to catch her breath and arrest the feeling of faintness.

It seemed against the natural way of things that he should be helping *her* thus, a woman less than half his age, yet his kindness and patience illustrated the depth of his devotion and made her sorry for her earlier cruelty. It would be some time before the bell for dinner would summon the professor away and she longed to recapture their former way of conversing about all manner of things.

Seated opposite as Rose reclined in an armchair, Ruskin observed how the golden glow of evening filled the room and alighted on her hair, putting him in mind of Constable landscapes and hayricks, a sacred country untouched by the suffocating industry of the city. How nice it would be never to see London again and have only one person to care for, he contemplated wistfully, the amber light bathing his love's usually wan face and lending it colour.

'I hardly know what I should do if it were not for kind friends keeping me abreast of all your activities at the university,' she lamented. 'In comparison, there is nothing to enlighten you about *my* life. What to tell you apart from what this or that doctor says about my health?'

'Do not imagine that I am ever too preoccupied to think of *you*. I still spend most of each waking hour wondering what you are doing and if you ever think of me,' he confessed.

Raising her leg, Rose placed her grass-stained cream leather boot on his knee and giggled, indicating that she wished him to remove it. Smiling at this unexpected intimacy, Ruskin knelt before her, unlacing one and then the other with considerable care.

Supremely grateful at being granted such a liberty, he held one of her stockinged feet in his hand, as cold as ice, and his smile turned to an expression full of earnest longing to bring her back to life. The warmth of his ardour was as great as her own morbid resignation, for in looking down upon him with sorrowful, helpless eyes and a gaze fixed more on the next world than the present she captivated him entirely.

Moving closer and taking her hands in his, he kissed them before resting his head on her knee that she might pet him like once she used to when he had a headache. And yet somehow it was not like formerly, or did he merely fancy that her actions had new meaning? Say that her fingers moved through his hair without sensuality and he would send all of heaven to the Devil, for in that one gesture Ruskin felt happiness such as he had not known in ten years.

Looking up solemnly he stole a kiss from her rosebud mouth, insisting boldly, 'You should *never* go home, except to mine.'

Whilst she felt her heart quicken when he pressed his lips against hers, she cowered at him voicing his feelings or displaying them so audaciously, ignoring all that she had said in so doing. Bewildered by the manner and intensity of his affection, she paused before answering in the attempt to collect her thoughts.

But still kneeling, he was unable to bear the wait and shook the arms of her chair like a beggar grappling in the dust for any coin she might deem to throw. 'Won't you answer me? You have a dreadful habit of *not*.'

'What can I say, except that it cannot end as you hope.'

'I sometimes think that having half your love is worse than having none at all,' he vented, rising to his feet impatiently.

'You do have *all*,' she disputed, reaching for his hand but failing to grasp it. 'I'm just not strong enough to be to you what you wish, or return the vehement love you offer me.'

'What I wish?' he repeated resentfully. 'I would take you for wife, for child, for queen, for any shape of fellow spirit your soul can wear if only you would be loyal to me.'

'I have never been anything *but* loyal,' Rose attested, 'but the love of my parents is the only kind that is a real possession to me, that I have any *right* to claim, and that I dare not lose or wound. If a human being can belong to anyone except God I believe a child belongs to their parents, however ignorant they may be.'

'What should you say if He wanted you to belong to me? Your father has convinced you that the love between a man and a woman is a sin when it's the most precious thing in the world. Don't you see, if you told me that you don't *want* to be mine I would leave this very moment? I'd be content to live on the other side of the world if it should not be well for you to come to me, but it must be at the word of your own lips.'

'It's not that I don't desire a new life but because I am broken,' Rose explained, pitying his steadfastness.

'*They* have broken you.'

Regarding him with her mournful blue eyes, she agreed, 'Perhaps, but marrying you would only give you false hope.'

'What uncanny foresight I had when I was a boy and wrote, "O what is Happiness?"' he scorned, moving towards the window where he observed the sunset peeping behind the treetops. '"That precious thing, rare, and in great request, yet seldom found, sought for in various ways in which it seems to be within the reach. Now try! Behold, it yet eludes the searcher's grasp and leads him hopeful on, then disappoints him."'

'How does your holiday go?' Georgiana asked a sombre-looking Ruskin on finding him alone in the library after dinner, one of the rare moments when he was not to be found in Rose's company.

'I lunge from being so happy I can barely walk on the ground to feeling as though I have stepped into the deepest abyss,' he responded darkly.

'Is Rose the same?'

'She's exhausted and can scarcely bring herself to eat more than a few green peas and a strawberry, hence why there's no point in her coming down for dinner,' he answered, rubbing his forehead as she perched herself on the arm of his chair confidentially. 'I know that she is gravely ill,' he went on, 'and fear that she will pass before I am ready.'

'I'm so sorry for you both,' she sighed heavily, resting her hand on his shoulder. 'Perhaps I should have spared you from seeing her.'

'Do not be grieved at bringing us together,' he rejected, looking up at her. 'It is much better as it *is* than as it was. I have had a taste of heaven that I would gladly purchase with the rest of my life. The good that you may be sure of having done me is in my having known, actually, the perfect joy of love. And this after ten years of agony and thirst.'

'You have fought a better fight than you yourself know,' she praised.

'But I am weary of the battle. Rose goes home tomorrow and, whilst I had hoped that these past few days with her might have lasted me a century, I'm already sick with pining for one minute more,' he faltered.

Not pressing him further, Georgiana simply held his hand until he composed himself. He felt no embarrassment at expressing himself thus, for no other friend ever matched her for sheer sympathy, nor her selflessly romantic wish to help him fulfil the dream of a lifetime.

'What will you do when she has gone?'

He shrugged, 'Lock myself in my room I suppose.'

Afraid that the encounter would result in another breakdown, she saw the need to encourage Ruskin to carry on without pausing to reflect on what had been. 'What about your Oxford lectures?'

'I can't face talking to anyone, let alone lecturing,' he dismissed. 'I prayed for Rose to be given to me yesterday morning, and just hours later she was standing in the garden beside me, mine. She will not marry me because I do not love God better than I do *her*, but today came my consolation. It is not her fault but her glory that she cannot love me better; I only wonder that she ever loved me at all.'

PARTING AT TOFT

S TEALING AWAY WITHOUT A WORD THE FOLLOWING HAZY
summer dawn when all Broadlands slumbered and the professor
dreamed of spending another day by her side, Rose continued on
her journey: not with any gladness on knowing how she would be missed,
but shamefaced at her cowardice in avoiding his inevitable appeals to
remain.

Leaving two notes upon the hall table, one for Ruskin, the other for
her hosts, she closed the door behind her as if relinquishing a final chance
of happiness, injuring the man she loved without fully realising the pain
she inflicted upon herself. Preferring to punish rather than redeem, flee
rather than yield, she knew no thought that was not riddled by doubt,
indecision and misgiving, her every action distancing her from the person
she had always sought to be.

Seeking detachment when she most needed comfort, the beauty
of the rejuvenating morning made the wrench all the greater, the sun
illuminating the landscape she had delighted in just hours before and

would perhaps never know again. As Ruskin said, summer days *were* more melancholy than cold and dreary ones when one had no hope.

Every day weaker and more debilitated, Rose decided to break the journey to Ireland by visiting relatives, namely her maternal aunt who had expressed a desire to see her. Whilst Rose stayed with friends in Cheshire, the professor, overwrought by the suddenness of her departure, returned straightway to his modest garret quarters at Herne Hill, where he wrote to Georgiana of his desperation.

> *"I prayed so hard all morning, from first light until I rose, that she might not be taken from me and that I might not have more horror of doubt ahead of me. Get her back for me and give me yet some days with bright morning and calm sunset. I am getting too old to wait. Can't you get her back for me again? I was so foolish and wrong to let her go…"*

As if in answer to his prayers that his recent paradisiacal time with Rose might be extended, if only by another hour, he was born again on being presented with two letters from her the next morning, begging him to join her at Toft: the greatest proof that she too was not easy on having to part and wanted to linger a while longer.

Leaving his work unfinished upon his desk, he raced to Euston station and, taking the first train, was determined to be with her by evening, forever indebted to Rose or God, he knew not which, for allotting him another dose of her sovereignly company.

No reason could have held him back, for he knew himself to be guilty of the most infinite weakness whenever Rose bade him do anything, while the fragility of her life increased his desire to grant her anything she desired, no matter the inconvenience or humiliation.

He cared not how much his self-respect had been bruised in the years spent pursuing Rose with his chivalrous, idealistic love, for how gladly he again rushed forth, as full of courage as a soldier with no armour or weaponry but only the steadfast conviction that justice would ultimately reward him with victory.

***

Evening church was over and Rose chose the longest path through the fields towards Toft Hall, a solitary figure absorbed in a regretful derision of her life. There had been something especially beautiful and poignant in the service, though the wish to do God's will remained very hard and perplexing, she reflected as she went, her head bent in contemplation and her feet sinking into the long, scented and dewy grass, restored to the most vibrant green after days of ceaseless rain. Why did God allow life to be so full of sorrow?

A whole troop of buttercups smiled at her as if in reassurance, each golden chalice throwing back the sunlight and enticing her to take a seat on the ground beside them. She did so and, gathering one of the deep crimson poppies and some of the orchises, white, purple and speckled lilac, she inhaled their scent and momentarily forgot the many unanswered questions which assaulted her.

Falling into a pleasant stupor, allowing her to take pleasure in the environment that Ruskin would shortly share, she was soon overcome with anger on contemplating how to broach what she had learned from her aunt in the interval since their last meeting, tainting everything that had gone before and everything to come.

The shameful revelation persecuted her and shook her faith in both God and the man she had spent a lifetime admiring, and she found herself tearing the flowers in her hands to pieces and sobbing until a little girl, whom she had noticed at church and reminded her of dear Emily, came upon her in the grass and brought her to her senses.

Toft Hall, a seventeenth-century stone manor house built as solidly as a fortress, had a central tower which put Ruskin in mind of an institution, while the harsh-looking slate roof sounded horribly tinny as the warm late summer rain pelted down upon it.

Though cows grazed in the parkland like a typical English idyll and most of the traditions of the Hall were upheld from the time the property had been built, it altogether lacked the charm of Broadlands.

Even as he alighted from the carriage and crunched the gravel beneath his feet, Ruskin feared that he had been deluded in thinking he could recreate the recent joy he and Rose had known in Hampshire.

His impressions worsened when his eyes fell upon the foreboding oak double door, featuring a large lion knocker which fairly growled at newcomers, and he approached the residence with a light tread for fear of disturbing the ominous guard.

Despite hardly knowing his new hosts, his relationship with Rose seemed to be an open secret, although the reserved Leycesters did not share the Cowper-Temples' relaxed approach to the romance, if so it could be called, and from the minute he arrived hardly ever left them alone for fear that their home should be the scene of scandal.

Passing the weekend in meaningless social activities irritated Ruskin, not least because he could only offer Rose the briefest words of affection whenever someone left a room, something which happened by chance rather than design.

He was therefore delighted when Rose invited him to accompany her to church that Sunday, for the walk would give them their first opportunity to talk openly and for him to fathom her reason for inviting him to Cheshire, something he was still mystified by given her coolness.

Wondering how long she intended to delay her return to Ireland, he saw Rose as a young woman misplaced, travelling from one relation or friend's house to another in order to avoid returning to her own. And yet *still* she would not venture with him to Brantwood, the place she surely belonged above all others.

Rose immediately dashed any such hopes and seemed keener to lecture him about religion rather than discuss love. Expressing her disappointment that he no longer habitually attended church and derided his going as a favour to her, she sought to persuade his restoration of faith by cajoling him with a dogmatic rhetoric which only offended him and made him think that he had rushed to her side under false pretences.

'You imagine that, by taking me by the hand and placing me on bended knees in prayer, my old beliefs will come flooding back, but you are sadly mistaken,' Ruskin disillusioned her as they approached the village church of St John the Evangelist, a building he considered ugly and lacking in all spirituality.

'Despite your protestations, here you are entering God's house,' she responded staunchly, her face and tone losing all compassion the more she hectored.

'It is my devotion to *you* that brings me and makes me want to hold your prayer book.'

'With my help, you *can* find God again,' she insisted, taking up his hands like a religious zealot.

He resented the loss of the tender woman she had been such a short while ago and fumed, 'There is only one thing *I* worship, and it is not an invisible being on high who makes judgements on us all.'

'He doesn't only judge us,' she argued, 'but shows us the path when we are lost. You aren't even loyal to atheism, having admitted that you *prayed* that I would send for you. You forget His graciousness in convincing me to do so.'

'I pray not in belief but from despair,' Ruskin responded, impassioned by the futility of explaining himself.

'Even though you repeatedly turn away from Him, I still believe you love Him,' Rose encouraged, clutching the cross around her neck and wringing it fanatically.

'The love I expend on you has taken everything I have and wastes and parches me like the enthusiasms of the old anchorites. I have managed to live all my life without sight of Him, yet I know not how long I could continue without a glimpse of *your* face. My life is no longer my own, as surely as yours is too much His.'

The conversation could not continue, for they had reached the open door of the church where the rector was preparing to greet them on the threshold. Neither Ruskin nor Rose were familiar to him, yet he greeted them as he did his usual congregation, with a beaming smile.

Observing how the newcomers stood arm in arm despite having just concluded a disagreement, the clergyman mistook them for a married couple, much to the professor's delight who reluctantly corrected him before ushering Rose inside.

This misunderstanding, and his companion's obvious embarrassment, prompted Ruskin to spend the duration of the service troubling over how far he was from such a reality. Misjudging Rose's wish to see him as an indication that she might welcome a reiteration of his long-standing proposal, he pressed a note into her hand on which he had written just two heartfelt words.

One look at her expression of horror told him how naive and unwanted his declaration was, however, for when Rose opened the note at the end of the last hymn she flushed scarlet in anger at what she considered his lack of respect in making such an overture in a place of worship, something that mattered greatly to her even if it was of no consequence to him.

As they walked back to Toft Hall after the service, she kicked the dust under her feet and railed, 'I shall leave tomorrow. Nothing would induce me to stay after such an insult.'

'Insult?' he repeated, bewildered. 'You sound just like your mother.'

Stopping in her tracks, her hackles rising, Rose returned, 'Well I might, when the worst of her sordid allegations about you have now been confirmed to me.'

'Kindly tell me, in the plainest language you know, the precise things you have heard said of me,' he begged humbly.

But her train of thought was muddled by rage and she swerved clear of his request. 'Why *must* you persist in trying to court me when I have asked you not to?'

Shocked at such a reaction, which he partly attributed to his views regarding religion, he stooped pitifully and gently retorted, 'Did not you encourage me by asking me to Cheshire?'

'You perceive any friendly gesture of mine as romantic encouragement,' she ridiculed, laughing in his face spitefully.

Baffled by another episode of change just when he thought they had reached an understanding, he interrogated, 'Did not you admit at Broadlands that your feelings were not confined to friendship? It *is* merciless to refuse marrying me simply because I do not love God better than I do *you*.'

'We go round in circles, but where does it get us? Accept that we cannot go on like this and leave me be when I go from this place.' Saying which, she turned and continued along the path unsteadily.

'I would if you'd only tell me why you have altered your manner towards me since last we met,' he called after her, pursuing her at a wary distance until the church was far behind them.

Raindrops fell upon his face as if to cool his temper and he observed that the summer was a distinctly English one, with only a few glimpses of glorious, constant sunshine before the inevitable return of gloom, stifling one by withdrawing light and warmth, just as Rose did; the clear, bright days, so deceptive, were all the more cherished for having led one to imagine that they would last forever.

'Speak plainly and utterly,' Ruskin demanded, frustrated on trailing behind Rose in silence.

Halting in the hope that she would do the same, when she turned he saw, for the first time, hatred in her eyes.

'Though my health is such that I thought it would be wrong to accept your proposal, I believed that we *had* found peace at Broadlands,' she related disconsolately. 'Yet soon afterwards I was shown several appalling, grotesque letters, written by yourself to my aunt, confessing your sin as a young man, the repulsive habit shared by Rousseau. It is *that* which made me invite you here, but the moment you arrived I found myself too shy to question you and chose to keep my disgust to myself. You have pressed me for the truth, so there it is.'

'Truth?' Ruskin scorned. 'In addressing your aunt, who offered to liaise between myself and your mother, I merely sought to illustrate that I am not, and never have been, impotent.'

Ignoring his explanation, she approached him as if to reinforce her resolve. 'What a relief to finally explain why I could *never*, even if I should recover enough health, contemplate marrying a man who so boastfully declares his failings and weaknesses to a lady he barely knows!'

'Your family burn my letters and ask me to write more,' he rejected, 'yet I'm the fool for having fallen into their trap, having always trusted that *you* would be wise enough to see through such devilish misrepresentations. Have you not known me long enough to judge my character for yourself?'

'You are, and have been, dear to me, but I *must* turn away from you, though I will not judge or condemn you.'

'That's precisely what you are doing, despite the fact that the sins of my youth are passed away and I know myself to be entirely worthy of you, although I am no saint,' he asserted with pride. '*You* are, but a cruel one. I have never tried to hide my faults; what good there is in me you have the power to learn if you will.'

'Your love to me, your great perceptions of all that is lovely, your gifts, *everything* that God has given you, make me recoil from you now,' Rose despaired, covering her eyes as if struggling to look on him. 'When I think of what you might have been, to Christ, to other human souls, to *me*! How the angels must have sorrowed and wept over you! How my heart is sorrowing still!'

'You talk as if I am beyond redemption.' Ruskin shook his head, resentful that he was allowing this young woman to appraise him.

'I am overpowered with the mysterious ghastliness of my discovery, nor do I wonder that your faith is shipwrecked! Better never to have known the ways of righteousness than, after you had known them, turn aside.' And she shook with the violence of her abhorrence.

'Your faith is the most unforgiving, unchristian kind I have ever witnessed,' he scorned.

'I cannot blot out one single stain, not if I could lay down my life for you; all I can do is to speak to you of Christ, for at His feet we might meet, in His love we might be drawn together again. In His forgiveness and atonement the horror of your sins might not be removed but turned into the joy of bringing you to Him, to be again as a little child.'

Perceiving the rift between them if he did not do as she asked, he made a martyr of himself. 'I am ready to do anything you ask if only *you* will absolve me. Will you forgive me and be to me as you were if I agree to love Him and repent as you say?'

'It would cleanse you of your past indeed,' she assured him, sceptical of his sincerity, 'but *have* you repented? Do you really believe in Christ and Eternity?'

Rose claimed not to judge, but did so mercilessly, addressing Ruskin in the most abrupt and unkind manner from thenceforward, nor did his attempt at atonement alter her determination to leave Cheshire the next day.

Though he insisted upon accompanying her on the train to Crewe, she became increasingly cross and fractious, ignoring his appeals to redeem their last few moments together and set aside all bitterness.

Seated opposite Ruskin in an otherwise empty first-class compartment, Rose rested her face against the glass, staring out of the window in order to avoid looking at him. He could hardly bear the silence, for every second seemed to damn their remaining time together, whilst hastening her imminent departure. Nor did she appreciate his gesture of apology when he presented her with a sketch of an olive branch.

'I don't want any more drawings or books written for me!' Rose spurned, discarding the highly detailed pencil drawing as carelessly as she might have thrown a confectionery wrapper onto the floor.

Leaving the work where it lay, he could not help but ask, 'Where does this wanton destruction come from? It is an experience for me to know what "possession" truly means.'

Overwhelmed with unconscious fury and the doubt thrown on their ever meeting again, Rose convinced herself that it *would* be better for them both if she broke off all contact finally. The professor, if not herself, still had a chance of finding someone else to love.

'I want you to forget me! I shan't see you again,' she continued, castigating him by repeating her parents' old arguments for mile after mile of the journey.

'No friend could have behaved more cruelly than you in forcing me to endure this farewell,' Ruskin could only respond, his sole comfort the certainty that she acted hysterically.

With neither of them knowing how to say goodbye, there was at least consolation in an end, however unpleasant, for neither of them wanted to live through another separation of uncertain length.

He feared for Rosie's state of mind as she continued to channel her mother's vindictiveness, transforming the sweet and gentle girl he had fallen in love with into a disturbed young woman who used the Bible and God to rail at him.

Nor did she have any awareness that her behaviour aroused the consternation of other travellers; everyone who passed through the carriage peered into their compartment to witness Rose's face contorted in the vehemence of the diatribe she directed at her companion. What had started out as a journey Ruskin wished to extend station by station became one that could not reach its destination soon enough.

With Rose bound for the Holyhead steamer, when the train pulled into the station at Crewe she stepped onto the platform without so much as saying goodbye and, calling to a porter to assist with her luggage, slammed the door behind her. Ruskin was too astonished to do anything but continue to watch her as she staggered away, half mad, half starved.

As the whistle blew and the locomotive began to fire up again, as set upon its course as his beloved, he leant out of the window, distraught at the sight of her wasted figure disappearing amidst the billowing steam, for she did not turn back or hesitate. The thought that *this* was the conclusion to their brief empyrean August was agonising.

As he settled back in his seat, regarding the drawing of the olive branch lying trodden and torn, he recalled her most evil words. Did she hate him or simply want to punish him for her own feebleness in conceding to the will of her parents, God and Christ?

He dug his fingernails into the palms of his hands until the pain distracted him. Christian or no, was she not crucifying him with no intention of taking him down from the cross? It was with this in mind that he scratched in his diary that night the words of Jesus, "It is finished."

On reaching Euston, the mental torment had worked its way to the professor's limbs and there was no going any further. Not only did his head ache, but his arms and legs were as tired as if he had been climbing Everest whilst carrying a pair of boulders.

Reserving a small room at the station hotel for an indefinite period, regardless of not having completed his next series of lectures, Ruskin found himself weeping and raging like the furies, for temptress Rose had slipped through his fingers again and who knew if she would condescend to beckon him for a third time? Or if he would be senseless enough to allow her.

Joan visited with the Burne-Joneses following receipt of a confused scrawl of events, yet he was too absorbed in what had just befallen him to benefit from either their sympathy or their company.

'It's good of you all to come and see me, but you shan't want to remain long, I assure you.'

'This place is enough to depress anyone,' Joan observed, appalled by the tired, damp-ridden suite of rooms with peeling wallpaper.

'The room is of no consequence, I am too grief-stricken to notice. It seems that it is my lot to bear all things.' And, sighing heavily, Ruskin pulled up the sheets to his chin as if intending to hide from the world.

'We all feel for you, but you can't stay at the Euston Hotel forever,' Joan censured, ready with matronly encouragement. 'Just *imagine* what your mother would have said.'

'All I seem to do is move from one hotel to another, it matters very little where it is.'

'Won't you come home with me?' she urged.

'And where pray is *home?*'

'Herne Hill, as you know very well. You would have been content to stay there forever as a boy, so it is sure to restore you now.'

'But it is not *my* home any longer,' he denied.

'That is a horrid thing to say, when you have always called it so before,' she reproached.

Ignoring this, Ruskin turned to Ned and, handing him the photograph of Rose he always carried, enquired, 'Did you ever think Rose like Swinburne's Dolores?'

'I can't say that it ever occurred to me,' the artist admitted, merely glancing at Rose's profile due to his resentment towards the woman who over and again caused so much distress.

Ruskin, consumed by frenzy, pointed to the photograph and recited, '"Cold eyelids, which hide, like a jewel, hard eyes that grow soft for an hour. Icy white limbs and a cruel red mouth like a venomous flower." I always said, if Rose hadn't a pretty nose and red lips, what should I care for her?'

'Speaking as your friend, I am glad that the lady of perplexity and pain has gone on her way,' Ned insisted. 'May there never be need to mention her sweet, sad name again!'

After almost a week in bed, spent by reading passages of poetry he interpreted to suit his own feelings, Ruskin finally ventured outside, not to look for light or joy but rather to add to his own cup of unhappiness the woes of others.

Touring the squalid neighbouring slums backing onto the railway line, the bleak environment, where no flowers grew nor sun seemed to penetrate, suited his mindset, nor did he consider himself much better off than the inhabitants, for the happiness of souls, he well knew, could not always be attributed to financial security on the one hand or poverty on the other. He had riches far beyond his needs and yet no love with whom to share them.

Knowing himself to be in the deepest and most unconquerable of mental declines, he reasoned that even the sanest of men would experience a bout of the blackest melancholy after the treatment he had received from Rose. The only way he could save himself from drowning in such wallowing was to accept his current psychopathy as a natural and temporary consequence of recent events.

To add further injury to his wounds, a letter arrived from Rose which, instead of being the apology he might have expected, was filled with the same defamations she had subjected him to on the train. Emphatically forbidding him to reply, his indignation told him that he was not yet insane enough to keep tolerating such behaviour and would surely expire if he did so for much longer.

Once again his survival instinct impelled him to carry on and leave behind his miserable lodgings in Euston – the thick, quiet despair on the personal question encouraging him to go forth with fire and sword on the universal one.

The only thing possible was to persevere in all that he had been endeavouring to do. He could not measure what else he would have to endure, nor what those who loved him might suffer on his behalf, yet there was so much dependent upon him that he believed strength would be given him to bear, and to carry out, what he must.

Persuaded to travel to Coniston with Joan in order to oversee essential repairs and alterations to Brantwood, residing at the Waterhead Hotel provided a welcome tonic while the house was overrun with workmen, for he could not feel comfortable in any place, least of all the one he had always hoped to share with another.

There were decisions to be made as to his preference for this or that fitting, wood or paint, yet his mind was too confused from recent brain fog to care. What did any of it matter if *she* would never see it?

The following Sunday he found himself attending church, a sinner among sinners. Yet stranger still was the occurrence that happened on leaving the service; passing through the burial ground where one day he would be at rest, he was interrupted by a messenger who thrust a packet from Rose into his hand.

As if she had somehow foreseen his desire to attend church, in order to ask for forgiveness or otherwise, he was disheartened to open it and discover his most recent letter enclosed, having been unable to uphold her request to remain silent when he was entitled to defend himself.

Doubly deflated when he saw that she had returned it unopened, he rowed to Brantwood as fast as his arms would steer him in order to find Joan and rage a little. So relieved was he to come across her in the kitchen, sorting through the first autumn bounty from the walled garden, that he sat upon the floor and cradled his head in his hands.

Shaking his head dejectedly he asked, 'What is one to do when the thing one has been praying for turns out to be not worth the prayer? But then perhaps Rose feels the same. She has been praying for me and finds that I am only an ordinary mortal.'

'She isn't solely to blame,' Joan reasoned. 'You have more cause to be angry with those who have driven her to this kind of fanaticism than reason to be angry with her.'

'I regret ever having stepped foot in church today.'

She looked up from what she was about and sighed. 'Whatever your motivation in going to church, Rose would still be pleased to know that you went.'

'Yes, among other deadlinesses, she has contrived to make me religious again,' he scorned, munching a carrot which Joan had just scraped clean.

'Although you're now endeavouring to attend church on Sundays, we all know that if at last you didn't get Rose that would be an end to your praying,' his cousin shrugged.

'Perhaps I shall keep it up regardless,' Ruskin denied, smiling at the jibe. 'The infinity of God is not mysterious, it's unfathomable. Not concealed, only incomprehensible. As incomprehensible as why people choose to eat Brussels sprouts.' Saying which, he shuddered at the sight of one of Joan's baskets filled to the brim with an early crop, causing her to laugh heartily.

'I have never been more amazed by your redoubtable spirit and perceive that you are glad to re-examine a lifetime of conflicting beliefs in Christianity,' she suggested, something Ruskin did not attempt to deny, for religion *did* offer him comfort at the worst of times, though he saw his need of it as no more than weakness.

With Rose vanished into the darkness again, vengeance gave Ruskin no solace, and thus he attempted to isolate their sorrowful parting at Crewe from those miraculous days when she had permitted him to hold her in his arms and kiss her as she rested: a week of perfect life that had flown by faster than he was prepared for, yet which had contained more meaning than all the summers of his existence.

Receiving no further word, he was still desperate to hear of Rose through mutual friends and requested that Mrs Cowper-Temple try her powers of persuasion:

"She returned my last letter unopened, so now I have no resource but you, as of old. Can't you get her to write to me again? My fault was letting her see that I still hoped, but she need never fear my having any more."

639

CRESSIDA AND TROILUS

ALTHOUGH HE DID NOT RECOVER HIS COMPOSURE AT once, Ruskin found himself ready for new work and challenges by the following spring when he began to reap the pleasures he had sown.

On fair days and foul, he took delight in the strenuous exertion of assisting Downs in the garden at Brantwood, working until every muscle in his body ached and his hands were as blistered as if he'd plunged them into acid: his moans of agony a means of venting the mental anguish it was not possible to express so violently in any other environment. In that peaceful, fruitful realm, where, set apart from railroads and steam engines, heaven and earth met, Ruskin reigned as gentle monarch, leading by example creatures who were never idle.

Having always found the pain of physical toil a cathartic one, he never felt more alive than when he took up pitchfork to plough the earth, or chop firewood with an axe he had to muster all his strength just to lift. Considering no man above sweating or getting dirt under his nails to create his own kingdom, there was no more satisfying an occupation than the manual exertion of perfecting one's dwelling place, not merely to suit himself but to make all who lived alongside him content and happy.

He also supervised the repair and reconstruction of the neglected, dilapidated harbour, with the idea of building a new lodge for Crawley and his family, for nothing gave him more delight than by showing his appreciation towards his most loyal staff whom he regarded as his own kin and would look after accordingly, to the end of their days if not his own.

Introducing himself to his new neighbours, Ruskin was soon established as a charming, if peculiar, middle-aged gentleman landowner within the larger community, all of whom were fascinated whenever they caught sight of his scrawny, lithe figure dressed in an old-fashioned frock coat with a worn velvet lapel. He strode with great haste, as if he had only a month to live and must set about things with urgency, whether on one of his walks along the quiet country lanes or when carrying out daily errands in the village – there being no charge or assignment too small or menial for him to take up, nor would he ever ask anyone to do that which he was not prepared to do himself.

The solitude he always claimed to have craved, yet secretly feared, he needn't have troubled himself about, for by the summer Joan and Arthur had installed themselves at Brantwood with their first child, Lily: a bonny baby as gentle-natured and amiable as her mother, who confirmed that the house was a new beginning.

As soon as the old harbour had been repaired with the help of Arthur, an enthusiastic sailor, boating became a favourite pastime and Ruskin made daily excursions to the hub of Coniston simply by rowing across to the opposite shore.

It was his habit to take a drink with the locals at the Black Bull, just across the road from the church of St Andrew where he continued to appear on Sundays, and for the first time in his life, despite perceiving that many considered him an unusual character, he felt a true sense of community, solidarity and belonging.

Refusing the Cowper-Temples' invitation to join them whilst they were hosting Rose, he tried to banish memories of their last encounter at Crewe whilst preserving those treasured few days at Broadlands.

Thinking of his love amidst the Hampshire landscape in which they had wandered not so long ago prompted him to dream that Rose gave herself to him as sweetly in body as Cressida to Troilus: increasing his torment tenfold when he awoke and filling him with a fatal longing for beautiful womanhood, for skin as pure and bright as the moon and lips never a lover had kissed.

The only thing that cooled his yearning was finding himself at Brantwood, a serene spot set apart from worldly or emotional struggles, positioned high above life's mysterious unknowns and imponderables. He was among the land and people he cherished and resigned himself to Shakespeare's truism, "To be wise and *love* exceeds man's might".

The gloom which Ruskin had been wrestling with for years was harder to shake off when once he was away from Coniston, however, and following the familiar pattern of residing at Oxford for the Michaelmas term, soon Christmas in London was upon him. Not that he could feel any particular gladness at the prospect of attending pantomimes and feigning merriment with the Severns, the new family of Herne Hill.

It made his heart glad to see his dear Joanna revel in the joys of family life in his former childhood sanctuary, yet it was all he could do not to allow jealousy to take root, it being strange and isolating whenever he recalled the Christmases of his youth in that very place and liken *those* to the first festivities of little Lily Severn whose experiences appeared a great deal happier than his own.

Exhausted from over-indulgent meals, lack of work and being cooped up by the hearth bouncing his goddaughter fondly on his knee, Ruskin went in search of Turner's Margate during the New Year, countless months having gone by without a single word from Rose, nor any prospect of another reconciliation.

He could not have said why he chose to go to Margate over returning to Brantwood, other than that it was the place the artist he admired above all others had gone whenever *he* wanted to be quit of people, a well-considered curative for a mind as crammed full of bittersweet memories as Turner's old cluttered studio on Queen Anne Street.

After selecting a modest, yet clean and decent inn with plenty of character for a few weeks, Ruskin occupied himself by taking bracing morning walks along the seafront where he attempted to recreate Turner's greatest landscapes, though it was hard to prevent the paper from flying away like a kite belonging to one of the children who so often interrupted his view and increased his sadness with their laughter and play.

Returning to the inn in time for luncheon, his face tingling from the biting January wind and his clothes permeated by the salty sea air, he would make himself comfortable in the bow-windowed parlour overlooking the beach as he tucked into a chop and some good cheese, yet everything tasted bland and he found that he had no appetite.

Loathing his own company as much as everyone else's back at Herne Hill, the pendulum between contentment and discontentment swung back and forth like a clock that never needed winding. Just like pilgrim Rose, he was a lost soul, unsure of where he belonged. When he had a city dwelling all he desired was a glimpse of the Lakes of England, but now that he had *them* only the sea would do.

Despite detesting what a bore he had become, he felt all the better for the sight of the crashing, tumultuous waves, and it was equally pleasant to look upon skies recommended to him by his late artist friend, who had quite rightly described the sunset over the Isle of Thanet as the loveliest in all Europe.

Along with the unique light which that part of Kent boasted, where the rays of the sun broke through the pink fleecy clouds in heaven-like shafts, the weather of that New Year was unpredictable, wild and at times tranquil enough to rejuvenate any man's senses and prepare him for whatever else was in store. As so often before, Ruskin resolved during those lonely days that nothing could come that he could not bear. However long Rose was kept from him and whatever she did to him, he would not fear, nor grieve, but *wait*.

SWEET BRIAR

K NOWING ONLY ISOLATION IN IRELAND, ROSE GREATLY regretted having spurned Ruskin so brutally all those months ago, and her health went into sharp decline upon realising the consequence of her remorseless attack.

This was coupled with disappointment that the man she had always revered after Christ, and far above her own father, had turned out to be just like any other, with weaknesses that threw her high opinions of him into jeopardy however much she hated to believe her mother.

Worn down from being in constant pain, she never felt so ill and exhausted as when the tidings of the season were finally over and the tedium of having to pass another Christmas at Harristown was at an end. They were almost unrecognisable to the people who used to sit around the table together laughing and playing games as Bruno slept contentedly at her feet, while Percy was almost as much of a ghost as her dear, sweet sister in her grave: his eyes and cheeks hollow with unhappiness, while his plain, nonchalant wife hardly ever participated in conversation, replying to questions with a single word and never enquiring anything in return.

Any dreams Rose had of finding a friend and confidant in her sister-in-law had been dashed the instant she had been introduced to the proud Lady Annette, whose sole interests consisted of hunting, entertaining and dressing in gowns from Paris, another shallow figure in a society and family in which she felt no sense of belonging.

Yes, if only in order to get away, Rose was glad to put herself in the hands of her Dublin doctor and be entirely under his care for as long as he liked. Her parents did not deny her attempt to find a remedy, however hopeless they considered it, for Percy, despite his weakness when it came to his own life, saw to it that they would never more try to control or interfere in her treatment.

The great churning, industrious city had grown considerably since she was a girl and she was inclined to tiptoe cautiously for fear of being pushed aside by the throngs of workmen pouring out of the factories and offices every evening only to find a numbing kind of solace in liquor. Desperate poverty rubbed shoulders with excessive wealth, making Rose question her own lifestyle, though it was far humbler than other members of her family.

Yet just the sight of the rippling, ice-cold Liffey reassured her and tamed her rising despondency, for she was glad to be standing there rather than by the streamlet flowing through Harristown. She saw the river as the soul of Dublin and crossed each bridge connecting left bank to right, careless of the hours she was absent and allowing her imagination to recall the many occasions when she and the professor had walked along the Thames: his philosophies and ideals flooding into her consciousness and imbuing her with a social awareness far greater than any religion ever could.

She was at least proud of her own sense of reality, for it seemed that other women of her class preferred to close their eyes to the extremes around them and the hardships so many suffered as a result of being born into inescapable destitution. Rose scorned the carefully defined limits of her mother and father's benevolence and felt a pang to think how much more *she* might have done to change things if only she had made a life with the professor. Didn't he always say how greatly his Irish Rose influenced him?

The physician's Georgian townhouse, accommodating his large, bustling family upstairs and his well-respected consulting practice on the ground floor, was situated on the salubrious Merrion Square, a familiar spot to Rose where she would take fresh air whenever the opportunity afforded.

Going to church every morning in a city where its inhabitants were as divided about religion as they were financially was nothing if not discordant with her beliefs, although the anonymity of city life suited her much better than the country.

Careful never to attract attention to herself through flamboyancy of dress or mixing in the social circles in which her mother had once desired her to reign, all the company Rose needed was an hour or so with Percy, who took tea with her most days at the Shelbourne: their closeness having remained from her sanatorium days, though they never discussed their parents or Ruskin, both recognising the pointlessness of regret unless one was either able or willing to change things.

The relentless, unfathomable pain she experienced gave her an unpleasant awareness of every fibre of her being, from her aching fingers when she held a pen, to joints as stiff and inflexible as an old woman's when she walked as little as a few hundred yards.

The weeks she spent in Dublin seemed more like waiting for death rather than recuperation and were passed in hollow observation of the metropolis she stood on the periphery of. There was a vividness to all she saw, however, and the more her body failed her in one way the keener she felt an intuitive love towards her brethren and country.

The sparrows and nightingales over St Stephen's Green, along with the jovial native accent of a newspaper boy calling out, were terrifically harmonious, mingling as they did with the sounds of Irish folk music played by street urchins who roamed the park in search of a generous patron touched by the music they remembered from their youth.

The mildness of the New Year, when the bright days made one forget that it was still winter and that hands would soon numb, allowed Rose to take up a corner bench in the park most afternoons, alone except for a few passing strangers.

Yet, no matter how long she tried to read the Ruskin volume on her lap, purchased from a Dublin bookshop the moment she arrived, it was not possible to retain any of his words like once she used to. Even on reaching the end, it was as though she had never turned the pages, for all she could think about was her own existence and what a waste it had been.

What had she learned from life? To expect nothing. To plant seeds and expect no flowers. To give and expect no thanks. To be grateful, to make a very little go for much, as the birds in the park did who found half-frozen crumbs and still sang on a winter's day. She had learned what suffering was, yet perhaps understood joy more fully because of it. How wrong she had been to chastise and punish her only friend!

The book in her hand only overwhelmed her with its beauty and wisdom, making her resentful of the life she had spurned. Born almost thirty years apart, what an unlikely couple she and the professor would have made, she mused in the chill twilight. And yet their affection defied all reason or norm and an intangible thread united them in spite of all they had faced, and which even now drew her back to him.

Didn't they both have the same way of seeing the world – nature *and* people? The same blind faith in being able to alter wrongs and restore values? Yes, she admitted forlornly, closing the volume and rising to leave before allowing herself any vain tears, she still loved and respected him beyond measure.

Knowing not if she had been made mad by illness or her parents, or whether insanity had been to blame all along, Rose nevertheless returned to the doctor's house with more certainty in her step, for she meant the doctor to admit that he was helpless to restore her health so that she might pack up her things and travel to London.

A desire to rekindle her friendship with Joan and re-establish a link with the professor compelled her to make yet another reckless action with no assured outcome, yet just the thought distracted her from the debilitating pain assaulting her brain and limbs and gave rise to the most miraculous feeling of elation.

The torture she must undergo in order to rise, get dressed and exist for another pointless twelve hours until the partial respite of bed called to her again! It would take Herculean fortitude to leave Ireland, she well knew, but if there was some prospect of fulfilment ahead she would brave anything. Surely Joan and Ruskin would grant her friendship again and pardon her erratic changeableness?

'Doctor Logan, I wonder if I might speak with you?' Rose asked timidly, entering his consulting room when his last patient had departed.

'Why of course, take a seat,' he offered, rising in a gentlemanly fashion and holding out a leather armchair on which all manner of ailments had been diagnosed.

'I was wondering if you perceive me to have made any progress in the months that I have been here?' she asked frankly. 'I have never asked you this before, but I feel that things cannot go on indefinitely without my confronting the peculiar situation in which I find myself. Namely, *what*, if anything, is to be done with me?'

The doctor sighed and, leaning his forearms on the desk, shook his head doubtfully. 'It greatly distresses me to admit that, like the long line of physicians you consulted before me, I am unable to find an adequate cause or solution to your ailing strength, nor can I suggest you remain here if you wish to go elsewhere in search of treatment. Rather selfishly, myself and my family have grown too fond of you to *prompt* you to leave, especially when I gather that you might be happier here than returning home.'

'That is certainly the case and I am most grateful for your professional attention and the warmth you have all shown towards me. I may not leave cured, but I am a deal happier and clearer in my mind than I was. For that reason I do not intend to return to Harristown, but plan to look up old friends in London.'

The physician repeated with some surprise, 'Friends?'

'You imagined I had none?' Rose baulked. 'Perhaps you mistake my enforced loneliness for something I have *chosen*.'

The doctor rose from his seat and stood looking out over the square where he had observed his patient go almost daily. He would be sorry to see her go and asked, 'Is it not true that you often choose to be alone when my house is full of companionship, Miss La Touche?'

'Your people are not *my* people, Doctor Logan,' she replied boldly.

'Save for your brother, you have nothing much to do with your own kind as I can see,' he continued, pressing her in the hope of gleaning a reaction more passionate than the sharp, defensive words which reminded him of the young lady's elegant, incisive mother, a woman who settled his account with more questions than he could provide answers.

But Rose had no intention of explaining herself and asked abruptly, 'If you are so concerned that I should have company, might you arrange a nurse to travel with me?'

'I advise you to think again,' he cautioned; 'the journey will almost certainly be too much for you.'

'I must go *somewhere*,' she denied, 'and I refuse to go home. Surely there is more hope of me being well among the people I wish to be with than those I emphatically do *not*?'

She pitied the physician for being faced with the limitations of his profession, for hadn't the dear, kind, useless man been incapable of fixing her because she was not inclined to save herself?

There was an occasion when her desire to live might have stopped the rot, when she could have risen one morning and steered her life on its rightful course, but she had let her body waste away to such an extent that it would make no difference how hard she thought herself out of it now.

Nonetheless, the idea that she might achieve absolution from the one she cherished most gave her a surprising energy, no matter if it hastened the end. The interval since she had abandoned Ruskin at the station had been bitterly unhappy, for she felt that her judgement had been more reprehensible than *his* crime and she could never get well while there was ill feeling between them.

"I wonder what Some People are about just now. Joanie, do you think I shall ever see him again? I sometimes wonder if you and your Arthur have thought at the bottom of your hearts that we weren't meant to be so far apart – or not? Do you think he has forgiven me for my behaviour at Crewe Station? I cannot help coming out with all this, for somehow a blight seems to have got at the very stalk of my life and I shall never grow out of it."

Ruskin returned to Herne Hill after the summer, bearded and all the brighter for an extensive European adventure, yet his good mood withered like the windblown flowers when he discovered that Rose had stationed herself in London several weeks ago and that Joan, who was soon to become a mother to a second child, had visited her on numerous occasions without once mentioning it in her letters.

With the change of season and climate came an initiation that troubled and perplexed him like the furies. Scratching his head impatiently when his cousin revealed her subterfuge one chill, quiet Sunday, he scorned Rose for yet another turnabout and Joan for allowing herself to become embroiled in it.

'And what is Rose doing with herself these days?'

'Trying to get well,' she answered carefully.

'Wandering the world in search of a health cure, you mean?'

Joan sighed before responding and, taking a seat beside Arthur, who continued to scan his art journal as though not paying any attention, explained, 'She has seen several doctors, yes, but has no real hope of improving. I'm not sure *that* was her motivation in travelling to London.'

'No, to plague me was the reason!' Ruskin assailed. 'She is always well enough to do that.'

'It took a great deal of effort for her to come,' Joan refuted, 'even accompanied by a nurse, for she is not strong enough to travel, or *be*, on her own.'

'Perhaps her parents made it a condition for fear that I would snatch her away,' he growled, throwing himself down in the armchair opposite.

'It has more to do with the fact that Rose and her mother are practically estranged; it would be inappropriate for her to stay in hotels alone.'

'That never stopped her before. I hear from George MacDonald that she is more a resident of the Shelbourne than Harristown.'

'She is indeed misplaced,' his cousin returned sadly, looking down.

And then it occurred to Ruskin to ask the most important question, 'Where is she staying *now*?'

'The Queen's Hotel,' came the quiet answer, for Joan was apprehensive of his reaction to Rose residing less than a mile away.

'The Queen's?' Ruskin jolted. 'Why must she come here and harass me? While it's obvious that she's manipulating *you* to just that end.'

'You are spoiling for an argument,' she observed, rising to go.

'Stay, I apologise for being fractious,' he atoned, taking hold of her arm as she brushed past him. 'Please be brave enough to tell me,' he pleaded, 'does Rose hate me now, as mad people do, or only not speak of me? I am always thinking she hates me. The idea has driven *me* mad all the time I've been away.'

'She is very sorry for her behaviour towards you.' And Joan handed him Rose's initial communication filled with remorse, while she and Arthur exchanged an anxious glance.

'This is all very interesting,' he dismissed, folding the letter and handing it back, 'but I still say she should address me, if only to give me some comfort, for the very beauty of the heavens and earth have tormented me since she has been silent. What does she want from me if she won't marry me? Absolution? No. *She* cannot be allowed to say in her heart, peace, when there is no peace.'

'That is because it is far from over between you,' his cousin reasoned.

'Rose seems appointed to break me down just when I am resigned to my fate or am coming to a leap.'

'And yet she has been at the root of all your best work, you always say so,' Joan contradicted, crossing her arms.

'Fie! You want me to be compassionate when another anniversary of my proposal has just passed? A day I ever recall with mortification due to its suspended conclusion.'

'I don't often venture my opinion,' Arthur interrupted, 'but it seems to me that if you both love one another enough to marry, then you ought to, and she should leave father and mother and cleave to *you!*'

'I appreciate you saying that,' he thanked, 'but I feel as though I have been slowly murdered for years. If Rosie does ever come to me I do not think she will complain of being too little loved, but *she* cannot remember my mother's final hours. Dearest Joanie, you have been a mother and a sister in one,' Ruskin said, taking up her hand and kissing it before turning to her husband. 'You do *know* how fortunate you are?'

'Indeed I do,' Arthur asserted, too used to such declarations to be offended or jealous.

'At least I am not so removed from Rose now that you are our intermediary again.'

'A role I continue to carry out faithfully. She has appointed me to tell you that she doesn't want to write to you, she wants to *see* you.'

'I guessed that from her choice of hotel, but you can say that I'll be damned if I see her illicitly after all that passed last time,' he avowed. '*I* have nothing to hide and nor can she if she wishes to put things right. Rose must tell her parents of her intention to meet with me before I will so much as *look* on her.'

The fashionable Queen's Hotel, standing on the brow of the hill, goaded Ruskin through the barred window of the garret *pied-à-terre* he occupied, leaving him unable to work or think of anything but Rose's proximity.

Though he had to strain in order to glimpse it, he tormented himself by standing upon a chair morning, noon and night simply in order to look upon her chosen dwelling, devoid of all the comforts of home.

Gracious enough to accompany Joan on the short stroll to The Queen's for her afternoon meeting the next day, his magnanimity stopped there and, refusing to enter even the lobby, he stubbornly went on his way, though his cousin had expected him to surrender.

His brow was as troubled as the skies overhead, his steps heavy and the hairs on the back of his neck on end as he speculated whether Rose was watching him from her window – his only consolation an immature delight on imagining her disappointment on seeing him walk away, for hadn't he a right to show his animosity?

More than a fortnight was wasted in such stupidity, and while the women had one another for company he would occupy himself by playing chess for several hours a day with the famed automaton at the Crystal Palace, a game he was hardly surprised to lose.

Were they discussing him over tea? Or, even worse, perhaps they barely mentioned him. Not for the first time, he found himself wildly envious of his cousin's ability to reconnect with Rose so effortlessly, but then *she* had not known an ounce of his grief.

His determination to stand firm was only exacerbated by the biblical texts Joan passed on to him from Rose each day, for what good was it to say, "Be strong and of courage. Fear not, for the Lord thy God is with thee whithersoever thou goest"?

He did not wonder that so many of his friends, who had witnessed the harm Rose had done, found it impossible to forgive her and advised him to save himself from being drawn into the familiar circle of joy followed by destruction. Yet still he found himself defending her whenever they said so much as a word against her.

Subsequently harangued with a stream of heartfelt letters from Rose, Ruskin promised himself that it would take more than that to change his mind, and so he persisted in his stubbornness until Mrs La Touche, concerned by reports of her daughter's refusal to eat until she saw him, wrote to Joan blessing their reunion in as curt a manner as possible.

However brief the content, it was still astonishing enough to prompt his cousin to rush home with the news. 'Rose's parents no longer oppose your contact with her, and you can see her as much as you both please,' she beamed, her face fairly falling when she perceived that, instead of being jubilant, Ruskin viewed the acquiescence as confirmation of the gravity of Rose's plight, a death warrant in disguise.

He would have liked to have received Mrs La Touche's condescending pardon with ambivalence, refusal even, being resentful of that woman holding any power over him, and yet he could not.

Distrustful after all the evil she had filled her daughter's head with, and conscious of the need to protect himself from any further emotional injury, he nevertheless gladly accepted the gift of being uninhibited to offer Rose the companionship she desired above all else.

'Dear Sweet Briar!' he exclaimed, finding her resting upon the sofa coddled in countless blankets which emphasised her slight frame.

He was shocked to find Rose more emaciated and wan than ever, and that she ate nothing apart from what she liked, chiefly an occasional sugared almond, a small heap of which sat untouched in a crystal dish on the tea table beside her.

'I am so glad to see you,' she smiled tenderly, for she was embarrassed that he should find her thus diminished.

'I had no idea how much strength it took for you to come here, or I should have called on you sooner,' he uttered apologetically, for he was mortified at his immature behaviour that past fortnight.

'My determination to have your forgiveness gave me boundless energy for the journey; it was only when I arrived that God asked for it back in lieu. But I don't mind a bit now that you are in the same room as me,' she proclaimed, holding out her hand. 'Speak to me as you used to do, that we may know each other's hearts again.'

Not ready to accept her overture without first reminding her of the pain she had inflicted, he continued to stand awkwardly in the middle of the floor, unsure how to proceed or protect himself from the boundless love she conjured up with one word.

Looking down at his broken Rose sorrowfully, he spoke with a power which surprised even himself, 'I thought, before I saw you, that you could never undo the evil you have done, but just seeing you brings me back to life and puts the past away as if it had not been.'

'Yes, though we have much to settle and forgive, I feel sure that there will be no more quarrelling or misunderstandings,' she announced with a sigh of the deepest relief. 'I came to make amends for all my inconsistencies and wrongs, though they were not always my fault.'

'You could not continue to blame your parents after your coming of age,' he denied.

'That is true, but nor could I shrug off my sense of duty to them, instilled in me from birth. The thing that always troubled me most about our friendship was the thought of disobedience.'

'Do you still say *friendship?*'

'It began as such and so it must end,' Rose confirmed regretfully. 'I am in search of reconciliation, but I want it with *everyone.*'

'And you shall have it so long as you promise never to leave me as you once did. You cannot drive me from your memory or heart any more than your parents can be excised from your conscience.' And he leant over her and kissed her golden head devotedly, just as he had a long time ago in the drawing room of Broadlands.

Falling into their old ways of frank discussion and silent interludes, proving the alignment of their sympathies despite the warring years which had shaken and finally restored their faith in one another, there was a serenity in the enormity and inevitability of Rose's demise, in the certain parting that would follow mellow evenings of inconsequential talk which mattered not but offered comfort, as if the end was further away than they both knew.

Ruskin's return walk to Herne Hill was short, yet enriched with memories of boyhood and the dawning realisation that he was akin to a man whose wife lay dying. This, coupled with knowing every house, fence, tree and imperfection along the road, was a peculiar sensation, for it was as though Rose had chosen the most poignant place in which to fade away that she might become part of the very landscape of his past.

'The relief of seeing her is very great,' he confided to Joan that evening, 'partly due to her showing me that she has not yet begun to tire of me, and that there *is* loyalty in her.'

'She sacrificed you because it was demanded of her, but in so doing sacrificed herself,' she observed.

'My poor Briar Rose, whose blighted leaves are dropping one by one, is dreadfully ill,' he agreed, 'and what hope there is of recovering her to any strength of mind or body depends on there being more harmony between her parents and me. If they refuse it, her fate, whatever it may be, shall be their causing, not mine. If they would only believe it, much as I love her, I most assuredly won't marry her unless her health changes, though I will never marry any other woman if *she* won't come to me.'

Ruskin's work, that of preparing for the next term at Oxford, was severely impaired by the distress of seeing Rose so undermined. An intense biliousness arrested his appetite, while zigzags of light interrupted his vision to such a degree that he could not read or write until he had rested each afternoon, something he resisted when he considered the number of lectures he still had to compose.

Although Rose meant to bring such sunshine into his life again, the sight of her wasting away before his eyes made each day of the next fortnight as black as the inferno and it was impossible to achieve anything with a clear mind. Nothing could rid him of the impermeable veil of sadness which clouded his judgement and got in the way of everything; a premature grief, but a grief nonetheless, as unshakeable and immeasurable as love itself.

TOIL IS THE LAW

T HE ONLY FRIENDS RUSKIN WAS GLAD TO BE REACQUAINTED
with when he returned to Oxford that Michaelmas were
Acland and the ailing Prince Leopold, the two people whom he
consistently grew to like and admire more rather than less.

Dreading the prospect of lunching with fifty or sixty others at the
vice chancellor's on his first day back, the professor no sooner deposited
his luggage than set off on a brisk morning walk in the opposite direction
– nimble when it came to clambering over country gates due to being in
better health, though his spirits were sadly depleted and none could know
the wrench he felt at having to leave his love behind in London.

Standing upon the very hilltop he recalled from his own days as a
student and transcending into a thick, quiet despair, he surveyed the
surrounding Oxfordshire plains through a pale and sunny mist, a skylark
singing sweetly over the furrows, just as it had then. And yet so much else
had changed, not least his own position at the university, a place he could
not quite decide if it was liberating or inhibitive to be a part of.

Oxford, city of spires, thinkers and dreamers, gave him a platform he was predestined to make use of, though he had not achieved nearly enough simply from fear of upsetting the hierarchy always looming over his shoulder.

He was firmly opposed to being prevented from teaching what he wanted, regardless if it should be seen to lie outside the subject of art, for without humanity an artist might as well be a gravedigger. Permission would have to be sought for the plan he had in mind, however, and he must carefully select the students who would be most altered and improved by the experience.

Taking his trusty sketchpad and pencil from his breast pocket as he sat upon a tree stump overlooking his familiar route from the university to Abingdon, he mused awhile before making an imaginary study of how the road before him, now sadly uncared for, might have looked twenty or thirty years before: long tall grasses dappled with abundant wild flowers either side, a mingling of daisies, buttercups, poppies and cornflowers each crying out to have a gentle hand fall upon them and caress them in promise that their humble corner of the earth would not be forgotten.

Was not the desire of the heart also the light of thine eyes? All scenes could be made rich by joyful human labour, even such a road as that, he considered fancifully. No air was ever sweet being silent, but only when filled with low currents of under-sound: triplets of birds, the murmur and chirp of insects, the deep-toned words of men and the wayward trebles of children. As he learned the art of life so he found that all lovely things were also necessary – the wild flowers by the wayside as well as the tended corn, the birds and creatures of the forest as well as the tended cattle – because man doth not live by bread alone.

The Ferry Hinksey Road was icy when twelve undergraduates, each wrapped up from their ears to their fingertips in woollens and scarves, all gathered around Ruskin to discover his agenda; bemused upon speculating the reason for having been summoned there, and on such an intemperate day.

The group ranged from the supremely athletic to aristocrats destined to become great landowners, or starry-eyed scholars who looked as though they were bound to come last in any competitive sport.

Included among the latter was the dandyish-looking, long-haired Oscar Wilde, tall enough to stand out in any crowd and strong enough to defend himself in a fight despite his effeminate manner. Not only was he the keenest to hear the professor but the most open-minded to act upon his words and stood close beside him accordingly.

'Here is my notion of what a country road should be...' Ruskin announced, intentionally baffling his audience who saw only a muddy, dilapidated, broken-down highway in urgent need of repair. 'Or rather, I intend to show you what I would have *instead*. I first noticed the appalling state of the route during my regular walks to the university, for despite the village appearing pretty, populated as it is by an Elizabethan manor and cottages bearing traditional thatched roofs, it is hardly better than a slum in terms of living conditions.'

The squalid misery was undeniable, the grey manor house long since having drifted into decay, while the shallow pit of brown peat-coloured water they stood before served as both the reservoir for the inhabitants and the drinking ground for the sheep and cattle.

'I think you'll agree that it's not hard to find inspiration in the swamp which makes the road from Upper to Lower Hinksey impassable for the villagers,' the professor decried, pointing out the areas most in need of improvement, 'while the regular flooding increases the risk of a cholera outbreak. I don't know a lovelier lane in all England and I want to bring it, by next spring, into the prettiest shape I can. I want to level where the water lodges, to get the ruts out of the rest and sow borders of wild flowers.'

Genuinely confused rather than prompted by impudence, one student raised his hand and asked, 'But why must *we* do it?'

'To set others an example. Words are not always enough, and perhaps it will take this grand gesture to show you the nobility of honest labour, the pleasures of *useful* muscular work and the benefits of doing some good for your fellow men. The highest reward for a man's toil is not what he gets for it, but what he *becomes* by it,' he illuminated powerfully, lifting up his gleaming pickaxe as the Duke of Marlborough might have encouraged his army by raising his sword prior to the Battle of Blenheim.

'How very Utopian,' someone else muttered.

Spiking the ground violently with the instrument, Ruskin surveyed his nonchalant soldiers, huddled together in order to defend themselves against the ferocious wind chill. 'If you want knowledge you must toil for it, if you want food you must toil for it, and if pleasure, you must toil for it. *Toil* is the law. And I believe the first test of a truly great man is in his humility and his understanding of not only what he can *say* but what he can *do*. Each of you look perplexed, but I brought you here to teach you about *life*, not art.'

'That isn't exactly what we subscribed for,' another young man grumbled, regretting the comment the moment it was uttered.

The professor ignored this remark, however, and removing his jacket and rolling up his shirtsleeves, as if oblivious to the cold, meant to shame them into joining him.

'It does seem wrong that many of you,' he chided, 'who have some of the best physiques out of all the young men at the college, only choose to spend your strength aimlessly on the cricket ground or river, without any result except that if one rows well one gets a pewter pot, or if one makes a good score one receives a cane-handled bat. I know you must think me an old windbag, but cannot you *see* that the bat and the racer's oar are merely children's toys? I may not be your ordinary kind of professor, but nor do I want my students to become ordinary men.'

Ruskin's chief assistant, Downs, handed out pickaxes and spades for each man, something that was met with considerable surprise, with most looking to their neighbour for influence, as if wary of being the first to accept the challenge and look a fool.

Yet Wilde, the flamboyant, nineteen-year-old who had remained at Ruskin's elbow throughout, wasted no time in stepping forward and, likewise removing his jacket and adapting his foppish attire as best he could, began digging the road alongside his revered leader.

'Thank you, Mr Wilde,' the professor appreciated sincerely, guessing that the others would soon follow his example.

Yet before the others had a chance, a fair-haired, athletic-looking young man, who shared rooms with Wilde, went over and nudged him in the ribs. 'Never thought I'd see you out of bed before midday, Oscar, let alone digging a road!'

'Today is an exception,' came the aloof rebuttal. 'I am humbled to be a digger and hope to have the privilege of pushing Mr Ruskin's sacred wheelbarrow.'

Though his roommate laughed at Wilde's ready wit, he and the other men who remained looking on were a good deal moved by the sentiment and needed no further persuasion to consider whether or not they might lose face by assisting in such a project.

Indulging their leader by placing their coats, hats and scarves onto the heap of clothing which he and Wilde had begun, they soon warmed themselves by breaking into a sweat and labouring long enough to take satisfaction from the improvement.

Always inviting "the diggers", as they were afterwards known among their university compatriots, to breakfast with him at his rooms in Corpus prior to commencing work, Ruskin regarded the men fondly before remarking, 'If, from my windows, I could have seen forty years ago, myself pass in the future, and my thoughts!'

Though it was not clear what exactly the professor meant, the students admired him for not merely expounding on his theories but straining alongside them through the mist, rain and sleet of that harsh winter, dressed in a blue frock coat with the ears of a blue cloth cap pulled down to shield the chill wind that was all the keener upon the open, unsheltered Oxfordshire plain.

'These diggings involve many questions, and are in fact a business I should like to take up wholly, with no lectures,' he paused to observe, seemingly ignorant that the men were being blown about in icy gusts that made the work nigh on impossible.

'Wholly?' Wilde repeated, mopping his brow theatrically.

'Yes, gutters want bridging, sloughs swallow up stones, banks won't slope steep enough. There's a new problem every day I'm here, and two if I'm not. Then there's how to get hammers enough, for you men go at them so hard that you sometimes break them in ten minutes! Thankfully my hammer is intact having broken a good lot of stones today and my own hands into the bargain,' he chuckled, examining his injured knuckles with pride.

The delicacy, sympathy and gentleness of his way, the fresh and penetrating things he said, the boyish fun, the earnestness and the interest he showed in all deep matters, combined to make a whole which his students had never seen equalled.

Believing the road-building enterprise at Ferry Hinksey to be the best lecture he had ever delivered at Oxford, for hours on end Ruskin continued with his spade until he felt as though the muscles in his arms would snap, or amused his pupils with jokes as he sat breaking stones: each of the men careless of their enemies on the neighbouring bank who, forming a dense crowd comprising other students and members of the press, mocked and ridiculed them.

The more they were lampooned and taunted, the more they went to work with gusto. Nor did Ruskin and his disciples view the many cartoons which their road-building inspired with anything other than hearty amusement, with the exception of Acland who was determined to protest on his friend's behalf and marched over to the journalists having prepared a written defence he urged them to print.

'Surely in an age of liberty and philanthropy,' the doctor began, fuming as Ruskin had never before witnessed, 'well-meaning men might be allowed to mend the muddy approaches of some humble dwellings of the poor without being held up to the public as persons only fit for the asylum?'

'But what are his students gaining from this odd little experiment?' a reporter quizzed, further inflaming Acland.

'Professor Ruskin, a man of no narrow sympathies, is as interested in the greatness of the educated youth of England as he is in the well-being of the poor,' he lauded, pointing his finger at those who muttered anything to the contrary. Reading from his prepared speech he went on, 'He has always passed his life almsgiving not fortune-hunting, in labouring for the honour of others not his own, and would far rather make people look to Turner than exhibit the skill of his own hand. He has lowered his rents and assured the comfortable lives of his poor tenants instead of taking from them all that he could. He loves a woodland walk better than a London street and would rather see a bird fly than shoot it. To the high-spirited youth of Oxford he has said, "Will, then, none of you, out of the abundance of your strength and of your leisure, do anything for the poor? Drain a swamp, repair a village byway, fix a garden wall, make pleasant with flowers one widow's plot?" Meanwhile, all the hacks of Oxford would prefer to wag their heads and talk of the sentimentality of Ruskin rather than offer him their support.'

But the person whom he praised cringed to hear such a profuse harangue being laid at the feet of journalists only for them to trample on it, and thus Ruskin dissuaded Acland, 'Nothing you say will stop them publishing their own nonsense,' leading him away from the smug band who continued to bluster.

'I hadn't finished what I was saying,' his friend griped.

'I'm sure they have more than enough to go on,' Ruskin assured, approaching the makeshift refreshment table presided over by Crawley and handing the doctor a steaming cup of tea.

'Have you *heard* what they are calling you all? Amateur navvies!'

'It's not that I don't appreciate your attempts at rationalising with them, it's just that I'm far more comfortable defending others than *being* defended. You see,' the professor observed, pointing at the press who scrambled to make notes and draw caricatures, 'our little group of wise hearts is better than a wilderness full of fools,' saying which he ravenously consumed a neat little crust-less sandwich with his dirty hands, a disarming contrast which Acland marvelled at.

The scornful crowd, who had been standing on the bank all morning sneering and preparing their newspaper columns, were just about to turn on their heels when, much to their chagrin, the royal carriage drew up and Prince Leopold alighted with Sir Robert Collins.

'Though there are many clever men who are indolent, you will never find a *great* man who is so,' the professor inspired his men during lunch, not having noticed the royal party making their way towards them. 'When I hear a young man spoken of as possessing genius, the first question I always ask about him is, "Does he work?"'

'Lord knows *I* am no genius, but I wish I could be permitted to help you,' His Royal Highness began, offering Ruskin his hand regretfully.

'You offer us assistance in more important ways than taking a spade or pickaxe to the ground,' he smiled, bowing to the prince and Sir Robert. 'You do know that you are likely to find yourselves depicted in a *Punch* cartoon simply for showing your support?'

'That is what I intended,' Leopold responded drolly. 'My mother is an avid reader of the magazine and my brother Bertie will be so pleased at having the attention diverted from *him* for a time.'

For two exhausting, yet oddly stimulating months as the Ferry Hinksey undertaking progressed in spite of all challenges and criticisms, Ruskin journeyed back and forth from Oxford to London to see his world-weary Rose, his dear one ever encouraging him to never lay down his tools until the work was completed.

As a lesson of biblical proportions he was delighted by the morals it instilled into those upper-class gentlemen, while Rosie relished his accounts of the project, no matter that she was not there to witness it.

'When I am well enough, I will go to Ferry Hinksey in my carriage,' she declared, no longer talking of her imminent departure from this life but, on the contrary, having begun to make plans.

'Nothing would please the men more. They have such a sense of pride that is wonderful to see. Haven't I always said that whenever men are rightly occupied, their amusement grows out of their work like the petals out of a blossoming flower, and when they are faithfully helpful and compassionate all their emotions become steady, deep, perpetual and vivifying to the soul, as the natural pulse to the body?'

'It is, as you say, far more than just a road,' she smiled, 'and although the maintenance of it may be forgotten when the group go their separate ways at the end of term, like all great miracles it will be remembered long afterwards.'

The undergraduates had been taught, under the knowledgeable guidance of Ruskin and Downs, how to drain a field, break stones, lay levels and manoeuvre a barrow over a narrow plank, until finally, after many weeks of back-breaking work, the great chasm, which the village inhabitants had once been forced to avoid by inconvenient circumnavigation, could be crossed uninhibited: the villagers admiring as they went an abundance of wild flowers sown along the banks just as the professor had first designed. The diggers all felt that they had been imparted with far more than road-making skills.

"'The dearest memories of my Oxford days are my walks and talks with you,'" Wilde wrote to Ruskin during the vacation, a letter the professor reluctantly read aloud to Rose, never liking compliments, "'for from you I learned nothing but what is good. How else could it be? There is in you something of prophet, of priest, and of poet, and to you the gods gave eloquence such as they have given to none other, so that your message might come to us with the fire of passion, and the marvel of music, making the deaf hear and the blind see.'"

A NORWOOD ROMANCE

THE TEDIUM OF TRAIN JOURNEYS ALWAYS PROVOKED A contemplative mood in Ruskin and the need to assess his broader direction in life, whether in Oxford, the place whence he departed, or London where he was bound.

In turn, these ponderances made way for speculating on all that might occur between himself and Rose before he took up the return ticket, and he became conscious of the countryside rushing past him as he sat still: his brain whirring faster than the locomotive or the decoupage clouds travelling in the opposite direction, a boundary to the infinite and all no traveller could reach.

It was this that prompted him to remember, with a rage that had sat in the pit of his stomach for years, his first and sole journey to Harristown when he had arrived to such fanfare only to be discarded by Maria La Touche like so much rubbish.

Just as church was a place to mark birth and passing, or a door was something to enter or leave by, so a train took you away from one place and pulled you towards another. Life, it appeared, was no different, for as Rose ebbed away, inching closer to the next world by the hour, the more he could claim her as his own in a new and wonderful sense.

She was no less his for the failure to take his name or lay her head upon his pillow, and he took comfort in the thought that death would sanctify those precious final days and wash away the bitter ones, leading him to dedicate the rest of his existence to the girl, woman, angel whose confidence in him had never failed, even during her abject silence. There would be many more years of quietude to endure he well knew, but at least they would not be unbearable due to their uncertainty.

Though he had long questioned Rose's love of hotels, Ruskin fully appreciated the discretion her large suite of rooms at The Queen's afforded, with evenings of reading Dickens by lamplight following afternoons spent indoors talking, playing chess or sketching: a quiet domesticity which, unlike the occasions when they had been hosted by mutual friends, offered an intimacy which neither of them had to break the charm of by recounting to a third party.

Rose's inability to walk further than the ugly Central Hill Baptist Chapel at the end of the road meant that the majority of their days were limited to the simplest but greatest pleasure in life, that of companionship, while she permitted, nay asked him, to liaise with her doctor as if he were her husband, never enquiring the diagnosis as if she had no desire to know how limited they were by time.

'How can you always have so much patience with me?' Rose enquired of the ever youthful professor as she paused to rest during the walk back from church one Sunday.

'Whatever do you mean?' Ruskin baulked.

'Well, I don't refer to my feeble walking,' she laughed in sarcastic self-chastisement, leaning upon his arm.

'I realised long ago that it was better to lose my pride than lose *you* because of it,' he answered frankly. 'I had thought that those sunny days at Broadlands would be my most prized with you, and yet these seemingly ordinary Norwood ones, with unsympathetic-looking churches and distastefully decorated hotel rooms, are all the more holy because of the reassurance they give me that I was not wrong to think that we would have lived well together. It is true that I could have made you happy?'

'Yes,' she answered simply, walking on, her hand gripping his arm more tightly than usual due to her increasing fatigue.

'Though work often prevents me from being by your side,' he patted her glove devotedly, 'I can't tell you how much it pleases me to think of you here in my old stomping ground, visiting Herne Hill and the Severns whenever you are able.'

'I'm afraid I'm not always sociable,' she confessed. 'Sometimes I just ask Joan if I can read up in your old nursery, for I feel almost as close to you there as when we're together.'

'The nursery? Where I sleep whenever I find myself too drained with emotion to take the train back to Oxford?'

'Yes,' she nodded tellingly.

'My sparse college rooms show me how alone I am in the world without you, whereas spending the night under my childhood roof offers me indescribable solace for knowing you are nearby, not to mention finding Joanna's kind face waiting for me at the door, no matter *how* late my arrival,' he explained, his heart bursting with a sentimentality he had longed to express for almost a decade.

'I like being there very much.'

'Fancy you reading up there in my old room. I'm so thankful! The views are not what they used to be before the railroads came. They were once quite lovely, with so much space and height in their sweep, taking in the Norwood hills, partly wooded and rough with furze, all the way to the rustic loveliness of Surrey and Kent.'

She smiled at the corners of her mouth and, looking into his face intently, replied, 'I do not go there for the view.'

It frustrated Arthur that his home appeared to be run expressly around Ruskin's comings and goings, and that he and Joan were no more the master and mistress than esteemed servants forever at the beck and call of the whims and desires of "The Professor", who kept extremely irregular hours due to visiting Rose whenever she requested. The lease of Herne Hill had not been so much a gift, but a bind tying the three of them together.

Ruskin never thought anything of keeping Joan up late in order to talk about Rose, a subject Arthur had heard far too much of since marrying Joan. He had never come across a man so vociferous about his feelings, something he found preposterous and weak in someone with a reputation to uphold. As ever, the professor found it beneficial to unburden himself of all his fears, chiefly Rose's passing, far worse to contemplate than his own mortality due to their story being so far from complete.

Yet Arthur's sympathy was exhausted and, believing his wife should prioritise their own family, he grew irritable and short-tempered, with no thought of the strain which Joan, who never considered herself, underwent in trying to please them both.

With the approach of Christmas, Ruskin awaited Rose's decision as to whether she would remain in London or travel to Ireland, something which only increased the tension at Herne Hill, although Joan refused to give her cousin any indication of her awkward predicament when he had much greater concerns.

'You know that I don't mean to be ungrateful by holding off accepting your kind invitation to spend Christmas with you?' Ruskin asked one morning as Joan was about to go out, her grocery basket on her arm. 'It's just that, if I get the opportunity to spend it with Rose, I feel I ought to seize it.'

'Oh *dear* John,' she exclaimed, holding back tears of pity and those of anger towards Arthur for not being more tolerant in light of the tragic circumstances afflicting her cousin. 'Don't bother about *us*. We should be delighted to have you here with us but gladder still to think of the two of you together. Do you really think she might stay?'

'I shall ask her,' he answered cheerfully, taking up his coat and walking out with her, oblivious as to the troubled look on her face belying her suspicion that he would again be forsaken.

***

Ruskin bustled into Rose's suite with armfuls of the handsomely wrapped presents she had asked him to collect from various shops in Mayfair. All morning he had rushed around like an errand boy, longing to be back beside his dear one's hearth, where she reclined on a sofa by the fire, enveloped in a pink cashmere shawl.

'I would give anything to have a Christmas all our own,' he announced as Rose approvingly inspected the ribbons and wrapping he had selected.

She sighed, 'And I, but I don't want to vex my parents when they have conceded so much. Can't we have a make-believe Christmas right here?'

'It seems my very life is spent eating mock turtle soup,' Ruskin replied petulantly, collapsing into the wing armchair opposite and causing her to giggle as she always did whenever he sulked.

'Oh please don't be disappointed, my love,' Rose urged, leaning forward and touching his knee persuasively. 'We could get a Christmas tree and a roast goose!'

Thrilled at hearing her address him with such affection, he buckled, '*And* a flaming pudding?'

'Yes, anything you like,' she agreed enthusiastically, despite knowing that she would hardly eat, for she so wanted to return a fraction of his devotion by creating an occasion that would live in his memory.

Both imagined the scene simultaneously, with a tender pang at the pretence. She would arrange everything beautifully, just as if it were their own home, with stockings hung on the mantle, candles on the Norwegian fir and carols aplenty – drinking one another's health with the joy of newly-weds. Presents too, but they were neither here nor there. To be together was all.

Ruskin would have believed himself to be walking through his own dream when he arrived at The Queen's Hotel for the fantasy Christmas morning Rose had spent days planning, only that everything was even nicer than he had imagined.

The room had been decorated with enough festive trimmings to make it appear like a magical forest, while Rose not only looked surprisingly well but utterly charming in a green silk dress with lace collar and tartan sash. Likewise, in honour of the occasion, he had exchanged his usual blue stock in favour of a cheery red one.

Catching a glimpse of the sprig of mistletoe behind his back, she struggled to her feet in order to permit him one sweet kiss, then, threading her arm through his, led him to the fireside where she had arranged a breakfast of tea and hot buttered muffins.

Wishing him, 'Merry Christmas', she proceeded to pour his tea like the doting wife she might have been, her hand trembling as she offered him the floral-sprig-decorated teacup.

'And to you,' he toasted before taking a sip. 'It is already by far the merriest of my life.'

'It has hardly begun,' she laughed.

'What a contrast to the Christmas when you were in London and I in Switzerland!' he recalled.

'When our thoughts crossed on seeing Venus? I so wanted to be with you and wrote and told you.'

'I still have that letter now,' Ruskin confessed, placing his hand on his breast pocket.

'Show me!' Rose cried in disbelief.

He passed it to her and her eyes moistened upon seeing her old handwriting and the confidence and honesty of her words.

'I haven't set eyes on it since the day you handed it back to me at the Royal Academy,' she upbraided.

'But you wouldn't take it,' he answered, keen to know why.

'No, because I meant every word. Taking it back would have been like denying it. "You needn't tell me that you have not forgotten me, yet I can't help saying that I *was* looking for a letter,"' she read, knowing that saying it aloud would carry even more meaning than when he had first received it. '"I wanted so much to know what you were doing and thinking this Christmas Day. I have always told you that I can see some things quite plain and I have been living in Switzerland with you all week. Am I not there with you still?"'

'And now we *are* together,' he declared ecstatically, clutching her arm and attempting to restore her earlier light-heartedness.

'Yes, and I am truly happy, for perhaps you don't consider how many hours I have to pass here alone, waiting for your return. It always feels like an age since you were last sitting here beside me.'

'I shall stay as long as you can put up with me,' he teased.

'That will be a very long time, I warn you.' And she kissed his cheek.

Glancing at the sash tied around her waist, he asked, 'You realise that you're wearing the tartan belonging to my clan?'

'Why of course, I ordered it especially!' And she stroked the silk, the texture of the slub a strangely pleasant one.

'A lovely, wifely thing to do,' he praised, taking up her hand. 'May I call you my little wife, just for today? And will you call me by my name?'

'You may call *me* whatever you wish, whilst I am too shy to call you anything,' she admitted, blushing guilelessly. 'Haven't I told you that it's as though we were still back in the schoolroom whenever I go to address you?'

He took no offence but laughed upon reminiscing on her former coquettish ways. 'You had very many pet names for me back then!'

'I suppose all my boldness vanished after my eighteenth birthday,' she ventured solemnly, for his proposal had changed everything.

The reminder pained him. 'I never meant to cause you distress, you must believe me. It was only ever my intention to love you, and I naively thought your parents would recognise the attachment that had developed between us. How I wish that I had waited until you were of age, with a right to judge your own feelings.'

'They would have been just the same,' she proclaimed. 'Your declaration threw me into much confusion certainly, but I knew even at eighteen what I wished.'

'I empathise with your parents for being opposed to you marrying a man so much older, though I have never been convinced that it was the main reason for their disapproval. Even *were* that so, after years of interrogating God for making our ages so divided, it occurred to me that some of the best and longest of marriages often possess a bond not unlike that of parent and child.'

672

'How so? I never perceived that between my own mother and father,' Rose replied cynically, her brow creased. 'Mama always said that my father was born at the age of forty and simply stayed that way.'

'I am merely referring to *happy* partnerships.'

'Oh,' came the return, for she fully accepted that her parents' marriage had been anything but. Intrigued to hear more of his theory, she prompted, 'Go on.'

Ruskin rested his palms together in thought and asked seriously, 'You'll agree that my mother was always matriarch at Denmark Hill?'

She nodded vigorously, giggling at her fond memories of the strict old lady by the fireside.

'My father had the exceedingly bad habit of yielding to my mother in large things and taking his own way in little ones, seeking her tenderness and approval much like a young boy. Although he was entirely his own man and single-minded by nature, he never rested with a decision if she was displeased with it. At the same time, my mother remained girlishly dependent upon *him*, a mutual respect and loyalty co-existing between them which brought them through the darkest of troubles and years of financial struggle. Nor can it be doubted that their ultimate success was a result of their union.'

'I suppose you're right,' Rose conceded.

'The difference in *our* ages has highlighted this to me,' he asserted, kneeling before her in his enthusiasm to explain his viewpoint, 'for the boundless, unshakeable love existing between us is far greater than the lust that fades as quickly as an English summer, and is the very essence of what a marriage *should* be. Are we not both of us utterly dependent upon each other for peace of mind and happiness?'

Her answer came not in words, for they had talked enough and, motioning him to settle down beside her, they spoke no more.

Practically as soon as they had exchanged their Christmas gifts, following a long dinner and more wine than was good for him, Ruskin turned melancholic on thinking of Rose's departure.

Why must she go just when they had crossed the boundary into adult love? He considered begging her not to leave him again, and should not have hesitated to do so had he not accepted how futile and provoking it would be.

He would have been far better off trying to enjoy that brief, wondrous occasion without dwelling so, but he could not alter his nature or quell his desire to keep her near him for as long as he could.

No matter how much he was used to her going away, the sense that there was not a day to be wasted troubled him far more than any previous parting, though he could rely upon a steady stream of the most tender and loving letters he had ever received to soothe his anxieties and encourage him to look to their next reunion.

Not having to doubt her love seemed wondrous after all their ruptures, like having God finally revealed after all his rage and loss of faith in Him. And yet, having leisure to hold Rose's hand or take it up and press it to his lips was more precious than even that, nor did he ask for anything more. Those simple, innocent gestures of worship were all that he desired, beautiful in their tenderness and symbolic of the great distance they had traversed in fully understanding one another. She was his and nothing could come between them anymore.

LXV
UNTO THIS LAST

R USKIN HAD JUST PASSED AND AVOIDED CELEBRATING HIS fifty-sixth birthday in February when a brief note arrived at Herne Hill from Mrs La Touche, the last person he expected to hear from, relating in an almost official tone her daughter's continuing decline and their intention to return to London in a further bid to seek medical intervention.

He was greatly surprised to be invited to call on Rose at their address on Curzon Street, the very backdrop of his first encounter with the lady and her daughter all those years ago, and it was only when he entered the fussy drawing room that he could truly appreciate the quiet normality of The Queen's Hotel: not ostentatious enough for the staff to be interested in or concerned by the affairs of their guests, nor too small for them to notice when anyone came and went.

Ruskin stood waiting for the lady who had once courted his favour uneasily, holding a brown paper parcel and not inclined to take a seat without being invited to do so. Taking in the familiar surroundings when the door opened, he was fairly sickened by the sight of Maria La Touche who glided in like a condescending duchess and held out her hand as she had on that first occasion, albeit with a less welcoming air.

He observed a great change in her after eight years of estrangement, for she looked incredibly severe and defiant. Her hair was turning white and her countenance could no longer be thought handsome due to being heavily lined, from anger rather than shame he surmised from her cold, righteous manner.

'It's been a long time, Mr Ruskin,' Mrs La Touche began formally, motioning him to take a seat.

Placing the packet, which had alerted his hostess's attention, by his feet, he was in no mood to be gracious or diplomatic, and coldly replied, 'Indeed, I never expected to be invited here again.'

'Come, all that is over,' she dismissed, smiling falsely. 'For some time now, my husband and I have granted Rose's wish to see you.'

'I believe I know the reason for you doing so now,' Ruskin confronted: 'because you are confident that my courtship will end not in marriage but in death.'

'You hold me responsible for not ending my resistance sooner?'

'To the end of my days, yes,' he nodded solemnly, 'for it is all *too* late, all vain and full of shadows.'

Mrs La Touche, deeply affronted at being addressed so abruptly in her own home, sat stiffly with her hands clenched together on her lap and paused a moment before retaliating, 'You speak to me thus when it is *my* daughter lying upstairs?'

'The woman I hoped to be my *wife*,' Ruskin returned pertinently.

'*Need* you persecute me more than life already has?' she appealed.

'And what about Rose who is entirely broken like her lover?'

But the lady did not see the truth of this statement, nor did she pity her former friend for a circumstance he had brought upon himself. Instead she went on matter-of-factly, 'She will remain in London for another week. I hoped to find another physician but everyone I've consulted says her condition is too desperate. Therefore, you may continue to see her as much as she pleases.'

'I finally have leave to look after her?' Ruskin asked contemptuously, though he was drained by arguing and knew that it would do no good. 'The dream of life too sorrowfully fulfilled.'

'Perhaps it's best that I bid you a good evening,' the lady concluded, rising and refusing to participate in further discussion casting pointless blame. She deeply regretted having engaged him at all, for she hardly knew her own conscience before he reminded her of it. It was unbearable to have him judge her, having once held him in such high regard, and she was annoyed with herself that curiosity finally got the better of her and made her ask, 'What is in the packet?'

'A Turner watercolour for Rose, that she might have something beautiful to look upon before she falls asleep and when she awakens.' Regarding her reproachfully he added, 'I assume presents are no longer forbidden?'

'Of course not,' Maria said, flinching.

'Then I shall take it to her.' And Ruskin rose, as glad to leave her presence as she was to see him go.

With his hand upon the door he hesitated and turned, however, for knowing that he might never have another opportunity to vent his animosity, he could not go without one final word of retribution. 'The night is far spent,' he observed sadly. 'Go on your way knowing that you have stained every stone of it with your daughter's blood.'

One look at Rose's slight figure, dwarfed by the large canopied bed, was enough to confirm to Ruskin that it was indeed futile for her to be subjected to any further treatment regimes, and that what she needed most was *love*.

'You see? Mama is quite defeated,' she murmured, half opening her eyes and holding out her arm as if her greatest cares had been resolved simply by him being there — more than that, his having leave to be with her.

'Yes,' he answered softly, taking up the chair beside the bed. 'Now please close your eyes and rest.'

Quietly unwrapping the Turner he hoped to delight her with when she awoke, he sat quietly observing the one he would have given all the Turners in the world to save: her hair tangled on the pillow, her cheeks hollow, and yet she was more divinely beautiful than ever, with a greater majesty than all Pre-Raphaelite heroines and saintlier than any book of hours.

He felt drawn to sketch her as she rested, the last portrait he would surely ever make, though the result would not tell the viewer whether the subject was a living girl or one already passed. It was not merely his way of distracting himself as he kept vigil, but a means of recording those final moments.

The sad picture he created could never prevent him from remembering the vivacious young Irish child who had so unexpectedly entered his life just when he most needed her, yet neither would he forget the invalid who lay before him, angelically shrouded in white bedclothes with a small silver cross around her neck.

He should have liked to have conveyed a fraction of Rose's sacred beauty, and might have were it not for the emotion running through his fingers and ruining any hope of accuracy. A tear rolled down his cheek unchecked until it threatened to smudge his work, forcing him to brush it away and continue with more focus.

Like the lock of Rose's hair or the incomplete map from that sunny day at Harristown, this too would be locked away in his desk drawer, never to be looked on apart from in solitary moments when he was at his loneliest and longed for her company, or when he tried so hard to recall her face that he feared forgetting it.

He had countless memories to reflect on, many of them miserable, others too glorious to ever capture on paper or preserve in a locket; yet objects became oddly meaningful to those left behind, and it was with this in mind that he carried on with the drawing until she grew too restless for him to continue.

Like anyone who loves feels frustration and rage on having to watch their dearest suffer without being able to comfort, so it disturbed Ruskin to his core on witnessing the pain afflicting Rose. She could not get comfortable, no matter if she turned left or right, right or left, and so she writhed continually, unable to find a position that did not increase every bone ache or nerve spasm.

Eventually she rolled onto her side with her knees tucked in front of her like a foetus in the womb, her eyes tight shut and her hands covering her ears so that she might not hear the nurse babbling away to her mother when they entered the room, breaking the welcome hush that Ruskin had brought with him.

Just to have peace! Rose thought vaguely as she perceived her mother beside the bed. She wished that everyone, save one person, would leave her to convene with her inner voice, the constant adviser urging her to drift away and stop her tongue from attempting speech, for it was too hard to think or formulate words.

All she longed for was sleep and his arms around her when her lids closed, his hold tighter than was comfortable but worth bearing, though she had not the strength to return the intensity of his embrace.

She lived within her waiting corpse and every breath was significant and painful in its rise and fall. The welcome oblivion prompted by opiates released her from agony to a degree, though it came with its own punishing disadvantages, increasing the feelings of weakness, confusion and nausea. Nor could the benefits of numbness last, for the dread of returning to feeling and sensation depressed her and drove her to maddening despair, increasing the crippling fatigue a hundredfold.

Ruskin could see that death alone would vanquish his dearest one and rescue her from such misery, for she clearly wished, from the things she voiced as she fell in and out of delirium, to be quit of life with an eagerness that wounded him far more for knowing that she loved him after all.

It was impossible to predict when she would pass – a day, a week, or months hence – but when she did it *would* be a blessing and not a tragedy, for didn't he feel her suffering more acutely than if it was his own?

Death was not a journey into an unknown land, it was a voyage home. Dear Rose was going, not to a strange country but to her Father's house, and there she would find her dear, sweet Emily.

Withdrawing from his pocket the poem Rosie had gifted him at Christmas, he read it slowly and carefully, considering it to be her most breathtaking composition, for it taught him to take solace in the fact that the great weight was shortly to be lifted.

"I heard a voice from far away

As I lay dull and sad
(For very grief I could not pray

To Him who makes us glad);
Yet, like the words a friend might say,

It stilled the pain I had.

He who hath balm for all our pain
Knows every grief of ours;

We shall not cry to Him in vain
In life's most hopeless hours.

Oh, doubting heart, look up again;
He will revive thy powers.

We weep for every vanished thing,
We call the winter long,

'Tis but the hush before the spring,
When all things wake in song,

And thou too shalt rejoice and sing.
Who now hast mourned so long.

We, when our earthly joys depart,
Turn from His love divine.

And let each vain regretful smart
Through all our souls entwine.

Oh, child, the God who knows each heart
Could heal this pain of thine.

The tears no longer dimmed my eyes,
I was no more oppressed;

Strong in God's strength I will arise,
And He will give me rest.

Touched with the Light of Paradise
Life's darkest hours are blest."

The questions regarding mortality had never been more obscure to Ruskin, for in order to see Rose in Paradise would not he have to believe in it? His own dying hours would surely be the sweeter for thinking that he need only close his eyes and fold his arms upon his chest in order to attain an everlasting union: his soul merging with hers to become one perfect, faultless entity, cleansed of all sin.

As Rose cried the cries of a martyr yearning to be released from torment, Ruskin saw each hour of the night until Mrs La Touche sent the nurse to say that he should retire for a few hours in the neighbouring room. He would have preferred to stay regardless had it not been for her insisting on taking up vigil.

There was no kindliness in her manner, and commencing sewing, as if she were in her drawing room and not beside her daughter's deathbed, she punctured with her blunt crewelwork needle the taut linen constrained within a hoop, only to look up and stare at him, bidding him, with her unfeeling eyes, to be gone.

He was loath to leave for Herne Hill in case he should be prevented from saying his farewell, but even the next bedchamber was too far, and within an hour of him retiring Rose was in severe distress at finding him absent, with neither Mrs La Touche or the nurse able to calm her. Left with no alternative, the women rapped on his door frantically and begged him to return.

Still dazed after being disturbed from an inadequate half-sleep, Ruskin re-entered Rose's chamber horrified to find his darling sitting up in bed wringing her hands and rocking to and fro. Talking nineteen to the dozen, despairing at the pain no medicine was able to diminish, she held out her arms and beckoned him.

With soothing words and abundant patience, he took a seat on the bed and succeeded in persuading her to lie down and rest in his arms, kissing her forehead as a father might a poorly infant and gently pressing her hand until she was quite calm again.

Without opening her eyes she murmured, 'John?'

'Yes,' he replied, astonished to finally hear her utter his Christian name. 'What is it, my dear one?'

'Will you stay until I fall asleep?'

'Of course, I will do anything you like.'

'"The Lord is my shepherd, therefore I feel no ill,"' she recited, grinding her teeth through an intense spasm, a shooting pain which radiated the length of her spine and down her legs. '"He leads me to the pastures green, and by the waters still."'

Words and omens, promises and prayers, have failed me too often for me to care about any of them now, he thought. *What is said of pearl gates, golden floors and the like, is as distinctly a work of fiction or romantic invention as any novel of Sir Walter Scott.* And yet he kept his scepticism to himself and put his hands together in order to please her.

As always when he prayed in times of crisis, the action lifted his spirits and encouraged him to continue praying intently as he stroked her forehead and rocked her gently as she lay cradled: a shared communion which proved unexpectedly restorative, with Rose drifting off to sleep more pacified than he had seen her for many an hour.

When Ruskin was quite sure that she was fast asleep, he too allowed himself to close his eyes, though he did not meet with tranquil visions when he succumbed to slumber but only that painful torturous dream of old: that he and Rose had married after all, in a surprise ceremony, with their friends and Joan looking on.

Even as they all regarded her admiringly in her white dress he knew that he was being tricked, and yet it all felt real enough for him to believe the mistake upon waking. Unlike the consciousness that takes one from stupor into reality, he remained convinced that such an event had taken place even as he walked back to Herne Hill to refresh himself the following morning, entering the house elatedly and believing himself to be a newly-wedded man until Joan gently disillusioned him.

Noticing the glance she and Arthur exchanged in concern, Ruskin recognised that his sanity was once again precariously balanced, and that with much more anxiety he would succumb to another attack which might even prevent him from seeing Rose.

It had stopped raining almost an hour before, yet droplets still clung to the nursery window panes, looking out over the rooftops of the inflated South London suburbia where terraces upon terraces were continually erected to satisfy growing demand.

Herne Hill hadn't been countryside since he was a boy, yet the changes continued to make Ruskin resentful, as if all Christendom would soon be sacrificed for the encroaching railways delivering carriages full of naive country folk to work in the airless, soporific factories and live in the cramped red-brick houses which were surely a poor exchange for clean air and unadulterated food.

Having reposed long enough in his rickety old iron bed, staring blankly at the ceiling and sometimes counting the cracks, Ruskin threw back the thin coverlet and shot up. A terrific draught had been caused by one of the windows having been blown open in the night and he noticed that the breeze had configured the melted wax of his bedside candle into an "R", a sign he tried to dismiss but which lingered in his mind all morning.

Pouring cold water from the jug on the nightstand and awakening himself more fully by splashing his face, after changing his clothes and breakfasting with the much too lively family downstairs another lamentable day began.

His legs were determined to return to Curzon Street, each step taking his memory back to those he had made prior to being introduced to Rose, then a girl with everything before her and no inkling of the life that would overwhelm and destroy her.

Still he could not help asking himself, as he had on so many other occasions, if he was to blame, yet the anger he felt towards Mrs La Touche told him that it was not so.

There were two kinds of parental love, he reflected: the one liberating, pure and selfless, the other ensnaring, destructive and ugly. He had witnessed and experienced both kinds and trusted that, had his romantic history turned out differently, he would have been a father clear-sighted enough to recognise if his own possessiveness warped and tainted the love for his child into something grotesque.

Ruskin loitered on all the familiar streets he and Rose had traversed countless times on their way to and from the Royal Academy, pausing to look up at the cold, grey, blank February sky as if searching for an answer but with no expectation of finding one.

The nausea he felt seemed to define the finality of his actions and the farewell he would soon make against his will, a bitter opportunity afforded by the person he despised above all others, save himself for harbouring such hatred towards the woman who had, after all, brought his dear one into the world.

His life would go on without Rose, that was *his* curse, yet any love he had ever realised would go to the grave with her. The lonely years stretched far, far in front of him, longer perhaps than the tumultuous time he had known her, yet the grief that would soon burst forth was endless.

It would not commence with her passing but would continue on indefinitely, as much a part of him as breathing. The only worsening of his suffering would be caused by the inability to find out anything about her, thereby forcing him to acknowledge the reality of bereavement. His work would come to a crashing halt and, despite having previously ridiculed those who, grief-stricken, turned to spiritualism, he would find himself open to anything that might allow him to keep Rose beside him always.

The acuteness of mourning would melt away as easily as snow on early spring flowers, though frost would blight their growth and make them bow their shrivelled heads in deference to nature's unpredictability, and he would be left with only a dull, chronic pain that would never leave him.

Without her surely everything would be meaningless: his mind insensitive to all external woes and his limbs powerless to shake off the indefatigable weariness emanating from perpetual sorrow. An unbearable void would open up, leaving him incapable of perceiving beauty, while, if he wasn't careful, all that he had ever worked for would be laid aside like some strange fossil.

As a writer feels a physical need to voice his thoughts on paper, or an artist a view in order to paint, so he needed Rose in order to feel any inspiration at all, to see the world and all its glories, whilst identifying the changes *he* in turn might inspire others to bring about.

It was a wound that would close, yes, but the scar would act as a reminder never to forget her, not for a single day. Keeping her memory alive was his only chance of being able to work, and if he didn't set himself *some* task he might as well be buried alongside her.

What was he thinking? He would never be permitted *that*. In death, just as in life, Rose would still be at the mercy of her parents. There would be no weeping beside her tomb, for she would be locked away in the La Touche mausoleum beside her sister where he could never reach them.

If only they had married she might have been laid to rest in an unmarked spot overlooking Lake Coniston: a tranquil hilltop on his own land where he could have taken himself on calm summer days when the irregular, capricious clouds were mirrored in the still water as surreally as the Venetian lagoons. There she would have been his forever.

The sky was covered with grey cloud, not rain cloud but a dry black veil which no ray of sunshine could pierce, as Ruskin approached the white townhouse with its shiny black door and railings.

He noticed that the La Touche carriage, with its two fine bays, was waiting outside: the cobbles below Rose's bedroom window densely laid with straw in order to mute the clattering sound of hooves.

Remaining on the opposite side of the street, strangely hesitant to approach, he watched as the door opened and Mrs La Touche came out, followed by the nurse and a footman carrying an insentient Rose in his arms. Wrapped up in blankets, she remained motionless, and Ruskin wondered if she had been drugged so as not to struggle at the prospect of being taken away without saying goodbye.

Having received no word of warning from Mrs La Touche as to this hurried departure, a great wave of paralysing consternation came over him as he looked on the scene as a stranger might, helpless upon realising that they were taking his poor Sweet Briar away to Ireland and that it meant never setting eyes on her again.

Just as she was preparing to disappear into the carriage beside her daughter, Mrs La Touche caught sight of Ruskin standing transfixed, his forlorn expression that of a man who has endured too much to comprehend the final scene or challenge its outcome.

She could not help pausing a moment as he removed his hat out of respect of her imminent loss as much as his own, for the gesture caused her to empathise with him for the first time since he had offered himself as her daughter's suitor.

Nodding courteously, Mrs La Touche was nonetheless opposed to greeting him or starting up conversation for risk of being delayed. After all, Rose was under her care and no explanations were required. Thus she settled back in the carriage opposite the nurse attending Rose and signalled to the driver.

Ruskin did not replace his hat, never mind the spots of rain falling, and, waiting on the pavement until he lost sight of the carriage, knew not whither to go or what to do having set aside the entire afternoon to keeping Rose company.

Finding his day unexpectedly empty and purposeless, as all days must be from thenceforth, he took the liberty of returning to Herne Hill the longest way he knew, once more passing locations he most associated with Rose, though doing so inevitably worsened the sense of loneliness and abandonment.

Cursing Saint Valentine as he went, the irony of that cruel February day would forever be imprinted on his mind, along with the sentimental greetings card and poem he had dedicated to Rose but which would ever remain undelivered.

"She sat beside me yesterday
With lip, and eye, so blandly smiling,
So full of soul, of life, of light,
So sweetly my lorn heart beguiling
That she had almost made me gay
Had almost charmed the thought away
(Which, like the poisoned desert wind,
Came sick and heavy o'er my mind)
That memory soon mine all would be,
And she would smile no more for me."

HAWTHORN BLOSSOMS

S UBJECTED TO AGAIN HAVING TO AWAIT MRS LA TOUCHE'S vague dispatches about Rose's health, increasingly sporadic as the spring advanced, Ruskin's friends were equally distant, as if no-one quite knew how to write to him.

Despite feeling as though he had spent the past two decades in limbo for one reason or another, he found that lingering more terrible than anything, for it seemed to possess and shadow him through and through.

Broken in will and thought after expecting the bad news to come every day for months, he began to think that Rose might rally and have one of her mysterious improvements, prompting him to look out for the post each day instead of dreading it.

The one thing he did not expect was a letter from Rose herself, not least because the envelope had not been addressed in her hand, though his heart sank on finding only a feeble pencil-written note begging him to go to her: "I am alone in Dublin under the care of doctors. My father has driven me mad and only you can save me."

688

'Oh God,' he uttered, knowing not how to help her.

'Don't tell me…?' Joan enquired, fearing the worst.

'No, it's not that. It's from Rose herself, begging me to deliver her from her father and the doctor he has placed her with in Dublin. But what can I do? I'm as paralysed as ever. It's horrifying to think that she's incarcerated in yet another institution when she might pass at any moment with no-one by her side.'

'You are, as you say, quite helpless,' she sighed.

'It is the *worst* possible outcome.' He shook his head, again glancing at the note. 'That they would take her away from *us*, only to wash their hands of her the moment she was back in Ireland. It turns me sick to the point of fever.'

'And you have every right to feel thus when *we* would gladly have nursed her,' his cousin agreed, reaching out across the table and resting her hand on his.

'Love was the only thing she needed and assuredly won't have where she is,' he vented, tears rising up but held back by anger.

'She knows that *you* love her and that you would be there if you *could*,' Joan consoled, though she knew her words carried no meaning just then.

It was a still, bright morning in May when the nurse, entering Rose's room, found her cold. Yet so peaceful was her countenance upon the pillow that the woman continued babbling away before she noticed that her patient had no need of her cheering words.

Rose had passed at dawn and the feeling of sadness which she had often felt on there being no-one at her bedside to offer comfort vanished entirely in her final moments. She found such perfect repose that, even though she lay awake through the long night, she was at rest in soul, body and mind.

She could not formulate ideas with any degree of cognition and, feeling that her heartbeat was growing fainter, thoughts seemed to pass before her, not as if she was thinking but as if they came down to her like one of her favourite psalms: "heaviness may endure for a night but joy will cometh in the morning".

The fervent belief that she would eventually be joined by the person who had loved her unfailingly, and that no more obstacles would stand in their way, offered Rose further solace, and in the delirium which accompanies final illness she momentarily opened her eyes and believed the professor to be sitting in the chair beside the bed.

The age she had first met him, with sandy hair and glinting blue eyes, he had smiled at her and recited her own verse, "'I heard a voice from far away, as I lay dull and sad. For very grief I could not pray to Him who makes us glad. Yet, like the words a friend might say, it stilled the pain I had.'" He spoke not with reluctance to see her go but with pure selflessness, holding her hand that she might have courage.

And she had no more pain. The fever, the spasms and the tiredness vanished, and Christ, and that blessed, blessed hope of Eternal Life, seemed near.

Percy, who felt his sister's passing keenest of all the La Touches, broke down when a messenger arrived at his home just a few miles from Harristown. Plagued with shame that he had been unable to steer Rose's course in another direction, he locked himself away in his study in order to vent his grief, along with indignation towards his mother who closed her letter forbidding him to send word to Ruskin.

No-one, especially not his wife, could understand the anger he tried to stifle in the hours preceding his sister's funeral, nor the resentment with which he regarded his parents as they effused their anguish when they all gathered in the house where Rose ought to have spent her last night surrounded by her family.

They had each failed Rose in their own way and *this* was the penalty, he judged, as they approached the small church of St Patrick standing adjacent to the entrance of the La Touches' vast domain. The place where he had married to please everyone but himself, Percy, no longer a conceited, carefree young man, stepped through the open door of the church and felt the full weight of bereavement and a crushing loss of faith.

The choir commenced singing, while he, acting alongside the young men of the estate as one of the pall-bearers, shared the burden of his sister's coffin, conducted to the nave with emotion concealed behind ceremony. Unlike those observing the scene, he preferred to keep his grief to himself.

The sight of Rose's small coffin, barely larger than a child's, adorned with abundant white roses, elicited a gasp from many in attendance, while sobs echoed in unison with the choir. Every seat was taken up with mourners from the estate, each recalling their own memories of the young woman who would visit them no more.

The infirm Mrs Casey; the shepherd boy who once rescued Rose on the moors, now a man with his own farm-holding; even the rector who had himself been inspired by Rose's grace, all bowed their heads and trusted in God's wisdom.

Maria and John La Touche, bereaved for the second time, were the subject of most interest and, seated in the family pew at the front of the church, were forced to share the silent accusation which the congregation placed upon their heads. Unsure whether paranoia or conscience led them to sense the disapproval focussed upon them, they did not look at anyone, least of all one another.

Rumours of Rose's love for Ruskin had circulated far and wide, and yet the man they wanted to share their grief with was not there. Instead, as the community joined together through hymn and prayer, weeping with no attempt at restraint, the young woman's lover remained oblivious to his great loss.

Maria was not sorry for her lapse of humanity, for what difference did one more error make besides the heap of wrongs she would answer for on her own day of judgement? She dwelt upon her present suffering rather than her failings as a mother and, regarding her husband out of the corner of her eye, considered only the consequences that this event would have upon their life at Harristown, Rose's death leaving them quite alone.

Ruskin, who would evermore retreat to Brantwood, was away into the meadows to see buttercup and clover when the news finally reached him on the day of Rose's funeral.

He was gathering wild flowers when Crawley approached him clutching a telegram: his loyal servant's face imbued with the deepest pity, telling him, without his even having to read the message, that that which he had dreaded most had occurred. The story of his wild Rose was ended, and this year the sweetly scented hawthorn blossoms would fall *over* her.

Although he had long expected it, he felt giddy in the head at first. The black font appeared too harsh and uncharitable to deliver such terrible tidings, and so he allowed the paper to fall from his hand and rest on the long grass before floating away on the gentle breeze.

The Psyche was aloft and her wings were broad and white, Ruskin thought on looking up to the beauty of the sky, which still gave him something to be thankful for, his life the richer for the memory of what came but could not stay.

Seeing the world in a new dimension, Rose's death was the seal of a great fountain of sorrow which would never ebb away; he could only fight through it by trying to go on, mechanically.

Even the flowers in his hand made him sad, but in the end there was nothing more fitting than gladness. The weight was gone, the gravestone heaved from off her, and the struggle with that which *was*, and yet was not herself, was over.

AUTHOR'S NOTE

THIS IS A WORK OF FICTION, WOVEN FROM THE TANGLED threads of one of the nineteenth-century's greatest minds, John Ruskin. The story highlights his complex relationships with family, friends and loved ones. All the main characters are based on real people and although some had a larger part to play than others, each impacted on Ruskin's turbulent emotional life and thus often inadvertently changed the course of his work and philosophy.

His beliefs not only altered English society, trade and politics, but influenced the likes of Mahatma Gandhi who became a disciple of Ruskin after reading his ground-breaking political economy essay, *Unto This Last*. When I became the youngest ever member of the Ruskin Society at the age of seventeen, much as I relished learning about the academic side of Ruskin's life, I yearned to discover the man behind the career and reputation (good and bad), something it has taken almost two decades of research to piece together from biographies and countless other sources. Fortunately, Ruskin was a prolific diarist and letter writer, as were many

693

of his friends and family, something which allowed me to form my own interpretation of his eventful personal history.

Whilst this novel is in essence a tribute to Ruskin, a man who did indeed "think with his heart", as Tolstoy observed, I have not steered away from his many failings, as he himself did not. Often considered self-centred and arrogant, he was also generous and fiercely loyal, an attribute which motivated the borrowed title of this book and refers largely, if not wholly, to his relationship with Rose La Touche. The title also reflects the themes of parental love such as Ruskin's intense relationship with his parents, along with the undying marital love he longs for and idealises on witnessing the mutual devotion between his parents, Margaret and John James, and his friends Thomas and Jane Carlyle.

Doubtless this portrait, which seeks to convey the many ups and downs of Ruskin's emotions, his flaws and obsessions, will be challenging and even at times uncomfortable, but I trust it will prove ultimately rewarding. Written so as you may not be aware where Ruskin's voice ends and the author's begins, I have attempted to suspend my own judgement of the characters and their actions, in order that you might form your own view of a man who was perhaps neither hero nor anti-hero.

The joy of the biographical fiction genre is that it allows the reader to follow three-dimensional characters who loved and lived, contradicted themselves and changed their minds, alternately prompting our admiration and frustration, just as friends or relations might. It was always my ambition to create a love story grounded in reality: one that consciously or unconsciously provokes each of us to examine our own relationships and allows us to truly feel that we know Ruskin. I won't say 'knew', for it is my greatest wish that Ruskin goes on living with you long after you lay this book aside.